Praise for

ROBIN HOBB'S
Spectacular Trilogies

THE LIVESHIP TRADERS TRILOGY

SHIP OF MAGIC
MAD SHIP
SHIP OF DESTINY

"A truly extraordinary saga . . . the characterizations are consistently superb, and [Hobb] animates everything with the love for and knowledge of the sea. If Patrick O'Brian were to turn to writing high fantasy, he might produce something like this. Kudos to the author, and encore!"
—*Booklist*

"Hobb gives us her usual marvelously coherent setting and intriguing, multidimensional characters who refuse to be pigeonholed. . . . A new series sure to please fantasy fans."
—*Publishers Weekly*

"Rich, complex . . . [Hobb's] plotting is complex but tightly controlled, and her descriptive powers match her excellent visual imagination. But her chief virtue is that she delineates character extremely well."
—*Interzone*

THE FARSEER TRILOGY

ASSASSIN'S APPRENTICE
"A gleaming debut in the crowded field of epic fantasies and Arthurian romances."
—*Publishers Weekly*

"An intriguing, controlled, and remarkably assured debut, at once satisfyingly self-contained yet leaving plenty of scope for future extensions and embellishments."
—*Kirkus Reviews*

ROYAL ASSASSIN

"*Royal Assassin* offers great rewards. Hobb continues to revitalize a genre that often seems all too generic, making it new in ways that range from the subtle to the shocking. And beneath all, that wise, deeply involved humanity."
—*Locus*

ASSASSIN'S QUEST

"An enthralling conclusion to this superb trilogy, displaying an exceptional combination of originality, magic, adventure, character, and drama."
—*Kirkus Reviews* (starred review)

THE TAWNY MAN TRILOGY

FOOL'S ERRAND

"A dazzling array of characters, many of them human, and all of them drawn in exquisite detail."
—*Booklist*

"Hobb's skills shine through in *Fool's Errand*. . . . Hobb draws people and events with clarity."
—*Kansas City Star*

"Hobb has created a world brimming with detail and complexity [and] once again proves herself a full master of the epic fantasy."
—*Tulsa World*

"Hobb's fans won't be disappointed with this latest installment. *Fool's Errand* lives up to the legacy of the Farseer trilogy."
—*Monroe News-Star*

bantam books

BY ROBIN HOBB

❧

Fool's Fate

ROBIN HOBB

BOOK III OF THE TAWNY MAN

bantam books NEW YORK TORONTO LONDON SYDNEY AUCKLAND

FOOL'S FATE
A Bantam Spectra Book

PUBLISHING HISTORY
Bantam hardcover edition published February 2004
Bantam mass market edition / December 2004

Published by Bantam Dell
A Division of Random House, Inc.
New York, New York

Library of Congress Catalog Card Number: 2443062217

ISBN 0-553-58246-1

Printed in the United States of America
Published simultaneously in Canada

OPM   10 9 8 7

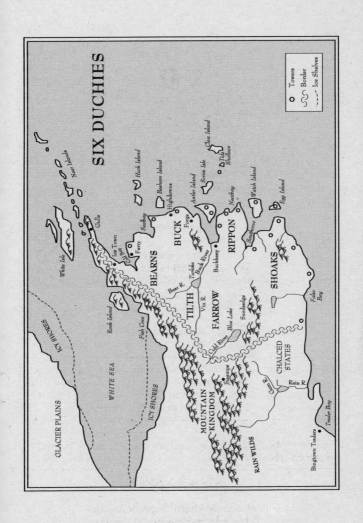

Fool's Fate

prologue

BATTLING FATE

The White Prophet's premise seems simple. He wished to set the world in a different path than the one it had rolled on through so many circuits of time. According to him, time always repeats itself, and in every repetition, people make most of the same foolish mistakes they've always made. They live from day to day, giving in to appetites and desires, convinced that what they do does not matter in the larger scheme of things.

According to the White Prophet, nothing could be further from the truth. Every small, unselfish action nudges the world into a better path. An accumulation of small acts can change the world. The fate of the world can pivot on one man's death. Or turn a different way because of his survival. And who was I to the White Prophet? I was his Catalyst. The Changer. I was the stone he would set to bump time's wheels out of its rut. A small pebble can turn a wheel out of its path, he told me, but warned me that it was seldom a pleasant experience for the pebble.

The White Prophet claimed that he had seen, not just the future, but many possible futures, and most of them were drearily similar. But in a very few cases, there was a difference, and that difference led to a shining realm of new possibilities.

The first difference was the existence of a Farseer heir, one who survived. That was me. Forcing me to survive, dragging me away from the deaths that constantly tried to eliminate me so that time's wheels could jolt back into their comfortable ruts, became his life's work. Death and near-death swallowed me, time after time, and each time he dragged me, battered and bruised, back from the brink to follow him again. He used me relentlessly, but not without regret.

And he succeeded in diverting fate from its preordained path into one that would be better for the world. So he said. But there were people who did not share his opinion, people who envisioned a future without a Farseer heir and without dragons. One of them decided to ensure that future by ridding herself of the fool who stood in her way.

chapter I

LIZARDS

Sometimes it seems unfair that events so old can reach
forward through the years, sinking claws into one's life
and twisting all that follows it. Yet perhaps that is the
ultimate justice: we are the sum of all we have done
added to the sum of all that has been done to us. There is
no escaping that, not for any of us.

So it was that everything that the Fool had ever said
to me and all the things he'd left unsaid combined. And
the sum was that I betrayed him. Yet I believed that I
acted in his best interests, and mine. He had foretold
that if we went to Aslevjal Island, he would die and
Death might make another snap of his jaws at me. He
promised to do all in his power to see that I survived, for
his grand scheme to change the future required it. But
with my latest brush with death still fresh in my memory,
I found his promises more threatening than reassuring.
He had also blithely informed me that once we were on
the island, I would have to choose between our
friendship and my loyalty to Prince Dutiful.

Perhaps I could have faced one of those things and
stood strong before it, but I doubt it. Any one of those
things was enough to unman me, and facing the sum of
them was simply beyond my strength.

*So I went to Chade. I told him what the Fool had
said. And my old mentor arranged that when we sailed
for the Out Islands, the Fool would not go with us.*

        ❧   ❧   ❧

Spring had come to Buckkeep Castle. The grim black
stone edifice still crouched suspiciously on the steep cliffs
above Buckkeep Town, but on the rolling hills behind the
keep, new green grass was pushing optimistically up
through the standing brown straw of last year's growth.
The bare-limbed forests were hazed with tiny green leaves
unfurling on every tree branch. The wintry mounds of dead
kelp on the black beaches at the foot of the cliffs had been
swept away by the tides. Migratory birds had returned, and
their songs rang challenges in the forested hills and along
the beaches where seabirds battled for choice nesting
nooks in the cliffs. Spring had even invaded the dim halls
and high-ceilinged chambers of the keep, for blossoming
branches and early-blooming flowers graced every alcove
and framed the entries of the gathering rooms.

     The warmer winds seemed to sweep my gloom away.
None of my problems and concerns had vanished, but
spring can dismiss a multitude of worries. My physical state
had improved; I felt more youthful than I had in my twenties. Not only was I building flesh and muscle again, but I
suddenly possessed the body that a fit man of my years
should have. The harsh healing I had undergone at the inexperienced hands of the coterie had inadvertently undone old damage as well. Abuse I had suffered at Galen's
hands in the course of his teaching me the Skill, injuries I
had taken as a warrior, and the deep scars from my torture
in Regal's dungeons had been erased. My headaches had
nearly ceased, my vision no longer blurred when I was
weary, and I did not ache in the chill of early morning. I
lived now in the body of a strong and healthy animal. Few

things are so exhilarating as good health on a clear spring morning.

I stood on the top of a tower and looked out over the wrinkling sea. Behind me, tubs of earth, freshly manured, held small fruit trees arrayed in blossoms of white and pale pink. Smaller pots held vines with swelling leaf buds. The long green leaves of bulb flowers thrust up like scouts sent to test the air. In some pots, only bare brown stalks showed, but the promise was there, each plant awaiting the return of warmer days. Interspersed with the pots were artfully arranged statuary and beckoning benches. Shielded candles awaited mellow summer nights to send their glow into the darkness. Queen Kettricken had restored the Queen's Garden to its former glory. This high retreat was her private territory. Its present simplicity reflected her Mountain roots, but its existence was a much older Buckkeep tradition.

I paced a restless turn around its perimeter path, and then forced myself to stand still. The boy was not late. I was early. That the minutes dragged was not his fault. Anticipation warred with reluctance as I awaited my first private meeting with Swift, Burrich's son. My queen had given me responsibility for Swift's instruction in both letters and weaponry. I dreaded the task. Not only was the boy Witted, but he was undeniably headstrong. Those two things, coupled with his intelligence, could carry him into trouble. The Queen had decreed that the Witted must be treated with respect, but many still believed that the best cure for Beast Magic was a noose, a knife, and a fire.

I understood the Queen's motive in entrusting Swift to me. His father, Burrich, had turned him out of his home when the boy would not give up the Wit. Yet the same Burrich had devoted years to raising me when I was a lad and abandoned by my royal father as a bastard that he dared not claim. It was fitting that I now do the same for Burrich's son, even if I could never let the boy know that I had once been FitzChivalry and his father's ward. So it was

that I awaited Swift, a skinny lad of ten summers, as nervously as if I faced the boy's father. I took a deep breath of
the cool morning air. The scent of the fruit tree blossoms
balmed it. I reminded myself that my task would not last
long. Very soon, I would accompany the Prince on his
quest to Aslevjal in the Out Islands. Surely I could endure
being the lad's instructor until then.

The Wit Magic makes one aware of other life, and so I
turned even before Swift pushed open the heavy door. He
shut it quietly behind him. Despite his long climb up the
steep stone stairs, he was not breathing hard. I remained
partially concealed by screening blossoms and studied him.
He was dressed in Buckkeep blue, in simple garments befit-
ting a page. Chade was right. He would make a fine axe-
man. The boy was thin, in the way of active boys of that
age, but the knobs of shoulders under his jerkin promised
his father's brawn. I doubted he would be tall, but he would
be wide enough to make up for it. Swift had his father's
black eyes and dark curling hair, but there was something
of Molly in the line of his jaw and the set of his eyes. Molly,
my lost love and Burrich's wife. I took a long, deep breath.
This might be more difficult than I had imagined.

I saw him become aware of me. I stood still, letting his
eyes seek me out. For a time we both stood, unspeaking.
Then he threaded his way through the meandering paths
until he stood before me. His bow was too carefully practiced to be graceful.

"My lord, I am Swift Witted. I was told to report to
you, and so I present myself."

I could see he had made an effort to learn his court
courtesies. Yet his blatant inclusion of his Beast Magic in
how he named himself seemed almost a rude challenge, as
if he tested whether the Queen's protection of the Witted
would hold here, alone with me. He met my gaze in a forth-
right way that most nobles would have found presumptu-
ous. Then again, I reminded myself, I was not a noble. I
told him so. "I am not 'my lord' to anyone, lad. I'm Tom

Badgerlock, a man-at-arms in the Queen's Guard. You may call me Master Badgerlock, and I shall call you Swift. Is that agreed?"

He blinked twice and then nodded. Abruptly, he recalled that that was not correct. "It is, sir. Master Badgerlock."

"Very well. Swift, do you know why you were sent to me?"

He bit his upper lip twice, swift successive nibbles, then took a deep breath and spoke, eyes lowered. "I suppose I've displeased someone." Then he flashed his gaze up to mine again. "But I don't know what I did, or to whom." Almost defiantly, he added, "I cannot help what I am. If it is because I am Witted, well, then, it isn't fair. Our queen has said that my magic should not make any difference in how I am treated."

My breath caught in my throat. His father looked at me from those dark eyes. The uncompromising honesty and the determination to speak the truth was all Burrich's. And yet, in his intemperate haste, I heard Molly's quick temper. For a moment, I was at a loss for words.

The boy interpreted my silence as displeasure and lowered his eyes. But the set of his shoulders was still square; he did not know of any fault he had committed, and he would not show any repentance until he did.

"You did not displease anyone, Swift. And you will find that to some at Buckkeep, your Wit matters not at all. That is not why we separated you from the other children. Rather, this change is for your benefit. Your knowledge of letters surpasses the other children of your age. We did not wish to thrust you into a group of youths much older than you. It was also decided that you could benefit from instruction in the use of a battle-axe. That, I believe, is why I was chosen to mentor you."

His head jerked and he looked up at me in confusion and dismay. "A battle-axe?"

I nodded, both to him and to myself. Chade was up to

his old tricks again. Plainly the boy had not been asked if he had any interest in learning to wield such a weapon. I put a smile on my face. "Certainly a battle-axe. Buckkeep's men-at-arms recall that your father fought excellently with the axe. As you inherit his build as well as his looks, it seems natural that his weapon of choice should be yours."

"I'm nothing like my father. Sir."

I nearly laughed aloud, not from joy, but because the boy had never looked more like Burrich than he did at that moment. It felt odd to look *down* at someone giving me his black scowl. But such an attitude was not appropriate to a boy of his years, so I coldly said, "You're like enough, in the Queen's and Councilor Chade's opinions. Do you dispute what they have decided for you?"

It all hovered in the balance. I saw the instant when he made his decision, and almost read the workings of his mind. He could refuse. Then he might be seen as ungrateful and sent back home to his father. Better to bow his head to a distasteful task and stay. And so he said, voice lowered, "No, sir. I accept what they have decided."

"That's good," I said with false heartiness.

But before I could continue, he informed me, "But I have a skill with a weapon already. The bow, sir. I had not spoken of it before, because I did not think it would be of interest to anyone. But if I'm to train as a fighter as well as a page, I already have a weapon of choice."

Interesting. I regarded him in silence for a moment. I'd seen enough of Burrich in him to suspect he would not idly boast of a skill he didn't possess. "Very well, then. You may show me your skills with a bow. But this time is set aside for other lessons. To that end, we've been given permission to use scrolls from the Buckkeep library. That's quite an honor for both of us." I waited for a response.

He bobbed a nod, and then recalling his manners, "Yes, sir."

"Good. Then meet me here tomorrow. We'll have an

hour of scrolls and writing, and then we'll go down to the weapons court." Again I awaited his reply.

"Yes, sir. Sir?"

"What is it?"

"I'm a good horseman, sir. I'm a bit rusty now. My father refused to let me be around his horses for the last year. But I'm a good horseman, as well."

"That's good to know, Swift." I knew what he had hoped. I watched his face, and saw the light in it dim at my neutral response. I had reacted almost reflexively. A boy of his age shouldn't be considering bonding with an animal. Yet as he lowered his head in disappointment, I felt my old loneliness echo down the years. So too had Burrich done all he could to protect me from bonding with a beast. Knowing the wisdom of it now didn't still the memory of my thrumming isolation. I cleared my throat and tried to keep my voice smoothly assured when I spoke. "Very well, then, Swift. Report to me here tomorrow. Oh, and wear your old clothes tomorrow. We'll be getting dirty and sweaty."

He looked stricken.

"Well? What is it, lad?"

"I . . . sir, I can't. I, that is, I don't have my old clothes anymore. Only the two sets the Queen gave me."

"What happened to them?"

"I . . . I burned them, sir." He suddenly sounded defiant. He met my eyes, jaw jutting.

I thought of asking him why. I didn't need to. It was obvious from his stance. He had made a show for himself of destroying all things that bound him to his past. I wondered if I should make him admit that aloud, then decided that nothing would be gained by it. Surely such a waste of useful garments was something that should shame him. I wondered how bitterly his differences with his father had run. Suddenly the day seemed a little less brightly blue. I shrugged, dismissing the matter. "Wear what you have, then," I said abruptly, and hoped I did not sound too harsh.

He stood there, staring at me, and I realized that I hadn't dismissed him. "You may go now, Swift. I will see you tomorrow."

"Yes, sir. Thank you, Master Badgerlock." He bowed, jerkily correct, and then hesitated again. "Sir? May I ask you a last question?"

"Certainly."

He looked all around us, almost suspiciously. "Why do we meet up here?"

"It's quiet. It's pleasant. When I was your age, I hated to be kept indoors on a spring day."

That brought a hesitant smile to his face. "So do I, sir. Nor do I like to be kept so isolated from animals. That is my magic calling me, I suppose."

I wished he had let it rest. "Perhaps it is. And perhaps you should think well before you answer it." This time I intended that he hear the rebuke in my voice.

He flinched, then looked indignant. "The Queen said that my magic was not to make a difference to anyone. That no one can treat me poorly because of it."

"That's true. But neither will people treat you well because of it. I counsel you to keep your magic a private matter, Swift. Do not parade it before people until you know them. If you wish to know how to best handle your Wit, I suggest you spend time with Web the Witted, when he tells his tales before the hearth in the evenings."

He was scowling before I was finished. I dismissed him curtly and he went. I thought I had read him well enough. His possession of the Wit had been the battle line drawn between him and his father. He had successfully defied Burrich and fled to Buckkeep, determined to live openly as a Witted one in Queen Kettricken's tolerant court. But if the boy thought that being Witted was all he needed to earn his place, well, I'd soon clear that cobweb from his mind. I'd not try to deprive him of his magic. But his flaunting of it, as one might shake a rag at a terrier to see what reaction he would win, distressed me. Sooner or later, he'd encounter a young noble happy to challenge him over the despised Beast Magic. The tolerance was a mandated thing, grudgingly given by many who still adhered to the old distaste for our gift. Swift's attitude made me doubly determined that he should not discover I was Witted. Bad enough that he cockily flaunted his own magic; I wouldn't have him betraying mine.

I gazed out once more over the wide spectacle of sea and sky. It was an exhilarating view, at once breathtaking and yet reassuringly familiar. And then I forced myself to stare down, over the low wall that stood between me and a plummet to my sure death below. I forced myself to stare down. Once, battered both physically and mentally by Galen the Skillmaster, I had tried to make that plunge from this very parapet. It had been Burrich's hand that had drawn me back. He had carried me down to his own rooms, treated my injuries, and then avenged them upon the Skillmaster. I still owed him for that. Perhaps teaching his son and keeping him safe at court would be the only repayment I could ever offer him. I fixed that thought in my heart to prop up my sagging enthusiasm for the task and left the tower top. I had another meeting to hasten to, and the sun told me that I was already nearly late for it.

Chade had let it be known that he was now instructing the young Prince in his heritage Skill Magic. I was both grateful and chagrined at this turn of events. The announcement meant that Prince Dutiful and Chade no longer had to meet secretly for that purpose. That the Prince took his half-wit servant with him to those lessons was regarded as a sort of eccentricity. No one in the court would have guessed that Thick was the Prince's fellow student, and far stronger in the Farseer's ancestral magic than any currently living Farseer. The chagrin came from the fact that I, the true Skill instructor, was the only one who still had to conceal his comings and goings from those meetings. Tom Badgerlock was who I was now, and that humble guardsman had no business knowing anything of the Farseer's magic.

So it was that I descended the steps from the Queen's Garden, and then hastened through the keep. From the servants' areas there were six possible entry points to the hidden spy labyrinth that meandered through the entrails of Buckkeep Castle. I took care that every day I used a different entry from the day before. Today I selected the one near the cook's larder. I waited until there was no one in the corridor when I entered the storeroom. I pushed my way through three racks of dangling sausages before dragging the panel open and stepping through into now familiar darkness.

I didn't waste time waiting for my eyes to adjust. This part of the maze had no illumination of any kind. The first few times I'd explored it, I carried a candle. Today I judged that I knew it well enough to traverse it in the dark. I counted my steps, then groped my way into a narrow staircase. At the top of it, I made a sharp right and saw thin fingers of spring sunlight filtering into the dusty corridor. Stooped, I hastened along it and soon reached a more familiar part of the warren. In a short time, I emerged from the side of the hearth in the Seawatch Tower. I pushed the panel back into place, then froze as I heard someone lifting the door latch. I barely had time to seek flimsy shelter in the long curtains that draped the tower windows before someone entered.

I held my breath, but it was only Chade, Dutiful, and Thick arriving for their lessons. I waited until the door was firmly closed behind them before stepping out into the room. I startled Thick, but Chade only observed, "You've cobwebs down your left cheek. Did you know?"

I wiped away the clinging stuff. "I'm surprised that it's only on my left cheek. Spring seems to have wakened a legion of spiders."

Chade nodded gravely to my observation. "I used to carry a feather duster with me, waving it before me as I went. It helped. Somewhat. Of course, in those days, it little mattered what I looked like when I arrived at my destination. I just didn't care for the sensation of little legs down the back of my neck."

Prince Dutiful smirked at the idea of the immaculately attired and coiffed Queen's councilor scuttling through the corridors. There had been a time when Lord Chade was a hidden resident of Buckkeep Castle, the royal assassin only, a man who concealed his pocked face and carried out the King's justice in the shadows. No longer. Now he strode majestically through the hallways, openly lauded as both diplomat and trusted adviser to the Queen. His elegant garb in shades of blue and green reflected that status, as did the gems that graced his throat and earlobes. His snowy hair and piercing green eyes seemed like carefully chosen accoutrements to his wardrobe. The scars that had so distressed him had faded with his years. I neither envied nor begrudged him his finery. Let the old man make up now for the deprivations of his youth. It harmed no one, and those who were dazzled by it often overlooked the rapier mind that was his real weapon.

In contrast, the Prince was garbed nearly as simply as I was. I attributed it to Queen Kettricken's austere Mountain Kingdom traditions and her innate thrift. At fifteen, Dutiful was shooting up. What sense was there in creating fine garments for everyday wear when he either outgrew them or tore out the shoulders while practicing on the weapons court? I studied the young man who stood grinning before me. His dark eyes and curling black hair mirrored his father's, but both his height and his developing jawline reminded me more of my father Chivalry's portrait.

The squat man accompanying him was a complete contrast. I estimated Thick to be in his late twenties. He had the small tight ears and protruding tongue of a simpleton. The Prince had garbed him in a blue tunic and leggings that matched his own, right down to the buck crest on the breast, but the tunic strained across the little man's

potbelly and the hose sagged comically at his knees and ankles. He cut an odd figure, both amusing and slightly repul-
sive, to those who could not sense, as I did, the Skill Magic
that burned in him like a smith's forge fire. He was learning
to control the Skill-music that served him in place of an
ordinary man's thoughts. It was less pervasive and hence
less annoying than it had once been, yet the strength of
his magic meant that he shared it with all of us, constantly.
I could block it, but that meant also blocking my sensitiv-
ity to most of the Skill, including Chade's and Dutiful's
weaker sendings. I could not block him and still teach
them, so for now I endured Thick's music.

Today it was made from the snickings of scissors and
the clack of a loom, with the high-pitched giggle of a
woman winding through it. "So. Had another fitting this
morning, did you?" I asked the Prince.

He was not dazzled. He knew how I had deduced it. He
nodded with weary tolerance. "Both Thick and I. It was a
long morning."

Thick nodded emphatically. "Stand on the stool.
Don't scratch. Don't move. While they poke Thick with
pins." He added the last severely, with a rebuking look at
the Prince.

Dutiful sighed. "That was an accident, Thick. She told
you to stand still."

"She's mean," Thick ventured in an undertone, and I
suspected he was close to the truth. Many of his nobles
found it difficult to accept the Prince's friendship with
Thick. For some reason, it affronted some servants even
more. I suspected some of them found small ways to vent
that displeasure.

"It's all done now, Thick," Dutiful consoled him.

We took our customary places around the immense
table. Since Chade had announced that he and the Prince
were beginning Skill-lessons together, this room of the
Seawatch Tower had been furnished well. Long curtains
framed the tall windows, now unshuttered to admit a

pleasant breeze. The stone walls and floor of the chamber
had been well scrubbed and the table and chairs oiled and
polished. There were proper scroll racks to hold Chade's
small library as well as a stoutly locked cabinet for those he
regarded as highly valuable or dangerous. A large writing
desk offered inkpots and freshly cut pens and a generous
supply of both paper and vellum. There was also a sideboard with bottles of wine, glasses, and other necessities
for the Prince's comfort. It had become a comfortable,
even indulgent room that reflected Chade's taste more
than Prince Dutiful's.

I enjoyed the change.

I surveyed the faces around me. Dutiful was looking at
me alertly. Thick was pursuing something inside his left
nostril. Chade was sitting bolt upright, fairly shivering
with energy. Whatever he had taken to bring him back to
alertness had done nothing for the threads of blood in his
eyes. The contrast with his green gaze was unsettling.

"What I'd like to do today . . . Thick. Please stop that."

He looked at me blankly, his finger still wedged in his
nose. "Can't. It's poking me in there."

Chade rubbed his brow, looking aside. "Give him a
handkerchief," he suggested to no one in particular.

Prince Dutiful was closest. "Here, blow your nose.
Maybe it will come out."

He handed Thick a square of embroidered linen.
Thick regarded it doubtfully for several seconds, and then
took it. Over the deafening sounds of his attempts to clear
his nose, I asked, "Last night, each of us was to try Skill-
walking in our dreams." I had been nervous about suggesting this, but I had felt both Dutiful and Chade were ready
to attempt it. Thick routinely forgot what he was to do in
the evenings, so I'd had small concern for him. When one
Skill-walked, one could leave one's own body and for a
short time experience life through someone else. I had
managed it several times, most often by accident. The Skill
scrolls had suggested that it was not only a good way to

gather information but also to locate those who were open enough to be used as King's Men, sources of strength to a Skill-user. Those sufficiently open sometimes proved to possess the Skill themselves. Chade had been enthused yesterday, but a glance at him today showed none of the triumph he would have displayed if he had managed the feat. Dutiful likewise looked gloomy. "So. No success?"

"I did it!" Thick exulted.

"You Skill-walked?" I was astounded.

"No-o-o. I got it out. See?" He displayed his greenish trophy trapped in the middle of the Prince's handkerchief. Chade turned aside with an exclamation of disgust.

Dutiful, being fifteen, laughed aloud. "Impressive, Thick. That's a big one. Looks like an old green salamander."

"Yah," Thick agreed with satisfaction. His mouth sagged wide with pleasure. "I dreamed a big blue lizard last night. Bigger than this!" His laughter, like a dog's huffy panting, joined the Prince's.

"My prince and future monarch," I reminded Dutiful sternly, "we have work to do." In reality, I was struggling to keep a straight face. It was good to see Dutiful laugh freely, even over something puerile. Since I had first met the boy, he had always seemed weighted by his station and his perpetual duties. This was the first time I had seen him acting like a youngster in springtime; I regretted my rebuke when the smile faded so abruptly from his face. With a gravity that far exceeded my own, he turned to Thick, seized the handkerchief and balled it up.

"No, Thick. Stop. Listen to me. You dreamed a big blue lizard? How big?"

The intensity of the Prince's question drew Chade's glance. But Thick was confused and offended by how quickly Dutiful's tone and attitude toward him had changed. His brow furrowed and both bottom lip and tongue jutted as a sulk settled onto his face. "That wasn't nice."

I recognized the phrase. We'd been working on Thick's

table manners. If he was to accompany us on the trip to Aslevjal, he had to learn at least a modicum of courtesy. Unfortunately, he seemed to recall the rules only when he could rebuke someone else with them.

"I'm sorry, Thick. You're right. Grabbing isn't nice. Now tell me about the big lizard you dreamed."

The Prince was smiling earnestly at Thick, but the change of topic was too fast for the little man. Thick shook his heavy head and turned away. He folded his stubby arms on his chest. "Na," he declined gruffly.

"Please, Thick," Dutiful began, but Chade interrupted. "Can't this wait, Dutiful? We've not that many days before we sail, and we still have so much ground to cover if we are to function as a Skill coterie." I knew the old man's anxiety. I shared it. The Skill might be essential to the Prince's success. Neither of us put much weight on his truly slaying some buried ice dragon. The true value of the Skill would be that Chade and I could gather information and convey it to Dutiful to smooth the path for his wedding negotiations. "No. This is important, Chade. I think. Well, it might be. Because I dreamed a big blue lizard last night, too. Actually, the creature I dreamed was a dragon."

A moment of silence held as we considered this. Then Chade hesitantly attempted, "Well, it should not surprise us if you and Thick share the same dream. You are so often Skill-linked throughout the day, why shouldn't it bleed over into the night?"

"Because I don't think I was asleep when it happened. I was trying to do the Skill-walking. Fi— Tom says it was easiest for him to bridge over to it from a light sleep. So I was in my bed, trying to be asleep but not too asleep, while reaching out with the Skill. And then I felt it."

"What?" Chade asked.

"I felt it looking for me. With its great big whirly silver eyes." Thick was the one who answered.

"Yes," the Prince confirmed slowly.

My heart sank.

"I don't understand," Chade said irritably. "Start at the beginning and report it properly." This was addressed to Dutiful. I understood the double prong of Chade's anger. Once again, the three of them had attempted an exercise, and both Thick and Dutiful had experienced some success while Chade had failed. Underscoring that was the mention of a dragon. There had been too many mentions of dragons lately: a frozen dragon for Dutiful to unearth and behead, the dragons the Bingtown contingent had bragged about (supposedly at the beck and call of the Bingtown Traders), and now a dragon intruding into our Skill-exercise. We knew far too little about any of them. We dared not dismiss them as legends and lies; too well we recalled the stone dragons that had rallied to the Six Duchies' defense sixteen years ago, yet we knew little about any of them.

"There's scarcely enough to report it," Dutiful replied. He took a breath, and despite his own words, began in the orderly way in which Chade had schooled both of us. "I had retired to my chambers, exactly as if I were going to sleep for the night. I was in my bed. There was a low fire in the hearth, and I was watching it, unfocusing my mind in a way that I hoped would invite sleep and yet leave me aware enough to reach out with the Skill. Twice I dozed off. Each time, I roused myself and tried to approach the exercise again. The third time, I tried reversing the process. I reached out with the Skill, held myself in readiness, and then tried to sink down into sleep." He cleared his throat and looked around at us. "Then I felt something big. Really big." He looked at me. "Like that time on the beach."

Thick was following the tale with his jaw ajar and his small round eyes bunched with thought. "A big fat blue lizard," he hazarded.

"No, Thick." Dutiful patiently kept his voice soft. "Not at first. At first, there was just this immense ... presence. And I longed to go toward it, and yet I feared to go toward it. Not because of any deliberate threat from it. On the contrary, it seemed...infinitely benign. Restful and safe. I was afraid to touch it for fear that...I'd lose any desire to come back. It seemed like the end of something. An edge, or a place where something different begins. No. Like something that lives in a place where something different begins." The Prince's voice trickled away.

"I don't understand. Talk sense," Chade demanded.

"It's as much sense as you can apply to it," I interceded quietly. "I know the sort of being, or feeling, or place, that the Prince is speaking about. I've encountered such, a time or two. Once, one helped us. But I had the feeling that one was an exception. Perhaps another one of them might have absorbed us and not even noticed. It's an incredibly attractive force, Chade. Warm and accepting, gentle as a mother's love."

The Prince frowned slightly and shook his head. "This one was strong. Protective and wise. Like a father," said Dutiful.

I held my tongue. I had long ago decided that those forces presented to us whatever it was that we most hungered for. My mother had given me up when I was very small. Dutiful had never known his father. Such things leave large gaps in a man.

"Why haven't you spoken of this before?" Chade asked testily.

Why, indeed? Because that encounter had seemed too personal to share. But now I excused myself, saying, "Because you would only have said to me what you just said. Talk sense. It's a phenomenon I can't explain. Perhaps even what I've said is just my rationalization of what I experienced. Recounting a dream; that's what it is like. Trying to make a story out of a series of events that defy logic."

Chade subsided, but he did not look content. I resigned myself to being wrung for more facts, thoughts, and impressions later.

"I want to tell about the big lizard," Thick observed sullenly to no one at all. He had reached a point at which he sometimes enjoyed being the center of attention. Obviously he felt that the Prince's tale had stolen his stage.

"Go ahead, Thick. You tell what you dreamed, and then I'll tell what I did." The Prince ceded him all attention.

Chade sat back in his chair with a noisy sigh. I turned my attention to Thick and watched his face brighten. He gave a wiggle like a stroked puppy, squinted thoughtfully, and then in a painstaking imitation of how he had frequently heard Dutiful and me report to Chade, began his account. "I went to bed last night. And I had my red blanket. Then, Thick was being almost asleep, going into the music. Then, I knew Dutiful was there. Sometimes Thick follows him to dreams. He has lots of good dreams, girl dreams..."

Thick's voice trailed off for a moment as he breathed through his open mouth, pondering. The Prince looked acutely uncomfortable, but both Chade and I managed to retain blandly interested expressions.

Thick abruptly resumed his tale. "Then, I thought, where is he? Maybe it's a game. He's hiding from Thick. So I go, 'Prince' and he goes, 'Be quiet.' So I am and Thick is small, and the music goes around and around me. Like hiding in the curtains. Then I peep, just a tiny peep. And it's a big fat lizard, blue, blue like my shirt, but shiny when she moves, like the knives in the kitchen. Then she says, 'Come out, come out. We can play a game.' But Prince says, 'Sh, no, don't,' so I don't, and then she gets mad and gets bigger. Her eyes go shiny and whirl round and round like that saucer I dropped. And then Thick thinks, 'But she's on the dream side. I'll go on the other side.' So I made the music get bigger and I woke up. And there wasn't a lizard but my red blanket was on the floor."

He finished his telling with a great gasp, having run out of breath, and looked from one of us to the other. I found myself giving Chade the tiniest of Skill-pokes. He glanced at me, but contrived to make it seem a chance thing. I felt tremendous pride in the old man when he said, "An excellent report, Thick. You've given me much to consider. Let us hear the Prince now and then I'll see if I have any questions for you."

Thick sat taller in his chair and his chest swelled with such pride that the fabric of his shirt strained across his round belly. His tongue still stuck out of his wide froggy grin, but his little eyes danced as he looked from Dutiful to me to be sure we had noticed his triumph. I wondered when impressing Chade had become so important to him, and then realized that this too was an imitation of his prince.

Dutiful wisely allowed Thick a moment or two to bask in our attention. "Thick has told you most of the story, but let me add a bit. I told you of a great presence. I was—well, not watching—I was experiencing her, or it I suppose, and being slowly drawn closer and closer. It wasn't frightening. I knew it was dangerous, but it was hard to care that I might be absorbed and lost forever. It just didn't seem to matter. Then the presence began to recede. I wanted to pursue it, but at that moment I became aware of something else watching me. And it did not feel so benign. My sensation was that while I'd been contemplating that presence, this other being had crept up on me.

"I looked around and saw that I was at the edge of a milky river, on a very small clay beach. A great forest of immense trees stood at my back. They were taller than towers and shaded the day to dusk. I didn't see anything else at first. Then I noticed a tiny creature, like a lizard, only plumper. It was on the wide leaf of a tree, watching me. Yet once I saw it, it began to grow. Or perhaps I shrank. I'm not sure. The forest grew bigger as well, until when the animal stepped down onto the clay, it was a dragon. Blue and silver, immense and beautiful. And she spoke to me, saying, 'So. You've seen me. Well, I don't care. But you will. You're one of his. Tell me. What do you know of a black dragon?' Then, and this part was very odd, I couldn't find myself. It was as if I had looked at her too hard and forgotten to remember that I existed. And then I decided I would be behind a tree, and I was."

"This doesn't sound like the Skill," Chade interrupted irritably. "It sounds like a dream."

"Exactly. And so I dismissed it when I awoke. I knew I had Skilled briefly, but I thought that then sleep had crept up on me, and all that followed was a dream. So, in this dream, in the odd way that dreams have, Thick was suddenly with me. I didn't know if he had seen the dragon, so I reached for him and told him to be quiet and hide from her. So we were hiding, and she became very angry, I think because she knew we were still there but hiding. Then suddenly Thick was gone. And it startled me so much that I opened my eyes." The Prince shrugged. "I was in my bedroom. I thought it had just been a very vivid dream."

"So it could have been, one that you and Thick shared," Chade replied. "I think we can leave this now and settle to our real business here."

"I think not," I said. Something in Chade's easy dismissal warned me that the old man did not want us to speak of this but I was willing to sacrifice part of my secret to discover his. "I think the dragon is real. Moreover, I think we have heard of her before. Tintaglia, the Bingtown dragon. The one that masked boy spoke of."

"Selden Vestrit." Dutiful supplied his name quietly. "Can dragons Skill, then? Why would she demand to know what we knew of a black dragon? Does she mean Icefyre?"

"Almost certainly she does. But that is the only one of your questions that I can answer." I turned reluctantly to face Chade's scowl. "She has touched my dreams before, with the same demand. That I tell her what I knew of a black dragon and an island. She knows of our quest, most likely from the Bingtown contingent that came to invite us so cordially to their war with Chalced. But I think that she only knows as much as they did. That there is a dragon trapped in ice, and that Dutiful goes to slay him."

Chade made a sound almost like a growl. "Then she'll know the name of the island as well. Aslevjal. It is only a matter of time before she discovers where that is. The Bingtown Traders are famous for doing just that: trading. If they want a chart that shows the way to Aslevjal, they'll obtain one."

I spread my hands, displaying a calm I didn't feel. "There is nothing we can do about that, Chade. We'll have to deal with whatever develops."

He pushed back his chair. "Well, I could deal with it better if I knew enough to expect it," he said. His voice rose as he did. He stalked to the window and stared out over the sea. Then he turned his head to glare at me over his shoulder. "What else have you not told me?"

Had we been alone then, I might have told him about how the dragon had threatened Nettle and how she had dismissed the creature. But I did not wish to speak of my daughter in Dutiful's presence, so I only shook my head. He turned back to gaze out over the sea.

"So we may have another enemy to face, besides the cold and ice of Aslevjal. Well. At least tell me how big is this creature? How strong?"

"I don't know. I've only seen her in dreams, and in my dreams, she shifted her size. I don't think we can be sure of anything she has shown us in dreams."

"Oh, well, that's useful," Chade replied, discouraged. He came back to the table and dropped into his chair. "Did you sense anything of this dragon last night?" he suddenly asked me.

"No. I didn't."

"But you did Skill-walk."

"Briefly." I'd visited Nettle. I wasn't going to discuss that here. He didn't seem to notice my reticence.

"I did neither. Despite my best efforts." His voice was as anguished as an injured child's. I met his eyes and saw, not just frustration there, but pain. He looked at me as if I had excluded him from some precious secret or wonderful adventure.

"Chade. It will come in time. Sometimes I think you try too hard." I spoke the words, but I wasn't sure of them. Yet I could not bring myself to say what I secretly suspected: that he had come to these lessons too late, and would never master the magic so long denied him.

"So you keep saying," he said hollowly.

And there seemed nothing to reply to that. For the remainder of our session, we worked through several exercises from one of the scrolls, but with limited success. Chade's discouragement seemed to have damped all his ability that day. With hands linked, he could receive the images and words I sent him, but when we separated and moved to different parts of the room, I could not reach him, nor could he touch minds with Dutiful or Thick. His growing frustration disrupted all of us. When Dutiful and Thick departed to their day's tasks, we had not only made no progress, but had failed to equal the previous day's level of Skill.

"Another day spent, and we are no closer to having a working coterie," Chade observed bitterly to me when we were alone in the room. He walked over to the sideboard and poured brandy for himself. When he gestured questioningly at me, I shook my head.

"No, thank you. I've not even broken my fast yet."

"Nor I."

"Chade, you look exhausted. I think an hour or two of rest and a solid meal would do you better than brandy."

"Find me two empty hours in my day, and I'll be happy to sleep," he offered without rancor. Chade walked to the window with his cup and gazed out over the water. "It all closes in on me, Fitz. We must have this alliance with the Out Islands. With Chalced and Bingtown warring, our trade to the south has dwindled to a trickle. If Chalced defeats Bingtown, as it well may, it will next turn its swords against us. We must ally with the Out Islands before Chalced does.

"Yet it isn't just the preparations for the journey. It's all the safeguards I must put in place to be sure Buckkeep runs smoothly while I am gone." He sipped from his cup then added, "In twelve days we depart for Aslevjal. Twelve days, when six weeks would scarcely be enough time for all I must arrange so that things will run smoothly in my absence."

I knew he was not speaking of things like Buckkeep's provisions and taxes and the training of the guard. There were others who routinely administered all such systems and reported directly to the Queen. Chade worried about his network of spies and informants. No one was certain how long our diplomatic mission to the Out Islands would take; let alone how much time would be consumed by the Prince's quest to Aslevjal. I still harbored a fading hope that his "slaying of the dragon" would be some strange Outislander ritual, but Chade was convinced there was an actual dragon carcass encased in glacial ice and that Dutiful would have to uncover it enough to sever the head and publicly present it to the Narcheska.

"Surely your apprentice can handle those matters in your absence." I kept my voice level. I had never confronted Chade over his choice of apprentice. I was still not ready to trust Lady Rosemary as a member of the Queen's court, let alone as an apprentice assassin. As a child, she had been Regal's tool, and the Pretender had used her ruthlessly against us. But now would be a poor time to reveal to Chade that I had discovered who his new apprentice was. His spirits were already low.

He shook his head irritably. "Some of my contacts trust only me. They will report to no one else. And the truth is that half of my knack is that I know when to ask more questions and which rumors to follow. No, Fitz, I must resign myself that though my apprentice will attempt to handle my affairs, there will be gaps in my knowledge-gathering when I return."

"You left Buckkeep Castle once before, during the Red Ship War. How did you manage then?"

"Ah, that was a very different situation. Then, I followed the threat, pursuing the intrigues to their hearts. This time, in truth, I will be present for a very critical negotiation. But there is still much happening here at Buckkeep that needs to be watched."

"The Piebalds," I filled in.

"Exactly. Among others. But they are still the ones I fear most, though they have been quiescent of late."

I knew what he meant. The absence of Piebald activity was not reassuring. I had killed the head of their organization, but I feared another would rise to take Laudwine's place. We had gone far to gain the respect and cooperation of the Witted community. Perhaps that mellowing would leech away the anger and hatred that the extremist Piebalds throve on. Our strategy had been that by offering amnesty to the Witted, we might steal the force that drove the Piebalds. If the Witted were welcomed by the Farseer Queen into common society, welcomed and even encouraged to declare their magic openly, then they would have less interest in overthrowing the Farseer reign. So we had hoped, and so it seemed to be working. But if it did not, then they might still move against the Prince, and attempt to discredit him with his own nobles by showing that he was Witted. A royal proclamation that the Wit Magic was no longer to be considered a taint could not undo generations of prejudice and mistrust. That, we hoped, would fall before the benign presence of Witted ones in the Queen's own court. Not just boys such as Swift, but men such as Web the Witted.

Chade still gazed out over the water, his eyes troubled.

I winced as I said them, but could not keep the words back. "Is there anything I could do to help?"

He swung his gaze to meet mine. "Do you offer that sincerely?"

His tone warned me. "I think I do. Why? What would you ask of me?"

"Let me send for Nettle. You needn't acknowledge her as your daughter. Just let me approach Burrich again about bringing her to court, and teaching her the Skill. I think there is still enough of his old oath to the Farseers left in his heart that if I told him she was needed by her prince, he'd let her come. And surely it would be a comfort to Swift, to have his sister close by."

"Oh, Chade." I shook my head. "Ask me anything else. Only leave my child in peace."

He shook his head and held his silence. For a time longer I stood by his side, but finally I accepted that silence as a dismissal. I left him standing there, staring out over the water, looking east and north, to the Out Islands.

chapter II

SONS

*Taker was the first man to call himself a king at
Buckkeep Castle. He came to these shores from the Out
Islands, a raider and looter, as so many others had come
before him. He saw in the timbered fort upon the cliffs
that overlooked the river an ideal location to establish a
permanent foothold in the land. So some say. Others tell
it that he was a cold, wet, and queasy sailor, anxious to
be off the ocean's heaving belly and onto shore again.
Whatever his initial motivation might have been, he
successfully attacked and seized the wooden castle on its
ancient stone foundation and became the first Farseer
king at Buckkeep. He burned his way in; henceforth, he
built all his further fortifications of Buckkeep from the
black stone so plentiful there. Thus, from the earliest
days, the Six Duchies ruling family has roots that reach
back to the Out Islands. They are not, of course, alone
in this. Six Duchies and Outislander folk have mingled
blood as often as they have shed one another's.*

                🙝 VENTURN'S "HISTORIES"

With only five days remaining until our departure date, the
journey began to seem real to me. Up to that point, I had

been able to push it out of my mind and consider it an abstract thing. I had prepared for it, but only as an eventuality. I had studied their writing symbols, and spent many of my evenings in a tavern frequented by Outislander traders and sailors. There I had worked on learning as much of the language as I could. Listening was my best technique for that. Outislander shared many roots with our own tongue, and after a number of evenings, it no longer rang so strange against my ears. I could not speak it well, but I could make myself understood and, more important, understand most of what I heard. I hoped that would be enough.

My lessons with Swift had progressed well. In some ways, I would miss the boy when we sailed. In others, I'd be just as glad to be free of him. True to his word, he was a superb bowman for a boy of ten. Once I'd alerted Cresswell to this, the Weaponsmaster had been very glad to take him in hand. "He's got a feel for it. He isn't one to stand and take a long and careful aim. With this lad, the arrow flies from his eye as much as from his bow. He'd be wasted on the axe. Let's build his strength instead, and move him into a longer and more powerful bow as he grows." So Cresswell evaluated him, and when I passed on his words to Chade, the old assassin agreed in part.

"We'll start him on the axe, as well," Chade directed me. "It cannot hurt him."

Less time with the boy was more of a relief than I cared to admit. He was a bright lad, and pleasant to deal with in all ways save two: he reminded me far too much of both Molly and Burrich, and he could not leave the topic of his magic alone. No matter what lesson I began with, he found a way to transform it to a discussion of the Wit. The depth of his ignorance appalled me; and yet I was not comfortable correcting his misconceptions. I decided to consult with Web about him.

Finding Web alone was the initial difficulty. Since he had first arrived at the Buckkeep court as a speaker and advocate for his people and their maligned magic, he had gained the respect of many who had once despised the Wit and those who practiced it. He was often referred to now as the Witmaster. The title that had once been a mockery of the Queen's acceptance of the outlawed magic was rapidly becoming an accepted honorific. Many sought his advice now, and not just on matters relating to his magic or his Old Blood people. Web was an affable man, interested in everyone and able to converse animatedly on almost any topic; but for all that he was not so much garrulous as an active listener. Folk react well to a man who hangs on their words. Even if he had not been our unofficial ambassador from the Witted folk of the realm, I think he would have become a court favorite. But this odd connection put him even more in regard, for if one wished to demonstrate to the Queen that one shared her politics about the Witted, how better than to invite Web to dine or partake of other amusement? Many nobles sought to curry the Queen's favor this way. I am sure that nothing in Web's previous experience had prepared him to be such a social novelty, and yet he took it in stride, as he seemed to do all things. Nor did it change him that I could tell. He was still as enraptured by the chatter of a serving girl as by the sophisticated discussions of the most elevated noble. I seldom saw him alone.

But there are still a few places where polite society does not follow a man. I was waiting for Web when he emerged from a backhouse. I greeted him and added, "I'd like to ask your advice on something. Have you time for a word or two, and a quiet stroll about the Women's Gardens?"

He raised one graying eyebrow in curiosity, then nodded. Without a word, he followed me as I led the way, easily matching his rolling sailor's gait to my stride. I'd always enjoyed the Women's Gardens, ever since I was a boy. They supply much of the herbs and fresh greens for Buckkeep's kitchens in summer, but are arranged to be a pleasure to stroll in as well as yielding a practical bounty. They are called the Women's Gardens for no other reason than that they are mostly tended by women; no one would look askance at our being there. I plucked several leafy new fronds of copper fennel as we passed and offered one to Web. Above us, a birch tree was uncurling its leaves. There were beds of rhubarb around the bench that we chose. Fat red nubs thrust through the earth. On a few plants, the crinkling leaves were opening to the light. The plants would need boxing soon, if the stems were to grow long enough to be useful. I mentioned this to Web.

He scratched his trimmed gray beard thoughtfully. There was a touch of merriment in his pale eyes as he asked me, "And rhubarb was what you wished to consult me about?" He put the end of the fennel stem between his teeth and nibbled at it as he waited for me to answer.

"No, of course not. And I know you are a busy man, so I will not keep you any longer than I must. I'm concerned about a boy who has been placed in my care for lessons and weapons training. His name is Swift, and he is the son of a man who was once the Stablemaster here at Buckkeep, Burrich. But he has parted ways with his father in a dispute over Swift's use of the Wit, and so calls himself Swift Witted now."

"Ah!" Web gave a great nod. "Yes, I know the lad. He often comes to the edge of the circle when I am telling tales at night, yet I do not recall that he has ever spoken to me."

"I see. Well, I have urged him not just to listen to you, but to talk with you, as well. I am troubled over how he sees his magic. And how he speaks of it. He is untrained in it, as his father did not approve of the Wit at all. Yet his ignorance does not make him cautious, but reckless. He reveals his Wit to all he meets, thrusting it under their noses and insisting they acknowledge it. I have warned him that, Queen's decree or no, there are many folk in Buckkeep who still find the Wit distasteful. He does not seem to grasp that a change in a law cannot force a change in people's hearts. He flaunts his Wit in a way that may be a danger to him. And soon I must leave him on his own, when I depart with the Prince. I have five days left in which to instill some caution in him."

I ran out of breath and Web commiserated. "I can see where that would make you very uncomfortable."

It was not the comment I would have expected, and for a moment I was taken aback. "It isn't just that I feel he endangers himself when he reveals his magic," I excused myself. "There is more to it. He speaks openly of choosing an animal to bond with, and soon. He has sought my aid in this, asking if I would take him through the stables. I've told him I don't think that is the proper way of doing it, that there must be more to such a bond than that, but he does not listen. He brushes me off, telling me that if I had the Wit Magic, I'd understand better his need to end his isolation." I tried to keep the irritation out of my voice as I added this last.

Web gave a small cough and a wry smile. "And I can see why that would be very galling to you, as well."

His words sent a shivering across my back. They were freighted with a weight of unspoken knowledge. I tried to ignore it. "That's why I've come to you, Web. Will you speak to him? I think you could best teach him how to accept his magic without letting it overwhelm him. You could speak to him about why he should wait to bond, and why he should be more conservative in how swiftly he shares the information that he is Witted. In short, you could teach him to carry his magic as a man would, with dignity and privacy."

Web leaned back on the bench. The fronds of his fennel danced as he chewed the stem thoughtfully. Then he said quietly, "All of those things, FitzChivalry, you could teach him as well as I, if you have a mind to." He regarded me steadily, and on this bright spring day, blue seemed to predominate over the gray in his eyes. His look was not cold and yet I felt pierced by ice. I took a slow and steadying breath. I kept still, hoping not to betray myself as I pondered how he could know. Who had told him? Chade? Kettricken? Dutiful?

His logic was relentless as he added, "Of course, your words would only carry weight with him if you told him that you too are Witted. And they would have the most effect if you told him your true name, as well, and your relationship to his father. Yet he might be a bit young to share that secret fully."

For two breaths longer, he regarded me, and then looked aside. I thought it was a mercy until he added, "Your wolf still looks out of your eyes. You think that if you stand perfectly still, no one will see you. That won't work with me, young man."

I rose. I longed to deny my name, yet his certainty was such that I knew I'd only look a fool in his eyes if I did so. And I did not want Master Web to consider me foolish. "I scarcely think myself a young man," I rebuked him. "And perhaps you are right. I shall speak to Swift myself."

"You're younger than I am," Web said to my retreating back. "And in more ways than years, Master Badgerlock." I paused and glanced back at him. "Swift is not the only one who needs to be instructed in his magic," he said in a voice pitched for my ears alone. "But I will not teach anyone who does not come to me and ask for it. Tell that to the lad, too. That he must come to me and ask. I will not impose learning on him."

I knew I was dismissed and again I walked away from him. Then I heard his voice lifted again, as if in casual observation. "Holly would love a day such as this. Clear skies and a light wind. How her hawk would soar!"

And there was the answer given to my unasked question, and I surmised that was a true show of mercy. He would not let me wonder who at Buckkeep had betrayed my secret, but told me plain that my true name had come to him from another source. Holly, widow to Black Rolf, who had tried to teach me the Wit so many years ago. I continued walking as if his words were no more than a pleasantry, but now I had to wonder a more unsettling thing. Had Holly passed her knowledge directly to Web, or had it traveled from tongue to tongue to reach him? How many Witted also knew who I really was? How pointed a piece of knowledge was that? How could it be used against the Farseer throne?

I went about my tasks that day with a distracted air. I had weapons drill with my guard company, and my preoccupation meant that I came away from it with more bruises than usual. There was also a final fitting for the new uniforms we all would wear. I had recently become a member of the newly created Prince's Guard. Chade had arranged that not only was I accepted to this elite group, but that my lot had been drawn to accompany the Prince on his quest. The uniform of the Prince's Guard was blue on blue, with the Farseer buck insignia on the breast. I hoped that mine would be finished in time for me to privately add the small extra pockets I would require. I had declared that I was no longer an assassin for the Farseer reign. That did not mean I had surrendered the tools of that trade.

I was fortunate that I had no meetings with Chade or Dutiful in the afternoon, for either one of them would have immediately sensed that something was amiss. I knew that I would tell Chade; it was information he definitely needed to have. But I did not wish to divulge it to him just yet. First, I would try to work it through in my mind, and see how it unfolded.

And the best way for me to do that, I knew, was to put my thoughts on other matters. When I went down to Buckkeep Town that evening, I decided to give myself a reprieve from the Outislander tavern and spend some time with Hap. I needed to tell my adopted son that I'd been "chosen" to accompany the Prince, and to make an early farewell to him in case there was no time for a later one. I hadn't seen the lad in some time, and there were few enough days left before I sailed that I decided I would be justified in begging a full evening of Hap's company from Master Gindast. I had been very pleased with his progress on his training since he had settled into the apprentices' quarters and earnestly devoted himself to his schooling. Master Gindast was one of the finest woodworkers in Buckkeep Town. I still counted myself fortunate that, with a nudge from Chade, he had agreed to apprentice Hap. If the boy acquitted himself well there, he had a bright future in any part of the Six Duchies where he chose to settle.

I arrived just as the apprentices were preparing for their evening meal. Master Gindast was not present, but one of the senior journeymen released Hap to me. I wondered at his surly granting of the wish, but put it down to some personal problem of his own. Yet Hap did not seem as delighted to see me as he might have. It took him a long time to fetch his cloak, and as we left, he walked silently beside me.

"Hap, is all well?" I asked him at last.

"I think it is," he replied in a low voice. "But doubtless you will disagree. I have given Master Gindast my word that I would regulate myself in this matter. It insults me that he still thought he needed to send word for you to come and rebuke me, as well."

"I have no idea what you are talking about," I told him, striving to keep my voice level even as my heart sank into my boots. I could not help but think that I had to sail in only a few days. Was whatever-this-was something I could mend in such a short space? Disturbed, I blurted my news. "My name was chosen from among the guards. Soon I leave with the Prince, to accompany him on his mission to the Out Islands. I came to tell you that, and to spend an evening with you before I had to leave."

He gave a snort of disgust, but I think it was aimed at himself. He had betrayed his problem to me, whereas if he had been a bit more circumspect, he could have kept it private. I think that outweighed any initial reaction to my news. I walked on beside him, waiting for him to speak.

The streets of Buckkeep Town were fairly quiet tonight. The light had begun to linger longer at the end of the bright spring days, but folk were also rising earlier and putting in more hours, and hence more likely to seek sleep while light was still in the sky. When Hap kept his silence, I finally offered, "The Dog and Whistle is down this way. It's a pleasant place for food and good beer. Shall we go?"

His eyes didn't meet mine as he countered me with, "I'd rather go to the Stuck Pig, if it's all the same to you."

"It isn't," I said in a determinedly pleasant voice. "It's too close to Jinna's house, and you know she goes there some evenings. You also know that she and I have come to a parting of the ways. I'd rather not encounter her tonight, if I can avoid it." The Stuck Pig, I had also belatedly discovered, was considered a gathering place for Witted folk, though no one made that accusation openly. It accounted for some of the tavern's shoddy reputation; the rest of it was because it was, in truth, a rather dirty and poorly kept place.

"Isn't your objection actually that you know Svanja lives close by there?" he asked me pointedly.

I suppressed a sigh. I turned my steps in the direction of the Stuck Pig. "I thought she had thrown you over for her sailor boy with his pretty gifts."

He flinched, but kept his voice level when he replied. "So it seemed to me, also. But after Reften went back to sea, she was free to seek me out and speak the truth of it. Her parents arranged and approve of that match. That arrangement is why they so disliked me."

"Then they thought you knew she was promised, and continued to see her anyway?"

"I suppose so." Again, that neutral voice.

"A shame she never thought to tell her parents she was deceiving you. Or to tell you of this Reften."

"It wasn't like that, Tom." A low growl of anger crept into his voice. "She didn't set out to deceive anyone. She thought, at first, that we would be only friends, and so there was no reason to tell me she was spoken for. After we began to have feelings for one another, she was afraid to speak, for fear I might think her faithless to him. But in reality, she had never given her heart to him; all he had received was her parents' word."

"And when he came back?"

He took a deep breath and refused to lose his temper. "It's complicated, Tom. Her mother's health is not good, and her heart is set on the match. Reften is the son of her childhood friend. And her father does not want to have to take back his word after he agreed to the marriage. He's a proud man. So, when Reften came back to town, she thought it best to pretend that all was well for the brief time he was here."

"And now that he is gone, she's come back to you."

"Yes." He bit the word off as if there were no more to say.

I set my hand to his shoulder as we walked. The muscles there were bunched, hard as stone. I asked the question that I had to ask. "And what will happen when he comes back to port again, with gifts and fond notions that she is his sweetheart?"

"Then she'll tell him that she loves me and is mine now," he said in a low voice. "Or I will." For a time we walked in his silence. He did not relax under my hand but at least he did not shrug it off. "You think I'm foolish," he said at last as we turned down the street that went past the Stuck Pig. "You think she is toying with me, and that when Reften comes home, she will again throw me aside."

I tried to make my voice say the hard words softly. "That does seem possible to me."

He sighed and his shoulder slouched under my hand. "To me, also. But what am I to do, Tom? I love her. Svanja and no other. She is the other half of me, and when we are together, we make a whole that I cannot doubt. Walking with you now and telling you of it, I sound gullible, even to myself. So I voice doubts, like your own. But when I am with her and she looks into my eyes, I know she is telling me the truth."

We tramped a bit farther in silence. Around us, the town was changing its pace, relaxing from the day's labors into a time for shared meals and family companionship. Tradesmen were closing their shutters for the evening. Smells of cooking wafted out of homes. Taverns beckoned to such as Hap and me. I wished vainly that we were simply going to sit down to a hearty meal together. I had thought him in safe waters, and had comforted myself with that whenever I thought of leaving Buckkeep. I asked a question both inevitable and foolish. "Is there any chance that you could stop seeing her for a time?"

"No." He answered without even drawing breath. He looked ahead as he spoke. "I can't, Tom. I can no more put her aside than I could give up breath or water or food."

Then I spoke my fear honestly. "I worry that while I am gone, you will get into trouble with this, Hap. Not just a fistfight with Reften over the girl, though that would be bad enough. Master Hartshorn has no fondness for either of us. If he believes you have compromised his daughter, he may seek revenge on you."

"I can deal with her father," he said gruffly, and I felt his shoulders stiffen again.

"How? Take a beating from him? Or beat him insensible? Remember, I've fought him, Hap. He'll neither cry for mercy, nor grant it. If the City Guard had not intervened, our fight would have continued until one of us was unconscious, or dead. Yet even if it doesn't come to that, there are other things he could do. He could go to Gindast and complain that his apprentice lacks morality. Gindast would take that seriously, would he not? From what you have said, your master is not well pleased with you just now. He could turn you out. Or Hartshorn could simply turn his own daughter out into the streets. Then what?"

"Then I take her in," Hap replied grimly. "And I care for her."

"How?"

"Somehow. I don't know how, I just know that I would!" The anger in his furious reply was not for me, but for himself, that he could not think of a way to refute the question. I judged that it was a good time to hold silence. My boy could not be dissuaded from his path. If I sought to do so, he'd only turn away from me to pursue her.

We walked on, and as we drew closer to the Stuck Pig, I had to ask, "You don't meet her openly, do you?"

"No," he answered reluctantly. "I walk past her house. She watches for me, but we pretend not to notice one another. But if she sees me, she makes an excuse of some kind and slips out later in the evening to meet me."

"At the Stuck Pig?"

"No, of course not. There's a place we discovered, where we can be alone."

And so I felt a part of their deception as I walked with Hap past Svanja's house. I hadn't known where she lived until now. As we passed the cottage, Svanja was sitting on the step with a small boy. I hadn't realized that she had siblings. She immediately rose and went inside with the child, as if snubbing Hap and me. We walked on to the Stuck Pig.

I was reluctant to enter, but Hap went ahead of me and so I followed. The innkeeper gave us a brusque nod. I was surprised he didn't order me out. The last time I'd been there, I'd brawled with Hartshorn and the City Guard had been called. Perhaps that was not so unusual an event there. From the way the inn boy greeted Hap, he'd become a regular. He took a corner table as if it were his accustomed place. I set out coin on the table, and in response we soon had two mugs of beer and two plates of indifferent fish stew. The bread that came with it was hard. Hap didn't appear to notice. We spoke little as we ate, and I sensed him tracking time, estimating how long it would take Svanja to make an excuse and then slip off to their meeting place.

"I was minded to give Gindast some money to hold for

you, so that you'd have funds of your own as you needed them while I'm gone."

Hap shook his head, mouth full. A moment later he said quietly, "That wouldn't work. Because if he was displeased with me for any reason, he'd withhold it."

"And you expect your master to be displeased with you?"

For a time he didn't answer. Then he said, "He thinks he needs to regulate me as if I were ten years old. My evenings should be my own, to do as I please. You've paid for my apprenticeship, and I do my work during the day. That should be all that concerns him. But no, he would have me sit about with the other apprentices, mending socks until his wife shouts at us to stop wasting candles and go to sleep. I don't need that sort of supervision, and I won't tolerate it."

"I see." We ate more insipid food in silence. I struggled with a decision. Hap was too proud to ask me to give the money to him directly. I could refuse him to express my disapproval. Certainly I didn't like what he was doing. I foresaw it would lead him to trouble . . . and if that trouble came while I was gone, he might need money to extricate himself. Certainly I'd seen enough of the Buckkeep Town gaol to know I didn't want my boy to spend time there, unable to pay a fine. Yet if I left him money, would I not perhaps be giving him enough rope to hang himself? Would it all go for gifts to impress his sweetheart and tavern meals and drink? It was possible.

It came down to this: did I trust this boy that I'd raised for the last seven years? He had already set aside much of what I had taught him. Yet so Burrich would have said of me at that age, if he had known how much I used the Wit. So would Chade have said, if he'd known of his private excursions into town. Yet here I sat, very much still the man they had made me. So much so that I would not show a purse of coins in a tavern so ill-reputed as this one. "Then I shall simply give you the money and trust you to be wise with it," I said quietly.

Hap's face lit up, and I knew it was for the trust I offered him, not the coins. "Thank you, Tom. I'll be careful with it."

After that, our meal went more pleasantly. We spoke of my upcoming trip. He asked how long I would be gone. I told him I didn't know. Hap asked if my journey would be dangerous. All had heard that the Prince was setting forth to kill a dragon in the Narcheska's honor. I mildly ridiculed the idea that we would find any such beast in the ice of the Out Islands. And I told him, truthfully, that I expected to be bored and uncomfortable for much of the journey, but not at risk. I was, after all, only a minor guardsman, honored to be chosen to accompany the Prince. Doubtless I would spend most of my time waiting for someone to tell me what to do. We laughed together over that, and I hoped he had taken my point: that obeying one's superior was not a childish limit, but a duty that any man could expect in his life. But if he saw it in that light, he made no mention of it.

We did not linger over our meal. The food didn't warrant it and I sensed that Hap was anticipating his assignation with Svanja. Whenever I thought of it, my heart sank, but I knew there was no turning him aside from it. So when our hasty meal was finished, we pushed away our greasy plates and left the Stuck Pig. We walked together for a short time, watching evening creep up on Buckkeep Town. When I was a boy, the streets would have been near empty at this hour. But Buckkeep Town had grown and the duskier trades of the city had increased. At a well-traversed crossroad women lingered on the streets, walking slowly. They eyed the passing men, speaking desultorily to one another as they waited to be approached. There Hap halted. "I have to go now," he said quietly.

I nodded, forbearing to make any comment. I took the purse I'd prepared out of my jerkin and slipped it to him.

"Don't carry it all about with you, but only what you think you'd need that day. Do you have a safe place to put the rest?"

"Thank you, Tom." He took it gravely, tucking it inside his shirt. "I do. At least, Svanja does. I'll have her keep it for me."

It took every bit of control and deception that I'd ever learned to keep my misgivings from showing in my eyes or on my face. I nodded as if I had no doubt all would be well. Then I embraced him briefly as he bid me to be careful on my journey, and we parted.

I found I did not want to return to Buckkeep Castle yet. It had been an unsettling day, between Web's words and Hap's news. And the food I had eaten at the Stuck Pig had more dismayed than satisfied my belly. I suspected it would not stay with me long. So I turned a different way from Hap lest he think I followed him and wandered for a time through the streets of Buckkeep. Restlessness vied with loneliness. I found myself passing the tailor shop that had once been a chandlery where Molly had worked. I shook my head at myself and deliberately set out for the docks. I wandered up and down them for a time, tallying to myself how many Out Island ships, how many from Bingtown or Jamaillia and beyond, and how many were our own vessels. The docks were longer and more crowded than my boyhood recollection of them, and the number of foreign ships was equal to our own. As I passed a vessel, I heard an Outislander shout a gruff jest to his fellows, and their raucous replies. I was pleased with myself that I could follow their words.

The ships that would bear us to the Out Islands were tied up at the main docks. I slowed to stare up at their bare rigging. The loading of them had ceased for the night, but men kept watch on their decks by lantern light. The ships looked large now; I knew how small they would become after a few days at sea. In addition to the ship that would carry the Prince and his selected entourage, there were three ships that would carry lesser nobles and their baggage, and a cargo of gifts and trade items. The ship Prince Dutiful would sail on was called the *Maiden's Chance*. She was an older ship, proven swift and seaworthy. Now that she had been scrubbed and her paint and canvas completely renewed, she looked like a new creation. As a merchant vessel, built for carrying cargo, speed had been traded for capacity and stability: her hull was as rounded as the belly of a pregnant sow. Her forecastle had been enlarged to provide adequate housing for her noble guests. She looked top-heavy to me and I wondered if her master approved of the changes that had been made for Dutiful's comfort. I would travel aboard her, along with the rest of the Prince's Guard. I wondered idly if Chade would wrangle quarters for me, or if I would have to make do with whatever space I could claim for myself as guardsmen usually did. Useless to wonder, I told myself. Whatever would be would be, and I'd have to deal with it as it came. I sourly wished there was no journey to make.

I could recall a time when a journey anywhere was something I anticipated eagerly. I'd awake on the day of departure at dawn, full of enthusiasm for the adventure to come. I'd be ready to depart when others were still crawling sleepily from their blankets.

I didn't know when I had lost that ebullience for travel, but it was definitely gone. I felt not excitement but a growing dread. Just the thought of the sea voyage to come, the days spent in cramped quarters as we sailed east and north, was enough to make me wish I could back out of the expedition. I did not even allow my mind to stray beyond it, into the doubtful welcome of the Outislanders and our extended stay in their cold and rocky region. Finding a dragon trapped in ice and chopping its head off was beyond my imagining. Near nightly, I muttered to myself over the Narcheska's strange choice of this task for the Prince to prove himself worthy of her hand. Over and over, I had tried to find a motive that would make it comprehensible. None came to me.

Now, as I walked the windy streets of Buckkeep, I prodded again at my greatest dread. Most of all, I feared that moment when the Fool would discover I had divulged his plans to Chade. Although I had done my best to mend my quarrel with the Fool, I had spent little time with him since then. In part, I avoided him lest some look or gesture of mine betray my treachery. Yet most of it was the Fool's doing.

Lord Golden, as he now styled himself, had recently changed his demeanor considerably. Previously, his wealth had allowed him to indulge himself in an extravagant wardrobe and exquisite possessions. Now, he flaunted it in ways more vulgar. He disposed of coin like a servant shaking dirt from a duster. In addition to his chambers in the keep, he now rented the entire upper floor of the Silver Key, a town inn much favored by the well-to-do. This fashionable establishment clung like a limpet to a steep site that would have been considered a poor building location in my boyhood days. Yet from that lofty perch, one could gaze far out over both the town and the water beyond.

Within that establishment, Lord Golden kept his own cook and staff. Rumors of the rare wines and exotic dishes he served made his table clearly superior to the Queen's own. While he dined with his chosen friends, the finest of Six Duchies minstrels and entertainers vied for his attention. It was not unusual to hear that he had invited a minstrel, a tumbler, and a juggler to perform simultaneously, in different corners of the dining chamber. Such meals were invariably preceded and followed by games of chance, with the stakes set sufficiently high that only the wealthiest and most spendthrift of young nobles could keep pace with him. He began his days late and his nights finished with the dawn.

It was also rumored that his palate was not the only sense he indulged. Whenever a ship that had stopped in

Bingtown or Jamaillia or the Pirate Isles docked, it was certain to bring him a visitor. Tattooed courtesans, former Jamaillian slaves, slender boys with painted eyes, women who wore battle dress, and hard-eyed sailors came to his door, stayed closeted within his chambers for a night or three, and then departed on the ships again. Some said they brought him the finest Smoke herbs, as well as cindin, a Jamaillian vice recently come to Buckkeep. Others said they came to provide indulgence for his other "Jamaillian tastes." Those who dared to ask about his guests received only an arch look or a coy refusal to answer.

Strange to say, his excesses seemed only to increase his popularity with a certain segment of the Six Duchies aristocracy. Many a noble youth was sternly called home from Buckkeep, or received a visit from a parent suddenly concerned about the amount of coin it was taking to keep a youngster at court. Amongst the more conservative, there was grumbling that the foreigner was leading Buckkeep's youth astray. But what I sensed more than disapproval was a salacious fascination with Lord Golden's excesses and immorality. One could trace the embroidery of the tales about him as they moved from tongue to tongue. Yet, at the base of each gossip tree was a root that could not be denied. Golden had moved into a realm of excess that no other had approached since Prince Regal had been alive.

I could not comprehend it and that troubled me greatly. In my lowly role of Tom Badgerlock, I could not call openly on such a lofty creature as Lord Golden, and he did not seek me out. Even when he spent the night in his Buckkeep Castle chambers, he filled them with guests and entertainers until the sky was graying. Some said he had shifted his dwelling to Buckkeep Town to be closer to those places that featured games of chance and depraved entertainment, but I suspected he had moved his lair to be away from Chade's observations, and that his foreign overnight guests were not for his physical amusement but rather spies and messengers from his friends to the south. What tidings did they bring him, I wondered, and why was he so intent on debasing his reputation and spending his fortune? What news did he give them to bear back to Bingtown and Jamaillia?

But those questions were like my ponderings on the Narcheska's motivation for setting Prince Dutiful to slay the dragon Icefyre. There were no clear answers, and they only kept my thoughts spinning wearily during hours that would have been better spent in sleep. I looked up at the latticed windows of the Silver Key. My feet had brought me here with no guidance from my head. The upper chambers were well lit this night, and I could glimpse passing guests within the opulent chambers. On the sole balcony, a woman and a young man conversed animatedly. I could hear the wine in their voices. They spoke quietly at first, but then their tones rose in altercation. I knelt down as if fastening my shoe and listened.

"I've a wonderful opportunity to empty Lord Verdant's purse, but only if I have the money to set on the table to wager. Give me what you owe me, now!" the young man demanded of her.

"I can't." The woman spoke in the careful diction of one who refuses to be drunk. "I don't have it, laddie. But I soon will. When Lord Golden pays me what he owes me from his gaming yesterday, I'll get your coin to you. Had I known you were going to be so usurious about it, I never would have borrowed it from you."

The young man gave a low cry between dismay and outrage. "When Lord Golden pays you his wager? That's as well as to say never. All know he's fallen behind in his debts. Had I known you were borrowing from me to wager against him, I'd never have loaned it."

"You flaunt your ignorance," she rebuked him after a moment of shocked silence. "All know his wealth is bottomless. When the next ship comes in from Jamaillia, he will have coin enough to pay us all."

From the shadows at the corner of the inn, I watched and listened intently.

"If the next ship comes in from Jamaillia...which I doubt, from the way the war is going for them...it would have to be the size of a mountain to bring enough coin to pay all he owes now! Haven't you heard that he is even behind on his rent, and that the landlord only lets him stay on because of the other business he brings here?"

At his words, the woman turned from him angrily, but he reached out to seize her wrist. "Listen, you stupid wench! I warn you, I won't wait long for what is owed me. You'd best find a way to pay me, and tonight." He looked her up and down and added huskily, "Not all of it need be in coin."

"Ah, Lady Heliotrope. There you are. I've been looking for you, you little minx! Have you been avoiding me?"

The leisurely tones of Lord Golden wafted down to me as he emerged onto the balcony. The light from behind him glanced off his gleaming hair and limned his slender form. He stepped to the edge of the balcony. Leaning lightly on the rail, he gazed out over the town below him. The man immediately released the woman's wrist and she stepped back from him with a toss of her head and went to join Lord Golden at his vantage point. She cocked her head at him and sounded like a tattling child as she complained, "Dear Lord Golden, Lord Capable has just told me that there is little chance you will pay me our wager. Do tell him how wrong he is!"

Lord Golden lifted one elegant shoulder. "How rumors do fly, if one is but a day or so late in honoring a friendly wager. Surely one should never bet more than one can afford to lose...or afford to do without until paid. Don't you agree, Lord Capable?"

"Or, perhaps, that one should not wager more than one can immediately afford to pay," Lord Capable suggested snidely.

"Dear, dear. Would not that limit our gaming to whatever a man could carry in his pockets? Small stakes, those. In any case, sweet lady, why do you think I was seeking you, if not to make good our bet? Here, I think, you will find a good part of what I owe you. I do hope you won't mind if it is in pearls rather than coin."

She tossed her head, dismissing the surly Lord Capable. "I don't mind at all. And if there are those that do, well, then they should simply be content to wait for crass coin. Gaming should not be about money, dear Lord Golden."

"Of course not. The risk is the relish, as I say, and the winning is the pleasure. Don't you agree, Capable?"

"And if I did not, would it do me any good?" Capable asked sourly. He and I had both noticed that the woman made no immediate effort to pay him *his* due.

Lord Golden laughed aloud, the melodic sound cutting the cool air of the spring night. "Of course not, dear fellow. Of course not! Now, I hope both of you will step within and sample a new wine with me. Standing out here in this chill wind, a man could catch his death of cold. Surely friends can find a warmer place to speak privately?"

The others had already turned to reenter the well-lit chamber. Yet Lord Golden paused a moment longer and gazed pensively at the spot where I had thought myself so well concealed. Then he inclined his head slightly to me before he turned and departed.

I waited a few moments longer, then stepped from the shadows. I felt annoyed with him because he had noticed me so effortlessly and because his offer to meet me somewhere else had been too vague for me to comprehend. Yet as much as I longed to sit down and talk with him, greater was my dread that he would uncover my treachery. Better, I decided, to avoid my friend than have to confront that in his eyes. I strode sullenly through the dark streets, alone. The night wind on the back of my neck chilled me as it pushed me back toward Buckkeep Castle.

chapter III

TREPIDATION

Then Hoquin was enraged with those who questioned his treatment of his Catalyst, and he resolved to make a show of his authority over her. "Child she may be," he declared. "And yet the burden is hers and it must be borne. And nothing must make her question her role, or sway her to save herself at the expense of condemning the world."

And then he required of her that she go to her parents, and deny them both, saying, "I have no mother, I have no father. I am only the Catalyst of the White Prophet Hoquin." And further she must say, "I give you back the name you gave me. I am Redda no longer, but Wild-eye, as Hoquin has made me." For he had named her thus for her one eye that always peered to one side.

This she did not wish to do. She wept as she went, she wept as she spoke the words, and she wept as she returned. For two days and two nights, the tears did not cease to flow from her eyes, and he allowed her this mourning. Then Hoquin said to her, "Wild-eye, cease your tears."

And she did. Because she must.

        ∝ SCRIBE CATEREN, OF THE WHITE PROPHET HOQUIN

When a journey is twelve days away, that can seem plenty of time to put all in readiness. Even at seven days away, it seems possible that all preparations will be completed on time. But as the days dwindle to five and four and then three, the passing hours burst like bubbles, and tasks that seemed simple suddenly become complex. I needed to pack all I would require to be assassin, spy, and Skillmaster, while appearing to carry only the ordinary gear of a guardsman. I had farewells to make, some simple and some difficult.

The only part of the trip that I could look forward to with pleasure was our eventual return to Buckkeep. Dread can weary a man more than honest labor, and mine built with each passing day. Three nights before we were to sail, I felt exhausted and half-sick with it. That tension woke me long before dawn and denied me any more sleep. I sat up. The embers in the tower room's fireplace illuminated little more than the shovel and poker leaning to one side of the hearth's mouth. Then my eyes slowly adjusted to the gloom of the windowless chamber. It was a place familiar to me from my days as the assassin's apprentice. Little had I thought that I would ever make it my own. I rose from Chade's old bed, leaving behind the nightmare-rucked blankets and the warmth of sleep.

I padded over to the fireplace and added a small log. I hung a pot of water from the hook and swung it over the low flames. I thought of putting on a kettle for tea but felt too weary still. I was too worried to sleep and too tired to admit that I was now awake for the day. It was a miserable place, one that had become achingly familiar as our departure date grew closer. I kindled a taper from the fire's dancing flames. I lit the waiting candles in the branched candelabrum on the scarred old worktable. The chair was cold beneath me as I sat down with a groan.

I sat at the worktable in my nightshirt and stared at the various charts I had assembled last night. They were all of Outislander origin, but so varied in size and composition that it was difficult to see their relationship to one another. It is their peculiar custom that charts of the sea can only be made on sea mammal or fish skin. I suspected these charts had been cured in urine, for they had a peculiar and clinging odor. Out Island custom also decrees that each island must be presented as one of their god's runes, on its own chart. This means that there were curious flourishes and fillips on the representations that had nothing to do with the island's physical characteristics. These additions had great significance to an Outislander, denoting what anchorage or currents might be present, and if the "luck" of an island were good, bad, or neutral. To me, the embellishments were only confusing. The four scrolls I had obtained were drawn by different hands and to different scales. I had spread them out on the table in their approximate relation to each other yet they still gave me only a hazy idea of the distance we would cross. I traced our route from chart to chart, with the burns and circles on the old table's top representing the unknown dangers and seas that lay between them.

We would sail first from Buckkeep Town to Skyrene. It was not the largest of the Out Islands, but it boasted the best port and the most arable land of the isles, and hence the largest population. Peottre, mother-brother to the Narcheska, had spoken of Zylig with disdain. He had explained to Chade and Kettricken that Zylig, the busiest Out Island port, had become a haven for all sorts of folk. Foreigners came there to visit and trade, and in Peottre's opinion, far too many stayed, bringing their crude customs with them. It was also a supply port for the vessels that came north to hunt sea mammals for hides and oil, and those rough crews had corrupted many an Outislander youth and maiden. He made Zylig sound like a dingy and dangerous port town with the flotsam and jetsam of humanity making up a good part of its population.

There we would dock first. Arkon Bloodblade's mothershouse was on the other side of Skyrene, but they had a stronghouse in Zylig for when they visited there. Here we would meet with the Hetgurd, a loose alliance of Outislander headmen, for a discussion of our quest. Chade and I were both leery of that event. Chade anticipated resistance to the marriage alliance, and perhaps to our quest. To some Outislanders, Icefyre was a guardian spirit to those islands. Our quest to chop off his head might not be well received.

When our meeting at Zylig was complete, we would transfer from our Six Duchies vessel to an Outislander ship, one more suited to the shallow waters we must next negotiate, with a captain and crew that knew the channels. They would take us to Wuislington on Mayle, the home island for Elliania and Peottre's Narwhal Clan. Dutiful would be presented to her family and welcomed to her mothershouse. There would be celebrations of the betrothal, and advice for the Prince on the task that lay before him. After our visits to their home village, we would return to Zylig and there take ship for Aslevjal and the dragon trapped in a glacier.

Impulsively, I swept the charts aside. Folding my arms, I put my brow down on my crossed wrists and stared into the darkness trapped there. My guts were cramped with dread. It wasn't just the voyage ahead. There were other hazards to be negotiated before we even set foot on the ship. The Skill coterie had still not mastered their magic. I suspected that despite my warnings Dutiful and his friend Lord Civil were using the Wit Magic, and that the Prince would be caught. Too often, the openly Witted were his companions these days. Even if the Queen had decreed there was no shame to possessing such magic, the common folk and her nobles still despised practitioners of the Beast Magic. He risked himself, and perhaps the betrothal negotiations. I had no idea how the Outislanders felt about the Wit Magic.

Around and around, my thoughts chased themselves with no escape from worry. Hap was still dangling after Svanja, and I dreaded leaving him to his own devices. The few times my dreams had brushed Nettle's, she had seemed both secretive and anxious. Swift seemed to become more intractable by the day. I'd be relieved to leave that responsibility, but worried what would become of him in my absence. I still hadn't told Chade that Web knew who I was, or discussed that information with Web. My desperate longing for someone to confide in only made me more aware of how isolated I had become. I missed my wolf Nighteyes as I would miss my heart's beating.

When my forehead thumped solidly against the table, I came back to wakefulness abruptly. The sleep that had evaded me in my bed had captured me sitting at the worktable. With a sigh, I sat up straight, rolled my shoulders, and resigned myself to the day. There were tasks to accomplish, and little time to do them in. Once we were on the ship, I'd have plenty of time to sleep, and even more time for fruitless worrying. Few things were as boring to me as an extended journey at sea.

I rose and stretched. It would soon be dawn. Time to get dressed and go to the Queen's Garden for the morning's lesson with Swift. The water in the pot had almost boiled away while I dozed. I mixed it with cold in the washbasin, made my ablutions, and dressed for the day. A plain leather tunic went on over my shirt and trousers of Buck blue. I pulled on soft boots and forced my cropped hair into a stubby warrior's tail.

After my session with Swift, I'd be meeting the Skill coterie for another shared lesson. I wasn't anticipating it with pleasure. As each day passed, we made improvement, but it was not sufficient to satisfy Chade. He saw his slow progress as failure. His frustration had become a palpable and discordant force whenever we came together. Yesterday, I had noticed that Thick feared to meet the old man's eyes and that Dutiful's pleasant expression had a fixed desperation to it. I had spoken privately to Chade, asking him to be more self-forgiving and more tolerant of the rest of the coterie's vulnerabilities. He had taken my request as a rebuke and only become more grimly self-contained in his fury. It had not lessened any of the tension.

"Fitz," someone said softly, and I spun, startled. The Fool stood framed in the doorway that was usually concealed by the wine rack. He could move more silently than anyone else I had ever known. Coupled with that, he was undetectable to my Wit-sense. Sensitive as I was to the presence of other living beings, he alone had the ability to take me completely by surprise. He knew it, and I think he enjoyed it. He smiled apologetically as he advanced into the room. His tawny hair was bound sleekly back and his face was innocent of Lord Golden's paint. Bared, his face was more bronzed than I had ever seen it. He wore Golden's foppish dressing gown but it seemed a bizarre costume when he dropped the lord's elaborate mannerisms.

Never before had I known him to venture here without an invitation. "What are you doing here?" I blurted out, and then added more courteously, "Though I am glad to see you."

"Ah. I had wondered if you would be. When I saw you lurking beneath my window, I thought you wanted to meet. I sent Chade an oblique message for you the next day, but heard no response. So I decided to make it easy for you."

"Yes. Well. Do come in." His sudden appearance, coupled with the disclosure that Chade had not relayed his message to me, rattled me. "It's not the best time for me; I'm supposed to be meeting Swift soon, in the Queen's Garden. But I've a few moments to spare. Er, should I put on the kettle for tea?"

"Yes, please. If you've the time. I don't wish to intrude. I know we've all much to do in these last few days." Then his words stopped abruptly and he stared at me, the smile fading from his face. "Listen to how awkward we've become. So polite and so careful not to give offense." He drew a long breath, then spoke with uncharacteristic bluntness. "After I sent a message and heard nothing back, the silence began to trouble me. I know we've had our differences lately. I thought we had mended them, but I began to have doubts. This morning, I decided I'd confront them. So here I am. Did you want to see me, Fitz? Why didn't you answer my message?"

His sudden change in tone further unbalanced me. "I didn't receive your message. Perhaps Chade misunderstood or forgot; he has had many concerns lately."

"And the other night, when you came to my window?" He walked over to the hearth, dippered fresh water into the kettle from the bucket and put it back over the flame. As he knelt to poke up the fire and add a bit of wood, I felt grateful I didn't have to meet his eyes.

"I was just strolling about Buckkeep Town, chewing over my own problems. I hadn't really planned to try to see you. My feet just carried me that way."

It sounded awkward and stupid, but he nodded quietly. The awareness of our mutual discomfort was a wall between us. I had done my best to patch our quarrel, but the memory of that rift was still fresh with both of us. Would he think I avoided his eyes to hide some hidden anger from him? Or would he guess at the guilt I tried to conceal?

"Your own problems?" he asked quietly as he rose, dusting his hands together, and I was glad to seize on the topic. Telling him of my woes with Hap seemed by far the safest thing we could discuss.

And so I confided my worries about my son to him, and in that telling, regained our familiarity. I found tea herbs for the bubbling water, and toasted some bread that was left over from my last night's repast. He listened well, as he bundled my charts and notes to one end of the table. By the time my words had run out, he was pouring steaming tea from a pot into two cups that I had set out. The ritual of putting out food reminded me of how easily we had always worked together. Yet somehow that hollowed me even more when I thought of how I deceived him. I wished to keep him away from Aslevjal because he believed he would die there; Chade aided me because he did not want the Fool interfering in the Prince's quest. Yet the result was the same. When the day came for us to sail, the Fool would suddenly discover that he was not to be one of the party. And it was my doing.

Thus my thoughts wrapped me, and silence fell as we took our places. He lifted his cup, sipped from it, and then said, "It isn't your fault, Fitz. He has made a decision and no words or acts of yours will change it now." For one brief instant, he seemed to be replying to my thoughts, and the hair stood up on the back of my neck because he knew me so well. Then he added, "Sometimes all a father can do is stand by and witness the disaster, and then pick up the pieces."

I found my tongue and replied, "My worry, Fool, is that I won't be here to witness it, or to pick up the pieces. What if he gets into real trouble, and there's no one to step in on his behalf?"

He held his teacup in both hands and looked at me over it. "Is there no one staying behind that you can ask to watch over him?"

I suppressed an impulsive urge to say, "How about you?" I shook my head. "No one that I know well enough. Kettricken will be here, of course, but it would hardly be appropriate to ask the Queen to play such a role to a guardsman's son. Even if Jinna and I were still on good terms, I no longer trust her judgment." In dismay, I added, "Sometimes it's a bit daunting to realize how few people I really trust. Or even know well, as Tom Badgerlock, I mean." I fell silent for a moment, considering that. Tom Badgerlock was a façade, a mask I wore daily, and yet I'd never been truly comfortable being him. I felt awkward deceiving good people such as Wim or Laurel. It made a barrier to any real friendship. "How do you do it?" I asked the Fool suddenly. "You shift who you are from year to year and place to place. Don't you ever feel regret that no one truly knows you as the person you were born?"

He shook his head slowly. "I am not the person I was born. Neither are you. I know no one who is. Truly, Fitz, all we ever know are facets of one another. Perhaps we feel as if we know one another well when we know several facets of that person. Father, son, brother, friend, lover, husband . . . a man can be all of those things, yet no one person knows him in all those roles. I watch you being Hap's father, and yet I do not know you as I knew my father, any more than I knew my father as his brother did. So. When I show myself in a different light, I do not make a pretense. Rather I bare a different aspect to the world than they have seen before. Truly, there is a place in my heart where I am forever the Fool and your playfellow. And within me there is a genuine Lord Golden, fond of good drink and well-prepared food and elegant clothing and witty speech. And so, when I show myself as him, I am deceiving no one, but only sharing a different part of myself."

"And Amber?" I asked quietly. Then I wondered that I dared venture the question.

He met my gaze levelly. "She is a facet of me. No more than that. And no less."

I wished I had not brought it up. I levered the conversation back into its old direction. "Well. That solves nothing for me, as far as finding someone to watch over Hap for me."

He nodded, and again there was a stiff little silence. I hated that we had become so self-conscious with one another but could not think how to change it. The Fool was still my old friend from my boyhood days. And he wasn't. Knowing that he had other "facets" reordered all my ideas of him. I felt trapped, wanting to stay and ease our friendship back into its old channel, yet also wanting to flee. He sensed it and excused me.

"Well, I regret that I came at a bad time. I know you have to meet Swift soon. Perhaps we shall have a chance to speak again before we sail."

"He can wait for me," I heard myself say suddenly. "It won't hurt him a bit."

"Thank you," he said.

And then again our conversation lapsed. He saved it by picking up one of the furled charts. "Is this Aslevjal?" he asked as he unrolled it on the table.

"No. That's Skyrene. Our first port of call is at Zylig."

"What's this over here?" He pointed to a curling bit of scrollwork on one shore of the island.

"Outislander ornamentation. I think. Or maybe it means a whirlpool, or a switching current or seaweed beds. I don't know. I think they see things differently from us."

"Undoubtedly so. Have you a chart of Aslevjal?"

"The smaller one, with the brown stain at one end."

He unrolled it next to the first, and glanced from one to the other. "I see what you mean," he murmured, tracing an impossibly lacy edge on the shoreline. "What do you think that is?"

"Melting glacier. At least, that is what Chade thinks."

"I wonder why he didn't give you my message."

I feigned ignorance. "As I said, perhaps he forgot. When I see him today, I'll ask him."

"Actually, I'd like to speak to him, as well. Privately. Perhaps I could come with you to your Skill-lesson today."

I felt extremely uncomfortable yet I could think of no way to wriggle out of inviting him. "That's not scheduled until afternoon today, after Swift's lessons and weapons practice."

He nodded, unconcerned. "That would be fine. I've things to tidy up in my chamber below." As if inviting me to ask why, he added, "I've nearly moved out of those rooms completely. There won't be much left for anyone to trouble about."

"So you intend to move to the Silver Key permanently?" I asked.

For a moment, his face went blank. I had surprised him. Then he shook his head slowly at me, smiling gently.

"You never believe a thing I tell you, do you, Fitz? Ah, well, perhaps that has sheltered us both through many a storm. No, my friend. I will leave my Buckkeep chambers empty when I go. And most of the wonderful possessions and furnishings in the Silver Key belong to others already, accepted as collateral for my debts. Which I don't intend to pay, of course. Once I leave Buckkeep Town, my creditors will descend like crows and pick those quarters bare. And that will be the end of Lord Golden. I won't be returning to Buckkeep. I won't be returning anywhere."

His voice did not quaver or shake. He spoke calmly and his eyes met mine. Yet his words left me feeling as if a horse had kicked me. He spoke like a man who knew he was going to die, a man tidying up all the loose ends of his life. I experienced a shift in perception. My awkwardness with him was because of our recent quarrel, and because I knew I deceived him. I did not fear his death, because I knew I had already prevented it. But his discomfort had a different root. He spoke to me as a man who knew he faced death would speak to an old friend who seemed indifferent to that fact. How callous I must have seemed to him, avoiding him all those days. Perhaps he had thought I was carefully severing the contact between us before his death could do it suddenly and painfully. The words burst from me, the only completely true thing I'd said to him that day. "Don't be stupid! I'm not going to let you die, Fool!" My throat suddenly closed. I picked up my cooling cup of tea and gulped from it hastily.

He caught his breath and then laughed, a sound like glass breaking. Tears stood in his eyes. "You believe that so thoroughly, don't you? Ah, Beloved. Of all the things I must bid farewell to, you are the one most difficult to lose. Forgive me that I have avoided you. Better, perhaps, that we make a space between us and become accustomed to it before fate forces that upon us."

I slammed my cup down. Tea splattered the table between us. "Stop talking like that! Eda and El in a tangle,

Fool! Is that why you've been squandering your fortune and living like some degenerate Jamaillian? Please tell me that you haven't spent all your windfall, that there is something left for . . . for you to come back to." And there my words halted, as I teetered at the edge of betraying myself.

He smiled strangely. "It's gone, Fitz. It's all gone, or else arranged to be bestowed. And getting rid of that much wealth has not only been a challenge, but a far greater pleasure than possessing it ever was. I've left papers that Malta is to go to Burrich. Can you imagine his face when someone hands her reins to him? I know he will value her and care for her. And for Patience, oh, you should have seen it before I sent it on its way! A cartload of scrolls and books on every imaginable topic. She'll never imagine where they came from. And I've provided for Garetha, my garden maid. I've bought her a cottage and a plot of earth to call her own, as well as left her the coin to keep herself well. That should cause a mild scandal; folks will wonder why Lord Golden left a garden girl so well endowed. But let them. She will understand and she won't care. And for Jofron, my Jhaampe friend? I've sent her a selection of fine woods and all of my carving tools. She'll value them, and recall me fondly, regardless of how abruptly I left her. She's made her reputation as a toymaker. Did you know that?"

As he divulged his generous mischief to me, he smiled and the shadow of imminent death nearly left his eyes. "Please stop talking like that," I begged him. "I promise you, I won't let you die."

"Make me no promises that can break us both, Fitz. Besides." He took a breath. "Even if you manage against all the foreordained grinding of fate to keep me alive, well, Lord Golden still must vanish. He's lived to the end of his usefulness. Once I leave here, I shall not be him again."

As he spoke on of how he'd dismantled his fortune and how his name would fade to obscurity, I felt sick. He had been determined and thorough. When we left him behind on the docks, we'd be leaving him in a difficult situation.

That Kettricken would provide for him, no matter how he had squandered his wealth, I had no doubt. I resolved to have a quiet word with her before we left, to prepare her to rescue him if need be. Then I reined my thoughts back to the conversation, for the Fool was watching me oddly.

I cleared my throat and tried to think of sensible words. "I think you are too pessimistic. If you have a coin or two left to your name, you'd best be frugal with it. Just in case I'm right and I keep you alive. And now I must go, for Swift will be waiting for me."

He nodded, rising as I did. "Will you come down to my old chambers when it is time for us to meet Chade for the Skill-lesson?"

"I suppose so," I concurred, trying not to sound reluctant.

He smiled faintly. "Good luck with Burrich's boy," he said, and left.

The teacups and charts were still on the table. I suddenly felt too weary to tidy them away, let alone hasten to my lesson with Swift. But I did, and when I arrived on the towertop garden, he was waiting for me in a square of crenellated sunlight, his back to a chill stone wall, idly playing on a pennywhistle. At his feet, several doves bobbed and pecked, and for a moment, my heart sank. As I approached, they all took flight, and the handful of grain that had drawn them scattered in their wind. Swift noticed the relief on my face. He took the whistle from his lips and looked up at me.

"You thought I was using the Wit to draw them in, and it scared you," he observed.

I made myself pause before answering him. "I was frightened for a moment," I agreed. "But not at the idea you might be using your Wit. Rather I feared that you were trying to establish a bond with one of them."

He shook his head slowly. "No. Not with a bird. I've touched minds with birds, and my thoughts glance off their minds like a stone skipping on moving water." Then he smiled condescendingly and added, "Not that I expect you to understand what I mean."

I reined myself to silence. Eventually I asked him, "Did you finish reading the scroll about King Slayer and the acquisition of Bearns?"

He nodded and we proceeded with the day's lessons, but his attitude still vexed me. I vented it on the practice court, insisting that he pick up an axe and try his strength against me before I would let him go to his bow lesson. The axes were heavier than I recalled, and even with the heads well muffled in leather wraps, the bruises from such a session are formidable. When he could no longer hold the weapon aloft, I let him go to Cresswell for his bow lesson. Then I punished myself for taking out my temper on the boy by finding a new partner, one seasoned to the axe. When I was well and truly aware of just how rusty my skills were, I left the courts and went briefly to the steams.

Cleansed of sweat and frustration, I ate a hasty meal of bread and soup in the guardroom. The talk there was loud and focused on the expedition, Outislander women and drink. Both were acclaimed strong and palatable. I tried to laugh at the jests, but the single-mindedness of the younger guards made me feel old and I was glad to excuse myself and hasten back to my workroom.

I took the secret passage from there down to the chamber I had occupied when I had been Lord Golden's servant. I listened carefully before I triggered the concealed door. All was quiet on the other side, and I hoped that the Fool was not there. But no sooner had I closed the portal to the hidden access than he opened the outer door of the room. I blinked at him. He wore a simple tunic and leggings, all in black, with low black shoes. The light from the window gilded his hair. Daylight reached past his silhouette into the tiny room and revealed my old cot heaped with possessions I had abandoned when I left his service. The wonderful sword he had given me nestled upon a mound of colorful and extravagant garments tailored for me. I gave the Fool a puzzled look. "Those are yours," he said quietly. "You should take them."

"I doubt I'd ever have occasion to dress in such styles again," I said, and then heard how hard a rejection that sounded.

"You never know," he said quietly, looking away. "Perhaps one day Lord FitzChivalry will again walk the halls of Buckkeep Castle. If he did, those colors and cuts would suit him remarkably well."

"I doubt any of that would ever come to be." That too sounded cold, so I tempered it with "But I thank you all the same. And I will take them, just in case." All the awkwardness fell on me again like a smothering curtain.

"And the sword," he reminded me. "Don't forget the sword. I know it's a bit showy for your taste but . . ."

"But it's still one of the finest weapons I've ever drawn. I'll treasure it." I tried to smooth over the slight of my first refusal. I saw now that by leaving it behind when I shifted my den, I'd hurt his feelings.

"Oh. And this. Best that this come back to you now, too." He reached to unfasten the carved wooden earring that Lord Golden always wore. I knew what was concealed within it: the freedom earring that had passed from Burrich's grandmother to Burrich, to my father, and eventually to me.

"No!" I gripped his wrist. "Stop this funeral rite! I've told you, I've no intention of letting you die."

He stood still. "Funeral rite," he whispered. Then he laughed. I could smell the apricot brandy on his breath.

"Take charge of yourself, Fool. This is so unlike you that I scarcely know how to talk to you anymore," I exclaimed in annoyance, feeling the anger that uneasiness can trigger in a man. "Can't we just relax and be ourselves in the days we have left?"

"The days we have left," he echoed. With a twist of his wrist, he effortlessly freed himself from my grip. I followed him back into his large and airy chamber. Stripped of his possessions, it seemed even larger. He went to the brandy decanter and poured more for himself, and then filled a small glass for me.

"In the days we have left before we sail," I expanded my words for him as I took the glass. I looked around the chamber. Necessities had been left in place: a table, chairs, a desk. All else was either gone or in the process of being cleared out. Rolled tapestries and rugs were fat sausages against the wall. His workroom stood open, bare and empty, all his secrets tidied away. I walked into the room, brandy in hand. My voice reverberated oddly as I said, "You've eradicated every trace of yourself."

He followed and we stood together looking out the window. "I like to leave things tidy. One must leave so many things incomplete in life that I take pleasure in finishing those I can."

"I've never known you to wallow in emotion like this before. It almost seems that you are enjoying this." I tried not to sound disgusted with him.

A strange smile twisted his mouth. Then he took a deep breath as if freed of something. "Ah, Fitz, in all the world, only you would say something like that to me. And perhaps you are right. There is drama in facing a definite end; I've never encountered these sensations before . . . yet, in a like situation, I think you would be untouched by them. You tried to explain to me once how the wolf always lived in the present and taught you to take every possible satisfaction you could from the time that you had. You learned that well. While I, who have always lived trying to define the future before I reach it, suddenly espy a place beyond which all is black. Blackness. That is what I dream of at night. And when I deliberately sit down and try to reach forward, to see where my path might go, that is all I see. Blackness."

I did not know what to say to him. I could see him trying to shake off his desperation as a dog might try to shake a wolf's grip from his throat. I took a sip of the brandy.

Apricots and the heady warmth of a summer day flooded me. I recalled our days at my cottage, the brandy on my tongue reawakening the pleasure of that simpler time. "This is very good," I said to him without thinking.

Startled, he stared at me. Then he abruptly blinked away tears and the smile he gave me was genuine. "Yes," he said quietly. "You are right. This is very good brandy, and nothing that is to come can change that. The future cannot take from us the days we have left . . . unless we let it."

He had passed some sort of crossroads within himself and was more at peace. I took another swallow of the brandy as I stared out over the hills behind Buckkeep. When I glanced at him, he was looking at me with a fondness I could not bear. He would not have looked at me so kindly if he knew how I deceived him. And yet his terror of the days to come only firmed in me my judgment that I had made the best decision for him. "A shame to rush this, but Chade and the others will be waiting."

He nodded gravely, lifted his glass in a small toast to me, and then tossed off the brandy. I followed his example and then had to stand still while the liquor spread heat throughout me. I took a deep breath, smelling and tasting apricots. "It is very good," I told him again.

He smiled small. "I'll leave all the remaining bottles to you," he offered very quietly, and then laughed when I glared at him. Yet his step seemed lighter as he followed me through the labyrinth of corridors and stairs that threaded between the walls of Buckkeep. As I moved through the dimness, I wondered how I truly would feel, did I know the hour and day of my death. Unlike Lord Golden, there would be very few possessions for me to disperse. I numbered my treasures to myself, thinking I owned nothing of significance to anyone but myself; then I realized abruptly it wasn't true. With a pang of selfish regret, I resolved to correct that. We reached the concealed entrance to the Seawatch Tower. I unseated the panel and we emerged from the hearth.

The others had already gathered so I had no opportunity for a private word to prepare Chade. Instead, as we stepped out, the Prince exclaimed with delight and came forward to welcome Lord Golden. Thick was more cautious, scowling suspiciously. Chade sent me one glance full of rebuke, and then smoothed his face and exchanged greetings with the Fool. But after that first moment of welcome, awkwardness ensued. Thick, unsettled by having a stranger in our midst, wandered aimlessly about the room instead of settling into his place at the table. I could almost see the Prince trying to fit Lord Golden, even dressed so simply, into the role of King Shrewd's Fool as he had heard the Queen tell the tale. Chade finally said, almost bluntly, "So, my dear fellow, what brings you here to join us? It's wonderful to see you, of course, but we've still much to learn and little time in which to learn it."

"I understand," the Fool replied. "But there is also little time for me to share with you what I know. So I came hoping for a bit of your time, privately, after the lesson."

"I think it's wonderful that you've come," the Prince broke in artlessly. "I think you should have been included from the first. You were the one who let us link our strength and go through you to heal Tom. You've as much a right to be a member of this coterie as anyone here."

The Fool looked touched by Dutiful's comments. He looked down at his hands, neatly gloved in black, rubbed his fingertips together almost idly, and then admitted, "I don't have any true Skill of my own. I only used what was left of the touch I'd taken from Verity. And my own knowledge of . . . Tom."

At the mention of his father's name, the Prince had perked up like a foxhound catching a scent. He leaned closer to the Fool, as if his knowledge of King Verity were something that could be absorbed from him. "Nonetheless," he assured Lord Golden, "I look forward to journeying with you. I think you may be a valuable member of this coterie, regardless of your level of Skill. Will you not join us for the day's lesson and let us explore the extent of your ability?"

I saw Chade torn. The Fool offered a possibility of greater power for the coterie, which Chade craved; but he feared the Fool's opposition to our basic mission to take the dragon's head. I wondered if there was an element of jealousy in how his eyes darted from the Fool to me. The Fool and I had always been close, and Chade knew he wielded a friend's sway over me. Yet now, more than ever, Chade desired to rule me.

His greed for the Skill won out. He added his voice to Dutiful's. "Please, Lord Golden, take a seat with us. If nothing else, you may find our efforts amusing."

"Well, then, I shall," the Fool declared almost gladly. He pulled out a chair and sat down expectantly. I wondered if any of the others could see the darker tides running behind the placid affability he presented to them. Chade and I took the chairs on either side of him while Dutiful persuaded Thick to come and join us at the table. When he was settled, four of us simultaneously took a deep breath and reached for that state of openness where we could all reach the Skill. As we did so, I had an insight both affirming and alarming. The Fool was an intruder here. In our short time of striving to become a coterie, we had achieved a unity. I had not perceived it until the Fool interrupted it. As I joined my awareness to Dutiful's and Thick's, I could feel Chade fluttering like a frantic butterfly at the edge of our union. Thick reached a reassuring hand to draw him into firmer contact with the rest of us. He belonged with us, but the Fool did not.

He was not so much a presence as an absence. I had noticed years ago that he was invisible to my Wit-sense. Now, as I deliberately reached toward him with the Skill, it was like trying to lift sun dazzle off a still pond.

"Lord Golden, do you avoid us?" Chade asked very softly.

"I am here," he replied. His words seemed to ripple softly in the room, as if I felt them as well as heard them.

"Give me your hand," Chade suggested. He set his own, palm up, on the table, outstretched toward my friend. It seemed as much a challenge as an invitation.

I felt a minuscule tickle of fear. It quivered along the Skill-bond between the Fool and me, letting me know that link still existed. Then the Fool lifted his gloved hand and set it in Chade's.

I could feel him then, but not in any way that is easy to describe. If our combined Skill was a quiet pool, then the Fool was a leaf floating upon it. "Reach for him," Chade suggested, and we all did. My awareness of the Fool's uneasiness grew stronger via our bond, but I did not think the others could sense that. They could almost touch him, but he parted before them and joined after them, as if they dragged their fingers through water. It disturbed his presence without making it accessible to them. His fear intensified. I reached along our bond surreptitiously, trying to discover what frightened him.

Possession. He did not wish to be touched in a way that might let another possess him. Belatedly I recalled what Regal and his coterie had once done to him. They had found him, through the link I shared with him, and taken a bit of his consciousness and used it against me, to spy upon me and gain knowledge of Molly's whereabouts. That betrayal still shamed and pained him. He still carried that burden of guilt for something that had happened so long ago. It stabbed deeper that soon he would know that I had betrayed him, as well.

It wasn't your fault. I offered him comfort through our link. He refused it. Then, as if from a distance and yet clear, his thoughts reached mine.

I knew it would happen. I'd foretold it myself, when I was a child. That the one closest to you would betray you. Yet I could not believe that it would be me. And so I fulfilled my own prophecy.

We all survived.

Barely.

"*Are you Skilling to one another?*" Chade asked testily. I both heard and felt his words.

I took a deeper breath and sank deeper into the Skill. "Yes," I breathed. "I can reach him. But only just. And only because we have been Skill-linked before."

"Would you have more than this?" The Fool's voice was less than a whisper. I discerned a challenge in his words, but could not understand it.

"Yes, please. Try," I bade him.

Beside me at the table, I was aware of the Fool making some small movement but my vision was unfocused on the room and I had no warning of his intentions until his hand settled on my wrist. His fingertips unerringly found their own faded gray fingerprints, left on my flesh so many years ago. His touch was gentle, but the sensation was an arrow in my heart. I physically spasmed, a speared fish, and then froze. The Fool ran through my veins, hot as liquor, cold as ice. For a flashing instant, we shared physical awareness. The intensity of it went beyond any joining I'd ever experienced. It was more intimate than a kiss and deeper than a knife thrust, beyond a Skill-link and beyond sexual coupling, even beyond my Wit-bond with Nighteyes. It was not a sharing, it was a becoming. Neither pain nor pleasure could encompass it. Worse, I felt myself turning and opening to it, as if it were my lover's mouth upon mine, yet I did not know if I would devour or be devoured. In another heartbeat, we would be one another, know one another more perfectly than two separate beings ever should.

He'd know my secret.

"No!" I cried before he could discover my plot against him. I wrenched myself free, mind and body. For a long time I fell, until I struck the cold stone floor. I rolled under the table to escape that touch, gasping. My time of blackness seemed to last for hours, yet it was only an instant before Chade dragged my curled body from under the table.

He propped me against his chest as he knelt beside me. Dimly I was aware of him demanding, "What happened? Are you hurt? What did you do to him, Fool?"

I heard a sob escape Thick. He alone, perhaps, had sensed what had transpired. A prickling shiver ran over my body. I could not see anything. Then I realized my eyes were tightly clenched shut, my body huddled in a ball. Knowing those things, it still took me a time to persuade myself I could change them. Just as I opened my eyes, the Fool's thought uncurled in my mind like a leaf opening to sunlight.

And I set no limits on that love.

"It's too much," I said brokenly. "No one can give that much. No one."

"Here's brandy," Dutiful said close by me. It was Chade who hauled me into a sitting position and put the cup to my lips. I gulped it as if it were water, then wheezed with the shock. When I managed to turn my head, the Fool was the only one still sitting in his chair at the table. His hands were gloved again, and the look he gave me was opaque. Thick crouched in a corner of the room, hugging himself and shivering. His Skill-music was his mother's song, a desperate attempt to comfort himself.

"What happened?" Chade demanded in a fierce voice. I still leaned against his chest, and I could feel the anger emanating from him like heat. I knew he directed his accusatory glare at the Fool, but I answered anyway.

"It was too intense. We formed a Skill-link that was so complete, I couldn't find myself. As if we'd become one being." I called it the Skill yet I was not sure that was a proper name for it. As well call a spark the sun. I took a deeper breath. "It scared me. So I broke free of it. I wasn't expecting anything like that." And those words were spoken as much to the Fool as to the others. I saw him hear them, but I think he took a different message from them than what I had intended.

"And it affected you not at all?" Chade demanded of him.

Dutiful helped me to my feet. I needed his aid. I sank down into a chair almost immediately. Yet it was not weariness I felt, but a loose energy. I could have scaled Buckkeep's highest tower, if I could have recalled how to make my knees bend.

"It affected me," the Fool said quietly. "But in a different way." He met my eyes and said, "It didn't frighten me."

"Shall we try it again?" Dutiful proposed innocently, and "No!" Chade, the Fool, and I all replied with varying degrees of emphasis.

"No," the Fool repeated more quietly in the tiny silence that followed. "For myself, I've learned enough today."

"Perhaps we all have," Chade concurred gruffly. He cleared his throat and went on. "It's time we dispersed to our own tasks anyway."

"We've still plenty of time," Dutiful protested.

"Ordinarily, yes, that would be so," Chade agreed. "But the days run away from us now. You've much to do to prepare for our journey, Dutiful. Rehearse your speech thanking the Outislanders for their welcome again. Remember, the *ch* is sounded toward the back of the throat."

"I've read it a hundred times now," Dutiful groaned.

"And when the time comes, the words must seem to come from your heart, not from a scroll."

Dutiful nodded grudgingly to this. He gave one longing look at the bright and breezy day outside the window.

"Off you both go, then," Chade told him, and it was suddenly clear he was dismissing both Thick and Dutiful.

Disappointment crossed the Prince's face. He turned to Lord Golden. "When we are at sea, and have more time and fewer tasks, I'd like to hear of your time with my father. If you wouldn't mind. I know that you cared for him when he ... at the end of his days."

"I did," the Fool replied gently. "And I'd be glad to share my memories of those days with you."

"Thank you," Dutiful replied. He went to the corner, and gently chivied Thick along, asking him what on earth had frightened him, for no one had been hurt. I was grateful that Thick had no intelligible answer to that.

They were nearly at the door when I recalled my earlier resolution. "Prince Dutiful, would you come to my workroom this evening? I've something for you."

He raised an eyebrow, but when I said no more, he replied, "I'll find time. I'll see you then."

Dutiful left with Thick trudging at his heels. But at the door, Thick turned and gave the Fool an oddly appraising look before he transferred his gaze to me. I wondered uneasily how much he had sensed of what had passed between the Fool and me. Then Thick was gone, shutting the door rather too firmly behind himself.

For a moment, I feared that Chade would demand to know more of what had happened. But before he could speak, the Fool said, "Prince Dutiful must not kill Icefyre. That is the most important thing that I must tell you, Chade. At all costs, the dragon's life must be preserved."

Chade had crossed to the bottles of spirits. He selected one, poured from it silently, and then turned back to us. "As the creature is frozen in a glacier, don't you think it might be a bit late to worry about preserving his life?" He sipped from his glass. "Or do you truly think that any beast could survive that long, bereft of warmth, water, and food?"

The Fool lifted his shoulders and shook his head. "What do any of us know of dragons? How long had the stone dragons slept before Fitz woke them? If they share any of their natures with true dragons, then perhaps some spark of life still glows within Icefyre."

"What do you know of Icefyre?" Chade demanded suspiciously. He came back to the table and sat down. I remained standing, watching the two of them.

"I know no more of him than you do, Chade."

"Then why forbid us the taking of his head, when you know the Narcheska has demanded this as a condition of the marriage? Or do you think the world would be set into a better path if our two realms remained at each other's throats for another century or two?"

I winced at his sarcasm. Never would I have mocked the Fool's stated goal to change the world. It shocked me that Chade did, and made me realize the depth of his antagonism.

"I've no love of strife, Chade Fallstar," the Fool replied softly. "Yet even a war amongst men is not the worst thing that can occur. Better war than that we do deeper, graver damage to our world itself. Especially when we have the briefest grasp at a chance to repair an almost irreparable wrong."

"Which is?"

"If Icefyre lives . . . and I concede it would be surpassing strange if he did . . . but if there is some spark of life in him yet, we must abandon all other quests to free him from the ice and restore him to full life."

"Why?"

"You haven't told him?" He swung an accusing gaze to me. I didn't meet it and he didn't wait for me to reply. "Tintaglia, the Bingtown dragon, is the sole adult female dragon in the world. With every passing year, it becomes more apparent that the young ones which emerged from their cases will remain stunted and weak, unable to hunt or fly. Dragons mate in flight. If the hatchlings never fly, they can never mate. Dragons will die out in the world. And this time, it will be forever. Unless there remains one fully formed male dragon. One who could rise to mate Tintaglia and sire a new generation of dragons."

I had told Chade all those things. Did he ask his question to test the Fool's frankness?

"You are telling me," Chade enunciated carefully, "that we must put peace between the Out Islands and the Six Duchies at risk for the sake of reviving dragons. And this will benefit us how?"

"It won't," the Fool admitted. "On the contrary. It will

present many drawbacks for men. And many adjustments. Dragons are an arrogant and aggressive species. They ignore boundaries and have no concept of 'ownership.' If a hungry dragon sees a cow in a pen, he'll eat it. To them, it's simple. The world provides and you take what you need from it."

Chade smiled archly. "Then perhaps I should do the same, on behalf of humanity. The world has provided us a time free of dragons. I think I shall take it."

I watched the Fool. He was not upset by Chade's words. For the space of two breaths he held his peace. Then he said, "As you will, sir. But when the time comes, that decision may not be yours. It may be mine. Or Fitz's." As Chade's eyes blazed with anger, he added, "And not only the world but humanity itself does need dragons."

"And why is that?" Chade demanded disdainfully.

"To keep the balance," the Fool replied. He glanced over at me, and then past me, out of the window, and his eyes went far and pensive. "Humanity fears no rivals. You have forgotten what it was to share the world with creatures as arrogantly superior as yourselves. You think to arrange the world to your liking. So you map the land and draw lines across it, claiming ownership simply because you can draw a picture of it. The plants that grow and the beasts that rove, you mark as your own, claiming not only what lives today, but what might grow tomorrow, to do with as you please. Then, in your conceit and aggression, you wage wars and slay one another over the lines you have imagined on the world's face."

"And I suppose dragons are better than we are because they don't do such things, because they simply take whatever they see. Free spirits, nature's creatures, possessing all the moral loftiness that comes from not being able to think."

The Fool shook his head, smiling. "No. Dragons are no better than humans. They are little different at all from men. They will hold up a mirror to humanity's selfishness.

They will remind you that all your talk of owning this and claiming that is no more than the snarling of a chained dog or a sparrow's challenge song. The reality of those claims lasts but for the instant of its sounding. Name it as you will, claim it as you will, the world does not belong to men. Men belong to the world. You will not own the earth that eventually your body will become, nor will it recall the name it once answered to."

Chade did not reply immediately. I thought he was stunned by the Fool's words, his view of reality reordered by them. But then he snorted disdainfully. "Pish. What you say only makes it plainer to me that no good will be worked for anyone by resurrecting this dragon." He rubbed his eyes wearily. "Oh, why do we bother with this fatuous debate? None of us know what we will find when we get there. It's all philosophical ramblings and nursery tales at this point. When I confront it, then I will think about what is best to do. There. Does that satisfy you?"

"I scarcely believe that my satisfaction matters to you." And as he spoke those odd words, the Fool sent a sidelong glance my way. But it was not a look to catch my eye, but rather one that pointed me out to Chade.

"You're right," Chade agreed smoothly. "It is not your satisfaction but Fitz's agreement that matters to me. Yet I know that if this decision falls to him alone, he would give your satisfaction much weight, even, perhaps, at the risk of Farseer fortunes." My old master gave me a speculative look, as if I were a spavined horse that might or might not last through another battle. The smile he gave me was almost desperate. "Yet I hope he will hear my concerns, as well." His gaze met mine. "When we confront it, then we will decide. Until then, the choice remains open. Is that acceptable?"

"Almost," the Fool replied. His voice was cool as he proposed, "Give us your promise, as a Farseer, that when the time comes, Fitz may do as his judgment bids him."

"My promise as a Farseer!" Chade was incensed.

"Exactly," the Fool replied calmly. "Unless your words are just an empty sop thrown to keep Fitz on the path to doing your will." He leaned back in his chair, his wrists and hands lax on the arms of it, perfectly at ease. For a moment, I recognized that slender man in black with his shining hair bound back. This was the boy the Fool had been, grown to a man. Then he turned his head to regard Chade more directly, and the familiarity was gone. His face was a sculpted silhouette of determination. I had never seen anyone challenge Chade so confidently.

I was shocked at the words Chade spoke then. His smile was very strange as his eyes went from me to the Fool and back again. It was my gaze he met as he said, "I give my word as a Farseer. I will not ask him to do anything against his will. There. Are you content, man?"

The Fool nodded slowly. "Oh, yes. I am content. For the decision will come to him, and that I see as clearly as anything that remains to me to see." He nodded to himself. "There are still things we must discuss, you and I, but once we are on board ship and under way, there will be time for that. But the day rushes on without us, and I still have much to do to prepare for my departure. Good day, Lord Fallstar."

A very slight smile hung about his mouth. His glance went from me to Chade. And then he made a most curious gesture. Sweeping his arms wide, he made a graceful bow to Chade, as if they had afforded one another some great courtesy. When he straightened he spoke to me. His tone was warmer. "It was good to have a few moments with you today, Fitz. I've missed you." Then he gave a sudden small sigh, as if he had recalled an unpleasant duty. I suspected that his predicted death had just pushed itself to the forefront of his mind. His smile faded. "Gentlemen, you will excuse me," he murmured. And he departed, exiting through the cramped panel concealed in the side of the hearth as gracefully as a lord departing a banquet.

I sat staring after him. Our recent Skill-encounter

rattled in my mind with his strange words and stranger gestures. He had clashed with Chade over something, and triumphed. Yet I was not quite sure what, if anything, had just been settled between them.

My old mentor spoke as if he could hear my thoughts. "He challenges me for your loyalty! How dare he? Me, who practically raised you! How can he think there would be any chance of us disagreeing, when we both know how much rests upon the successful completion of this quest? My word as a Farseer, indeed! And what does he think you are, when all is said and done?"

He turned and put the question to me as if he expected an unthinking assent from me. "Perhaps," I said quietly, "he believes that he is the White Prophet and I am his Catalyst." Then I took a stronger breath and spoke a question of my own. "How can the two of you quarrel over my loyalty, as if I had no thought of my own to give to any decision I might make?" I gave a snort of disgust. "I would not think a horse or a dog as mindless a game piece as you both seem to think I am."

He was staring past me out of the window when he spoke, and I do not think he truly considered the import of his words. "Not a horse or a dog, Fitz, no. I'd never think of you that way. No. You're a sword. So you were made to be, by me, a weapon to be wielded. And he thinks you fit his hand the best." The old man snorted in contempt. "The man is, still, a fool." He looked at me and nodded. "You were wise to tell me of his plans. It is good we shall be leaving him behind."

There seemed nothing to say to that. I left the Seawatch Tower, going as I had come through the dark maze hidden within the walls of Buckkeep. I had seen both my friend and my mentor more clearly today than I liked. I wondered if the Fool's touch on my wrist had been a demonstration for both Chade and me of the influence he had over me. And yet, and yet, it had not felt that way. Had he not asked me first if I wished for it? Still, it had felt as if it were a thing he wished to display to me. Yet had it been only circumstances that had made him reveal it to Chade, as well? Or had his intent been that I see clearly how Chade regarded me, how he assumed he could always depend on me to do his will? I shook my head. Could the Fool imagine I did not already know that? I clenched my teeth. There would come a moment when the Fool realized Chade and I had conspired against him, a moment when he knew how I had held my tongue today.

I went back to my workroom, and I did not like any of the thoughts I took there with me.

As I pushed open the door, I instantly knew that the Fool had been there before me. He'd left his gift on the table beside my chair. I walked over to it and ran a finger down Nighteyes' spine. My wolf was in his prime in the carving. A dead rabbit sprawled between his forepaws. His head was lifted, his dark eyes regarding me intelligently, patiently.

I picked it up. I had seen the Fool begin the carving when he sat at the table in my cabin. I had never guessed what it might be, had almost forgotten that he had promised to show it to me when it was finished. I touched the points of Nighteyes' pricked ears. Then I sat down in the chair and stared into the fire, my wolf cradled in my hands.

chapter IV

AN EXCHANGE OF WEAPONS

Weaponsmaster Hod ascended to that title after long service as journeyman to Weaponsmaster Crend. Her years in that position were well spent, for she became familiar not only with the use of each weapon, but the manufacture of good blades. Indeed, there are still some who say that her primary talent was in the creation of fine weapons, and that Buckkeep would have been better served to give another the title of Weaponsmaster and keep her at her forge. King Shrewd, however, did not see it that way. Upon Crend's death, she was immediately moved into his position, and oversaw the training of all Buckkeep's men-at-arms. She served the Farseer reign well, ultimately giving her life in battle for then King-in-Waiting Verity.

                              ❧ FEDWREN'S "CHRONICLES"

The Fool's carefully planned disposal of his possessions sparked in me a sudden desire to sort out my own belongings. That night, instead of packing, I sat on the corner of Chade's old bed, surrounded by all I owned. If I had been inclined to the Fool's fatalistic melancholy, perhaps it would have saddened me. Instead, I found myself grinning at the paucity of it. Even Gilly the ferret nosing through my trove seemed unimpressed.

The stack of clothing from the Fool's chamber and the marvelous sword with the overdecorated hilt comprised most of it. My clothing from my days in the cottage had largely been consigned to the rag heap near the worktable. I possessed two new uniforms as a Prince's Guard. One was already carefully packed in a sea chest at the foot of my bed with my other changes of clothing. Concealed beneath them were a number of small packages of poisons, sedatives, and restoratives that Chade and I had prepared. On the bed beside me, various small tools, lockpicks, and other handy oddments were in a small roll that could be concealed inside my shirt. I added it to the sea chest. I sorted through the rest of my strange collection as I waited for Dutiful.

The carving of Nighteyes was on the mantel over the hearth. I would not risk it on the journey with me. There was a charm necklace that Jinna the hedge-witch had made for me, when we were on friendlier terms. I'd never wear it again, and yet I was oddly reluctant to dispose of it. I set it with the clothing Lord Golden had inflicted on me. The little fox pin that Kettricken had given me rode where it always did, inside my shirt above my heart. I had no intention of parting from that. To one side I had placed a few items for Hap. Most were small things I'd made or acquired when he was a child: a spinning top, a jumping jack, and the like. I packed them carefully into a box with an acorn carved on the lid. I'd give them to him when I bid him farewell.

In the center of my bed was the bundle of carved feathers I'd taken from the Others beach. Once, I had tried to give them to the Fool, to try in his carved wooden crown. I was certain they would fit. But he had given them a single glance and rejected them. I unrolled the soft leather I'd wrapped them in, considered each of them briefly, and then wrapped them again. For a time I debated what to do with them. Then I tucked them into the corner of the sea chest. Into it also went my needles and various weights of thread for them. Extra shoes and smallclothes. A razor. Mug, bowl, and spoon for the ship.

And that was it. There was nothing else to pack, and precious little else in the world that belonged to me. There was my horse, Myblack, but she had little interest in me beyond doing what she must. She preferred her own kind, and would not miss me at all. A stable boy would exercise her regularly, and as long as Hands was in charge of Buckkeep's stables, I had no fear that she would be neglected or ill-used.

Gilly emerged from the heap of clothing and came romping across the bed to challenge me. "Small chance you'll miss me, either," I told him as he menaced my hand playfully. There were plenty of mice and rats in the walls of Buckkeep to keep him well fed. He'd probably enjoy having the whole bed to himself. He already believed that the pillow belonged to him. My gaze wandered over the room. Chade had taken possession of all the scrolls I'd brought back from my cabin. He'd sorted them, adding the harmless ones to the Buckkeep library and securing in his cabinets any that told too many truths too plainly. I felt no sense of loss.

I carried the armload of clothing over to one of Chade's old wardrobes, intending to stuff it all inside. Then my conscience smote me, and I carefully shook out and folded each garment before putting it away. In the process, I realized that, taken individually, many of the garments were not as ostentatious as I had imagined them. I added the warmly lined cloak to my sea chest. When all of the clothing was stored or packed, I set the jeweled sword on top of the chest. It would go with me. Despite its showy hilt, it was well made and finely balanced. Like the man who had given it to me, its glittering appearance obscured its true purpose.

There was a courteous tap and the wine rack swung

out of the way. As Dutiful stepped wearily into the room, Gilly leaped from the bed and sprang to confront him, menacing him with white teeth as he made abortive springs at his feet.

"Yes, I'm glad to see you, too," Dutiful greeted him and swept the little animal up in one hand. He scratched the ferret's throat gently and then set him down. Gilly immediately attacked his feet. Being careful not to tread upon him, Dutiful came into the room, saying, "You had something extra for me to pack?" With a heavy sigh, he dropped down on the bed beside me. "I'm so tired of packing," he confided. "I hope it's something small."

"It's on the table," I told him. "And it's not small."

As he walked toward the worktable, I knew a moment of intense regret and would have undone the gift if I could. How could it possibly mean to this boy what it had to me? He looked at it, and then looked up at me, shock on his face. "I don't understand. You're giving me a sword?"

I stood up. "It's your father's sword. Verity gave it to me, when last we parted. It's yours, now," I said quietly.

The look that overtook Dutiful's face in that moment erased any regret I might have felt. He put out a hand toward it, drew it back, and then looked at me. Incredulous wonder shone in his face. I smiled.

"I said it was yours. Pick it up and get the feel of it. I've just cleaned and sharpened it, so be careful."

He reached his hand down and set it on the hilt. I waited, watching, for him to lift it and discover its exquisite balance. But he drew his hand back.

"No." The word shocked me. Then, "Wait here. Please. Just wait." And then he turned and fled the room. I heard the scuff of his running footsteps fade in the hidden corridor.

His reaction puzzled me. He had seemed so delighted at first. I walked over and looked again at the blade. Freshly oiled and wiped, it gleamed. It was both beautiful and elegant, yet there was nothing in its design that would interfere with its intended function. It was a tool for killing other men. It had been made for Verity by Hod, the same Weaponsmaster who had taught me to wield both blade and pike. When Verity had gone on his quest, she had gone with him, and died for him. It was a sword worthy of a king. Why had Dutiful rejected it?

I was sitting before the hearth, a cup of hot tea between my two hands, when he returned. He carried a long, wrapped bundle with him. He was talking and untying the leather thongs that bound it as he came through the door. "I don't know why I didn't think of this a long time ago, when my mother first told me who you were. I guess because it was given to me so long ago, and then my mother put it away for me. Here!"

The wrappings fell away from it and he flourished it aloft. Grinning widely, he suddenly reversed his grip on it, and proffered it to me, the hilt resting on his left forearm. He grinned at me, his eyes blazing with delight and anticipation. "Take it, FitzChivalry Farseer. Your father's sword."

A shiver ran over me, standing up every hair on my body. I set the teacup aside and came slowly to my feet. "Chivalry's sword?"

"Yes." I had not thought his grin could grow wider, but it did.

I stared at it. Yes. Even without his words, I would have known it. This blade was the elder brother to the one Verity had carried. It resembled the other sword, but this one was slightly more ornate and longer, designed for a man taller than Verity. There was a stylized buck on the cross-guard. It was, I suddenly knew, a sword made for a prince who would be king. I knew I could never bear it. I longed for it all the same. "Where did you get it?" I asked breathlessly.

"Patience had it, of course. She'd left it at Withywoods when she came to Buckkeep. Then, when she was 'sorting the clutter,' as she put it, after the end of the Red Ship War, when she was moving her household to Tradeford, she came across it. In a closet. 'Just as well I never took it to Buckkeep,' she told me when she gave it to me. 'Regal would have taken it and sold it. Or kept it for himself.'"

It was so like Patience that I had to smile. A king's sword, amongst her "clutter."

"Take it!" Dutiful commanded me eagerly, and I had to. I had to feel, at least once, how my hand would fit where my father's had rested. As I took it from him, it felt near weightless. It perched in my hand like a bird. The moment I relieved Dutiful of it, he stepped to the table and took up Verity's sword. I heard his exclamation of satisfaction, and grinned as he gripped it two-handed and swept it through the air. These blades were proper swords, as fit to shear through flesh as skewer some vulnerable point. For a time, we were both like boys as we moved the blades in a variety of ways, from the small shifts of the hand and wrist that would block and divert an opponent's thrust to a reckless overhand slash by Dutiful that stopped just short of the scrolls on the tabletop.

Chivalry's blade fit me. There was satisfaction in that, even as I realized how woefully unworthy my skills were to a weapon such as this. I was little more than competent with a sword. I wondered how the abdicated king would have felt to know that his only son was defter with an axe than with a sword, and more inclined to use poison than either of those. It was a disheartening line of thought, but before I could give in to that blight, Dutiful was at my side, comparing his blade to mine.

"Chivalry's is longer!"

"He was taller than Verity. Yet this blade, I think, is lighter. Verity had the brawn to put behind a heavy stroke, and so I think Hod made his weapon. It will be interesting to see which weapon fits you best when you are grown."

He took my meaning instantly. "Fitz. I gave you that sword to keep. I mean it."

I nodded. "And I thank you for that thought. But I shall have to be satisfied with the intention in place of the reality. This is a king's sword, Dutiful. It's not for a guardsman, let alone an assassin, or a bastard. See, look here, on the hilt. The Farseer buck, large and plain. It's on Verity's too, but smaller. Even so, I wrapped the hilt in leather to disguise it in the years after the Red Ship War. Anyone who had seen it would have known it couldn't properly belong to me. This would be even more obvious." Regretfully and respectfully, I set it down on the worktable.

Dutiful deposited Verity's blade carefully beside it. A stubborn look came over his face. "How can I take my father's sword from you, if you won't take Chivalry's from me? My father gave you that blade. He meant you to have it."

"I'm sure he did, at that moment. And for many years, it has served me well. To see it in your hands will serve me even better. I know that Verity would agree with me. For now, Chivalry's blade we should both set aside. When you are crowned, your nobles will expect to see the king's sword on your hip."

Dutiful scowled in thought. "Didn't King Shrewd have a sword? What became of it?"

"Doubtless he did. As to what became of it, I've no idea. Perhaps Patience had the right of it; perhaps Regal sold it or carried it off for other scavengers to steal after he died. In any case, it's gone. When the time comes for you to ascend the throne, I think you should carry the king's sword. And when you sail for Aslevjal, I think you should wear your father's sword."

"I shall. But won't folk wonder where I got it?"

"I doubt it. We'll have Chade put out some tale that he has been holding it for you. Folk love stories of that sort. They'll be happy to accept it."

He nodded thoughtfully, then said slowly, "It takes some of the pleasure from it, that you cannot carry Chivalry's sword as openly as I shall carry this one."

"For me also," I replied with painful honesty. "Would that I could, Dutiful. But that is simply how it is. I've a sword given to me by Lord Golden, also of a quality that exceeds my skill. I'll carry that. If I ever lift a blade to defend you, it had better be an axe."

He looked down, pondering. Then he set his hand to the hilt of Chivalry's sword. "Until the day when you give this sword back to me, on the day I am crowned, I wish it to remain here with you." He took a breath. "And when I take your father's sword from you, I will return my father's sword to you."

That was a gesture I could not refuse.

Soon he left as he had come, taking Verity's sword with him. I made myself a fresh cup of tea and sat considering my father's blade. I tried to think what it meant to me, but encountered only a curious absence inside myself. Even my recent discovery that he had not ignored me, but had Skill-watched me through his brother's eyes, did not make up for his physical absence in my life. Perhaps he had loved me from afar, but Burrich had been the one to discipline me and Chade the one to teach me. I looked at the blade and groped for a sense of connection, for any emotion at all, but could not find one. By the time I had finished my tea, I still had no answer, nor was I completely certain what my question was. But I had resolved that I would find time to see Hap again before I departed.

I went to bed, successfully claiming the pillow from Gilly. Nonetheless, I slept badly, and even that poor rest was interrupted. Nettle edged into my dreams like a child reluctantly seeking comfort. It was a peculiar contrast. In my dream, I was crossing a steep scree slope from my sojourn in the mountains. I had crossed this avalanche-prone incline carrying the Fool's lax body. I was not so burdened in my dream, but the mountainside seemed steeper and the fall eternal. Loose pebbles shifted treacherously under my feet. At any moment I might go sliding off the face of the mountain like the small stones rattling past me. My muscles ached with tension and sweat streamed down my back. Then I caught a flash of motion at the corner of my eye. I turned my head slowly, for I dared risk no swift movement. I discovered Nettle sitting calmly uphill from me, watching my agonized progress.

She sat amongst grass and wildflowers. Her gown was green and her hair decked with tiny daisies. Even to my father's eyes, she looked more woman than child, but she sat like a little girl, her knees drawn up under her chin and her arms clasped around her legs. Her feet were bare and her eyes troubled.

Such was our dichotomy. I still struggled to retain my footing on the unstable slope. In her dream, adjoining mine, she sat in a mountain meadow. Her presence forced me to admit that I dreamed, and yet I could not surrender the exertion of my nightmare. I did not know if I feared I would be swept to my death or thrust into wakefulness. So, "What is it?" I called to her as I continued my inching progress across the mountain's face. It mattered not how many steps I took: solid ground remained ever distant, while Nettle kept her place above me.

"My secret," she said quietly. "It gnaws at me. So I have come to ask your advice."

She paused but I did not reply. I did not want to know her secret, or to offer advice. I could not commit myself to helping her. Despite the dream, I knew I was leaving Buckkeep soon. Even if I stayed, I could not venture into her life without the risk of destroying it. Better to remain a vague dream-thing on the edge of her reality. Despite my silence, she spoke to me.

"If someone gives her word to keep silent about a thing, not realizing how much pain it will bring, not just to herself but to others, is she bound to keep her word?"

That was too grave a question to leave unanswered. "You know the answer to that," I panted. "A woman's word is her word. She keeps it, or it is worth nothing."

"But I did not know the trouble it would cause when I gave it. Nim goes about like half a creature. I did not know that Mama would blame Papa, or that Papa would take to drink over it, blaming himself more deeply than she does."

I halted. It was dangerous to do so, but I turned to face her. Her words had plummeted me into a deeper danger than the chasm that yawned below me. I spoke carefully. "And you think you've found a way around the word you gave. To tell me what you promised not to tell them."

She lowered her forehead to her knees. Her voice was muffled when she spoke. "You said you knew Papa, long ago. I do not know who you truly are; but perhaps you know him still. You could speak to him. The last time Swift ran away, you told me when he and Papa were safely on their way home to us. Oh, please, Shadow Wolf! I don't know what your connection to my family is, but I know it exists. In trying to aid Swift, I have nearly torn us apart. I have no one else to turn to. And I never promised Swift that I would not tell you."

I looked down at my feet. She had changed me into her image of me. Her dream was devouring mine. Now I was a man-wolf. My black claws dug into the loose gravel. Moving on all fours, with my weight lower, I clawed my way up the slope toward her. When I was close enough to see the dried salt track of tears on her cheeks, I growled, "Tell me what?"

It was all the permission she needed. "They think Swift ran away to sea, for so we made it seem, he and I. Oh, do not look at me like that! You don't know what it was like around here! Papa was a perpetual storm cloud and Swift near as bad. Poor Nim slunk around like a whipped dog, ashamed to win praise from Papa because his twin could not share it. And Mama, Mama was like a madwoman, every night demanding to know what ailed them, and both of them refusing to answer. There was no peace in our house anymore, no peace at all. So when Swift came to me and asked me to help him slip away, it seemed the wise thing to do."

"And what sort of aid did you give him?"

"I gave him money, money that was mine, to use as I pleased, money I had earned myself helping with the Gossoin's lambing last spring. Mama often sent him to town, to make deliveries of honey or candles. I thought up the plan for him, that he would start asking neighbors and folk in town about boats and fishing and the sea. And then, at the last, I wrote a letter and signed Papa's name as I have become accustomed to doing for him. His eyes...Papa can still write, but his hand wanders for he cannot see the letters he is forming. So, of late, I have written things for him, the papers when he sells a horse and such. Everyone says that my hand is just like his; probably because he taught me to make my letters. So..."

"So you wrote a letter for Swift saying that his father had released him and that he could go forth and do as he pleased with his life." I spoke slowly. Every word she spoke burdened me more. Burrich and Molly quarreled, and he took to drink again. His sight was failing him, and he believed he had driven his son away. Hearing these things rent me, for I knew I could not mend any of them.

"It can be difficult for a boy to find any sort of work if folk think he is a runaway apprentice or a lad whose work still belongs to his father." She spoke the words hesitantly, trying to excuse her forgery. I dared not look at her. "Mama packed up six racks of candles and sent Swift into town to deliver them and to bring back the money. When he said good-bye to me, I knew he meant to take that opportunity. He never came back." Around her, flowers bloomed and a tiny bee buzzed from one to the next, seeking nectar.

I slowly worked through her words. "He stole the candle money to travel on?" My estimate of Swift dropped.

"It wasn't...it wasn't exactly stealing. He'd always helped with the hives. And he needed it!"

I shook my head slowly. It disappointed me that she found excuses for him. But then, I'd never had a little brother. Perhaps it was a thing all sisters did.

"Won't you help me?" she asked piteously when my silence grew long.

"I can't," I said helplessly. "I can't."

"Why not?"

"How could I?" I was completely in her dream now. The meadow grass was firm beneath my feet. A spring day in the hills surrounded me. The bee buzzed past my ear, and I flicked it away. I knew my nightmare still lurked behind me. If I stepped back two paces, I'd be on that treacherous slope again.

"Talk to Papa for me. Tell him it wasn't his fault Swift went away."

"I can't talk to your papa. I'm far, far away. Only in dreams can we reach across distances like this."

"Can't you visit his dreams, as you do mine? Can't you talk to him there?"

"No. I can't." Long ago, my father had sealed Burrich off from all other Skill-users. Burrich himself had told me that. Chivalry had been able to draw strength from him for Skilling, and the bond between them meant that Chivalry would be vulnerable through Burrich to other Skill-users. Dimly I wondered, did that mean that at one time Burrich had had some level of Skill ability? Or did it only mean that the two men were so close that Chivalry could take strength from him for Skilling?

"Why not? You come to my dreams. And you were friends long ago; you said so. Please. He can't go on as he is. It's killing him. And my mother." She added softly, "I think you owe him this."

A bee from Nettle's flowers buzzed past my face and I swiped at it. I decided I needed to end this contact swiftly. She was drawing too many conclusions about her father and me. "I cannot come to your father's dreams, Nettle. But there may be something I can do. I may be able to speak to someone, someone who can find Swift and send him home again." Even as I said the words, my heart sank. As annoying as Swift was, I knew what it would mean to the boy to be sent back to Burrich; I hardened my will. It truly wasn't my problem. Swift was Burrich's son, and they must sort it out themselves.

"Then you know where Swift is? You've seen him? Is he well, is he safe? A thousand times I've thought of him, so young and alone and out in the world. I never should have let him talk me into this! Tell me about him."

"He's fine," I said shortly. The bee buzzed past my ear again. I felt it settle on the back of my neck. I tried to paw it off me, but an instant later, I was bowed under the weight of a sizable animal on my back. I yelped and struggled, but before I could draw breath, I was dangling from the dragon's jaws. She gave me a shake, not to kill but to caution. I stopped struggling and hung there. Her teeth gripped the scruff of my neck, not piercing either hide or flesh but paralyzing me.

As Nettle surged indignantly to her feet, reaching for me, the dragon lifted me higher. I dangled above Nettle and then was swung out over the chasm from my earlier nightmare.

"Ah-ah!" the dragon cautioned us both. "Resist and I drop him. Wolves do not fly." Her words did not come from her mouth and throat, but penetrated my thoughts, a mind-to-mind touch.

Nettle froze. "What do you want?" she growled. Her dark eyes had gone flinty.

"He knows," Tintaglia replied, giving me a small shake. I felt it unhinge every bone in my spine. "I want to know all that you know of a black dragon buried in ice. I want to know all you know of an island humans name Aslevjal."

"I know nothing of such things!" Nettle replied angrily. Her hands had knotted into fists. "Let him go."

"Very well." The dragon released me, and for a heart-stopping instant, I plummeted. Then her head shot out on her snakelike neck and she caught me up again. This time her jaws encompassed my ribs. She squeezed me, demonstrating how easily she could crush me. Then she eased the pressure and asked me, "And what do you know, little wolf thing?"

"Nothing!" I gasped, and then choked out every bit of air in my lungs as she crushed me. It would be quick, I told myself. I would not have to maintain my lie long. She wasn't a patient creature; she'd kill me swiftly. I glanced back to take a last look at my daughter.

Nettle stood, suddenly larger than she had been. Then she flung her arms wide. Her hair tossed in a wind that only she felt, and then haloed out around her face. She threw her head back. "This is a *dream*!" she shouted. "And it is *my* dream! I cast you out of it!" The last she spoke as single words, uttered with all the command of a queen. For the first time, I comprehended the strength of my daughter's Skill. Her ability to shape dreams and command that which happened in them was a manifestation of her Skill-talent.

Tintaglia flung me spinning out over an infinite void. Beneath me I saw, not the rocky chasm of my dream, but a vast emptiness without color or end. I had one whirling glimpse of the dragon writhing as Nettle dwindled her back to the size of a bee. Then I clenched my eyes shut against the dizzying fall. Even as I drew painful breath to scream, Nettle spoke softly by my ear. "It's only a dream, Shadow Wolf. And it belongs to me. In my dreams, you will never come to harm. Open your eyes, now. Awake to your own world."

An instant before I awoke, I felt the comforting resistance of bedding beneath me and when I opened my eyes to the darkness of my workroom, I was not in panic. Nettle had taken the terror from the nightmare. For a moment, I felt relief. I drew a deep breath, and as I surrendered to sleep once more, I felt a drowsy amazement at my daughter's odd Skill-strength. But as I tugged my blanket back over my shoulder and reclaimed half the pillow from the ferret, the earlier portion of my dream dragged me back to wakefulness. Swift had lied. Burrich hadn't discarded him. Worse, his leaving had thrown the family into turmoil.

I lay still, eyes closed, wishing vainly to sleep. Instead, I mapped out what I must do. The boy must be sent home, but I didn't want to be the one to do it. He'd demand to know how I knew he had lied. So. I'd tell Chade that Burrich had not released Swift from his household. That would involve admitting to Chade that I'd had more Skill-contact with Nettle. Well, it couldn't be helped, I told myself grumpily. All my secrets seemed intent on leaking out and becoming known.

So I made my resolution and tried to persuade myself that was the best I could do. I tried not to imagine Burrich going back to drinking every night, or Molly driven to distraction not only by her husband's dive into the bottle but by her son's vanishing. I tried not to wonder how much Burrich's vision had faded. Enough that he had either not tried to track his son, or had failed in the effort.

I was up at dawn. I got bread and milk and bacon in the guardroom, and carried it out to the Women's Garden to eat it. I sat listening to the birdcalls and smelling the new day's warmth touching the earth. Such things have always been a deep comfort to me. This morning, they affirmed that the goodness of the earth always goes on and made me wish that I could stay to watch the summer grow strong and the fruit swell on the trees.

I felt her before I saw her. Starling wore a morning robe of pale blue. Her hair was loose upon her shoulders, and her graceful narrow feet were in simple sandals. She carried a steaming mug between both her hands. I watched her and wished that things could have been simpler between us. When she noticed me sitting silently on the bench beneath the tree, she gaped in feigned astonishment, then changed her expression to a smile as she came to join me. She sat down, kicked her feet free of her sandals, and curled her legs on the bench between us.

"Well, good morning," she greeted me. There was mild

surprise in her eyes. "I nearly didn't recognize you, Fitz. You look as if you've lost ten years."

"Tom," I reminded her gently, well knowing that she had dropped my old name to rattle me. "And I feel as if you are right. Perhaps the daily routine of a guardsman was what I needed all along."

She made a skeptical noise in her throat, and took a sip from her mug. When she looked up, she added sourly, "I notice you don't think the same is true for me?"

"What, that you'd do better as a guardsman?" I asked her innocently. Then, as she pretended a kick at me, I added, "Starling, you always look like Starling to me. Neither older nor younger than I expect you to be, but always Starling."

She furrowed her brow for a moment, then shrugged and laughed. "I never know if you mean the things you say as compliments or not." Then she leaned closer to me, sniffing the air near me. "Musk? Are you wearing musk these days, Tom Badgerlock? If you are interested in attracting female companionship . . . ?"

"No, I wear no musk. I've just been sleeping with a ferret."

I had replied with honesty, and her whoop of laughter startled me. A moment later, I was grinning with her as she shook her head at me. She shifted on the bench so that her sun-warmed thigh pressed against mine. "That is so like you, Fitz. So like you." She gave a sigh of contentment, and then asked lazily, "Then, can I surmise that you have ended your mourning and bonded again?"

Her words dimmed the summer morning for me. I cleared my throat and spoke carefully. "No. I doubt that I ever will. Nighteyes and I fit together like a knife and a sheath." I looked out over the chamomile bed and said quietly, "After him, there can be no other. It would be a disservice to whatever creature I joined, for he would be only a substitute, and never genuinely my partner."

She read more into my words than I intended. She put

her arm along the back of the bench. Pillowing her head on it, she looked up at the sky through the tree branches that shaded us. I finished the milk I had brought with me and set the cup aside. I was about to excuse myself for my morning lesson with Swift when she asked, "Have you ever thought of taking Molly back, then?"

"What?"

She lifted her head. "You loved the girl. At least, so you've always maintained. And she had your child, at great cost to herself. You know that she could have shaken it from her body if she had chosen. That she didn't means that she felt something deep for you. You should go to her. Take her back."

"Molly and I were a long time ago. She is married to Burrich. They built a life together. They have six children of their own," I pointed out stiffly.

"So?" She brought her gaze to meet mine. "I saw him when he came to Buckkeep to fetch Swift home. He was closemouthed and grim when I greeted him. And he was old. He walks with a hitch and his eyes are clouding." She shook her head over him. "If you decided to take Molly back from him, he could offer you no competition."

"I would never do that!"

She sipped from her mug, looking at me steadily over the rim. "I know that," she said when she took the cup from her lips. "Even though he took her from you."

"They both think I'm dead!" I pointed out to her, my voice harsher than I'd intended.

"Are you sure you're not?" she asked flippantly. Then, at the look on my face, her eyes softened. "Oh, Fitz. You never do anything for yourself, do you? Never take what you want." She leaned closer to me. "Do you think Molly would have thanked you for your decision? Do you truly think you had the right to decide for her?" She leaned back a little, watching my face. "You gave her and the child away as if you were finding a good home for a puppy. Why?"

I'd answered that question so many times I didn't even

need to think. "He was the better man for her. That was true then; it's true now."

"Is it? I wonder if Molly would agree."

"And how is your husband today?" I asked her roughly. Her glance went opaque. "Who knows? He's gone trout fishing in the hills with Lord and Lady Redoaks. As you know, I've never enjoyed that kind of outing." Then, glancing aside, she added, "But their lovely daughter Ivy apparently does. I've heard that she leaped at the chance to make the trip."

She did not need to explain it to me. I took her hand. "Starling. I'm sorry."

She took a breath. "Are you? It matters little to me. I've his name and his holdings to enjoy. And he leaves me the freedom of my minstrel ways, to come and go as I please." She cocked her head at me. "I've been thinking of joining Dutiful's entourage for the journey to the Out Islands. What do you think of that?"

My heart lurched at the thought. Oh, no. "I think that it would be far worse than going trout fishing. I expect to be uncomfortable and cold for much of it. And Out Island food is terrible. If they give you lard, honey, and bone marrow mixed together, you've had the height of their cuisine."

She stood gracefully. "Fish paste," she said. "You've forgotten their fish paste. Fish paste on everything." She stood looking down on me. Then she reached a hand and pushed several strands of hair back from my face. Her fingertips walked the scar down my face. "Someday," she said quietly. "Someday you'll realize that we were the perfect match, you and I. That in all of your days and places, I was the only one who truly understood you and loved you despite it."

I gaped at her. In all our years together, she'd never said the word "love" to me.

She slid her fingers under my chin and closed my mouth for me. "We should have breakfast together more often," she suggested. Then she strolled away, sipping from her cup as she went, knowing that I watched her go.

"Well. At least you can make me forget all of my other problems for a time," I observed quietly to myself. Then I took my mug back to the kitchen and headed for the Queen's Garden. Perhaps it was my conversation with Starling, for when I walked out on the tower top and found the boy feeding the doves, I was direct.

"You lied," I said before he could even give me "good morning." "Your father never sent you away. You ran off. And you stole money to do it."

He gaped at me. His face went white. "Who... how did...?"

"How do I know? If I answer that question for you, I'll answer it for Chade and the Queen, as well. Do you want them to know what I know?"

I prayed I had his measure. When he gulped and shook his head suddenly and silently, I knew I had. Given the chance to run home, with no one here the wiser as to how he had shamed himself, he'd take it.

"Your family is worried sick about you. You've no right to leave people who love you in suspense about your fate. Pack up and go, boy, just as you came. Here." Impulsively I took my purse from my belt. "There's enough here to see you safely home, and pay back what you took. See that you do."

He couldn't meet my eyes. "Yessir."

When he didn't reach for the purse, I took his hand in mine, turned it palm up and put the sack into it. When I let go of his hand, he still stood staring up at me. I pointed at the door to the stairwell. He turned, stunned, and stumbled toward the door. With his hand on it, he halted. "You don't understand what it's like for me there," he whispered feebly.

"Yes. I do. Far better than you might imagine. Go home, bow your head to your father's discipline, and serve your family until you reach your majority, as an honest boy should. Didn't your parents raise you? Didn't they give you life, put food on your plate, clothes on your back, shoes on your feet? Then it is only right that your labor belongs to them, until you are legally a man. Then you can openly go your own way. You will have years after that to discover your magic, years of your own, rightfully earned, to live as you please. Your Wit can wait until then."

He halted by the door and leaned his head against it for a moment. "No. My magic won't wait."

"It will have to!" I told him harshly. "Now go home, Swift. Leave today."

He ducked his head, pushed the door open and left, shutting it behind him. I listened to his fading footsteps on the stair and felt his presence fade from my Wit-sense. Then I let out my breath in a long sigh. I had sent him to do a hard thing. I hoped Burrich's son had the spine to do it. I hoped, without real belief, that the boy's return would be enough to mend the family. I wandered over to the parapet wall and stood staring down at the rocks below.

chapter V

DEPARTURES

Do not disdain those who find that their strongest Skill-talent is in the fashioning of dreams. It is a talent most often manifested among Solos. These lone Skill-users, while not as effective as a coterie, can employ their unique talents to serve their monarchs in ways both subtle and effective. Ominous dreams sent to an enemy lord can make him reconsider his actions, while dreams of victory and glory can fortify the courage of any military leader. Dreams can be rewards, and in some cases can offer balm to those who are discouraged or weary at heart.

                TREEKNEE'S "LESSER USES OF THE SKILL"

That evening I told Chade that Swift had become desperately homesick and that I'd sent him home in the hopes that he could mend things with Burrich. The old man nodded distractedly: the boy was the least of his concerns.

I also told him of my conversation with Web, finishing with "He knows who I am. I think he has since he arrived here."

Chade's reaction to that was more emphatic. "Damn!

Why must you start coming unraveled now, when I have so much else to deal with?"

"I don't think I'm unraveling," I said stiffly. "Rather I think that this is knowledge that someone has possessed all along, and now it has come round to bite us. What do you suggest I do?"

"Do? What can you do?" he demanded testily. "It's known, boy. All we can do is hope that Web truly has as much goodwill toward us as he appears to have. And that the knowledge is not widespread amongst the Witted." He thumped a leather case to settle the scrolls inside and then began to tie it shut. "Holly, you say?" he asked after a moment. "You think Holly told Web?"

"So he seemed to imply."

"And when is the last time you saw her?"

"Years ago, when I lived among the Witted. She was Rolf's wife."

"I know that! My wits aren't failing me that badly." He pondered while he rolled the next scroll up. "There isn't time," he finally announced. "I'd send you off to see this Holly if there was, to discover how many people she has told. But there just isn't time. So, think with me, Fitz. How will they use this?"

"I'm not sure that Web intends to use it at all. The way he said it was as if he wished to help me; I felt no threat from him, nor even that he was holding my secret over my head. It was more as if he were urging me toward honesty with Swift as the best way to break through to him."

"Hm," the old man replied thoughtfully, tying the last case shut. "Push the teapot this way." Then, as he poured, "Web is a puzzle, isn't he? The man knows a great deal, and it isn't just those Witted tales he tells. I would not call him an educated man, yet, as he puts it, anything he has ever decided he needed to know, he's found a way to learn." Chade's gaze went distant as he spoke. Plainly he had spent some time pondering Web's significance. "I did not like Civil's proposal that Dutiful have a 'Witted coterie' as he did not have a Skilled one. No public mention has been made of such a thing. Yet, nonetheless, it seems to have come into existence. There is Civil Bresinga with his cat, that minstrel Cockle, and Web. All plan to accompany us on this voyage. And I sense, though the Prince is reluctant to speak of it, that they are a 'coterie' of sorts. There is a closeness when all of them are in the room that excludes me. Web is plainly the heart stone of the group. He is more like a priest than a leader; that is, he does not command, but he counsels them, and speaks often of serving 'the spirit of the world' or 'the divine.' He has no qualms that such words may make him appear foolish. If he had ambitions, he'd be a dangerous man. With what he knows, he could bring all of us tumbling down. The very few times he has spoken to me, it has been in a very indirect way. I feel as if he is urging us toward an action, but he does not tell us what it is that he hopes we will do. Hm."

"So." I ticked the possibilities off on my fingers. "Maybe Web simply wanted me to be honest with Swift. Well, with the boy gone, that's no longer an issue. But perhaps he wants me to reveal to all who I really am. Or perhaps he wants the Farseers to admit that the Prince is Witted. Or, if the two things were presented at once, it would be as good as saying that the Wit runs in the Farseer blood." And then my tongue froze. Did the Wit truly run in the Farseer line? The last prince to have definitely had it was the Piebald Prince, and he had left no issue. The crown had passed to a different Farseer bloodline. So, perhaps I had gotten the Wit from my Mountain-bred mother. And passed it on when Verity had usurped my body for the conception of Dutiful. That was a little bit of the puzzle that I'd never given Chade, nor did I ever intend to. Dutiful, I was convinced, was the son of Verity's spirit. Yet now I wondered uncomfortably if by the use of my body, Verity had passed on some of my tainted magic to his son.

"Fitz," Chade said, and I started at his voice, my thoughts having carried me so far afield. "Don't worry so. If

Web meant to do us harm, there'd be little advantage in tipping his hand. He's going with us on the Prince's quest, so we can keep an eye on him. And talk to him. You, especially, should seek him out. Pretend you wish to learn more of the Wit. That will win him over to you."

I sighed softly. I was sick of deception. I said as much to Chade. He snorted callously.

"You were born for deception, Fitz. Born for it. Just as I was, just as all bastards are. We're tricky things, sons but not heirs, royal but not princes. I would have thought that by now you would have accepted that."

I only said, "I'll try to get to know Web better on the voyage and see what he's about."

Chade nodded sagely. "A ship's a good place to do that. Little for men to do but talk on a voyage. And if he proves to be a danger to us . . . well."

He didn't have to say that many mishaps could befall a man at sea. I wished he had said nothing at all. But he was talking on.

"Did you put it into Starling's head to go with us? For she asked. Gave the Queen a long-winded speech about how a minstrel should go to bring home a clean telling of the Prince's adventure."

"Not I. Did the Queen give her permission?"

"I refused it, saying that all the places on the Prince's ship were already spoken for, and that the minstrel Cockle had already claimed a spot. Why? Do you think she'd be useful?"

"No. I fear this may be like the last quest I went on; the less truth that comes home with us, the better." I was relieved that Chade had refused Starling, and yet some sneaking part of me was mildly disappointed. That feeling shamed me too much to examine it closely.

The next day, I managed to see Hap. It was only a brief visit, and we talked while he worked. One of the journeymen was doing an inlay project, and had asked Hap to do the sanding of the pieced bits. It looked deadly dull to me, but Hap seemed absorbed in the work when I approached him. He smiled wearily when I greeted him, and gravely accepted the small gifts and mementos I'd brought him. When I asked how he was, he didn't pretend to misunderstand. "Svanja and I are still together, her parents still don't know, and I'm still juggling that with my duties as an apprentice. But I think I'm managing it. My hope is that if I apply myself here, I can make journeyman quickly. Once I have that status, I think I can present myself to Svanja's father as a likely marriage prospect for his daughter." He sighed. "I'm so tired of the sneaking about, Tom. I think Svanja relishes it, that it makes it more exciting for her. But for me, well, I like things settled and done right. Once I'm a journeyman, I can make everything as it should be."

I bit my tongue before saying that apprenticeships lasted years, not months. We both knew that. What mattered was that Hap was not shirking his training, but delving into it in the hopes of realizing his dreams. What more could I ask of him? So I embraced my son and told him I would be thinking of him. The hug he returned me was fierce. "I won't shame you, Tom. I promise I won't shame you."

With the rest of the guardsmen, I loaded my sea chest onto a wagon and followed it down to the docks. Buckkeep Town was decked for Spring Fest. Flowers garlanded door lintels and banners fluttered. The doors to taverns and common houses stood open, with song and the smell of holiday food wafting from them. Some of the men grumbled about missing the holiday but the first day of spring was a fortuitous day for beginning a journey.

Tomorrow morning, we'd make a show of escorting the Prince aboard. Today we boarded the *Maiden's Chance* and jostled companionably for space on the lower deck allotted to us. Our area was dark, airless, and thick with the stink of men in close quarters and the bilge below us. I hit my head twice on the low joists, and after that walked hunched. We would be crowded cheek by jowl, with little privacy and no quiet. The smoke-darkened timbers seemed to breathe out a miasma of oppressiveness. The water lapped loudly against the outside of the hull as if to remind me that only a plank of wood stood between the cold, wet sea and me.

I stowed my gear quickly, already anxious to be out of there. I little cared where my trunk was lashed down; I resolved to spend as much time above deck in the open air as I could. About half the guard were veterans of this sort of journey. They made much of the fact that we had an area separate from the working sailors, whom they despised as drunks, thieves, and brawlers. Personally, I suspected the seamen regarded the guardsmen in much the same light.

I settled my belongings quickly and headed up to the deck. I could not linger there, for it was crowded with sailors and passengers, all with some task in mind that involved pushing past me. Crates were being lifted from the docks and swung overhead before being guided down through the hatches and stowed belowdecks. The sailors who weren't shouting at each other were swearing loudly about the landsmen in their way.

Once on the docks again, I breathed a sigh of relief. All too soon, I'd be trapped aboard that ship with no opportunity to escape. But as I came down the gangway, my relief evaporated. On the dock stood the Fool as Lord Golden, fuming. A retinue of servants bearing boxes, crates, bags, and packages of all descriptions stood behind him. Blocking him was a harassed scribe with a scroll. He was shaking his head, his eyes nearly shut, as Lord Golden harangued him.

"Well, obviously there has been a mistake! What seems to elude you is that the error is not mine. For months, it has been settled that I am to accompany the Prince on his quest! Who better can advise him than a man like me who has traveled far and experienced many cultures? So take yourself out of my way! I myself shall select a suitable cabin, as you insist that none has been allotted to me, and move my comforts into it while you trot about and discover who is responsible for this gross error."

The scribe had never paused in his head-shaking and when he spoke, I was certain he was repeating words he'd already uttered. "Lord Golden, I humbly regret any error that has been made. My list came directly from Lord Chade's hands, and my instructions were most explicit. Only those listed here are to be settled aboard the Prince's ship. Nor am I allowed to leave my post here, to run and ask if some mistake has been made. My orders are quite clear on that." As if hoping to be rid of Golden, he added, "Perhaps you have been assigned to one of the accompanying vessels."

Lord Golden gave an exasperated sigh. As he turned to his servant, his eyes seemed to skate past me, but for the tiniest instant, our gazes met. "Put that down!" he commanded the man, and the servant lowered a box to the ground with relief. Lord Golden promptly sat down on it. As he crossed his green-hosed legs, he gestured imperiously at all of his other servants. "All of you! Set your burdens down where you are."

"But...you're blocking the...Please, Lord Golden..."

He ignored the scribe's anguish. "Here I shall remain until this matter is resolved," he announced in a wounded voice. He crossed his arms on his chest. Lifting his chin, Lord Golden gazed out over the waters as if nothing else in the world concerned him at all.

The scribe darted a look past him. His servants and equipment formed an effective blockade of the dock. Other passengers were beginning to clog the docks behind him, and longshoremen with barrows and tubs of supplies were gathering, too. The scribe took a breath and tried to summon authority. "Sir, you will have to remove yourself and your belongings until this is resolved."

"I shall not. So I suggest you send a runner to Lord Chade and have him give you the authority to let me board. For nothing less will satisfy me."

My heart sank. I knew that Lord Golden's remark was intended more for me than for the scribe. He had seen me.

He expected I would hasten back to Buckkeep Castle and drop a word in Chade's ear that would bring a speedy solution to his quandary. He did not yet suspect that his difficulty was of my making, and that even if I regretted it, Chade would stand firm. As I turned away from the milling spectacle he was creating, I saw him give me the ghost of a wink. No doubt he thought that Lord Golden's grand departure from Buckkeep Town would become one of the town's legends.

I wanted to see no more of it. As I trudged up the steep streets that led back to the castle, I told myself there was no reason to agonize. Lord Golden would sit there until evicted from the spot. No worse than that. And when we sailed tomorrow without him, well, he'd remain safely in Buckkeep whilst the rest of us went off to whatever discomfort and boredom the journey could offer us. No worse than that.

Nonetheless, the rest of the day dragged for me. After days of last-minute rushing, I found my final hours empty. There was nothing left to do. My space in the guard barracks was empty of all save the clothing and weapon I would wear on the morrow. The Prince's Guard would go forth handsomely. Leggings, shirt, and overtunic were all of Buckkeep blue. The Farseer buck was embroidered on the breast. My new boots had been made to my feet and didn't pinch. I'd already greased them well against wet. Although it was spring, the cloaks we'd been given were of thick wool against the expected cold of the Out Islands. The Fool's gift sword laid out atop my colors seemed like a rebuke. I left it there, safe as anything was safe in a barracks where a man's honor was most of what he possessed in the world.

In my tower workroom, it was much the same. If Chade had noticed that Chivalry's sword now hung over the mantelpiece, he'd chosen not to comment on it. I moved ineffectually around the room, putting away the things that Chade had left scattered from his packing. The charts of the Out Islands and all other writings that Chade thought might be needed had already been packed. For lack of anything else to do, I lay on the bed and teased the ferret. But soon even Gilly tired of that. He went off to hunt rats. I took myself off to the steams, scrubbed myself raw, and then shaved twice. Afterward, I went to my barracks and got into the narrow bed there. The rest of the long room was quiet and nearly deserted. Only a few old hands had chosen an early bed as I had. The others were out and about Buckkeep Town, bidding the taverns and whores farewell. I pulled the blankets around me and stared up at the shadowed ceiling.

I wondered how hard the Fool would try to follow us. Chade had assured me that he wouldn't be able to get passage out of Buckkeep Town. He'd have to travel to a different port, and pay a lot of money to persuade a ship's captain to sail after us. Lord Golden wouldn't have that money. After his recent escapades, I doubted he'd find any friends willing to loan him any. He'd be stuck.

And furious with me, I decided. He had a keen mind. He'd soon deduce who had been behind his abandonment. He would know that I had chosen his life over what he perceived as his destiny. He'd feel no gratitude. His Catalyst was supposed to aid him in changing the course of the world, not thwart him.

I closed my eyes and sighed. It took me several tries to compose myself. When finally I floated just beneath the surface of sleep, I reached out for Nettle. This time, she was sitting in an oak tree, wearing a gown of butterfly wings. I looked up at her from the knoll beneath the tree. I was the man-wolf, as I always was in her dreams. "All those dead butterflies," I said sorrowfully, shaking my head at her.

"Don't be silly. It's only a dream." She stood up on the branch and leaped. I reared onto my hind legs and opened my arms to catch her, but the butterflies of her gown all fluttered simultaneously, and she floated, light as thistledown, and landed on her feet beside me. She wore one large yellow butterfly in her hair like a hair ribbon. It slowly fanned its wings. The color of her gown shifted in waves as the butterflies wafted their wings lazily.

"Ew. Don't all the little legs tickle?"

"No. It's a dream, remember? You don't have to keep the unpleasant parts."

"You never have nightmares, do you?" I asked in admiration.

"I think that I used to, when I was very small. But I don't anymore. Why would anyone stay in a dream that didn't please her?"

"Not all of us can control our dreams the way you can, child. You should count it as a blessing."

"Do you have nightmares?"

"Sometimes. Don't you recall where you found me last time, crossing that talus slope?"

"Oh. Yes, I remember that. But I thought it was something you liked to do. Some men like doing dangerous things, you know."

"Perhaps. But some of us have had our fill of that, and would avoid nightmares if we could."

She nodded slowly. "My mother has terrible nightmares sometimes. Even when I go into them and tell her to come out, she won't. She either won't or can't see me. And my father . . . I know he has bad dreams, because sometimes he shouts aloud. But I can't find my way into his dreams at all." She stopped for a moment's thought. "I think that's why he started drinking again. When he's drunk, he passes out instead of falling asleep. Do you think he could be hiding from his nightmares?"

"I don't know," I said, and wished she had not told me such things. "I bring you news that may ease both of them, however. Swift is on his way back home."

She clasped her hands together and took a deep breath. "Oh, thank you, Shadow Wolf. I knew you could help me."

I tried to be stern. "I wouldn't have to help you if you'd used common sense. Swift is far too young to be out and about on his own. You shouldn't have helped him run away."

"I know that, now. But I didn't then. Why can't real life be like dreams? In a dream, if something starts to go wrong, you can simply change it." She lifted her hands to her shoulders and smoothed them down the front of her gown. Suddenly, she was wearing a dress of poppy petals. "See? No tickly legs now. You just have to tell the parts you don't like to go away."

"Like you sent away the dragon?"

"The dragon?"

"You know who I mean. Tintaglia. She appears small at first, as a lizard or a bee, and then becomes larger until you vanquish her."

"Oh. Her." She knit her brow. "She only comes when you do. I thought she was a part of your dream."

"No. She's not a part of anyone's dream. She's as real as you and me." It suddenly disturbed me that Nettle had not perceived that. Had our dream conversations exposed her to a greater danger than I knew?

"Who is she, then, when she is awake?"

"I told you. She's a dragon."

"There's no such thing as dragons," she declared with a laugh, shocking me into momentary silence.

"You don't believe in dragons? Then who saved the Six Duchies from the Red Ship raiders?"

"Soldiers and sailors, mostly, I suppose. It hardly matters anyway, does it? It happened so long ago."

"It matters a great deal to some of us," I muttered. "Especially to the ones who were there."

"I'm sure it does. Yet I've noticed that few if any can tell a straight tale of exactly what happened to save the Six Duchies. Just that they saw the dragons in the distance and that the next thing they knew, the Red Ships were sinking or broken. And the dragons were almost out of sight."

"Dragons have a strange effect upon people's memories," I explained to her. "They...they seem to absorb them as they pass over people. Like a cloth wiping up spilled beer."

She grinned up at me. "So, if that's true, why doesn't Tintaglia have that effect on us? How is it we can remember her being in our dreams?"

I held up a warning hand. "Let's not use her name anymore. I've no wish to encounter her again. As to why we can remember her, well, I think it is because she comes to us as a dream creature rather than in the flesh. Or it could be that she does not take our memories because she is a creature of flesh and blood, instead of..."

I recalled to whom I was speaking and halted. I was telling her too much. If I did not guard my tongue, soon I'd be telling her about Skill-carving dragons from memory stone, and how those creatures were the Elderlings of tale and song.

"Go on," she urged me. "If Tintaglia is not of flesh and blood, then what else could she be? And why does she always ask us about a black dragon? Are you going to say that he is real, too?"

"I don't know," I said cautiously. "I don't even know if he exists at all. Let's not talk of that, just now." I had felt nervous ever since she had mentioned Tintaglia's name. The word seemed to shimmer in the air, as betraying as the smoke from a cook fire.

But if there was any truth to the old summoning magic of a name, we were spared that night. I bade her farewell. Somehow, in leaving her dream I reentered my old nightmare. The sliding pebbles of the steep slope promptly rolled away under my feet. I was falling, falling to my death. I heard Nettle's outflung cry of "Change it to flying, Shadow Wolf! Make it a flying dream instead," but I did not know how to heed her. Instead, I jerked upright in my narrow cot in the barracks.

Morning was near, and most of the beds were filled now. Yet there was still a small time left for sleep. I tried to find it, but could not, and arose earlier than usual. None of my fellows were stirring. I put on my new uniform, and spent some time trying to persuade my hair to stay out of my face. I had shorn it for grief at Nighteyes' death, and it had not yet grown enough to stay bound back in a warrior's tail. I tied it back into a ridiculous stub, knowing it would soon pull free to hang about my face and brow.

I went to the guardroom and ate heartily of a lavish breakfast the kitchens had prepared for us. I knew I was bidding farewell to land food for a time, and availed myself of hot meat, fresh bread, and porridge with honey and cream. Meals on the ship would depend on the weather, and most of it would be salted, dried, and plainly cooked. If the water were rough and the cook judged fire too dangerous, we'd get cold food and hard bread. The prospect did not cheer me.

I returned to the barracks to find most of the guard stirring to wakefulness. I watched the rest of the men-at-arms don their blue tunics and complain about the weight of wool cloaks on a warm spring day. Chade had never admitted it, but there were a half-dozen of our company who, I suspected, were as much spies as guardsmen. There was a quiet watchfulness about them that made me think they saw more than they seemed to.

Riddle, a youngster of about twenty, was most emphatically not. He was as excited as I was jaded. A dozen times he consulted his mirror, paying particular attention to a rather new mustache. He was the one who insisted on loaning me pomade for my hair, saying he could not allow me to set forth on such an important day looking like a shaggy-haired farmer. He himself, dressed for display and seated on his bunk, tapped his feet impatiently on the floor and kept up a constant stream of chatter, everything from teasing me about the ornate hilt on my sword to demanding whether I knew if it was true that dragons could be slain only with an arrow to the eye. His loose energy was as annoying as a pacing dog. I was relieved when Longwick, our newly appointed captain, tersely ordered us to form up outside.

Not that the order meant imminent departure. It meant only that it was time for us to stand in formation and wait. Guardsmen spend more time waiting than they ever do in drill or fighting. This morning was no exception. Before we were ordered to move, I'd listened to a very detailed account of all three of Hest's liaisons of the night before, while Riddle helpfully asked detailed questions. When we did get the order to move, it was only as far as the courtyard in front of the main doors. Here we formed up around the Prince's horse and groom, and waited some more. Servants and lackeys who, like ourselves, were dressed and deployed to show their master's importance, soon joined us. Some held horse's heads, some leashed dogs, and some, like us, merely stood, armed and attired and waiting.

Eventually the Prince and his entourage emerged. Thick was at his heels and Sada, the woman who tended him on such occasions, was right behind him. Dutiful spared no glance for me today; I was as faceless as the rest. The Queen and her men preceded us, while Councilor Chade and his escort came immediately behind us. I spotted Civil, with his cat by his side, chatting with Web as they found their places in the procession. Despite Chade's objection, the Queen had announced that several of her "Old Blood friends" would travel with the Prince. The court reaction had been mixed, with some saying that we'd soon see if Old Blood Magic was good for anything and others muttering that at least it got the beast-magickers out of Buckkeep.

Behind them came the favored nobles who would accompany the Prince, both to curry favor with him and to investigate trading opportunities in the Out Islands. Behind them trailed those who would bid us farewell and then enjoy Spring Fest. But although I craned my neck, I saw no sign of Lord Golden as the procession formed up. By the time Dutiful was up and mounted and we were striding out of the gate, it seemed as if all of Buckkeep Castle were following us. I was grateful to be in the forefront, for by the time all passed, the road would be a trampled mire of mud and manure.

We reached the ships but could not simply load and depart. There were speeches and presentations of flowers and last-minute gifts. I had half-expected to find Lord Golden and his baggage and servants still camped out on the docks but there was no sign of them. I wondered uneasily what had happened. He was a resourceful man. Had he managed to find a way aboard the ship?

I sweated through the formalities. Then we moved aboard the ship, flanking the Prince, who went to his cabin, where he would receive farewell visits from the nobles who were not accompanying him, while those who were to be passengers boarded the ship and settled. Some of us were stationed outside the Prince's cabin, but the rest, including myself, were sent belowdecks, to be out of the way.

I spent most of that miserable afternoon sitting on my sea chest. Above me, the planks resounded with the noise of people coming and going. Somewhere a dog barked in a continuous frenzy. It was like being stuck inside a cask while someone beat on the outside of it. A dim, smelly cask, I amended to myself, with the rising stink of the bilges, elbow to elbow with men who thought they had to shout to be heard. I tried to distract myself by wondering what had become of the Fool, but that only increased my sensation of suffocation. I bowed my chin down to my chest, closed my eyes, and tried to be alone.

It didn't work.

Riddle perched on my sea chest beside me. "Eda's tits, but it stinks down here! Think it'll get worse when we're under way and the bilge is sloshing around?"

"Probably." I didn't want to think of that before it

happened. I'd traveled by sea before, but on those voyages, I'd slept on the deck, or at least had free access to it. Here, in the confined darkness, even the rhythmic swaying of the ship against its mooring was giving me a headache.

"Well." He kicked his heels against the chest, sending the vibration up my spine into my head. "I never have been to sea before. Have you?"

"Once or twice. On little boats, where I had light and air. Not like this."

"Oh. Ever been to the Out Islands?"

"No."

"Are you all right, Tom?"

"Not really. Too much to drink and not enough sleep last night."

It was a lie but it worked. He grinned, gave me a friendly jostle that made me snarl, and then left me alone. The bustle and noise pressed me from all sides. I was miserable and frightened and I wished I hadn't eaten all the sweet pastries at breakfast. No one was paying attention to me. My collar was too tight, and Sada had already left the ship, so she couldn't fix it for me.

"Thick," I whispered, recognizing the source of my woe. I sat up straight, drew a deep breath of the foul air, and tried not to retch. Then I reached for him. *Hey, little man. Are you all right?*

No.

Where are you?

In a little room. There's a round window and the floor moves.

You're better off than me. I've got no window at all.

The floor moves.

I know. But we'll be fine. Soon all the extra people will get off the boat, and the sailors will throw the lines free and we'll set off on our adventure. Won't that be fun?

No. I want to go home.

Oh, it'll be better once we get under way. You'll see.

No it won't. The floor moves. And Sada said I'd get sea-sick.

I wished someone had thought to tell Sada to speak positively of the journey to come.

Is Sada coming with us, then? Is she on board?

No. Only me, by myself. Because Sada gets horribly sick on ships. She felt very sorry for me, that I had to go. She said every day on a ship is like a year to her. And there's nothing to do except be sick, and vomit and vomit and vomit.

Unfortunately, Thick was right. It was late afternoon before the well-wishers were escorted from the ship. I managed to get up on the deck, but only briefly, for the captain cursed all the guard, ordering us to get back down below, to give his crew room to work. My glimpse of the crowd on the docks did not show me the Fool. I had dreaded to meet his accusing stare, but it worried me even more not to see him there. Then I was herded belowdecks with the rest and the hatches were closed over us, cutting off what little light and air we'd had before. I perched on my sea chest again. The resinous smell of the ship's tarry timbers intensified. Overhead, the captain ordered the ship's boats to tow us away from the dock. The sounds changed as we began to move through the water. The captain shouted incomprehensible commands, and I heard the pattering of bare feet as sailors rushed to obey them.

I heard the ship's boats called back and taken in. The vessel gave a sort of dip and then the rhythm of the motions changed again. I judged that our canvas had caught the wind. This was it. We were finally under way. Someone took pity on us down below and opened the hatch a crack, which taunted more than comforted. I stared at the skinny band of light.

"I'm already bored," Riddle confided to me. He stood next to me, carving on the heavy planks of the hull.

I made a noise at him. He went on carving.

Well, Tom Badgerlock, we're under way. How do you fare down below?

The Prince sounded cheery, but what could one expect of a fifteen-year-old, off on a sea voyage to slay a dragon and win the hand of a narcheska? I could sense Chade in the background, and pictured him at a table next to the Prince, Dutiful's fingers lightly touching the back of his hand. I sighed. We still had a lot of work to do to make the Skill coterie work. *I'm already bored. And Thick seems distressed.*

Ah. I was hoping you'd appreciate a task. I'll send a man to your captain. Thick is at the afterrail, and could use some company. You'll be joining him. That was unmistakably Chade, speaking through the Prince.

Is he sick already?

Not quite yet. But he has convinced himself that he will be.

Well, at least it would get me out into the air, I thought sourly.

A short time later, Captain Longwick called out my name. When I reported to him, he informed me that I was to tend the Prince's man Thick, who was indisposed on the afterdeck. The men who overheard my orders chivied me for being nursemaid to a half-wit. I grinned and replied that being abovedecks watching over one simpleton was far better than being trapped belowdecks with a troop of them. I climbed the ladder and emerged into the fresh sea air.

I found Thick on the afterdeck, holding on to the railing and staring dolorously back at Buckkeep. The black castle on top of the rocky cliffs was dwindling behind us. Civil stood near the little man, his hunting cat at his heels. Neither he nor the cat looked pleased to be there, and as Thick leaned out over the railing and made retching noises, the cat flattened his ears.

"Here's Tom Badgerlock, Thick. You'll be fine now, won't you?" Civil gave me a brief nod, nobleman to guardsman. As always, he stared at me searchingly. He knew I was not what I seemed. I'd saved his life from the Piebalds back in Buckkeep Town. He had to wonder at how I'd suddenly appeared and come to his aid. He'd have to keep wondering, just as I had to wonder how much Laudwine had told him about Lord Golden and me. We'd never spoken of it, nor did I intend to now. I made my eyes opaque and bowed.

"I'm here to assume my duties, sir." My tone was neutrally respectful.

"I'm very glad to see you. Well, farewell, Thick. You're in good hands, now. I'm going back into the cabin. I'm sure you'll feel better soon."

"I'm going to die," Thick replied dismally. "I'm going to puke my guts out and die."

Civil gave me a sympathetic look. I pretended not to see it as I took my place at the railing alongside Thick. He leaned far out again, forcing gagging sounds from his throat. I held on to the back of his jacket. Ah, yes. The adventure of travel by sea.

chapter VI

VOYAGE OF DREAMS

. . . despised Beast Magic's other uses. The ignorant believe that the Wit can only be used to give humans the power to speak to animals [words obscured by scorching] and shape-changing for evil intent. Gunrody Lian, the last man to admit openly at Buckkeep Court that he had [large fragment burned away] for healing the mind as well. From beasts too he claimed they could harvest the instinctive knowledge of curative herbs, as well as a wariness against [This portion ends here. Next scorched fragment of scroll begins:] . . . set hands to her head and held her steady and looked in her eyes. So he stood over her while the ghastly surgery was done, and she never looked away from him, nor cried out in agony. This I myself saw but . . . [Again, into the scorched edge of the scroll. The next three words may be:] dared not tell.

       FALLSTAR'S ATTEMPT TO RE-CREATE THE WIT
SCROLL BY SKILLMASTER LEFTWELL, FROM THE BURNED
FRAGMENTS DISCOVERED IN A WALL OF BUCKKEEP CASTLE

I managed to get all the way to the next morning before I vomited myself. I lost count of how many times I held on to Thick while he leaned far over the railing and retched hopelessly at the sea. The taunting of the sailors did not help matters, and if I had dared leave his side, I'd have taken some satisfaction from one or two of them. It was not congenial mockery of a landsman with no stomach for the sea. There was an ugly undercurrent to it, like crows drawn to torment a single eagle. Thick was different, a dimwit with a clumsy body, and they gleefully delighted in his misery as proof that he was inferior to them. Even when a few other miserable souls joined us at the railing, Thick took the brunt of their teasing.

It diminished briefly when the Prince and Chade took an evening stroll out on the decks. The Prince seemed invigorated by the sea air and his freedom from Buckkeep. As he stood by Thick and spoke to him in low tones, Chade contrived to set his hand on the railing touching mine. His back was to me and he appeared to be nodding to the Prince's conversation with his man.

How is he?

Sick as a dog and miserable. Chade, the sailors' mockery makes it worse.

I feared as much. But if the Prince notices and rebukes them, the captain will come down on them, as well. You know what will follow.

Yes. They'll find every private opportunity to make life hell for Thick.

Exactly. So try to ignore it for now. I expect it will wear off once they become accustomed to seeing him about the ship. Anything you need?

A blanket or two. And a bucket of fresh water, so he can wash his mouth out.

So I remained at Thick's side through the long and weary night, to protect him lest the taunting become physical as well as to keep him from falling overboard in his misery. Twice I tried to take him inside the cabin. Each time we did not get more than three steps from the railing before he was retching. Even when there was nothing left in his belly for him to bring up, he refused to go inside. The sea grew rougher as the night progressed, and by dawn we had a wind-driven rain soaking us as well as the flying spray from the tips of the whitecaps. Wet and cold, he still refused to budge from the railing. "You can puke in a bucket," I told him. "Inside, where it's warm!"

"No, no, I'm too sick to move," he groaned repeatedly. He had fixed his mind on his seasickness, and was determined to be miserable. I could think of no way to deal with it, except to let him follow it to its extreme and then be done with it. Surely, when he was miserable enough, he'd go inside.

Shortly after dawn, Riddle brought food for me. I was beginning to suspect that perhaps the naïve and affable young man truly was in Chade's employ and assigned to assist me. If so, I wished he wasn't, yet I was grateful for the pannikin of mush he brought me. Thick was hungry, despite his nausea, and we shared the food. That was a mistake, for the sight of it leaving Thick shortly after that inspired my own belly to be parted from what I had eaten.

That seemed to be the only thing that cheered Thick that morning.

"See. Everyone's going to be sick. We should go back to Buckkeep now."

"We can't, little man. We must go on, to the Out Islands, so the Prince can slay a dragon and win the Narcheska's hand."

Thick sighed heavily. He was beginning to shake with the cold despite the blankets that swaddled him. "I don't even like her. I don't think Prince likes her, either. She can keep her hand. Let's just go home."

At the moment, I agreed with him but dared not say so.

He went on. "I hate this ship, and I wish I'd never come."

Odd, how a man can become so accustomed to something that he no longer senses it. It was only when Thick spoke the words aloud that I realized how deeply they echoed his wild Skilling song. All night it had battered my walls, a song made of flapping canvas, creaking lines and timbers, and the slap of the waves against the hull. Thick had transformed them into a song of resentment and fear, of misery and cold and boredom. He had taken every negative emotion that a sailor might feel for a ship, and was blasting it out in an anthem of anger. I could put my walls up and remain unaffected by it. Some of the sailors that crewed the *Maiden's Chance* were not so fortunate. Not all were sensitive to the Skill, yet for those who were, the unrest would be acute. And in the close quarters, it would quickly affect their fellows.

I spent a few moments watching the crew at work. The current watch moved among their tasks effectively but resentfully. Their competence had an angry edge to it, and the mate who drove them from task to task watched with an eagle's eye for the slightest sign of slackness or idleness. The congeniality I had glimpsed when they were loading the ship was gone, and I sensed their discord building.

Like a nest of hornets that felt the thud of the axe echoing from the tree trunk below, they were stirred to a buzzing anger that had, as yet, no target. Yet if their general fury continued to mount, we could well be faced with brawls or, worse, a mutiny. I was watching a pot come to a seething boil, knowing that if I did nothing, we'd all be scalded.

Thick. Your music is very loud right now. And very scary. Can you make it different? Calm. Soft like your Mothersong?

"I can't!" He moaned the words as he Skilled them. "I'm too sick."

Thick, you're frightening the sailors. They don't know where the song comes from. They can't hear it, but some of them can feel it, a little bit. It's making them upset.

"I don't care. They're mean to me anyway. They should make this ship go back."

They can't, Thick. They have to obey the captain, and the captain has to do what the Prince tells him. And the Prince must go to the Out Islands.

"Prince should make them go back. I'll get off and stay at Buckkeep."

But Thick, we need you.

"I'm dying, I think. We should go back." And with that thought, his Skill-music swept to a crescendo of fear and despair. Nearby, a team of sailors had been hauling on a line to put on yet more canvas. Their loose trousers flapped in the constant wind, but they didn't seem to notice it. Muscles bulged in their bare arms as they methodically hauled the sheets into place. But as Thick's despondent song soaked them their rhythm faltered. The front man took more weight than he could manage, and stumbled forward with an angry shout. In an instant, the sailors had regained control of the line, but I had seen enough.

I sought the Prince with my mind. He was playing Stones in his cabin with Civil. Swiftly I relayed my problem to him. Can you pass this on to Chade?

Not easily. He's right here, watching the play, but so are Web and his boy.

Web has a boy?

That Swift boy.

Swift Witted is on board?

Do you know him? He came on board with Web and seems to serve him as a page serves a master. Why? Is that important?

Only to me, I thought. I grimaced with frustration. Later. But as soon as you can, tell Chade. Can you reach to Thick and calm him?

I'll try. Drat! You distracted me and Civil just won!

I think this is more important than a game of Stones! I replied testily and broke the contact. Thick was sitting on the deck at my feet, his eyes closed, swaying miserably, his music a queasy accompaniment to the rhythm of his body. It was not the only thing making me feel sick. I'd promised Nettle that her brother was on his way back to her. He wasn't. What was I to say to her? I set it aside as something I couldn't solve right now. Instead I crouched down beside Thick.

"Listen to me," I said quietly. "The sailors don't understand your music and it frightens them. If it goes on much longer, they might—"

And there I halted. I didn't want to make him fear the sailors. Fear is a solid foundation for hate. "Please, Thick," I said helplessly, but he only stared stubbornly out over the waves.

The morning passed while I waited for Chade to come and help me. I suspected that Dutiful Skilled a reassurance to him, but Thick stolidly ignored it. I stared at our wake, watching the other Buckkeep ships that trailed us. Three carracks followed us like a row of fat ducklings. There were two smaller vessels, pinnaces that would serve as communication vessels between the larger ships, enabling traveling nobles to exchange messages and visit one another as the voyage progressed. The smaller boats could use oars as well as sails, and could be used to maneuver the heavier ships in and out of crowded harbors. It was a substantial flotilla for Buckkeep to dispatch to the Out Islands.

The rain dwindled to a drizzle and then ceased, but the sun still hid behind the clouds. The wind was a constant. I tried to be positive about it for Thick. "See how swiftly it drives us over the water. Soon enough, we'll reach the Out Islands, and think how exciting it will be to see a new place!"

But Thick only replied, "It's pushing us farther and farther from home. Take me back now." Riddle brought us a noon meal of hard bread, dried fish, and watery beer. I think he was glad to be out on the deck. The guard was expected to stay below and out of the sailors' way. No one had said that the more they kept us separate, the less chance there was for fighting, but we all knew it. I spoke little, but Riddle chatted anyway, letting me know that the guardsmen below were also out of sorts. Some were seasick who swore they had never been bothered by that ailment before. That was not good news to me. I ate, and I managed to keep my food down, but I couldn't persuade Thick even to nibble on the sea bread. Riddle took our dishes and left us alone again. When Chade and the Prince finally appeared, my impatience and anger had been worn away to a dull resignation. While the Prince spoke to Thick, Chade swiftly conveyed to me how difficult it had been for the Prince and him to get out of the cabin alone. In addition to Web, Civil, and Swift, no less than three other nobles had come to his cabin to visit and lingered to talk long. As Chade had pointed out earlier, there was little else to occupy the time, and the nobles who had accompanied the Prince had done so to ingratiate themselves with him. They'd take advantage of every moment.

"So. When are we to work in Skill-lessons?" I asked him very softly.

He scowled. "I doubt that we'll manage much time for those. But I'll see what can be done."

Dutiful didn't have any more success with Thick than I had. Thick stared out sullenly over the ship's wake while the Prince spoke earnestly to him.

"Well. At least we managed to get away without Lord Golden," I observed to Chade.

He shook his head. "And that was far more difficult than I expected it to be. I imagine you heard of his blocking the docks in an attempt to board. He only gave up on that when the City Guard arrived and arrested him."

"You had him arrested?" I was horrified.

"Now, lad, be easy. He's a nobleman and his offense is a fairly trivial one; he'll be treated far better than you were. And they'll only hold him two or three days; just long enough for all the Out Island–bound ships to be gone. It seemed the easiest way to deal with him. I didn't want him coming up to Buckkeep Castle and confronting me, or begging a favor of the Queen."

"She knows why we did this, doesn't she?"

"She does. She doesn't like it, however. She feels a great debt to the Fool. But don't worry. I left enough hurdles that it will be difficult if not impossible for Lord Golden to get an audience with her."

I had not thought my spirits could sink lower, but now they did. I hated to think of the Fool imprisoned and then snubbed by Buckkeep's royalty. I knew how Chade would have worked it: a word there, a hint, a rumor that Lord Golden was not in the Queen's graces anymore. By the time he was out of the gaol, he'd be a social outcast. A penniless social outcast, with outstanding debts.

I'd only meant to leave him safely behind, not put him into such a position. I said as much to Chade.

"Oh, don't worry about him, Fitz. Sometimes you behave as if no one can manage without you. He's a very capable, very resourceful creature. He'll cope. If I'd done any less, he'd be on our heels right now."

And that too was true but scarcely comforting.

"Thick's seasickness can't go on much longer," Chade observed optimistically. "And when it passes, I'll put it about that Thick has become attached to you. That will give you good reason to be at his side, and sometimes in his chamber adjacent to the Prince's. Perhaps we shall have more time to confer that way."

"Perhaps," I said dully. Despite the Prince's conversation with Thick, I sensed no lessening of his discordant music. It wore on my spirits. By an effort of will, I could convince myself that Thick's nausea was not mine, but it was a constant effort.

"Are you sure you don't want to come back to the cabin?" Dutiful was asking him.

"No. The floor goes up and down."

The Prince was puzzled. "The deck moves up and down here, too."

It was Thick's turn to be confused. "No it doesn't. The boat goes up and down on the water. It's not as bad."

"I see." I saw Dutiful surrender any hope of explaining it to Thick. "In either case, you'll soon get used to it and the seasickness will go away."

"No it won't," Thick replied darkly. "Sada said that everyone will say that, but it isn't true. She got sick every time she went on a boat and it never went away. So she wouldn't come with me."

I was beginning to dislike Sada and I'd never even met the woman.

"Well. Sada is wrong," Chade declared briskly.

"No she isn't," Thick replied stubbornly. "See. I'm still sick." And he leaned out over the railing again, retching dryly.

"He'll get over it," Chade said, but he did not sound as confident as he had.

"Do you have any herbs that might help him?" I asked. "Ginger, perhaps?"

Chade halted. "An excellent idea, Badgerlock. And I do believe I have some. I'll have the cook make him a strong ginger tea and send it up to you."

When the tea arrived, it smelled as much of valerian and sleepbalm as it did of ginger. I approved of Chade's thought. Sleep might be the best cure for Thick's determined seasickness. When I offered it to him, I firmly told him that it was a well-known sailor's antidote to seasickness, and that it was certain to work for him. He still regarded it doubtfully; I suppose my words did not carry as much weight as Sada's opinion. He sipped it, decided he liked the ginger, and downed the whole cup. Unfortunately, a moment later he spewed it up just as swiftly as it had gone down. Some of it went up his nose, the ginger scalding the sensitive skin, and that made him adamantly refuse to try any more, even in tiny sips.

I had been on board for two days. Already it seemed like six months.

The sun eventually broke through the clouds, but the wind and flying spray snatched away whatever warmth it promised. Huddled in a damp wool blanket, Thick fell into a fitful sleep. He twitched and moaned through nightmares swept with his song of seasickness. I sat beside him on the wet deck, sorting my worries into useless piles. It was there that Web found me.

I looked up at him and he nodded gravely down at me. Then he stood by the rail and lifted his eyes. I followed his gaze to a seabird sweeping lazy arcs across the sky behind us. I had never met the creature, but I knew she must be Risk. The Wit-bond between man and bird seemed a thing woven of blue sky and wild water, at once calm and free. I basked in the edges of their shared pleasure in the day, trying to ignore how it whetted the edge of my loneliness. Here was the Wit Magic at its most natural, a mutual bond of pleasure and respect between man and beast. His heart flew with her. I could sense their communion and imagine how she shared her joyous flight with him.

It was only when my muscles relaxed that I realized how tense I had been. Thick sank into a deeper sleep and some of the frown eased from his face. The wind in his Skill-song took on a less ominous note. The calm that emanated from Web had touched us both, but my awareness of that came slowly. His warm serenity pooled around me, diluting my anxiety and weariness. If this was the Wit, he was using it in a way I'd never experienced before. This was as simple and natural as the warmth of breath. I found myself smiling up at him and he returned the smile, his teeth flashing white through his beard.

"It's a fine day for prayer. But then, most days are."

"That's what you were doing? Praying?" At his nod, I asked, "For what do you petition the gods?"

He raised his brows. "Petition?"

"Isn't that what prayer is? Begging the gods to give you what you want?"

He laughed, his voice deep as a booming wind, but kinder. "I suppose that is how some men pray. Not I. Not anymore."

"What do you mean?"

"Oh, I think that children pray so, to find a lost doll or that Father will bring home a good haul of fish, or that no one will discover a forgotten chore. Children think they know what is best for themselves, and do not fear to ask the divine for it. But I have been a man for many years, and I should be shamed if I did not know better by now."

I eased my back into a more comfortable position against the railing. I suppose if you are used to the swaying of a ship, it might be restful. My muscles constantly fought against it, and I was beginning to ache in every limb. "So. How does a man pray, then?"

He looked on me with amusement, then levered himself down to sit beside me. "Don't you know? How do you pray, then?"

"I don't." And then I rethought, and laughed aloud. "Unless I'm terrified. Then I suppose I pray as a child does. 'Get me out of this, and I'll never be so stupid again. Just let me live.'"

He laughed with me. "Well, it looks as if, so far, your prayers have been granted. And have you kept your promise to the divine?"

I shook my head, smiling ruefully. "I'm afraid not. I just find a new direction to be foolish in."

"Exactly. So do we all. Hence, I've learned I am not wise enough to ask the divine for anything."

"So. How do you pray then, if you are not asking for something?"

"Ah. Well, prayer for me is more listening than asking. And, after all these years, I find I have but one prayer left. It has taken me a lifetime to find my prayer, and I think it is the same one that all men find, if they but ponder on it long enough."

"And that is?"

"Think about it," he bade me with a smile. He stood slowly and gazed out over the water. Behind us, the sails of the following ships were puffed out like the throats of courting pigeons. They were, in their way, a lovely sight. "I've always loved the sea. I was on boats since before I could speak. It saddens me that your friend's experience of it must be so uncomfortable. Please tell him that it will pass."

"I've tried. I don't think he can believe me."

"A pity. Well, best of luck to you, then. Perhaps when he wakes, he'll feel better."

He began to walk away, but I remembered abruptly that I had other business with him. I came to my feet and called after him. "Web? Did Swift come aboard with you? The boy we spoke of before?"

He halted and turned to my question. "Yes. Why do you ask?"

I beckoned him closer and he came. "You recall that he is the boy that I asked you to talk with, the one who is Witted?"

"Of course. That was why I was so pleased when he came to me and offered to be my 'page' if I would take him on and teach him. As if I even knew what a page is supposed to do!" He laughed at such nonsense, and then sobered at my serious face. "What is it?"

"I had sent him home. I discovered that he did not have his parents' permission to be at Buckkeep at all. They think that he has run away, and are greatly grieved by his disappearance."

Web stood still and silent, digesting this news, his face showing no expression. Then he shook his head regretfully. "It must be a terrible thing for someone you love to vanish, and leave you always wondering what became of him."

An image of Patience sprang into my mind; I wondered if he had intended that his words prick me. Perhaps not, but the possible criticism made me irritable all the same. "I told Swift to go home. He owes his parents his labor until he either reaches his majority or is released by them."

"So some say," Web said, in a tone that indicated he might disagree. "But there are ways parents can betray a child, and then I think the youngster owes them nothing. I think that children who are mistreated are wise to leave as swiftly as they can."

"Mistreated? I knew Swift's father for many years. Yes, he will give a lad a cuff or a sharp word, if the boy has earned it. But if Swift claims he was beaten or neglected at home, then I fear that he lies. That is not Burrich's way." My heart sank that the boy could have spoken so of his father.

Web shook his head slowly. He glanced at Thick to assure himself that the man was still sleeping and spoke softly. "There are other types of neglect and deprivation. To deny what unfolds inside someone, to forbid the magic that comes unbidden, to impose ignorance in a way that invites danger, to say to a child, 'You must not be what you are.' That is wrong." His voice was gentle but the condemnation was without compassion.

"He raises his son as he was raised," I replied stiffly. It felt odd to defend him, for I had so often railed against Burrich for what he had done to me.

"And he learned nothing. Not from having to deal with his own ignorance, not from what it did to the first lad he treated so. I try to pity him, but when I consider all that could have been, had you been properly educated from the time you were small—"

"He did well by me!" I snapped. "He took me to his side when no one else would have me, and I'll not hear ill spoken of him."

Web took a step back from me. A shadow passed over his face. "Murder in your eyes," he muttered.

The words were like being doused with cold water. But before I could ask what he meant by them, he nodded to me gravely. "Perhaps we shall speak again of this. Later." And he turned and paced away from me. I recognized his walk. It was not flight. It was how Burrich would withdraw from an animal that had learned viciousness from bad treatment and had to be slowly retrained. It shamed me.

Slowly I sat down beside Thick again. I leaned back against the railing and closed my eyes. Perhaps I could doze a bit while he slept. But it seemed I had no sooner closed my eyes than his nightmare threatened me. Closing my eyes was like venturing downstairs into the noisy, smoky common room of a cheap inn. Thick's nauseous music swirled up into my mind, while his fears amplified the roll of the ship into a terrifying series of plunges and leaps without a pattern. I opened my eyes. Enduring sleeplessness was better than being swallowed by that bad dream.

Riddle brought me a pan of salty stew and a mug of watery beer while Thick still dozed. He'd brought his own rations as well, probably to enjoy eating on deck rather than in the cramped hold below. When I started to waken Thick to share the food, Riddle stopped me. "Let the poor moron sleep. If he's fortunate enough to be able to, he's the envy of every guardsman below."

"And why is that?"

He lifted one shoulder in a hapless shrug. "I can't say. Perhaps it's just the close quarters. But tempers are tight, and no one's sleeping well. Half of them are avoiding food for fear it won't stay down, and some of them are seasoned travelers. If you do manage to doze off, someone shouting out in a dream wakes you. Perhaps in a few days things will settle down. Right now, I'd rather stand in a pit surrounded by snarling dogs than go back down there. There were two fistfights just a moment ago, over who got fed first."

I nodded sagely, trying to conceal my anxiety. "I'm sure things will settle in a day or so. The first few days of a voyage are always difficult." I was lying through my teeth. Usually the first few days were the best, while the journey was still a novelty and before the tedium set in. Thick's dreams were poisoning the guards' sleep. I tried to be congenial while waiting for Riddle to leave. As soon as he took our empty dishes and departed, I leaned over and shook Thick awake. He sat up with a wail like a startled child.

"Shush, now. You're not hurt. Thick, listen to me. No, shush and listen. This is important. You have to stop your music, or at least make it quieter."

His face was wrinkled like a prune, with anger and

hurt feelings that I had so roughly awakened him. Tears stood in his little round eyes. "I can't!" he wailed. "I'm going to die!"

The men working on deck turned scowling faces our way. One muttered angrily and made a sign against ill luck toward us. On some level, they knew the source of their uneasiness. He snuffled and sulked as I talked to him, but firmly resisted any suggestion that he could either dampen his song, or overcome his seasickness and fear. I became fully aware of the strength of his wild Skilling only when I tried to reach the Prince through the cacophony of Thick's emotions. Chade and the Prince had probably increased the strength of their walls without even noticing they were doing so. Skilling to them was like shouting into a blizzard.

When Dutiful realized how difficult it was for him to understand me, I felt panic touch him. He was in the midst of a meal and could not graciously leave. Even so, he found some way to make Chade aware of our crisis. They brought the meal to a hasty end and hastened out on deck to us.

By then, Thick had dozed off again. Chade spoke quietly. "I can mix a powerful sleeping draught and we can force it down him."

The Prince winced. "I'd rather not. Thick does not soon forget ill-treatment. Besides, what would we gain from it? He sleeps now, and still his song is enough to torment the dead."

"Perhaps if I put him into a very deep sleep—" Chade ventured uncertainly.

"We'd be risking his life," I interrupted. "With no assurance that his song would stop."

"We have only one option," the Prince said quietly. "Turn back and take him home. Put him off the ship."

"We can't!" Chade was aghast. "We'll lose too many days. And we may need Thick's strength, when we actually confront the dragon."

"Lord Chade, we are seeing the full effects of Thick's strength now. And we are seeing that it is not disciplined, nor controlled by us." There was a new note in the Prince's voice, a monarch's tone. It reminded me of Verity, and his carefully weighted words. It made me smile and that earned me an odd frown from the Prince. I hastened to clarify my own thoughts.

"Right now, Thick's strength is not governed, not even by him. He does not intend us ill, but his music threatens us all. Think what sort of damage he might do, were he provoked to true anger. Or badly hurt. Even if we can cure his seasickness and calm his song, Thick will remain a double-edged blade. Unless we can find a sure discipline for his strength, he can threaten us when he is unsettled. Perhaps we would be wiser to go back and put him ashore."

"We can't go back!" Chade insisted. Then, as both Dutiful and I stared at him, he pleaded, "Let me have one more night to ponder. I'm sure I'll think of a solution. And give him one more night to become accustomed to the ship. Perhaps by dawn, his sickness might have passed."

"Very well," Dutiful replied after a moment. Again, there was that note in his voice. I wondered how he was learning it, or if he was simply growing into his role as ruler. In either case, I was glad to hear it. I was not sure if his decision to grant Chade one more day was a wise one or not. Yet it was his decision and he had made it with confidence. That was a thing to value.

When Thick awoke, he was sick again. I suspected that his prolonged hunger had as much to do with his weakness now as his seasickness did. He was sore from retching, for the muscles of his belly ached and his throat was raw. I could not persuade him to take anything except water, and that he accepted reluctantly. The day was neither cold nor warm, but Thick shivered in his damp clothes. They chafed him, but my suggestion that we go into his cabin and change or get warm met angry resistance. I longed to simply pick him up and drag him there, but knew he would scream and fight me, and that his music would become wild and violent. Yet I feared that he might soon slip into a real illness.

The slow hours passed miserably, and not just for us. Twice I heard the mate explode in anger at his bad-humored crew. The second time, he threatened a man with a lashing if he didn't show a more respectful face. I could feel the tension building aboard the ship.

In late evening the rain returned as a pervasive misting. I felt as if I had not been dry for a week. I put my blanket over Thick, hoping the weight of wool would be good for some warmth. He was dozing fitfully on the deck, twitching in his sleep like a dog with nightmares. I had often heard the jest "You can't die from seasickness, but you wish you could." Now I wondered if it was wrong. How long could his body accept this treatment?

My Wit made me aware of Web before his silhouette lumbered out of the dim light of the ship's lantern to stand over me. "You're a faithful man, Tom Badgerlock," he observed as he hunkered down beside me. "This can't be pleasant duty, but you've not left his side even for a moment."

His praise both warmed me and made me uncomfortable. "It's my responsibility," I replied, letting his compliment slide past me.

"And you take it seriously."

"Burrich taught me that," I said, a bit testily.

Web laughed easily. "And he taught you to hang on to a grievance like a pit dog hanging on to a bull's nose. Let it go, FitzChivalry Farseer. I'll say no more of the man."

"I wish you would not bandy that name about so casually," I said after a moment of heavy quiet.

"It belongs to you. It's a piece of you that is missing. You should take it back."

"He's dead. And better left that way, for the sake of all I hold dear."

"Is it truly for them, or is it for yourself?" he asked of the night.

I wasn't looking at him. I was staring out over the

stern, watching the other ships that trailed us through the watery night. They were black hulks, their sails blotting out the stars behind them. The lanterns they bore rose and fell with them, distant moving stars. "Web, what do you want of me?" I asked him at last.

"Only to make you think," he answered soothingly. "Not to make you angry, though I seem to excel at that. Or perhaps your anger is always there, festering inside you, and I am the knife that lances the boil and lets it burst forth."

I shook my head at him silently, not caring if he could or could not see me. I had other things to deal with right now, and wished I were alone.

As if he could read my thoughts, he added, "And tonight I did not even intend to start you on your thinking path. Actually, I came here to offer you respite. I'll sit vigil with Thick, if you wish to take a few hours to yourself. I doubt you've slept deeply since you took up this watch."

I longed to move about freely on my own, to see what the temper was on the rest of the ship. Even more than that, I longed for a little unguarded sleep. The offer was incredibly attractive. It therefore made me immediately suspicious.

"Why?"

Web smiled. "Is it that unusual for people to be nice to you?"

His question jolted me in an odd way. I took a breath. "Sometimes it seems that way, I suppose."

I rose slowly, for I had stiffened in the night chill. Thick muttered in his uneasy rest. I raised my arms over my head and rolled my shoulders as I arrowed a swift thought to Dutiful. *Web is offering to take over my watch of Thick for a time. May I allow this?*

Of course. He seemed almost surprised that I had asked.

But then, sometimes my prince trusted too easily. *Please let Chade know.*

I felt Dutiful's agreement. I spoke aloud to Web, at the

end of my stretch. "Thank you. I'll take you up on your offer, very gratefully."

I watched him settle himself carefully beside Thick
and take the smallest seapipes I'd ever seen from inside his
shirt. Seapipes are probably the most common musical instrument in any fleet, for they withstand both bad weather
and careless handling. It takes little to learn to play a simple tune on them, yet a talented player can entertain like a
Buckkeep minstrel with them. I wasn't surprised to see
them in Web's hands. He'd been a fisherman; he probably
still was, in many ways.

He waved me away. As I departed, I heard a breathy
sigh of music. He was playing, very softly, a child's tune on
his pipes. Had he instinctively known that might soothe
Thick? I wondered why I hadn't thought of music as a way
to comfort him. I sighed. I was becoming too set in my
ways. I needed to remember how to be flexible.

I went to the galley in hopes of begging something hot
to eat. Instead I got hard bread and a piece of cheese no
bigger than two fingers. The cook let me know I could consider myself fortunate for being allowed that. She didn't
have food to waste, she didn't, not aboard this top-heavy,
overpopulated tub. I had hoped for washwater, just enough
to splash the salt from my hands and face, but she told me I
hadn't a prayer of that. I'd had my share for the day, hadn't
I? I should take what I was issued and be happy with it.
Guardsmen. No idea what life aboard a vessel required of a
man in self-discipline.

I retreated from her sharp tongue. I longed to stay
abovedecks to eat, but I was out of my territory there, and
the sailors were in a mood to prove it to me. So I went below, down to where the rest of the guard snored and muttered and played cards by the swinging light of a lantern.
Our days at sea had not improved the smell of our quarters.
I found that Riddle had not exaggerated the ill humor of
the men. The comments of one man on "the returning
nursemaid" would have been enough justification for a

fight if I'd wanted one. I didn't, and managed to shed his insults, eat my food hastily, and dig my blanket out of my sea chest. Finding a place to stretch out was impossible. Prone guardsmen littered the floor. I curled up in their midst. I would have preferred to sleep with my back to a wall, but there was no hope of that. I eased off my boots and loosened my belt. The man next to me muttered nastily and rolled over as I tried to settle on the deck and cover most of myself with my blanket. I closed my eyes and breathed out, reaching desperately for unconsciousness, grateful for the opportunity to close my eyes and sleep. At least in my dreams I could escape this nightmare.

But as I crossed the dim territory between wakefulness and sleep, I recognized that perhaps I held the solution to my problems. Instead of wallowing my way into full sleep, I slid sideways through it, seeking Nettle.

My task was harder than I had expected. Thick's music was here, and finding my way through it was like blundering through brambles in a fog. No sooner did I think of that than the sounds sprouted tendrils and thorns. Music should not hurt a man, but this did. I staggered through a fog of sickness, hunger, and thirst, my spine tight with cold and my head pounding with the discordant music that snatched and dragged at me. After a time I halted. "It's a dream," I said to myself, and the brambles writhed mockingly at my words. As I stood still, pondering my situation, they began to wrap around my legs. "It's a dream," I said again. "It can't hurt me." But my words did not prevail. I felt the thorns bite through my leggings into my flesh as I staggered forward. They tightened their grip and held me fast.

I halted again, fighting for calm. What had begun as Thick's Skill-suggestion was now my own nightmare. I straightened up against the weight of the thorny vines trying to pull me down, reached to my hip and drew Verity's sword. I slashed at the brambles and they gave way, wriggling away like severed snakes. Encouraged, I gave the sword a blade of flame that singed the writhing plants and lit my way through the encroaching fog. "Go uphill," I told myself. "Only the valleys are full of mist. The hilltops will be clean and bare." And it was so.

When I finally struggled clear of Thick's Skill-fog, I found myself at the edges of Nettle's dream. I stood staring up at a glass tower on the hilltop above me. I recognized the tale. The hillside above me was littered with tangling threads. As I waded in, they clung like spiderweb. I knew that Nettle was aware of me. Nonetheless, she left me to my own devices, and I floundered through the ankle-deep tangle that represented all the broken promises her false lovers had made to the princess. In the old tale, only a true-hearted man could tread such a path without falling.

In the dream, I had become the wolf. All four of my legs were soon bound by the clinging stuff and I must needs stop and chew myself clear of it. For some reason, the thread tasted of anise, a pleasant enough flavor in moderation, but choking by the mouthful. When I finally reached the glass tower and looked up at her, my chest was wet and my jaws dripped saliva. I gave myself a shake, droplets flying, and then asked her, "Aren't you going to invite me to come up?"

She did not reply. She leaned on the parapet of her balcony and stared out over the countryside. I looked behind me, down to where the brambles waved above the banked fog in the deep valleys. Was the fog creeping closer? When Nettle continued to ignore me, I trotted around the base of the tower. In the old tale, there was no door and Nettle had re-created it faithfully. Did that mean she had had a lover who had been faithless to her? My heart turned over in me and for a moment I forgot the purpose of my visit. When I had circled the tower, I sat down on my haunches and looked up at the figure on the balcony. "Who has betrayed you?" I asked her.

She continued to stare out and I thought she would

not answer. But then, without looking down at me, she replied, "Everyone. Go away."

"How can I help you if I go away?"

"You can't help me. You've told me that often enough. So you might as well just go away and leave me alone. Like everyone else."

"Who has gone away and left you alone?"

That brought me a furious glare. She spoke in a low voice full of hurt. "I don't know why I thought you might remember! My brother, for one. My brother Swift, who you said would soon be coming home to us. Well, he hasn't! And then my stupid father decided to go look for him. As if a man with fogged eyes can go look for anything! And we told him not to go, but he did. And something happened, we don't know what, but his horse came home without him. So I went out on my horse, despite my mother shrieking at me that I wasn't to leave, and I tracked his horse's trail back and found Papa by the side of the road, bruised and bloody and trying to crawl home dragging one leg. So I brought him home, and then my mother scolded me again for disobeying her. And now my father is in bed and all he does is lie there and stare at the wall and not speak to anyone. My mother forbade any of us from bringing him any brandy. So he won't talk to us or tell us what happened. Which makes my mother furious at all of us. As if it were my fault."

Halfway through this tirade, her tears had begun to stream down her face. They dripped from her chin and ran over her hands and trickled down the wall of the tower. Slowly they solidified into opal strands of misery. I reared up on my hind legs and clawed at them, but they were too smooth and too shallow for me to gain any purchase. I sat down again. I felt hollow and old. I tried to tell myself that the misery in Molly's home had nothing to do with me, that I had not caused it and could not cure it. And yet, the roots of it ran deep, did they not?

After a time, she looked down at me and laughed

bitterly. "Well, Shadow Wolf? Aren't you going to say you can't help me with that? Isn't that what you always say?" When I could think of no reply, she added in an accusing tone, "I don't know why I even speak to you. You lied to me. You said my brother was coming home."

"I thought he was," I replied, finding words at last. "I went to him and I told him to go home. I thought he had."

"Well, perhaps he tried to. Perhaps he started this way, and was killed by robbers, or fell in a river and drowned. I don't suppose you ever considered that ten is a bit young to be out on the roads alone? I suppose you never thought that it might have been kinder if you had brought him home safely to us, instead of 'sending' him? But no, that might have been inconvenient to you."

"Nettle. Stop. Let me speak. Swift is safe. Alive and safe. He is still here, with me." I paused and tried to breathe. The inevitability of what must follow those words sickened me. *Here it comes, Burrich,* I thought to myself. *All the pain I ever tried to save you. All tied up in a tidy package of misery for you and your family.*

For Nettle asked, as I knew she must, "And where is 'safe with you'? And how do I know he is safe? How do I know you are a true thing at all? Perhaps you are like the rest of this dream, a thing I made. Look at you, man-wolf! You are not real and you offer me false hope."

"I am not real as you see me," I replied slowly. "But I am real. And once upon a time, your father knew me."

"'Once upon a time,'" she said scornfully. "Another tale from Shadow Wolf. Take your silly stories away." She took a shuddering breath and fresh tears started down her face. "I'm not a child any longer. Your stupid stories can't help me."

So I knew I had lost her. Lost her trust, lost her friendship. Lost my chance of knowing my child as a child. Terrible sadness welled up in me, but it was laced with the music of brambles growing. I glanced behind me. The thorn vines and fog had crept higher. Was it just my own dream threat-

ening me, or had Thick's music become even more menacing? I didn't know. "And I came here seeking your help," I
reminded myself bitterly.

"My help?" Nettle asked in a choked voice.

I had spoken without thinking. "I know I don't have
the right to ask you for anything."

"No. You don't." She was looking past me. "What is
that, anyway?"

"A dream. A nightmare, actually."

"I thought your nightmares were about falling." She
sounded intrigued.

"That's not my nightmare. It belongs to someone else.
He is . . . It's a very strong nightmare. Strong enough to
spread out from him and take over the dreams of other people. It's threatening lives. And I don't think the man
whose dream it is can control it."

"Just wake him up, then." She offered the solution disdainfully.

"That might help, for a little time. But I need a more
permanent solution." For a brief moment, I considered
telling her that the man's nightmare endangered Swift, as
well. I pushed the thought aside. There was no use frightening her, especially when I wasn't sure she could help me.

"What did you think I could do about it?"

"I thought you could help me go into his dream and
change it. Make it pleasant and calm. Convince him that
what is happening to him won't kill him, that he'll be fine.
Then his dreams might be calmer. And we could all rest."

"How could I do that?" And then, more sharply, "And
why should I do that? What do you offer me in exchange,
Shadow Wolf?"

I did not like that it had come down to barter, but I had
only myself to blame. It was cruelest of all that the only
thing I had to offer her would bring pain and guilt for her
father. I spoke slowly. "As to how, you are very strong in the
magic that lets one person walk into another person's
dreams and change them. Strong enough, perhaps, to shape

my friend's dream for him, even though he himself is also very strong in magic. And very frightened."

"I have no magic."

I ignored her words. "As for why...I have told you that Swift is with me, and safe. You doubt me. I don't blame you, for it appears I have failed you in my earlier assurance. But I will give you words, to say to your father. They will...they will be hard for him to hear. But when he hears them, he will know that what I say is true. That your brother is alive and well. And with me."

"Tell me the words, then."

For one brief Chade-ish moment, I thought of demanding that first she help me with Thick's dreaming. Then I harshly rejected that notion. My daughter owed me exactly what I had given her: nothing. Perhaps there was also the fear that if I did not speak to her then, I would lose my courage. Uttering those words was like touching my tongue to a glowing coal. I spoke them. "Tell him that you dreamed of a wolf with porcupine quills in his muzzle. And that the wolf said to you, 'As once you did, so I do now. I shelter and guide your son. I will put my life between him and any harm, and when my task is done, I will bring him safely home to you.'"

I had cloaked my message as best I could, under the circumstances. Nettle still struck far too close to the truth when she eagerly asked, "My father cared for your son, years ago?"

Some decisions are easier if you don't allow yourself time to think. "Yes," I lied to my daughter. "Exactly."

I watched her mull this for a moment. Slowly her tower of glass began to melt into water. It flowed, warm and harmless, past my feet until her balcony had descended to the ground. She offered me her hand to help her climb over the railing. I took it, touching and yet not touching my daughter for the first time in her life. Her tanned fingers rested briefly on my black-clawed paw. Then she stood clear of me and looked down at the fog and creeping briars that were ascending the hillside toward us.

"You know I've never done anything like this before?"

"Neither have I," I admitted.

"Before we go into his dream, tell me something about him," she suggested. The fog and bramble crept ever closer. Whatever I told her about Thick would be too much, and yet for her to enter his dream ignorant might be dangerous to all. I could not control what Thick revealed to her in the context of the dream. For one fleeting second, I wondered if I should have consulted Chade or Dutiful before seeking Nettle's aid. Then I smiled grimly to myself. I was Skillmaster, was I not? In that capacity, this decision was mine alone.

And so I told my daughter that Thick was simple, a man with the mind and heart of a child, and the strength of an army when it came to Skill Magic. I even told her that he served the Farseer Prince, and that he journeyed with him on a ship. I told her how his powerful Skill-music and now his dreams were undermining morale on the ship. I told her of his conviction that he would always be seasick and that he would likely die from it. And as I told her these things, the thorns grew and twined toward us, and I watched her quickly drawing her own conclusions from what I said; that I was on board the ship also, and therefore that her brother was with me, on a sea voyage with the Farseer Prince. Rural as her home was, I wondered how much she had heard of the Narcheska and the Prince's quest. I didn't have to wonder long. She put the tale together for herself.

"So that is the black dragon that the silver dragon keeps asking you about. The one the Prince goes to slay."

"Don't speak her name," I begged her.

She gave me a disdainful look that mocked my foolish fears. Then, "Here it comes," she said quietly. And the brambles engulfed us.

They made a crackling sound as they rose around our

ankles and then our knees, like fire racing up a tree. The thorns bit into our flesh and then a dense fog swirled up about us, choking and menacing.

"What is this?" Nettle exclaimed in annoyance. Then, as the fog stole her from my sight, she exclaimed, "Stop it. Shadow Wolf, stop it right now! This is all yours; you made this mess. Let go of it!"

And she wrested my dream from me. It was rather like having someone snatch away your blankets. But most jarring for me was that it evoked a memory I both did and did not recognize: another time and an older woman, prying something fascinating and shiny from my chubby-fisted grasp, while saying, "No, Keppet. Not for little boys."

I was breathless in the sudden banishment of my dream, but in the next instant we literally plunged into Thick's. The fog and brambles vanished, and the cold salt water closed over my head. I was drowning. No matter how I struggled I could not get to the top of the water. Then a hand gripped mine, and as Nettle hauled me up to stand beside her, she exclaimed irritably, "You are so gullible! It's a dream, and that's all it is. Now it's my dream, and in my dream we can walk on the waves. Come on."

She said it and it was so. Still, I held on to her hand and walked beside her. All around us, the water stretched out, glittering shoreless from horizon to horizon. Thick's music was the wind blowing all around us. I squinted out over the water, wondering how we would ever find Thick in the trackless waves, but Nettle squeezed my hand and announced clearly through Thick's wild song, "We're very close to him now."

And that too was so. A few steps more and she dropped to her knees with an exclamation of pity. The blinding sunlight on the water hid whatever she stared at. I knelt beside her and felt my heart break.

He knew it too well. He must have seen it, sometime. The drowned kitten floated just beneath the water. Too young even for his eyes to be opened, he dangled weightlessly in the sea's grip. His fur floated around him, but as Nettle reached in to grip him by the scruff of the neck and pull him out, his coat sleeked suddenly flat with the water. He dangled from her hand, water streaming from his tail and paws and dribbling from his nose and open red mouth. She cupped the little creature fearlessly in her hand. She bent over him intently, experimentally flexing the small rib cage between her thumb and forefingers. Then she held the tiny face close to hers and blew a sudden puff of air into the open red mouth. In those moments, she was entirely Burrich's daughter. So I had seen him clear birth mucus from a newborn puppy's throat.

"You're all right now," she told the kitten authoritatively. She stroked the tiny creature, and in the wake of her hand, his fur was dry and soft. He was striped orange and white, I suddenly saw. A moment before, I thought he had been black. "You're alive and safe, and I will not let any evil befall you. And you know that you can trust me. Because I love you."

At her words, my throat closed up and choked me. I wondered how she knew them to say. All my life, without knowing it, I had wanted someone to say those words to me, and have them be true and believable. It was like watching someone give to another the gift you had always longed for. And yet, I did not feel bitterness or envy. All I felt was wonder that, at sixteen, she would have that in her to give to another. Even if I could have found Thick in his dream, even if someone had told me those were the words I must say, the words he most desperately needed to hear, I could not have said them and made them true as she did. She was my daughter, blood of my blood, and yet the wonder and amazement she made me feel at that moment made her a creation entirely apart from me.

The kitten stirred in her hand. It looked about blindly. When the little red mouth opened wide, I was prepared for a yowl. Instead, it questioned in a hoarse little voice, "Mam?"

"No," Nettle replied. My daughter was braver than I.

She did not even consider the easy lie. "But someone like her." Nettle looked around the seascape as if noticing it for the first time. "And this is not a good place for someone like you. Let's change it, shall we? Where do you like to be?"

His answers surprised me. She coaxed the information from him, detail by detail. When they were finished, we sat, doll-sized, in the center of an immense bed. In the distance, I could make out the hazy walls of a traveling wagon such as many puppeteer families and street performers lived in when they traveled from town to town. It smelled of the dried peppers and braided onions that were roped across one corner of the ceiling. Now I recognized the music around us, not just as Thick's Mothersong, but also the elements that comprised it: the steady breathing of a sleeping woman, the creak of wheels, and the slow-paced thudding of a team's hoofbeats, woven as a backdrop for a woman's humming and a childish tune on a whistle. It was a song of safety and acceptance and content. "I like it here," Nettle told him when they were finished. "Perhaps, if you don't mind, I'll come and visit you here again. Would that be all right?"

The kitten purred, and then curled up, not sleeping, but simply being safe in the middle of the huge bed. Nettle stood up to go. I think that was when I realized that I was watching Thick's dream but was no longer part of it. I had vanished from it, along with all other discordant and dangerous elements. I had no place in his mother's world.

"Farewell for now," Nettle told him. And added, "Now remember how easy it is to come here. When you decide to sleep, all you have to do is think of this cushion." She touched one of the many brightly embroidered pillows on the bed. "Remember this, and when you dream, you'll come straight here. Can you do that?"

The kitten rumbled a purr in response, and then Thick's dream began to fade around me. In a moment, I stood again on the hillside by the melted glass tower. The brambles and fog had vanished, leaving a vista of green valleys and shining rivers threading through them.

"You didn't tell him he wouldn't be seasick anymore," I suddenly remembered. Then I winced at how ungrateful my words sounded. Nettle scowled at me and I saw the weariness in her eyes.

"Do you think it was easy to find all those things and assemble them around him? He kept trying to change it all back into cold seawater." She rubbed her eyes. "I'm sleeping, and yet I suspect I'm going to wake exhausted."

"I apologize," I answered gravely. "Well do I know that magic can take a toll. I spoke without thinking."

"Magic," she snorted. "This dream-shaping is not magic. It is just a thing I can do."

And with that thought, she left me. I pushed from my mind the dread of what might be said when she gave Burrich my words. There was nothing I could do about any of that. I sat down at the base of her tower, but without Nettle to anchor it, the dream was already fading. I sank through it into a dreamless sleep of my own.

chapter VII

VOYAGE

Do not make the error of thinking of the Out Islands as a kingdom under a sole monarch, such as we have in the Six Duchies, or even as an alliance of peoples such as we see in the Mountain Kingdom. Not even the individual islands, small as they may seem, are under the sole command of any single lord or noble. In fact, there are no "nobles or lords" recognized among the Outislanders. Men have status according to their prowess as warriors and the richness of the spoils they bring back. Some have the backing of their matriarchal clans to enhance whatever reputation they may claim by force of arms. Clans hold territory on the islands, it is true, but these lands are the matriarchal farmlands and gathering beaches, owned by the women and passed down through their daughters.

Towns, especially harbor towns, belong to no single clan and mob law is generally the rule in them. The City Guard will not come to your aid if you are robbed or assaulted in an Out Island town. Each man is expected to enforce the respect others should give him. Cry out for help and you will be judged weak and beneath notice. Sometimes, however, the dominant clan in the area may

have a "stronghouse" in the town and set itself up in
judgment over disputes there.

 The Outislanders do not build castles and forts such
as we have in the Six Duchies. A siege is more likely to
be conducted by enemy vessels taking control of a harbor
or river mouth rather than by a land force attempting to
seize land. It is not unusual, however, to find one or two
clan "stronghouses" in each major town. These are
fortified structures built to withstand attack and often
having deep cellars with not only a well for water but
also substantial storage for food. These "stronghouses"
usually belonged to the dominant clan in each town, and
were designed more for shelter from civil strife than to
withstand foreign attack.

     ❧ SHELLBYE'S "OUT ISLAND TRAVELS"

When I awoke, I could feel that the ship was calmer. I had
not slept for many hours, but I felt rested. About me on the
deck, men still sprawled, immersed in slumber as if they
had not slept well in days, as was the case.

 I rose carefully, bundling my blanket in my arms and
stepping through the prone bodies. I put my blanket back
into my sea chest, changed into a cleaner shirt, and then
went back on deck. Night was venturing toward morning.
The clouds had rained themselves out, and fading stars
showed through their rent curtains. The canvas had been
reset to take advantage of a kindlier wind. The barefoot
sailors moved in quiet competence on the deck. It felt like
the dawn after a storm.

 I found Thick curled up and sleeping, the lines of his
face slack and peaceful, his breathing hoarse and steady.
Nearby, Web dozed; his head drooped forward onto his bent
knees. My eyes could barely make out the dark shape of a
seabird perched on the railing. It was a gull of some sort,
larger than the average. I caught the bright glint of Risk's
eye, and nodded to her in affable greeting as I approached

slowly, giving Web time to open his eyes and lift his head. He smiled at me.

"He seems to be resting better. Perhaps the worst is over."

"I hope so," I replied. Cautiously I opened myself to Thick's music. It was no longer a storm of Skill, but was still as constant as the shushing waves. His Mothersong had become dominant in it again, but I heard also the trace of a kitten purring, and a reassuring echo of Nettle's voice promising him that he was loved and safe. That unsettled me a bit; I wondered if I only heard it because I had witnessed the change, or if Chade and the Prince would also detect her words and voice.

"You look more rested, as well," Web observed, his voice abruptly recalling me to my manners and myself.

"Yes, I am. And I thank you."

He extended a hand to me, and I took it, helping him onto his feet. Once upright, he released my hand and rolled his shoulders to limberness again. On the railing, his bird waddled a step or two closer. In the gathering light, I marked the deep yellow of her beak and feet. Somewhere in Burrich's tutelage, I seemed to recall that bright colors were indicative of a well-nourished bird. This creature gleamed with health. As if aware of my admiration, she turned her head and carefully preened a long flight feather through her bill. Then, as effortlessly as a cat lofts into a chair, she rose from the railing, her cupped wings catching the wind and lifting her in flight.

"Show-off," Web muttered. He smiled at me. It came to me that Wit-partners take the same inane pride in one another that parents do in their children. I smiled back, commiserating.

"Ah. That looks genuine. In time, my friend, I think you will come to trust me. Tell me when you do."

I gave a small sigh. It would have been courteous to insist that I already trusted him, but I did not think I could lie well enough to deceive him. So I simply nodded. Then, as he turned to go, I remembered Swift. "I've another favor I would ask of you," I said awkwardly.

He turned back to me, sincere pleasure in his face. "I'll take that as an indication of progress."

"Could you ask Swift to give me some of his time today? I'd like to talk to him."

Web cocked his head like a gull regarding a dubious clamshell. "Are you going to browbeat him about returning to his father?"

I considered. Was I? "No. I'm only going to tell him that I regard it as essential to my honor that he return safely to Buckkeep. And that I expect him to keep up his lessons with me while on this journey." Oh, that would please Chade, I thought sourly. My time already was stretched thin, and I was taking up yet another task.

Web smiled warmly. "It would please me greatly to send him to you to hear those things," he replied. He offered me a sailor's brief bow before he departed, and I nodded back.

A Skilled suggestion from me meant that the Prince rose early and was on the deck beside Thick when he finally stirred. A servant had brought up a small basket, with warm bread and a pot of hot tea in it. The smell of it made me aware I was ravenous. He set it on the deck near Thick and then the Prince dismissed him. We stood silently staring out over the sea, waiting for Thick to awaken.

When did his music change? When I awoke this morning, I could not believe how relaxed and rested I felt. It took me some time before I realized what the change was.

It's such a relief, isn't it? I wanted to say more, but dared not. I could not admit to the Prince that I had tampered with Thick's dreams, because I wasn't really the one who had done it. I doubted that Thick had even been aware I was there.

Thick's awakening saved me. He coughed, and then opened his eyes. He looked up at Dutiful and me and a slow smile spread over his face. "Nettle fixed my dream for me," he said. Before either Dutiful or I could respond to his words, he went off in a fit of coughing. Then, "I don't feel good. My throat hurts."

I seized the opportunity to divert the conversation. "It's probably from all the retching you've done. Look, Thick, Dutiful has brought you tea and fresh bread. The tea will ease your throat. Shall I pour you some?"

His only reply was another spell of coughing. I crouched down beside him and touched his cheek. His face was warm, but he had just awakened and he was still wrapped in wool blankets. It didn't mean he had a fever. He pushed the blankets away irritably, and then sat shivering in his wrinkled, damp clothing. He looked miserable and his music began to swirl discordantly.

The Prince took action. "Badgerlock, bring that basket. Thick, you are coming back into the cabin with me. Immediately."

"I don't want to," he groaned, then shocked me by slowly standing up. He staggered a step, then looked out over the rolling waves and seemed to recall. "I'm seasick."

"That's why I want to take you to the cabin. You'll get better there," the Prince told him.

"No I won't," Thick insisted, but all the same when Dutiful started off toward the cabin, he slowly fell in behind him. His gait was unsteady, as much from weakness as from the gentle shifting of the deck. I stepped up to take his arm and escorted him, the laden basket on my other arm. He wobbled along beside me. We stopped twice for coughing spells, and by the time we reached the door of the Prince's cabin, my concern had become worry.

Dutiful's chamber was more elaborate and better furnished than his bedchamber at home. Obviously someone else had designed it to a Buckkeep idea of what a prince merited. It had a bank of windows that looked out onto the wake behind the ship. There were rich carpets over the polished deck, and heavy furniture that was well anchored against the sway of the ship. I would probably have been more impressed if I had lingered there longer, but Thick arrowed for his own small room that opened off the main chamber. It was far more modest, little more than a closet the size of his bunk with a space beneath it for storing personal items. The architect of the ship had probably intended it for a valet rather than a bedchamber for the Prince's pet simpleton. Thick immediately crumpled onto the bed. He moaned and muttered as I shook him out of his stained and sweaty clothing. When I covered him with a light blanket, he clutched it to himself and complained, teeth chattering, of the cold. I fetched him a stuffed coverlet from the foot of the Prince's own bed. I was certain of his fever now.

The pot of tea had cooled a bit, but I poured a cup for Thick and sat by him while he drank it. At my Skilled suggestion, the Prince sent for willow bark tea for his fever and raspberry root syrup for his cough. When the servant finally brought them, it took me some time to coax Thick to accept them. But his stubbornness seemed to have been eroded by the fever, and he gave way to me.

The room was so small that I could not shut the door while I was sitting on the edge of his bed, so it remained open and I idly watched the flow of people through my prince's chamber as I tended our simpleton. I found little of interest until Dutiful's "Witted coterie" arrived. They were Civil, Web, the minstrel Cockle, and Swift. Dutiful was seated at the table, softly rehearsing his Outislander speech, when they came in. As the servant admitted them and then was dismissed, he pushed the scroll aside with apparent relief. Civil's cat padded in at his heels and immediately made himself comfortable on the Prince's bed. No one seemed to take any notice of him.

Web glanced at me, bemused, before he greeted the Prince. "All's fair aloft, Prince Dutiful." I thought it was an odd courtesy, until it dawned on me that he was relaying the word from his bird, Risk. "No ships save our own are in sight."

"Excellent." The Prince smiled his approval before he turned his attention to the others. "How fares your cat today, Civil?"

Civil held up his hand. His sleeve fell back to expose a raised red scratch the length of his forearm. "Bored. And irritated with the confinement. He'll be glad when we see land again." All the Witted ones laughed indulgently together, as parents would over a child's willfulness. I marked how comfortable they all seemed in the Prince's presence. Only Swift seemed to retain any stiffness, and that could have been due to either his awareness of me or the age difference between him and the rest of the company. So had Verity's closest nobles been with him, I recalled, and thought to myself that the casual affection of those men was more valuable than the way Regal's hangers-on used to bow and scrape to him.

So it did not seem overly odd when Web turned to look at me and then asked Dutiful, "And has Tom Badgerlock come to join us today, my prince?"

Two questions rode in his words. Was I there to admit my Wit and possibly my identity, and would I be joining their "coterie"? I held my breath as Dutiful answered, "Not exactly, Web. He tends my man Thick. I understand you kept watch by him during the night to allow Badgerlock some rest, and for that I thank you. Yet now Thick has taken a cough from his night exposure and is feverish. He finds Badgerlock's company soothing, and so the man has agreed to sit with him."

"Ah. I see. Well, Thick, I'm sorry to hear you are ill." As he spoke, Web came to peep in through the door. At the table behind him, the rest of the coterie continued their quiet conversation. Swift watched Web anxiously. Thick, huddled in his blankets and staring at the wall, seemed only mildly aware of him. Even his Skill-music seemed subdued and muted, as if he lacked the energy to drive it. When Thick made no response, Web touched me softly on the shoulder and said quietly, "I'll be happy to take a watch beside him tonight, too, if you'd like the rest. In the meanwhile..." He turned from me and gestured at Swift, whose face clouded with sudden apprehension. "I'll leave my 'page' here with you. Doubtless you two have much to discuss, and if there are any errands that can be run for Thick's comfort, I'm sure Swift will be glad to fetch for you. Isn't that right, lad?"

Swift was in an untenable position and he knew it. He came to heel like a whipped dog and stood beside Web, eyes downcast.

"Yes, sir," he replied softly. He lifted his gaze to me and I didn't like what I saw there. It was fear coupled with dislike and I did not feel I had done anything to justify either of those emotions.

"Swift," Web said, drawing the boy's eyes back to him. He went on quietly, in a voice pitched for our ears alone. "It will be fine. Trust me. Tom wishes to be sure you will continue your education while you are aboard this ship. That is all."

"Actually, there is more," I said unwillingly. That made both of them stare at me. Web lifted a brow. "I've given a promise," I said slowly. "To your family, Swift. I promised that I'd put my life between you and anything that threatened you. I've promised that I'll do my best to see you safely home, when all this is over."

"What if I don't want to go home when all this is over?" Swift asked me insolently, his voice rising. I felt more than saw the Prince become aware of the conversation. And then the boy added, indignantly, "Wait! How did you talk to my father? There wasn't time for you to send a messenger and then get a reply before we left. You're lying."

I drew a slow breath through my nostrils. When I could speak calmly, I replied, keeping my voice pitched low. "No. I am not lying. I sent my promise to your family. I didn't say they had replied. I still consider it just as binding."

"There wasn't time," he protested, but more quietly. Web looked at him disapprovingly. I scowled. Web flicked a disapproving glance at me, but I met it steadily. I'd promised to keep the boy alive and return him home. That didn't mean I had to tolerate his insults gladly.

"I suppose this may be a long voyage for both of you," Web observed. "I'll leave you to each other's company, and hope you both learn to make the best of it. I believe you each have something to offer the other. But you'll only value it if you discover it for yourselves."

"I'm cold," Thick moaned, rescuing me from Web's lecture.

"There's your first errand," I told Swift brusquely. "Ask the Prince's serving man where you can find two more blankets for Thick. Wool ones. And bring him a big mug of water, as well."

I think it offended his dignity to fetch things for a half-wit, but he found it preferable to remaining in my company. As Swift scuttled off, Web gave a sigh.

"Truth between the two of you," he advised me. "It's going to be your only bridge to reaching that boy, Tom. And he needs you to reach him. I'm only realizing that now. He ran from his home, and he ran from you. He has to stop running or he'll never learn to stand and face down his problems."

So, he thought I was one of Swift's problems? I looked away. "I'll deal with him," I said.

Web sighed wearily as he replied, "I'll leave him to you, then."

Web returned to the table and the Witted coterie's conversation. After a time, they all left. The Prince resumed rehearsing his speech. By the time Swift returned with blankets and a mug of water for Thick, I'd combed through the Prince's collection of scrolls and selected several I thought would benefit Swift. To my surprise, I found some I hadn't seen before; Chade must have acquired them just before we sailed. They dealt with Out Island society and customs. I chose the simpler ones for Swift.

I made Thick as comfortable as I could. His fever was rising. The hotter he became the more fantastic the music he Skilled. He still hadn't taken in any food, but at least he'd lost the will to fight me as I held the mug to his mouth and made sure that he drank it all. I settled him again, tucking the blankets snugly around him, and wondering how the heat of a fever could make a man think he was cold.

When I finished, I glanced up to find Swift looking at us in distaste. "He smells funny," the boy complained to my reproving glance.

"He's sick." I pointed at the floor as I resumed my seat at the edge of Thick's bed. "Sit there. And read aloud to us, quietly, from that scroll. No, the one with the frayed edge, there. Yes, that one."

"What is it?" he asked needlessly as he untied the scroll and opened it.

"It's a description of the history and people of the Out Islands."

"Why do I need to read this?"

I ticked the reasons off on my fingers. "Because you need to practice your reading. Because we are going there, and it behooves you to know something about the people there so you don't shame your prince. Because the history of the Six Duchies is entwined with that of the Out Islands. And because I said so."

He lowered his eyes but I sensed no mellowing toward me. I had to prompt him again before he began reading it. But once he began, I think he interested himself. The rise and fall of his boyish voice was soothing. I let my thoughts float on the sound, barely taking in the sense of the words.

He was still reading when Chade entered. Ostensibly, I paid no attention to the old man while he conferred quietly with the Prince. Then Dutiful's Skill touched me.

Chade would like you to dismiss Swift for a time, so we could speak freely here.

A moment.

I nodded as if to myself over whatever Swift had just read. When he drew breath, I reached out to touch his shoulder. "That's enough for today. You can go. But I will be here tomorrow, and so should you be. I'll expect you."

"Yes, sir." There was no anticipation, no resignation in his voice. Just a flat acknowledgment. I suppressed a sigh. He went to the Prince, made his courtesy, and was dismissed. At a Skill-nudge from me, Dutiful let him know that he thought education a desirable advantage for every man, and that he too wished to see Swift at his lessons every day. He received the same lackluster assent that I had, and then Swift went on his way.

The door had scarcely closed behind him before Chade was at my side. "How is he?" he asked gravely as he touched Thick's face.

"Feverish and coughing. He has taken water but no food."

Chade sat down heavily on the edge of the bed. He felt Thick's throat just under his jaw and then slipped his hand inside his collar, assessing his fever. "For how long," he asked me, "has he been fasting?"

"It has been at least three days since he took any substantial food that stayed with him."

Chade breathed out noisily. "Well, that is where we must begin. Get nourishment into him. Salty broths, thick with soft meat and vegetables."

I nodded, but Thick groaned and turned his face to the wall. His music had an odd floating quality to it. It seemed to fade into a distance, as if it were leaking into a place I could not access.

Chade's hand on my wrist distracted me. *What did you do to him, last night? Did you cause this sickness, do you think?*

His query shocked me and I answered it aloud. "No.

No, I think this is just the result of his seasickness, his nights on deck in the rain, and the lack of food."

Thick had, perhaps, been aware of our Skilling. He rolled his head toward us and looked at me balefully. Then his eyes sank shut again.

Chade moved away, motioning for me to follow. He sank down onto a well-padded bench built beneath one of the windows and indicated I should sit close beside him. The Prince had been setting out game pieces for Stones. Now he lifted his gaze to regard us curiously.

"Strange, that speaking softly may be the best way to keep this private." Chade pointed out the window as if bidding me observe something. I leaned forward and nodded. He smiled, and spoke quietly near my ear. "I could not sleep last night. I've been practicing Skill-exercises, on my own. I fancy that I've become more attuned to it. Thick's music was strong and wild. Then, I sensed something… someone. You, I thought. But there was another presence, one I thought I had glimpsed before. It grew stronger, more masterful; then Thick's music calmed."

A part of me was astounded that Chade was strong enough in the Skill to have witnessed anything. I didn't think fast enough and I was silent for too long before I asked innocently, "Another presence?"

Chade smiled toothily. "Nettle, I think. You are bringing her into the coterie this way?"

"Not really," I said. And it was like a wall collapsing, this surrendering of my secret to Chade. I resented it, and yet I could not deny the relief that I felt to speak of it. I was tired of my secrets, I realized abruptly. Too tired to protect them anymore. Let him know of Nettle and her strength. It didn't mean I'd allow her to be used. "I asked a favor of her. I needed to let her know that Swift was safe and that I'd watch over him. Before we left Buckkeep, I'd told her that he was coming home, because that was what I believed. When I discovered he'd come aboard with Web, well…I couldn't leave her in suspense, wondering if her brother were dead in a ditch somewhere."

"Of course not," Chade murmured. His eyes glinted with hunger for information. I fed it.

"In return, I asked that she soothe Thick's nightmare. She seems very Skilled at controlling her own dreams. Last night, she proved capable of controlling someone else's."

I watched his face as avidly as he watched mine. I saw him ponder the possible uses of such a thing; saw sparks kindle as he recognized how powerful a weapon it could be. To take control of the images in a man's mind, to guide his unguarded thoughts into channels grim and daunting, or uplifting and lovely . . . what could not be done with such a tool? One could craze a man with nightly terrors, inspire a wedding alliance based on romantic dreams, or poison an alliance with suspicions.

"No," I said quietly. "Nettle is unaware of the power of what she does. She does not even know it is the Skill she plies. I will not bring her into the coterie, Chade." And then I told the most cunningly crafted lie I could swiftly fashion. Had he been aware of it, Chade would have been proud of me. "She will work best for us as a Solo, incognizant of the full import of what she does. She will remain more tractable so. Even as I was, when I worked as an unknowing youth."

He nodded gravely, not bothering to deny the truth of it. I saw then a blind spot in my mentor. He had loved me, and yet still used me, and still permitted me to be used. Perhaps, just as he had been used. He did not guess that I would shield Nettle from such a fate. "I'm glad you have come to see that that is for the best," he said approvingly.

"What's out there?" the Prince asked curiously. He rose to come and stare out the window. Chade replied some nonsense about us playing tricks with our eyes, seeing first the ships as moving upon the water and then blinking, to make the water move beneath the ships.

"And what was it that you wished to speak to us privately about?" the Prince asked curiously.

Chade took a breath and I almost saw him scrabble for a topic. "I think this is an excellent arrangement. With both Thick and Fitz here, we have access to our entire coterie. I think it would be well if we let it be known that Thick has grown very attached to Fitz and wishes him near. With that excuse, it will not seem so odd for an ordinary guardsman to attend his prince so closely, even after Thick's health improves."

"I thought we had already discussed that?" the Prince queried.

"Did we? Well. I suppose we did. Excuse an old man's wandering mind, my prince."

Dutiful made a small and skeptical noise. I made a tactful retreat to Thick's bedside.

His fever had in no way abated. Chade called a servant and commanded the foods he thought would be most helpful for Thick. I thought of the surly cook I'd encountered and pitied the boy sent with the order. He returned far too soon with a cup of hot water with a piece of salt meat in the bottom of it. Chade fumed at that, and sent a second serving man with terse and precise orders. I coaxed plain water into Thick, and listened anxiously as his breathing grew more hoarse.

The food arrived. The cook's second effort was much better than her first, and I managed to spoon some of it down Thick. His throat was sore and swallowing pained him, so the meal was a very slow one. She had also, at Chade's direction, sent food for me so that I could eat without leaving his side. That became the regular pattern of my meals. It was nice to be able to eat at my leisure without competing with the rest of the guardsmen, but at the same time, it isolated me from any talk save Thick's, Chade's, and Dutiful's. I had hoped to get a solid night of sleep my first night in the Prince's cabin. Thick had settled and did not toss or moan. I dared to hope that he had found his own peace. My pallet spanned the threshold to his closet. I closed my eyes, longing to find my own rest, but instead breathed deep, centered myself, and dove into Thick's dream.

He wasn't alone. Kitten-Thick nestled in the middle of a big bed upon his cushion while Nettle moved quietly around the tiny room. She seemed to be busy with evening tasks. She hummed as she tidied away discarded clothing and then set foodstuffs into cupboards. When she was finished, the little room was neat and bright. "There," she told the watchful kitten. "You see. All is well. Everything is where it should be and as it should be. And you are safe. Sweet dreams, little one." She stood on her tiptoes to blow out the lamp. I had a sudden odd realization. I had known she was Nettle, but perceived her through Thick's eyes as a short, stout woman with long graying hair bundled into a knot and deep lines in her face. His mother, I realized, and knew then that she had borne him very late in her life. She looked more of an age to be his grandmother.

Then Thick's dream retreated from me, as if I gazed at a lighted window from a distance. I looked around me. We were on the hillside, the melted tower above me and a bramble of dead briars surrounding me. Nettle stood at my side. "I do this for him, not you," she said bluntly. "No soul should have to endure dreams so plagued with fear."

"You're angry at me?" I asked her slowly. I dreaded her answer.

She did not look at me. From nowhere, a cold wind blew between us. She spoke through it. "What did they really mean, those words you told me to say to my father? Are you truly a callous beast, Shadow Wolf, that you gave me words to pierce his heart?"

Yes. No. I lacked a truthful answer to give her. I tried to say, I would never want to hurt him. But was that true? He had taken Molly to be his own. They had believed me dead; neither of them had intended me ill. But he had taken her from me, all the same. And raised my daughter,

in safety and health. Yes. That was true, and I was grateful
to him for that. But not grateful that she would always see
his face when she heard the word "papa." "You asked me
for those words," I said, and then heard how harsh I
sounded.

"And just like the wishes granted in old tales, you gave
me what I wanted and it has broken my heart."

"What happened?" I asked unwillingly.

She didn't want to tell me, and yet she did. "I told him
I'd had a dream, and that in the dream, a wolf with porcupine quills in his nose had promised to watch over Swift
and bring him safely home to us. And I said the words you
gave me. 'As once you did, so I do now. I shelter and guide
your son. I will put my life between him and any harm,
and when my task is done, I will bring him safely home
to you.'"

"And?"

"My mother was kneading bread, and she told me not
to speak of Swift if all I could talk was moonshine and foolishness. But her back was to the table where I sat with my
father. She did not see his eyes widen at my words. For a
time, he just stared at me, with his eyes showing the whites
all around them. Then he fell from the chair to the floor
and lay there, staring like a corpse. I thought he was struck
dead. My brothers and I carried him to his bed, fearing the
worst. My mother was terrified, demanding of him where
he hurt. But he did not answer. He only put his hands over
his eyes, curled up like a beaten child, and began to weep.

"He wept all day today, and did not say a word to any
of us. As night fell, I heard him get up. I came to the edge
of my loft and looked down. He was dressed for travel. My
mother was holding to his arm, begging him not to go out.
But he said to her, 'Woman, you've no idea what we have
done, and I haven't the courage to tell you. I'm a coward.
I've always been a coward.' Then he shook her off and left."

For a terrible flashing instant, I imagined Molly
spurned and abandoned. It was devastating.

"Where did he go?" I managed to ask her.

"I suspect he's coming to you. Wherever you are." Her words were curt, and yet I heard hope in them, hope that someone knew where her father was bound and why. I had to take it from her.

"That cannot be. But I think I know where he has gone, and I think he will come back to you soon." Buckkeep, I thought to myself. Burrich was a direct man. He'd go to Buckkeep, hoping to corner Chade and question him. He'd get Kettricken instead. And she would tell him. Just as she had told Dutiful who I really was. Because she believed in telling people the truth, even if it hurt them.

While I was still pondering that scene, Nettle spoke again. "What have I done?" she asked me. It was not a rhetorical question. "I thought I was so clever. I thought I could bargain with you, and get my brother safely home. Instead . . . what have I done? What are you? Do you wish us ill? Do you hate my father?" Then, with even more dread she asked, "Is my brother in your power somehow?"

"Please don't fear me. You have no reason to fear me," I said hastily, and then wondered if it was true. "Swift is safe, and I promise I will do all in my power to bring him home to you as soon as I can." I paused, wondering what I could safely tell her. She was no fool, this daughter of mine. Too many hints and she'd unravel the whole mystery. Like as not, then I'd lose her forever. "I knew your father, a long time ago. We were close. But I made decisions that went against his rules, and so we parted. For a long time, he has believed I was dead. With your words, he knows I am not. And, because I never came back to him, he now believes he did me a great wrong. He didn't. But if you know your father at all, you will know that it is what he believes in that regard that will drive him."

"You knew my father a long time ago? Did you know my mother then, too?"

"I knew him long before you were born." Not quite a lie, but a deception nonetheless. I let her mislead herself.

"And so my words meant nothing to my mother," Nettle softly concluded after a moment.

"Yes," I confirmed. Then, gingerly I asked, "Is she all right?"

"Of course not!" I felt her impatience with my stupidity. "She stood outside the house and shouted after him when he left, and then ranted to all of us that she never should have married such a stiff-necked man. A dozen times she asked me what I said, and a dozen times I told her of my 'dream.' I came so close to telling her all I knew of you. But that would not have helped, would it? For she never knew you."

For one chill instant, I saw it through Nettle's eyes. Molly stood in the road. In her struggle to restrain Burrich, her hair had come loose. It curled as it ever had, brushing against her shoulders as she shook her fist after him. Her youngest son, little more than six, clutched at her skirts, sobbing in terror at this wild spectacle of his father abandoning his mother. The sun was setting, tingeing the landscape with blood. "You blind old fool!" Molly shrieked after her husband, and the flung words rattled against me like stones. "You'll be lost or robbed! You'll never come home to us!" But the fading clatter of galloping hooves was her only reply.

Then Nettle turned away from the scalding memory of it, and I found we were no longer on the hill with the melted tower. Instead, we were in a loft. My wolf ears on top of my head nearly brushed the low rafters. She was sitting up in her bed, her knees clutched to her chest. Beyond the curtain that screened us from the rest of the attic, I could hear her brothers breathing. One shifted in his sleep and cried out restlessly. No one dreamed peacefully in this house tonight.

I desperately wanted to beg her to say no word of me to Molly. I dared not, for then she would be certain that I lied. I wondered how strongly she already suspected a link between her mother and myself. I did not answer her directly.

"I don't think your father will be gone long. When he returns home, will you tell me, to put my mind at rest?"

"*If* he comes home," she said in a low voice, and I suddenly knew that Molly had voiced aloud the family's very real fears. Now Nettle spoke reluctantly, as if to speak the truth made it more real. "He has already been robbed and beaten once when he was traveling alone seeking for Swift. He has never admitted it to us, but we all know that is what befell him. Nevertheless, he has once more set out alone."

"That's Burrich," I said. I dared not voice aloud what I hoped in my heart: that he had ridden a horse that he knew well. Although he would never use his Wit to speak to his mount, that did not prevent the animals he worked with from communicating with him.

"That's my father," she agreed, both with pride and sorrow. And then the walls of the room began to run like inked letters when tears fall on them. She was the last sight to fade from my dream. When I came to myself, I was staring up at a darkened corner of the Prince's cabin, seeing nothing.

In the tedious days and nights that followed, Thick's condition changed little, for better or worse. He would rally for a day and a night, and then slip back into fever and coughing. His real illness had chased away his fear of seasickness, but there was no comfort for me in that. More than once, I sought Nettle's aid in banishing Thick's fever-dreams before they could unsettle the crew. Sailors are a superstitious lot. Under Thick's influence, they shared a nightmare and, when they compared their night's recollections, decided it was a warning from the gods. It only happened once, but was nearly enough to set off a mutiny.

I worked more closely and more often on Skill-dreams with Nettle than I desired. She did not speak of Burrich and I did not ask, though I know we both counted the days that he had been gone. I knew that if she had had tidings of him, she would share them. His absence in her life left a place for me. Unwillingly, I felt our bond grow stronger, until I carried a constant awareness of her with me at all times. She taught me, without realizing, how to slip behind Thick's dreams and manipulate them, gently guiding them into consoling images. I could not do it as well as she did. Mine was more a suggestion to him, while she simply set the dream right.

Twice I felt Chade observing us. It grated on me, but there was nothing I could do about it since to acknowledge him would have made Nettle aware of him, as well. Yet, in ignoring him, I profited as well, for he grew bolder and I saw my old mentor grow stronger in the Skill. Did he not realize it, or did he conceal it from me? I wondered, but did not betray that wondering to him.

I have never found sea travel enthralling. One watery seascape is much like any other. After a few days, the Prince's cabin seemed almost as cramped, confining, and stuffy as the hold my fellow guardsmen shared. The monotonous food, the endless rocking, and my anxiety for Thick hollowed me. Our diminished coterie made little progress in our Skill-lessons.

Swift continued to come to me daily. He read aloud, earning knowledge of the Out Islands and refreshing mine as he did so. At the end of each session, I would question him to be sure the knowledge was settling into his mind and not simply passing through his eyes and out of his mouth. He had a good head for holding information, and asked a few questions of his own. Swift was seldom gracious but he was obedient to his teacher, and for now that was all I asked. Thick seemed to find Swift's presence soothing, for he would relax, and some of the lines would smooth from his brow as he listened. He spoke little and breathed hoarsely and would sometimes go off into coughing fits. The process of coaxing spoonfuls of broth into him exhausted both of us. The rounded paunch he had recently gained dwindled, and dark hollows showed under his small eyes. He was as sick a creature as I've ever seen, and his acceptance of his misery was heart-wrenching. In his own mind, he was dying, and not even in his dreams could I completely vanquish that notion.

Nor could Dutiful aid me in that. The Prince did his best, and he was truly fond of Thick. But Dutiful was fifteen, and a boy in many ways still. Moreover, he was a boy being courted by his nobles, who daily devised distractions that would put him in their company. Freed of Kettricken's austere traditions, they plied him with entertainment and flattery. Smaller boats shuttled between the ships of our betrothal fleet, not only bringing nobles to visit Dutiful but often carrying Chade and him off to the other vessels for wine and poetry and song. Such trips were meant to divert his attention from the ennui of the uneventful voyage and they succeeded only too well, but it behooved Dutiful to distribute his favors and attentions amongst his nobles. The success of his reign would be built upon the alliances he forged now. He could scarcely have refused to go. Yet all the same, it bothered me to see how easily his attention could be drawn away from his ill servant.

Web was my sole comfort. He came every day, offering quietly to keep watch by Thick while I took some time for myself. I could not completely relax my vigil, of course. I maintained a Skill-awareness of Thick lest he sweep us all into some wild and fearful dream. But I could at least leave the confines of the cabin to stroll briefly on the deck and feel some wind in my face. This arrangement, however, kept me from having time alone with Web. It was not just for Chade's ends that I longed to speak with him. More and more, his quiet competency and kindness impressed me. I had a sense that he courted me, not as Dutiful's nobles courted the Prince, but as Burrich had insinuated himself into the presence of a horse he wished to retrain. And it worked, despite my being aware of it. With every passing day, I felt less wariness and caution toward him. It no longer seemed a threat that he knew who I really was, but almost a comfort. I harbored a host of questions I longed to ask him: How many of the Old Blood knew that FitzChivalry still lived? How many knew I was he? Yet I dared not voice such questions in Thick's hearing, even when he wandered in his fever-dreams. There was no telling how he might repeat such words, aloud or in dreams.

Very late one evening, when the Prince and Chade had returned from some entertainment, I waited until Dutiful had dismissed his servants. He and Chade sat with glasses of wine, talking quietly on the cushioned bench beneath the window that looked out over our wake from our dimly lit cabin. I rose and left Thick's side and, going to the table, beckoned them. Weary as they both were from a long session of Stones with Lord Excellent, they were still intrigued enough to immediately join me. I spoke to Dutiful without a preamble. "Has Web ever confided to you that he knows I am FitzChivalry?"

The look of astonishment on his face was answer enough.

"Did he need to know that?" Chade grumbled at me.

"Is there a reason to keep such knowledge from me?" the Prince replied for me, more sharply than I would have expected.

"Only that this bit of intrigue has nothing to do with our present mission. I would keep your mind focused on the matters that most concern us, Prince Dutiful." Chade's voice was restrained.

"Perhaps, Councilor Chade, you could let me decide which matters concern me?" The asperity in Dutiful's voice warned me that this was a topic that had been discussed before.

"Then there is no sign that anyone else in your 'Witted coterie' knows who I am?"

The Prince hesitated before replying slowly. "None. There has been talk, from time to time, of the Witted Bastard. And when I think back, Web has initiated it. But he brings it up in the same manner in which he teaches us Witted history and traditions. He speaks of a topic, and then asks us questions that lead us deeper into understanding it.

He has never spoken of FitzChivalry as other than an historic figure."

A little unnerving, to hear of myself as an "historic figure." Chade spoke before I became too uncomfortable.

"Then Web teaches your Witted coterie formally? History, traditions . . . what else?"

"Courtesy. He tells us old fables of Witted folk and beasts. And how to prepare before beginning a Search for an animal partner. I think that what he teaches are things that the others have known from childhood, but he teaches them for my benefit and Swift's. Yet when he tells tales, the others listen closely, especially the minstrel Cockle. I think he possesses much lore that was on the verge of being lost, and he speaks it to us that we may keep it safe and pass it on in our turn."

I nodded to that. "When persecution broke up the Witted communities, the Witted had to conceal their traditions and knowledge. It would be inevitable that less of it was passed on to their children."

"Why, do you think, does Web speak of FitzChivalry?" Chade asked speculatively.

I watched Dutiful think it through, in the same way Chade had taught me to ponder any man's action. What could he gain by it? Who did it threaten? "It could be that he suspects that I know. Yet I don't think that is it. I think he poses it to the Wit coterie to make them consider, 'What is the difference between a ruler who is Witted or unWitted?' What would it have meant for the Six Duchies if Fitz had come to power at that time instead of being executed for his magic? What might it mean for the Six Duchies if it ever becomes safe for me to reveal that I am Old Blood? And also, how does it benefit my people, all my people, to have an Old Blood ruler? And how can my Wit coterie assist me in my reign?"

"In your reign?" Chade asked sharply. "Do their ambitions run that far ahead of us? They had spoken of aiding you on this quest, to show the Six Duchies that the Wit can be put to a good cause. Do they think to continue as advisers beyond this task?"

Dutiful frowned at Chade. "Well, of course."

When the old man knit his brows in irritation, I intervened. "It seems natural to me that they would, especially if their efforts do assist the Prince in his quest. To use them and then cast them aside afterward is not the sort of political wisdom you have taught me over the years."

Chade was still scowling. "Well . . . I suppose . . . if they truly proved to be of any value, they would expect some compensation."

The Prince spoke levelly, but I could sense him holding his temper. "And what would you expect them to ask in return if they were a Skill coterie aiding me?" He sounded so like Chade as he set his trap question that I almost laughed aloud.

Chade bristled. "But that would be entirely different. The Skill is your hereditary magic, as well as being vastly more powerful than the Wit. That you would bond with your Skill coterie and accept both counsel and companionship from them would be expected." Then he stopped speaking abruptly.

Dutiful nodded slowly. "Old Blood is also my hereditary magic. And I suspect there is far more to it than we know. And, yes, Chade, I do feel a bond of both companionship and trust with those who share that magic. It is, as you said, to be expected."

Chade opened his mouth to speak, then shut it again. After an instant, he opened his mouth, but again subsided. Irritation vied with admiration when he said quietly, "Very well. I follow your logic. I do not necessarily agree with the conclusion, but I follow it."

"That is all I ask," the Prince replied and in his words I heard the echo of the monarch he would be.

Chade turned his beetling gaze on me. "Why did you bring this up?" he asked me crossly, as if I had sought to precipitate a quarrel between them.

"Because I need to know what it is that Web seeks from me. I sense that he courts me, that he tries to draw me closer into his confidence. Why?"

There is no true silence on board a ship. Always there are the ongoing conversations between wood and water, canvas and wind. Those voices were the only ones in the cabin for a time. Then Dutiful gave a small snort. "Unlikely as you think it, Fitz, perhaps he only wishes to be your friend. I see nothing here for him to gain."

"He holds a secret," Chade said sourly. "There is always power in holding a secret."

"And danger," the Prince countered. "Revealing this secret is as dangerous to Web as it is to Fitz. Think what would follow if he revealed it. Would it not undermine my reign? Would not some of the nobles turn on my mother the Queen, angered that she had kept this secret from them and preserved Fitz's life?" In a lower voice he added, "Do not forget that in revealing to Fitz that he knew his identity, Web put himself at risk, also. This is a secret that some men would kill to preserve."

I watched Chade sift it through his mind. "Truly, the threat is to your reign as much as to Fitz," he conceded worriedly. "Right now, you are correct. It benefits Web most to keep the secret a secret. As long as your reign is amiable toward the Witted, they have no interest in deposing you. But if you ever turned against them? What then?"

"What then, indeed?" the Prince scoffed. "Chade, ask yourself as you have so often asked me, 'What would happen next?' If my mother and I were overthrown, who would seize power? Why, those who had overthrown us. And they would be the enemy of the Witted, a harsher enemy than Old Blood has had to confront in my lifetime. No. I think Fitz's secret is safe. More, I think he should set aside his wariness and become Web's friend."

I nodded, wondering why such an idea made me so uneasy.

"I still see little benefit in this Witted coterie," Chade muttered.

"Do you not? Then why do you ask me each day what Web's bird has seen? Does it not ease your mind to know that all the ships she has shown Web have been honest merchant or fishing vessels? And think what tidings she gave us today. She has flown over the harbor and town of Zylig, and Web has looked down on it through the bird's eyes. She has seen no massing of folk as for battle or treachery. True, the city is swelled with people, but it seems to flaunt a festive air. Do you not take comfort in that?"

"I suppose. But it is a thin comfort, given that treachery is so easy to disguise."

Thick rolled over muttering, and I made that my excuse to leave them. Not long after, Chade departed for his own cabin, the Prince went to his bed, and I made up my pallet beside Thick's bunk. I thought of Web and Risk, and tried to imagine seeing the ocean and the Out Islands through a bird's eyes. It would be a marvel and a wonder. Yet before my imagination could capture me completely, a wave of longing for Nighteyes swept over me. That night, I dreamed my own dreams, and they were of wolves hunting in the summer-seared hills.

chapter VIII

THE HETGURD

This is how it was. Eda and El coupled in the darkness, but he did not find favor with her. Then she gave birth to the land, and the outrush of her waters which accompanied that birth was the sea. The land was shapeless, clay and still, until Eda took it in her hands. One at a time, she molded the runes of her secret name, and El's too did she fashion. She spelled out the god name with the God's Runes, setting them in careful order in the ocean. And all this El watched.

But when he would have taken up clay of his own to fashion his own runes, Eda would not give any over to him. "You gave me but a rush of fluid from your body as seed to make all this. The flesh of it came from me. So take back only what was yours to start with, and be content with it."

El was little content with that. So he made for himself men, and gave them ships and put them on the sea's face. Laughing to himself, he said, "There are too many for her to watch them all. Soon they will walk on her land and shape it to my liking, so it spells my name instead of hers."

But Eda had already thought before him. And when El's men came to land, they found Eda's women,

*already walking on it and ordering the growing of fruit
and grain and the proliferation of the cattle. And the
women would not suffer the men to shape the lands, nor
even to abide on them for long. Instead, the women said
to the men, "We will let you give us the brine of your
loins, with which we will shape flesh to follow ours. But
never will the land that Eda bore belong to your sons,
but only to our daughters."*

❧ BIRTH OF THE WORLD,
AS TOLD BY OUT ISLAND BARDS

Despite Chade's misgivings, Web's bird had shown him accurately what we could expect. The next morning, the
lookout cried out his sighting, and by afternoon the nearest
islets of the Out Islands were streaming past on our port
side. Green-banked islands, tiny houses, and small fishing
vessels enlivened a view that had been watery for too long.
I tried to convince Thick to rise and come on deck to see
how close we were to the end of our journey but he refused
to be tempted. When he spoke, his words were slow and
measured. "It won't be home," he moaned. "We're too far
from home, and we'll never get back there again. Never."
Coughing, he turned away from me.

Yet even his sour attitude could not dampen my relief.
I convinced myself that once he was on shore, he would regain both his health and spirits. The knowledge that we
were close to getting off that cramped vessel made every
moment stretch into a day. It was only the next afternoon
that we sighted Zylig harbor, but it seemed a month had
passed. When small boats rowed out to greet us and guide
our ships through the narrow channel to their harbor, I
longed to be on deck with Chade and Prince Dutiful.

Instead, I paced the Prince's cabin, staring out the frustrating view from the aft windows. I could hear our captain
bellowing and the thunder of the sailors' feet on the deck.
Chade and Prince Dutiful and his contingent of nobles and

his Witted coterie were all up on the deck, looking on as the ship approached Zylig. I felt like a dog chained in the kennel while the hounds streamed off to the hunt. I felt the change in the ship's movements as our canvas was lowered and the towlines of our pilot boats took up their slack. When they had us in position, the Out Island guides brought us about so that our stern now faced Zylig. As I heard the splash of our anchor, I stared restlessly out at the foreign city that awaited us. The other Six Duchies ships were being maneuvered into anchorage nearby.

I do not think there is anything so ponderously slow as a ship coming into port, save perhaps the process of unloading. Suddenly the water about our ships swarmed with small craft, their oars dipping and rising as if they were many-legged water bugs. One, grander than the rest, soon bore Prince Dutiful, Chade, a selected entourage, and a handful of his guards away from the ship. I watched them go, certain they had completely forgotten about Thick and me. Then there was a tap at the door. It was Riddle, freshly attired in his guard's uniform. His eyes shone with excitement.

"I'm to watch your half-wit while you get yourself ready. There's a boat waiting to take you and him and the rest of the guard ashore. Step lively now. Everyone else is ready to go."

So they had not forgotten me, but neither had they served me with much warning of their plans. I took Riddle at his word, leaving him with Thick while I went below. The guards' area was deserted. The others had donned their clean uniforms as soon as we'd approached harbor. Those who hadn't accompanied the Prince lined the railing on deck, eager to be away. I changed swiftly and hurried back to the Prince's quarters. Harrying Thick into clean clothing was not going to be pleasant or easy, but when I arrived, I found that Riddle had already undertaken that task.

Thick swayed on the edge of his bunk. His blue tunic and trousers hung on his wasted frame. Until I saw him dressed, I had not realized how much flesh he had lost. Riddle knelt by the bunk, good-naturedly trying to chivy him into his shoes. Thick was moaning feebly and making vaguely helpful motions. His face was crumpled with misery. If I had doubted it at all before, I was now certain that Riddle was one of Chade's men. No ordinary guardsman would have undertaken that task.

"I'll finish that," I told him, and could not keep the brusqueness from my voice. I could not have said why I felt protective of the small man looking at me blearily from his little round eyes, but I did.

"Thick," I told him as I finished getting his shoes on. "We're going ashore. Once we're on solid ground again, you're going to feel much better. You'll see."

"No I won't," he promised me. He coughed again and the rattle in it frightened me. Nonetheless, I found a cloak for him and heaved him to his feet. He staggered along beside me as we left the cabin. Out on the deck in the fresh wind for the first time in days, he shivered and clutched his cloak tightly around him. The sun shone brightly, but the day was not as warm as a summer day in Buck. Snow still owned the peaks of the higher hills, and the wind carried its chill to us.

The Outislanders provided our transportation to shore. Getting Thick from the deck into the dancing boat below required both Riddle and myself. I silently cursed at those guards who laughed at our predicament. At their oars, the Outislanders discussed us freely in their own tongue, unaware that I understood the disdain they expressed for a prince who chose an idiot as his companion. Once settled on the seat beside Thick, I had to put my arm around him to settle him against the terrors of a small, open boat. He wept, the round tears rolling down his cheeks as our little dory rose and fell with every passing wave. I blinked at the bright sunlight glancing off the moving water and stared stolidly at the wharves and houses of Zylig as the straining sailors rowed us to our destination.

It was not an inspiring view. Peottre Blackwater's disdain for the city was not misplaced. Zylig offered all the worst aspects of a lively port. Wharves and docks jutted haphazardly into the bay. Vessels of every description crowded them. Most were fat-hulled greasy whale-hunters, with a permanent reek of oil and butchery clinging to them. A few were merchanters from the Six Duchies. I saw one that looked Chalcedean and one that could have been Jamaillian. Moving amongst them were the small fishing boats that daily fed the bustling town, and even smaller craft that were hawking smoked fish, dried seaweed, and other provisions to the outward-bound vessels. Masts forested the skyline and the docked ships grew taller as we approached them.

Beyond them, I caught glimpses of warehouses, sailors' inns, and supply stores. Stone structures predominated over wood. Narrow streets, some little more than trails, meandered amongst the crowded little buildings. At one end of the bay where the water ran shallower and rocky, unfit for anchorage, little stone houses clustered by the water. Rowboats were pulled out above the tideline, and spread fish hung like laundry drying from poles. Smoking fires in trenches beneath the fish added flavor as they preserved the catch. I glimpsed a pack of children racing along the beach, shrieking raucously in some wild game.

The section of the town we were approaching seemed recently built. In contrast to the rest of the settlement, the streets were wide and straight. Timber supplemented the native stone, and most of the structures were taller. Some had windows of swirled glass in the upper stories. I recalled hearing that the Six Duchies dragons had visited this port city, bringing death and destruction to our enemies. The structures in this area were all of an age, the streets straight and well cobbled. It was strange to see this orderly section amongst the haphazard port town and I wondered what it had looked like before Verity-as-Dragon had paid a call here. Stranger still to think that the destruction of war could result in such rebuilt tidiness.

Above the harbor, the land rose in rocky hillsides. Dark evergreens hunched in sheltered areas. Cart tracks wound among the hillsides where sheep and goats grazed. Smoke wandered up through the tree cover from scarcely visible huts. Mountains and taller hills, crowned still with snow, loomed beyond them.

We had arrived on a low tide, and the docks towered above us, supported on thick timbers crusted with barnacles and black mussels. The rungs of the ladder up to the dock were still wet from the retreating tide, and festoons of seaweed hung from them. The Prince and several boatloads of nobles had already disembarked. More Buckkeep noblemen were unloading as we approached. Grudgingly they gave way to us, to allow the Prince's Guard to clamber up the ladders onto the docks and form up to escort Dutiful to his welcome.

I was the last out of the tippy little boat, having shoved a moaning Thick ahead of me up the slippery ladder. Once on the docks, I moved us away from the edge and looked around me. The Prince, flanked by his advisers, was being greeted by the Hetgurd. I was left standing to one side with Thick, unsure of what was expected of me. I needed to get him to a place where he would be comfortable and out of the public eye. I wondered uneasily if it would not have been wiser for me to remain on the ship with him. The open looks of disgust and dismay that he was receiving did not indicate a warm welcome for us. Evidently the Outislanders shared the Mountain opinion of children that were born less than perfect. If Thick had been born in Zylig, his life would not have lasted a day.

My status as both bastard and assassin had often left me lurking in the shadows at official proceedings so I did not feel slighted. If I had been alone, I would have known that my task was to mingle and observe while being nondescript. But here, in a foreign land, saddled with a sick

and miserable simpleton and clad in a guard's uniform,
I could do neither. So I stood awkwardly at the edge of
the crowd, my arm supporting Thick, and listened to the
exchange of carefully phrased greetings, welcome, and
thanks. The Prince seemed to be acquitting himself well,
but the look of concentration on his face warned me not to
distract him with a Skill-query. Those who had come to
meet him represented a variety of clans, judging from the
differing animal sigils featured in their jewelry and tattoos.
Most were men, richly attired in the lush furs and heavy
jewelry that signified both rank and wealth among the
Outislanders; but there were four women also. They wore
woven wool garments trimmed with fur, and I wondered if
this was to show the wealth of their land holdings. The
Narcheska's father, Arkon Bloodblade, was there, along
with at least six others displaying the boar of his clan. Peottre Blackwater accompanied him, his narwhal an ivory
carving on a gold chain around his neck. It seemed odd to
me that I saw no other narwhal sigils. That was the Narcheska's maternal clan, and among the Outislanders, her significant family line. We were here to finalize the terms of
the marriage between Dutiful and her. Surely it was a momentous occasion for her clan. Why did only Peottre come
to represent them? Did the rest oppose this alliance?

The formalities of greeting satisfied at length, the
Prince and his entourage were escorted away. The guard
formed up without me and marched off behind him. For a
moment I feared that Thick and I would be left standing on
the docks. Just as I was wondering if I could bribe someone
to take us back to the ship, an old man approached us. He
wore a collar of wolf fur and sported the boar sigil of Bloodblade's clan, but did not seem as prosperous as the other
men. He obviously believed he could speak my language, for
I could understand about one word in four of his barbarously
mangled Duchy tongue. Fearing to insult him by asking him
to speak Outislander, I waited and finally grasped that the

Boar Clan had appointed him to guide Thick and me to our lodging.

He made no offer to assist me with Thick. In fact, he assiduously avoided getting any closer to him than was absolutely necessary, as if the little man's mental deficiency were a contagion that might leap to him like a plague of lice. I felt it as a slur, but counseled myself to patience. He walked briskly ahead of us, and did not slacken his pace, even though he often had to halt completely to wait for us. Obviously, he did not wish to share the gawking stares we attracted. We made a strange sight, me in my guard's uniform and poor miserable Thick, swathed in a cloak and staggering along under my arm.

Our guide led us through the reconstructed part of town and then up a steeper, narrower road. Thick's breath was a moaning wheeze. "How much farther?" I demanded of our guide, calling the words to him as he hastened ahead of us.

He turned abruptly, scowling, and made a brusque motion for me to keep my voice down. He gestured up the street at an old building, all of stone and much larger than the houses we had passed in the lower part of town. It was rectangular, with a peaked roof of slates, and three stories high. Windows interrupted the stonework at regular intervals. It was a plain and functional building, stoutly built and probably amongst the oldest structures in the town. I nodded, unspeaking. A boar, his tusks and tail lifted defiantly, was etched into the stone above the entry. So. We would be housed in the Boar Clan's stronghouse.

By the time we reached the courtyard around the building, our guide was practically chewing his mustache in his teeth-gnashing impatience at our slow pace. I no longer cared. When he opened a side door and gestured to me to hurry, I slowly drew myself up to my full height and glared down at him. In my best Outislander, and all too aware of how poor my accent was, I told him, "It is not the pleasure of the Prince's companion that we hurry. I serve at his command, not yours."

I saw uncertainty wash over the man's face as he wondered if he had offended someone of a much higher rank than he knew. He was somewhat more courteous as he showed us up two steep flights of stairs and into a chamber that looked out over the town and the harbor through a swirl of thick glass. By then I'd had enough of him. I gauged him as a lesser lackey to some minor Boar war leader. As such, I dismissed him brusquely once we were inside, and shut the door even though he lingered in the hallway.

I sat Thick down on the bed and then assessed the room quickly. There was a door that connected to another, much grander chamber. I decided that we had been put in a servant's room adjacent to the Prince's quarters. The bed was adequate, the furnishings simple in Thick's small room. Even so, it seemed a palace after his closet on the ship. "Sit there," I told Thick. "Don't go to sleep yet."

"Where are we? I want to go home," he mumbled. I ignored him and stole through into the Prince's chamber. There I helped myself to a pitcher of washwater and a basin and drying cloths. There was a platter of food on the table. I was not sure exactly what it was, but took several pieces of a dark, sticky stuff cut in squares, and an oily-looking cake covered with seed. I also took a bottle of what I thought was wine and a cup.

Thick had toppled over on his bed. Painstakingly I hauled him upright again. Despite his groaning protests I made him wash his face and hands. I wished that I had a tub to put him in, for he smelled strongly of his days of sickness. Then I forced food down him, and a glass of the wine. He complained and sniveled until he hiccuped. Once I felt him marshal his Skill-strength against me, but it was a weak and childish swipe that did not even challenge my walls. I pulled off his tunic and shoes and put him to bed. "The room is still moving," he muttered petulantly. Then he closed his eyes and was still. A few moments later he gave a great sigh, stretched out in the bed, and fell into a true sleep. I closed my own eyes and cautiously tiptoed into his dream. The kitten slept in a tiny curled ball upon the embroidered pillow. He felt safe. I opened my eyes, suddenly so weary that I could have cast myself down on the floor and slept where I fell.

I didn't. Instead I used what was left of the clean water. I sampled the food, found it unpalatable and ate it anyway. The oily one was probably intended to be some sort of sweet; the other tasted strongly of fish paste. The "wine" was something fermented from fruit; other than that, I had few ideas about it. It didn't quite take away the fish taste from my mouth.

Then, armed with the basin of soiled water, I left the chamber to venture out into our lodgings. If anyone questioned me, I was simply looking for a place to dump the slops.

The building was as much stronghold as clan residence. We were on the highest floor, and I heard no sounds of other occupants. The interior walls featured carved and painted boars and tusk motifs. The other doors on the hall were not locked. They seemed to alternate between small chambers such as Thick had and larger ones, more generously furnished. None of them met the Buckkeep standard for guest housing even for lesser nobles. I reserved judgment on that. I doubted they intended to insult us; I knew the Outislanders had different customs for hospitality than the Six Duchies did. Generally speaking, houseguests were expected to provide their own victuals and comforts. We had come here knowing that. The wine and food in the Prince's room seemed to be a nod to the Six Duchies hospitality the Narcheska's entourage had enjoyed at Buckkeep. There were no signs of any servants on this upper floor, and I doubted that any would be supplied to us.

The next floor down seemed much the same. These rooms smelled as if they had been recently used; odors of smoke, food, and, in one case, wet dog lingered in them. I wondered if they had been vacated for our use. The chambers here were slightly smaller, and the windows were of oiled skin rather than glass. Heavy wooden shutters, some bearing the old scars of arrows, offered protection from any determined assault. Evidently the highest chambers were accorded to those of highest ranks; very different from the Six Duchies, where servants were given the upper rooms so that nobility need not climb too many flights of steps. I had just closed a door when I heard footsteps coming up the stairs. An ant trail of servants suddenly appeared, bearing belongings, comforts, and victuals for their Six Duchies masters. They halted in confusion, milling in the hallway, and one asked me, "How do we know which chamber is for whom?"

"I've no idea," I replied pleasantly. "I'm not even certain where we are to dump slops."

I slipped away from them, leaving them to sort out the rooms, suspecting that the best ones would go to the nobles with the most aggressive servants. On the ground floor I found a back door that led out to a waste pit behind the privies and dumped my water there. Another door led down a corridor to a large kitchen where several young Outislander men were tending a large roast on a spit, chopping potatoes and onions, and kneading bread. They seemed intent on their tasks and all but ignored me as I peered in at them. A quick tour of the outside of the building showed me that a second, much grander door led to a large open hall that made up much of the ground floor of the building. These doors stood open to admit both light and air. Within, I glimpsed what was undoubtedly the welcome gathering for the Prince. I abandoned my basin in the deep grass at one end of the building, and hastily straightened my uniform and smoothed back my hair into a tail.

Unnoticed, I slipped into the back of the room. My fellow guardsmen were ranged against the wall. They looked as alert as men do when they are stiflingly bored and ignored. In truth, there seemed little for them to guard against.

The large room was long and low ceilinged. The main part of it was taken up with benches, all of a height and all full of seated men. There was no throne or dais of any kind. Nor were the benches oriented to focus attention on one person. Rather, they ringed the room, leaving the center open. A bowed old kaempra, or war leader, of the Fox Clan was speaking. His short jacket was fringed with the tips of foxtails, white as his unruly hair. He was missing three fingers on his sword hand, but wore a necklace of his enemies' fingerbones to compensate. He tugged at them nervously as he spoke, glancing often at Bloodblade as if reluctant to give offense and yet too angry to keep silent. I only caught his closing words. "No one clan can speak for all of us! No one clan has the right to bring bad luck down on us all."

As I watched, the Fox kaempra nodded gravely to each corner of the room and then retired to his bench. Another man stood and made his way to the center and began speaking. I saw the Prince and Lord Chade seated amongst the nobles who attended him in one section of the benches. His Wit coterie was ranged behind him. The Hetgurd, for so I recognized this assembly, the gathering of the war leaders of the clans, had accorded my prince no indication of his rank. Here, he was seated as a warrior leader among his warriors, just as the other clan war leaders were. This was a gathering of equals, come together to discuss the Narcheska's betrothal. Did they see him so? I tried not to scowl at the thought.

All this I grasped in the time it took my eyes to adjust to the dimness of the hall after the summer sunshine outside. I found a piece of wall to lean on next to Riddle in the back row of guardsmen. Riddle spoke out of the side of his mouth. "Not like us at all, my friend. No feast or gifts or songs to welcome our prince. Just a how-d'ye-do greeting on the docks and then they brought him straight here and began discussing the betrothal. Right to business for these people. Some don't like the idea of one of their women leaving her motherland to go live in the Six Duchies. They think it's unnatural and probably bad luck. But most don't care much about that, one way or another. They seem to think that would be Clan Narwhal's bad luck, not theirs. The real sticking point is the dragon-slaying bit."

I nodded to his swift summary. Chade had a good man in Riddle. I wondered where he had recruited him and then focused my attention on the man who was speaking. I noticed now that he stood in the middle of a ring painted on the floor. It was intricate and stylized, and yet still recognizable as a serpent grasping its own tail. The man did not give his name before he began speaking. Perhaps he assumed that everyone knew it, or perhaps the only important part of his identity was the sea otter tattooed on his forehead. He spoke simply, without anger, as if explaining something obvious to rather stupid children.

"Icefyre is not a cow that belongs to any one of us. He is not cattle to be offered as part of a bride price. Even less does he belong to the foreigner Prince. How then can he offer the head of a creature that does not belong to him as payment to the Blackwater mothershouse of the Narwhal Clan? We can only see his promise in one of two ways. Either he has made his offer in ignorance, or it is an affront to us."

He paused then and made a strange gesture with his hand. In a moment its meaning was made clear as Prince Dutiful slowly stood and then came to join him in the speaker's circle. "No, Kaempra Otter." Dutiful addressed him as war leader for his clan. "It was not ignorance. It was not intended as affront. The Narcheska presented this deed to me as a challenge to prove myself worthy of her." The Prince lifted his hands and let them fall helplessly. "What could I do but accept it? If a woman issued such a challenge to you, saying before your gathered warriors, 'Accept it or admit cowardice,' what would you do? What would any of you do?"

Many heads in the assembly nodded to this. Dutiful nodded gravely back to them and then added, "So what am I to do now? My word has been given, before your warriors and mine, in the hall of my parents. I have said I will attempt to do this thing. I know of no honorable way to unsay such words. Is there a custom here, among the people of the Narcheska, that allows a man to call back the words that have issued from his mouth?"

The Prince moved his hands, imitating the same gesture that the Otter Kaempra had used to cede him the speaker's circle. He bowed to the four corners of the hall, and then retreated to his bench again. As he took his seat, Otter spoke again.

"If this was the manner of your accepting the challenge, then I will take no affront toward you. I reserve what I think of Clan Blackwater's daughter for issuing such a challenge. Regardless of the circumstances."

I had previously noticed Peottre Blackwater sitting almost by himself on one of the front benches. He scowled at the Otter's remark but made no indication that he wished to speak. The Narcheska's father, Arkon Bloodblade, sat a small distance away from Peottre, his Boar warriors ranked about him. Arkon's brow remained smooth, as if the rebuke had nothing to do with him, and perhaps by his lights that was correct. The Otter had rebuked Elliania as a daughter of the Blackwater family of the Narwhal Clan. Arkon Bloodblade was a Boar. Here, within his own people, he assumed the role that they expected of him. He was only the Narcheska's father. Her mother's brother, Peottre Blackwater, was responsible for the quality of her upbringing.

When the silence had stretched enough that it was obvious no one would offer a defense for what the Narcheska had done, the Otter leader cleared his throat. "It is true that as a man you cannot call back your word, Prince of the Farseer Buck Clan. You have said you will try to do this thing, and I will concede that you must do it, or be judged no man at all.

"Yet that does not release us of the Out Islands of our duties. Icefyre is ours. What do our great mothers tell us? He came to us, in the years before years were counted, and asked asylum from his grief. Our wisewomen granted it to him. And in return for our sheltering, he promised that his protection should be ours. We know the power of his spirit and the invulnerability of his flesh, and fear little that you shall slay him. But if, by some strange twist of fate, you manage to do him injury, on whom will his anger fall after he has killed you? On us." He turned slowly in a circle as he spoke, including all the clans as he warned them, "If Icefyre is ours, we also belong to him. Like a kin pledge we should see the debt woven between us. If his blood is shed, must not we shed blood in return? If, as his kin, we fail to come to his aid, cannot he exact from us the blood price ten times over, according to our law? This prince must honor his word as a man. That is so. But after, must not war come to us again, regardless of whether he lives or dies?"

I saw Arkon Bloodblade draw a long slow breath. I noted now what I had not before, that he held his hand in a certain way, open yet with the fingers pointing toward his sternum. Several men, I now saw, were making the same gesture. A request to speak? Yes, for when the Otter warrior made the now familiar gesture, Bloodblade stood and came to take the man's place in the circle.

"None of us want war again. Not here in the God's Runes, nor in the Prince's farmers' fields across the water. Yet a man's word must be satisfied. And though we all be men here, there is a woman's will in this, as well. What warrior can stand before a woman's will? What sword can cut her stubbornness? To women Eda has given the islands themselves, and we walk upon them only by her leave. It is not for men to set aside the challenge of a woman, lest our own mothers say, 'You do not respect the flesh you sprang from. Walk no more on the earth that Eda has granted us. Be abandoned by us, with only water under your keel and never sand under your feet.' Is that easier than war? We are caught between a man's word and a woman's will. Neither can be broken without disgrace to all."

I had understood Bloodblade's words but the full import of their meaning escaped me. Obviously there was custom here we were not familiar with, and I questioned what we had blundered into with our matchmaking. Bleakly I wondered if we had not fallen into a trap. Was the Blackwater family of the Narwhal Clan intent on kindling war between the Six Duchies and the Out Islands? Had their offer of the Narcheska been a sham, to draw us into a situation in which, regardless of the outcome, we had invited bloodshed yet again to our shores?

I studied Peottre Blackwater's face. His expression was stolid and still, his eyes turned inward. He seemed impassive to the dilemma his sister-daughter had set us, and yet I felt he was not. I sensed rather that we balanced on the knife blade that had already cut deep into him. He looked, I suddenly thought, like a man without choices. A man who could no longer hope, because he knows that no action of his own can save him. He was waiting. He did not plan or plot. He had already done the task he had set out to do. Now he could only wait to see how other men would carry it out. I was certain I was right, and yet what I could not understand or even imagine was *why*. Why had he done it? Or, as her father had said, was it beyond his control, the will of a woman who might be younger than he was and dependent on him, and yet controlled who might walk on the earth of his mother-holdings?

I looked around me. There were simply too many differences between us, I decided. How could the Six Duchies ever make a peace with the Out Islands when our customs varied so widely? Yet, tradition had it that the Farseer line had its roots in the Out Islands, that Taker, the first Farseer monarch, had begun his life as an Out Island raider who had seen the log fortress that Buckkeep once was and decided to make it his own. Our lines and our ways had diverged far since those days. Peace and prosperity depended on our finding some common ground.

The likelihood of that did not seem great.

I lifted my eyes to find the Prince's gaze fixed on me. I had not wanted to distract him before. Now I sent him a reassuring thought. *Thick is resting in his chamber upstairs. He ate and drank before he went to sleep.*

I wish I could be doing the same. They did not give me so much as a chance to wash my face before they convened the Hetgurd. And now it shows no sign of ending.

Patience, my prince. They'll end this eventually. Even Outislanders must eat, drink, and sleep sometime.

Do they piss, do you think? That's starting to be a very immediate concern to me. I've thought of excusing myself quietly, but don't know how it would be interpreted if I stood and walked out now.

The hair stood up on the back of my neck as I felt a fumbling Skill-touch. *Thick?*

It was Chade. I saw Dutiful start to reach out his hand, to touch Chade and add his strength to the old man's. I stopped him. *No. Don't. Let him try it on his own. Chade, can you hear us?*

Barely.

Thick is asleep upstairs. He ate and drank before he fell asleep.

Good. I sensed the effort he put into that brief reply. Nonetheless, I was grinning. He was doing it.

Stop. Silly grin, he scolded me. He looked around the room gravely. *Bad situation. Need time to think. Need to stop this before it goes too far without us.*

I made my face solemn. The expression was far more in keeping with that of those around me. Arkon Bloodblade was surrendering the speaking circle to a man who wore an Eagle badge. They paused to clasp wrists in a warrior's greeting before the Eagle entered the circle. The Eagle Kaempra was an old man, possibly the oldest man in the assembly. Gray and white streaked his thinning hair, yet he still moved like a warrior. He stared around at us accusingly, and then spoke abruptly, the ends of his words softened by his missing teeth.

"Doubtless a man must do what he has said he will do. It wastes our day to even discuss that. And men must honor their kinship bonds. If this foreign prince came here and said, 'I have promised a woman that I would kill Orig of the Eagle Clan,' all of you would say, 'Then you must try, if you have promised to do it.' But we would also say, 'But know that some of us have kinship bonds with Orig. And we will kill you before we let you do this thing.' And we would expect the Prince to accept that as obviously correct, also." His slow gaze traveled the assembly disdainfully. "I smell merchants and traders here, who used to be warriors and honorable men. Shall we sniff after Six Duchies goods like a dog groveling after a bitch? Will you trade your own kin for brandy and summer apples and red wheat? Not this Eagle."

He gave a snort of contempt for all who thought there was any need of more discussion. He left the circle and crabbed back to his seat amongst his warriors. A silence fell as we all pondered his words. Some exchanged glances; I sensed the old man had cut close to the bone. There were many here uneasy at the thought of letting the Prince kill their dragon, but they were also hungry for peace and trade. War with the Six Duchies had cut them off from all trade from points south of us. Now the Chalcedean quarrel with the Bingtown Traders was throttling that route. If they did not gain free trade with the Six Duchies, they would have to forgo all goods and luxuries that warmer countries could provide for them. It was not a thought to relish. Yet no one there could oppose the Eagle's stance without taking the name of greedy trader to himself.

We have to end this somehow. Now, before anyone adds their spoken approval to his words. Chade's thin Skilling sounded desperate.

No one else stepped forward into the speaking circle.

No one had a solution to offer. The longer the silence stretched, the more charged the room became. I knew Chade was right. We needed time to think of a diplomatic solution to our position. And if there wasn't one, we still needed time to discover how many of the Outislander clans would actively oppose us and how many would simply disapprove. Given the disapproval of the other clans, would the Narcheska persist in her challenge to Dutiful or would she withdraw it? Could she honorably recall it? Here we were, not even a full day on this island's soil and already we seemed on the verge of confrontation.

Adding to my discomfort was that I was becoming aware of Dutiful's need to urinate. I started to shield myself from his Skill, and then had a different idea. I recalled how Thick's uneasiness aboard the ship had spread to infect the sailors. I wondered if Dutiful's current discomfort could be used in a like manner.

I opened myself to his unwitting sending, amplified it, and then sent my Skill-questing out through the room. None of the Outislanders that I touched had any strong aptitude for the Skill, but many were susceptible to its influence in varying degrees. Once Verity had used a similar technique to baffle Red Ship navigators, convincing them that they'd already passed key landmarks and thus sending their ships onto the rocks. Now I used it to end this Hetgurd gathering by reminding every man my Skill could touch of his urgent need to empty his bladder.

All around the room, men began to shift in their seats. *Doing?* Chade demanded.

Ending this meeting, I told him grimly.

Ah! I felt Dutiful's sudden comprehension, and then felt him join his persuasion to mine.

Who is in charge? I asked him.

No one. They share authority here. Or so they say. Dutiful obviously thought it a poor system.

Bear opened meeting, Chade told me tersely. I felt him draw my attention to a man who wore a bear's-tooth necklace. I was suddenly aware of how much strength it was taking from Chade for him to do this feeble Skilling.

Don't tax yourself, I warned him.

Know my own strength! His reply was angry but even from where I stood, I could see his shoulders drooping.

I singled out the Bear and focused my attention on him. Fortunately for me, he had little wall against the Skill and a full bladder. I pressed urgency on him and he suddenly stood up. He came forward to claim the speaking circle. The others ceded it to him with hand motions of giving.

"We need to ponder on this. All of us," he suggested. "Let us go apart, to talk with our own clans and see what thoughts they have for us. Tomorrow, let us gather again and speak of what we have learned and thought. Do any think this is wise?"

A forest of hands rose in spiraling gestures of assent.

"Then let our meeting be over for this day," the Bear suggested.

And just that quickly, it was over. Men stood immediately and began moving toward the door. There was no ceremony to it, no precedence for those of higher rank, just a push of men toward the exit, some with a greater insistence than others.

Tell your captain that you must check on your ward. That, until he is fit, I have commanded that you continue to tend him. We'll soon join you upstairs.

I obeyed my prince's command. When Longwick released me, I retrieved the washing basin I'd left outside the door and returned to Thick's chamber. He had not stirred that I could see. I felt his forehead. He was still feverish, but it did not burn as it had aboard the ship. Nonetheless, I roused him and coaxed him to drink water. He took little urging to down a whole mug of it, and then settled back into the bed again. I was relieved. Here, in this strange room and away from the perspective of his sickbed on the ship, I could truly see how wasted Thick was. Well, he would recover now. He had all he needed: quiet, a bed, food and drink. Soon he would be better. I tried to convince myself that my hope was a fact.

I heard Prince Dutiful and Chade conversing in the hall with someone. I stood and went to the door, ear pressed to it. I heard Dutiful pleading weariness, and then the closing of the door of the next chamber. His servants must have been waiting for him there. Again, there was a murmur of conversation, and then I heard him dismiss them. A little time passed and then the connecting door opened and Dutiful wandered in. He held a small black square of the food in his hand. He looked depressed. He held the food up and asked me, "Any idea what this is?"

"Not really, but it has fish paste in it. Maybe seaweed, too. The cakes with the seeds are sweet. Oily but sweet."

Dutiful regarded the food in his hand with distaste, then gave the shrug of a fifteen-year-old who hasn't been fed for several hours and ate it. He licked his fingers. "It's not bad, as long as you expect it to taste like fish."

"Old fish," I observed.

He didn't reply. He'd crossed over to where Thick slept. He stood looking down on him. He shook his head slowly.

"This is so unfair to him. Do you think he's getting better now?"

"I hope so."

"His music has become so much quieter, it worries me. Sometimes I feel as if Thick himself goes away from us when his fever rises."

I opened myself to Thick's music. Dutiful was right. It did seem less intense. "Well, he's sick. It takes strength and energy to Skill." I didn't want to worry about him just now. "Chade surprised me today."

"Did he? You must have known that he would keep at it until he could do at least that much. Nothing stops the old man once he has decided to do something." He turned away from me and headed toward the connecting door. Then he paused. "Did you want any of that stuff to eat?"

"No, thank you. You go ahead."

He spoke over his shoulder. He vanished for a moment into his own room, then returned with one hand stacked with the fish cakes. He bit into one of the squares, made a dismal face, and then quickly ate the rest of it. He looked around the room hungrily. "Didn't anyone bring us food yet?"

"You're eating it, I think."

"No. This is just an Out Island nod because we fed them. I know Chade told servants to find fresh food and buy it for us."

"Are you saying that Boar Clan isn't going to feed us?"

"They may. They may not. Chade seems to think we should act as if we don't expect it. Then, if they offer us food, we can accept it as a gift. And if they don't, we don't seem grasping or weak."

"Have you informed your nobles of their customs?"

He nodded. "Many of them came here as much to form new trading alliances and see what other opportunities the Out Islands offered as to support me in my courtship of the Narcheska. So they are just as glad to move about Zylig, seeing what is for sale here and what people might want to buy. But we'll have to feed my guard, the servants, and of course my Wit coterie. I thought Chade had arranged provisions."

"The Hetgurd seem to accord you little respect," I said worriedly.

"I do not think they truly understand what I am. It is a foreign concept to them, that a boy of my years, unproven as a warrior, is assured the ruling of such a large territory. Here, men do not claim sovereignty over an area of land, but instead show strength by the warriors they can command. In some ways, I am seen more as a son of my mother's house. Queen Kettricken was in power when we defeated them at the end of the Red Ship War. They are in awe of that, that she not only kept the homelands safe but that she launched war against them in the form of the dragons she called down on them. That is how it is told here."

"You seem to have learned a great deal in a very short time."

He nodded, pleased with himself. "Some of it comes from putting together what I hear here with what I experienced of the Outislanders at Buckkeep. Some from the reading I did on the way here." He gave a small sigh. "And it is not as useful as I hoped it would be. If they offer us hospitality, I mean, feed us, then we can see it as welcome, that they know it is our custom and honor it. Or we can see it as insult, that we are too weak to feed ourselves and too foolish to have come prepared. But no matter how we 'see' it, we can't be certain how they meant it."

"Like your dragon-slaying. Do you come to kill a beast and thus prove yourself a worthy mate for the Narcheska? Or do you come to kill the dragon that is the guardian of their land, proving that you can take whatever you want from them?"

Dutiful paled slightly. "I hadn't thought of it that way."

"Nor had I. But some of them do. And, it brings us back to that one essential question. Why? Why did the Narcheska choose this particular task for you?"

"Then you think it has significance to her besides my being willing to risk my life just to marry her?"

For a moment all I could do was stare at him. Had I ever been that young? "Well, of course it does. Don't you think so?"

"Civil had said that she probably wanted 'proof of my love.' He said that girls were often like that, asking men to do things that were dangerous or illegal or next to impossible, simply to prove their love."

I made a mental note of that. I wondered what Civil had been asked to do and by whom, and if it had related to the Farseer monarchy or was merely a boyish deed of derring-do that some girl had demanded of him.

"Well, I doubt it would be anything that romantically

frivolous with the Narcheska. How could she possibly think that you loved her, after the way she has treated you? And she's certainly given no sign of being fond of your company."

For a flashing moment, he stared at me with stricken eyes. Then he smoothed his expression so completely that I wondered if I had been mistaken. Surely the Prince could not be infatuated with the girl. They had nothing in common, and after he had accidentally insulted her, she had treated him as less than a whipped dog whining after her. I looked at him. A boy can believe almost anything when he is fifteen. Dutiful gave a slight snort. "No. She has certainly given me no sign of even tolerating my company. Think on it. She did not journey here with her father and uncle to meet us and offer us welcome to these islands. She is the one who thought up this ridiculous quest, but I notice she is nowhere in sight when it must be justified to her countrymen. Perhaps you are right. Perhaps it has nothing to do with me proving my love for her, or even proving my courage. Perhaps all along it was only to present a stumbling block to our marriage." In a glum voice, he added, "Perhaps she hopes I'll die in the attempt."

"If we press forward with the task, it may block more than your marriage. It may send both our countries back to war."

Chade entered on those words. He looked both worried and weary. He cast a disparaging look around the small chamber and observed, "Well, I see Thick has been afforded a chamber almost as lush as that allotted to Prince Dutiful and me. Is there anything to eat and drink?"

"Nothing I'd recommend," I observed.

"Fish and grease cakes," Prince Dutiful offered.

Chade winced. "Is that what the local market offers? I'll send a man to bring us provisions from the ship. Foreign food will not ride well with me after this day. Come. Let us allow Thick some rest." He spoke over his shoulder as he led us through the connecting door to the Prince's room.

As he sat down on Dutiful's bed, he added, "I do not approve of your putting the Skill to such a low use, Fitz. And yet, I must admit, you extricated us from a difficult situation. Please consult with me before you use it in such a way again."

It was both a rebuke and a compliment. I nodded, but Dutiful snorted. "Consult with *you*? Am not I to have any say in these matters?"

Chade recovered well. "Of course you are. I am merely conveying to Fitz that in matters of diplomacy, he should not assume that he knows best which course we should set."

The Prince opened his mouth to speak, but at that moment there came a rap at the hall door. At a gesture from Chade, I retreated to Thick's room, drew the connecting door nearly closed, and stood at an angle that allowed me to view a slice of the room without being easily observed. Chade lifted his voice and asked, "Who is there?"

The visitor interpreted that as permission to enter. The door opened, and as I set my muscles in readiness, Peottre Blackwater came in. He closed the door behind him, and then swept a Buckkeep bow to the Prince and Chade. "I have come to tell you that there is no need for you or any of your nobles to venture forth in search of food and drink. It is the pleasure of Clans Boar and Narwhal to provide for you as generously as you did for our folk when we visited your Six Duchies."

The words were spoken perfectly. It was a well-rehearsed speech. Chade's response was as practiced. "It is a gracious offer, but our people have already seen to their own provisions."

Peottre looked distinctly uncomfortable for a moment, but then admitted, "We have already informed your nobles of our invitation, and are honored that all have accepted it."

Outwardly, both Chade and the Prince maintained a stiff silence, but the Prince's anguished worry rang in my mind. *I should have cautioned all of them not to accept any offer of hospitality that was not conveyed through me. Will we be seen as weaklings now?*

Peottre's gaze moved worriedly from Chade's face to the Prince's. He seemed to sense he had misstepped. Then, "May I speak for a time with you?" he asked.

"Lord Blackwater, you are welcome to call upon me at any time," the Prince assured him reflexively.

A very slight smile twitched Peottre's face. "Well you know that I am no 'lord,' Prince Dutiful, but only a kaempra of the Narwhal Clan. And even as that, I stand in the Hetgurd assembly with no warriors at my back. They tolerate me more for the sake of my sister's husband, Arkon Bloodblade, than for any respect toward me. Our clan has fallen on very hard times in every way except the richness of our motherlands and the honor of our bloodlines."

I privately wondered in what other ways a clan could experience hardship, but Peottre was still speaking. "I was not unprepared for what we heard from the Hetgurd this afternoon. In truth, ever since the Narcheska proposed her challenge, I have expected it. Arkon Bloodblade too saw that there were those who would be disgruntled by the test she has proposed for the Prince. I wanted to tell you that we are not unprepared for this. We have made plans against it. The hospitality we offer, within this stronghouse, is but one safeguard we have put in place. We had hoped opposition would not be voiced so soon, nor by such a respected kaempra as the Eagle Kaempra. It is our great good fortune that the Bear Kaempra, who is allied with Boar, saw fit to dismiss the assembly so abruptly. Otherwise, discussion might have gone too far for us to mend it."

"You might have warned us of this opposition, Kaempra Peottre, before we faced the Hetgurd," Chade observed quietly, but the Prince cut through his words with "So you think it can be mended? How?"

I winced at his eagerness. Chade was right. The man deserved a rebuke for having led us into a trap, not an unquestioning acceptance of his aid in getting out of it.

"It will take time, but not too long—days rather than months. Since we returned from your country, we have spent much in both wealth and influence to buy allies. I speak bluntly, of course, of what cannot be openly acknowledged. Those who have agreed to support us must not swing too quickly to our side, but must seem to be persuaded by the arguments that Clan Boar will present in our favor. So, I wish to counsel you both to patience and to wariness while the Hetgurd is swayed."

"Wariness?" Chade queried sharply. *Assassins?* His unspoken fear reached me clearly.

"This is not the right word," Peottre apologized. "Sometimes, it seems, what one language says in one word another has many for. I would ask you to be . . . not as seen. Not as visible. Not as easy to find or to speak to."

"Unavailable?" the Prince suggested.

Peottre smiled slightly and shrugged. "If that is how you would say it. We have a saying here, 'It is difficult to insult the man you don't speak to.' That is what I suggest. That the Farseer Buck Clan avoids giving offense by being . . . unavailable."

"While we trust Boar Clan to speak for us?" Chade asked. He allowed a trace of skepticism into his voice. "And what are we to do in the meanwhile?"

Peottre smiled. I was not in the best position to observe him, but I thought I had glimpsed a look of relief that we seemed inclined to accept his advice. "I would suggest that we remove you completely from Zylig. All expect that you will visit the mothershouse of the Narcheska. It was almost surprising to the Hetgurd that you came here first. So, I suggest that tomorrow you board the Boar vessel *Tusker* and sail with us to Wuislington, the motherlands of Narwhal Clan. There, you shall be welcomed and provided for, just as you welcomed and provided for us at Buckkeep. I have reported to my mothershouse of your customs in this regard. They find them unusual, but will concede the fairness of feeding you as you fed us."

He could not conceal his hope as he offered this suggestion. His eagerness alarmed me. Did he shoo us away from danger, or lure us into it? I felt the same query cross Chade's mind as he said, "But we have only arrived here today, and we are weary from the sea. The Prince's man, Thick, does not fare well on the waves. He has taken ill and needs his rest. We cannot think of leaving tomorrow."

I knew that we could, and that he was considering the cost of it even now. He but said these words to Peottre to see what the man would reply. For a moment, I almost pitied the Outislander. He could not know that Chade and the Prince were sharing their thoughts, let alone that I stood around the corner not only hearing his every word but also supporting their observations with mine. I saw dismay blossom behind his eyes, and confirmed to both Dutiful and Chade that I believed his discomfort was genuine as he exclaimed, "But you must! Leave the man here with someone to tend to him. He will be safe here in the Boar stronghouse. To do murder in a clan's stronghouse is a terrible insult to their mothershouse and the Boar Clan is powerful. No one will consider it."

"But they might consider it if he ventured outside the stronghouse? Or if I went out tonight, seeking a meal perhaps?" The velvet courtesy of Chade's tone did not quite mask the razor edge of his question.

From my concealment, I could see that Peottre regretted his hasty words. He considered lying and then boldly pushed that aside in favor of blunt truth. "You must have known it could come to this. You are not fools, either of you. I have seen you study men and balance the bargain you offer this one against what that one desires. I have seen you offer both honey and the spur to move others to your will. You would have come here knowing what Icefyre means to some of us. You would have anticipated this opposition."

I felt Chade caution Dutiful to silence as he spoke out severely on his behalf. "Opposition, yes. Even a muttering of war. A threat of murder to the Prince's man, or the Prince himself, no. Dutiful is the sole heir to the Farseer crown. You are not a fool, either. You know what that means. We have extended him as far into danger as we will risk him in allowing him to embark on this ridiculous quest. Now you admit that murder may hang over him, simply because he seeks to keep his word to your sister-daughter. The stakes for this alliance have become too high, Peottre. I will not wager the Prince's life for the sake of this betrothal. The Narcheska's demand has never made sense to me. Give us one good reason why we should proceed."

The Prince was seething. His Skilled objections to Chade's high-handedness drowned out my own thoughts. I thought I knew what Chade was doing, yet the only emotion I could experience was the Prince's affront that Chade would imply he would retreat from his word. Even Thick turned over with a heavy moan under the Prince's Skill-onslaught.

Peottre's glance darted to the Prince. Even without the Skill, he could read a young man's spirit. "Because Prince Dutiful had said he will do it. To back away from his word now and flee home would make him seem both cowardly and weak. It might stave off war, but it would invite raiding again. You know our saying, I am sure: 'A coward owns nothing for long.'"

In the Six Duchies we say, "Fear is the only thing that a man cannot take from a coward." I supposed that it meant the same thing. That if our prince showed a cowardly nature, so all the Six Duchies would be judged, and the Outislanders would see us as ripe to be raided again.

Silence! Glare all you wish, but still your tongue! Chade's command to Dutiful was as strong a bit of Skilling as I had ever experienced from him. Even more astonishing was the private command he arrowed solely to me. *Watch Peottre's face, Fitz.* I felt what it cost Chade in strength, yet he kept his voice steady as he said coolly, "Kaempra Narwhal. You mistake me. I did not say the Prince would go back on his word to set the dragon's head before your narcheska. He has given his word, and a Farseer does not go back on his word. But once he has done that deed, I see no need to waste my prince's bloodline on a woman who would connive to send him into such danger, from her own people as well as from a dragon. He will do this, but we will feel no duty to wed him to the Narcheska afterward."

I had done as Chade bade me, but there was no reading the succession of expressions that flitted over Peottre's visage. Astonishment, of course, followed by confoundment. I knew what Chade desired to discover. What did Peottre and the Narcheska seek most strongly: the death of the dragon or an alliance with the Farseers? Yet we were no closer to an answer when Peottre stammered out, "But is not that what the Six Duchies most desires? To create goodwill and an alliance by this marriage?"

"The Narcheska is not the only woman of high stature in the Out Islands," Chade replied dismissively. Dutiful had grown very still. I could sense the racing of his thoughts, but not hear them. "Certainly Prince Dutiful can find a woman from amongst your people who does not frivolously risk his life. And if not, there are other alliances to be had. Do you think Chalced would not value such an arrangement with the Six Duchies? Here is an old Six Duchies saying for you to ponder: 'There is more than one fish in the sea.'"

Peottre was still struggling to grasp the sudden change in situation. "But why risk the Prince's life in slaying the dragon if there is no reward for doing so?" he asked bewilderedly.

It was finally Dutiful's turn to speak. Chade fed him the words, but I think the Prince would have known them for himself even without the prompting. "To remind the Out Islands that what a Farseer says he will do, he does. A few years have passed since my father roused his Elderling allies and destroyed most of this city. Perhaps the best way for us to stave off war between the Six Duchies and the Out Islands is not with a wedding. Perhaps the best way is to remind your countrymen, again, that what we say we will do, we do." The Prince's voice was soft and even. He spoke, not man to man, but as a king.

Even a warrior such as Peottre was not immune to such an assumption. He took less offense at my young prince's words than he would if one of his fellow kaempras had spoken so to him. I saw him uncertain of his footing, yet I could not have said if he was dismayed at the thought that his sister-daughter might not be wed to the Prince, or relieved. "Truly, it must seem that we have resorted to trickery in tempting you to swear to such a task. And now that you have discovered the full import of your promise, you must feel twice tricked. It is a hero's task that Elliania has laid upon you. You have sworn to do it. Did I desire to indulge in trickery, I would remind you that you had given your word, as well, to wed her. I might ask if you were not, as a Farseer, bound as tightly there to do as you had said you would do. But I release you from that without quibbling. You feel yourself betrayed by us. I cannot deny that it appears that way. I am certain that you recognize that if you perform this task and then refuse the Narcheska's hand, you will shame us in proportion to the glory that you will have won for yourself. Her name will become a word for the faithless trickery of a woman. I do not relish such a prospect. Nonetheless, I bow to your right to take such a stance. Nor will I bring blood-vengeance against you, but will hold my sword and acknowledge that you had a right to feel yourself wronged."

From my place of concealment, I shook my head. What Peottre said obviously filled him with great emotion, yet I knew I was missing the full import of his words. Our traditions were simply too different. One thing I did know, and an instant later the Prince echoed my thought even as he looked at Peottre consideringly. *Well, I have not bettered the situation. We both stand affronted by the other's behavior now. How can I improve this? Draw a sword and challenge him right now?*

Don't be a fool! Chade's rebuke was as sharp as if Dutiful had been serious. *Accept his offer of transport aboard the* Tusker *to Wuislington. We knew we would have to make that journey; as well to appear to concede it to him. Perhaps we may learn more when we are there. This riddle must be unraveled, and I would have you away from the Hetgurd and any assassination attempts until I know more.*

Prince Dutiful lowered his head slightly. I knew it was at Chade's suggestion, but it must have appeared to Peottre that he perhaps regretted the tenor of his earlier words. "We are pleased to accept your hospitality this night, Peottre Blackwater. And we will take passage on the *Tusker* tomorrow, to Wuislington."

The relief that Peottre felt at Dutiful's words was palpable. "I myself will vouch for the safety of your folk while we are gone from them."

Dutiful shook his head slowly. His mind was racing. If Peottre were seeking to separate him from his guard and advisers, he would not allow it. "My nobles will, of course, remain here. As they are not of the Farseer line, I suspect that they will not be seen as of my clan and appropriate targets for vengeance. But certain of my entourage must accompany me. My guard, and my advisers. I am sure that you understand."

What of Thick? He is still very sick. I asked the question urgently.

I cannot leave you behind, and I will not trust him to the dubious care he would receive from another. Hard as it will be for him, he must travel with us. He is a member of my Skill coterie. Besides. Think of the havoc he could wreak in our absence did he go back to his old nightmares.

"Farseer Prince of the Six Duchies, in that I think we can accommodate you." In his eagerness to be certain of our assent, Peottre almost babbled the words.

The conversation had moved into safer channels. In a

short time, Peottre escorted them downstairs to a meal. Chade loudly observed to the Prince that they must arrange that a substantial meal be sent upstairs to Thick, to hasten his recovery. Peottre assured them that this would be done, and then I heard them leave. When they were clear of the Prince's room, I let out my pent breath, rolled my shoulders, and moved to check on Thick. He slept on, peacefully unaware that on the morrow he would be carted off to yet another miserable sea voyage. I looked down on him and sent calming thoughts into his dreams. Then I sat down by the door and awaited, without enthusiasm, whatever Outislander victuals would be sent up to me.

chapter IX

MOTHERSHOUSE

Bowsrin was kaempra for the Badger Clan at that time. His ships were fleet, his warriors strong, and he raided well, bringing back brandy and silver and tools of iron. He was nearly a hero before he shamed his clan.

He desired a woman of the Gull Clan. He went to her mothershouse with gifts, but she did not accept them. Her sister did, and he lay with her, but it was not enough for him. He went away and raided for a year and returned to the Badger mothershouse with much wealth, but no pride in his heart, for he was eaten up with unworthy lust.

His warriors were good fighters but foolish in heart, for they listened to his command when he took them to raid the Gull Clan mothershouse. Their warriors were away and the women in the field when Bowsrin's ships came to their shore. Kaempra Bowsrin and his warriors killed their old men and some of their nearly grown boys, and took the women on the bare earth, despite how they fought. Some died rather than be forced. Bowsrin stayed there for seventeen days, and every day that he was there, he forced the Gull Clan daughter Serferet to accept his body. Finally she died of it. Then they left, to return to their own mothershouse.

*The moon changed and then the Badger
mothershouse received tidings of what their kaempra had
done. They were shamed. They drove their men from
their lands, telling them never to return. Seventeen of
their sons the women gave to the Gull Clan, to do with
whatever they wished, in atonement for Bowsrin's evil.
And the mothershouses of all clans banned Bowsrin and
his men from the land, and any man who offered them
any comfort was to share their fate.*

*In less than a year, the sea ate him and his men.
And Clan Gull used his forfeited sister-sons, not as
slaves, but as warriors to defend their shores and as men
to raise up more sons and daughters for Gull Clan. And
the women of the mothershouses were at peace with one
another again.*

❧ OUTISLANDER CAUTIONARY TALE,
FROM BARD OMBIR

The next day we took ship for the island of Mayle. Prince
Dutiful and Chade met briefly with the convened Hetgurd
to announce this decision to them. The Prince gave a brief
speech in which he said he had chosen to recognize the
conflict as a Hetgurd matter. As a man, he could not call
back the word he had given, but he would give them the
chance to discuss this challenge and reach a consensus on
what their will was. He spoke with dignity and calm,
Chade told me later, and his willingness to concede that
it was a matter only the Hetgurd could settle seemed to
soothe many of the ruffled feathers. Even Eagle spoke well
of it, saying that a man who was willing to face a challenge
squarely was a man anyone could respect, regardless of
where he was birthed.

The Prince's nobles received the tidings of his departure with varying degrees of surprise and dismay. It was
conveyed to them as a slight change in our schedule. Most
had not planned to accompany the Prince to his fiancée's

mothershouse; they had been told back in Buckkeep that such a large delegation of folk would not be easily welcomed there. They had expected to stay in Zylig and establish connections for future trade negotiations. For the most part, they were content to remain on Skyrene and court trading partners. Arkon Bloodblade, kaempra of the Boar Clan and the Narcheska's father, quietly assured us that he would remain with his warriors to ensure their stay was pleasant, and to further advance our cause with the Hetgurd.

Chade told me later that he had strongly suggested to our nobles that they continue to enjoy the hospitality of the Boar stronghouse rather than investigate the hospitality of the local inns. He also suggested that they display their own heraldic devices when they went out and about amongst the Outislanders, just as the clansmen sported their animal sigils. I doubt that he told the Six Duchies nobles there would be more safety for them if they were not seen as part of the Farseer Buck Clan, as the Outislanders thought of the Prince's family.

The *Tusker* was an Outislander vessel, far less comfortable than the *Maiden's Chance* had been. She bobbed more in the waves, I noted as I watched the others board, but her shallower draft was more suitable for the interisland channels that we would be navigating than the *Maiden's* deeper hull. Some of the channels, I was told, were barely passable at a low tide, and during certain tides that came only once or twice a year a man could walk from island to island on foot. We would traverse several of these channels before once more crossing open water to the Narcheska's home island and her village of Wuislington.

It was a cruel thing to do to Thick. I let him sleep as long as possible before I awakened him to a hot meal of familiar foods brought from the *Maiden's Chance*. I urged him to eat and drink well and spoke only of pleasant things. I concealed from him that we would be embarking on yet another voyage. He was unhappy about having to wash and dress, wanting only to go back to his bed. I longed to be able to let him, for I was convinced it would have been best for his health. But we could not safely leave him behind in Zylig.

Even when we stood on the docks with the Prince's guardsmen, his Wit coterie, Chade, and Prince Dutiful, watching the cargo of bridal gifts being loaded onto the *Tusker*, Thick thought we had only come out on a morning's stroll. The boat was tied alongside the dock. At least, I told myself grimly, boarding would present no problem. I was wrong. He watched the others walk up the gangway and on board with no qualms, but when it was his turn, he stopped dead beside me. "No."

"Don't you want to see the Outislander ship, Thick? Everyone else has gone on board to look around. I've heard it is very different from our ship. Let's go and see it."

He looked at me for a moment in silence. "No," he said. His little eyes were beginning to narrow in suspicion.

Further deception was useless. "Thick, we have to go on board. It's going to sail soon, to take the Prince to the Narcheska's home. We have to go with him."

Around us, activity on the docks had halted. All else had been in readiness, and all the others were aboard. The ship waited only for Thick and me. Men from other ships and passersby stared at Thick's strangeness avidly, with varying degrees of revulsion on their faces. Sailors from the *Tusker* waited to haul the planks of the walkway on board and cast off lines. They stared at us in annoyance, waiting. I sensed from them that we humiliated them by our very presence. Why could not we get on board and out of sight belowdecks? Time to act. I took his upper arm firmly. "Thick, we have to get on board now."

"No!" He bellowed the word suddenly as he slapped at me wildly, and both his fear and his fury struck me in a wild wave of Skill. I staggered aside from him, bringing a general guffaw from those who had halted to watch us. In

truth, it must have looked strange to them, that the petulant slap of a half-wit had nearly driven me to my knees.

I hate to recall what followed. I had no choice but to
force him. But Thick's terror left him no choice either. We
fought it out on the docks, my physical size and strength
and the stoutness of my well-practiced walls against his
Skill and awkward fighting abilities.

Both Chade and Prince Dutiful were instantly aware
of my dilemma, of course. I sensed the Prince trying to
reach Thick and calm him, but the red haze of his anger
acted as efficiently as any Skill-wall. I could not feel
Chade's presence at all; I think his effort of the day before
had drained him. The first time I seized Thick with the intent of simply lifting him off his feet and carrying him
aboard, his Skill flooded into me. The skin-to-skin contact
left me vulnerable. It was his fear that he flung at me, and I
nearly wet myself with the terror he woke in me. Ancient
memories of moments when death's jaws had closed
around me rushed through me. I felt the teeth of a Forged
One sink into my shoulder and an arrow thudded home in
my back. I had lifted him to my shoulder, and I sagged to
my knees, under the weight of his terror rather than his
body. This elicited a fresh roar of laughter from the onlookers. Thick broke free of me and then stood there, crying
out wildly and wordlessly, at bay, unable to flee, for now a
circle of jeering men ringed us.

The mockery around us grew and battered me more effectively than Thick's flailing fists. I could not grasp hold of
him without risking the integrity of my walls, nor did I dare
lower my walls against Thick's onslaught to allow my own
Skill to have its full effect. So I made futile efforts at herding him aboard, closing off his escape whenever he tried to
dart past me down the docks. When I stepped toward him,
he would step back, closer to the gangplank, and the circle
of men there would give way. Then he would dart at me,
hand outstretched, knowing that if he touched me, my walls
would fall before him. And I would be forced to give ground

to avoid his reaching hand. And all the while, men laughed and shouted to their comrades in their harsh tongue, to come and see a Duchyman who could not fight a half-wit.

In the end, it was Web who saved me. Perhaps the excited cries of the sailors on the *Tusker* brought him to the railing. The bulky sailor pushed his way past the gawkers and came down the gangway toward us. "Thick, Thick, Thick," he said calmingly. "Come now, man. There's no need for this. No need at all."

I had known that the Wit could be used to *repel* someone. Who has not leaped back from the clashing teeth of a dog or narrowly avoided the swipe of a cat's claws? It is not just the threat that forces one to give ground, but the force of the creature's anger that pushes its challenger back. I think that for a Witted one, to learn to repel is as instinctive as knowing how to flee danger. I had never stopped to think that there might be another complementary force, one that calmed and beckoned.

I did not have a word for what Web exuded toward Thick. I was not his target, yet I was still peripherally aware of it. It settled my hackles and calmed my thundering heart. Almost without my volition, my shoulders lowered and my jaw unclenched. I saw a wondering look come over Thick's face. His mouth sagged open and his tongue, which was never completely inside it, protruded even more as his little eyes drooped almost closed. Web spoke softly. "Easy, my friend. Relax. Come now, come with me."

There is a look a kitten gets when its mother lifts it by the nape of its neck. That look was on Thick's face as Web's big hand settled on his arm. "Don't look," Web suggested to him. "Eyes on me, now," and Thick obeyed him, looking up at Web's face as the Witmaster led him aboard the ship as easily as a lad leads a bull by the ring in its nose. I was left trembling, the sweat drying down my spine. The blood rushed to my face at the taunting of the men that accompanied my boarding of the ship. Most of them spoke Six Duchies in a rudimentary way. That they used it now was deliberate, to be sure I understood their scorn. I could not pretend to ignore them, for I could not control the blood that reddened my face with shame. I had no place I could vent my anger as I stalked after Web. I heard the planks taken up behind me as soon as I was on board. I didn't look back, but trailed after Web and Thick toward a tentlike structure on the deck of the ship.

The accommodations were far cruder than those on the *Maiden's Chance* had been. On the foredeck, there was a permanent cabin with wooden walls, such as I was accustomed to seeing on a ship. I was to learn it was divided into two chambers. The larger of these had been given over to the Prince and Chade, and the Wit coterie crowded into the smaller one. This temporary cabin on the aft deck was for the guardsmen. The walls were made of heavy leather stretched on poles with the entire structure lashed down to pegs set in the deck. These shelters were a concession to our Six Duchies sensibilities; the Outislanders themselves preferred an open deck as best for hauling freight or fighting. A look at the faces of my fellow guardsmen persuaded me of how little welcome Thick would be amongst them. After my shameful performance on the dock, I was little higher in their regard. Web was trying to get Thick to sit down on one of the sea chests that had been brought from the *Maiden's Chance*.

"No," I told him quietly. "The Prince prefers that Thick be housed close at hand to him. We should take him to the other cabin."

"It's even more crowded than this one," Web explained, but I only shook my head.

"The other cabin," I insisted, and he relented. Thick went with him, still with that glazed look of trust on his face. I followed, feeling as exhausted as if I'd spent a morning in sword training. It was only later that I realized it was Web's own pallet he settled Thick onto. Civil sat in the corner on a smaller pallet, his snarling cat on his lap. The minstrel Cockle was disconsolately inspecting three broken strings on a small harp. Swift was looking everywhere but at me. I could feel his dismay that this half-man had been brought right into his living space. The silence in the tiny room was thicker than butter.

Once Thick had settled on the pallet, Web smoothed a callused hand over his sweaty brow. Thick stared up at us in puzzlement for a moment and then closed his eyes, weary as a child. His breathing was hoarse as sleep claimed him. After the buffeting he'd dealt me, I longed to join him there, but Web was taking my arm.

"Come," he said. "We have to talk, you and I."

I would have resisted him if I could, but when he set his hand on my shoulder, my defiance melted. I let him steer me out onto the deck. I heard the jesting shouts of the sailors when I reappeared, but Web chose to ignore them as he steered me to a rail. "Here," he said, and from his hip took a leather flask and unstoppered it. The scent of brandy reached me. "A bit of this down you, and then take some deep breaths. You look like a man who has bled half to death."

I did not think I needed the brandy until I took some and felt its heat run through me.

Fitz?

The Prince's worried query reached me as a whisper. I realized abruptly how tightly I was still holding my walls. Gingerly I eased them down, and then reached back to Dutiful. *"I'm fine. Web has Thick settled now."*

"That's right. I do. But you scarcely need to tell me that."

Give me a moment, my Prince, to gather myself. I had not even realized that I had spoken aloud the thought I'd previously Skilled to Dutiful. "I know. I'm a bit rattled, I suppose."

"Yes, you are. What I don't understand is why. But I have my suspicions. The simple man is very important to the Prince, isn't he? And it has something to do with how he could stop a warrior in his prime from forcing him to do a thing he didn't wish to do. What made you flinch before his touch? When I touched him, nothing happened to me."

I handed him back his flask. "Not my secret," I said bluntly.

"I see." He took a mouthful of his brandy. He looked aloft pensively. Risk did a lazy loop around our ship, waiting for us. Canvas blossomed suddenly on the mast. A moment later, it bellied in the wind and I felt our ship dip and then gather speed. "Short journey, they tell me. Three days, four at most. If we'd taken the *Maiden's Chance*, she would have had to sail around the whole cluster of islands, and then we would have had to put her at harbor on one of the other islands and still take another shallow-draft vessel to reach Wuislington."

I nodded sagely to that, not knowing if it was true or not. Perhaps his bird had told him. More likely, it was sailor's gossip, gained by his own ready ears.

As if it were a logical continuation, he asked, "If I were to guess this secret, would you tell me I'd got it right?"

I gave a short sigh. Only now that the struggle was over did I realize how weary I was. And how strong Thick had been when driven by his fear and anger to apply all his strength to me. I hoped he had not burned reserves he could not afford. His sickness had already drained much of his vigor. He had thought himself in a life-or-death struggle with me; of that I had no doubt. Concern for him suddenly filled me.

"Tom?" Web pressed me, and with a start I recalled his question.

"It's not my secret," I repeated doggedly. Hopelessness was welling up in me like blood from a puncture wound. I recognized it as Thick's. That didn't help. I'd have to quell it somehow, before it could affect the rest of the people on the ship.

Can you handle him for us?

The assent I sent to the Prince was an acknowledgment

of his request rather than a confirmation that I could accomplish it.

Web was offering me his flask again. I took it, swigged from it, and then said, "I have to go back to Thick. It's not good for him to be left alone."

"I think I see that," he agreed as he took the flask back from me. "I wish I was sure whether you were protector or gaoler to him. Well, Tom Badgerlock, when you judge that it's safe for me to be the one to stay with him, you let me know. You look as if you could use a bit of rest yourself."

I nodded without replying and I left him there and went to the little chamber allotted to the Wit coterie. All the other folk had fled, probably made uncomfortable by the strength of the emotions emanating from Thick on a swelling Skill tide. He slept, but it was from exhaustion, not peace. I looked down on his face, seeing a simplicity there that was not childish or even simple. His cheeks were flushed and tiny beads of sweat stood on his forehead. His fever was back and his breathing was raspy. I sat on the floor by his pallet. I was ashamed of what we were doing to him. It wasn't right and we knew it, Chade and Dutiful and I. Then I gave in to my weariness and lay down at his side.

I gave myself three breaths to center myself and gather my Skill. Then I closed my eyes and put my arm lightly across Thick in order to deepen our Skill-connection. I had expected him to have his walls up against me, but he was defenseless. I slipped into a dream in which a lost kitten paddled desperately in a boiling sea. I drew him from the water as Nettle had done and took him back to the wagon and the bed and the cushion. I promised him that he was safe and felt his anxiety ease a little. But even in his dreams, he recognized me. "But you made me!" the kitten suddenly cried out. "You made me come on a boat again!"

I had expected anger and defiance, or even an attack following those words. What I received was worse. He cried. The kitten wept inconsolably, in a small child's

voice. I felt the gulf of his disappointment that I could betray him so. He had trusted me. I picked him up and held
him, but still he cried, and I could not comfort him, for I
was at the base of his sorrow.

I was not expecting Nettle. It was not night, and I
doubted that she was sleeping. I suppose I had always assumed that she could only Skill when she slept. A foolish
notion, but there it was. As I sat rocking the tiny creature
that was Thick, I felt her presence beside me. *Give him to
me*, she said with a woman's weariness at a man's incompe-
tence. Guilty at my relief, I let her take him from me. I
faded into the background of his dream, and felt his tension ease as I retreated from him. It hurt that he found my
presence upsetting, but I could not blame him.

After a time, I found myself sitting at the base of the
melted tower. It seemed a very forsaken place. The dead
brambles coated the steep hillsides all around it, and the
only sound was the wind soughing through their branches.
I waited.

Nettle came. *Why this?* she asked, sweeping an arm at
the desolation that surrounded us.

It seemed appropriate, I replied dispiritedly.

She gave a snort of contempt and then, with a wave,
made the dead brambles into deep summer grasses. The
tower became a circle of broken stone on the hillside, with
flowering vines wandering over it. She seated herself on a
sun-warmed stone, shook out her red skirts over her bare
feet, and asked, *Are you always this dramatic?*

I suspect I am.

*It must be exhausting to be around you. You're the second
most emotional man I know.*

The first being?

My father. He came home yesterday.

I caught my breath, and tried to be casual as I asked, *And?*

*And he had gone to Buckkeep Castle. That is as much as
he told us. He looks as if he has aged a decade and yet sometimes
I catch him gazing across the room and smiling. Despite his*

fogged eyes, he keeps staring at me, as if he has never seen me before. Mother says she feels as if he keeps saying farewell to her. He comes to her and puts his arms around her and holds her as if she might be snatched away at any moment. It is hard to describe how he behaves; as if some heavy task is finally finished, and yet he also acts like a man preparing for a journey.

What has he told you? I tried to keep her from sensing my dread.

Nothing. And no more than that to my mother, or so she says. He brought gifts for all of us when he came back. Jumping jacks for my smallest brothers, and cleverly carved puzzle boxes for the older boys. For my mother and me, little boxes with necklaces of wooden beads inside them, not roughly shaped but each carved like a jewel. And a horse, the loveliest little mare I've ever seen.

I waited, knowing what I would hear next and yet praying it would not be said.

And he himself now wears an earring, a sphere carved from wood. I've never seen him wear an earring before. I didn't even know his ear was pierced for one.

I wondered if they had talked, Lord Golden and Burrich. Perhaps the Fool had merely left those gifts with Queen Kettricken to be passed on to Burrich. I wondered so many things and could ask none of them. *What are you doing right now?* I asked her instead.

Dipping tapers. The most boring and stupid task that exists. For a moment, she was silent. Then, *I've a message for you.*

My heart stopped at those words. *Oh?*

If I dream of the wolf again, my father says, I'm to tell him, You should have come home a long time ago.

Tell him . . . A thousand messages flitted through my mind. What could I say to a man I hadn't seen in sixteen years? Tell him that he needn't fear I'll take anything away from him? Tell him that I love still as I have always loved? No. Not that. Tell him I forgive him. No, for he never knowingly wronged me. Those words could only increase whatever burden he put upon himself. There were a thousand things I longed to say and none I dared send through Nettle.

Tell him? Nettle prompted me, avidly curious.

Tell him I was speechless. And grateful to him. As I have been for many years.

It seemed inadequate, and yet I forced myself to say no more. I would not be impetuous. I would think long and hard before I gave any real message to Nettle to relay to Burrich. I did not know how much she knew or guessed. I did not even know how much Burrich knew of all that had befallen me since last we parted. Better to regret unsaid words than repent of words I could never call back.

Who are you?

I owed her at least that much. A name to call me by. There was only one that seemed right to give her. *Changer. My name is Changer.*

She nodded, both disappointed and pleased. In another place and time, my Wit warned me that others were near me. I pulled away from the dream and she reluctantly let me go. I eased back into my own flesh. For a time longer, I kept my eyes closed while opening all my other senses. I was in the cabin, Thick breathing heavily beside me. I smelled the oil the minstrel used on the wood of his harp and then heard Swift whisper, "Why is he sleeping now?"

"I'm not," I said quietly. I eased my arm away from Thick lest I awake him and then sat up slowly. "I was just getting Thick settled. He is still very sick. I wish we didn't have to bring him on this voyage."

Swift was still looking at me oddly. Cockle the minstrel was moving very softly, wiping the frame of his repaired harp with oil. I stood, head bent beneath the low ceiling, and looked at Burrich's son. Much as he wished to avoid me, I had a duty. "Are you busy with anything right now?" I asked Swift.

He looked at Cockle as if expecting the minstrel to speak for him. When he remained silent, Swift replied quietly, "Cockle was going to play some Six Duchies songs for the Outislanders. I was going to listen to them."

I took a breath. I needed to pull this boy closer to me if I was going to keep my word to Nettle. Yet I'd already alienated him by trying to send him home. Too firm a rein on him now would not gain his trust. So I said, "Much can be learned from a minstrel's songs. Listen, also, to what the Outislanders say and sing, and do your best to gain a few words of their language. Later, we will speak of what you learned."

"Thank you," he said stiffly. It was as hard for him to express gratitude as it was for him to acknowledge I had authority over him. I would not push for that, yet. So I nodded to him and let him leave. Cockle swept me a minstrel's gracious bow at the door and for an instant our eyes met. The friendliness there surprised me, until he bade me farewell with, "It's rare to find a man-at-arms who values learning, and rarer still to find one who recognizes that minstrels can be a source of it. I thank you, sir."

"It is I who thank you. My prince has asked me to educate the lad. Perhaps you can show him that gaining knowledge need not be painful." In the blink of an eye, I made a second decision. "I'll join you, if I would not be intruding."

He flourished me another bow. "I'd be honored."

Swift had gone ahead of us, and he did not look pleased when he saw me accompanying the musician.

The Outislander sailors were like any sailors I've ever known anywhere. Any sort of entertainment was preferable to the daily tedium of the ship. Those not currently on duty soon gathered to hear Cockle sing. It was a fine setting for the minstrel, standing on the bare deck with the wind in his hair and the sun at his back. The men who gathered to hear him brought their own handiwork with them, much as women would have brought their embroidery or knitting. One worked a tatter of old rope into a knotted mat; another carved lazily at a bit of hardwood. The intentness with which they listened confirmed what I had suspected. By choice or by chance, most of Peottre's crew had a working knowledge of Duchy tongue. Even those of the crew working the sails nearby had one ear for the music.

Cockle gave them several traditional Six Duchies ballads that memorialized the Farseer monarchs. Wise enough a man was he to avoid any of the songs that had to do with our long feud with the Out Islands. I wouldn't have to sit through the Antler Island Tower song today. Swift appeared to pay good attention to the songs. His attention was most deeply snared when Cockle told an Old Blood fable in song. I watched the Outislander sailors as Cockle sang it and wondered if I'd see the same disgust and resentment that many Six Duchies people showed when such songs were sung. I didn't. Instead, the sailors seemed to accept it as a strange song of foreign magic.

When he had finished, one of the Outislander sailors stood with a broad grin that wrinkled the boar tattoo on his cheek. He'd set aside his whittling and now he brushed the fine curls of clinging wood from his chest and trousers. "You think that magic is strong?" he challenged us. "I know a stronger, and best you know it, too, for face it you might."

With one bare foot, he nudged the shipmate who sat on the deck beside him. Plainly embarrassed at the circle of listeners, this man nonetheless tugged free a little carved whistle that hung inside his shirt on a string around his neck and played a simple, wailing tune on it, while his fellow, with more drama than voice, hoarsely sang us a tale of the Black Man of Aslevjal. He sang in Outislander, and in the special accents that their bards used, making the song even harder for me to follow. The Black Man stalked the island, and woe to any who came there with unworthy intents. He was the dragon's guardian, or perhaps he was the dragon in human form. Black as the dragon was black, "something" as the dragon was "something," strong as the wind and as unslayable, and unforgiving as ice was he. He would gnaw the bones of the cowardly, and slice the flesh of the rash, he would—

"To your duty!" Peottre suddenly interjected into our circle. His command was good-naturedly severe, reminding us that he was acting captain on this ship as well as our host. The sailor stopped barking the song and looked at him askance. I sensed a tension there; the boar proclaimed that this was Arkon Bloodblade's warrior. Most of the crew was marked as Bloodblade's, loaned to Peottre for this task. Peottre gave a tiny shake of his head at the sailor, as much rebuke as warning, and the man lowered his shoulders.

"At what task, then, in our hours of rest?" he still asked, a hint of bravado in his tone.

Peottre spoke mildly but his stance said he would tolerate no defiance. "Your duty, Rutor, is to rest in these hours, so that when you are called to work, you come fresh to the task. Rest, then, and leave entertaining our guests to me."

Behind him, both Chade and the Prince had emerged from their cabin to watch curiously. Web stood behind them. I wondered if Peottre had heard the man's song and excused himself abruptly from their company. I reached to them both. *Do we know a tale of the Black Man on Aslevjal Island? One who guards the dragon, perhaps? For that is the song that Peottre has just silenced.*

I know nothing. I will ask Chade in a quiet moment.

Chade? I attempted a direct contact.

There was no response. He did not even shift his eyes toward me.

I think he attempted too much yesterday.

Has he taken any teas today? I asked suspiciously. Skill-effort such as Chade had expended yesterday could well leave a novice exhausted, yet the old man was moving as spryly as ever. Elfbark? I wondered jealously. Denied to me but used by him?

He has some foul brew nearly every morning. I've no idea what is in it.

I quashed the thought before I could betray myself to the Prince. I did resolve to purloin a pinch of Chade's tea herbs if I could and determine what he was using. The old man was too careless with his health. He would burn his life away while trying to spend it in our cause.

I had no such opportunity. The remaining days of our brief voyage passed uneventfully. I was kept occupied with Thick's care and Swift's education. These two actually merged, for when Thick awoke from a long sleep, he was weak and fretful, yet would not tolerate me looking after him. He was willing to accept Swift's attentions, however. The boy was understandably reluctant. Caring for a sick man is tedious and can be unpleasant. Swift also felt the ingrained abhorrence that many Six Duchies folk feel toward the malformed. My disapproval did not shake this from him, but Web's calm acceptance of Thick's differences gradually swayed the boy. Web's ability to teach Swift by example made me feel a clumsy and thoughtless guardian. I wanted so badly to do well by Swift, as well as Burrich had done by Nettle, and yet I repeatedly failed even to win his trust.

Days can be long when one feels useless. I had little time with Chade or the Prince. There was no casual way to be alone with either of them on the crowded ship, so communication was limited to the use of the Skill. I tried to reach to Chade as little as possible, hoping that a time of rest would rebuild his ability. The Prince relayed to me that Chade knew nothing of a Black Man on Aslevjal Island. Peottre kept the sailor who had sung of him extremely busy, so he was not available as a source for me. Isolated from Chade and the Prince and rejected by Thick, I felt lonely and incapable of discovering peace anywhere. My heart yearned out to old memories, to my simple romance with Molly and the effortless friendship I had once shared with the Fool. Nighteyes came often to my mind, for Web and his bird were very much in evidence and Civil's cat trailed him everywhere on the ship. I had lost the passionate attachments I had formed in my youth, and lost too the heart to seek others. As for Nettle, and Burrich's invitation for me to "come home" . . . my heart ached with longing to do just that, but I knew it was a time that I longed to return to, not a place, and neither Eda nor El offers that to a man. When we sailed into a tiny harbor, no more than a bite out of a small island's coast, and Peottre shouted with pleasure to see his home, envy flooded me.

Web stepped up to the ship's railing beside me, disturbing my fine wallow in melancholy. "I left Swift helping Thick get his shoes on. He'll be glad to be ashore again, though he doesn't admit it. He's not even really seasick anymore. It's his lung ailment that weakens him now. That, and homesickness."

"I know. And little I can do about either on this ship. Once we're ashore, I hope to find him a comfortable place and offer him quiet, rest, and good food. They're usually the best hope one has for such illness."

Web nodded in companionable silence as we drew closer to the shore. A single figure, a girl in blowing russet skirts, stood on a headland watching us approach. Sheep and goats grazed the rocky pasturage around her and on the rolling hillsides behind her. Inland, we glimpsed threads of rising smoke from cottages that snuggled tight amongst the furze. A single dock on stone pilings reached out into the tiny bay to greet us. I saw no sign of a town. As I watched, the girl on the headland lifted her arms over her head and waved them three times. I thought she was greeting us, but perhaps she signaled folk at the settlement, for a short time later people came down the path to the shore. Some stood on the dock, awaiting us. Others, youngsters, ran along the beach, shouting excitedly to one another.

Our crew sailed the ship right up to the dock in a brash display of seamanship. The tossed lines were caught and made fast, checking our motion. In a matter of moments, it seemed, our canvas was taken down and stowed. On the deck, Peottre surprised me by offering gruff thanks to the Boar crew who had sailed the ship. It made me aware yet again that we were dealing with an alliance of two clans, not one. Obviously, both Peottre and the crewmen regarded this as a great favor and possible debt between the clans.

That was made even clearer to me in the manner in which we disembarked. Peottre went first, and as he stepped onto the dock, he made a grave obeisance to the women gathered to greet him. There were men there as well, but they stood behind the women, and it was only after Peottre had been warmly received by the older women of his clan that he walked past them to the men to exchange greetings. Few of them, I noted, were of warrior age, and those who were bore the disabling scars of that trade. There were a few oldsters, and a milling group of boys in their early teens. I frowned to myself, and then tried to pass my thought to Chade. *Either their men don't see fit to greet us, or they are concealed from us somewhere.*

His returned thought was thin as a thread of smoke. *Or they were decimated in the Red Ship War. Some clans took heavy losses.*

I could sense that he strained to reach me and let the contact lapse. He had other things on his mind just now. It was more my Wit than my Skill that picked up the Prince's restlessness and disappointment. The reason for that was plain. Elliania was not among those who had come to meet us. *Don't let it bother you,* I counseled him. *We don't know enough of their customs in this regard to know what her absence means. Don't assume it is a slight.*

Bother me? I'd hardly noticed. This is about the alliance, Fitz, not about some girl and her ploys. The sharpness of his retort betrayed his lie. I sighed to myself. Fifteen. All I could do was thank Eda that I'd never have to be that age again.

Peottre must have advised Chade of their custom in this regard, for he and all our party remained standing on the deck until a young woman in her early twenties lifted her clear voice and invited the Son of the Buck Clan of the Farseer Holdings to descend from the ship with his folk.

"That's our signal," Web said quietly. "Swift will have Thick ready to leave. Shall we go?"

I nodded, and then asked, as if I had a right to, "What does Risk show you? Does she see armed men anywhere about?"

He smiled a tight smile. "If she had, don't you think I would have told you? My neck would be in as much danger as yours. No, all she sees is what we ourselves have noted. A quiet orderly settlement in the peace of the early day. And a very fruitful valley, just beyond those hills."

So we joined the others and trooped off the boat to stand a respectful distance behind our prince as he was welcomed to Elliania Blackwater's mothershouse and holdings. The words of the greeting were simple, and in their simplicity I heard ritual. By this act of greeting and granting permission to come ashore, the women asserted both their ownership over the land and their authority over any people who set foot in Wuislington. Despite this, I was still surprised when a similar ritual of welcoming was offered to the Boar Clan members who disembarked behind us. As they replied to the welcome, I heard what had eluded me before. In accepting the welcome, they also pledged on the honor of their mothershouse that each man would be responsible for the good conduct of all the others. The penalty for violating the hospitality was not specifically spoken. A moment later, the sense of such a ritual came to me. In a nation of sea raiders, there must be some safeguard that made their own homes inviolable to other raiders in their absence. I suspected some ancient alliance of the women of the various clans was at work here, and wondered what punishment a man's own mothershouse would mete out to him for transgressing the welcome of another clan's.

Greetings finished, the women of the Narwhal mothershouse led the Prince and his party away. His guard followed them, and then came Web, Swift, and I with Thick. The lad walked before us while Web and I supported Thick. Behind us came the Boar crew, talking of beer and women and making jests about the four of us. Above us, Risk wheeled in the clear blue sky. Beach gravel crunched under our feet on the well-tended road.

I had expected Wuislington to be larger and closer to the water. As the Boar sailors, impatient with our plodding progress, passed us, Web engaged one in conversation. The man was plainly eager to hasten on with his fellows, and just as obviously reluctant to be seen in the company of the half-wit and his keepers. So his response was brief but courteous, as Web always seemed to bring out courtesy in those he spoke to. He explained that the harbor was good but not excellent. There was little current to worry about, but when the prevailing winds blew they were strong and cold enough "to scour the flesh from a man's bones!" Wuislington was built in a sheltered dip of the land, just beyond the next rise, where the wind blew over it rather than through it.

So we found it to be. The town was cupped in a sheltering palm of land. We followed the road down into it, and the day seemed to grow stiller and warmer as we descended. The town below us was well planned. The wood-and-stone mothershouse was the largest structure, towering as stronghouse over the simpler cottages and huts of the town. An immense painted narwhal decorated the slated roof of the house. Behind the mothershouse was a cultivated green that reminded me of the Women's Gardens at Buckkeep Castle. The streets of the town were laid out in concentric rings around it, with most of the markets and tradesmen's homes at the section nearest to the sea road. All this we saw before our closeness to it hid it from us.

The Prince's party had long vanished from our sight, but Riddle came back to us, puffing slightly from trotting. "I'm to show you to your lodging," he explained.

"We won't be housed with the Prince, then?" I asked uneasily.

"They'll be housed as guests in the mothershouse, along with his minstrel and companions. There is special housing for warriors of visiting clans, outside the stronghouse. Men of other clans may be guests there during the day, but warriors are not permitted to spend the night within the stronghouse. The Prince's Guard will be housed away from him. We don't like it, but Lord Chade has told Captain Longwick to accept it. And a cottage has been arranged for Thick. The Prince orders that you take lodging with him." Riddle looked uncomfortable. In a quieter voice, as if offering apology, he added, "I'll make sure your sea chest is brought there. And his things, as well."

"Thanks."

I didn't have to ask. Thick's difference made him unacceptable as a guest in the mothershouse. Well, at least they had been wise enough not to put us in with the guards. Nonetheless, it was becoming taxing to me to share Thick's outcast status. Little as I liked the intrigues of the Farseer Court, when I was too far removed from Dutiful and Chade, I felt ill at ease. I knew we were in danger here, but the greatest danger is always the one we are ignorant of. I wanted to hear what Chade heard, to know moment by moment how our negotiation was unfolding. Yet Chade could not demand that we be housed closer to the Prince, and someone had to remain with Thick. I was the logical choice. It all made sense, which didn't decrease the frustration I felt.

They did not insult us. The one-room stone cottage was clean, even though it smelled of disuse. Obviously it had not been inhabited for some months, yet there was wood in the hod and pots for cooking. The water cask was brimming with cold fresh water. There was a table and chairs, and a bed with two blankets on it in the corner. Sunlight lay across the floor in a fall from the single window. I'd stayed in worse places.

Thick said little as we settled him onto the bed. He was wheezing from the walk and his cheeks were red, but it was not the flush of health but the mark of a sick man who had overexerted himself. I pulled the shoes from his feet and then tucked the blankets around him. I suspected that the nights would be chilly here even in summer, and wondered if the two coverings would be enough to keep him comfortable.

"Do you need any help here?" Web asked me. Swift stood impatiently by the door, looking toward the mothershouse, two streets away.

"Not from you, but I'll need Swift for a time." I had expected the look of dismay the boy gave me. It didn't dampen my resolve. I took coin from my purse. "Go to the market. I have no idea what you'll find there. Be very polite, but get us something to eat. Meat and vegetables for a soup. Fresh bread if they have it. Fruit. Cheese, fish. Whatever this will buy."

By his face, he was torn between nervousness and a boy's eagerness to explore a new place. I set the money on his palm and hoped the Outislanders would accept Six Duchies coins.

"Then," I added, and saw him wince. "Go back to the ship. Riddle will see to our chests, but I want you to get extra bedding from the bunks there. Enough to make up pallets for you and me, as well as extra blankets for Thick."

"But I'm to stay in the mothershouse, with the Prince and Web and all . . ." His voice dribbled away in disappointment as I shook my head.

"I'll need you here, Swift."

He glanced at Web as if seeking his support. The Witmaster's face remained calm and neutral. "Are you sure there is no way I can be of assistance?" he asked me again.

"Actually." And I was suddenly almost frozen by how difficult it was to ask. "If you wouldn't mind coming back later, I'd enjoy a few hours to myself. Unless the Prince needs you elsewhere."

"I will do that. Thank you for asking." His second comment was genuine, not an idle courtesy. I let a moment pass in silence as I handled his words. He praised me for finally being able to ask a favor of him. When I met his eyes, I realized how long that silence had been but his face was as calm and patient as ever. Again I had that feeling he was stalking me, not as a hunter stalks prey but as a trainer befriends a wary animal.

"Thank you," I managed.

"And perhaps I'll accompany Swift to the market, for I am as curious to see this town as he is. I promise we won't dawdle, however. Do you think a sweet pastry might tempt Thick to eat, if we chanced upon a bakery?"

"Yes." Thick's voice was wavering as he replied, but I took heart from this show of interest. "And cheese," he added hopefully.

"Pastries and cheese should probably be what you look for first," I amended. I turned to Thick with a smile but his eyes wandered away from me. I was still unforgiven. I knew I'd have to do it at least two more times, for our journey back to Zylig and then for the ship that would take us to Aslevjal. I could not make myself face the thought of the eventual journey home. It seemed hopelessly far away now.

Web and Swift left, the boy chattering happily and the man responding as eagerly. In truth, I was relieved to see them go together. A boy in a strange town might easily give unintentional offense or be in danger. Nonetheless, I felt abandoned as I watched them walk away.

I backed away from the gulf of self-pity that beckoned me by putting my mind on the folks I cared about. I tried not to wonder what had befallen Hap or the Fool since I had left Buckkeep Town. Hap was a sensible lad. I had to trust him. And the Fool had managed his own life, or lives, for many years with no help from me. Yet it still made me uncomfortable to know that somewhere back in the Six Duchies, he was probably furious at me. I caught myself tracing the silvery fingerprints his Skill-touch had left on my wrist. I had no sense of him, but nonetheless put both my hands behind my back. I wondered again what he had said to Burrich, or if he had seen him at all.

Useless thoughts, but there was little else to occupy me. Thick watched me as I drifted idly around the small cottage. I offered him a dipper of cold water from the cask, but he refused it. I drank, tasting the difference of this island in its water. It tasted mossy and sweet. Probably pond water, I thought. I decided to build a small fire on the hearth in case Web and Swift brought back uncooked meat.

Time passed very slowly. Riddle and another guardsman came with our trunks from the ship. I took brewing herbs from my trunk. I filled the heavy kettle and set it on the hearth to heat, more to be doing something than because I wanted a cup of tea. I mixed the herbs to be sweet and calming, chamomile and fennel and raspberry root. Thick watched me suspiciously when I poured the hot water, but I didn't offer him the first cup. Instead I put a chair by the window where I could look out over the sheep on the grassy hillside above the town. I drank my tea and tried to find the satisfaction I had once taken in peace and solitude.

When I offered Thick the second cup, he accepted it. Perhaps my drinking the first one had reassured him that I didn't intend to drug or poison him, I thought wearily. Web and Swift returned, their arms full of bundles and the lad's cheeks pink from the walk and fresh air. Thick slowly levered himself to an upright position to eye what they had brought. "Did you find a strawberry tart and yellow cheese?" he asked hopefully.

"Well, no, but look what we did find," Web invited him as he unloaded his trove onto the table. "Sticks of smoked red fish, both salty and sweet. Little rolls of bread, with seeds sprinkled on top. And here's a grass basket full of berries for you. I've never seen any like this. The women called them mouseberries, for the mice stuff their tunnels full of them to dry for the winter. They're a bit sour, but we did find some goat cheese to go with them. These funny orange roots they said to roast in the coals and then eat the insides with salt. And lastly, these, which aren't as hot as when we bought them but still smell good to me."

The last items were pasties about the size of a man's fist. Web carried them in a sack of twisted and woven grass lined with wide fronds of seaweed. As he set them out on the table, I smelled fish. The pasties were stuffed with chunks of white fish in rich and greasy gravy. It heartened me when Thick tottered out of his bed to come to the table for one. He ate one hurriedly, pausing only when his coughing fits forced him to, and a second one more slowly, with another cup of tea to wash it down. He coughed so heavily and for so long after his tea that I feared he was choking, but at last he took a deeper breath and looked round at us with watery eyes. "I'm so tired," he said in a trembling voice, and no sooner did Swift help him back to bed than he nodded off to sleep.

Swift had enlivened our meal with his discussion of the town with Web. I had kept quiet while we ate, listening to the boy's observations. He had a quick eye and an inquisitive mind. It seemed that most of the market folk had been friendly enough after they'd seen his coins. I suspected that Web's genial curiosity had once more worked for him. One woman had even told him that the morning's low tide would be a good time for gathering the sweet little clams from the beaches. Web mentioned this, and then wandered into a tale of clamming with his mother when he was a youngster, and from there to other tales of his childhood. Both Swift and I were fascinated by them.

We shared another mug of the tea I'd made, and just as the afternoon began to seem companionable and pleasant, Riddle arrived at the door. "Lord Chade sent me to say you're to go up to the mothershouse for a welcome," he announced from the door.

"You'd best go, then," I told Web and Swift reluctantly.

"You, too," Riddle informed me. "I'm to stay with the prince's half-wit."

I gave him a look. "Thick," I said quietly. "His name is Thick."

It was the first time I'd ever rebuked Riddle for anything. He just looked at me, and I could not tell if he was hurt or offended. "Thick," he amended. "I'm to stay with Thick. You know I didn't mean anything by that, Tom Badgerlock," he added almost petulantly.

"I know. But it hurts Thick's feelings."

"Oh." Riddle glanced suddenly at the sleeping man, as if startled to learn he had feelings. "Oh."

I took pity on him. "There's food on the table, and hot water for tea if you want."

He nodded, and I sensed that we'd made peace. I took a moment to smooth my hair back and put on a fresh shirt. Then I took a comb to Swift, much to his disgust, and was dismayed at the knots in the boy's hair. "You need to do this every morning. I'm sure your father taught you better than to go about looking like a half-shed mountain pony."

He gave me a sharp look. "That's the very words he uses!" he exclaimed, and I excused my own slip, saying, "It's a common saying in Buck, lad. Let's look at you, now. Well, you'll do. Washing a bit more often wouldn't hurt you either, but we've no time for it now. Let's go."

I felt a pang of sympathy for Riddle as we left him sitting alone at the table.

chapter X

THE NARCHESKA

*This is their custom regarding marriage: it is binding only
so long as the woman wishes to be bound by it. The
woman chooses the man, although the man may court a
woman he finds desirable, with gifts and deeds of war
done in her honor. If an Outislander woman accepts a
man's courtship, it does not mean she has bound herself
to him, only that she may welcome him into her bed.
Their dalliances may last a week, a year, or a lifetime. It
is entirely of the woman's choosing. All things that are
kept under a roof belong to the woman, as does all that
comes from the earth which her mothershouse claims.
Her children belong to her clan, and are commonly
disciplined and taught by her brothers and uncles rather
than by their father. While the man lives on her land or
in her mothershouse, his labor is hers to command. All
in all, it baffles this traveler why a man would willingly
submit to such a minor role, but Outislanders seem
likewise baffled by our arrangements, asking me
sometimes, "Why do your women willingly leave the
wealth of their own families to become servants in a
man's home?"*

      "AN ACCOUNT OF TRAVEL IN A BARBAROUS LAND,"
BY SCRIBE FEDWREN

The mothershouse of the Narwhal Clan was both fortification and home. It was by far the oldest structure in Wuislington. The stout wall that surrounded its grounds and garden were the first line of defense. If invaders pushed the defenders back, they could retreat to the mothershouse itself. Scorch marks on its stone walls and timbers showed that it had stood even against fire. There were no apertures at all in the lower story, the second boasted arrow slits, and only the third had real windows and these featured stout shutters that would have defied any missiles. Yet it was not a castle in our tradition. There was no place to bring sheep or for an entire village to take shelter, nor a place for great stores of food. I suspected it was intended to defy raiders who would come and go with a tide rather than to withstand a significant siege. It was one more way in which the Outislanders differed from our folk and our way of thinking.

Two young men wearing the Narwhal badge nodded us past the gate in the wall. Inside, the road had crushed shell added to the beach gravel that paved it, giving it a gleaming opalescence that sparkled underfoot. The door of the mothershouse, carved with narwhals, stood open wide enough to admit three men abreast. Within, all was dimness and torchlight. It was almost like entering a cave.

We paused inside the entrance to let our eyes adjust. The air was thick with the aromas of long human habitation. There were food smells, stews and smoked meat and spilled wine, and the odor of cured hides and gathered people. It could have been a stench, but it was not. Rather, it was a homey smell, of safety and family.

The entrance gave immediately onto a great room, with supporting pillars as the only dividers. There were three hearths, all with cook fires on them. The stone-flagged floor was strewn with fresh rushes. Benches and shelves ran around the walls. The lower benches were wide, and the rolled sleeping skins proclaimed that these were beds by night and seating and tables by day. The

higher, shallower shelves above the benches held foodstuffs and personal possessions. Most of the light in the
room came from the hearths, though there were ineffectual
candles in sconces on many of the pillars. In the far left
corner, a wide staircase wound up into the dimness. It was
·the only access I could see to the upper regions of the
house. It made sense. Even if an attacking force gained
control of this level of the mothershouse, the folk above
would have only one entrance to defend. Invaders would
pay dearly to gain the upper floors of the mothershouse.

All this I saw through the gathered people. Folk of
every age were clustered everywhere and there was a sense
of anticipation in the air. We were obviously late. At the
end of the long room, before the largest hearth, Prince Dutiful waited. Ranged on his side of the hearth were Chade
and his Wit coterie, and beyond them, his guard drawn up
in three rows. The Narwhal Clan folk parted to make way
for us to assume our correct positions. Web and Swift advanced to stand with Cockle the minstrel and Civil and his
Wit-cat. I took a place at the end of the front row of
guardsmen.

Elliania was not there. Those gathered on the other
side of the hearth were mostly women. Peottre was the only
adult man in his prime. There were a few old grandfathers,
four lads about the Narcheska's age, and then six or seven
boys ranging down to toddlers clinging to their mothers'
skirts. Had the Red Ship War so decimated the Narwhal
Clan?

The Boar warriors from the ship were present, but they
stood in a group off to one side, witnesses to rather than
participants in whatever was about to happen. The people
who crowded the rest of the room were almost entirely
Narwhal Clan, as evinced by their jewelry, clothing adorn-
ments, and tattoos. The exceptions seemed to be almost
entirely males standing alongside women, and were probably men who had married into the clan or were partners in

a less formal arrangement with a Narwhal woman. I saw bears, otters, and one eagle amongst them.

Without exception, the women were strikingly arrayed. Those who did not wear jewelry of gold or silver or precious stone were still bedecked with ornaments of shell, feather, and seeds. The artful arrangement of hair had not been neglected, and added substantially to the height of several women. Unlike Buckkeep, where the women seemed to shift their finery in mysteriously feminine coordination, I saw a wide variety of styles. The only unifying theme to the beaded or embroidered or woven patterns of their dress seemed to be the brightness of the colors and the narwhal motif.

Those in the first circle, I surmised, were relatives of the Narcheska, while those who stood closest to the hearth would be her most immediate family. They were almost all women. All of the Narwhal women shared an intent, almost fierce air. The tension in that part of the room was palpable. I wondered which one was her mother, and wondered too what we awaited.

Absolute silence fell. Then four Narwhal clansmen carried a wizened little woman down the stairs and into the hall. She rode in a chair fashioned from twisty pieces of gleaming willow wood and cushioned with bearskins. Her thin white hair was braided and pinned in a crown to her head. Her eyes were very black and bright. She wore a red robe and the narwhal motif was repeated in tiny ivory buttons sewn all over it. The men set her chair down, not on the floor, but upon a heavy table where she could remain seated and still look out over all those who had gathered in her house. With a small whimper of complaint, the old woman straightened herself in the chair, sitting tall and gazing at the folk who had gathered. Her pink tongue wet her wrinkled lips. Heavy fur slippers dangled on her skinny feet.

"Well! Here we all are!" she proclaimed.

She spoke the words in Outislander, loudly, as old folks

who are going deaf are prone to do. She did not seem as mindful of the formality of the situation, nor as tense as the other women.

The Great Mother of the Narwhal Clan leaned forward, her gnarled hands gripping the twisted wood of the chair arms. "So. Send him out, then. Who seeks to court our Elliania, our Narcheska of the Narwhals? Where is the warrior bold enough to seek the mothers' permission to bed with our daughter?"

I am sure those were not the words Dutiful had been told to expect. His face was the color of beetroot as he stepped forward. He made a warrior's obeisance before the old woman and spoke in clear Outislander as he proclaimed, "I stand before the mothers of the Narwhal Clan, and seek permission to join my line with yours."

She stared at him for a moment and then scowled, not at him, but at one of the young men who had borne her chair. "What is a Six Duchies slave doing here? Is he a gift? And why is he trying to speak our language and doing such a horrible job of it? Cut his tongue out if he attempts it again!"

There was a sudden silence, broken by a wild whoop of laughter from someone in the back of the room, quickly muffled. Somehow Dutiful kept his aplomb, and was wise enough not to attempt to explain himself to the incensed Great Mother. A woman from the Narcheska's contingent stepped to the Mother's side and stood on tiptoe, whispering frantically to her. The Mother waved her off irritably.

"Stop all that hissing and spitting, Almata! You know I can't hear a word when you talk like that! Where is Peottre?" She glanced around as if she'd misplaced a shoe, then lifted her eyes and scowled at Peottre. "There he is! You know that I hear him best. What is he doing way over there? Get here, you insolent rascal, and explain to me what this is about!"

There would have been a sweet humor to watching the old woman order the seasoned warrior about if his face had not betrayed such worry. He strode over to her, went down briefly on one knee, and then stood up. She lifted one rootlike hand and settled it on his shoulder. "What is this about?" she demanded.

"Oerttre," he said quietly. I suspect his deep voice reached her old ears better than the woman's shrill whisper had. "It's about Oerttre. Remember?"

"Oerttre," she said, and her eyes brimmed suddenly with tears. She looked around the room. "And Kossi? Little Kossi, too? Is she here, then? Come home to us at last?"

"No," Peottre said shortly. "They're not here, neither one of them. And that is what this is about. Remember? We talked about it in the garden, this morning. Remember?" He nodded at her slowly, encouraging her.

She watched his face and nodded slowly with him, and then stopped. She shook her head once. "No," she cried out in a low voice. "I don't remember. The alyssum has stopped blooming, and the plums may be sour this year. I remember we spoke of that. But... no. Peottre, was it important?"

"It was, Great Mother. It is. Very important."

She looked troubled and then suddenly angry. "Important, important! Important, says a man, but what do men know?" Her old voice, cracked and shrill, rose in anger and derision. Her thin hand slapped her thigh in disgust. "Bedding and blood-shedding, that is all they know, that is all they think is important. What do they know of the sheep to shear and the gardens to be harvested, what do they know of how many barrels of salt fish for the winter and how many casks of sweet lard? Important? Well, if it's important, let Oerttre handle it. She is the Mother now, and I should be allowed to rest." She lifted her hand from Peottre's shoulder and gripped the arms of her chair. "I need my time to rest!" she complained piteously.

"Yes, Great Mother. Yes, you do. And you should take it now and I will see that all is handled as it should be. I promise." And with these words, Elliania emerged from the shadows at the top of the stairs and hurried down to us. Her lightly shod feet seemed to skim each riser. Half of her hair was pinned up with tiny star pins; the rest flew loose to her shoulders. It did not look intentional. Behind her on the stairs, two young women started to follow her, then halted in horror, whispering to one another. I suspected they had been readying her for her appearance, and she had bolted free of them when she heard the raised voices.

I recognized her bearing more than her form as people parted to let her through. Like Dutiful, she had grown taller in the months since I had last seen her, and all her childish plumpness had melted away, replaced by woman's flesh. As she came past the row of her female relatives, I was not the only Six Duchies man who gasped. Her gown covered her shoulders and back but left bare her proudly uptilting breasts. Had she rouged her nipples, to make them stand so pink? I wondered, and felt my flesh stir in response. An instant later, I had flung up my walls and, *Guard your thoughts*, I chided Dutiful. He must have heard me, yet he did not flinch. He stared at the Narcheska's bared breasts as if he had never seen a woman's breasts, and in all likelihood, that was possible.

She did not spare a glance for him and his gawking but went straight to the Great Mother. "I will deal with this, Peottre," she said in her new woman's voice. Then she spoke to the men who had carried the Great Mother's chair. "You have heard our Great Mother. She requires her time of rest. Let us all thank her for gracing our gathering this evening, and wish her calm sleep and easy bones."

There was a murmur of response, echoing the Narcheska's good-night to the Great Mother, and then the young men took up the old woman's chair and carried her off. The Narcheska stood straight and silent, turning to watch after her until she disappeared into the shadows at the top of the stair. She took a deep breath. The Prince was now staring at her back, at the knob at the top of her spine bared by her upswept hair and her graceful neck above it.

The seamstresses had cut it well, I thought to myself. Not even the edge of her tattoos peeped over it. I saw Chade give Dutiful a tiny jab in the ribs. The young man started as if waking from a dream and discovered a sudden interest in Peottre's feet. Peottre was staring at him flatly, as if he were an ill-mannered dog that might steal meat from the table if he were not watched.

I saw the Narcheska square her shoulders. She turned back to face us all. Her eyes roved over the assembly. The ornament in her hair was made from narwhal's horn. I have no idea how they had wrought that iridescent blue upon it. The tiny star pins sparkled around it, and I no longer had any doubt that the carving that Prince Dutiful had found upon the Treasure Beach had presaged this moment. I was no closer to knowing what that meant, and had no time to think upon it.

Somehow the Narcheska had found a smile. It was a bit wry at the corners as she gave a small laugh and a shrug. "I've forgotten what I'm supposed to say now. Will someone speak the Mother's words for me?" Then, before anyone could reply to her request, she let her gaze come to meet Dutiful's. He had blushed before; now he burned as he met her eyes. She ignored his fluster and spoke calmly. "You see, we combine two of our traditions tonight. By chance, it is my time to show myself as a blooded woman before my clan. And on this very day you are come here, to offer yourself as mate to me."

His lips moved. I think they muttered the words "blooded woman" but no sound came forth.

She laughed, but the lightness had gone out of it. It was brittle as ice shards breaking. "Have you no ceremony among your folk for this? A boy bloodies his sword to become a man, no? In his ability to kill, he announces that he is now complete. But a woman has no need of a sword. Eda herself bloodies us, and announces us as complete. What a man can take with a sword, a woman can give by her flesh alone. Life." She set both her ringless hands on her flat belly. "I have shed my first woman's blood. I can bring forth life from within me. I stand before you all, a woman now."

There was a muttered response of "Welcome, Elliania, Narwhal Clan woman." I sensed that she had stepped back into the ritual and taken up the words, too. Peottre had retreated into the row of her clansmen. Women came to stand around her, and there was a formalized greeting that passed between every woman of the Narwhal Clan and Elliania. A group of wide-eyed girls, hair loose upon their shoulders, stood in a cluster, watching her. One, taller than the others and close to being a woman herself, pointed at Dutiful and said something approving to two of her fellows. They giggled and drew closer to her, whispering and nudging one another. I sensed that these girls had been Elliania's playmates and companions, but that Elliania had stepped apart from them now and into the ranks of the women. The effortless way in which she had assumed command of the situation told me that she had, in many ways, been a woman amongst them for a long time. This ceremony was the formal recognition that her body was starting to catch up with her spirit.

When every woman had greeted her, Elliania stepped back out of the circle of firelight from the hearth. A stillness came over the crowd, replacing the murmur of comment and welcome. For a brief time, I felt their awkwardness. Peottre shifted on his feet, then forced himself to stand still. Dutiful remained where he had been, and I sensed that these minutes were passing like hours for him.

Finally, the same young woman who had whispered to the Great Mother stepped forward. A faint blush suffused her cheeks. Obviously, she felt she was stepping above her station, but no one else had offered to take charge. She cleared her throat, but there was still a tremor in her voice as she said, "I am Almata, a daughter of the Mothers of the Narwhal Clan. I am cousin to the Narcheska Elliania, and six years her senior. Unworthy as I am, I will speak for the Great Mother."

She paused a moment, as if to allow time for someone to challenge her in this role. There were older women present, but none of them spoke. A few gave tiny, encouraging nods. Most looked heartsick. Almata took a deep breath, visibly steadied herself, and spoke again.

"We are gathered in our mothershouse because one not of our clan has come among us, seeking to join his lines to ours. He asks, not just for any woman, but for our Narcheska Elliania, she whose daughters will in turn be Narcheska and Mother and Great Mother to us all. Stand forth, warrior. Who seeks to court our Elliania, our Narcheska of the Narwhals? Where is the warrior bold enough to seek the mothers' permission to bed with our daughter, and give her daughters to raise up as Mothers of the Narwhal Clan?"

Dutiful took a shuddering breath. He should not have; he should have been steadier than that, and yet I could not blame him. All could sense that something was awry here tonight, and it was something more than foreigners intruding on an Outislander ceremony. I had a sense of people stretching to close a gap, of trying to mend a tragedy by retreating to tradition. Yet there was no space left for us to be cautious. Dutiful's voice was steady as he proclaimed, "I come. I would have the Narcheska Elliania of the Narwhal Clan as the mother of my children."

"And how will you provide for her and the children that you will give her? What will you contribute to the Narwhal Clan, that we should let your bloodlines mingle with ours?"

And suddenly we were on solid ground. Chade had prepared well for this. Riddle nudged me, and I stepped aside almost in rhythm with the other guards. Behind them was a canvas-draped heap. Longwick dragged the cover from it, and each guardsman in turn took up an item and brought it forward as Chade announced what it was. Dutiful stood silent and proud as his gifts were presented to both Almata and the Narcheska, as well he might be. Nothing had been spared.

Some of the trove had come with us, hastily transferred from the *Maiden's Chance* to the *Tusker*. Casks of brandy from Shoaks, a bale of ermine skins from the Mountain Kingdom, and colored glass beads from Tilth, wrought into a tapestry that could be hung over a window. Silver earrings, Kettricken's own handiwork. Cotton, linen, and fine woolen cloth from Bearns were among the offerings. Other gifts were merely mentioned as promises, cargo to be brought from Zylig on the next trip. The reading of that list took some time. The labor of three skilled smiths for three years. A bull and twelve cows of our finest bloodlines. Six brace of oxen, and a team of matched horses. Hunting hounds and two merlins, trained to be lady's birds. And some things that Chade offered on Prince Dutiful's behalf were only dreams yet, trade and peace between the Six Duchies and the Out Islands, gifts of wheat when their fishing harvest was poor, good iron, and the freedom to trade in all the Six Duchies ports. It was a long list and I felt the day's weariness catch up with me as Chade catalogued it for them.

But all weariness left me when Chade concluded and Almata spoke again. "This is the offer made to our clan. Mothers, daughters, and sisters, what say you? Do any speak against him?"

Silence followed her words. It evidently expressed approval, for Almata nodded gravely. Then she turned to Elliania. "Cousin, Woman of the Narwhal Clan, Elliania the Narcheska, what is your will? Do you desire this man? Will you take him as yours?"

The muscles stood out in Peottre's neck as the slender young woman stepped forward. Dutiful held out a hand, palm up. She stood beside him, shoulder to shoulder, and placed her hand flat upon his. When she turned to look at him, and as their eyes met, my lad blushed again. "I will take him," she replied gravely. A part of me noted that she did not reply as to whether she desired him or not. She took a deeper breath and said, more loudly, "I will take him, and he will bed me, and we will give daughters to the mothershouse. If he performs the task that I have already named to him. If he can bring here, to this hearth, the head of the dragon Icefyre, then he may call me wife."

Peottre's eyes flickered shut and then open again. He forced himself to watch as his sister-daughter sold herself. His shoulders moved once in what might have been a sob denied. Almata held a hand out and someone placed a long strip of leather in it. She stepped forward and continued speaking as she bound Dutiful's and Elliania's wrists together.

"This binds you as your words have bound you. While she accepts you, bed with no other, Dutiful, or that woman's life is forfeit to Elliania's knife. While he pleases you, Elliania, bed with no other, or that man must face the challenge of Dutiful's sword. Now, mingle your blood upon the hearthstones of our mothershouse, in offering to Eda for the children she may send you."

I had no desire to watch, but I did. First the knife was offered to Dutiful. He betrayed no pain as he sliced his forearm until it bled freely. He cupped his bound hand and waited for blood to trickle past the leather strip and into his palm. Elliania did likewise, her face grave and somehow impassive, as if she had transgressed into an area so far beyond disgrace that nothing could move her now. When each hand cupped a small amount of blood, Almata guided their hands into a clasp. Then they knelt and each left a palm print of the mingled blood on the hearthstone. When they turned to face the gathered folk again, Almata freed their hands of the leather cord, and offered it to Dutiful, who accepted it gravely. Almata moved to stand behind them, a hand on each of their shoulders. She tried to put a note of joy into her voice, but it sounded flat to me as she announced, "They stand before you, joined and bound by their words. Wish them well, my people." The murmur of approval that rose from the gathered folk was more as if they applauded a deed of great courage than if they had just witnessed the happy joining of a loving couple. Elliania bowed her head before it, Sacrifice for them in some way I did not yet comprehend.

I'm married? Wonder, dismay, and outrage mingled in Dutiful's flung Skill-thought.

Not until you give her a dragon's head, I warned him.

Not until we hold the real ceremony in Buckkeep Castle, Chade comforted him.

The Prince looked dazed.

All around us, the hall erupted into activity. Boards were brought out, and then food to grace them. Outislander minstrels struck up a song upon their windy instruments. True to their tradition, the minstrels so twisted the words to fit the tune that I could scarce understand it. I noticed that two of them came to greet Cockle and invite him to their corner of the hall. Their welcome seemed genuine, and again I was struck by the universal understanding that seems to exist amongst musicians.

Dutiful Skill-shared with me the words Elliania said quietly to him. "Now you must hold my hand and walk with me as I present you to my older cousins. Remember, they are my elders. Although I am the Narcheska, I still owe them the deference due my elders. So do you." She spoke as if instructing a child.

"I'll try not to humiliate you," he replied, rather stiffly. His words did not please me and yet I could not completely blame him for saying them.

"Then smile. And keep quiet, as befits a warrior in a mothershouse that is not his own," she retorted. She took his hand and let it be obvious that she led him. Rather as one might lead a prize bull by the ring in his nose, I thought to myself. The women did not come to meet him. Instead, Elliania took him from group to group. At each, he made the warrior's obeisance accepted in the Out Islands, that is, he offered his sword hand, empty and now bloodied, wrist up, to them while bowing his head. They smiled upon him, and offered comments to the Narcheska upon

her choice. I sensed that in another time and place, the
words would have been lighthearted and teasing. But at
this ceremony and with this man, the compliments offered
to her were moderate and well mannered. Instead of reliev-
ing the tension of the formal pledging, they prolonged it.

Seeing the other groups of warriors dispersing
throughout the feast, Chade dismissed us from our ranks.
Ears and eyes open, he cautioned me as I wended my way
through the throng.

Always, I replied to him. He did not need to suggest
that I keep the Prince in sight. Until I knew what was behind this façade, I had no idea who might or might not
wish him harm. And so I drifted about the wedding feast,
never too far from my prince and keeping a light Skill-
contact with him.

The gathering was very different from any Buckkeep
celebration. There was no seating of the guests according
to rank or favor. Instead, the food was set out and people
helped themselves to it and wandered the room as they ate
it. There was roast mutton on spits kept warm near the
hearth, and trays heaped with fowl cooked whole. I sampled from a platter of smoked candlefish, seasoned and
crisp and remarkably tasty. Outislander breads seemed to
be dark and unleavened, cooked in huge flat rounds. Diners
tore off a piece of an appropriate size and then heaped it
with sliced and pickled vegetables, or dipped it in fish oil
and salt. All the flavors of the foods seemed overly strong
to me, and much of it was pickled or smoked or salted.
Only the mutton and the chicken were freshly killed, and
even those had been seasoned with some sort of seaweed.

The eating and drinking, the talking and the music and
some sort of juggling contest, with betting, all happened simultaneously. The roar of raised voices was near deafening.
After a time, I became aware of something else. Young
Outislander women of the Narwhal Clan were approaching
not just our guardsmen but even Civil and Cockle. I saw

several guards grinning fatuously as their young partners led them outside or up the shadowy staircase.

Are they deliberately luring Dutiful's guard away? I Skilled anxiously to Chade.

Here, it is a woman's prerogative, he replied. *They do not have the same customs regarding chastity. The guardsmen were warned to be cautious but not cool. The Prince's warriors and companions are expected to be available for the evening but only if they are invited; it would be a breach of hospitality if they approached a woman who had not first signaled her interest. If you have not noticed, there is a lack of men here, and far fewer children than there should be for this many women. An empty womb filled on a wedding night foretells a lucky child, here.*

Was there a reason I was not told of this before now?

Does it bother you?

After a moment of surreptitious peering, I located my old mentor. He was sitting on one of the bed benches, nibbling on a fowl's leg and conversing with a woman half his age. I caught a glimpse of Civil and his cat disappearing into the upper reaches of the house. The woman who led him was at least five years older than he was, but he did not look intimidated. I had no time to wonder or worry where Swift had vanished to; surely he was too young to be of any interest to these viragos. In that moment I realized that Dutiful was leaving the mothershouse in the company of a gaggle of the Narcheska's girlish friends. Elliania did not look particularly pleased, even though she still held his hand and led him out of the door.

It was not easy to follow him. A woman with a tray of sweets stepped between me and the door. I managed to feign a thick-witted indifference to her offering of more than the sticky confections as I helped myself to a handful in a boorish display of greed and ate them in two mouthfuls. Somehow this flattered her, and she set the tray aside and followed me as I ate them. She was still at my elbow when I reached the door. "Where's the backhouse?" I asked her, and when she did not understand the Six Duchies euphemism,

I mimed what I sought. With a puzzled look, she pointed out a low building to me and returned to the feasting. As I walked toward it, I cast a wide glance for Dutiful. There were several couples in the courtyard, in various stages of dalliance, and two boys carrying water from the well back into the mothershouse. Where had he gone?

I saw him at last, not far away, sitting beside Elliania on a grassy rise near some young apple trees. The other girls had settled around them in a ring. These were girls not yet women, as their loose hair proclaimed. I guessed that their ages ranged from ten to fifteen or so. *Doubtless, before this night, they were Elliania's playmates for years. Now she has left their companionship behind her with her change to woman's status.*

Not quite, Dutiful informed me sourly. *They have evaluated me as if I were a horse bought cheap at the fair. "If he is a warrior, where are his scars?" "Did he not have a clan? Why does his face not bear her tattoo?" They tease her, and one of them is quite a nasty little vixen. Lestra is her name, and she is Elliania's older cousin. She is mocking Elliania, saying that perhaps she is a woman and even wed in name, but that she doubts that she has ever been kissed. Lestra claims to have been kissed several times, quite thoroughly, even though she has not bled yet. Fitz, have the girls no shame or reticence in this land?*

I grasped it on an intuitive level. *Dutiful, it is a driving-out. Elliania is no longer one of them, and so they will peck and tease her tonight. Doubtless it would have happened in any case; it may even be seen as a part of her womanhood ceremony.* And then, needlessly, I added, *Be careful. Follow her lead, lest you shame her somehow.*

I have no idea what she wants of me, he replied helplessly. *She glares at me out of the corner of her eye, and yet holds to my hand as if it were a line thrown to her in wild water.*

As clearly as if I sat beside him, the words reached me through our Skill-link. The girl who flung the challenge was taller than Elliania, and perchance older. I knew enough of women to know that age alone did not determine their blood time. Indeed, save for her loose hair, I would have guessed her a woman already. Lestra spoke saucily, taunting Elliania with, "So. You'll bind him to you, so no one else can have him, but you dare not even kiss him!"

"Perhaps I do not wish to kiss him yet. Perhaps I intend to wait until he has proven himself worthy of me."

Lestra shook her head. She had little bells wired into her hair and I heard the jingle of her mane as she said mockingly, "No, Elliania, we know you well. As a girl you were always the most meek and least daring of us. I daresay you are the same as a woman. You don't dare kiss him, and he is too timid a man to take one for himself. He is a smooth-cheeked boy, masquerading as a man. Isn't that true, 'Prince'? You are as timid as she is. Perhaps I could teach you to be bolder. He does not even look at her breasts! Or perhaps they are so small, he cannot see them."

I did not envy Dutiful. I had no advice to offer him. I sat myself down on the low stone wall that marked the edge of the young orchard. I lifted my hands to my face and rubbed my cheeks, as a man does when he has had too much to drink and seeks to drive the tingle from his face. I hoped folk would think me drunk and leave me sitting. I did not relish watching Dutiful go through his dilemma, but I dared not leave him. I sagged my shoulders and set my head as if staring into the distance while watching out of the corner of my eye.

Dutiful made an effort, speaking stiffly. "Perhaps I respect Narcheska Elliania too much to take what she has not offered." I could feel his steely determination not to look at her breasts as he said this. His awareness of them, bared and warm so near him, was taking its toll.

He could not see the look Elliania cast to one side. That answer had not pleased her.

"But you don't respect me, do you?" the little minx taunted him.

"No," he replied shortly. "I do not think that I do."

"Then there is no problem. Show your boldness and

kiss me!" Lestra commanded him triumphantly. "And I will tell her if she is missing anything worth having." As if to force him to the act, she leaned forward suddenly, thrusting her face at him, even as one sly hand flew toward his groin. "What's this?" she crowed mischievously as Dutiful shot to his feet with an exclamation of outrage. "There's more than a kiss he has waiting for you, Elliania. Look at it! An army of one has pitched a tent for you there! Will the siege last long?"

"Stop it, Lestra!" Elliania snarled. She too had come to her feet. Her cheeks blazed with color and she did not look at Dutiful but scowled at her enemy. Her bared breasts rose and fell with her angry breath.

"Why? You've obviously no intent of doing anything interesting with him. Why shouldn't I take him? By rights, he should be mine, just as by rights I should be Narcheska. And will be, when he takes you off to be a lesser woman in his own mothershouse."

Several of the girls gasped, but Elliania's eyes only blazed hotter.

"That is among the oldest of the lies you tell, Lestra! Your great-grandmother was the younger twin. Both midwives said so."

"First out of the womb is not always oldest, Elliania. So many say. Your great-grandmother was a mewling, sickly kitten of a babe. Mine was the hearty, healthy child. Your great-grandmother had no right to be Narcheska, nor did her daughter, or her granddaughter, or you!"

"Sickly? Indeed! Then how is it that she lives still, as Great Mother! Take back your lie, Lestra, or I will cram it down your throat." Elliania spoke in a flat, ugly voice. It carried well. I was not the only one who had turned to watch the quarrel. When Dutiful stepped forward, mouth open to speak, Elliania put her hand flat in the center of his chest and thrust him back. The young girls formed into a ring now around the potential combatants and he found himself outside it. He looked toward me as if for help.

Don't intervene, I think. Elliania has made it plain that she doesn't want you to.

I hoped my advice was good. Even as I attempted to Skill the situation to Chade, I saw Peottre. He had probably been lurking just out of my line of sight at the building's corner. He strolled over to the low wall where I sat and leaned one hip on it casually. "He should stay out of that," he said to me casually.

I swung my head and regarded him blearily. "Who?"

He stared at me levelly. "Your prince. He should leave this to Elliania to settle. It's woman's business, and she won't welcome his interference. You should convey that to him, if you can."

Peottre says, Step back from it. Let Elliania settle it.

What? Dutiful demanded in consternation.

Why is Peottre speaking to you? Chade demanded.

I don't know!

To Peottre, I said, "I'm just his guardsman, sir. I don't advise the Prince."

"You're his bodyguard," Peottre replied pleasantly. "Or his . . . what would it be in your language? His chaperon? As I am for Elliania. You're good, but you're not invisible. I've seen you watching him."

"I'm his guardsman. I'm supposed to guard him," I protested, letting the words slur a little. I wished I'd thought to have a glass of wine. The smell of spirits can be very convincing.

He was no longer looking at me. I turned to stare up the hill. There was a shout behind me from the door of the mothershouse, and I heard other people emerging. The two girls had gone into a clinch. With apparent ease, Lestra threw Elliania onto the ground on her back. Even at that distance, I heard her breath whoosh out of her. Peottre made a frustrated sound and he twitched in that small way that experienced fighters do when they are watching a prized student compete. As Lestra flung herself on top of Elliania, the smaller girl suddenly drew her knees up to her chest and firmly kicked her opponent in her midsection. Lestra shot backward, landing badly. Elliania rolled to her knees and, careless of her fine gown and coiffed hair, flung herself on top of Lestra. Every muscle in Peottre's neck and arms was taut, but he did not move. I came to my feet to gain a better vantage and gawked, just as the other Buckkeep guardsmen were doing. The Outislanders who had emerged to watch the struggle were interested, but not intent. Evidently, for girls or women to wrestle in this manner was not shocking to them.

By sitting high on Lestra's chest, her knees on her arms, Elliania had effectively pinned the larger girl to the earth. Lestra was kicking and struggling, but the Narcheska had gripped a handful of her loose hair to fix her head to the ground. With her free hand, she rubbed a handful of dirt into Lestra's mouth. "Let honest earth cleanse the lie from your lips!" she shouted triumphantly. Dutiful stood back from them, his mouth ajar. He was aware of the wild jiggle of Elliania's bared breasts as her chest heaved with exertion. I sensed he was as horrified at his physical reaction to that as he was by the girls' struggle. All around them, the other girls leaped and yelled, encouraging the combatants.

With a wild shriek, Lestra tore her head free of Elliania's grasp, leaving her clutching a goodly handful of hair. Elliania slapped her, hard, and then seized her by the throat. "Call me Narcheska, or you will not draw another breath!" she shouted at her.

"Narcheska! Narcheska!" the older girl shrieked, and then she began to sob wildly, more from frustration and humiliation than pain.

Elliania put her hand flat to Lestra's face and pushed up off it as she stood. "Leave her alone!" she warned two of the girls who stepped forward to aid the loser. "Let her lie there and be glad that I didn't have my knife. I am a woman now. From now on, my knife will answer anyone who dares to dispute that I am Narcheska. From now on, my knife will answer anyone who dares to touch the man I have claimed for myself."

I glanced at Peottre. His grin was hard, showing every tooth he had. Elliania reached Dutiful in two strides. He stood gawking down at his disheveled bride. As casually as I would seize a horse's mane to mount him, she reached up and gripped his warrior's tail. As she pulled his face down to hers, she commanded him, "You will kiss me now."

An instant before their mouths met, he snatched his Skill-awareness away from me. Yet neither I nor any man watching needed the Skill to sense the fervor in that kiss. She locked her mouth to his, and as his arms came awkwardly around her to draw her closer, she leaned into his embrace, deliberately brushing her bared breasts against his chest. Then she broke the kiss, and while Dutiful drew an uneven breath, she met his eyes and reminded him, "Icefyre's head. On my mothers' hearth. Before you may call me wife." Then, from within the circle of his embrace, she looked at her old playmates and announced, "You girls may stay here and play if you wish. I'm taking my husband back inside to the feasting."

She stepped clear of his arms, and took his hand again. He followed her docilely, grinning vapidly. Lestra was sitting up, alone, staring after them with fury and shame. There were approving whoops from several women and some envious groans from the watching men as she triumphantly led her prize past them. I glanced at Peottre. He looked stunned. Then his eyes came to mine. "She had to do that," he told me sternly. "To make her point with the other girls. That's why she did it. To establish herself in their eyes as a woman, and to make clear her claim to him."

"I could see that," I agreed mildly. But I did not believe him. I suspected that something had just happened that was outside his plan for Elliania and Dutiful. It made it all the more essential for me to discover just what his true intent was.

The rest of the evening seemed bland. Eating, drinking,

and listening to Outislander bards could not compare to the claiming of power that I had just witnessed. I found a meat pie and a mug of ale and took it to a quiet corner. I pretended to be absorbed in it as I Skilled to Chade all that I had witnessed.

This is moving more swiftly than I had dared hope, he Skilled in return. *And yet I mistrust it. Does she truly want him as husband, or was it only to establish that what she claimed, no one can take from her? Does she hope lust will spur him to kill the dragon for her?*

I felt foolish as I told him, *This is the first time I have realized that if she becomes his bride and moves to his house, some will say she has forfeited her place here. Lestra spoke of her becoming a "lesser woman in his mothershouse." What did it mean?*

Chade's reply came reluctantly. *I think the idiom is the same used for a woman captured in a raid, but taken as a wife rather than a slave. Her children have no clan. It is like being a bastard, somewhat.*

Then why would she agree to this? Why would Peottre allow it? And if she is not the Narcheska when she comes to Buckkeep and remains there, do we gain any advantage by this wedding? Chade, this does not make sense to me.

There is still too much that is not clear here, Fitz. I sense an unseen current in all this. Stay alert.

And so I did, through the long evening and longer night. The sun lingered as it does in that northern clime, so that night was just a long twilight. When the time came for the bridal couple to retire, it was Dutiful who announced that he would remain below in the common room "lest any say that I have taken what I have not earned." It added another awkward moment to the day, and I saw a puff-lipped Lestra gloating about it with her cohorts. The couple parted at the foot of the staircase, Elliania ascending and Dutiful going off to take a seat beside Chade. This night, he would sleep within the mothershouse, as befitted a man properly wedded to a woman of the clan, but down here on the bed boards, not above with Elliania. His guards were dismissed for the night, to return to the warriors' housing or warmer welcomes, so long as their partners bedded them outside the mothershouse walls. I longed to move closer to Chade and Dutiful and have some quiet talk with them, but I knew it would look odd. Instead, I decided that it was time for me to return to my own lodgings.

I had not gone far when I heard footsteps crunching on the pathway behind me. Glancing back, I saw Web. Beside him slogged a weary Swift. The tops of his cheeks were very pink and I suspected the boy had overindulged in wine. Web nodded to me, and I slackened my pace to allow them to catch up with me. "Quite an occasion," I remarked idly to Web when he walked beside me.

"Yes. I think the Outislanders now regard our prince as wed to their narcheska. I thought this was only to confirm the betrothal before her mother's hearth." There was a note of question in his statement.

"I don't think they make any distinction between couples marrying and couples announcing that they will marry. Here, where property and children belong to the women, marriage is seen in a different light."

He nodded slowly. "No woman ever has to wonder if a babe is truly hers," he observed.

"Does it make that great a difference that the children belong more to the woman than they do the husband?" Swift asked curiously. His words were not slurred, but when he spoke, I could smell the wine on his breath.

"I think it depends on the man," Web answered gravely. After that, we walked for a time in silence. Whether I would or no, my thoughts wandered to Nettle and Molly and Burrich and me. To whom did she belong now?

As we drew near the cottage, the town around us was silent. Any folk who were not at the wedding festivities in the mothershouse were long abed. I opened the door quietly. Thick needed all the rest he could get; I did not wish to wake him. The slice of light that we admitted to the cottage showed me Riddle lying on the floor beside Thick's bed. One eye was open and his hand was on his bared blade arranged beside him. When he saw who it was, he closed his eyes and lapsed back into sleep.

I remained standing motionless by the door. There was another intruder in the cottage, one whose presence Riddle had not noticed. Large and round as a fat cat, yet masked like a ferret, he crouched on the table, his bushy striped tail sticking straight up behind him. He looked at us with round eyes over the hunk of our cheese that he clutched in his front paws. The marks of his sharp teeth were clearly visible in it.

"What is it?" I breathed to Web.

"I think they call it a robber-rat, though rat it is clearly not. I've never seen the like of it before," he replied as softly.

The robber-rat stared past us both, his entire attention fixed on Swift. Like a whisper against my senses, I became aware of the Wit flowing between the two. There was a smile on Swift's face. He stepped forward, pushing between Web and me to do so. I lifted a hand to reach after him, but before I could do so, Web's hand fell on the boy's shoulder. He jerked Swift back, startling the robber-rat with the abruptness of his move. Aloud, he told the creature, "Take the cheese and go." Then, in the harshest voice I'd ever heard him use, he demanded of Swift, "What did you think you were doing? Have you not heard one word of anything I've tried to teach you?"

Robber-rat and cheese were gone in a flicker of motion, vanishing through the open window with a flick of striped tail.

Swift gave a cry of disappointment and tried to wrench himself free of Web's grip. The stout man's hand held him firm. The boy was angry, mostly I think in response to Web's visible anger with him. "All I did was greet him! I liked the feel of him. I could sense that we would go well together. And I wanted—"

"You wanted him like a child wants a bright toy on a tinker's tray!" Web spoke severely and there was no mistaking the condemnation in his voice as he released Swift's shoulder. "Because he was sleek and swift and clever. And he is as young and foolish as you are. And as curious. You felt him reach back to you not because he was seeking a partner but because you intrigued him. That is not a basis for a Wit-bond. And you are not old enough or mature enough to be seeking a partner. If you attempt that again, I will punish you, just as I would punish any child who deliberately put himself or a playmate into danger."

Riddle had sat up and was regarding the discussion with open-mouthed astonishment. It was no secret to anyone that both Web and Swift were part of Dutiful's Witted coterie. I shuddered to think how close I had come to betraying myself as Old Blood. Even Thick had opened one sleepy eye to scowl at the argument.

Swift flung himself disconsolately into a chair. "Danger," he muttered. "What danger? Is it dangerous that I might have someone that cared about me, at last?"

"Danger that you would bond with a creature you know nothing about? Has he a mate and kits at home? Would you take him from them, or remain here on this island when we sailed? What does he eat and how often? Would you stay here with him for his life span, or take him away from all others of his kind when we left here, condemning him to remain forever mateless? You took no thought for him, Swift, nor for anything beyond the connection of the moment. You're like a drunk, bedding a young girl tonight with no thoughts for the morrow. It is not a behavior I can excuse. No true Old Blood would."

Swift glared at him. Riddle spoke thoughtlessly into the tense silence. "I did not know the Witted had any rules about bonding with animals. I thought they could bond with any creature, for an hour or a year."

"A false perception," Web said heavily, "that many folk not of Old Blood have about us. It is bound to happen, when one people must keep their ways secret and unseen. But it leads to the idea that we use animals and then discard them. It makes it easier for folk to think we would bid a bear savage a man's family, or send a wolf to kill a flock of sheep. The Wit-bond is not a man taking mastery over an animal. It is a joining founded on mutual respect, for life. Do you understand that, Swift?"

"I meant no harm," he replied stiffly. There was no repentance or apology in his voice.

"Neither does the child who plays with fire and burns a cottage down. Meaning no harm is not enough, Swift. If you would be Old Blood, then you must respect our rules and ways all the time, not just when it suits you."

"And if I don't?" Swift asked sullenly.

"Then call yourself a Piebald, for that is what you will be." Web drew in a heavy breath and then sighed it out. "Or an outcast," he said softly. I felt that he tried not to look at me as he spoke those last words. "Why any man would wish to remain apart from his own, I do not know."

chapter XI

WUISLINGTON

The attachment that the women have to their clan lands is remarkable. They often refer to tales that the earth itself is made from Eda's flesh and bones while the sea belongs to El. All land belongs to the women of the clan; the men born into a clan may tend the land and help with the harvest, but the women determine the distribution of the harvest and also decree what crops will be planted and where and in what proportions. It is not merely a matter of ownership, but a matter of Eda's worship.

Men may be buried anywhere, and most often are given to the sea. But all women must be buried within their own clan fields. The graves are honored for seven years, during which time the burial field is left fallow. After that, they are plowed again, and the first harvest from such a field is served in a special feast.

While the Outislander men are wanderers and may remain away from their home ports for years, the women tend to stay close to the lands of their birth. In marriage, they expect their husbands to reside with them. If an Outislander woman dies away from her clan lands, extraordinary efforts will be made to return her body to her clan fields. To do otherwise is both great shame and serious sacrilege for the woman's clan. The clans will *willingly go to war to repatriate a woman's body to her home.*

❧ "AN ACCOUNT OF TRAVEL IN A BARBAROUS LAND," BY SCRIBE FEDWREN

We were guests at Wuislington at the Narcheska's mothershouse for twelve days. It was a strange hospitality they offered us. Chade and Prince Dutiful were allotted sleeping space on the benches in the lower level of the house. The Witted coterie was housed alongside the guardsmen outside the walls. Thick and I continued in our cottage, with Swift and Riddle as frequent visitors. Every day, Chade sent two of the guards into the village to purchase victuals. They brought a share to us in the cottage, some to the guards, and the rest back to the mothershouse. Although Blackwater had promised to feed us, Chade had chosen this tactic shrewdly. To be seen as dependent on the Narwhal mothershouse largesse would be seen as a weakness and a foolish lack of planning.

There were good aspects to our extended stay. Thick began to recover his health. He still coughed and was short of breath if he went for a walk, but he slept more naturally, took an interest in his surroundings, ate and drank, and generally recovered some of his spirits. He still held it against me that I had forced him to travel there in a ship and that he would eventually have to leave in the same way. Every effort at casual conversation that I made always seemed to lead us back to that bone of contention. Sometimes it seemed easier not to speak to him at all, but then I sensed his anger for me as a simmering displeasure. I hated that things had become uncomfortable between us when I had worked so hard to gain his trust. When I said as much to Chade during one of our brief meetings, he dismissed it as necessary. "It would be far worse if he blamed it on Dutiful, you see. In this, you will have to be the whipping boy, Fitz." I knew it was so, and yet his words were no comfort.

Riddle spent several hours daily with Thick, usually when Chade wanted me to keep an unobtrusive eye on Dutiful. Web and Swift often came to the cottage. Swift seemed chastened by Web's rebuke and appeared generally more respectful to both Web and myself. I kept the lad busy with daily lessons and demanded that he practice his bow as well as his swordsmanship. Thick would come to sit outside the cottage and watch our mock battles in the sheep enclosure. He always cheered for Swift, bellowing his pleasure every time the boy landed a blow with the bound swords we used. I confess that bruised my feelings as much as Swift's thwacks bruised my flesh. It was my own skills more than his that I wished to keep sharp, but teaching the boy not only gave me an excuse to practice, it also allowed me to demonstrate my proficiency to the Outislanders. They did not gather to watch, but from time to time I would glimpse a lad or two perched on a nearby wall, eyeing us. I resolved that if I must be spied upon, I would see that the reports of me were that I was not easy prey. I did not think that their scrutiny was casual curiosity.

I felt constantly watched in that place. Wherever I went, always it seemed there was someone nearby, idly lingering. I could not have pointed to a single boy or old woman who spied on me, and yet there were always eyes on my back. I felt too a sense of danger to Thick. It was in the glances he received whenever we went out, and in the reaction of the folk we encountered. They drew back from him as if he carried contagion, and stared after us as if he were a two-headed calf. Even Thick seemed aware of it. I realized that, without consciously thinking of it, he seemed to use the Skill to be less noticed. It was not like his blast of "You don't see me!" that had once nearly laid me low, but more a constant announcement of his unimportance. I stored the knowledge away as something worth discussing with Chade.

I had little true time with my old mentor, and the Skill-messages I relayed to him were brief. We all felt it was more important that he use his Skill-strength in being available to Dutiful. Chade had also decided that as Peottre Blackwater had already discerned that I was a bodyguard for the Prince, there was no harm in my more openly pursuing that role. "As long as he does not realize you are any more than that," Chade cautioned me.

I tried to be an unobtrusive observer and guard to the Prince. Although Dutiful never complained I think he was uncomfortable with my constant lurking presence. The rest of the settlement regarded Dutiful and Elliania as a married couple now. There was no effort to chaperone them in any way. Only Peottre's presence, as subtle as a standing stone, reminded us that some in the Narcheska's family would see that their relationship remained chaste until Dutiful had fulfilled his end of the bargain. I think Peottre and I watched one another as much as we watched Dutiful and the Narcheska. In a strange way, we became partners.

I discovered in that time one of the reasons why the Narcheska was held in such regard by all of the clans, not just Narwhal. This was a culture in which women owned the land and what it produced. I had assumed the wealth of the clan was in its sheep. It was only when I trailed Dutiful and Elliania on one of their hikes across the rocky hills of the island that I came to discover its true wealth. They crested a ridge, with Peottre a discreet distance away from them and me a distant fourth. As I too reached the rise and then looked down into the next valley, I gasped.

There were three lakes in the valley, and two of them steamed even in the height of the summer day. Greenery was lush all around them, as were the precisely planted and tended fields that patchworked the valley. As I followed them down into the valley, the constant cooling wind faded. I walked down into cupped warmth and the smell of mineral-rich water. The boulders and stones had been cleared from the fields to neatly divide the crops as stone fences. Not only did the crops grow better in this warmer valley, but there I saw plants and trees that I would have judged too tender to flourish this far north. Here, in the harsh Out Islands, was an island mellowed by bubbling hot springs into an oasis of gentle warmth and plenty. No wonder the winning of the Narcheska was seen as such a prize. An alliance with she who controlled the food produced here was a valuable thing indeed in these harsh lands.

Yet I also had to note that, even in the midst of the summer, many of the fields were left fallow, and workers on the land were not as numerous as I would have expected. Again, the women and girls outnumbered the men and boys, and few of the males were in their prime years. It presented a mystery to me. Here were women, wealthy in land and lacking the workers to farm it. Why were there not more men courting here from other clans, seeking to contribute children to this island of plenty?

One early evening, Dutiful and Elliania were jumping two of the scrawny little island ponies that her people used for a multitude of tasks on Mayle. Their course was a stony meadow at the gently sloping base of a hill littered with boulders, and their makeshift jumps were cut saplings laid across paired boulders. The little ponies amazed me with how high they could leap when badgered into jumping. Sheep had cropped the grass short and scrub brush fringed the meadow. The deepening blue of the sky arched over us, and soon the first stars would show. They were riding bareback, and Dutiful had already taken two tumbles from his scrawny and willful steed in his attempts to keep pace with his fearless consort. The girl was wholeheartedly enjoying herself. She rode astraddle; her yellow skirts bunched and blossomed around her legs. From the knee down, her legs were bare, even her feet. Her cheeks were flushed, her hair wild, and she rode with a disregard for everything except showing the Prince she could excel him at this. The first time he fell, Elliania had ridden on, her mocking laughter reaching all of us. The second time, she actually rode back to see if he was injured while Peottre caught the nasty little beast and led it back to them. Most of my attention was focused on Dutiful; I felt proud of him for how genial he had been about both falls.

These ponies are as skinny and bony as calves. Trying to keep a seat on one is more bruising than taking the fall when it hops sideways.

Elliania seems to manage it well enough, I pointed out teasingly. At the look he shot me, I hastily added, *It doesn't look easy. I think she admires your tenacity.*

I think she admires my bruises, the little vixen. I caught a note of fondness in the epithet. As if to distract me from that, the Prince added, *Glance to your left and tell me if you see someone behind the boulders at the edge of the scrub brush.*

I flicked my eyes that way without turning my head. Something was there. I was not sure if it was a person or a large animal crouched there. The Prince remounted, and clung to his seat while the pony did a series of wild crow-hops across the meadow. His mount was obviously weary of the game, but Elliania's merry laughter rewarded Dutiful's efforts to stay on top. He cleared the jump that had previously defeated him, and she saluted him with a flourish. Her enjoyment of the spectacle seemed genuine, and a glance at Peottre showed that a grudging smile lit even his dour face. I joined my laughter to theirs and walked closer to them.

Ride toward that area and take a tumble. And when you do, make sure the pony flees toward the boulders.

He Skilled a disgusted groan at me, but did as I asked. And when the pony bolted, I sprang up and raced after it full speed, deliberately more chasing him than attempting to catch the creature. Together we flushed a woman, clad all in moss green and brown from her hiding place. She fled with no pretense of doing anything else, and I recognized not only how she moved but the very faint scent of her that I caught. Much as I longed to chase after her, I did not. Instead I Skilled what I now knew to both Chade and Dutiful.

That was Henja! The Narcheska's servant from Buck-keep. She's here on the island, spying on us.

Neither replied to me save with a wave of dread.

I was deliberately awkward at catching the pony. Finally Peottre came to help me. "We gave that old woman quite a fright!" I observed to him as I herded the pony toward him.

He seized the recalcitrant little animal by the forelock and looked up at the sky. He never met my gaze. "It grows dark. We are fortunate the Prince did not take a worse fall and severely injure himself." Then, to our wards, "We should go back now. The ponies are tired of jumping and night draws on."

I wondered if he had tried to warn me of a worse danger to the Prince than falling from a pony's back. I took him around again. "Do you think that poor old woman is all right? Should we look for her? She seemed quite frightened. I wonder what she was doing behind those boulders."

Face and voice impassive, he replied, "She was probably just gathering kindling. Or herbs or roots. I do not think we need bother about her." He lifted his voice. "Elliania! The time for fun is over. We should return to the mothershouse."

I saw Elliania's face when you made Henja run. The Narcheska was startled. And now she is frightened.

The brusque nod she gave to Peottre's words confirmed the Prince's opinion. She slid immediately from her pony's back, and then lifted the hackamore from his head, turning him loose on the hillside. Peottre did the same for the beast the Prince had been riding, and suddenly I found myself walking back to the mothershouse alongside them. Elliania and Dutiful led the way, and the silence between them contrasted sadly with their earlier merriment. My heart was heavy for him. He was learning to love this Outislander girl, but every time they drew closer to one another, the damned politics of throne and power wedged them apart. I felt a sudden rush of anger, and spoke rashly.

"That was Henja, wasn't it? That woman hiding in the bushes. She was the Narcheska's servant in Buckkeep Castle, if I recall correctly."

I give the man credit for his composure. Although he could not look at me, his voice was calm. "I doubt it. She left our service before we departed Buckkeep. We both believed she might be happier in the Six Duchies, and thus were glad to release her."

"Perhaps she returned to Wuislington on her own. Perhaps she became homesick."

"This is not her home; she is not of our mothershouse," Peottre announced firmly.

"How odd." I was determined to be relentless. As a mere guardsman, I would not be expected to possess tact, only curiosity. "I thought that in this country, the mother's family was all-important; anyone attending the Narcheska would be of her mother's line."

"Ordinarily, yes." Peottre's voice was growing stiffer. "No woman of the family could be spared at the time we sailed. So we hired her."

"I see." I shrugged. "I have wondered, why do not Elliania's mother and sisters attend her now? Are they dead?"

He shuddered as if I'd stuck a dart in him. "No. They aren't." Bitterness came into his voice. "Her two older brothers are. They died in Kebal Rawbread's war. Her mother and her younger sister live but they are ... detained elsewhere, on an important matter. If they could be here with her now, they would."

"Oh, I'm sure of that," I replied blandly. I was convinced of the truth of every word he had uttered, and just as certain that I did not have the entire truth.

Late that night, while Thick slept heavily, I Skilled as much to Chade. I tried to keep my thoughts to the old man private and separate from my Skill-link to the Prince. I could sense his restless sleep. The undercurrent of the boy's frustration and impatience set my nerves on edge. I tried to set his emotions aside as I communicated to Chade all that had passed between Peottre and me. Chade was annoyed with my bluntness with Peottre even as he was avidly interested in the man's responses. *There are designs within designs here, like one of the Fool's wooden puzzle balls. I am convinced that he and the Narcheska have an agenda of their own, and that not all in her mothershouse know of it. Some do. Almata for example. And the Narcheska's great-grandmother has been told, but I do not think she can hold the significance in her mind. Lestra and her mother interest me. Lestra stands to become narcheska when Elliania goes off to Buckkeep to wed Dutiful. Yet, she seems to vie with Elliania for Dutiful's attention, and I suspect her mother encourages it. Does she grasp that eventually becoming Queen of the Six Duchies might be a loftier ambition than stealing the narcheska title from Elliania? I do not think Lestra and her mother attach any importance to Elliania's demand for the dragon's head. I think that Lestra's ambitions should give both Elliania and Peottre concern, yet they seem to remain aloof, their thoughts elsewhere. Elliania only drives Lestra off when the challenge becomes too blatant to ignore.*

Like their fistfight on the night of the wedding?

Betrothal, Fitz. Betrothal. We do not recognize that ceremony as a true wedding. The Prince must be wed at home, in Buckkeep, and the marriage must be consummated. But no, not just that confrontation. Lestra has made several attempts at him since then, usually when the Narcheska is not about.

Does Elliania know?

How could she?

He might tell her, I speculated. *I wonder what would happen if she knew?*

I have no desire to find out. The situation is quite complicated enough as it is. Perhaps this is just a rivalry between girl cousins. I wish I understood Henja's role in all this. Is she just some dotty old woman? Or more? Are you quite sure it was she?

Quite. It had not been just my eyes that confirmed it, but I would not tell Chade I had scented her, and that enough of the wolf remained in me to be certain of that sense.

Our conversation had wearied Chade and I let him go to his rest. I checked to be sure the cottage door was latched, and then regretfully closed the window shutters, as well. I did not like sleeping in such a tightly closed place. I always slept best when I could feel air moving freely on my face, but after my sighting of Henja that day, I would not give anyone the opportunity to have a clear shot at me.

Such was my frame of mind as I settled myself for sleep, and the next morning, I tried to use it to account for my nightmares. Yet it was not fair to call my dreams that. There was nothing of terror in them, only uneasiness, and a vividness that was not Skill-walking, but something else. I dreamed of the Fool as he had been once, not as Lord Golden but as a pale, frail lad with colorless eyes. In that guise, he bestrode the stone dragon behind Girl-on-a-Dragon, and together they rose into the blue skies. But then suddenly he became Lord Golden, and as he rode behind the carved and soulless girl that was a part of the dragon sculpture that he had called back to wakefulness and life, a black-and-white cloak fluttered out on the wind behind him. His hair was pulled back sleek and tight from his face and bound back like a warrior's tail. His expression was so set and stern that he looked as soulless as the Girl whose slender waist he clasped. His hands were bare, I saw in surprise, for it had been a very long time since I had seen him do anything ungloved. Higher they rose into the sky, and higher still, and then suddenly he lifted his hand and pointed, and the Girl kneed the dragon to fly in the direction of that slender, pointing finger. Then clouds cloaked them as if mist enfolded them. I stirred from sleep to find my own fingers set to my wrist in the pale prints he had once left there. I shifted in my bedding but could not seem to come back to full wakefulness. Pulling my blanket more tightly around me, I surrendered to sleep again.

And then I did Skill-walk in my dreams, to a most disturbing scene. Nettle sat and chatted with Tintaglia on a grassy hillside. I knew it was a dream of Nettle's making, for never had flowers blossomed so brightly, nor bloomed so evenly throughout the grass. It reminded me of a carefully worked tapestry. The dragon was the size of a horse, and crouched in a way that was not quite threatening. I stepped into the dream. Nettle's back was very straight and her voice nearly brittle as she demanded of the dragon, "And what has any of that to do with me?"

And in a silent aside to me, *Why did you delay? Didn't you feel me summoning you?*

"I can hear that, you know," Tintaglia pointed out calmly. "And he did not hear you summoning him because I did not wish him to. So, you see, you are quite alone, if I decide you are." The dragon suddenly turned her cold gaze on me. Beauty had fled her reptile eyes, leaving them spinning gems of fury. "A fact that does not escape you, either, I assume."

"What do you want?" I demanded of her.

"You know what I want. I want to know what you know of a black dragon. Is he real? Does another dragon, grown and whole, still exist in the world?"

"I don't know," I answered her truthfully. I could feel her mind plucking at mine, trying to get past the words I gave her to see if I was hiding anything. It was like having cold rat feet run over you in a prison cell at night. Then she seized that memory and tried to turn it against me. I slammed my walls tighter. Unfortunately that meant that Nettle was also outside them. They both became like shadows dimly cast on a wavering curtain.

Tintaglia spoke, and her voice reached me like a whisper of doom. "Accept that your kind will serve mine. It is the natural order of things. Serve me in this and I will see that you and yours prosper. Defy me, and you and yours will be swept aside." Suddenly the image of the dragon loomed large and towered over Nettle. "Or devoured," she offered knowingly.

Dread prickled at me. On some fundamental level, the dragon associated me with Nettle. Was it simply that she had always reached me through my daughter, or did she sense our kinship? Did it matter? My daughter was in danger, and it was my fault. Again. And I had no idea how to protect her.

It did not matter. A moment ago the flower-studded meadow had reminded me of a tapestry. Then Nettle abruptly stood up, bent and seized her dream, then shook it as if she sought to shake dust from a rug. The dragon's presence was flung from it and went spinning off into nothingness, dwindling as it went. In that nothingness, Nettle stood and wadded up her dream and tucked it into her apron pocket. I no longer knew where or what I was in her dream, but she sent the words to me. *You'll have to learn to stand up to her and drive her off, not just curl up in a ball and hide. Remember, Shadow Wolf, that you are a wolf. Not a mouse. Or so I thought.* She began to fade.

Wait! The Prince Skilled with desperate determination. In some way I did not understand, he caught at her and detained her. *Who are you?*

Nettle's shock went through me like a wave. She struggled a moment, but when his grip held, she demanded, *Who am I? Who are you, who dare to intrude here so rudely? Let go of me.*

Dutiful did not react well to her rebuke. *Who am I? I am the Prince of all the Six Duchies. I go wherever I will.*

For a moment, she was stunned to silence. Then, *You are the Prince?* Her disbelief was as evident as her scorn.

Yes, I am. And now you will stop wasting my time and tell me who you are! I winced at the snap of command in his voice. A terrible silent void stretched all around me. Then Nettle reacted as I had known she would.

Oh. Well, of course I will, since you ask me so nicely. Prince Mannerless, I am Queen I-Doubt-It-Very-Much of the Seven Dungheaps. And perhaps you go "wherever you will," but when the where belongs to me, I will that you do not ever go there. Changer, you should cultivate nicer friends.

I saw what she had done. In the pause, she had seen

exactly how he had fastened himself to her. And now, effortlessly, she shook herself free of him. And vanished.

I jolted awake with her disdain rattling against me like flung pebbles. Torn between awe for my daughter and dread for the dragon, I tried to recover myself. I needed to think what I could do. Instead, Chade pushed his way into my mind.

We need to talk. Privately. His Skill trembled with excitement.

Privately? Are you sure you know what the word means? Why, tonight of all nights, did he have to spy on me?

Not privately. Dutiful was furious with both of us as he broke in on our Skilling. *Who is she? How long has this been going on? I demand to know. How dare you train another Skilled one and keep her existence concealed from me!*

Go back to sleep! Thick's ponderous Skilling was between a moan and a command. *Go back to sleep and stop shouting. It was only Nettle and her dragon. Go back to sleep.*

Everyone knows of her except me? This is intolerable. Dutiful's Skilling held fury and frustration, and that terrible sense of betrayal when one discovers one has been excluded from a secret. *I demand to know who she is. Right now.*

I fenced my thoughts tightly and prayed, even though I knew it would avail me nothing.

Chade? The Prince drove him out of his silence.

I do not know, my lord. The old man lied gracefully and without remorse. I both damned and admired him.

FitzChivalry.

There is a power to the naming of a man by his true name. I shuddered at the impact, and then swiftly begged, *Do not call me by that name. Not here, not now, lest the dragon be listening.* It was not the dragon I feared, but my daughter. Too many bits of my secrets were falling into her hands.

Tell me, Tom.

Not this way. If we must speak of this, let us speak voice to ear only. Near me in the dark, Thick pulled his blankets up over his head, groaning.

Meet me now. The Prince's voice was grim.

This isn't wise, Chade counseled us both. *Let it wait until morning, my prince. There is no sense in inviting questions by summoning a man-at-arms to you in the middle of the night.*

No. Now. What was truly unwise was for both of you to deceive me about this Nettle person. I will know now what is going on behind my back and why. It was almost as if I were in the mothershouse by the bed-benches. I could feel how his anger chased the chill from his bared chest as he threw his covers aside, sense how furiously he thrust his feet into his shoes.

Give me time to dress then, Chade conceded wearily.

No. Stay where you are, Councilor Chade. You say you know nothing? Then there is no sense in your bothering to come. I'll meet Fitz . . . Tom alone for this.

His anger roared like a fire now, and yet he still had refrained from saying my name. In some corner of my mind, I admired his restraint. But the greater part of my thoughts was taken up with a dilemma. This was my prince that was angry with me, and to his way of thinking, he was justified. How would I react to his questions? Who was I to him tonight? Friend, mentor, uncle, or subject? I became aware that Thick was sitting up on his blankets, watching me dress.

"I'll only be gone a short time. You'll be fine here alone," I reassured him even as I wondered if that was so.

I don't want to leave Thick alone here, I Skilled to the Prince, hoping this excuse would spare me.

Then bring him. The Prince bit off his succinct order.

"Do you want to come?"

"I heard him," Thick replied wearily. He heaved a huge sigh. "You're always making me go places I don't want to go," he complained as he rummaged for clothing in the dark.

I felt a year had passed before he was dressed. He huffily refused any offer of assistance from me. Together we finally left the cottage and wound our way through the

village. The odd twilight that passes for night in that part
of the world lent its gray aspect to the world. It was oddly
restful to my eyes and I finally identified the sensations.
These dimmed colors reminded me of how Nighteyes had
perceived the world on the evenings and dawns when we
had hunted together. It was a gentle light, and undistracted
by color, the eye was free to pick up the small movements
of game. I walked light as the wind, but Thick shuffled disconsolately along beside me. Every now and then, he
coughed. I reminded myself that he was still not completely well and tried to find patience with his slow pace.

Little bats flickered through the air over the town. I
caught the furtive glide of a robber-rat as it slunk from a
rain barrel to a doorstep. I wondered if it was the same one
that Swift had tried to befriend, then put it out of my mind.
We were drawing closer to the mothershouse. The courtyard was deserted. They posted no guard here, though they
kept a lookout over the coast and harbor. Evidently they
feared no attacks from within their own folk. I wondered
then if Peottre had told me all he knew of Henja. Certainly
he and the Narcheska seemed wary of the woman and he
had said she was an outsider. Why, then, did he not post a
guard against her?

I led Thick away from the main door. We approached
the mothershouse from behind, past the stone walls and
hedges that confined the sheep. Around the corner of a
shed, the Prince was waiting for us near some bushes beside
the privies. He shifted restlessly as he watched us approach,
and I sensed his impatience. I lifted a silent hand to gesture
to him to join us in the concealment of the hedge. Then:

Don't come to me. Stand still. No, hide. Or go away.

I halted, confused by the Prince's sudden command.
And then I saw what had rattled him. Elliania wore a cloak
over her nightgown as she leaned out from the door and
glanced around. I barely had time to put a hand on Thick's
chest and urge him back out of sight behind the hedge line.

The little man angrily slapped my hand from his chest. "I heard him," he complained to me as I shushed him in vain.

We have to be very quiet, Thick. The Prince doesn't want Elliania to know we are here.

Why not?

He just doesn't, that's all. We need to hide here and be very quiet. I crouched down on the earth behind the hedge and patted the ground by me invitingly. Thick, hunched in the grayness, scowled down at me. I longed simply to take him home but I was sure Elliania would hear his shuffling tread if we tried to leave. It was better to wait. Surely she wouldn't be long. She probably only needed to use the backhouse. I peered around the trunks of the hedge through a gap in the branches. *Come join us here before she sees you,* I Skill-suggested to the Prince.

No. She's seen me. Go away. I'll talk to you later. Then, disbelieving, I felt him raise his Skill-walls against me. He had grown stronger. It was by the Wit that I sensed him, poised and quivering in her steady-eyed regard as she came to him in the dusky light of a sun that scraped along the edge of the horizon, refusing to set.

I felt a lurch of dismay as I saw how swiftly she went to him and how close she stood to him in the dimness. This was not the first time these two had met clandestinely. I wanted to turn my eyes away and yet I stared avidly, peering at them through the bushes. Her words barely reached me. "I heard the door open and close, and when I looked out the window, I saw you waiting here."

"I couldn't sleep." He reached out as if to take her hands, but then dropped his hands back to his sides. I felt more than saw the sharp glance he sent in my direction. *Go away. I'll speak to you tomorrow.* His Skill-sending to me was tight and small. I doubted that even Thick was aware of it. Royal command was in his tone. He expected me to obey him.

I can't. You know this is dangerous. Send her back to her room, Dutiful.

I had no sense that he had received my thought. He had closed himself off to focus only on the girl. Behind me, Thick stood up, yawning and gaping. "I'm going back," he announced sleepily.

Sshh. No. We have to stay here and be very quiet. Don't talk out loud. I peered at the young couple anxiously, but if Elliania had heard Thick, she gave no sign. I wondered uneasily where Peottre was, and what he would do to Dutiful if he found them together like this.

Thick sighed heavily. He crouched back down, and then sat flat on the ground. *This is stupid. I want to go back to bed.*

Elliania glanced down at Dutiful's hands at his side, and then, cocking her head, looked up at his face. "So. Who are you waiting for?" Her eyes narrowed. "Lestra? Did she invite you to meet her here?"

A very odd smile appeared on Dutiful's face. Was he pleased that he had pricked her to jealousy? He spoke more softly than she did, but I could watch his lips form the words. "Lestra? Why would I wait by moonlight for Lestra?"

"There is no moon tonight," Elliania pointed out sharply. "And as for why Lestra, why, because she would willingly give you her body to use as you wished. More for the sake of spiting me than because she found you handsome."

He crossed his arms on his chest. I wondered if he did so to hold in his satisfaction or to keep from taking her in his arms. She was slender as a willow, and her night braids fell to her hips. I could almost smell the warmth of her rising up to him. "So. Do you think she finds me handsome?"

"Who knows? She likes odd things. She has a cat with a crooked tail and too many toes. She thinks it's pretty." She shrugged. "But she would tell you that you were handsome, simply to win you."

"Would she? But perhaps I don't want Lestra to win me. She is pretty, but perhaps I don't want Lestra at all," he suggested to her.

All the night held its breath as she looked up at him. I saw the rise and fall of her breasts as she took a deeper breath, daring herself. "Then what do you want?" she asked, soft as a breeze.

He didn't try to take her in his arms. I think she would have resisted that. Instead, he freed one hand from his crossed arms and, with the tip of one finger, lifted her chin. He leaned forward, bending down to take the kiss he stole from her. Stole? But she did not flee. Instead, she rose on her toes as only their mouths touched in the soft dimness.

I felt a lecherous old man, sprawled in the darkness of the hedge, spying on them. I knew he plunged himself into danger, that they both took foolish chances, but my heart leaped at the thought that my lad might know love as well as an arranged marriage. When their kiss finally broke, I hoped he would send her back to her bedchamber. I wanted him to have this moment, but I also knew that I'd have to intervene if it looked like their experiment was going to venture past a kiss. I cringed at the thought, but steeled myself to the necessity of it.

With dread, I heard her breathless question. "A kiss. That was all you wanted?"

"It is all I'll take now," he countered. His chest was rising and falling as if he'd run a race. "I'll wait until I've earned more to take more."

An uncertain smile crossed her face. "You need not earn it if I choose to give myself to you."

"But . . . you said you would not be my wife until I brought you the dragon's head."

"In my land, a woman gives herself where she will. It is different from being married. Or a wife, as you call it. Once a girl is a woman, she can take whatever man she wishes into her bedskins. It does not mean she is wed to each of them." She glanced aside and added carefully, "You would be my first. Some consider that more special than to be vowed to one another. It would not make me your wife, of course. I will not be wife or wedded to you until you have brought the dragon's head here, to my mothershouse."

"I would like you to be my first, as well," Dutiful said carefully. Then, as if uttering the words were as difficult as dragging a tree up by the roots, he added, "But not now. Not until I've done what I've said I'd do."

She was shocked, but not that he would keep his promise. "Your first? Truly? You've known no woman yet?"

It took him a long moment to admit it. "It is the custom of my land, though not all follow it. To wait until we are wed." He spoke stiffly, as if fearing she would mock him for his chastity.

"I would like to be your first," she admitted. She stepped closer to him, and this time his arms settled around her. She melted her body against him as his mouth found hers.

My Wit made me aware of Peottre before they were. Engrossed as they were, I doubt either of them would have been aware of a herd of sheep passing around them, but I came to my feet as I saw the old warrior step around the corner of the mothershouse. His sword was on his hip and his eyes were dangerous. "Elliania."

She leaped back out of Dutiful's embrace. One guilty hand wiped her mouth as if to conceal the kiss she had taken. I give Dutiful full credit that he stood his ground. He swung his head to look steadily at Peottre. There was nothing of remorse or disgrace in his stance, nor anything of boyishness. He looked like a man interrupted while kissing a woman who belonged to him. I held my breath, wondering if I would better or worsen the situation by stepping into plain view.

The silence was as still and watchful as the night. The gaze held between Peottre and Dutiful. It was a measuring look, not quite a challenge. When Peottre spoke, his words were for Elliania. "You should go back to your bedchamber."

At his suggestion, she spun and fled. Her bare feet were silent on the dust of the courtyard. Even after she was gone, Dutiful and Peottre continued to regard one another. At last Peottre spoke. "The dragon's head. You promised. As a man, you gave your word."

Dutiful inclined his head once, gravely. "I did. As a man, I promised."

Peottre started to turn away. Dutiful spoke again.

"What Elliania offered me, she offered as a woman, not as the Narcheska. Is she free to offer that, by your customs?"

Peottre's spine stiffened. He turned slowly and spoke unwillingly. "Who else can offer that to you, save a woman? Her body belongs to her. She can share that with you. But she will not truly be your wife until you bring her the head of Icefyre."

"Ah."

Again, Peottre slowly turned to go, and again Dutiful's voice stopped him.

"Then she is more free than I am. My body and my seed belong to the Six Duchies. I am not free to share it where I would choose, but only with my wife. That is our custom." I almost heard him swallow. "I would that she knew that. That, by our customs, I cannot accept what she offers, except dishonorably." His voice dropped, and his next words were a request. "I would ask that she not tempt or taunt me with what I cannot honorably take. I am a man but . . . I am a man." His explanation was both awkward and honest.

So was Peottre's response. There was grudging respect in his voice as he said, "I will see that she knows that."

"Will she . . . will she think less of me? Will she think me less of a man?"

"*I* do not. And I will see that she understands what it costs a man to hold back from such an offer." He stood looking at Dutiful as if seeing him for the first time. When he spoke, there was great sadness in his words. "You *are* a man. You would be a good match for my sister-daughter. The granddaughters of your mother would enrich my line."

He spoke the last as if it were a proverb rather than something that he could truly hope for. Then he turned and silently left.

I saw Dutiful draw a deep breath and sigh it out again. I dreaded that he would reach for me with the Skill, but he did not. Instead, head bowed, he walked back into Elliania's mothershouse.

Thick had fallen asleep sitting on the ground, his head bowed heavily onto his chest. He moaned lightly as I gently shook him to wakefulness and helped him to his feet. "I want to go home," he muttered as he tottered down the road beside me.

"Me, too," I told him. And yet it was not Buckkeep that came to my mind, but a meadow overlooking the sea, and a girl in bright red skirts who beckoned me. A time, rather than a place. No road led there anymore.

chapter XII

COUSINS

The toothy spires of the dragon's isle cup the glacier in its
    maw
As the gaping mouth of a dying man wells blood.
Young man, will you go there?
Will you climb the ice to win the regard of your fellow
    warriors?
Dare you cross the crevasses, seen and unseen?
Dare you brave the winds that sing of Icefyre, asleep
    within the ice?
He will burn your bones with cold, he will. The icy wind
    is his fiery breath.
With it he will blacken the skin of your face until it peels
    from the sore pink flesh beneath it.
Young man, will you venture there?
To win the favor of a woman, will you walk beneath the
    ice on the wet black stones that see no sky?
Will you find the secret cavern that gapes only when the
    tide retreats?
Will you count your own heartbeats to mark the passing
    of time until the sea waves return to grind you to a
    smear of blood against the deep blue ice above you?

     ❰ "THE DRAGON'S WELCOME," OUTISLANDER SONG,
                  TRANSLATION BY BADGERLOCK

The very next day, we were told that all the issues regarding the Prince's killing Icefyre had been resolved. We would return to Zylig to accept the Hetgurd's terms, and then depart for Aslevjal and our dragon hunt. I wondered briefly if the sudden plans for sailing had anything to do with the night scene I had witnessed, but then watched the releasing of a bird that carried tidings of our departure, and decided that the news had doubtless been borne to us on the same wings.

The ensuing bustle spared me an uncomfortable interview with the Prince, but plunged me into misery of a different sort. Thick was completely opposed to getting back onto a ship. It was useless to tell him that this was the only way he would eventually get home. In moments like that, I glimpsed the limits of his mind and logic. Thick had developed since he had come to us, becoming not only more free with his words but more sophisticated in how he used them. He was like a plant finally granted sunlight as he revealed more understanding and potential than I had suspected from the shuffling half-wit servant in Chade's tower. And yet, he would always carry his differences with him. Sometimes he became a frightened and rebellious child, and at such times, reasoning with him did us no good. In the end, Chade resorted to a strong soporific the night before we were to sail, which required me to keep a vigil on his dreams all that night. They were uneasy ones that I soothed as best I could. It filled me with misgivings that Nettle did not come to help me, even though in another sense I was glad she did not.

Thick was still soddenly asleep when we loaded him into a handcart to transport him to the ship the next day. I felt a fool trundling him over the bumpy roads and down to the docks, but Web walked alongside me and talked as casually as if this were an everyday occurrence.

Our departure seemed to be more of an event than our arrival. Two ships awaited us. I noticed that the entire Six Duchies contingent was loaded on the Boar ship as before.

The Narcheska and Peottre and the few folk accompanying them embarked onto a smaller, older vessel, flying a banner with a narwhal on it. The Great Mother came down to see her off and to offer a blessing to her. I understand there was other ceremony as well but I saw little of it, for Thick began to stir restlessly in his bunk and I judged it best to stay close by him lest he awake and decide to get off the ship.

I sat by his bunk in the tiny cabin allotted to us and tried to Skill peace and security into his dreams. The movement of the waves and the sound of the ship leaked in despite my best efforts. With a start and a cry he came awake and sat up, staring around the cabin with eyes both wild and groggy. "It's a bad dream!" he wailed.

"No," I had to tell him. "It's real. But I promise I'll keep you safe, Thick. I promise."

"You can't promise that! No one can promise that on a boat!" he accused me. I had put my arm around him comfortingly when he first sat up. Now he flung himself away from me. He huddled back into his blankets, rolled to face the wall, and began to sob uncontrollably.

"Thick," I began helplessly. Never had I felt so cruel, never so wrong in anything I had ever done.

"Go away!" Despite my walls, the Skill-command in his words snapped my head back on my spine. I found myself on my feet, groping toward the door of the minuscule cabin we'd share with the Wit coterie. I forced myself to halt.

"Is there anyone you want to be with you?" I asked hopelessly.

"No! You all hate me! You all trick me and poison me and make me go on the ocean to kill me. Go away!"

I was glad enough to do so, for his Skill pushed at me like a strong, cold wind. As I went out of the low cabin door, I stood upright too soon and slammed the top of my head into the doorjamb. The jolt was enough to dizzy me as

I staggered the rest of the way onto the deck. Thick's cruel laugh was like a second blow.

I soon learned it was not an accident. Perhaps the first one had been, but in the days of our journey, Thick managed enough Skill-stumbles for me that any thought of coincidence soon vanished. If I was aware of him, I could sometimes counter it, but if he saw me first, I'd only know of it when I felt the boat seem to lurch under me. I'd try to catch my balance, and instead stumble to the deck or walk into a railing.

But at that time, I dismissed it as my own clumsiness.

I went to find Chade and Dutiful. We had a greater degree of privacy on that journey than we had previously had on all our travels. Peottre and the Narcheska and her guards were on the other vessel. The Boar clansmen who operated our vessel seemed little interested in how we socialized, and fewer pretenses were needed.

So it was that I went directly to the Prince's cabin and knocked. Chade admitted me. I found them both well settled, including a meal set out on a table. It was Outislander fare, but at least there was plenty of it. The wine with it was of a decent quality, and I was pleased when a nod from Dutiful invited me to join them.

"How is Thick?" he asked without preamble. It was a relief, almost, to give a detailed report on that, for I had dreaded that he would immediately demand that I explain Nettle. I detailed the small man's discomfort and unhappiness and ended up with "Regardless of his Skill-strength, I do not see how we can force him to continue. With every ship we embark on, he dislikes me more and becomes more intractable. We risk stirring an enmity in him that we can never quell, one that will make him set his Skill against all our endeavors. If it can safely be done, I propose that we leave him on Zylig while we go on to Aslevjal."

Chade set his glass down with a thud. "You know it can't be done, so why ask it?" I knew his irritation masked his own guilt and regret when he added, "I swear, I never thought it would be so hard on him. Is there no way to make him understand the importance of what we do?"

"The Prince might be able to convey it to him. Thick is so angry with me right now, I don't think he'll truly hear anything I say."

"He isn't the only one who is angry with you," Dutiful observed coolly. The calmness with which he addressed me warned me that his anger had gone very deep indeed. He controlled it now as a man controls his blade. Waiting for an opening.

"Shall I leave you two alone to discuss this?" Chade rose a shade too hastily.

"Oh, no. As you know nothing of Nettle and her dragon, I'm sure this will be as enlightening to you as it is to me."

Chade sank slowly back into his chair, his retreat severed by the Prince's sarcasm. I knew abruptly that the old man was not going to help me at all. That, if anything, Chade relished my being cornered this way.

"Who is Nettle?" Dutiful's question was blunt.

So was my answer. "My daughter. Though she does not know it."

He leaned back in his chair as if I'd doused him with cold water. There was a long moment of silence. Chade, damn him, lifted his hand to cover his mouth, but not before I'd seen his smile. I shot him a look of pure fury. He dropped his hand and grinned openly.

"I see," Dutiful said after a time. Then, as if it were the most important conclusion he could reach, "I have a cousin. A girl cousin! How old is she? How is it that I've never met her? Or have I? When was she last at court? Who is her lady mother?"

I could not find my tongue, but I hated Chade speaking for me. "She has never been to court, my prince. Her mother is a candlemaker. Her father...the man she thinks is her father is Burrich, formerly the Stablemaster at Buckkeep

Castle. She is sixteen now, I believe." He halted there, as if to give the Prince time to puzzle it out.

"Swift's father? Then . . . is Swift your son? You spoke of having a foster son, but—"

"Swift is Burrich's son. And Nettle's half-brother." I took a long breath, and heard myself ask, "Have you any brandy? Wine isn't enough for this tale."

"I can see that." He stood up and fetched it for me, more nephew than prince in that moment, and ready to be enraptured by ancient family history. It was hard for me to tell that old tale, and somehow Chade nodding sympathetically made it worse. When the convoluted connections were finally all traced for him, Dutiful sat shaking his head.

"What a mare's nest you made of it, FitzChivalry. With this piece in place, the tale my mother told me of your life makes much more sense. And how you must hate Molly and Burrich, that they could both set you aside and faithlessly forget you and find comfort in one another."

It shocked me that he could speak of it that way. "No," I said firmly. "That isn't how it was. They believed me dead. There was nothing faithless about them going on living. And, if she had to give herself to someone, then . . . then I am glad that she chose a man worthy of her. And that he finally found a bit of happiness for himself. And that together they protected my child." It was getting harder to speak as my throat tightened. I loosened it with a slug of brandy, and then wheezed in a breath.

"He was the better man for her," I managed to add. I had told myself that so often, through the years.

"I wonder if she would have thought so," the Prince mused, and then, at the look on my face, added hastily, "I beg your pardon. It's not my place to wonder such things. But . . . but I am still shocked that my mother allowed this. Often she has spoken with me, forcefully, about how much rests on me as the sole heir to the throne."

"She gave way to Fitz's feelings in that. Against my

counsel," Chade explained. I could hear the satisfaction he took in finally vindicating himself.

"I see. Well, actually, I don't see, but for now the question is, how have you been teaching her to Skill? Did you live near her before or . . . ?"

"I haven't been teaching her. What she knows of it, she has mastered on her own."

"But I was told that was horribly dangerous!" Dutiful's shock seemed to deepen. "How could you allow her to be risked this way, knowing all she means to the Farseer throne?" That question was for me, and then he accusingly demanded of Chade, "Did you prevent her coming to court? Was this your doing, some silly effort at protecting the Farseer name?"

"Not at all, my prince," he denied smoothly. He turned his calm gaze on me and told Dutiful, "Many times, I have asked Fitz to allow Nettle to be brought to Buckkeep, so that she could both learn her own importance to the Farseer line and be instructed in the Skill. But, again, this was an area in which FitzChivalry's feelings had their way. Against the counsel of both the Queen and myself."

The Prince took several deep breaths. Then, "This is unbelievable," he said quietly. "And intolerable. It will be remedied. I'll do it myself."

"Do what?" I demanded.

"Tell that girl who she is! And have her brought to court and treated as befits her birth. See her educated in all things, including the Skill. My cousin is being raised as a country girl, dipping candles and feeding chickens! What if the Farseer throne required her? I still cannot grasp that my mother allowed this!"

Is there anything more chilling than looking at a righteous fifteen-year-old and realizing he has the power to unravel your entire life? I felt queasy with vulnerability. "You have no idea what that would do to my life," I pleaded quietly.

"No. I don't," he admitted easily, but with growing

outrage. "And neither do you. You go around making these monumental decisions about what other people should know or not know about their own lives. But you don't really have any more idea how it will turn out than I do! You just do what you think is safest and then crawl around hoping no one will find out and blame you later if things go wrong!" He was building up to a frenzy, and I suddenly suspected that this was not entirely about Nettle.

"What are you so angry about?" I asked bluntly. "This is nothing to do with you."

"*Nothing* to do with me? Nothing to do with *me*?" He stood up, nearly knocking his chair over. "How can Nettle be nothing to do with me? Do not we share a grandfather? Is not she a Farseer born, and possessed of the Skill Magic? Do you know—" He choked for a moment, and then visibly composed himself. In a softer voice he asked, "Have you no idea what it would have meant to me to grow up with a peer? Someone of my blood, someone closer to my own age that I could talk to? Someone who would have to shoulder a share of the responsibility for the Farseer reign, so that it wouldn't always have had to be only on me?" He glanced aside, staring as if he could see through the wall of the cabin and gave an odd little snort. "It could be her here in this cabin, promised to an Outislander spouse instead of me. If my mother and Chade had had two Farseers to spend to buy us peace, who knows . . ."

The thought made my blood cold. I didn't want to tell him that was exactly what I had tried to protect Nettle from. I did give him one truth. "It had never occurred to me to look at it from your point of view. It had never occurred to me that it would have an effect on you at all."

"Well, it has. And it does." He suddenly shifted his focus to Chade. "And you too have been negligent beyond all tolerance. This girl is the heir to the Farseer throne, after me. That should be documented and witnessed; it should have been done before I left port! If anything befalls me, if I die trying to chop up this frozen dragon, there will be chaos as all try to suggest who should be—"

"It has been done, my prince. Many years ago. And the documents kept safe. In that, I have not been negligent." Chade seemed incensed that Dutiful could even think such a thing.

"It would have been nice to know that. Can either of you explain to me why it was so important to keep this information from me?" He glared from Chade to me, but his stare settled on me as he observed, "It seems to me that you have gone about for a lot of your life, making decisions for other people, doing what you thought was best without consulting them about what they wanted at all. And you aren't always right!"

I kept my temper. "That's the trouble with making a decision. You never know if it's right until after you've done it. But it is what adults are supposed to do. Make decisions. And then live with them."

He was silent for a time. Then he said, after a moment, "And if I made an adult decision to tell Nettle who she is? To right at least that much of the wrong we have done her?"

I took a breath. "I'm asking you not to do that. It isn't something that should just be dropped on her, all of a piece."

He was quiet for a longer time and then asked wryly, "Have I any other secret relatives who will come popping into my life when I least expect it?"

"None that I know of," I replied seriously. Then, more formally, "My prince, please. Let me be the one to tell her, if she must be told."

"It's certainly a task you deserve," he observed, and Chade, who had been solemn for a few moments, smiled again. Dutiful seemed almost wistful as he added, "She seems strong in the Skill. Think how it could be, if she were here now. We'd have her to rely on, and perhaps Thick could have stayed safely at home."

"Actually, she works well with Thick. She's excellent at calming him and has gained a lot of his trust. She is the one who disarmed his nightmares for us on our voyage to Zylig. But in reply to what you said, no, my prince. Thick is too strong and too volatile to be left on his own anywhere now. And that is a thing that we must eventually deal with. The more we teach him, the more dangerous he becomes."

"I think the best remedy for Thick's willfulness is to take him home and put him back in his familiar life. I expect that he'll regain a more even temperament then. Unfortunately, I have to find and kill a dragon before we can do that."

I was relieved to leave the topic of Nettle, and yet there was one more chink in the wall to close. "My prince. Swift knows nothing of all this, of Nettle's being my daughter and only half-sister to him. I'd like to keep it that way."

"Ah, yes. Of course, when you decided to keep this a secret, you never wondered how it might affect other children that might come along."

"You are right. I didn't," I admitted stiffly.

"Well, I'll keep silent. For now. But you might want to consider how you would feel if you were only now discovering who your parents were." He cocked his head at me. "Think about it. What if it was suddenly revealed to you that you weren't Chivalry's son but Verity's? Or Regal's? Or Chade's? How much gratitude would you feel toward those who had known all along and 'protected' you from the truth?"

The cold chasm of doubt yawned briefly before me, even as I rejected such wild ideas. Yes, Chade was capable of such deception, but my logic denied the possibility. Still, Dutiful had succeeded in his goal. He had stirred in me the anger I would have felt at being deceived for so long. "I'd probably hate them," I admitted. I met his eyes squarely as I added, "And that is yet another reason why I don't wish Nettle to know."

The Prince pursed his lips and then nodded briefly. It wasn't a promise to keep my secret, but more an acknowledgment of the complexities of revealing it. That was as much as he was going to give me. I hoped he'd leave the subject now, but with a slight scowl, he asked suddenly, "And why is Queen I-Doubt-It-Very-Much consorting with the Bingtown dragon? Is she in league with Tintaglia?"

"No, my prince!" I was shocked that he could think such a thing of her. "Tintaglia found her through stalking my thoughts, or so I believe. When we Skill strongly, I think the dragon can perceive us. Or, as you and Thick discovered, when you are dream-walking. Tintaglia knows something of who I am from the Bingtown delegation's visit to Buckkeep. We were careless of our Skilling then, and I think she marked me. She knows that I visit Nettle. I think that she seeks to threaten Nettle as a way to wring information out of me. She wants to know what we know about the black dragon, Icefyre. As all the young dragons that hatched in the Rain Wilds are feeble, he may be her only hope of a mate. And thus her only hope of perpetuating her kind."

"And we have no way to protect Nettle."

A note of pride crept into my voice as I said, "She has proven herself very capable against the dragon. She has defended herself, and me, better than I could have hoped to do."

He measured me with his eyes. "And doubtless she will continue to do so. As long as the dragon remains a threat that only comes into her dreams. But we do not know much of this Tintaglia. If, as has been suggested, the black dragon is her only hope of a mate, then she may become very desperate, indeed. Nettle may be able to defend herself in her dreams; how will she fare against a dragon alighting in front of her home? Will Burrich's home stand against a dragon's fury?"

That was an image I didn't want to consider. "She only

seems to find Nettle at night in her dreams. It may be that she does not know where Nettle actually is."

"Or it may only be that she chooses to stay close to the young dragons. For now. And that tomorrow night, or an hour hence, driven by desperation, she may take wing to Nettle's home." He set the heels of his hands to his temples and, eyes closed, rubbed them. When he opened his eyes, he shook his head at me. "I·cannot believe that you never considered this. What are we to do?" He did not wait for an answer, but turned to Chade. "Have we messenger birds aboard?"

"Of course, my prince."

"I will send a message to my mother. Nettle must be taken to safety in Buckkeep…oh, this is foolish. It would be far swifter to Skill to her, warn her of her danger, and send her to my mother." He lifted his hands to his eyes, rubbed them, and then gave a heavy sigh as he lowered them. "I'm sorry, FitzChivalry," he said, softly and sincerely. "If she were not in·danger, perhaps I could leave things as they are. But I cannot. I'm shocked that you would consider doing so."

I bowed my head. I received his words with a strange sensation, not anger or dismay, but a sense of the inevitable at last winning its way. A shiver ran over me, standing up the hair on my hands and arms. An image of the Fool, smiling in satisfaction, came into my mind. I glanced down to see that I was once more tracing his fingerprints on my wrist. I felt like someone who had just been maneuvered into making a fatal move in a game of Stones. Or like a wolf, brought to bay at last. It was too immense a change to regret or fear. One could only stand frozen, awaiting the avalanche of consequences that must follow it.

"FitzChivalry," Chade said after a moment or two of my silence. I could hear the concern in his voice and the kindly look he gave me almost hurt.

"Burrich knows," I said awkwardly. "That I'm alive. I sent him a message through Nettle, one only he would understand. Because I had given Nettle my word, and I needed Burrich to know that his son . . . that Swift was safe and with us. Burrich went to Kettricken. And, perhaps he spoke with the Fool, as well. So . . . he knows." I took a deep breath. "He may even be expecting something like this, a summons to the court. He must suspect that Nettle has the Skill. How else would she have received knowledge of Swift's safety from me? He was King's Man to Chivalry. He knows what the Skill is. Would that Chivalry had not sealed him off from it. Would that I could touch minds with him, now. Though I do not think I would have the courage . . ."

"Burrich was King's Man to Chivalry?" Dutiful rocked back in his chair, balancing it on the two back legs. He looked from one of us to the other in consternation.

"He loaned Prince Chivalry strength for Skilling," I confirmed.

Dutiful shook his head slowly. "Another thing that has never been mentioned to me." He crashed his chair back down onto the deck. "What will it take?" he demanded angrily. "What must happen here, to rattle all the secrets out of you two?"

"That wasn't a secret," Chade said heavily. "Only a bit of ancient history, long forgotten as it seemed of little import to the present. Fitz, you are sure that Burrich is sealed?"

"Yes. I tried to get through to him any number of times. I've even tried to borrow Skill strength from him, that time in the mountains. Nothing. He's opaque. Even Nettle has tried to get into his dreams, and she cannot. Whatever Chivalry did to Burrich, he did thoroughly."

"Interesting. We should try to rediscover how Chivalry sealed him. If ever we need to eliminate Thick's Skill as a threat, that might be one way to do it. Seal him." Chade spoke the words in his considering way, with no thought that anyone might find them offensive.

"Enough!" the Prince snapped at him, and we both

flinched, surprised at his intensity. He crossed his arms on his chest and shook his head. "You two sit here like puppeteers and consider from afar other peoples' lives and how you will manipulate them." He swung his gaze slowly from Chade to me, forcing both of us to meet his eyes. He was young and vulnerable, and suddenly wise as prey in facing us. "Do you know how frightening you are sometimes? How can I sit here and look at how you have shaped Nettle's life, and not wonder what kinks you have knowingly put in mine? You, Chade, speak so calmly of sealing Thick to the Skill. Must not I wonder, would they join their strengths and do that to me, if I somehow became a threat to their plans?"

I was shocked that he grouped us together so, and yet, chilling as his words were, I could not deny them. Here he was, on his way to a quest he did not desire to win a bride he had not chosen. I dared not look at Chade, for how would the Prince interpret our exchanging a private glance just then? I looked at my brandy glass instead and, lifting it between two fingers, rocked the liquid, and then swirled it, as so often I had seen Verity doing when he pondered something. Whatever answers he might have glimpsed in the dancing liquor, they eluded me.

I heard the slow scrape of Chade's chair as he pushed it back from the table, and ventured a glance that way. He stood, older than he had been ten minutes ago, and slowly walked around the table. As the Prince twisted in his chair to look up at him, puzzled, the old assassin went ponderously down on one knee, and then two, before him. He bowed his head and spoke to the floor.

"My prince," he said brokenly. And then, "My king you will be. That is my only plan. Never would I lift a hand to harm you, no, nor cause others to do so. Take from me now, if you will, the oath of fealty that others will only formally swear to you when you are fully crowned. For you have had it from me since the moment you were birthed. Nay, from the instant you were conceived."

Tears stung my eyes.

Dutiful put his hands on his hips and leaned forward. He spoke to the back of Chade's head. "And you lied to me. 'I know nothing of this Nettle and dragon.' " His mimicry of Chade's innocence was excellent. "Isn't that what you said?"

A long silence ensued. I pitied the old man's knees on the floor. Chade drew a deep breath and spoke grudgingly. "I don't think it's fair to count it as a lie when we both know I'm lying. A man in my position is sometimes supposed to lie to his lord. So that his lord can speak truthfully when asked what he was told about a subject."

"Oh, get up." There was both disgust and weary amusement in the Prince's voice. "You convolute the facts until neither of us knows what you are talking about. You could swear fealty a thousand times to me, but if tomorrow you thought a good purging would aid me in some way, you'd slip me an emetic." He stood up and held out a hand. Chade took it and Dutiful drew him to his feet. The old assassin straightened his back with a groan, and then came around the table to take his seat again. He seemed unchastened by either the Prince's blunt words or the failure of his own dramatics.

I was left wondering what I had just witnessed. Not for the first time, I realized how different the relationship was between the old assassin and this boy and what it had been like between us when I was growing up. And that, I thought, was the answer in a nutshell. When Chade and I sat and talked, we sat and talked as tradesmen do, unabashed by the dirty secrets of our business. We should not speak like that before the Prince, I decided. He was not an assassin, and should not be included in our more nefarious enterprises. We should not lie about them to him, but perhaps we should refrain from rubbing his nose in them.

Perhaps that was what he had been reminding us about. I shook my head in quiet admiration. Kingliness was blossoming in him, as naturally as a hound pup exploring a trail. Already, he knew how to move us and use us. I did not feel demeaned by that, but reassured.

Almost immediately, he took that comfort from me. "FitzChivalry, I expect you to speak to Nettle tonight when she dreams. Tell her it is my command that she go to Buckkeep Castle and seek asylum with my mother. That should convince her I am who I say I am. Will you do that?"

"Must I phrase it like that?" I asked reluctantly.

"Well . . . perhaps you can modify it. Oh, tell her whatever you like, so long as she goes to Buckkeep immediately and understands that the danger to her is real. I will write a brief message to my mother and send it by bird, just to be sure all understand that this is not to be disputed." He stood, heaving a great sigh. "And now I am going to sleep, in a real bed behind a closed door instead of displayed on a plank in a common room like a choice game trophy. I can't remember when I've been this tired."

I was glad to leave the cabin. I took a turn about the deck. The wind was fresh, Risk swept the sky ahead of our ship, and the day was fine. I could not tell if I dreaded or anticipated the task before me. Dutiful had not said that I must tell Nettle she was my daughter. Yet sending her to Buckkeep Castle was setting her on the path to that knowledge. I shook my head. I no longer knew what I hoped for. I knew one thing I dreaded, however. The Prince's words about Tintaglia had shaken me. Had I been too serene about Nettle's ability to foil the dragon? Could the beast know where she lived?

The day passed slowly for me. I checked on Thick twice. He remained in his bunk, his face turned to the wall, insisting he was sick. In truth, I suspected he was becoming accustomed to sea voyages despite himself. When I told him he didn't seem sick to me and perhaps he'd enjoy coming out on deck, he nearly succeeded in making himself puke on my feet with his wild retching. Instead, he went off in a fit of genuine coughing, throaty and deep, and I decided I was wiser to leave the little man in peace. On my way out, I "accidentally" clipped my shoulder on the door-frame. Thick laughed.

Nursing my new bruise, I went out on the deck. Out on the foredeck, I found Riddle with a square of canvas and a handful of beach pebbles, trying to teach the Stone game to two of the crewmen. I left that unsettling sight, and found Swift with Civil. His cat had climbed one of the masts and they were trying to persuade him to come down, much to the annoyance of our captain and the amusement of several Outislanders.

Risk lighted in the rigging just out of the cat's reach and teased him, with partially uplifted wings and squawks, until Web came to order her to cease and aid in getting the cat down.

And so the day went, and the dreaded and longed-for nightfall came. I returned to the cabin I shared with Thick. Swift had brought him his dinner, and the empty dishes on the floor seemed to indicate his appetite was intact. I stacked them and set them aside, only to stumble over them a moment later. A low chuckle from Thick was the only sign he had witnessed my clumsiness. When I offered him good night, he ignored me.

He had the sole bunk. I lay down in my blankets on the floor and spent a good amount of time trying to find enough calmness to approach sleep and that suspended place between sleep and wakefulness where I could dream-walk. It was wasted time. No matter how I sought Nettle, I could not find her. It worried me enough that I could not sleep, but made fruitless forays into dream-walks for most of the night. But the more I looked for her, the more she wasn't there.

In the darkness of the stuffy little cabin, I told myself that if something had befallen Nettle, surely I would know of it. We were Skill-linked. Surely she would have cried out to me if she had been in danger. I consoled myself that my daughter had blocked me from her dreams before; and she had been irritated with me for "allowing" the Prince into our shared place the last time we had visited. Perhaps this was my punishment from her. But, as I lay in the darkness and stared at black, it came to me that the last time I had seen Tintaglia, the dragon had claimed she could block me from Nettle if she chose to. What had the dragon said to Nettle? "You are quite alone, if I decide you are." Where was my daughter right now? Trapped in a nightmare, tormented by a dragon? No, I promised myself. Nettle had shown she could competently defend herself there. I cursed the logic Chade had taught me, for it said that then the dragon, to gain what she wanted, would shift the battlefield to one more to her liking. Such as physically hunting down my daughter.

How fast could a dragon fly? Fast enough to get from the Rain Wild River to Buck in a single night? Surely not. But I did not know, I could not be sure. I shifted on the wooden floor and struggled with the short blankets.

When morning came at last, I rose, sandy-eyed, and lurched to my feet. Somehow I tangled my feet in the blankets and slipped, banging my shins. Thick appeared to sleep through my cursing. I left the cabin and went directly to report to the Prince. He listened in grim silence. Neither he nor Chade told me how foolish I had been to leave my daughter defenseless against a dragon in the name of protecting her. The Prince merely said, "Let us hope she is only angry with you. The bird flew yesterday. And as soon as he reaches Buckkeep, my mother will not be slow in sending for Nettle. I told her the danger was great, and not to waste time. We have done all we can, FitzChivalry."

It was a pale comfort. When I was not imagining the dragon feasting on Nettle's tender flesh, I was imagining Burrich's reaction to a company of Queen's Guard sent to his home to fetch Nettle back to Buckkeep Castle. I passed the voyage in a misery of suspense with little to distract me save Thick's sullen and subtle revenges on me. The second time I scraped my knuckles reaching for the doorknob, I turned on him.

"I know you're doing this, Thick. I don't think it's fair. It's not my fault you are on this voyage."

He sat up slowly, swinging his bare legs over the side of his bunk. "Then whose fault is it, huh? Who made me come on this boat, when I'm going to die from it?"

I saw my error. I could not tell him I was only doing the Prince's bidding. Chade was right. In this, I had to take the blame. I sighed. "I brought you onto the ship, Thick. Because we need your help if we are going to slay the dragon." I put all the warmth and excitement into my voice that I could muster. "Don't you want to help the Prince? Don't you want to be part of the adventure we're having?"

He squinted at me as if I were crazy. "Adventure? Puking and eating fishy food? Going up and down, up and down, all the time? Going around people who wonder why I'm not dead?" He crossed his stubby arms on his chest. "I heard adventures in stories. Adventures have golden coins and magic and beautiful girls to kiss. Adventures aren't puking!"

At the moment I was inclined to agree with him. As I left the cabin, I stumbled over the doorstep. "Thick!" I remonstrated.

"I didn't do it!" he claimed, but he laughed all the same.

The little ships flew over the white-tipped waves, and the winds favored us. Even so, the voyage seemed interminable to me. By day I tried to oversee Swift's lessons and be sure that Thick was not neglected without too many minor injuries to myself. By night, I struggled to reach my daughter, and found nothing. By the time we put into port at Zylig, I felt a tottering wreck and possibly looked as bad. Web came to stand beside me at the railing as I watched our approach to the town.

"I won't ask you your secrets," he said quietly. "But I'll

offer to help you bear whatever it is you're bearing, in any way I can."

"Thank you, but you've already eased much of it. I know I've been impatient with Swift these last few days, and that you've been helping him with his lessons. And I know too that you've visited Thick often and kept boredom away from him. That's as much help as anyone can give me right now. Thank you."

"Very well, then," he said regretfully, and patted me on the shoulder and left.

Our stay in Zylig dragged for me. We spent our nights in the stronghouse there, and I spent many of my days there also. Thick's cough lingered still, but I do not think he was as sick as he claimed to be. Tedious as it was for me to linger near his sickroom, I still judged it to be for the best, for on the two occasions I did persuade him to venture outside, the looks he received were not kindly. Thick was like a crippled chick in a flock of healthy birds; any excuse would have sufficed to peck him to bits. He did not feel kindly toward me, and yet I was not comfortable leaving him alone. Although he did not ever ask me to stay with him, whenever I left the chamber he was in, he would find an excuse to follow me, or to call for me a few minutes later.

The first time that Web came at Chade's suggestion to spend time with Thick, I thought it was the old man deliberately throwing us together. But then Chade summoned me and sent me out in the evening, garbed as an Outislander, right down to the owl tattoo he hastily marked on my cheek. With paint and pitch he put a twisting scar in my lower lip to explain my taciturn ways and guttural speech. He gave me enough Outislander coin to sit and drink their miserable beer in their overheated taverns for an evening. After that, I went out several more times, each time dressed as a trader from another clan. Zylig was a major trading town; no one remarked on an unfamiliar face in a noisy inn. My function was to sit and listen to gossip and tales. The negotiations with the Hetgurd had stirred all sorts of interests. Outislander bards were tipped well to sing every song they knew of Aslevjal and Icefyre, and many a family tale was traded to impress cronies around the inn fire. I listened well, and distilled gossip and legend down to common factors likely to be true.

There was definitely something frozen in the ice of Aslevjal Island, but it had been almost a generation since anyone had seen it clearly. Men told their fathers' stories of visiting the island. Some had camped on the beach and trekked over the glacier for a glimpse. Others had visited at the lowest tides of the years, when the retreating waters bared an under-ice passage on the south side of the island. By all accounts it was treacherous, for once one was in channels walled with blue ice, it was easy to become lost or to miscalculate the time and tides and stay too long. Then the returning sea trapped the unwary, never to release his bones. For those wise and strong and sly enough, the under-ice tunnel led to a huge cavern, where one might speak with the trapped dragon and beg a boon of him. Some had received prowess as hunters, others luck with women, and others had won fecundity for their mothers-houses. So the tales went.

They spoke too of leaving an offering for the Black Man of Aslevjal. Some spoke as if he were a hermit, others as if he were a spirit guardian of the dragon. All agreed he was dangerous, and that it was wise to mollify him with a gift. Some said raw red meat was the best offering; others contended his goodwill could be purchased with packets of tea herbs, bright beads, or honey.

Twice I heard the island mentioned in connection with the Red Ship War. There was less talk of this; few dwell long on tales of wars that were not gloriously won. I gathered that during the war, Kebal Rawbread and the Pale Woman had wished to establish a stronghold on Aslevjal. No one spoke of why, but many captured Six Duchies folk had been borne there, to work out the rest of their days

as slaves. It seemed that Rawbread had made slaves too of
the kin of any Outislanders who opposed his war. They had
been Forged by him, and carried off to Aslevjal Island,
never to be seen or heard from again. Thus the island had
gained an aura of shame and misery that vied with its legendary dragon. Few wished to make a pilgrimage there to
prove their mettle anymore.

All of these things I held in my mind, and reported
them in detail to both Chade and Dutiful. In late-evening
talks, my old mentor and I tried to see how these things
might help or hinder us in our quest. Sometimes I felt we
only discussed these nebulous rumors because there was so
little that we knew for certain.

Dutiful had two long meetings with the Hetgurd, each
lasting several days. The end result of them was that they
had set the terms of our dragon hunt as if it were some sort
of wrestling or shooting contest. What had Chade chewing
his tongue was that the Boar Clan had arranged this negotiation and bound us to it without consulting him at all. Although I did not witness it, I heard that Arkon Bloodblade
was surprised when the Prince, with cold courtesy, expressed dismay at the terms.

"We cannot change what he agreed to for us," Chade
told me grimly. "But it was worthwhile to see Bloodblade's
face when Dutiful told him, 'My word is mine, and I am the
only man who can give it. Never again presume to speak
for me.'"

This he told me over brandy, in the same room in the
stronghouse we had originally occupied. Thick and Dutiful
were in the adjoining room. I could hear only the tone of
their conversation: Dutiful was calmly explaining why
Thick must board the ship the next day and Thick's voice
was varying from a child's whine to a man's angry refusal. It
did not sound as if it were going well. But, given what
Bloodblade had committed us to, I did not think any of it
could go much worse than it had.

Our nobles had done well in our absence, better than I

had expected. Trading alliances between varying clans and Six Duchies houses were already being formalized. Displaying their own insignia had seemed to distance them sufficiently from the Buck of the Farseers to allow them to approach the varying clans without prejudice. Dutiful dined with his nobles almost every night, and each evening seemed to bring news of more trade negotiations. If the Prince was able to present a dragon head to the Narcheska, we would have succeeded in our goal. The Six Duchies and the Out Islands would be so tied together with marriage and trade that future wars would not profit anyone.

But the Hetgurd seemed determined it would not be easy for us. The Farseer Prince would be allowed to challenge the dragon, but the Hetgurd had set the rules for the confrontation. When we departed for Aslevjal, we would not be taking the Prince's Guard with him, but only a set number of warriors. Dutiful's Wit coterie took up most of that count, and so far he had refused to consider Chade's suggestion that he leave his Witted allies and take hardened fighters instead. As Dutiful had challenged her, the Narcheska would be accompanying us. We assumed that meant Peottre as well, and perhaps a few warriors from Narwhal or Boar clans, though their help had not been promised to us. A boat selected by the Hetgurd would transport us to Aslevjal. It would also transport the six Hetgurd representatives, who would see that we adhered to their rules. They would be warriors, selected from six different clans other than Boar or Narwhal clans. They would be allowed to defend themselves, if the dragon threatened them, but otherwise not harm him or assist us in any way. What we took with us would be limited to what the ship could carry, and once we were ashore, we'd be carrying it on our backs.

"I'm surprised they didn't specify the Prince must fight the dragon in single combat."

"They came close to it," Chade said sourly. "He is supposed to be the first man to challenge the beast. And it was strongly suggested that he should attempt to deal the death blow, if there is one. They are warriors enough to know that in the heat of a battle, no one can say which blow will actually do the deed. One of their bards will be accompanying us, as witness. Just what we needed." He scratched a whiskery cheek wearily. "Not that we are greatly concerned about any of that. As I've said from the start, I think this is more a case of digging something out of the ice than battling any living creatures. I had looked forward to having a larger workforce for that part of this business." He coughed slightly and looked mildly pleased with himself as he said, "But perhaps I have something that will serve us as well as the extra men would have."

"How many men is Dutiful allowed?"

"Twelve. And we make up the count of them far too quickly. You and me, Web, Civil, Cockle, Riddle, Thick, Longwick, and four guardsmen." He shook his head. "I wish Dutiful would consider leaving at least Civil and Cockle here. Two more seasoned warriors can make all the difference in a situation."

"What of Swift? Is he staying here, then?" I could not decide if I felt relief or uneasiness at the thought.

"No, we'll take him. But as he's a boy yet, he doesn't count toward our quota of warriors."

"And we leave tomorrow?"

Chade nodded. "Longwick has spent the last week gathering provisions for us. Most of what we brought of Six Duchies victuals has been used; I'm afraid we'll be eating the local provender. He has sorted through what we had and acquired what we need for a party of twelve. I've already warned him that there will be a cat to feed as well as the rest of us. We will all carry weapons, regardless of whether we've been trained in them or not. An axe for you?"

I nodded. "And one for Swift. He has his own bow and arrows, but as you said before, an axe for chopping ice may be more to the point."

Chade sighed. "And that is where my invention runs

out. I have no idea what we'll be facing, Fitz. We'll have food and tents and weapons and some tools. But beyond that, I've no idea what we'll need." He poured himself a stingy dollop of brandy. "I'll not deny that I take pleasure in knowing that Peottre is just as dismayed by all this as I am. He and the Narcheska will be accompanying us. Bloodblade is coming on the ship, but I don't think he's staying for the dragon-slaying." He smirked sarcastically as he called it that, doubting it would be any such thing. "It's damnably inconvenient all round, this giving a task the rules of a contest. They've limited us to two message birds as well, but to be used only to summon the ship back when we are ready to leave the island. They'll be in the keeping of our chaperones."

His words pushed my mind in another direction. "Do you suppose the bird you sent has reached Kettricken yet?"

He gave me a pitying look. "You know there's no way for us to tell. Wind or storms, a hawk . . . so many things can delay or stop a bird. A message bird flies only toward its home and mate. There is no way for Kettricken to send word back to us." Delicately he added, "Have you thought of trying to reach Burrich?"

"Last night," I replied. To his lifted eyebrow, I replied, "Nothing. I felt like a moth battering at a lantern glass. I can't reach him. Years ago, I used to be able to catch glimpses of them, of Molly and Burrich. Not a mind-to-mind touch, but . . . well, it's no use. That's gone. I suspect that Nettle was my focus for it, though I did not see through her eyes."

"Interesting," he said softly, and I knew he was squirreling away that bit of information for possible future use. "But you cannot reach Nettle?"

"No." I boxed the word in, refusing to let any emotion ride on it. I reached across the table and picked up the brandy bottle.

"Go easy on that," Chade warned me.

"I'm nowhere near drunk," I retorted irritably.

"I didn't say you were," he responded mildly. "But we haven't much left. And we may want it more on Aslevjal than we do here."

I set the bottle down as Dutiful came back into the room. Thick trailed him, a sullen look on his face. "I'm not going," Thick announced as he came in.

"Yes you are," Dutiful responded stubbornly.

"Not."

"Are."

"Enough!" Chade interjected as if they were seven-year-olds.

"Not!" Thick breathed as he sat down with a thump at the table.

"Yes you are," Dutiful insisted. "Unless you want to stay here all by yourself. All alone, with no one to talk to. All by yourself, just sitting in this room until we come back."

Thick thrust out his chin, lower lip, and tongue all at once. He crossed his short thick arms on his chest and cast Dutiful a measuring glance. "I don't care. Not alone, anyway. I'll just talk to Nettle. She'll tell me stories."

I sat up with a jolt. "You can talk to Nettle."

He glared at me, as if he had just realized that in needling Dutiful he had given something away to me. He swung his feet. "Maybe. But you can't."

I knew I could not afford to lose my temper with him, or push him too hard.

"Because you are stopping me from talking to her?"

"No. She just doesn't want to talk to you." He measured me as he said this, perhaps to see if this idea bothered me more than the thought that he could block me from her. He was right. It did. I sent a tiny, private plea to Dutiful. *Find out for me. Is she safe?*

Thick's eyes flickered from me to Dutiful and back again. The Prince kept silent. He knew as well as I did that we had been caught Skilling. Anything he said to Thick right now would be suspect. And the little man had not been pleased with Dutiful to begin with. I picked at that thought. "So. You're not going with us when we leave, Thick?"

"No. No more ships."

It was cruel. I did it anyway. "Then how are you going to get home? Going on a ship is the only way to get home."

He looked doubtful. "You aren't going home. You're going to that dragon island."

"To start with, yes. But after that, we're going home."

"And you'll come back here and get Thick first."

"Maybe," Dutiful conceded.

"Maybe, if we are still alive," Chade embroidered. "We had been counting on your help. If you stay here and we go on without you..." The old man shrugged. "The dragon may kill all of us."

"Serve you right," Thick replied darkly. But I thought we had put a crack in his resolve. He seemed to be thinking as he sat scowling at his pudgy hands clasped at the table's edge.

Chade spoke slowly and consideringly. "If Nettle is telling Thick stories to keep him company, then I don't think she is in any great danger, Fitz."

If he had hoped to provoke a comment from Thick, he failed. The little man gave a disgusted *hmph* and settled back in his chair, arms crossed firmly on his chest.

"Let it go," I suggested softly to all of them. When I tried to think why Nettle might be so angry with me as to break off all contact, there were far too many reasons. Yet, I told myself sternly, to know she was alive and angry with me was preferable to thinking that a dragon might have decimated her and her family. I longed for certainty about the situation, and knew I would not get it. In my heart, I wished speed to the messenger bird we had sent. If Nettle must be angry, let her at least be angry in a safe place.

Little else was said that evening. Three of us went over our packing, and Chade spent time muttering worriedly over a cargo manifest. Thick made a great show of not packing. At one point, Dutiful began to gather up Thick's clothes and stuff them into a bag, but when Thick dumped it out on the floor again, they both left them there. They were still there when we all went to bed.

I did not sleep well. Now that I knew Nettle was purposely ignoring me, I could find and feel the shape of her barrier. More annoying was knowing that Thick was observing me as I groped, and taking pleasure in my inability to break through it. If he had not, perhaps I would have made a more serious effort to get into Nettle's dreams. Instead, I gave it up and tried to slide into true sleep. Instead, I had a restless night of brief dreams of all the people I'd hurt or failed, from Burrich to Patience, with the most vivid ones being of the Fool's accusing stare.

We arose before the sun the next morning. We broke our fast in near silence, with Thick in a simmering sulk, waiting for us to entreat or order him to move. By tacit consent, none of us did. What brief words we shared were spoken past him. We loaded up our individual bags. Riddle arrived to help us carry our gear. Chade let the guardsman take his pack but Prince Dutiful insisted on carrying his own. And we left.

∽   ∽   ∽

Riddle walked a step behind Chade, carrying his pack. Longwick and the other four guardsmen followed us. I did not know any of them well. Hest, a youngster, I liked well enough. Churry and Drub were close friends and seasoned warriors. All I knew of Deft was that he lived up to his name when the dice were in his hands. The rest of the guard would be left behind with our nobles, and our diminished party was to form up on the docks. As we walked through the cobbled streets, I asked, "And if Thick doesn't come after us, what then?"

"Leave him," Dutiful replied grimly.

"You know we can't," I pointed out, and he grunted in reply.

"I could go back and drag him along," Riddle offered doubtfully. I winced to think of that, and Chade shook his head mutely.

It might come to that, I observed privately to them. *I can't do it, because his Skill can knock me to my knees. But someone unSkilled and insensitive to Thick's power might be able to force him physically. Look at the times when other servants mistreated him, taking his coins. Of course, we'd have to deal with his anger about that in the days to come, but at least he would be with us.*

Let's wait and see, the Prince replied grimly.

As we neared the docks, people grew more numerous, until we realized a crowd had gathered to watch our departure. The *Tusker* had been loaded since yesterday, and awaited only our boarding and the morning turn of tide to depart. There was a strange mood amongst the Outislanders. It was as if they had turned out to watch a competition of champions, and we were not the favored ones. No one hurled rotten vegetables or insults, but the knowing silence was almost as hard a pelting. Closer to the ship, our own nobles had gathered to wish us farewell and good luck. They clustered about the Prince, wishing him well, and as I waited obediently behind him, it struck me how little they realized of his quest and what it might mean. There was good-natured joking with him, and hearty wishes for good fortune, but none of his nobles looked particularly worried for him.

As we boarded, with still no sign of Thick, my heart sank and my belly knotted with fear. We could not leave him here alone, no matter how annoyed Dutiful might be with him. There was not just the fear of what he might do in our absence, but my worry over what might be done to him, stripped of the Prince's protection. Would the Six Duchies nobles care much what became of a half-wit lackey in Dutiful's absence? I leaned on the railing, and stared over the head of the crowd milling on the docks, up to the stronghouse. Web came to lean beside me. "Well. Looking forward to the voyage?"

I smiled bitterly. "The only voyage I'm looking forward to is the one that takes us home."

"I haven't seen Thick come aboard yet."

"I know. We're still waiting for him. He was reluctant to get on another boat, but we're hoping he'll come on his own."

Web nodded slowly and sagely to that, and then wandered off. I stood, fretting and chewing the side of my thumb.

Thick? Are you coming? The ship will leave soon.

Leave me alone, Dogstink!

He flung the name with intense anger, so that I almost smelled the image he hurled at me. On the edges of his fury, I could feel his fear and hurt that we would so abandon him. Our departure had agitated and worried him, but I still suspected his stubbornness would win out.

Time and tide wait for no man, Thick. Decide soon. Because when the waters are right, the ship has to leave. And after that, even if you let us know you've changed your mind and want to come, it will be too late. We won't be able to come back for you.

Don't care. And with that, he slammed his walls so tight that it felt like a physical slap. I was left feeling that I'd made the situation worse.

Too soon, I saw the final preparations for our departure begin. A late arrival of cargo from the *Maiden's Chance* came on board. There were a number of small casks, and I smiled, wondering if Chade had recalled a stash of brandy on the other ship. Weaponry and tools came aboard as well, as we filled up the odd corners of the hold with anything Chade thought might be helpful. But finally, it was time to depart. Well-wishers who had followed the Prince on board were leaving. The Hetgurd representatives arrived with their gear. All the last-minute cargo was stowed out of the way and the small boats that would tow us out of the harbor and into open water were manned and waiting. Web came to stand anxiously beside me at the railing.

"I don't think he's coming," I said quietly. I felt ill. "I'll go and speak to the Prince. We'll have to send someone after him."

"I already have," Web replied grimly.

"You did? What did Prince Dutiful say?" I hadn't seen any of our guardsmen depart from the ship.

"Oh. No, not spoken to him," Web replied distractedly. "I sent someone. Swift." More to himself, he muttered, "I hope this isn't an unfair test. I think he can do it. But perhaps I should have gone myself."

"Swift?" Mentally I measured the growing lad against Thick, and shook my head. "He'll never be able to do it. Thick is awkward, but he's surprisingly strong when he's roused. He might do the boy harm. I'd best go after them."

Web seized me by the arm. "No! Don't go! Look. He's done it. They're coming now!"

The relief in his voice was as if Swift had conquered some monumental task. Perhaps, in all justice, he had. I watched them come, the short man trudging along by the slight boy. Swift carried Thick's pack and held his hand protectively. That shocked me, but even at this distance, the boy's attitude was visible. His head was up and wary, and he met the eyes of every man they passed, as if challenging him to mock the half-wit or delay their progress. It was as great a display of courage as I'd ever seen, and my evaluation of the boy soared. It would have taxed my will to lead Thick by the hand through that throng, yet on they came. As they got closer and I could see the expression on Thick's face, I realized that more was at work here than simply sending a boy to bid him come.

"What is it?" I asked Web in a low voice.

"It's the Old Blood. As well you know." He spoke softly, not turning to look at me. "It works best Wit to Wit as you would say. But even on those who have no Wit, one can exert a drawing closer. I've had Swift practicing. Today was a sterner test than I wished to set him. But he's done well."

"Yes. I can see that he has." There was a look of trust on Thick's face as the boy led him toward the boarding plank. He hesitated there, halting. Then Swift spoke softly to him and, still holding the little man's hand, led him up the gangway. I debated before next I spoke, but curiosity dragged the words from me. "I know how to push someone away from me with the Wit. I think I've always known how to do that. But how do you draw someone closer with it?"

"Ah. Well. The pushing-away might come by instinct. Usually the drawing-close does, too. I would have thought you knew it; now I understand why you've never used it with Thick." He cocked his head and looked at me appraisingly. "Sometimes, the things you don't know baffle me. As if you'd forgotten or somehow lost some part of yourself." I think he saw the uneasiness that his words woke in me, for he suddenly changed his tone and spoke in generality. "I think all creatures use that drawing force, to some extent, with their young or when they wish to attract a mate. Perhaps you've used it without realizing it. But, you see, that is why a man given this magic should make an effort to learn about it. To be aware of how he's using it." He let a silence fall, then added, "I'll offer again to teach you what you need to know."

"I have to go and see to Thick and get him settled." I turned hastily to go.

"Yes. I know that you do. You've many tasks and duties, and I won't claim to know all that you do for our prince. I'm sure that at any moment of the day, you can find some reason to be too busy for this. But a man makes time for what is important in his life. So. I'll be hoping that you'll come to me. This is the last time I'll make the offer. Now it's up to you to accept it."

And before I could hurry away, he turned and quietly left me there. Overhead, Risk lifted off from our mast with a lonely cry that rode down the wind. Lines were tossed, the planks were pulled in, and in the little boats men leaned to their oars to pull us away from the docks and out to where the wind could catch us. I promised myself that I'd find the time, today, to speak to Web about privately learning about my magic. I hoped I didn't lie.

But nothing is ever simple. With the Narcheska, her father Arkon Bloodblade, and her uncle Peottre on board, most of Dutiful's and Chade's social time was taken up with one or another of them. I had little private conversation with either of them. Instead, as before, I was confined to Thick's companionship. As he was miserable, he saw no reason why I shouldn't be also. The minor bruises and scrapes he had given me on the previous voyage were renewed, and there was little I could do about it. Putting up walls against his subtle Skill-influence would have reduced my awareness of Chade and Dutiful. So I endured.

To make it worse, the water we crossed was nasty. We battled currents and tides that always seemed to oppose us. For two days of our journey, our ship rocked badly and Thick was genuinely seasick, as were Cockle, Swift, and Civil. The rest of us ate little and moved from one handhold to another. I glimpsed a very pale Narcheska taking a walk on the deck on Peottre's arm. Neither of them looked as if they were enjoying themselves. The slow days crawled by.

I did not find an opportunity to discuss the Wit with Web. From time to time, I would recall my intention, but it always seemed to come to me at a moment when a dozen other things wanted my attention. I tried to pretend it was circumstance that kept me from approaching him. In reality, I could not name what held me back.

Our destination finally appeared on the horizon. Even from a distance, Aslevjal looked a dismal place. It is among the northernmost of the Out Islands, a toothy isle of grim visage. Summer never really triumphs there. The milder days of summer's brief visit are not sufficient to melt the snow of the previous winter on its mountains. Most of the island is locked under the glacier that squats within the pronged hold of its peaks. Some say it is actually two islands, bridged by the ice of the glacier, but I do not know the basis for that belief. Low tide bares black sand beaches around it like a dreary skirt. A barren and stony stretch of beach and a bit of cliff are permanently exposed at one end of it. In other places, rocky stretches thrust up through the glacier's pale coat. I could not tell if the cloudiness around the island was the ice smoking in the sunlight or snow blown by the continuous north wind we were encountering.

Our approach was slow as both wind and water seemed to oppose us. We tacked painfully toward the island. I was at the railing when Dutiful and the Narcheska, accompanied by Chade and Peottre, came out to look at the island. Dutiful scowled at it. "It does not look like a place where any creature would willingly reside, let alone something the size of a dragon. Why would a dragon be there?"

The Narcheska shook her head and spoke softly. "I do not know. I only know that our legends say that he is there. So, thither we must go." She pulled her wool cloak more closely around her. The wind seemed to carry the island's icy bite to us.

In the afternoon, we rounded a headland and turned back toward Aslevjal's sole bay. Our spies' reports had told us it was a deserted place, with the remnants of a dock and a few stone structures tumbling into disrepair. Yet I glimpsed a patch of bright color on the exposed cliff above the beach. Even as I stared at it, trying to resolve what it was, a figure emerged from it. I decided it was a tent or some sort of shelter. A man came to stand on the tip of the cliff. His black-and-white hooded cloak struggled and flapped around him. He lifted no hand in greeting, but only stood there and awaited us.

"Who is that?" Chade demanded of Peottre when the lookout's cries to the captain had brought them back onto the deck.

"I do not know," the man replied. Dread was heavy in his voice.

"Perhaps it is the legendary Black Man of the island," Bloodblade suggested. He leaned forward avidly, studying the solitary figure on the bluffs. "I've always wondered if the tales were true."

"I don't want to find out," the Narcheska commented quietly. Her eyes were huge. As we drew closer to the bay, the railing became crowded as we all stared toward our destination and the solitary ominous figure that awaited us there. It was only when we dropped anchor in the bay and our small boats prepared to ferry us and our supplies to shore that he moved. He came down to the beach, and stood at the high-tide line. Even before he threw back his hood, something in my heart turned over. I felt sick with dread.

The Fool awaited me.

chapter XIII

ASLEVJAL

"Forging" was perhaps the most effective weapon that the Outislanders turned against us during the Red Ship War. The technique for "Forging" is still unknown to us, but the dreadful results are all too familiar to many. The name comes from the village of Forge, an iron-mining town that first suffered this horrendous attack. Red Ship raiders attacked in the night, killing or taking hostage most of the population. A "ransom note" to Buckkeep Castle demanded gold, under the threat of releasing the hostages. This made no sense to then King Shrewd, who declined to pay. The Red Ship raiders lived up to their threat, releasing their apparently unharmed hostages and sailing off into the night.

But it swiftly became apparent that, by some arcane magic, the villagers were no longer themselves. Although they knew who they were and what families they belonged to, they no longer seemed to care. Morality and ethics had been stolen from them. They thought only of satisfying their own immediate wants, and did not hesitate to steal, murder, and rape to do so. Some were "captured" by their families and vain efforts were made to restore them to themselves. None ever recovered.

> *Forging was a tactic used repeatedly during the war.*
> *It had the effect of leaving a resident, hostile army on our*
> *soil, made up of our own loved ones, at no emotional or*
> *financial cost to Kebal Rawbread and his raiders. Killing*
> *the Forged ones was a demoralizing and dehumanizing*
> *task that fell to our own folk. The scars remain to this*
> *day. The town of Forge has never been rebuilt.*
>
> ✎ FEDWREN'S "HISTORY OF THE RED SHIP WAR"

I was in the first small boat that touched the shore of Aslevjal, along with the other guardsmen. Moments later, the boat carrying Chade and Dutiful, the Narcheska, Peottre, and Arkon Bloodblade nosed into the sand. We stepped into the shallow water to seize the boat's gunwales, and on the next rising wave, we ran it up onto the shore so that its passengers could step out onto dry sand. The whole time, I was aware of the Fool standing on the lip of the land that overlooked the beach, watching us. He was still, but the cold wind seemed to speak for him. It whipped his cloak and long golden hair with a snapping, muttering sound. He had abandoned the face powder that had lightened his skin, as well as the Jamaillian cosmetic touches that had branded him a foreigner. The rich brown of his skin over the sculpted bones of his face and his tawny mane made him a creature out of a tale. The stark black-and-white of his garb erased every trace of indolent Lord Golden. I wondered if anyone besides Chade and myself had identified him yet. I tried to exchange a look with him, but he stared through me. He spoke only when the Prince stepped out of the boat onto the shore. He swept him a bow.

"I've hot tea waiting for you," he called down. His voice carried through the ceaseless hushing of the wind. That was all he said. Then he made a gesture toward his tent and turned his steps that way.

"Do you know him? Who is that?" Arkon Bloodblade demanded. His hand rested lightly on the hilt of his sword.

"I've known him for a long time," Chade replied heavily. "But how he came to be here, or why, I've no idea."

The Prince was trying not to gape after him. He sent me a glance but I looked hastily at the ground.

Was that Lord Golden? It was a genuine question from Dutiful. The change in the man's appearance was enough that he was uncertain.

No. Nor is it the Fool. But they are facets of whoever that is.

Stop being dramatic. This last from Chade, grumbled in annoyance to both of us. Aloud, he said, "He is no threat to us. I will deal with him. Guardsmen, remain here and assist with the unloading of the cargo. I want it all carried up above the tideline, and well secured against damp."

So neatly Chade banished me. He'd keep me separated from the Fool until he discovered what was going on. I thought of ignoring the order and following him up to the Fool's tent. Then Riddle gave me a nudge. "Looks like you'd better be ready to help them."

Thick was coming ashore in the boat with the Wit coterie. He had a white-knuckled grip on the side of the boat and his eyes were clenched tightly shut. Web had a hand lightly on his shoulder, but Thick was hunched against his touch. I sighed and went to take charge of him. Another small boat was putting out from the ship, bearing the warriors of the Hetgurd.

Evening was falling before all the cargo was removed from the ship and canvas securely roped over it. I'd had a quick look at the small casks that Chade had loaded at the last minute. They were not brandy. One was leaking a powdery substance. With both dread and anticipation, I recognized Chade's experimental powder for creating explosions. Was this why he had not more strenuously objected when the Hetgurd had deprived us of our manpower? How did he intend to use this stuff?

I pondered that as our temporary home took shape. Longwick was a good commander. He kept our small force,

Wit coterie and guardsmen alike, in steady motion. He chose a location on the highest clear ground the hill offered us, with a clear view of the surrounding area. Our tents were set up in tidy rows, a waste pit was dug, and the beach scoured for driftwood. Water was fetched from an icy stream of snowmelt that flowed from the glacier and past our camp. Hest, the youngest guard at about twenty, was put on general watch and Drub, a grizzled warrior muscled like a bear, was given the cooking duties. Deft and Churry were told to sleep now to relieve Hest later. Riddle was assigned to be at the Prince's convenience, shadowing him wherever he went. And as I expected, I was assigned to keep watch over the Prince's man, Thick. The Wit coterie members, nominally under Longwick's command now, were given lesser chores about the camp before he let them disperse to explore the beach. It was a strange experience for some of them, I am sure, especially for a young noble like Civil, but to his credit the lad did his work willingly and ceded Longwick the respect his position demanded. Several times I saw him cast a disapproving gaze toward the Fool's colorful tent, but he kept his reservations to himself. Chade and the Prince had accepted the Fool's hospitality, along with the Narcheska, Peottre Blackwater, and Arkon Bloodblade.

Thick chose to sit miserably hunched in the tent he would share with Web, Swift, and me. Not far away, our cook fire burned and Drub tended the simmering kettle that held our evening's porridge. I had set a smaller pot at the edge of the fire to heat water for tea. I foresaw that soon fuel would be a problem on this treeless island. I paced restlessly outside the tent, waiting for the kettle to boil, feeling like a tethered dog while the others roamed.

The Hetgurd warriors had set up their shelters in a separate row from ours, and brought ashore their own supplies. Each man had pitched his own small tent. I spied on them surreptitiously. These were not young warriors, but seasoned veterans. I did not know their names. I had been told that for this duty, their own names did not matter, but only their clan membership, and that was proclaimed in their tattoos. The Bear, hulking and dark as his namesake, seemed to be their leader. The Owl was a thinner, older man: their poet and bard. A Raven was as dark haired as his bird mentor, and as bright eyed. The Seal was a short, heavyset man who was missing two fingers from his left hand. There was a Fox who was the youngest of the group. He seemed petulant and unhappy at being on Aslevjal. The Eagle was a tall, rangy man of middle years. He was their watchman tonight, standing and keeping guard while the others sat cross-legged about their fire, eating and talking quietly. He caught me staring at him and returned my gaze expressionlessly.

I sensed no animosity from any of them. They had a duty to see that we adhered to the rules the Hetgurd had set for us, yet they did not seem opposed to our task. Rather they were like men awaiting some contest of champions. On the ship, they had mingled freely with us, and their poet had struck up an amusingly competitive friendship with Cockle. Now that we were ashore, they might set stiffer boundaries, but I doubted those would last more than a night or two. There were too few of us, and the landscape was too bleak.

Two slightly grander tents had been set up alongside the Fool's colorful one. The Narcheska and Peottre would share one, and Chade and the Prince had the other. I had seen little of any of them since we landed. The Fool had welcomed them to his tent, but I did not know what had passed there. Not so much as a Skill-hint had Chade or the Prince sent me. I'd helped to set up the larger tents beside the Fool's, but the low murmur of conversation from inside that structure had been as tantalizing and insubstantial as the wafting scent of spice tea.

Now, as evening asserted a slow dominance over the land, the Fool and Dutiful's Wit coterie were all on board the ship, enjoying the farewell meal with Arkon Bloodblade.

Neither he nor his Boar warriors would be staying with us. I wished I knew the logic of that. Was he disassociating the Boar Clan from a foolish Narwhal endeavor, or was it simply a matter of granting Peottre command of the quest? I scowled and kicked at the cold soil. There was too much I didn't know. I wanted to scout the area at least but Thick had steadfastly refused to reboard the boat, even when tempted with a sumptuous meal, remaining on the island to share our plain rations and useless sentry duty. Scuffing footsteps on the near-frozen earth turned my head. Riddle gave us a wide wave and a big smile as he approached.

"Exciting place, this. If you like snow, grass, and sand." He crouched down by the fire and held his hands out to it.

"I thought you'd gone back to the ship for the night, with the Prince."

"No. He dismissed me, saying he'd have no need of me there. And I was just as happy to stay. Standing about watching others eat is not my idea of entertainment. What occupies you this evening?"

"The usual. Keeping Thick company. I'm making him tea right now."

Riddle spoke quietly. "If you'd like, I can stay here and make his tea when the water boils. Might give you a chance to stretch your legs and explore a bit."

I received the offer with gratitude. Turning to our tent, I asked, "Would you mind if I took a short walk, Thick? Riddle will make the tea for you."

The little man pulled a blanket closer around his shoulders. "Don't care," he replied sullenly. He was hoarse from coughing.

"Well, then. If you're sure you don't want to come? If you got up and moved around a bit, you'd soon feel warmer. Truly, it isn't that cold here, Thick."

"Nnph." He turned his face away from me. Riddle nodded commiseration to me and, with a toss of his head, bade me leave.

As I walked away, I heard him say, "Come on, Thick,

buck up. Play us a tune on your whistle. That'll keep the dark at bay."

To my surprise, Thick took his suggestion. As I walked slowly away, I heard the tentative sounds of Thick's Mothersong. I literally felt Thick's attention focus on it, and felt an easing in the Skilled hostility he had been sending me. It was like putting down a heavy pack. Even though the tune was frequently broken as Thick stopped to catch his breath, I hoped that his interest in playing indicated he was recovering. I wished I could likewise soften the discomfort I felt hovering between the Fool and me. Not a word had we spoken, nor even stood within a speaking distance, and yet I felt his outrage like a cold wind on my skin. I wished he had stayed ashore tonight in his tent; it would have been a good time for quiet words with him. But he had been invited to share the farewell meal aboard the ship. I wondered who had issued the invitation: the Prince, because he was intrigued, or Chade because he wished to keep the tawny man where he could watch him.

I walked the beach in the deepening twilight, and found it much as Chade's spy had reported it. The tide was retreating, baring more of the beach. Barnacle-encrusted pilings leaned at odd angles in a double row projecting from the swallowing water, hinting at a one-time dock. At some time, there had been stone cottages along the shore, but they had been tumbled into ruin. Knee-high walls remained, in a row like tooth sockets in an empty skull. The rest of the stone walls were scattered both inside and around the structures. I frowned. The destruction was too complete. Had this little settlement been raided by someone intent on not just killing the inhabitants but on making it uninhabitable? It was as if someone had tried to obliterate it.

I climbed the low bluff above the shingle of the beach. A rocky meadow of tufty grasses greeted me, shadows creeping up from the roots as the color left the day. There were no trees, only tough and twisted bushes scattered through it. It might be summer, but the glacier crouching above us breathed winter year-round. I waded through the ungrazed grasses, the seed heads whispering against my leggings. Then, without warning, I came to the edge of a quarry. Had it been any darker, I would probably have tumbled right into it and taken a bad fall. I stood on the edge and looked down. A few feet down, the sod sides gave way to black stone walls, thinly veined with silver. A shiver ran over me. Memory stone had been mined here, just as it had in the immense quarry in the mountains where Verity's dragon had been carved from the stuff. The water that had collected in the bottom of the quarry was a second, starless night sky below me. Two large stones, the clean angles of their lines proclaiming the handiwork of men, were bare islands jutting from the water.

I backed slowly away from the edge and walked back to the camp. I wanted to speak to Chade and the Prince, but felt a greater urge to discuss this with the Fool. Standing at the edge of the bluff, I looked out over the bay at the *Tusker* rocking gently at anchor, the landing boats clustered around her. Tomorrow, she would depart, taking Arkon Bloodblade back to Zylig. The rest of us would remain here and begin our search for the dragon frozen beneath the glacier. The waves lapping methodically at the beach should have been soothing. Instead, the sea seemed relentless, intent on slowly devouring the land. I had never felt that way about it before.

A large animal breached briefly near the shore. I froze, trying to make out what it was. It vanished beneath the next wave, and was again bared as the wave retreated. In the moments it was exposed, it was perfectly motionless. I squinted at it, but it was a black shape against black water, and I could make out nothing save that it was as large as a small whale. I scowled at the idea of a creature that large in shallow water. It should not be this close to shore, unless it was dead and washed up by the tide. My Wit-sense told me that a low level of life still lurked in it, in a fuzzy, unfocused way. Yet I did not sense the defeat or resignation of a dying creature.

I stood on the beach, and watched as the falling waves gradually revealed not only the amorphous shape of a large animal, but several large black blocks of stone, gleaming wet in the moonlight. I forgot all else as the waves slowly lost their grasp on the shore and fell back. The creature that was gradually exposed was familiar in an eerie way. Once one has seen a supine dragon, one never forgets it. My heart began to beat faster. Could this be the answer to our riddle?

I think I've found your dragon, Dutiful. Make an excuse to come on deck and look toward the shore. It's being exposed as the tide retreats. There's a stone dragon here, in the tide zone.

My Skilling had not been confined to Dutiful. It reached Chade, as well. In a short time, Dutiful and the rest of the dinner gathering came out onto the deck. They stared toward shore, but I doubted they could see the creature as clearly as I did, for the lantern light on the ship now silhouetted it for me. And in that extra light, and with the retreat of the waves, I saw my error. What had appeared to be a dragon were actually several huge blocks of stone, set close together but not quite touching one another. I saw his head on his front paws, his neck and shoulders, three segments of back and hind legs, and then a number of dwindling sections of tail. Fused together, they would have formed a dragon. Exposed on the wet sand, they reminded me of a child's puzzle blocks.

Is this our dragon? Did she want the stone head taken back to her home hearth? I asked.

Linked to Dutiful, I saw him point and ask a similar question of Peottre. But it was Arkon Bloodblade who laughed and shook his head. My link with Dutiful conveyed Bloodblade's answer as clearly as if I stood on the deck beside them. "No, no, what you see there was one of the Pale Woman's follies. She had her slaves quarrying stone here. She insisted that only the black stone from this island could be ballast for her white ships. It looks as if some slaves were put to carving it, too. For what, we'll probably never—"

"It's late." Peottre's voice cut in abruptly. "And you sail with the morning tide, brother. Let us have one more good night of sleep on board, in beds, before we face the hardship of the island tomorrow. I recommend an early bed for you, too, Prince Dutiful. Tomorrow we must start early on the trail to where the true dragon is said to await us. It will be an arduous trip. Rest is wisest for all of us."

"A wise suggestion from a wise head. I'll wish you good luck and good night, then." Arkon acceded quickly to Peottre's suggestion.

Well. That was neatly turned, Chade observed as the men dispersed from the deck. *Arkon must have realized he was telling tales that Peottre didn't wish shared. See what else you can discover there, Fitz.*

How did the Fool react to that tale? I demanded of him.

I really didn't notice. Chade's reply was brusque.

How did the Fool get here? Why is he here? Why are you keeping him where I can't talk to him? I could no longer suppress the question, nor completely conceal my annoyance that they had not yet shared the answers with me.

Oh, don't sulk. Chade dismissed my irritation. *He's told us little enough. You know how he is. Let it ride until tomorrow, Fitz, when we're all on shore together and you can quiz him as much as you wish. Doubtless he'll be more open with you than he is with us. As to why I've kept him close to us, it's more to keep him away from the Hetgurd warriors than from you. He's already revealed that he will do all he can to persuade us not to slay the dragon. And he's been sufficiently puzzling, charming, and mysterious to intrigue Peottre and Bloodblade, but I think the Narcheska still fears him. She does not meet his eyes.*

The Prince broke in on Chade's thoughts. *Initially the Hetgurd men thought he was some kind of a cheat on our part, a secret ally we'd smuggled in. When we pointed out that we had no way of knowing the terms that the Hetgurd would set for us, they admitted that didn't seem likely.*

How did the Narcheska and Peottre react to his claim that he would help the dragon? I demanded of them both.

Chade's thoughts seemed well considered. *They reacted strangely. I expected that Peottre and the Narcheska would resent him, but Peottre seems relieved, almost glad to see him here. As for me, I am grateful he said no more than he did. And I'm asking you to keep any discussions you have with him out of earshot of Peottre or the Narcheska. If they discover how long you have been friends, they may well think that you are opposed to our quest as well.*

There was a warning for me in Chade's thought, a slight testing of my loyalty. I ignored it. *I'll wait and talk to him privately,* I told Chade.

Yes. You will. His words fell between confirmation and command.

The folk on the ship were already dispersing toward their beds. I glanced back at our camp. It looked as if almost everyone had already gone to bed. The fire had burned low. I hadn't even eaten my share of the evening rations. Hot porridge would probably seem a treat before this quest was over, but for now it did not entice me.

The sea had retreated enough now that I could walk around the entire dragon without getting more than ankle-wet. I knew I'd regret my soggy shoes in the morning, but if there was something to discover about this stone creature, now was my best opportunity. No Skill coterie had carved this being, but the minions of the Pale Woman. I thought I knew why. I had long suspected that Regal and Skillmaster Galen had sold off portions of the Skill library. Had Kebal Rawbread, the war leader of the Outislanders during the Red Ship War, come to possess them? Had he and his ally, the Pale Woman, attempted to create dragons of their own to battle our Six Duchies? I was almost certain it was so.

I came close to the gleaming wet stone, noticing that neither seaweed nor barnacles clung to it. It was as clean and black as the day it had been shaped. Gingerly, I set a hand to it. It was cold, wet, and hard, and it hummed with Wit under my touch. Just as the drowsing stone dragons had. And yet it was different. I could not decide how until I touched the adjacent block. It too harbored that hidden seething of life. And yet the two were different things. Cautiously, fearing some arcane trap, I ventured toward them with my Skill. There was nothing there. I ran my hand along the wet surface where neither seaweed nor barnacle clung. And then there was suddenly something, a confusion of voices lifted in agitation, and then nothing again.

I turned my head slowly, and then realized how foolish that was. The Skill-furor I had sensed was not a conversation muffled by distance or a barrier. As gingerly as if I caressed a hot coal, I slid my fingertips over the wet stone before me. Again, I received a confused impression of many voices, all speaking at once, at a great distance from me. I wiped my hand reflexively down the front of my shirt and stepped away. Uneasily, I examined the thought that had come to me.

This was memory stone. Although quarried on this island, it was unmistakably the same sort of stone that Verity had used to carve his dragon. All of the dragons I had encountered in the Stone Garden in the Mountain Kingdom had originally been carved from this stuff, some by Skill coteries seeking to store permanently their memories and being; others, perhaps, by Elderlings. The dragons I had seen had been shaped as much by the memories and thoughts poured into them as by the tools the carvers had wielded. Those dragons had eventually completely absorbed the people who had created them. I had witnessed Verity's passing into his dragon. It had demanded all of his memories and life force as well as Kettle's to satiate and saturate the stone, waking it to life. The old woman had sacrificed herself as willingly as Verity had. She had been the last of her Skill coterie, a lone woman who had outlived her time and her monarch, but returned nonetheless to serve the Farseer line. Kettle's extended years and Verity's passions had been barely enough to rouse the dragon. I knew that well. Verity had taken a bit of me for his dragon, and later I had impetuously fed other memories into the Girl-on-a-Dragon carving. I had felt the pull of a stone dragon's voracity. It would have been easy to let Girl-on-a-Dragon take all of me; it would have been a release, of a sort.

Or perhaps an imprisonment. What happened to a stone dragon that did not have enough memories to take life and flight? I had seen what had happened to Girl-on-a-Dragon. She had remained there in the quarry, mired in unformed stone. In her case, I did not think it had been lack of memories, but her creator's lack of willingness to surrender individuality to the whole. The leader of the coterie who had carved her had tried to hold back, and isolate her memories into the figure of the Girl astride the dragon rather than release them into the sculpture as a whole. Or so Kettle had told me, when I asked her why that statue had not taken life and flown away. She had told me the tale to warn me away from Verity's dragon, I think; to help me understand that the dragon would not be content with any less than all of me.

I wished Kettle stood beside me now, to tell me this dragon's story. But I suspected I knew it. The stone had not been shaped as a whole, but worked in blocks. Nor had the carvers put their own memories into the stone. Instead, I suspected that I stood by a dark memorial to the Red Ship War. What had become of the memories and emotions of the Forged folk? The disjointed clues came together in this disjointed creature. Blocks of memory stone had been ballast in the holds of White Ships. Had the Pale Woman and Kebal Rawbread learned the magic of waking a stone dragon from a purloined and sold Skill scroll? What had stopped them, then, from creating an Out Island dragon to ravage the coast of the Six Duchies? Had they lacked the willingness to sacrifice their own lives to give life to their creation? Had they thought they could create a dragon from the memories they had stolen from the Six Duchies folk?

Here before me was the evidence of their failure to grasp the fundamental reason why a coterie might journey to Jhaampe and beyond to create a stone dragon. They could steal the memories of Six Duchies folk and imprison them in stone forever. But they could not Forge from those memories the singleness of purpose that was required to breathe life into a dragon. Not even all the coteries that set out for the Mountains succeeded in that goal. Some had taken Mountain women as wives and settled down to end their lives in love. Others who had gone to carve their dragons had failed. It was not an easy task, even for a single-minded Skill coterie. A dragon filled with the memories of divergent folk forced into a single stone, a dragon born of terror and anger and hopelessness, would have been an insane creature if ever they'd managed to wake it.

Had that been what Kebal Rawbread and the Pale Woman had intended?

There had been a time when plunging myself into a stone dragon had been very tempting, indeed. I could still recall my hurt that Verity had excluded me from the creation of his. In retrospect, as a man grown, I could understand why. Sometimes, when Nighteyes had still been alive, I had toyed with the idea. What sort of a dragon could we two have made? I had wondered. And now, willing or no, I was part of a coterie again. Yet I had never considered that at some time Dutiful, Thick, Chade, and I might wish to make a dragon of ourselves. We were a coterie born more of chance than intent. I could not imagine us finding the devotion and purpose to carve a dragon, let alone the will to simultaneously end our human lives and memorialize our joining in a dragon.

I turned and slowly walked away from the shaped

stone. I tried not to wonder about the Forged memories imprisoned in it. Was awareness imprisoned in the rock? If
not, exactly what was it?

I reached again for Dutiful and Chade. *I think I've
found some of the memories and feelings Forged away from Six
Duchies folk during the war.*

What? Chade was incredulous.

When I had explained, a long moment of aghast horror lingered between us. Then Dutiful asked hesitantly,
Can we free them?

*For what purpose? Most of the people they belonged to are
long dead. Some may have died at my hand, for all I know. Besides, I have no idea whether it can be done, let alone how.* The
more I thought on it, the uneasier I became.

Chade's thought was full of calm resignation. *For now,
we must leave it as it is. Perhaps after we have dealt with this
dragon, Peottre will be more willing to share what he knows. Or
perhaps we can arrange for a Six Duchies ship to come here,
quietly, and take home what is ours.* I felt his mental shrug.
Whatever it is.

❦   ❦   ❦

The cook fire near our tent had burned down to a faded red
eye in the night. I poked at it a bit, pushing in the last nub
ends of the firewood, and woke a pale flame or two. There
was lukewarm tea in my weary kettle and a scraping of porridge in the bottom of the pot. Riddle himself had gone, either to watch duty or to his own blankets. I crawled into
the tent's low entry and found my sea chest by touch in the
dark. Thick was a shape huddled beneath blankets. I tried
not to wake him as I rummaged for my cup. I was startled
when he spoke into the darkness. "This is a bad place. I
didn't want to be here."

Privately, I agreed with him. Aloud I said, "It seems
wild and barren to me, but no worse than many a place I've

been. None of us really wanted to come here. But we'll make the best of it and do what we must."

He coughed, and then said, "This is the worst place I've ever been. And you brought me here." He coughed again, and I could feel how weary he was of coughing.

"Are you warm enough?" I asked guiltily. "Do you want one of my blankets?"

"I'm cold. I'm cold inside and outside, just like this place. The cold is eating me. The cold will eat us all to bones."

"I'm going to warm up the tea. Do you want some?"

"Maybe. If there was honey?"

"No." Then, I gave way to temptation. "There might be. Here's my blanket. I'll put the tea on to get warm again while I see if anyone has any honey."

"I suppose," he said dubiously.

I tucked the blanket around him. It was the closest we had been to one another in days. "I don't like it when you're angry at me, Thick. I didn't want to come here, or to bring you here. It was just a thing we had to do. To help our prince."

He made no reply and I sensed no lessening in his coldness toward me, but at least he didn't strike out at me. I knew who might have honey. I left the tent and headed up the hill to where the larger tents for the Narcheska and the Prince had been pitched. Between them, and slightly above them, the Fool's multicolored dwelling billowed softly in the wind. Amid the deepening darkness, it seemed to gleam from within.

I hesitated outside it. The flap was tied securely shut. Once before, when I was a boy, I had entered the Fool's private chambers, uninvited. I had lived to regret that intrusion, not only because it posed more mysteries than it solved, but also because it had made a small crack in the trust we had shared. Without ever uttering them, the Fool had taught me well the rules that governed retaining his friendship. He answered only the questions he wished to answer about himself, and any prying by me was regarded as an infringement of his privacy. This included efforts by me to find out anything about him other than what he had chosen to tell me himself. And so, I paused there, in the wind sweeping past me from the island's ice pack, and wondered if I wanted to take this chance. Were there not already too many cracks in our much-tested friendship?

Then I stooped and untied the door flap and slipped inside.

The tent was made from a fabric I didn't know, some sort of silk perhaps, but so tightly woven that no breath of air stirred inside it. The glow had come from a tiny brazier, set in a small pit dug in the floor of the chamber. The silk walls caught the heat it generated and held it well, while the light seemed multiplied by the sheen of the fabric. Even so, it was not bright inside the tent: rather it was lit warmly and intimately. A thin rug covered the rest of the floor, and a simple sleeping pallet of wool blankets was in one corner. To my wolf's nose, it smelled of the Fool's perfumes. In another corner was a small kit of clothing and a few significant items. I saw that he had brought the featherless Rooster Crown. Somehow it did not surprise me. The feathers from Others Island, the ones I had thought would fit in the crown, were in my sea chest. Some things are too significant to leave unattended.

He had a meager supply of foodstuffs and a single cooking pot; obviously he had relied on our arrival for his long-term survival. I saw no sort of weapon amongst his things; the only knives were ones suitable for cooking. I wondered what ship he had found that had dropped him off here, and why he had not supplied himself better. Among his victuals I found a small pot of honey. I took it.

There was no scrap of paper to leave him a note. All I had wanted to say to him was that I had not wanted him to come here to die, and that was why I had done what I could to thwart him. In the end, I moved the Rooster Crown into the middle of his bed. I turned the simple wooden circlet in my hands, the dim light catching for an instant in one rooster's sparkling gem eye. The Fool would know that I had set it there, and why. I did not want him to think, even for a moment, that I had tried to conceal this visit. As I left, I retied the tent flap with my knots.

Thick had almost dozed off, but when I poured tea and added sweetening to it, he sat up to take the mug from me. I had been generous with the honey. He drank off half of it, and sighed heavily. "That's better."

"Do you want more?" It would leave little for me, but I wouldn't lose any opportunity to regain his favor.

"A little bit. Please."

I sensed a lowering of the wall. "Give me your mug, then." As I poured and sweetened the brew, I said, "You know, Thick, I've missed us being friends. I'm really tired of your being angry with me."

"I am, too," he admitted as he took the mug from me. "And it's harder than I thought it would be."

"Is it? Then why do it?"

"To help Nettle be angry with you."

"Ah." I did not let myself dwell on that, but only commented, "She probably made it sound like a very good idea."

"Ya," he drawled sadly.

I nodded slowly. "But she's all right, isn't she? She's not hurt or in danger?"

"She's angry. 'Cause she had to leave her home. Because of the dragon. So that was scary for me, and I told her she could come here, because we're going to cut a dragon's head off. But she said, don't worry; my papa will kill the dragon for me. So, she's safe."

My head swam. It was definite then. The message bird had reached Buckkeep, and the Queen had acted swiftly to take Nettle into shelter. And someone, Kettricken or Burrich, had told her that she was my daughter. Why they had done it now or how they had phrased the words suddenly did not matter. Nettle knew. And she was angry with me, but had still found a way to send me a message through Thick, that told me that she knew who I was, and that I had believed I had done what I did to protect her. All the things I felt seemed to conflict with one another. I wondered if she knew all of what I was, or only that there was another man who had fathered her, and by his bloodline exposed her to danger. Had anyone explained the Skill to her? Did she know I was Witted? I had wanted to tell her myself that I was her father, if I had ever decided that she must know. Would it have been easier for her, or harder? I did not know. There was so much I did not know, and so much that she did not know about me.

Then another aspect of it washed over me like a wave. If Nettle was in Buckkeep, and if she would open her mind to our Skilling, we could communicate with the Queen and tell her all that was going on. A strange little thrill washed through me. Prince Dutiful had a working coterie now.

I came out of my reverie when Thick handed the mug back to me. It was empty. "Are you a little warmer now?" I asked him.

"A little," he admitted.

"So am I," I told him, but it had nothing to do with how cold the night was. There are moments that leave a man's heart pumping so strong and free that no chill can touch him. I felt alive and completed, vindicated in all I had done. Thick huddled back into his bed, my blanket still clutched around his shoulders. I didn't mind. I spoke cautiously. "If Nettle comes to your dreams tonight, will you tell her—" That I love her. No. It was far too soon to say such words, and when I spoke them, she should hear them first from me. Now they would be empty utterances from a shadow father she had never met. No. "Will you tell her to let the Queen know we are all well, and safely arrived at the island?" Deliberately I kept the message a general one. I had no assurance that the dragon Tintaglia could not listen in on what passed between Thick and Nettle.

"Nettle doesn't like the Queen. She is too nice, with lots of pretty skirts for Nettle and pretty smells and shiny things. She isn't Nettle's mother! But she makes her stay close and only lets her out with a guard. Nettle hates that. And she's had enough of lessons, thank you very much!"

Despite my worries, I smiled. I did not like to think that Nettle would clash with Kettricken, but in retrospect I saw it as inevitable. It was the way Nettle's words came out in Thick's voice. And it was a relief that too many skirts and lessons were Nettle's greatest threat right now. I felt almost fatuously happy despite all the ways it would complicate my life.

Thick was going to sleep but I wished to think awhile longer. I went out to the dying fire, closing the tent flap behind me. I scraped the leftover porridge from the kettle and ate it. As last man to eat, it fell to me to clean the pot for tomorrow. I scrubbed it out with sand and seawater and never once felt the cold water or the rough sand. My thoughts were elsewhere. Would Kettricken have put her in my old room? Did my daughter now wear the jewels and garb of a princess? I poured what was left of the tea into my cup and dumped out the dregs from the pot. But when I went to sweeten my brew, I could not find the pot of honey in the dark. So I drank it as it was, thick and bitter and delicious with the change that had visited my life that night.

chapter XIV

THE BLACK MAN

*Just as a Skill coterie may use its talents to influence the
waking mind of others and persuade their target that
certain things are true, so a Skill dreamer uses his Skill
upon his own sleeping mind to create a world which is, to
him, as real as our waking one. The Skill dreamer in a
sense turns the Skill against his own thoughts. Whereas
most of us have no control over what we dream at night,
the Skill dreamer is more likely never to have experienced
random dreams and may even have difficulty in
perceiving what one would be like or that other people
dream in such a fashion.*

∼ "SKILL DREAMING"—SKILLMASTER SOLICITY

I slept well, without dreams of any kind, and woke to the
sound of the waves against the beach. Dawn had barely
found us, but already both guardsmen and Hetgurd warriors
were up and about. I splashed my face in the icy stream. The
incoming tide had covered the carved dragon, but now that
I knew it was there, I could feel it as a sort of Wit-humming
from beneath the waves. I glanced out toward the anchored
ships. I wanted to ask Web what he thought of the dragon,
and yet I felt guilty at the thought. I hadn't kept faith with

him; I hadn't come to allow him to teach me. Did I have the right to ask him to use his knowledge for my benefit, when I would not learn it for myself? I knew how I would react to Swift's behaving so. I grimly reminded myself that there was only so much time in a day, and of late every moment in mine seemed to have been spoken for.

I checked on the tent where Thick slept on. Coward that I was, I decided to leave him in peace. I wandered over to the guards' cook fire, where the porridge was just beginning to boil. Longwick had no immediate task for me. I glanced out at the anchored ships, but saw no signs of life there. They had probably stayed up late talking. I visited the quarry again. By the light of day, I thought I glimpsed bones and the round of a human skull under the rainwater, but the sides of the quarry were steep and I had no desire to investigate. Whatever had happened there had happened long ago. My own problems were more immediate. I drifted over to where the Hetgurd men had their tents. They were gathered outside them, and at first I thought they were having breakfast from a stone table. Then, as I ventured closer, I realized that the sporadic conversation was an ongoing argument. I halted where I was, making a show of scratching and stretching while gazing seaward. Then I went down on one knee as if adjusting my shoe, all the while listening closely. They were muttering their complaints to one another, so it was not easy to understand them. When I had heard enough to realize that they had left an offering for the Black Man at the traditional spot, on this stone table, and that it had not been taken, I stood up and ventured near.

With an oafish smile on my face and using my broadest Six Duchies accent, I asked them brokenly if they knew when the Narcheska's party might come ashore. A broad man with a stylized bear on his cheek told me that they would arrive when they arrived. I nodded pleasantly with the slightly unfocused look of a man who is not certain of what has just been said to him. Then, nodding at the stone table, I asked what they were having for dinner. I took three steps toward it before two men stepped in between the table and me to block my access to it.

The Bear explained to me that this was not a meal, but an offering, and that I should probably go down to my own fellows and eat with them, as they had no use for beggars here. I peered at him, my mouth movements echoing his as if puzzling out his words, and then smiled broadly and wished them all a good evening and left. I'd had my glimpse of the stone table. On it was a clay pot, a small loaf of dark bread, and a dish of salted fish doused in oil. It had not looked appetizing, even to my morning hunger, and I scarcely blamed the Black Man for leaving it untouched. Their distress over this apparent rejection was interesting to me. From their words, they had expected some island denizen to come and stealthily take the offering. That he had not worried them. These were hardened warriors, selected by the Hetgurd to be single-minded in their task. Most warriors I had been around were pragmatic about matters of religion and superstition. They might make a "good luck" toss of the salt, but only a few cared much for omens such as the wind catching it and blowing it aside. My evaluation was that these men had expected the Black Man to accept their gifts and, by that acceptance, signal his permission for them to be here. He had not, and that unsettled them. I wondered how much that would affect their attitude toward our quest.

As I walked back to my tent, I reflected that this belief of theirs indicated that in the past, someone or something had accepted such offerings. Was there someone actually living on the island; or was it more likely some creature like the robber-rat that Swift had wanted to befriend that had taken the food?

I found Thick waking. He seemed a trifle more kindly disposed toward me this day, and accepted my aid in getting himself warmly dressed. He had one coughing spell that left him red-cheeked and breathless. It troubled me more than I let show. Lingering coughs could take down large warriors, and Thick was neither big nor hearty. He had been battling this lung ailment too long, and now faced a time of living in a drafty tent in a chilly spring. But I said nothing of my worries to him as we walked over to the fire for our share of hot porridge and tea.

Riddle and the other guardsmen were in that bitter good humor that is typical of men facing a difficult and perhaps unpleasant task. They traded crude jests, complained about the food, and made disparaging remarks about our Hetgurd "nannies." Longwick sat a little apart from us and, when the food was finished, found tasks to occupy the others. He had accepted that my duties for the Crown were supervising Thick, and offered me no other chores. So I took the little man for a walk. He had no comments on the quarry or the icy stream, no observations on the blue glacier crouching above us. But as I deliberately led him on a stroll along the beach and past the submerged dragon, he shook his head and told me solemnly, "This isn't a good place." He looked around slowly and then added, "Bad things happened here. And it feels like it's now."

I would have liked to probe that comment, but he then lifted a stubby arm to point at the ships. "Here they come!" he cried, and he was right. The small boats, laden with passengers, were headed toward the shore. We stood and watched them come. Peottre, Bloodblade, and the Narcheska rode in one. Chade, the Prince, Civil, his cat, and Web were in the second. The Fool, Swift, and Cockle were in the last one. Cockle seemed in high spirits, explaining something with much hand-waving while Swift was grinning and obviously enjoying himself. I gave a small sigh and then smiled to myself. So swiftly had my Fool won them over with his charm. I wished he had not come; I feared his prophecies concerning himself. At the same time, I could not deny that I was glad he was here. I had missed him.

By the time the boats reached shore, Thick and I were

not the only ones waiting for them. Riddle and one of the other guardsmen ran Peottre's boat up beyond the waves' reach. Longwick and I did the same for the Prince's, and then the Fool's. He disembarked without even a glance that would betray he knew me. By the time everyone stood on the sand, the Hetgurd men surrounded Arkon Blood-blade. They made no attempt to lower their voices as they explained to him that the Black Man had not accepted their offering. In light of that, they suggested we should all recognize that our mission here was deeply offensive to him. The Narcheska should change her mind and release the Prince from his task.

I had known they were upset. I didn't realize it was that important to them, I added after I had Skilled to Chade and the Prince the morning's event at the stone table. Neither one glanced at me as I relayed my information. They waited courteously, standing well back from the discussion around Bloodblade and Peottre. The Narcheska herself stood apart from the men, staring out over the water. She looked as if she were carved from stone: determination and resignation were etched into her face.

The Black Man discussion continued, but I was distracted from it by the Fool. He had approached, chatting amiably with Cockle and Swift. The layered black-and-white of his garments put me so in mind of him in the days when he had been King Shrewd's jester that I felt my throat close. He glanced my way once, a mere flicker of his brandy eyes. Then I saw his attention snag on the conversation the Hetgurd guard was having with Peottre and Bloodblade. It was like watching a hunting dog stiffen to a scent. He focused himself on them and drew near, careless of whether it would be seen as rude.

The conversation had become an argument, and the Out Island tongue they used had become so swift and guttural with anger that I could scarcely follow it. Peottre stepped back from the group and crossed his arms on his chest. He turned his head sideways and looked away from them, but as he did so, he clapped one hand loudly on his sword scabbard. It was not a gesture that would have been used in the Six Duchies, but its meaning was still plain to me. If anyone wished to argue further with him, they'd argue blade to blade. The circle of Hetgurd men turned their eyes away from him, plainly rejecting the challenge. Instead, they closed around Bloodblade, who gestured wide his helplessness and then flapped an arm at his daughter, shrugging as if to say that the ways of all women were beyond any man's reasoning. That seemed to settle something.

The Hetgurd man with the bear tattoo stepped away from the others and advanced to the Narcheska. She did not look at him as he came though I am sure she was aware of him. Instead she looked out over the waters, past the ship to the horizon. The wind blew past her, stirring the edges of the hooded blue cloak she wore and tugging at her embroidered skirts. It lifted them enough to reveal her sealskin boots and the wool leggings tucked into them. She ignored the breeze's liberty as easily as she ignored the waiting Bear. He cleared his throat, but was forced to speak before she turned to him.

"Narcheska Elliania, I would have a word with you."

Even when she turned to look at him, her look was the only acknowledgment she gave him. He accepted it as permission to speak to her. His words were clear and formal, and I think he intended that all should hear and understand them. The Owl drew closer to them as they spoke, probably to witness their words for posterity. Bards do not believe in privacy.

"I am sure that you heard us speaking just now. But I shall state it plainly. Last night, we left out the offering for the Black Man, as is customary when visiting this place, for any reason. This morning it remained on the stone table, untouched. Long has it been said that no man can buy the Black Man's approval with gifts, but when he takes them, he gives you permission to risk your life here. This morning,

we knew that he did not even cede that much to us. Narcheska, we have come here with you, knowing already that the
challenge you gave your suitor was inappropriate. You did
not listen to us. Will you pay attention now to what the
Black Man himself has shown us? We are not welcome here.
Many of us expected him to be angry with you. We did not
expect he would withhold his permission even from those
who come to see that your challenge to the dragon is a fair
one. You place not just your husband and yourself in danger,
but all who are here. And should you achieve your end, we
now fear that the displeasure of the gods will fall, not just on
you, but on all who witness the deed."

I saw her blink, and perhaps the color in her cheeks
heightened. Only her stillness proclaimed that she listened
to him as she stared into the distance. He spoke on more
quietly but his words carried clearly. "Withdraw the challenge, Narcheska. Replace it, if you wish, with one more
fitting. Demand a whale's spear from him, or the teeth of a
bear, killed by him alone. Pit him against any creature that
is right and proper for a man to hunt, but let us all leave
this island and the dragon it protects. Icefyre is not for a
man to kill, Narcheska. Not even for love of you."

I thought he would convince her, right up to his last
words. But they were uttered with such disdain that even I
felt the sting of them. She did not turn her eyes toward him
as she spoke. "My challenge stands." She spoke those words
to the sea. But then she turned to face Dutiful and added,
"Because it must. For the honor of Narwhal Clan."

She spoke the last words almost as if they were an
apology, as if she regretted them but had to say them anyway. Dutiful gave a single slow nod, an acceptance of the
challenge and her assertion that it must stand. It was an act
of faith between them, and I think I perceived then what
Chade seemed to have known for some time; that if those
two could learn to go in harness, they would be a powerful
pair.

The Bear clenched his fists at his side, and thrust out

his jaw. The Owl nodded jerkily to himself, as if to fix the moment in his memory.

The Narcheska turned to Peottre and said, "Should not we be preparing to leave now? It is a long and arduous journey, I am told, to where the dragon is under the ice."

Peottre nodded gravely. "As soon as we have bidden your father farewell."

To me, it sounded like a dismissal; yet Arkon Bloodblade did not seem insulted, but relieved. "We must sail with this tide," he agreed.

"Witness!" the Bear shouted angrily. All turned to his cry. "Witness that if we die here, we who have come at the Hetgurd's request, witness that if we die here, then Clan Narwhal and Clan Boar owe our mothershouses blood-gold. For we are not here by our choice, nor do we seek this conflict. If we fall to the gods' displeasure, then do not let our families cry in vain for justice."

A silence fell after his words. Then, "Witness," Peottre conceded gruffly, and "Witness," Arkon Bloodblade echoed him.

I sensed an Out Island custom with which I was not familiar. Chade seemed aware of my confusion. I felt his uneasiness as he told me, *He has bound them both. Whatever disgrace or bad luck may come from our actions here will belong to the Boar and the Narwhal clans. The Bear has claimed everyone here as a witness to this.*

It seemed to me that the Bear was almost discomfited by how easily Peottre and Bloodblade had accepted his gambit. He clenched his fists several times, but when no one deigned to notice that, he turned and walked away from them. The Owl followed him. I suspected that they had expected a challenge that they could have settled with swords or fists, and that their concession had actually forced him and the other Hetgurd companions to proceed with their mission.

The process of bidding farewell to the Narcheska's father proceeded grudgingly after that. The formal farewells involved the Hetgurd men, Chade, the Prince, Peottre, and the Narcheska. The rest of us were left standing as informal witnesses. Thick was wandering idly about on the beach, overturning rocks and poking at the tiny crabs he disturbed there. I pretended to be maneuvering to keep an eye on him as I edged closer and closer to the Fool. He appeared to be aware of my efforts, for he walked a little apart from Swift and Cockle. When I stood within hearing distance of a soft word, I said quietly, "So. Despite all my efforts, you contrived to get here. How did you do it?"

Although we are of a height, he still somehow managed to look down coolly on me. There was stillness in his face that bespoke a great anger. I thought he was not going to speak to me. Then, "I flew," he said coldly. He stood, not looking at me, breathing quietly. I felt somewhat encouraged that he had not stalked away but wondered if that was merely because he did not wish to call attention to our speaking. I ignored his mockery of my question.

"How can you be angry at me? You know why I did it. You said that if you came here you would die here. So I arranged that you would not come here."

For a time, he was silent. We both watched Arkon Bloodblade pushed off in a small boat. Two of his Boar warriors took the oars and leaned into them heartily. Their expressions proclaimed that they were happy to be leaving this island. The Fool gave me a sideways glance. His eyes had darkened to the color of strong tea in a glass. Clean of powder and paint, his face was a smooth golden brown. "You should have respected that I knew what I had to do," he rebuked me.

"If you knew that I was going to my death, would not you try to stop me?"

It was the wrong question to ask him, and I knew that almost as soon as I had asked it. He stared out at the ship in the harbor where sailors labored with the anchor chain and the sails and spoke in a low voice, his lips scarcely moving. "On the contrary. Many times I have known that faith or your own stubbornness would endanger your life, but I have always respected your decisions to do so."

Then he turned and walked slowly away from me. Swift sent me an odd glance, then hurried off to follow him. I noticed Civil looking after them with an expression of distaste. I heard the crunch of footsteps on beach gravel, and turned to find Web approaching me. It was hard for me to meet his eyes. I still felt oddly guilty, as if I had insulted him by refusing his offer of lessons. If he felt anything of the kind, he concealed it well. He gestured after the Fool and Swift with his chin. "You know him, don't you?"

"Of course." The question surprised me. "He's Lord Golden, from Buckkeep. Didn't you recognize him?"

"No, I didn't. Not at first. It wasn't until Lord Chade called him 'Lord Golden' that I perceived any similarity. But even when I was told his name, I felt that I did not truly know him at all. Yet I think that you do. He is an odd creature. Can you sense him?"

I knew what he meant. The Fool had never left any impression on my Wit-sense. "No. And he has no scent."

"Ah." That was all he said, but I suspected that I had given him much to ponder.

I looked down at my feet on the gravelly sand. "Web. I'm sorry. I keep intending to find time to spend with you, but I never seem to manage it. It isn't that I'm not interested, or that I disdain what you have to teach. It just seems that so many things come between me and what I would like to be doing."

"Like now," he replied with a grin. He raised his eyebrows and looked at Thick. The little man was hunkered down beside a piece of driftwood that he had overturned. His attention on the sand fleas and small crabs he had exposed was so intense that he was ignoring the waves that were nearly lapping about his feet. If I didn't intervene soon, he would have wet shoes and spend the rest of the day in misery. I exchanged an understanding glance with Web, and hurried down the beach toward my charge.

Even before the ship was out of sight, Longwick was issuing orders to his men. With the casual precision of the veteran soldier, he set them to breaking up our provisions into manageable loads. From the number of packs he was preparing, it was obvious he expected all to share in the task of transporting our goods to our next campsite. Thick had left off poking about on the beach and now sat disconsolately in the door of our tent, a blanket draped around his shoulders. The day was not truly that cold. I wondered anxiously if he was starting to burn with fever again. I went to confer with Longwick.

"How far do we expect to journey today?" I tilted my head toward Thick to explain my concern to him.

Longwick followed my gesture and scowled worriedly at my concern. "I've been told it's a three-day journey to where the dragon is trapped in the ice. But I'm sure you know that such measurements of distance mean nothing. A one-day journey for a seasoned traveler with a light pack can be a three-day trek for a courtier with a full load." He lifted his eyes to scan the clear skies and then the icy peaks of the island speculatively. "It's not going to be a pleasant journey for any of us," he opined. "It's always winter when you're crossing a glacier."

I thanked him and left. The other men had moved to strike their tents, but Thick had not budged from ours. I tried to put on a pleasant expression, but my heart sank at the thought of the task before me. If he had hated me for putting him onto a ship, how was he going to feel about me after I had dragged him on a hike across a glacier? "Time to pack up, Thick," I informed him cheerfully.

"Why?"

"Well, if we're going to slay the dragon, we have to go to where the dragon is."

"I don't want to slay the dragon."

"Well, we won't actually be the ones to slay the dragon. That will be up to the Prince. We'll just be there to help him."

"I don't want to go-oo." He dragged the word out mournfully. But to my relief, he stood and stepped out of the tent as if expecting me to take it down immediately.

"I know, Thick. I don't want to go hiking through all that snow and ice, either. But we have to. We're King's Men, and that is what we do. Now, before we take down the tent, we both have to dress more warmly. Shall we do that?"

"We don't have a king."

"Prince Dutiful will be King someday. And when he is, we'll still be his. So, we are King's Men, even now. But you can say you're a Prince's Man if you like that better."

"I don't like snow and ice." Grudgingly, he moved back into the tent and looked about it helplessly.

"I'll get out your things," I assured him, and proceeded to do so. I've been many things in my days, and serving as valet to the little man did not strike me as so strange as it might have at one time. I laid out his clothes and then stuffed him into them. It was like dressing a large child. He complained of his sleeves dragging up inside the second shirt I put on him, and then his boots were too tight with the extra stockings. By the time I had him dressed, I felt sweaty and smothered myself. I sent him outside, warning him to stay away from the water, as I added a layer to my own clothes and then repacked my and Thick's belongings.

I had to smile when I realized that I was dreading the hike because of the way the cold always made my scars ache. Because of my recent Skill-healing, I had no scars now, I reminded myself; at least not the bone and muscle deep ones that seemed to twist pain deep into me. Those had been replaced with superficial markings on my skin to pretend they were still there. I rolled my shoulders, proving to myself that my flesh no longer pulled against a deep scar in my back. It was a good feeling, and I found myself grinning as I dragged our packed gear out of the tent and then dismantled the tent itself.

I hauled our things to where Longwick was supervising

the parceling out of packs. A single small tent was still pitched there. The commander had decided to establish a cache of supplies here on the beach, and was discussing with Chade whether he should leave one or two men to guard it. Chade wanted to leave only one, in order to have a larger force with us. Longwick was courteously but stubbornly holding out for two. "For there is an unsettling feel to this island, sir. And we both know that guardsmen are prone to superstition. The Hetgurd men have been telling tales of a Black Man; and now my own men are muttering that, yes, they might have glimpsed a mysterious shadow lurking at the edge of the camp last night. A man alone would be prey to such thoughts. Two will play dice and talk and keep a better eye on our supplies."

In the end, Longwick won his point and Chade conceded to leaving two men behind. Churry and Drub would remain with our cache. That settled, Chade turned to me and asked, "Is the Prince's man Thick ready for the journey, Badgerlock?"

"As ready as I could make him, Lord Chade." *But he's not happy about it.*

Are any of us? "Excellent. I've a few extra items that we shall want when we reach the dragon. Longwick has divided them for easier carrying."

"As you will, Lord Chade." I bowed to him. He hurried off as Longwick issued me a small cask of Chade's explosive powder to add to my pack. I groaned to myself, for it proved heavier than I had expected. We were taking only two of them with us. The other one had been entrusted to Riddle's load. The rest would remain with our cached supplies.

One man would have been ready to leave shortly after Bloodblade's ship had sailed. But when one readies a company of men to travel anywhere, it is a different tale. The sun had reached noon before we were all packed and assembled. I noticed that the Fool struck his elaborate pavilion rapidly, with no help from anyone. Whatever it was made from, it packed down to an amazingly small load. He shouldered it all himself, and I would have been surprised, save that I had always known that he was much stronger than his slight frame would suggest. He moved amongst us but was not a part of either party. The Hetgurd men regarded him with the wariness that many warriors reserve for the God-touched. They did not disdain him, but felt it wiser neither to notice nor be noticed by him. The other guardsmen seemed to feel he was no business of theirs, and certainly did not want to be recruited to help carry his possessions or otherwise serve him. Cockle watched him curiously from afar, scenting a story but not strongly enough to be drawn in yet. Only Swift seemed uninhibitedly fascinated by the Fool. He dropped his own pack to the ground and perched on it while he chattered away at him. The Fool has ever had a clever way of talking, and Swift's ready laughter seemed to feed his wit. Web watched the two interact with something like approval on his face. It was only then that it dawned on me that this was the first time Swift had shown an easy friendliness toward anyone. I wondered how the Fool had melted his reserve, even as I noticed Civil regarding them with distaste. When Civil glanced up to find my eyes on him, he looked away, but I could sense his uneasiness bubbling just under the surface. I wondered if I could find a way to have a quiet word with him and calm his fears. Plainly he recalled his first impression of Lord Golden when we had guested at his home. It was easy to divine his worries now: he thought that the Fool was easing the lad toward seduction. I wanted to intervene before Civil muttered a word of that suspicion to anyone, for I suspected the Outislanders would be far less than tolerant of such behavior, God-touched or not.

Longwick distributed metal-shod walking staves to all of us, an item I would never have thought of packing. But it soon became apparent that Peottre was the real source of this equipment when Chade summoned all of us to listen to him before we left the beach.

Both he and the Narcheska were as heavily burdened

as any among us. She waited alongside three sleds, also provided by Blackwater, which were already loaded with much
of our supplies. Her long outer coat was all of snowy white
fox. She wore a bright little cap, woven of many colors, and
her glory of black hair was tucked completely out of sight
under it. Her loose boots were soled with scraped walrus
hide and the tops were of deerskin with the hair left on.
Leather bindings laced them around her legs to the knee.
But for the solemn look on her face, she looked as if she
had been prepared as a snow bride. Peottre was bulky as he
lumbered beside her in black wolf and bearskin trousers.
More than any Witted one I had ever known, he looked
like a shape-changer out of a beast-tale. His many layers of
clothing had enlarged him to an almost laughable size. Yet
all were solemn as he spoke to us, anxious to catch every
word.

"I know where the dragon sleeps," he said. "I have
been there twice before. Yet, even so, it will be difficult for
me to lead you there. On a glacier, knowing where something is does not mean I know the way to it. Glaciers are
not like stone and earth, which remain the same year after
year, and the glacier we shall cross here is among the most
restless in the world. Glaciers sleep and they walk, they
groan to wakefulness, cracking wide their yawns. And then
they sleep, and the blowing snow bridges over the gaping
crevasses, hiding their danger from all but the most wary
walker.

"To fall into one is little different from being swallowed by a snow demon. Down you will go into darkness,
and that is an end of you. We will mourn you, but we will
go on."

His eyes passed slowly over all of us as he said this, and
I was not the only man who suppressed a shiver.

"Follow me," Peottre went on. "Not just in where I go,
but in my very tread. And even then, do not trust the ice
beneath you. Once we venture out onto the glacier's face,
probe every step you take. One man, two men, three men

may pass safely right in front of you, and then the crust may betray you. Probe ahead with your staff, before every step you take. You will grow weary of doing this. But stop doing it only if you have also grown weary of your life." Again, his measuring glance passed over all of us. Again he nodded. Then he said, "Follow me."

And with no more ado, he turned and led us up the beach. The Narcheska fell in right behind him. Behind her went the Prince and then Chade. Lord Golden claimed the next spot and no one challenged him for it. Then went the Wit coterie, entrusted with one sled, and the Hetgurd witnesses, and finally Longwick and Hest pulling the second sled, and Deft and Riddle pulling the third. I came second to last, with Thick stumping stolidly along behind me. I had shifted part of his pack's load to mine, but left him enough of a burden not to hurt his pride. I soon regretted it, and vowed that on the morrow he would walk unencumbered. Even in the best of times, his stubby legs and wide girth would have made this trek difficult for him. Burdened with both a pack and a nagging cough, he simply could not keep the pace Peottre set. By the time we reached the lip of the glacier, there was a gap between the main party and the two of us. The diligent probing of each step began, and I thought that would slow them enough that we would catch up. I had not taken into account that Thick had taken Peottre's warnings deeply to heart. He prodded the ice before him at every step as if he were spearing fish. He was soon panting with the effort, but my offers to probe for both of us were stoutly refused.

"I don't want to be swallowed by an ice demon," he told me sulkily.

Can you see our path? Dutiful Skilled back to me.

Very clearly. Don't be concerned for us. If we need you to wait for us, I'll let you know. At least all the probing Thick is doing is keeping him warm.

Too warm. Too much work! Thick complained.

"Just tap with the stave. You don't have to stab the ground."

"Yes I do," Thick refuted my words. I decided that words were futile and let him do as he wished, though it taxed my patience to dawdle along in front of him at a pace he could match. It bored me, and gave me far too much time to ponder our situation. I did not like how events were unfolding, and yet I could not say precisely what bothered me. Perhaps it was as Thick had said: bad things had happened in this place, and it felt as if they were happening now.

The wind was a constant, but the skies were clear and blue. At intervals, I saw old rods poking out of the snow, some tied with scraps of bright fabric. I judged that they marked the path that Peottre followed. He often paused to straighten one, or to attach a fresh ribbon-banner. Even so, the advance party went more swiftly than Thick and I did. I watched them draw away from us and grow smaller until they had dwindled to little puppets doing an odd poking dance in a line as they ventured across the ice field. Our shadows slowly became longer and thinner, pale blue on the crystallized ice and snow. The surface we walked across did not seem like either true ice or true snow to me. There was a thin layer of real snow, but beneath that were compacted darning needles of ice and we walked upon their tips.

At some point, I realized that I had resolved I would find time to speak with the Fool that evening, and to the winds with whatever anyone else might think of it. Almost on the heels of that thought, I felt a thin tendril of Skill from Chade. Quietly and privately he asked me, *Lad, are you still mine?*

He should have been proud of the answer I gave him. I am sure he could not have come up with a better one on such short notice. *As much as I ever was,* I replied.

I felt his grim chuckle in my mind. *Ah. Well, at least you do not lie to me. What did he say to you?*

The Fool?

Who else?

We only spoke of why I had tried to leave him behind. To preserve his life. I gathered that he did not think that a sufficient reason.

He probably thought I put you up to it, to keep him clear of the dragon until it's unearthed and beheaded. A pause. *The Narcheska weeps as she walks. She has not looked back at us to betray the tears on her cheeks, but I hear it in how she breathes. Twice she has wiped her face with her mitten, and then loudly spoken of how the light off the ice makes her eyes water. Think this through with me, Fitz. Why would she weep?*

I don't know. The hike is arduous, but she did not strike me as a woman who would weep over heavy work. Perhaps she fears the disapproval of the Black Man, or fears that she has put her family and her father's family into disfavor with the Hetgurd by—

Hush! Thick's irritated Skilling cut through my thoughts. *She is sad, so she cries. Now stop being loud and listen! Listen and stop breaking the music!*

Chade and I instantly muffled our thoughts. Both of us had believed our Skilling was small and private. I was sure that he now wondered, just as I did, if the Prince had been aware of our conversation. Then I wondered why Chade had been keeping it private from him. I trudged on, watching the ever-dwindling figures of Peottre's group. They were headed over the lip of a wind-sculpted ridge and would soon be out of sight. Peottre had spoken truth about the restlessness of this ice. Some stretches were swept as smooth as a sugar-topped cake; others looked like the same cake after it had been dropped. The trail in the snow was plain now, but I knew that as the sun sank, uneven shadows might make it more difficult to follow them. I glanced back at Thick in annoyance. He was walking more slowly than ever.

Irritated as much by his command that we hush as by his slowness, I turned my back on him and walked briskly away. I did not neglect, however, to probe the snow before me at every step. I thought he would look up and realize that I was leaving him behind. But when I glanced back, he was still strolling ponderously along. I stared back to him in exasperation, and then something in his movements caught my eye. It was like a dance. He would probe the snow with his staff, prod, prod, prod, and then take a single large swaying step. Again he would probe the snow, prod, prod, prod, and then stride forward again on the other foot. I lowered my barriers to hear his ever-present music. Usually, I could recognize the elements that he incorporated into it. But today each step was made in time to a sighing sweep like wind, while the prod, prod, prod of his staff kept time to a deep and steady percussion. I sealed myself from his music, and listened with my ears, but could find no parallel sounds on this island.

While I had paused, Thick had nearly caught up to me. He looked up from his scrutiny of the snow before his feet to find me watching him. He scowled at me, and then glanced past me. His frown deepened. "They're gone! Why weren't you watching them? Now they're gone, and we don't know where they went!"

"It's all right, Thick," I told him. "I can still see their trail. And see, there's a rod with a rag on it at the top of the rise. We'll catch up to them. But only if we hurry." I tried not to betray my worry that night was coming on and the shadows deepening. I did not want to be caught out on the face of the glacier, alone.

He lifted his stubby arm suddenly, to point jabbingly at the ridge. "Look! It's all right! There's one of them!"

My gaze followed his pointing finger, suspecting that the Prince had sent someone back to stand upon the ridge and guide us. Thick was right. There was someone there. But even at that distance, and in the fading light, I knew he was not one of our party. He moved swiftly and oddly, yet in a way that I could not pinpoint, his gait was familiar. I saw no more of him than his silhouette as he hastened over the ridge. Then he was gone. I felt cold dread creep through my blood. I Skilled my frantic thought to Chade and Dutiful. *The Black Man! I think the Black Man is following you!*

An instant later, I regretted my panic. Dutiful could not conceal his amusement. *There's no one behind us that I can see, Fitz. Only snow and shadows. Are you nearly to the top of the ridge?*

We haven't even begun to climb it yet. Thick is distracted and moving slowly.

Not distracted! Again, I was jolted by how easily Thick had picked up thoughts I had not intended for him. *Listening to the music, that's all. Except that you keep breaking it.*

Chade's Skilling was like oil on water. *I've asked Peottre if we'll be stopping for the night soon and he says we will. Once you crest the ridge, you should see us easily. He has already pointed out our campsite to me. As there is no sort of shelter at all, you won't have any difficulty spotting our cook fires.*

Cook fires? Food soon?

Yes, Thick, food soon. Probably almost as soon as you get here. I've brought some sweets with me from the ship. I'll share them with you, if you get here before I've eaten them all.

I had to admire Dutiful's cunning, even as I shook my head at it. It distracted Thick from his "music" and he consented to follow in my footsteps and let me do the snow probing. I thought that Peottre's caution was a bit exaggerated anyway. Surely if the entire party had already passed over a section of glacier, it would withstand one more crossing. And that proved to be true. We climbed the ridge in their tracks, stopping several times to allow Thick to finish coughing and catch his breath.

When we crested the ridge, I could instantly see their campsite below. The snow staves were posted at intervals around it, with bright ribbons attached to the tops. Evidently Peottre had established what he considered a safe area for the party. The larger tents for the Prince and Narcheska had already sprung up like mushrooms. In the dimming light, the Fool's colorful one was like a blossom cast on the snow. Illuminated from within, the bright panels gleamed like stained-glass windows. What had seemed random designs suddenly resolved into dragons and serpents cavorting. Well, he had declared his allegiance clearly.

There were two small campfires for the drab tents of the rest of our group. The Hetgurd men had pitched their tents a little away from ours, and kindled their own tiny fire, as if to proclaim to the gods that they were not of our party and did not deserve to share our fate.

I saw no sign of the Black Man, or any place where one might have hidden. Yet this did not dismiss my concerns but only heightened them.

As we made our way down to the camp, we encountered our first fissure in the glacier. It was a narrow, snaking crack, no more than that, and I simply stepped over it. Thick halted, staring down at the depths that shaded from pale blue to black. "Come on," I encouraged him. "It's not far to camp. I think I can smell the food they're cooking."

"That's deep." He lifted his eyes from his contemplation of it. "Peottre was right. It could swallow me and gulp me down, snap!" He stepped back from it.

"No it can't. It's all right, Thick. It's not something alive; it's just a crack in the ice. Come on."

He took a deep breath, and then coughed. When he was finished, he said, "No. I'm going back."

"You can't, Thick. It will be dark soon. It's only a crack. Just step over it."

"No." He shook his head on his short neck, his chin brushing his collar. "It's dangerous."

In the end, I stepped back over it and took his hand to persuade him to cross. I nearly slipped and fell when his awkward and exaggerated leap over it took me off guard in mid-stride. As I tottered, for one breathless moment I imagined myself wedged in the crack, out of reach of helping hands and yet preserved from slipping further. Thick sensed my fear and comforted me with "See, I told you it was dangerous. You nearly fell in and died."

"Let's just go down to the camp," I suggested.

As promised, they had hot food waiting for us. Riddle and Hest had finished eating already. They were conversing quietly with Longwick as he directed a watch schedule for the night. I settled Thick on top of my pack beside the fire and fetched food that Deft ladled out for both of us. Supper was a stew made from salt meat, and it suffered from that, as well as a too-brief cooking time. I grinned briefly at myself as I pondered how swiftly I had once again become accustomed to Buckkeep's succulent fare. Had I forgotten how to subsist on a guard's rations? There had been times in my life when I'd had far worse to eat at the end of a long, cold day, or nothing at all. I took another bite. That thought should have made the tough meat taste better, but it didn't. I glanced surreptitiously at Thick, expecting he would soon complain about it. But he was staring at the fire wearily, his bowl balanced precariously on his knee. "You should eat, Thick," I reminded him, and he started as if from a dream. I caught the bowl before it tipped enough to spill and handed it back to him. He ate, but wearily, not showing any of his usual enthusiasm for food, and stopping often to cough. It worried me. I finished my food hastily and rose, leaving Thick watching the dwindling flames of the small fire and chewing methodically.

Chade and Dutiful were at the other campfire with the rest of Dutiful's Wit coterie. There was talk there, and even some laughter, and for a moment I envied their companionship. It took me a moment to realize that the Fool was not there. He was probably within his own tent already. And then I noticed the other absence. Peottre and the Narcheska were also missing from the gathering. I glanced at the tent pitched for them. It was dark and still. Did they sleep already? Well, perhaps that was the best idea. Doubtless Peottre would rouse us all early to travel on.

I think Chade noticed me standing idly at the edges of the firelight. He left the circle of light as if going to relieve himself and I followed noiselessly. I stood beside him in the blackness and spoke quietly. "I'm concerned about Thick. He seems oddly distracted. From one moment to the next, his temper changes from irritable to frightened to elated."

Chade nodded slowly. "There is something about this island . . . I have no name for it, and yet it tugs at me. I feel dread and worry, beyond what I should feel, and then the feelings go. This land seems to speak to me through my Skill. And if it can reach one as feeble as me in that talent, how must it speak to Thick?"

I heard bitterness in the self-deprecation of his magic. "You grow stronger in the Skill every day," I assured him. "But I think perhaps you are right. I've felt nameless worry nibbling at me all day. Such, at times, is my nature. But this does seem more formless than usual. Could it have anything to do with the memories trapped in the stone?"

He made a sound of resignation. "How could we possibly know? All we can do for Thick is see that he eats and sleeps well at night."

"He is growing stronger in the Skill."

"I've noticed that. It makes my own paltry ability seem all the more meager."

"Time, Chade. It will come with time and patience. You're doing well, for someone who began so late and has not been long in training."

"Time. Time is the only thing we have, when all is said and done, and yet we never have enough of it. You can be calm about it; you've had as much of magic as you've ever wanted, and more, all your life. While I've had to claw and scratch for a tiny shred of it at the end of my days. Where is the justice of fate, when a half-wit has in abundance and values not at all that which I so desperately lack?" He turned on me. "Why did you always have so much Skill, bursts of it, and never wanted with your whole heart to master it as I have longed to do all my life?"

He was starting to frighten me. "Chade. I think this place preys on our minds, finding both our fears and our despairs. Set your walls against it, and trust only your logic."

"Humph. I have never been prey to my emotions. But this time would be better spent in rest than in talk, by either of us. Care for Thick as best you can. I'll watch over the Prince. He too seems prey to a darker mood than is usual for him." He rubbed his gloved hands together. "I'm old, Fitz. Old. And tired. And cold. I shall be glad when all of this is over and we are safely on our way home again."

"And I," I agreed heartily. "But I had another bit of news I wished to share with you. Odd, isn't it? Once I thought Skilling was private and secret. Yet, still I must seek you out to whisper to you. I don't think Thick is ready for me to ask this favor of him. He still resents and blames me. It might come better from you or the Prince."

"What?" Chade demanded impatiently. He shifted restlessly and I knew the cold was biting into his skinny old bones.

"Nettle has gone to Buckkeep Castle. I think our bird must have reached the Queen and she sent someone to Burrich. She's gone to the castle for safety's sake. And she knows that the threat to her is connected to our quest for the dragon's head." I could not quite bring myself to tell Chade that she now knew I was her father. I wanted to be clear on just how much Burrich had told her before that secret ceased being a secret.

Chade grasped the implications immediately. "And Thick speaks to Nettle in his dreams. We can communicate with Buckkeep and the Queen."

"Almost. I think we need to approach it cautiously. Thick is still not pleased with me, and might make mischief if he knew it would upset me. And Nettle is angry with me, also. I cannot reach her directly, and I don't know how much heed she would give to messages from me that went through Thick."

He gave a disgruntled noise. "Too late you fall in with my plans for her. Fitz, I do not relish rebuking you. But if you had allowed us to bring Nettle in as soon as we knew her potential, she would never have been in danger. Nor would quarrels between you and her have crippled us in this way. Either the Prince or I could reach her instead of you, if she had been properly prepared to use her magic. We could have had communication with Buckkeep Castle all this time."

It was childish of me. I pointed it out anyway. "You would probably have brought her here with us, for the sake of mustering strength for the Prince."

He sighed, as if confronting a stubborn pupil who refused to concede a point. Which he was, I suppose. "As you will have it, Fitz. But, I beg you, do not charge into this development like a bull harried by bees. Let her settle at Buckkeep for a few days, while the Prince and I consult on how much she should know of who she is and how best to approach her through Thick. It may require some preparation of Thick as well."

Relief flowed through me. I had feared that Chade would be the one to charge in like a bull. "I will do as you say. Go slowly."

"There's a good lad," Chade replied absently. I knew that his thoughts had already wandered afar to how these new playing pieces could be deployed on the game board.

And so we parted for the night.

chapter XV

CIVIL

Hoquin was the White Prophet and Wild Eye his
Catalyst in the years that Sardus Chif held power in the
Edge Lands. Famine had ruled there even longer than
Sardus Chif, and some said it was a punishment on the
land because Sardus Prex, mother of Sardus Chif, had
burned every sacred grove in wild mourning and fury at
the Leaf God when her consort, Slevm, died of pox.
Since then, the rains had all but ceased, and that was
because there were no sacred leaves for the rains to
wash. For the rains only fall for holy duty, not to slake
the thirst of men or their children.

Hoquin believed that his call as White Prophet was
to restore the fertility of the Edge Lands, and he believed
that to do this, water must come. So he made his
Catalyst to study water and how it might be brought to
the Edge Lands, from deep wells or dug canals or prayers
and offerings for rainfall. Often he asked her what she
would change to bring water to her people's lands, but
never did she have an answer to please him.

Wild Eye had no care for water. She had been born
in the dry years and lived in the dry years and knew only
the dry years and their ways. What she cared for were
thippi-fruits, the little soft-fleshed many-seeded pomes

*that grow low to the earth in the shelter of the claw
brambles in the ravines of the foothills. When she was
supposed to be at her chores, she would slip away up to
the foothills and go to the bramble thickets, returning
with her skirts and hair thick with claw seed and her
mouth purple from thippi-fruit. This angered Hoquin the
White, and often he beat her for her inattention to her
duties.*

*Then, around their cottage, where had been only
dusty earth, the claw brambles began to grow. Their
tangling thorns sheltered the soil from the sun and
beneath them came in the thippi-fruit vines. In the
season when the thippi-fruit died back, greygrass grew,
and rabbits came to live beneath the brambles and eat the
greygrass. Then Wild Eye caught and cooked the rabbits
for the White Prophet.*

❧ SCRIBE CATEREN, OF THE WHITE PROPHET HOQUIN

Despite Chade's suggestion, I did not go immediately to my
blankets. I returned to the fire, where Thick sat staring at
the remaining embers and shivering as the cold of the glacier crept up into him. I rousted him from there and saw
him off to bed in the tent we would share with Riddle and
Hest. The tight quarters were welcome for the body
warmth that would be shared. He settled in, gave a huge
sigh that ended in a coughing fit, then sighed again and
dropped into sleep. I wondered if he would be conversing
with Nettle tonight. Perhaps in the morning I'd have the
courage to ask him. For now, I'd be content knowing she
was safe at Buckkeep.

I left the tent and went out under the stars. The fires
had died out almost completely. Longwick would keep a
few coals going in a firepot but we didn't have enough fuel
to keep them burning constantly. There was a dim light
from Dutiful's tent; probably a small lantern still burned
in there. The Fool's tent was likewise illuminated, glowing

like a jewel in the night. I walked quietly over the snow to it.

I halted outside it when I heard soft voices from within. I could not make out the words, but I recognized the speakers. Swift said something, and the Fool replied teasingly. The boy chuckled. It sounded peaceful and friendly. I felt a strange twinge of exclusion, and almost retreated to my tent. Then I rebuked myself for jealousy. So the Fool had befriended the boy. Very likely, it was the best thing that could happen to Swift. As I could not knock to announce myself, I cleared my throat loudly, and then stooped to lift the tent flap. A slice of light fell on the snow. "May I come in?"

There was the tiniest of pauses, and then, "If you wish. Try to leave the snow and ice outside."

He knew me too well. I brushed the damp snow from my leggings, and then shook it from my feet. Crouching, I entered and let the tent flap fall closed behind me.

The Fool had always had the unique talent of creating a small world for himself when he wished to retreat. The tent was no exception. When I had visited it before, it had been charming, but empty. Now he occupied it and filled it with his presence. A small metal firepot in the center of the floor burned near smokelessly. A smell of cooking, something spicy, lingered in the air. Swift sat cross-legged on a tasseled cushion while the Fool was half-reclined on his pallet. Two arrows, one a dull gray, the other brightly painted and obviously the Fool's work, rested across Swift's knees.

"Did you require me, sir?" Swift asked quickly. I could hear his reluctance to leave in his voice.

I shook my head. "I didn't even know you were here," I replied.

As the Fool sat up, I saw what had made Swift laugh. A tiny marionette dangled from his hand, with five fine black threads going to each of the Fool's fingertips. I had to smile. He had carved a tiny jester, done in black-and-white. The pallid face was his own, as it had been when he was a boy. White down hair floated around the little face. A twitch of one long finger set the creature's head to nodding at me. "So what brings you here, Tom Badgerlock?" the Fool and his puppet asked me. A shift of his finger made the little jester cock his head inquiringly at me.

"Fellowship," I replied after a moment's pondering. I sat down on the opposite side of the fire from Swift. The boy gave me a resentful look and then glanced away.

The Fool's face was neutral. "I see. Welcome." But there was no warmth in the words; I was an intruder. An awkward silence fell and I perceived in full the mistake I had made. The lad knew nothing of the connection between the Fool and me. I could not speak freely. Indeed, I could suddenly think of nothing at all to say. The boy sat staring glumly at the fire, obviously waiting for me to leave. The Fool began to unfasten the marionette from his fingertips, one string at a time.

"I've never seen a tent like this. Is it from Jamaillia?" Even to me, my query sounded like a polite nothing said to a chance acquaintance.

"The Rain Wilds, actually. The fabric is Elderling-made, I suspect, but I chose the patterns sewn into it."

"Elderling-made?" Swift sat up with the avidity of a boy who senses a tale. A very faint smile played about the Fool's mouth. I suspected that he had seen the quickening of interest in my face, too.

"So the Rain Wild people say. Those who live far up the Rain Wild River. They say that once there were great cities there, and that the cities were the homes of the Elderlings. What exactly or who the Elderlings were is harder to tell. But in some places, buried deep in the muck of the Rain Wild swamps, there are cities of stone. Sometimes, one can find a way into them and, within whatever chambers have remained dry and intact, discover the treasures of another time and people. Some of the items they rescue are magical, with uses and abilities that not even the Rain

Wilders completely understand. At other times, they find things that are just as we might make ourselves, but of a different quality."

"Like this arrow?" Swift held up the gray arrow. "You said it came from the Rain Wilds. I've never seen wood such as this."

The Fool's eyes flickered to me and then away. "It's wizardwood, a very rare wood. Even more rare than the fabric of this tent, which is finer than silk, and stronger than silk. I can crush all the fabric into a wad I could hold concealed inside my hand, yet stretched over the poles of the tent, it is sturdy, and so strongly woven that it holds warmth in and wind out."

Swift reached out to run a wondering finger down one wall. "It's nice in here. Warmer than I had thought a tent could be. And I like the dragons on the walls."

"So do I," the Fool said. He reclined on his pallet again as he stared into the firepot. The tiny flames found twin homes in his eyes. I leaned back, away from the light, and studied him. There were planes and angles to his face that had never been there when we were children. His hair had seemed to gain substance with color. It no longer floated wildly around his face when it was loose, as it was now. Sleek as a horse's mane but far finer, it hung to his shoulders. "The dragons are why I am here."

For a fraction of a moment, his eyes flickered to mine. I crossed my arms on my chest and leaned back deeper into the shadows.

"There are dragons in the Rain Wilds," he went on, speaking to Swift. "But only one that is hearty and strong. Tintaglia is her name."

The boy edged even closer to him. "Then the Bingtown Traders spoke truth? They have a dragon?"

The Fool cocked his head as if considering the answer. Again, that ghost of a smile bent his mouth. Then he shook his head. "That is not something I would say. Rather, I would say that there is a dragon in the Rain Wilds, and

Bingtown falls within the territory she claims as her own. She is a magnificent creature, blue as good steel and silver as a gleaming ring."

"Have you seen her, your own self?"

"Indeed I have." The Fool smiled at the boy's wonder. "And had words with her."

Swift drew his breath in. He seemed to have forgotten my hulking presence. Yet I wondered to which of us the Fool spoke as he said, "This tent is one of the gifts she persuaded the Rain Wild folk to give me."

"Why did she ask them to give you gifts?"

"She told them to give me gifts because she knew that I would serve her purpose unswervingly. For we have known each other, in other days and shapes."

"What do you mean?" The boy suspected he was being teased. I feared he was not.

"I am not the first of my kind to have dealings with dragonkind. And she has all the memories of her race. They cascade through her mind like bright beads sliding on a string. Back they go, past the serpent she was once to the egg that serpent came from, to the dragon that laid that egg, to the serpent that dragon was, to the egg that serpent hatched from, to the dragon that laid that egg, to the serpent that dragon—"

"Enough!" the boy laughed breathlessly. The Fool's tongue juggled the words like pins.

"Back to where she knew another such as I. And perhaps, had I a dragon's memory, I might have been able to say to her, 'Ah, yes, I do recall, and that is exactly how it was. Such a pleasure to meet you again.' But I have not a dragon's memory. And so I had to take her word for it that I was as trustworthy a fellow as she was ever likely to meet."

His words had fallen into the artful cadence of the storyteller. The boy was enraptured. "And what is her purpose that you shall serve?" Swift asked eagerly.

"Ah!" The Fool swept his hair back from his face, then stretched, but suddenly his long forefinger was pointing unerringly at me. "He knows. For he has promised to help me. Haven't you, Badgerlock?"

Frantically, I scrambled through my memories. Had I promised to aid him? Or had I only said that I would decide when the time came for it? I smiled, and with a wittiness I did not feel, I replied, "When the time comes, I'll serve my purpose."

I knew he marked my distancing from his words, but he smiled as if I had agreed and said, "As shall we all. Even young Swift, Burrich's son and Molly's son."

"Why do you name me so?" In that instant, the boy was stung. "My father is nothing to me. Nothing!"

"Whatever he is to you, you are still son to him. Perhaps you can deny him, but you cannot make him deny you. Some ties cannot be severed by a word. Some ties simply are. Such ties are what bind the world and time together."

"Nothing binds me to him," the boy insisted sullenly. A little time passed. He perceived he had broken the string of the story, and that the Fool was not going to knot it back together for him. After a pause, he conceded, asking again, "What is the dragon's purpose in your being here?"

"Oh, you know what it is!" The Fool sat up. "You've heard what was said back on the beach, and I know how swiftly gossip travels in a small group like this. You have come to slay the dragon. I am here to see that you don't."

"Unless it's a righteous battle. Unless the dragon attacks us first."

The Fool shook his head. "No. I am simply here to see that the dragon survives."

Swift's eyes traveled from the Fool to me and back again. He spoke hesitantly. "Then you are our enemy here? To battle us if we try to kill the dragon? But there is only one of you! How can you think to challenge us?"

"I challenge no one. I make no one my enemy, though some may consider me theirs. Swift, it is simply as I say it is. I am here to see that no one slays the dragon under the ice."

The boy shifted uncomfortably. I could almost see the thought pass through his mind, and when he spoke it, he sounded so like Burrich that it nearly broke my heart. "I am sworn to serve my prince." He took a breath, but when he spoke his voice was still troubled. "If you oppose him, sir, then I must oppose you."

The Fool had kept his eyes fixed on the boy's face all the while. "I am sure you will, if you believe it is the right thing to do," he said quietly. "And if that is so when the time comes, well, that will be soon enough for us to be opponents. I am sure you will respect the duty of my heart just as I respect yours. For now, however, we travel all together in the same direction, and I see no reason why we should not share what Tom Badgerlock came to seek here. Fellowship."

Again Swift's eyes traveled between us. "Then you are friends, you two?"

"For many years," I said, at almost the same instant that the Fool said, "Far more than friends, I would say."

It was at precisely that moment that Civil Bresinga flung open the tent flap and thrust his head inside. "I feared as much!" he declared angrily. Swift looked up at him, his mouth a round O of surprise. The Fool gave an exasperated sigh. I was the first to find my tongue.

"Your fears are groundless," I said quietly, while Swift, entirely mistaking Civil's declaration, retorted, "I would never be disloyal to my prince, no matter who tempted me!"

That comment, I think, threw Civil into complete confusion. Now totally uncertain of what was going on, he contemptuously ordered, "Swift, come out from there, and go to bed in your own blankets." Then, to the Fool, "And don't believe this is the end of this. I'll be taking my concerns to the Prince."

On the heels of his words, before the Fool or I could

respond, we heard Riddle's voice ring out in challenge. "Hold where you are! Who goes there?"

I thrust Swift out of the way to bolt out of the tent. I nearly knocked Civil over as I passed him, not that I would have regretted it much. I sensed him following me, and knew that Swift and the Fool would, also. By the time I reached Riddle's sentry post, most of the camp had tumbled out of their blankets to see what the uproar was about.

"Who goes there?" Riddle shouted again, his uncertainty making him more angry and challenging.

"Where?" I demanded as I came up beside him, and he lifted a finger to point.

"There," he said quietly, and then I saw the man's shadow. Or was it the man himself? The uneven surface of the blown snow on the glacier and the feeble light of the fire quarreled with the deep gray of the northern night, making it hard to tell substance from shade. The snowy mountains above us cast a second, deeper shadow across the reach of snow. I squinted. Someone stood at the far edge of the dwindled fire's reach. I saw no more than his silhouette, but I was certain it was the man I had glimpsed earlier in the day. Behind me, I heard Peottre gasp, "The Black Man!" He spoke with dread, and the spreading mutter among the Hetgurd men who had also roused was uneasy. The Fool was suddenly beside me, his long fingers gripping my forearm hard. He breathed his words, and I doubt any heard them save me. "What is he?"

"Come forward and show yourself!" Riddle commanded him. His drawn sword was in his hand as he stepped out of our circle and into the darkness. Longwick had thrust a torch into the dwindled embers of the fire. As the pitch took flame, and he lifted it aloft, however, the man simply was no longer there. Just as a shadow vanishes when light comes too close to it, so had he disappeared.

His appearance had roused the camp, but it was his disappearance that threw us into chaos. Everyone spoke at once. Riddle and the other guards ran forward to examine the place where the man had stood even as Chade shouted at them not to tread on the snow there. By the time Chade and I reached the spot, they had already trampled over whatever sign he might have left. Longwick lifted the torch higher, but we saw no definite footprints either approaching or leaving that spot. It was within the boundaries that Peottre had staked out for the camp, and our own trails crossed and overcrossed there.

One of the Outislanders was praying loudly to El. Never have I heard anything so unnerving as a hardened warrior praying to a god known for his merciless heart. It was a harsh prayer, one that promised gifts and sacrifices if El would only turn his attention elsewhere. Web looked shocked by it and Peottre's face was pale even in the torchlight. The Narcheska looked as if she had been carved from ivory, so still and stunned were her features.

"Perhaps it was only a trick of the light and shadows," Cockle suggested, but no one took him seriously. The Hetgurders offered no suggestions, but spoke low and swift amongst themselves. They sounded worried. Peottre too held his silence.

"Whatever or whoever it was, he's gone now," Chade declared at last. "Let us get what sleep is left to us tonight. Longwick, double the guard. And build up the fires."

The Hetgurd contingent, perhaps not trusting our sentries, set a guard of their own. They also spread an otter skin on the snow at the edge of our encampment and once more set out offerings on it. I saw Peottre shepherd the Narcheska back to their tent, but doubted he would sleep any more this night. I wondered why he appeared so badly rattled, and wished that I knew more of this "Black Man" and the traditions surrounding him.

I thought Chade would want to speak to me, but he only gave me an accusing glare. I thought at first that he wished that I had done more to apprehend the visitor; then realized it was because the Fool still stood beside me. I started to move away from him, then irritably checked my own action. I would determine where I wished to be, not Chade. I met his gaze levelly and kept my face devoid of expression. Nonetheless, he gave his head a small shake before he turned aside to accompany Dutiful back to their tent.

I was made aware of Swift's fears when he spoke from beside me. "What should I do now?" I heard both unadmitted fear and dread in his voice and I tried to think what would have reassured me at that age, and went back to Burrich's wisdom. Give him a task.

"Follow the Prince and stay at his side. I think it best if you sleep in his tent tonight, for you've a keen set of ears and the Wit to warn you if any should approach the tent from outside. Remind them of that, and let them know I suggested you be his guard tonight. Now go quickly, get your blankets and join them before they're abed."

He looked at me, mouth agape for an instant. Then he flashed me a look of pure gratitude. His eyes met mine, without resentment or restraint, and he said, "You know I'm loyal to my prince."

"I do." I confirmed it for him. I wondered if Burrich's face had shone like that the first time Chivalry had proclaimed that he belonged to him. I suddenly felt he was too cheaply bought, this son of Burrich. If he had half the loyalty and courage of his father, then Dutiful had acquired a jewel indeed. As Swift ran off into the darkened camp, I turned to the sound of footsteps behind me. Web approached, with Civil a scant two steps behind him. As if he could read my thoughts, he said, "The boy will be a good man."

"If he's allowed to grow that way, without interference or the creation of unnatural appetites," Civil appended to his words. He stepped into the circle, and never have I seen a man more ready to fight. His cat was a snowy ghost at his heels. I didn't want this. I didn't want the allegations and I didn't want the fight. I saw no way to avoid any of it. The Fool spoke before I could.

"You willfully persist in laboring under that misapprehension," he said quietly. "Yet if it must be said to you yet again, then I shall. I am no threat to that boy. What passed between us at your mother's home was a subterfuge, designed to make my quick departure easily explained. You are not a simpleton. You have seen that both Tom Badgerlock and I serve the Prince, in ways that no one has fully explained to you. Nor will anyone. So set that hope aside. This is as much as you get from me, and I speak it plainly. I feel no physical attraction to that boy, and I have no designs on his flesh. The same is true of how I feel toward you."

That should have put him at ease, if that had been his true concern. But it wasn't, of course. I could tell it by the way his Wit-cat flattened his ears. Civil spoke in a low voice. "And she who was affianced to me, Sydel? Will you say you felt no physical attraction to her and never had any designs on her flesh when you ruined the trust that was between us?"

The silence and cold that closed tight around us was not entirely of the glacier's making. I had seldom seen the Fool weigh his words so carefully. I became aware that Cockle stood just outside our circle, witnessing our words, and those who had started to return to their tents had also halted to watch this play. I wondered what the minstrel would make of what he had already heard, let alone what the Fool might say next. "Sydel was a lovely child when last I saw her," the Fool said quietly. "And like a child, she was given to quick turns of fantasy and fascination. I took advantage of her interest in me. I admit that. And I have told you already why I did so. But I did not ruin the trust between you. Only the two of you could do that, and that is indeed what you did. Some time has passed and perhaps, if you look back now, you will see that the trust she gave you was just that: the trust of a child, not the love of a young woman. I would wager that she had known few other young men besides you; she did not truly choose you, Civil. You were simply there and her parents approved. And when I came along and she perceived there might be a choice—"

"Don't try to blame it all on me!" Civil's voice was a low growl. His cat echoed it. "You seduced her and stole her from me. And then you cast her aside, and left her to her shame."

"I . . ." The Fool's shock was palpable to me. He seemed at a loss for words. But when he spoke, his voice was firm and in control again. "You are wrong. All that passed between Sydel and me, you saw. Such, of course, was my intent! There were no private moments between us, and certainly no seduction. I left her, certainly, but I did not shame her."

Civil shook his head, a bit wildly. The more calmly the Fool spoke, the more agitated the lad seemed to become. "No! No, you ruined everything between us, with your loathsome appetites! And now you will say it was some sort of game or ruse. You shattered my mother's dreams for us, and humiliated her father so that he cannot bear to be in the same room with her. All this for a jest? No. No, I refuse to believe it."

I felt queasy. I had been a part of that deception. We had guested in Civil Bresinga's home, in guise of enjoying the hunting there while actually tracking Prince Dutiful and the Piebalds who had taken him. When we needed to depart abruptly on the Prince's trail, Lord Golden had created a reason for Lady Bresinga to welcome our departure. He had made blatant advances toward Lady Sydel, Civil's fiancée, turning her young head with his wealth and charm and flattery. When Civil had attempted to intervene, he had drunkenly informed the young man that he too would be welcome to share Lord Golden's bed. We had done it for the Prince's sake, that we might more swiftly follow him and leave no one wondering why we departed so suddenly. But the trail of destruction we had left behind us sickened me now. I suddenly feared where this must lead. *My prince,*

I fear I must beg your intervention between Civil and the Fool. They quarrel, and I think Civil will take it to blows.

"I am sorry," the Fool said, and he put a depth of feeling into those words that could leave no one doubting his sincerity. He halted, then offered, "Truly, Civil, it is never too late. If you love the girl as you seem to, then go to her when you return to the Six Duchies and tell her so. Give her time to become a woman and see if she reciprocates your feelings. If she does, take joy in one another. If she does not, well, then know that it would not have lasted between you, regardless of whether I had come along or not."

It wasn't what Civil wanted to hear. His face went from scarlet to white, and he suddenly shrieked out, "I demand satisfaction of you!" And he launched himself at the Fool.

An instant too late, Web reached for his shoulder. A moment too late, I tried to block him. He pounced on the Fool like a cat on a mouse, and together they went rolling into the snow. Civil snarled like a cat as he fought. Something Web did, I think, restrained Civil's cat from leaping into the fray. I stepped forward to intervene, but felt the Prince inside my mind as he arrived, half-clothed, on the scene.

Let them have it out, Fitz. Better that the two of them settle it than that you become involved and we suddenly have the whole party taking sides. This has festered long with Civil and words will not suffice to settle it.

But the Fool doesn't fight. Never have I seen him fight!

Nonetheless. And this from Chade, with a grim sort of satisfaction. *He will now.*

I think they expected to see Civil triumph quickly. There, I knew the Fool better. Slight he might appear, but even when I was in fighting trim, he had always seemed able to pit his strength against mine. Once, when I was injured, he had carried me through the snow back to his home. His tumbler's tricks had always demanded strength as well as agility. So I knew he had the power to defeat

Civil if he chose. What I feared was that he would choose not to do so. And my fears were well grounded. Civil straddled the Fool. I winced to the solid sound of Civil's fists striking him, chest and shoulder and jaw.

Stop this! I begged the Prince. *Command them to stop!*

Let them finish it and let it be over, Chade suggested, and I glowered at him, thinking he had other reasons why he would see the Fool defeated before the men who had so swiftly gathered.

Then I'll stop it! But as I stepped forward, I saw that the tide of the battle had already turned. The Fool had writhed beneath Civil until he had his hip under him. He caught one of Civil's legs in the crook of his knee. Then by some twisting trick, the Fool suddenly unseated him and reversed their positions. In the next instant, he had flung himself on top of Civil. I was shocked even as I waited to see the Fool take his revenge.

He didn't. He caught Civil's flailing arms and restrained them, seemingly without effort. Dark red blood was running from one of the Fool's nostrils. It dripped down onto Civil as the lad struggled. The Fool's grip only tightened, and I saw how reluctantly he twisted down on one of Civil's elbows until the young man grunted with pain. Nearby, his cat snarled savagely. Web's touch on his back looked effortless, but the cat seemed to strain against iron restraints.

The Fool held the struggling young man down. I could sense Civil's outrage that the tawny man did so without apparent effort. When one has insulted someone's manliness, he does not expect to be easily mastered by the man. "It's done." The Fool spoke firmly, not just to Civil but to all of us. "It's over. I won't discuss this with you again."

Suddenly Civil went limp. The Fool held him down an instant longer, then pushed himself up off his prone body, took a staggering step, and then drew himself up straight. Just as he began to walk away, Civil rolled to his feet and sprang at him. I leaped forward at the same instant that the Fool, without so much as a glance back, moved lithely to one side. Civil and I were suddenly chest to chest in the night, the boy gawking up at me as I stared him down. He stumbled back a step, then he spun and hissed the insult at the Fool. "You say he isn't your lover, yet he stands ready to fight your battles for you."

Like a ship under full sail, the Fool seethed through the snowy night to stand aggressively close to the boy. He spoke flatly. "He is not my lover. He is far more than that to me, far more precious. I am the White Prophet and he is my Catalyst, and we are come here to change the course of time. I am here to see that Icefyre lives."

Peottre had ghosted up to the edge of the circle. In the dimness, he shuddered as if he had just taken an arrow. The Hetgurd men, gathered for the pleasure of watching a fight, suddenly muttered amongst themselves. But I had no time to watch them. Civil was like a crouching cat with a lashing tail. All his attention was focused on the Fool as he growled, "I don't care what you call yourself or him. I know what you are!"

He all but spat the final words and again he sprang. But this time the Fool met his onslaught. Civil went in swinging heavy blows but the Fool swayed around them and stepped in to seize Civil by the body. He did not push him away, but pulled him forward, increasing his momentum so that the boy slammed face first into the crystallized snow. The Fool followed him down. He pinioned him again, wrapping one arm around the boy's throat and winding the other under Civil's arm and up, so that his right arm was bent up behind him. Civil was cursing wildly and close to tears when the Fool hoarsely warned him, "We can do this as many times as you like. Struggle and you'll dislocate your shoulder. That is true, I promise you. Let me know when you are calm and ready to give this up."

I feared the boy would be stupid enough to hurt himself. The Fool, his weight spread flat on the snow, held him down and let him struggle. Twice Civil flung himself back against the Fool's grip. Each time I heard him grunt with pain. Finally, having proven the Fool's words to himself, he lay still. But he was far from calm. He panted and cursed and then shouted, "It was all your fault! You can't deny it. You ruined everything, everything. And now my mother is dead and I have nothing. Nothing. Sydel is shamed and I cannot go to her and offer her marriage, for I have nothing, and her father blames my family for his daughter's fall. He will not let me see her. If you had not come there, none of it would have happened. I'd still have my life."

"And the Prince would be dead. Or worse." Without realizing it, I had edged closer to the combatants. I wondered if anyone else heard the Fool's low comment.

With a moan of defeat, Civil dropped his face into the snow. He lay still. The Fool did not make him speak his surrender. Instead, he released his hold from the boy and got up. I winced for the pain he must feel.

The Fool spoke between gasps for breath. "It wasn't me. I didn't kill your mother. Or shame her. That was the Piebalds. Blame them. Not me. And don't fix blame on a young girl who did nothing more terrible than flirt with a stranger. Forgive her . . . and yourself. You were trapped and used. Both of you."

And the Fool's perceptive words lanced into Civil's soul, and his pain poured forth into the night. Wit and Skill, I felt it, like some hot, foul poison rushing out of him. When the Fool turned away, the young man didn't spring after him, but curled on his side in the snow, gagging with sorrow. His cat gave a low rumble of distress, and, released by Web, rushed to his side. The Fool stood well clear of them both. Panting, he dragged his sleeve across his face, and then shook his head at how he had marked the snowy white of it with the deep scarlet of his blood. He took several steps away from them, and then bent over, hands on his knees, taking deep panting breaths of the cold air.

The Prince finally spoke. "Let this be an end to it now, right here. We are a small party and can ill afford any divisions amongst us. Civil, you made your challenge and this will have to be your satisfaction. Lord Golden, you are here on my tolerance. You have openly avowed that you oppose my mission. I accept that, just as I accept the conscience that puts the Hetgurd watchers among us. But if you carry any ill will against Civil because of this, my tolerance will end. We will put you out of our company to make your own way."

I felt those last words as a threat. I went to the Fool's side and waited while he caught his breath. Web had gone to Civil and crouched in the snow beside him. He lay there, hugging his cat as if he were a child's comforting doll. Web's voice was a low rumble as he spoke to him. I could not catch the words. Swift stood, caught in between, staring from one combatant to the other. I took the Fool's arm and started moving him toward his tent. Now that it was over, he seemed half-stunned. "Follow your prince, son," I told Swift as I passed him. "It's done for now. We'll talk later."

He nodded, staring as we passed. The Fool stumbled a little and I firmed my grip on him. Behind us, I heard Longwick berating the guards for being distracted from their duty. Slowly, the camp dispersed back to their beds.

I put the Fool inside his tent, and then went back out, his kerchief in my hand, to gather up a pack of snow for him. When I returned, he had added a bit of oil to the tiny firepot, and the renewed flames danced higher, sending rippling shadows of color across the silken walls. He set a tiny kettle upon it as I watched, and then sat back on his pallet, pinching his nostrils shut with one bloody hand. His nose had almost stopped bleeding but his face was starting to darken where Civil's fists had landed. He leaned back gingerly as if the entire left side of his body were sore.

"Try this," I told him. I sat down beside him and gently pressed the cold compress against the side of his face. He turned away from it.

"Please don't! It's icy and I'm already too cold," he

complained. Wearily he added, "I'm too cold all the time in this place."

"Nevertheless," I told him relentlessly. "Just until your nose stops bleeding. And it will keep your face from swelling too much. You'll probably have a black eye anyway."

"Please, Fitz," he protested feebly and reached up, bare-handed, to seize my wrist in the same moment that my fingertips brushed his cheek.

The impact of that mutual touch blinded me for an instant, just as if I had stepped out of a dim stable into full direct sunlight. I twitched away from him, the snow bundle falling to the tent floor, and blinked, but the image of what I had seen was imprinted on the inside of my eyelids. I cannot say how I knew what it was I had glimpsed. Perhaps something in that closed circle of touching told me. I drew a shaky breath and reached recklessly toward his face with outstretched fingers.

"I can heal you," I told him, amazed and breathless with the discovery. The knowledge of my newfound power rushed through my blood, hot as whiskey. "I see what is wrong, the bits that are broken and how the blood pools under your skin where it should not. Fool, I can use the Skill and heal you."

Again he seized my wrist, but this time it was to hold my hand wide of his face. Again, I felt jolted by that sense of connection as his Skill-imbued fingertips made contact with my skin. He shifted his grip quickly to the cuff of my sleeve. "No," he said quietly, but a smile played over his swollen face. "Did you learn nothing from the 'healing' that we put you through? I have no reserves to burn for the sake of a swift healing. I'll let my own body mend itself, in its own way and time." He let go of my wrist. "But thank you," he added quietly, "for offering."

A shudder ran over me, as when a horse shakes flies from his coat. I blinked at him, feeling as if I had just awakened. The temptation was slower to fade. There was, I thought wryly, much of Chade in me. Knowing that I could do a thing made me itch to do it. Looking at his bruised face was like looking at a picture hung crooked on a wall. The impulse to right it was instinctive. I sighed. Resolutely, I crossed my arms on my chest and leaned back from him.

"You see it, don't you?" he asked me.

I nodded, and then he shocked me, for his mind was on something completely different. "Word must be sent to the Queen, somehow. Sydel, I think, is innocent. She deserves rescue, and after the misery I have helped cause her, I hope she receives it. I dare not guess which of her parents is the Piebald who worked with Laudwine. Perhaps both did. Sydel is shamed for accidentally falling in with our plans. And Civil is no longer seen as an appropriate match for her, for he has sided with the Farseers."

Of course. The connections were all there, plain to see when the Fool pointed them out. I reconsidered her parents' apparent reaction to "Lord Golden's" interest in their daughter. Her mother had seemed avid to take advantage of it; her father more cautious. Had they seen him as someone who could give the Piebalds access to Buckkeep society? As a benefactor whose wealth might forward their cause?

"Why didn't Civil just tell Dutiful, months ago?" I felt outraged. My prince had forgiven Civil, had welcomed him back as a comrade and friend, and he had held back from us this key piece of information.

The Fool shook his head. "I don't think Dutiful realizes the full implications, even now. Perhaps some part of him suspects, but he doesn't dare let himself see it. He is true Old Blood, not Piebald. What they did is so monstrous by his standards that he cannot imagine Sydel being connected to such a plot." He leaned over and picked up the snowbag from the floor, regarded it dolefully, and then put it gingerly to the swollen side of his face. "I'm so tired of being cold," he remarked. One-handed, he opened a small wooden box at the end of his pallet, and took out a cup and a bowl that nested together. From beneath them, he took a small cloth bag and shook herbs from it into the cup and bowl. He went on. "It's the only way I can make the pieces fit. Sydel is disgraced in her father's eyes; the engagement is broken. Civil assumes her father caught her in my bed. It is the only explanation he can imagine, and so he blames me for ruining all that was between them. But that isn't it at all. One or both of her parents are Piebalds. They used their close ties with the Bresinga household to intercept messages meant for Civil and return their own. They saw to it that the Prince was hosted invisibly within that household. The gift of the cat for Dutiful was probably delivered through them. The plan for Civil was that he'd wed their daughter, bringing his family's wealth and position to the Piebald cause. Then she failed them, by flirting with me. And we were the mechanism for the whole downfall of that first Piebald plan. That is how she is disgraced." He gave a sigh, leaned back on his bedding, and moved the kerchief to a different spot on his face. "It's small comfort to have worked it out now."

"I'll see that Kettricken knows of it," I promised him without telling him how I'd attempt to do that.

"But if we have set one puzzle to rest tonight, we've only encountered a greater one. Who is he, what is he?" The Fool's voice was musing.

"The Black Man?"

"Of course."

I shrugged. "Some recluse living on the island, accepting tribute from superstitious folk and ambushing those who don't leave him gifts. That's the simplest explanation." Chade's teaching was that the simplest explanation was often likely to be the right one.

The Fool shook his head slowly. The look he gave me was incredulous. "No. Surely you cannot believe that. Never have I felt a man so hung about with portents . . . not since I first encountered you have I felt such a tingle of . . . of significance. He is important, Fitz, vastly important. Perhaps the most important person we have ever met. Didn't you feel his consequence, hanging like mist in the air?" He held the snow away from his face and leaned forward eagerly. A single scarlet final drop hung from the tip of his nose. I gestured at it and he wiped it carelessly on his bloodstained sleeve.

"No. I felt nothing like that. In fact—Oh, Eda and El! Why does it come to me only now? I could not see him when the sentry shouted, and when he was pointed out to me, I thought I saw but his shadow. Because I didn't sense him with my Wit. Not at all. He was as blank as a Forged One . . . He's Forged, Fool. And that means there is no predicting what he might do."

A chill went over me despite the coziness of the tent. It had been many years since I'd had to deal with Forged Ones, but the unmerciful memories had not faded. One of my tasks as Chade's apprentice assassin had been to kill as many of them as I could, by whatever means was most expeditious. The deaths I had dealt to Six Duchies folk haunted me still, even though I knew there had been no alternative. Forging stole all humanity from its victims and was irreversible.

"Forged? Oh, surely not!" The Fool's astounded reaction broke my moment of introspection. He shook his head. "No, Fitz. Not Forged. Almost the opposite, if such a thing is possible. I felt in him the weight of a hundred lifetimes, the significance of a dozen heroes. He . . . displaces fate. Much as you do."

"I don't understand," I said uneasily. I hated it when the Fool spoke like this. He loved it.

He leaned forward, eyes gleaming with enthusiasm. As he spoke, he lifted the kettle from the oil flame and poured steaming water into the cup and a bowl. Ginger and cinnamon wafted toward me. "All of time, every sliced instant of it, is rich with vertices of choices. One becomes accustomed to that, to the point at which sometimes even I have to stop and remind myself that I am making choices, even when I do not seem to be. Every indrawn breath is a choice. But sometimes one is reminded of that forcibly, sometimes I meet a person so laden with possibilities and potential that the mere existence of such a being is a jolt to reality. You are like that, still, to me. The sheer improbability of your existence took my breath away. I have discovered relatively few possible futures in which you exist at all. In most of them, you died as a child. In others... well, I do not think I need to tell you all the ways in which you have died in other times. How many times have you been snatched from the jaws of death, in the most unlikely ways? I promise you, Fitz, in other times that parallel ours, you have met your deaths at those moments. Yet here you are, with me still, defying the odds by existing. And by your existence, with every breath you take, you change all time. You are like a wedge driven into dry wood. With every beat of your heart, you are pounded deeper into 'what might be' and as you advance, you crack the future open, and expose a hundred, a thousand new possibilities, each branching into another hundred, another thousand." He paused for breath. Noting my disgruntled expression, he laughed aloud. "Well. Like it or not, you do, my Catalyst. And so also did he feel to me tonight, the Black Man! So many possibilities shimmered around him that I could scarcely see him. He is even more unlikely than you are!" He drew a black kerchief out of his sleeve and wiped all traces of blood from his face, and then his hands. Carefully enfolding the bloody side, he tucked it into his sleeve again. Then he leaned back on his cushions, his eyes staring into the dim shadows at the peak of his tent. "And I have not a clue as to who or what he is. I've never glimpsed him before. What does that mean? Was it only with our coming here that his influence on the future became possible?"

He picked up the steaming bowl and offered it to me, excusing it with "I only brought one cup. Traveling light, you know." I took it from him, welcoming the warmth against my hands. With an odd jolt, I reminded myself that in the Six Duchies it was summer. Summer seemed an

impotent thing here in the Out Islands, camped on a glacier. He picked up the cup and, looking around, frowned
slightly. "You took my honey, didn't you? You don't happen
to have it with you, do you? It brings out the flavor of the
ginger and makes the tea more warming."

"Sorry. I left it in my tent . . . no, that's not quite true. I
left it outside by the fire last night, and this morning it was
gone." I halted, feeling as if I'd just heard a key turn in a
lock. "Or taken," I amended. "Fool, the Outislanders left
gifts for the Black Man. He didn't take any of them, but
honey was one of the things offered. And yours was missing
this morning."

"You think he took mine? You think that he supposed
it an offering left by you?"

The excitement he manifested was out of proportion, I
thought, to my speculation. I took a sip of the tea he had
made. The ginger was heat. I felt it spread comfortingly
through my belly even as his words unnerved me. "More
likely someone in our own camp took it. How could he
creep amongst our very tents, unseen?"

"Unseen and unfelt," he corrected me. "You said he is
invisible to your Wit. Likely the same is true for the other
Witted ones. So. I think he took the honey. And with it,
bound his fate to ours. It connects us, you see, Fitz." He
drank from his cup, his eyes near closing in enjoyment of
the warm liquid as he did so. When he set the cup down,
he had nearly drained it. He reached for a bright yellow
coverlet that looked as insubstantial as the stuff of his tent
walls and draped it around his shoulders, then kicked off
his loose boots and pulled his narrow feet up under him. "It
connects him to both of us. I think it might be highly significant. Do you see that it could change the outcome of
our mission here? Especially if I let it be known that the
Black Man had accepted our offering."

My mind raced through the possibilities. Would such
an announcement win the Outislanders to his side? Turn
the Narcheska and Peottre against him? Where did it leave

me, not only in relation to them but in terms of how Chade saw me? The answers were not comforting. "It could create a greater division in our party than there is now."

He lifted his cup and drank the rest of the tea before answering. "No. It would only expose the division that already exists." He looked at me and his expression was almost pitying. "This is the culmination of my life's work, Fitz. You cannot expect me to refuse any weapon, any advantage, that fate gives me. If I must die on this cold and forsaken island, at least let me die knowing I've achieved my aim."

I drank off the tea in the bowl and set it down beside his cup. I spoke firmly. "I'm not going to stay here and listen to this . . . nonsense. I don't believe any of it."

But I did. And it tightened my guts more than any cold or danger I'd ever faced.

"And you think that if you refuse to believe it, it can't come to pass? *That* is nonsense, Fitz. Accept it, and let's make the best of what time we have left." There was such terrible calm in his voice that I suddenly wanted to strike him. If death was truly lurking in wait for him, he should not be so placid and accepting of it. He should fight it, he should be *made* to fight it.

I drew a deep breath. "No. I won't believe it and I won't accept it." A thought came to me and I tried to speak it jokingly, but it came out as a threat. "Remember what I am to you, White Prophet. I'm the Catalyst. I am Changer. And I can change things, even the things that *you* think are fixed."

Halfway through my jest, I saw emotion transform his face. I would have halted my words, but once begun, they seemed to proceed of their own accord. The expression on his face was so stark, it was as if I stared at his bared skull bones. "What are you saying?" he demanded in a horrified whisper.

I looked away from him. I had to. "Only what you've been telling me for most of our lives. You may be the

Prophet and foretell things. But I'm the Catalyst. I change things. Perhaps even what you've foretold."

"Fitz. Please."

The words drew my gaze back to him. "What?"

He was breathing through his mouth as if he'd run a race and lost. "Don't do this," he begged me. "Don't try to stop me from doing what I must do. I thought I'd made you understand it, back there on the beach. I could have run away from this. I could have stayed in Buckkeep, or gone back to Bingtown, or even gone home. Or back to where home once was. But I didn't. I'm here. I'm facing it. I'm afraid and I don't deny that. And I know this will be hard for you. But it is what I've been aimed toward, all these years. You understand duty to family and king. You understand it all too well. Please see that this, now, is my duty to what I am. If you set out to defeat me, simply for the sake of keeping me alive, you will render all my life meaningless. All we have gone through up to now will be for nothing. You'll be condemning me to live out my years knowing that I failed. Would you do that to me?"

He gave me a piteous look. I gave him a few moments to calm before I spoke quietly. "So. You are saying, if I see something killing you, I'm to let it happen? Even if I can prevent it?"

Suddenly he seemed confused. "I suppose so . . ."

"What if it's the wrong thing? What if I see a bear killing you, and you're supposed to die in an avalanche? And I do nothing, so you die in the wrong way, and it's still all for nothing."

He looked at me blankly for a moment. "But that . . . No. I think you'll know. When the time comes, I think you'll know what—"

"And if I don't? If I make a mistake, what then?"

"I don't . . ." He faltered to a halt.

I pounced. "Do you see how stupid this is? I cannot possibly stand by and watch you die, Fool. I know that and you know that. You'd be asking me to be profoundly different from who I am. You'd be making the change, not me. And didn't you once tell me that precipitating the change was my task, not yours? So don't ask it of me. If fate demands that you be dead, well, then I'll probably be dead too. At that point, I doubt if it will matter much to either of us." I stood abruptly. "And that's the last that we're saying about this. This is a discussion that I choose not to have. It's late, and I'm tired. I'm going to bed."

The change that came over his face shocked me. I saw naked relief in his eyes. I think then I understood just how much he truly feared what he felt he had to face. That he had not revealed it to anyone was as great a show of courage as I have ever known. As I lifted the tent flap, he spoke again. "Fitz. I've really missed you. Don't go. Sleep here tonight. Please."

So I did.

chapter XVI

ELFBARK

Elfbark, more accurately called delventree bark, is a potent stimulant with the unfortunate additional effect of making the user prey to feelings of despondency and fearfulness. For this reason, it is often used by slave-owners in Chalced to increase the hours that a slave can work while at the same time dampening his spirit. Taken steadily over a long period it is addictive, and some say that even taken sporadically the herb can permanently alter a man's temperament, making him suspicious and defensive even with his closest companions, while eroding his sense of self-worth. Yet even with all these disadvantages, there are times when the risks are worth it for the stamina it may confer in times of necessity. It is less volatile a drug than either carris seed or cindin, in that those two may lead to wild surges of emotion and false euphoria that may prompt actions both foolish and dangerous.

The best quality of elfbark is obtained from the new branch tips of very old trees. Incise laterally along the twig and then around it at each end of the cut. Slip a fingernail or knife point under the bark edge and carefully loosen it from the branch. The freed bark will immediately curl into a cylinder. Store it thus in a pouch

*in a cool dry place until the bark has dried enough to be
grated into a powder, which can be infused as a tea.*

*If the need is immediate, a tea can be made from
the freshly harvested bark, but it is far more difficult to
judge the strength of the herb's potency from the color of
that tea.*

✎ RAICHAL'S "TABLE OF HERBS"

I emerged from the Fool's tent very early, before the rest of
the camp was astir. I had slept poorly, besieged by formless
nightmares. Toward dawn, I lay awake and wished that I
possessed Nettle's skill for mastering such uneasy dreams.
That put me in mind of her. I wished to speak with Chade
and Dutiful privately, without even Thick listening in. I
walked to the edge of our camp area to relieve myself. Deft
was on guard duty, and gave me a passing nod. I went directly to the Prince's tent, walking softly. I had forgotten
that I had assigned Swift guard duty there. The boy was
watchful as a fox, for as I drew close, the tent flap lifted
slightly, baring not only his vigilant eyes but also the point
of an arrow set in his bow.

"It's me," I said hastily, and was relieved when he eased
the bow and lowered the quarrel. I cudgeled my brain for
an errand to send him on, and then fell back on suggesting
he fetch some clean snow to melt for washwater for the
Prince, reminding him not to venture beyond the flagged
boundaries of the camp.

As soon as he trudged off, bucket in hand, I slipped inside the dim tent. "Are you awake?" I asked quietly.

Dutiful sighed heavily. "I am now. I feel as if I've been
awake for most of the night. Lord Chade?"

A muffled grunt was his only reply. Chade had the
blankets pulled up over his head.

"This is important, and I have to talk fast, before Swift
comes back," I warned them.

Chade lifted the covers a small crack. "Talk, then." He

yawned tremendously. "I am too old for this camping out in the snow after hiking all day," he muttered venomously, as if it were all my fault.

"I talked with the Fool last night, after he and Civil fought."

"Ah, yes. And we spoke with Civil. Or Civil spoke at us. For quite a long time. I had had no idea that your charade at Galekeep had been so convincing. Civil is quite distressed that we allow Swift to spend time with Lord Golden," Chade replied grumpily.

Dutiful snickered when I scowled. "The truth is that Civil would rather believe that than the truth. The Fool charted it out for me. He thinks that Sydel's parents, or at least one of them, were the traitors who sold Dutiful to the Piebalds. I suspect that her father is the one who broke the engagement between them, and that perhaps he did so more because Civil had opposed the Piebalds than because Sydel had behaved foolishly."

I was rewarded by Chade poking his nose out of his blankets. I watched him ponder, turning the pieces to see if they fit. After a moment, he said almost grudgingly, "Yes. He could be right. Sydel's parents would have been well positioned for all that was done. Would that I had an extra message bird, to send these tidings to the Queen! But I have just the one for Buckkeep, and one for the Hetgurd, to bring them back to fetch us. There are no birds to spare."

I raised an eyebrow at him. "Thick and Nettle?" I asked bluntly. I wondered if he had kept the Prince in ignorance.

Chade shook his head, tangling his white hair against his blankets. "No. That link is not ready to bear tidings as heavy as this. Think of the consequences if the message were incorrectly interpreted, or if the girl refused to believe Thick's tidings. No. That arrangement must be trained and tested, with simple messages, both sent and received, before we can rely on it for serious purposes." He sighed heavily, the sound an unuttered rebuke to me. "Thick will sleep in our tent tonight. Before he dozes off, Dutiful will ask him to convey greetings to Nettle, and to pass on some simple message to the Queen, one that will provoke a response from her. The creation of that will take some thought. If it goes well, then we will try a more weighty message the next night. But only when we are certain that messages are being relayed accurately will we pass on our suspicions of a traitor." He nodded to himself, and then rolled his head to look at the Prince. "Agreed?"

"Agreed." Dutiful gave a small sigh of his own. "Let us hope that Queen I-Highly-Doubt-It will be receptive to communicating with me via the Skill." And he too gave me a pointed look that placed the blame squarely on my doorstep that he and his cousin did not already know one another.

"I did what I thought best," I said stiffly.

And Chade, ever one to seize an advantage, agreed smoothly with "Of course you did. You always act from high motives, Fitz. But next time it is up to you to make a significant decision based on what you 'think is best,' you may remember this, and reflect that perhaps I have a few more years of experience than you do. Perhaps the next time, you will give my opinion of the matter a bit more weight."

"I will keep your advice in mind," I agreed, and this time my words were formally cool as well as stiff. Never had I thought to have my loyalty tugged between Chade and the Fool as if it were a rag desired by two puppies. Each had conceded that the decision would be mine, but apparently neither trusted me to make it without prompting. And then Swift returned with a pot packed full of snow so I excused myself and left. The Prince watched me go with thoughtful eyes but I felt no touch of his mind on mine.

By that time, the rest of the camp was well astir. Peottre had arisen early, Riddle told me, and had gone ahead to scout out the first part of our journey. He did not like the balmy breeze, heavy with moisture, that blew over the snowy ground. Even Thick was up and blundering about in the tent, scattering the contents of his pack in an effort to find fresh clothing. When I told him that we were traveling light and would both wear what we had on the day before, he looked quite displeased. I reminded him that when he first came into the Prince's service, he had had but one set of clothing to his name. At that, he knit his brows as if thinking deeply, then shook his head and said he did not recall such a time. I did not think the point worth arguing. I bundled him into his outer clothes and got him out of the tent so our guardsmen could strike it.

I found food for us, plain porridge and a bit of salt fish. He wasn't pleased with the breakfast and neither was I, but it was all that we had. Then I busied myself lightening his pack into mine. All the while I spoke to him encouragingly about the day's travel, saying that now that we knew how to walk over this glacier, we would do better and keep up with the others. He nodded, but in an unconvinced way that made my heart sink.

With a casualness I didn't feel, I observed, "I didn't sleep well last night. Bad dreams. But doubtless you had Nettle for company, and soothing dreams to welcome you."

"Nah." He pulled off his mitten to scratch his nose, and then spent a few moments putting it back on. "Bad dreams were everywhere last night," he observed darkly. "Nettle couldn't change them. When I called her, she just told me, 'Come away from there, don't look at that.' But I couldn't, because they were everywhere. I walked and walked and walked through the snow, but the dreams just kept coming up to me and looking at me." He took off his mitten and poked thoughtfully at his nose. "One had maggots in his nose. Like boogies, but wriggly. It made me think I had maggots in *my* nose."

"No, Thick, your nose is fine. Don't think about it. Come, let's walk around and see what everyone else is doing."

We were among the first to be ready to depart. I was

anxious to be on the move, for the clear sky had filled with low clouds. The wind was damp, and the prospect of either snow or rain was daunting to me. The others seemed to be taking a very long time to get ready, even though Peottre prowled through the camp casting anxious looks at the sky and beseeching us to get an early start. Thick began to complain of being too tired to hike and too bound up with layers of clothing. To distract him, I took him with me to watch the Fool take down his tent. Swift was already there, helping him. The lad's pack, quiver, and bow were neatly stacked to one side as he followed the Fool's instructions for dismantling the wooden poles that had supported the tent's airy fabric. I noted in passing that the peculiar arrow I had seen him holding the day before was now in his quiver.

The tent collapsed swiftly. The poles disassembled into pieces no longer than a good arrow. I had thought his little oil pot for his fire was heavy clay, but when I picked it up out of curiosity, it felt light and almost porous. The airy coverlets crushed down into a bundle the size of a small cushion. When all had been stowed, the Fool's pack was sizable and probably heavier than mine, even with Thick's belongings in it. Nevertheless, he shouldered into its harness and hefted it onto his back without a grunt. Never before had I seen a camp so neatly and swiftly stowed, and my admiration for Elderling skill at devising such things increased.

"The Elderlings made such marvelous things, and then they vanished. I've always wondered what made an end of them." I was not trying to start a conversation so much as distract Thick. He was rubbing at his nose again.

"When the dragons perished, the Elderlings perished with them. The one could not exist without the other." The Fool spoke as if he observed that leaves were green and the sky blue, as if that were a fact everyone accepted.

Before I could comment on that astonishing statement,

Thick dropped his hand from his nose and asked, "What's an Elderling?"

"No one really knows," I told him, and then the look on the Fool's face stopped me. He looked as if he would burst with it if I didn't give him a chance to tell. I wondered when he had acquired the knowledge and why he chose now to share it. Swift, sensing excitement, drew closer.

"The Elderlings were an old people, Thick. Old not just in how long ago they prospered, but old in how many years they numbered to a life. I suspect that for some of them, memory reached back beyond even the long spans of their own lives, back into the lives of their forebears."

Thick's brow was furrowed as he endeavored to understand. Swift was already enraptured in the tale. I interrupted. "Do you know these things, or do you guess?"

He pondered this for a moment. "I am as sure of these things as I can be, without either an Elderling or a dragon to consult."

Now it was my turn to look puzzled. "A dragon? Why would you consult a dragon about the Elderlings?"

"They are . . . intertwined." The Fool appeared to choose his word carefully. "In all I have read or heard, we never find one without the other. It seems that they create one another, or are necessary to one another's being somehow. I cannot explain it, I can only observe it."

"So, if you succeed in bringing back the dragons, you restore the Elderlings as well?" I asked recklessly.

"Perhaps." He smiled uncertainly. "I don't know. But I do not think it would be an evil thing if that happened."

And that was as much talk as we had time for. Peottre had returned and he wanted us on the move as swiftly as possible. The Prince called for Thick, and we hurried to him. Chade sent me a brief scowl. *What was that long conversation about?*

Elderlings, I replied, well aware that both Dutiful and Thick were sharing our thoughts. *Lord Golden believes that*

if he can restore dragons to the world, the Elderlings would re-
turn, as well. He feels there is some link between them, though
he cannot explain what it might be.

And that was all?

Yes. The brevity of my reply let him know I resented
his prying. I wondered if Dutiful's Skill-silence meant he
approved or disapproved of Chade's attitude. Then I told
myself it didn't matter. If the time came when it was truly
up to me whether the dragon lived or died, then I would
decide. Until then, I refused to torment myself with it, or
to sever my friendship with either of them.

Peottre formed us up for the day's journey. Today, we
took our places right behind the Prince's company. He
warned us that the mellow wind now sweeping over the
glacier ahead of us could make the surface unpredictable.
We would follow the old established trail, looking for the
poles and banners that marked it, but should remember
that conditions changed and the trail was not absolutely
trustworthy. Snow could blow across recent fissures, making it look like sound ground. He cautioned us again to be
sure of our every step. Then, staves in hand, we moved out
in a line. For the first part of the march, Thick and I kept up
well enough. He coughed, but not as much as he had, and
he trudged along gamely. Peottre moved us more slowly
today, plunging his stave ahead of us before every step he
took. He was correct about the treacherous weather. Although the warmer breeze soon had us loosening our hoods
and collars, it sculpted the damp snow into fantastic
shapes. The bluish shadows cast by the icy forms imparted
a dreamlike quality to the frozen land we traversed.

Twice, Peottre turned us aside from his chosen path.
The first time, he prodded the snow, only to have the
crusty surface suddenly give way beneath the pressure. The
top of the snow sagged, then collapsed and fell into a deep
hollow before us. The winds had sculpted an airy bridge
out of the frozen crystals, too fragile to bear any creature's

weight. He turned us and took us around the revealed chasm.

Our second detour came in the afternoon. By then, Thick had grown weary and discouraged. The damp snow clung heavily to our leggings and boots, and before long the main party outdistanced us, until we followed in their trodden path. We had just crested a long, low ridge when we met them all coming back toward us. Peottre had found very soft snow, his stave sinking into it to the depth of a short man, and had turned back, to seek a better route. It had been a weary climb, and Thick muttered curses as we turned and followed them back down into the trough of icy landscape.

The summer daylight bouncing off the blue and white snow dazzled our eyes. We squinted until the tears came and our brows ached with the tension. And still Peottre urged us onward.

We hiked far longer that second day, both in distance and time. The sun began its slow roll along the horizon, and still we pushed on. Thick and I followed at a substantial distance, and I soon began to wonder if Peottre would ever stop for the night. Twice Thick had stopped and refused to go on. He was tired, the damp snow was soaking through his boots and leggings, he was cold, he was hungry, and he was thirsty. He was a litany of my own complaints, and listening to him whine them only seemed to make them more unbearable. It was hard enough to talk myself into going on without prodding him along as well. His music today was a dull thudding of percussion against me, a steady and relentless rain of blows made of the crunch of our feet on the crusty snow and the keen sound of staves driving into crystalline snow.

If I walked in front of him, Thick lagged far behind, so I had to walk behind him, enduring his methodically slow poking of the snow in front of him. As the evening shadows lengthened, it became a tedious repetition of the day before. As I seethed along behind him, one slow step after another, the situation seemed to become more and more intolerable. My anger grew, slowly but steadily, like a fire methodically fed coal one lump at a time. When had I been thrust into this role? Why did I endure it? Why had Chade chosen me for this demeaning role? It had to be a punishment, a deliberate humiliation. I had been a warrior for the Farseers once. Now, in retaliation that I had taken my freedom, Chade humiliated me by making me nurse-maid to a fat, smelly moron. I tried to recall all the logical reasons, to ask myself who else should be the watchdog for one so powerfully Skilled as Thick, and yet I could no longer convince myself of the necessity of my loathsome task. My thoughts spiraled down, down into an ever-deeper chasm of frustration and anger and resentment. With an effort, I controlled myself. In a sugary voice, I coaxed him along. "Please move along a bit faster, Thick. Look. They've begun to set up the camp. Don't you want to get to the camp and get dry and warm?"

He turned his head to glare at me. "You say nice words. But I know what you are thinking at me. Like knives and rocks and big knobby sticks. Well, you made me come here. And if you try to hurt me, I'll hurt you back even worse. Because I'm stronger than you. I'm stronger, and I don't have to obey you."

Foolishly, he had warned me: I threw up my Skill-walls as I readied my own strength against him. In the moment before Thick's Skill-blast hit me, I became aware that all my animosity toward him had died, like a fire suddenly smothered under a wet blanket. His attack hit me, an iron hammer on an anvil of cheese. He had not touched me, and then I felt as if he had crushed my body in his grip. I staggered and then fell into the snow, feeling that the very blood must burst out through my skin, as Thick suddenly demanded, "Why are we mad? What are we doing?"

It was a child's wail of dismay. He must have thrown up his walls against me, and experienced the same loss of anger that I had. He waddled through the snow toward where I had fallen as the long-threatened rain began to pelt us. I rolled away from his touch, knowing that he meant well, but fearful that if he touched me, my walls would fall before him. "I'm not hurt, Thick. Really, I'm not. I'm just a bit sick." And stunned. And rattled. And aching as if I'd been flung from a horse. I got my knees under me and lurched to my feet. "No, Thick, don't touch me. But listen. Listen. Someone is trying to trick us. Someone is using our own magic to put bad thoughts in our heads. Someone we don't know." I knew it with sudden certainty. Someone was employing the Skill against us.

"Someone we don't know," he said dully. Dimly, I was aware of Dutiful trying to Skill to me. Doubtless they had felt some shadow impact of Thick's attack on me. I ventured to drop my walls for an instant, to Skill to them, *Be wary! Guard your thoughts!* And then I slammed my defenses tight against the insidious fingering of Skill that had attempted to once again infiltrate my mind. I knew that I should try to strike back, or at least follow the Skill-thread back to them. It took every bit of courage I possessed to drop my walls. I reached out wildly, Skilling in all directions to see who had been poisoning my mind against Thick.

I felt nothing and no one. Chade and Dutiful and Thick were there, walled against me. I thought of groping toward Nettle, and decided against it. My attackers might not know of her; I would not show her to them. I drew a shuddering breath, and then once more threw up my Skillwalls. I felt only marginally safer. We had an unknown enemy. I would not rest until I had uncovered all I could about them.

"It's the same ones that made my bad dreams, too," Thick announced decisively.

"I don't know. Maybe."

"I know. Yes. It's them, the bad-dream makers." Thick nodded emphatically.

The rain was coming down steadily, shushing against

the snow around us. I hoped the others had already put the tents up and that there would be some sort of dry shelter awaiting us when we arrived. All day long, the wet had crept up me from the damp snow. Now it drenched down on me, completing my misery. "Come on, Thick. Let's get to the camp," I suggested, and we lurched forward through the snow that packed unevenly under our feet. "Keep your Skill-walls up," I cautioned him as we slogged along. "Someone was trying to make us think bad thoughts about each other. They don't know that we are friends. They tried to make us hurt each other."

Thick looked at me dolefully. "Sometimes we are friends. Sometimes we fight."

It was true. Just as it was true that I did resent always being his caretaker. They had found my resentment and irritation with Thick and fed it, just as Verity had used to seek for fear or arrogance in our enemies, and feed it until our foes made some deadly mistake. It had been a subtle and well-planned attack by someone who had touched my mind enough to sense the feelings I hid from all others. That was unnerving.

"Sometimes we fight," I admitted to Thick. "But not to really hurt each other. We disagree. Friends often disagree. But we don't try to hurt each other. Even when we're angry with each other, we don't try to hurt each other. Because we are friends."

Thick gave a sudden, deep sigh. "I did try to hurt you. Back on the boat, I made you bump your head a lot. I'm sorry, now."

It was the most sincere apology I'd ever received in my life. I had to reciprocate. "And I'm sorry that I had to make you come here, on a boat."

"I think I forgive you. But I'll get angry with you again if you put me on a boat to go home."

"That's fair," I said after a moment. I tried to keep the dread and discouragement from my voice.

Thick shocked me when he halted and suddenly took

my hand. Even through my Skill-walls, I felt the steady warmth of his regard. "I always got angry at my mum when she washed my ears," he told me. "But she knew I loved her. I love you too, Tom. You gave me a whistle. And pink sugar cake. I'll try not to be mean to you anymore."

The simple words caught me off guard. He stood, lips and tongue pushed out, his round little eyes peering at me from under his knit cap. He was a toadish little man, and his nose was running. It had been a long time since I'd been offered love on such a simple and honest basis. Strangely enough, it woke the wolf in me. I could almost see the slow, accepting wag of Nighteyes' tail. We were pack. "I love you too, Thick. Come on. Let's get out of the wet."

The rain turned colder and was sleet by the time we staggered into camp. Chade came to meet us. As soon as he was within earshot of a whisper, I warned him, "Keep your walls up. Someone tried to fog us with Skill, much as Verity used the Skill to confuse and confound our enemy during the time of the Red Ship War. It . . . they sought to turn Thick and me against each other. And very nearly succeeded."

"Who is behind it?" Chade demanded, as if he thought I would actually know.

"The bad-dream people," Thick told him earnestly. I shrugged at Chade's scowl. It was as good an answer as any that I had.

Camp that night was a miserable place. Everything was either wet or damp. The tiny fires we could have allowed ourselves from our precious fuel wouldn't burn. Peottre once more set boundaries for our camp and then risked himself to reconnoiter to select tomorrow's route for us. A dim glow, as from a single candle, came from the Narcheska's tent. The Fool's was a gorgeous, beckoning blossom in the night, and I longed simply to go there, but Chade had demanded my presence and I recognized the need for my full report to him.

The Prince's tent was made smaller by the spread of wet clothing. No one even pretended it would dry by morning. Chade and the Prince had already changed into fresh clothing. A fat candle in a metal cup tried sadly to heat a small kettle of snow water. I took Thick's coat and boots outside to shake the wet clumps of snow from them while he put on a long wool shirt and dry socks. Somehow, stepping outside again made the bite of the wet wind worse. I took Thick's garments back into the tent and found drying space for them on the floor. Tomorrow would be a miserable hike when we had to redon our damp garments. Well, there was no help for it, I thought bitterly. Still, "This is not like any quest to slay a monstrous beast for a fair damsel that I've ever heard a minstrel sing," I observed sourly as I reentered the tent.

"No," Thick agreed sadly. "There should be swords and blood. Not stupid wet snow."

"I don't think you'd like swords and blood any better than the wet snow, Thick," the Prince observed glumly, but at the moment I tended to agree with Thick. One savage battle already seemed preferable to this endless slogging. With my luck, I'd probably get both before the end.

"We have an enemy," I announced to them. "One that knows how to use the Skill against us."

"So you said," Chade observed. "But Dutiful and I have conferred and we've felt nothing of that." He poured the lukewarm water over tea herbs, scowling skeptically as he did so.

That confounded me for a moment. I had expected that if anyone chose to attack us, they would make an attempt against the whole coterie. I said as much and then added, "Why would they target only Thick and me? We appear to be amongst the lowliest of your servants."

"Anyone aware of the Skill must be aware that Thick is not what he seems to be, nor you. Perhaps they realized Thick's strength and sought to get rid of it by having you two destroy each other."

"But why not strike immediately against the Prince and his trusted adviser? Why not turn you against each other, and sow discord at the top of the command rather than work from the bottom up?"

"It would be nice to know that," Chade conceded after a moment's pondering. "But we don't. Indeed, all we have is that you and Thick felt you were under attack. The Prince and I felt nothing, until you two turned on one another."

"That was rather impressive," Dutiful added, rubbing his temples wearily. He suddenly gave a huge yawn. "I wish this was over and done with," he said softly. "I'm tired, I'm cold, and I have no real heart for the task I must do."

"That could be a Skill-influence, subtly applied to you," I warned him. "Your father used the Skill that way, to confound the steersmen of the Red Ships and send them onto the rocks."

The Prince shook his head. "My walls are up and tight. No, this comes from within me." He watched Chade pour some yellowish tea from the pot, scowl, and return it to steep some more.

"It's not a Skill-influence," Chade concurred bitterly. "It's the damn Fool, talking to the Wit coterie and the Hetgurd folk, stirring up sympathy for the dragon and preying on the Hetgurd superstitions. Hold to your resolve, my prince. Remember, you gave the Narcheska your word that you would lay the dragon's head on her mothers' hearth for her."

"That you did," Peottre observed heavily as he lifted the tent flap. "May I come in?"

"Yes, you may," Dutiful replied. "And yes, I recall what I promised. But I never promised to take joy in the doing of it."

My Wit had warned me that someone had approached the tent, but I had expected it to be Swift or Riddle. I wondered why the Outislander had come, and hoped he would not hold his tidings until I had departed. But the nod he gave me seemed to concede my right to be there. Nor did he offer any ominous words of danger on the path ahead, but instead gave a hard smile as he said, "Today was little joy for any of us. And tomorrow will be as wearying. After such a cold and wet day, I thought I would share with you our cure for such a miserable journey." He sighed heavily. "This weather will not make our task any easier. The rain eats into the snow, weakening places that once were sound. Tomorrow, we must be wary of avalanche as well as crevasses as we cross the saddle of the island."

As he spoke, he was unwrapping a dark cake from a stained square of fabric. I was hungry and my nose was keen. Whatever it was, it had been soaked in brandy to preserve it. He broke a piece from it, revealing raisins, bits of suet, and what was probably dried apple. The brandy smell grew stronger. Thick sat up eagerly, but warily. I was still shielded from his Skill, but his worry reached me faintly. Fish oil. Would it taste of fish oil?

Peottre seemed to notice my avid stare, for he grinned as he offered me the first chunk. "You look to be the one coldest and wettest still," he observed. It was true, since the others had already changed to drier clothing. I took it gratefully. As I bit into it, he said, "These cakes are what our warriors call 'courage cake.' We make them with dark thick honey, dried fruits, and strengthening herbs, and then all is soaked in brandy to make it keep well. A man can fight a day or travel two on but a handful of this."

The sweetness and brandy-echo filled my mouth. As I swallowed, I caught a familiar aftertaste. The bitterness of elfbark had been cloaked by the cloying sweetness of the honey, suet, and fruit. I knew I should warn Chade, even as my weary body shouted in anticipation of the surge of energy it would bring.

Then the world went dead around me.

I do not know how else to describe it. The first time I encountered Forged folk was also the first time I was aware that I had the Wit Magic. I had never realized that I had an extra sense of the kinship of all creatures until I saw living beings that made no imprint on that sense. Forging removed one from the intertwining net of life, made humans into individual unconnected things that ate and raped and existed with absolutely no empathy or sympathy for other living creatures. Only in meeting them had I discovered how the Wit connected me to all living things.

This was a similar experience, but its antithesis. I had thought of the Skill as a magic that only linked me to other Skill-users. Now I was suddenly severed from all the myriad tiny connections it made to all folk. The great voice of the human world, the constant murmur of other thoughts and minds around me, was stilled. I blinked and hastily probed an ear with my finger, wondering for a fraction of a second what had happened to me. I saw, I heard, I smelled, I touched, and the taste of the food lingered still in my mouth, but some other sense, unnamed and unknown until that instant, had been completely quenched in me by that single bite. I made a sudden prodigious effort to reach Chade and Dutiful with the Skill but it was like asking a frozen hand to grip. I remembered how once that sense had been triggered, but now it was a numbed place inside me.

Smiling, Peottre had handed Thick a chunk of the cake. The little man had his mouth open wide and his hand was traveling toward it. I lunged to catch his wrist and pulled it away from him. He moved his mouth after it, snapping at the treat in a gesture that would have been comical if it were not such a threat to the coterie. "Elfbark!" My deprivation of the Skill made me shout the word, as if mere voice alone could not convey such a warning.

I immediately moderated my tone, behaving as if my remark were intended for Thick alone. "No, Thick! You know the herb makes you sick. Let me have that and I promise that I'll find you something else good to eat. No, Thick, please."

"What herb? I'm not sick! It's mine, it's mine! You said

we were friends and wouldn't hurt each other. Let go! Not fair, it's not polite to grab!"

In his love of sweets, he struggled with me for it. I dared not let him have even a taste. Never had I had such a strong reaction to the herb. I felt the rush of its energy through me, and wondered how deeply would I fall into the inevitable trough of despair that followed elfbark use. Then I had scooped the handful of cake from his grasp. He sat down flat on the floor, gave one angry sob, and then went off in a coughing fit. I handed the cake hastily to Chade with the improvised warning, "I wouldn't eat this in front of him, sir. I know how he is about sweets. If he sees you having some without him, well, I'd predict a disruption that would deafen us all."

I wondered if Chade and Dutiful reached toward me with the Skill. I wondered if Thick tried to make me stumble into the fire in revenge. But I felt absolutely nothing. No touch of them brushed against my senses. My Wit knew they were still there, and that was a comfort. But the Skill-threads that had run amongst us were all severed. Peottre scowled, looking on the verge of affront. Chade reacted more swiftly than I could have hoped, saying, "Ah, yes, I recall what an effect it had on you last time, Thick. It wouldn't be good for you, now, don't fuss, there's a good fellow. I'm sure we can find something just as nice for you." He turned to Peottre with a conspiratorial wink. "The Prince's good fellow stayed awake a day and a night, and then fell into such a black mood that nothing could cheer him for several days. Not the sort of thing to invite on such an expedition as ours. Come, Thick, don't scowl like that. I think Prince Dutiful has some sugar barley sticks that he has been saving for you."

The Prince was already rummaging in his pack and Chade hastily took the mashed handful of cake from me, deftly returned it to the rest of the cake and wrapped it up again. He tucked it immediately into his pack. "I'm sure the Prince and I will enjoy a bit of this later, perhaps after

Thick has fallen asleep," he confided to Peottre in a low-ered voice. "I, for one, will appreciate what an herb like elf-bark can do for an old man. I wasn't aware that it was used in the Out Islands."

"Elfbark?" Did Peottre feign his ignorance? "We have no plant by such an odd name. There are herbs in the cake but each mothershouse has her own recipe for it, and the ingredients are jealously guarded. But I can tell you that this is from my own home, the same mothershouse the Narcheska shares. This 'courage cake' has been a food that has sustained the Narwhal Clan for generations."

"Doubtless it is!" Chade exclaimed delightedly. "And I look forward to trying it, later tonight. Or perhaps early to-morrow morning, to have its invigoration with me for the day after a sound night's sleep. Poor Tom, I know what an effect elfbark has on you! You may enjoy it, but I doubt you'll get a wink of sleep tonight. I've told you before not to indulge in it at evening. But, well, there's no talking to you on that topic, is there?"

I essayed a grin I didn't feel. "That's true, Lord Chade, sir. No matter how long you might lecture me, doubtless I'd not hear a word you said." A tiny change in his eyes sug-gested he understood me only too well.

He poured weak tea for himself, sipped it, and then coughed loudly, nearly gagging, and vigorously thumping himself on the chest. In a wheezing voice, he added, "You are dismissed, Tom Badgerlock. Get yourself a bit of food, but please report back here before you sleep. I think Thick will wish to sleep here tonight."

"Yes, my lord." His mimed action had not been lost on me.

I left the tent, and by a roundabout route, walked to the far corner of the camp. The rain had stopped, but the wind still blew. At the outskirts of camp, I thrust two fin-gers down my throat and tried desperately to gag up the bite of cake I'd eaten. It didn't work. I'd fasted too long and my belly had taken it down too swiftly. What little I brought up left me shuddering with its bitterness. I ate a handful of wet snow to try to clear the bile from my mouth, kicked loose snow over my vomit, and went shaking back toward the tents. More than mere cold chilled me. I think that once a man has experienced the insidious treachery of poison, he never fully recovers from it. To know that you have taken something into your body, to be aware that it is working changes, debilitating changes, with every beat of your heart, is an excursion into horror that is hard to describe. I had tasted the elfbark and I already felt its impact. What if there had been other drugs in there, ones I had not tasted, working damage I did not yet suspect? I tried to rein my mind away from that precipice. It made no sense, I told myself. The cake had been a gift from Peottre, delivered without apparent guile. We were here to accomplish his mission of slaying the dragon; why would he attempt to poison one of us? Yet I could not quite dismiss it as a perverse twist of luck that he had fed me such a form of the herb strong enough to obliterate my magic.

I was cold and wet and shaky. I didn't want to join the guardsmen in our tent until I had finished calming myself. In a sort of instinctive retreat to safety, I found myself outside the Fool's tent. I fumbled with cold hands at the tent flap. "Lord Golden," I called softly, belatedly recalling that he might have other guests.

There must have been some note in my voice that alerted him to my distress. He flung the flap open and beckoned me hastily in. Then, "Stand still. Don't drip everywhere." He had already changed out of his hiking clothes. He looked warm and dry in a long black robe. I envied him.

"Peottre fed me a bit of cake. It had elfbark in it, and I've lost my Skill Magic." The words tumbled from me, broken by my chattering teeth.

"Take off your wet things." He had begun rummaging in his pack almost as soon as I entered. Now he dragged out a long coppery garment. "This will probably fit you. It's warmer than it looks. How could elfbark steal all your magic in one bite? It's never affected you that way before."

I shook my head. "It just did. And someone is attacking Thick and me with the Skill, trying to make us hate each other. It nearly worked, until I thought Thick was going to attack me with the Skill, so I put up my walls and then I could suddenly think my own thoughts and I knew that I didn't really resent having to nursemaid him all the time. It's not really his fault, and even if I don't like having to do it, I shouldn't take it out on him, should I? If anything, I should be angry with Chade, not Thick. He's the one who has put me in this position, and I think that half of it is that he's trying to keep me so busy that I'm separated from you and therefore won't be influenced by you. Because he wants me simply to follow his orders and not to think—"

"Stop!" the Fool exclaimed, alarmed. I halted in mid-word. I opened my mouth to ask what was wrong, but he held up both hands. "Fitz. Listen to yourself. I've never heard you rattle on that way. It's...disturbing."

"It's the elfbark." I shivered with the restless energy that coursed through me. The last of my wet clothing slapped onto the pile and I gratefully accepted the garment he held out to me, then flinched at its chill weight in my hands. "It's cold. It's cold as iron! What is this made from, fish scales?"

"Just trust me and put it on. It warms quickly."

I had little choice. I pulled it over my head and it slithered down my body. The long robe reached almost to my feet. I shifted my shoulders in its grip and it suddenly relaxed. "That's strange. It felt tight across my shoulders and chest, and then, when I flexed my shoulders, it just settled onto me. Look. It even reaches to my wrists. It's like unimaginably fine chain metal. Is this more Elderling magic? Is this from the Rain Wilds? I wonder how they made it, and from what? Look at the way the color shifts when I move."

"Fitz. Stop chattering like that. It's unnerving." The Fool had taken possession of my wet clothes. As he lifted them, a fine trickle of water ran out of them. "I'm putting these outside to drain. It's hopeless to expect them to dry by morning. Do you have others?"

"Yes. In my pack, but I left that in the Prince's tent. I left the keg of Chade's explosion powder there, too. And Thick's things were mostly in my pack, but that's all right as he is there and he'll need them. So it's good that they are already there." I heard myself babbling and managed to stop talking before he commanded me to.

For a few moments longer, I shivered, and then I felt the robe returning the warmth of my body to me. With a sigh, I sank down onto the Fool's blankets and drew my icy feet up under me. A moment later, I had unfolded myself and restlessly tried a new position. The Fool reentered the tent and regarded me curiously as I stood and paced a turn around his tiny candle. "What is it?"

"It's like ants running under my skin." I pulled my straggling hair back off my face and refastened my warrior's tail. "I can't sit still. I can't stop talking and thinking, and I can't really think in any sort of order, if that makes any sense at all." My hands suddenly felt too large for me. I systematically popped each of my knuckles, and then shook my hands loose again. I looked up to find the Fool staring at me, his teeth gritted. "I'm sorry," I apologized hastily. "I can't help it."

"That's obvious," he muttered. Then, more clearly he added, "I wish I had some way to help you, but giving you herbs to calm you might not be the best solution. I fear too the plunge in spirits that must follow this wild flight you're on. Never have I seen you so besieged by restlessness. If the pit of bleak despair that follows elfbark is as deep as this craze is lofty, I fear for us all."

I saw by his face that he was serious. "I dread it, too. That is, I know I should dread it, but I simply can't focus on it right now. Too many other thoughts overwhelm me.

How will I dry my clothes before tomorrow, and I was supposed to report back to Chade later, yet I do not think I should wander through the camp in this robe, however warm it is. Yet I cringe at the thought of putting my wet clothing back on, even for the brief walk back to Dutiful's tent. I left my pack there, with all my dry things in it. Thick's things are in it, too. But that's good, because Thick is there and he'll need them."

"Hush," he begged me, interrupting the outpour of my thoughts. "Hush, please, Fitz, and let me try to think. Always before, elfbark has done no more than dampen your talent, and that was passing. Do we dare hope that this will wear off and your magic return?"

I shrugged wildly. "I don't know. I don't think we can judge anything about this by what elfbark has done to me before. Did I tell you how close Thick came to eating it as well?"

"No. You didn't." The Fool spoke carefully, as if I were slightly mad, and perhaps I was at that time. "Would you try to do this for me? Leave your hair and your mouth alone. Fold your hands in your lap and tell me what happened to you today. The whole day, please."

I had not realized that I was tugging at my lower lip until he mentioned it. I folded my hands in my lap and made an effort to report to him as if he were Chade. I watched his face grow graver as I spoke and I knew that my words rattled out like hailstones, and that my tale was disjointed, told in bits and patches as I wove the events back and forth in my mind. Before I had finished, I was up and pacing the small confines of his tent. I could not master my agitation. A sudden inspiration came over me. "Here!" I cried, advancing on him, my bared wrist thrust out to him. "Let us test it and see if my Skill is as gone as I think it is. Touch me. Try to reach into me with the Skill as you once did."

He stared up at me, his face gone slack with astonishment. Then a sickly smile of disbelief spread over his face. "You're *asking* me to do this?"

"Of course. Yes. Let's find out how bad it is. If you can still reach me, then perhaps my Skill will come back to me as the herb wears off. Let's try it." I sat down beside him, and set my forearm, wrist up, on top of his knee. He looked at his faded fingerprints on my wrist and then gave me a sideways look.

"No." He drew back from me. "You are not yourself tonight, Fitz. This is not something you would ordinarily allow, let alone request. No."

"What, are you scared?" I challenged him. "Go ahead. What can we lose?"

"Respect for one another. That I would do such a thing when you were as good as drunk. No, Fitz. Stop tempting me."

"Don't worry. I'll remember, tomorrow, that I suggested this. I need to know. Is my magic dead in me?" In some isolated corner of my soul, I felt alarm. I wanted to stop and think, but the anxiety wouldn't let me. *Do it now, do something now, do anything now.* The drive to be doing, doing anything, was a pressing need that could not be denied.

I reached out and took hold of his slender wrist. His hand was ungloved and unresisting. As if fitting together a wooden puzzle, I set his hand to my wrist. His cool fingertips fell into alignment with the scars he had left on me. I waited. I felt nothing. I looked at him quizzically.

He had closed his eyes. A moment later, he opened them. They were deep gold and devastated as he said in disbelief, "Nothing. I feel the warmth of your wrist under my fingers. I reach for you, but you are not there. And that is all."

My heart lurched sideways in my chest. I instantly tried to deny what we had just established. "Well. Doesn't prove anything, I suppose. We've never tried this before, so what do we know of what to expect? Nothing. Nothing at all. Tomorrow, I may awaken and find the Skill as strong in me as ever."

"Or not," the Fool suggested quietly, watching my face. His fingers still rested on my wrist. "Perhaps we shall never connect in this way again."

"Or not," I agreed. "Perhaps I shall wake just as isolated and deaf as I am at this moment. Perhaps." I stood up, pulling my wrist from his loose clasp. "Well. It's no use thinking about it and worrying about it, is it? As well to fret over whether it will be wet or dry tomorrow. What will be will be." I paused, thinking I should keep still, but then the question burst out anyway. "Do you think Peottre did this to me purposely? Do you think he knew that elfbark can destroy the Skill? And how does he know that I have the magic at all? And, if he wants me to help the Prince kill the dragon, why would he disable me? Unless he doesn't really want us to kill Icefyre. Maybe he's lured us here so the Prince will fail. But that makes no sense. Does it?"

He looked battered by my onslaught of questions. "Can you be quiet, Fitz?" he asked me earnestly, and after a moment's thought, I shook my head.

"I don't think so." I shifted restively as I spoke. I was suddenly miserable. I could not find a comfortable position in which to be still. I was aware that I was sleepy but could not recall how to let go of wakefulness. I suddenly wanted all of it to go away and leave me in peace. I dropped my head into my hands and covered my eyes. "All my life, I've done everything wrong."

"It's going to be a long night," the Fool observed woefully.

chapter XVII

ICEFYRE

Now, this is the tale of Yysal Sealshoes and the dragon
Icefyre, and what befell her in the years when Wisal was
the Great Mother of her mothershouse. Wisal took a
dislike to a young man that Yysal had brought home to
her bedding, and she gave her reasons three: he was
bandy-legged and hollow-chested, and all know those are
traits that may be passed on to children, and Wisal did
not wish her mothershouse to be full of his bandy-legged
weaklings. His hair was red, which Wisal also did not
desire in her descendants; and whenever spring came to
the islands and the willow trees drooped with tiny furry
tails, the man sneezed and wept and coughed and was no
use at all for the spring chores. And so, when Yysal went
forth one summer day to gather crowberries from the
upper slopes of their mountain, Wisal told the other
women to gather clods of earth and rocks small enough
to sting but not cause major injury and drive Yysal's
bedmate away. This her sisters and mother and aunts did
with a good will, for none of them liked the way he
simpered at them whenever Yysal was absent.

When Yysal returned and found her bedmate fled,
she wept and she ranted and finally she vowed she would
go to the dragon and ask for vengeance on her own kin.

*All know that is a great sin against a mothershouse, and
yet she was so wroth, she would not listen to reason, nor
accept the hearty, black-haired young warrior they offered
her in place of her pale, scrawny stripling. And so she
went to Aslevjal, and waited for the tide of the year, and
then slipped under the icy shelves of the glacier to go deep
within its heart and beg of the dragon her evil wish..*

*Deep beneath the icy cap that domes the island, she
beached her tiny boat on a silty shore. She lifted her torch
but did not pause to wonder at the beauties of Icefyre's
blue ice tomb. Instead, she climbed out immediately and
made her way through the twisting blue tunnels to where
she might look up at the dragon encased in the ice. And
there she melted a hollow in the ice with the blood of the
lamb she had brought with her, and begged him to make
barren all the women who had driven her bedmate away
from her side.*

❧ BADGERLOCK'S TRANSLATION OF AN
OUT ISLAND BARD'S SONG

I recall the rest of that night and the following day and
night as one recalls fever dreams. My mind shies away from
remembering the misery I endured. "It was all in your
mind," Chade told me sometime later, and it stung that he
dismissed so lightly all that I had endured. *All of life,* I
wanted to tell him, *is in our minds. Where else does it take
place, where else do we add up what it means to us and subtract
what we have lost? An event is just an event until some person
attaches meaning to it.*

I survived it. Anyone who makes a difference between
such an herb and a poison has never been plunged into
such depths as I sounded. At some point that night, Chade
sent Riddle looking for me. He draped a blanket around me
and hurried me, barefoot and clad in the ridiculous Elderling robe, back to the Prince's tent. There, if I recall correctly, I spent several hours telling Chade just how much I

despised myself. Dutiful later told me that he had never lived through such a tiresome recounting of any man's imagined sins. I recall that several times he tried to reason with me. I spoke openly of killing myself, a fleeting notion that I had often considered but never before uttered. Dutiful was disgusted at such a maudlin fancy and Chade pointed out to me that it would be a selfish act that would not correct any of my stupidity. I think he was more than a bit weary of me by then.

And yet, it was not my fault. It was the despondency of the drug, not any rational consideration by me, that kept me talking through the night and on into dawn. By morning, Dutiful knew far more of my youthful excesses than I had ever planned on divulging to him. If he had ever been tempted to experiment with elfbark or carris seed, I am sure that long evening cured him of his curiosity.

When Thick could stand no more of my overemotional account, Riddle was summoned to escort him to the Witted coterie's tent, where Web took him in hand and settled him for the night. Chade and Dutiful had planned to attempt to contact Nettle with the Skill that night, but my indisposition made it impossible for them to focus. Before Thick fled, they made an attempt as a coterie to reach me with the Skill. They had no more luck than the Fool had. When I told Chade about that encounter, his face darkened and I knew he disapproved that I had even attempted that experiment with the tawny man.

The next day, both Riddle and Web walked with Thick and me. I am sure that Riddle was assigned the task by Chade, but I think Web came for me. To this day, I wonder what Thick told him to make him think it necessary that he attend me. I walked in a silent black despair, through an endless torment of bright ice and gently blowing snow. Riddle and Thick walked ahead of us, speaking little. Web came right behind me, and said not a word all day. Summer had regained its grip and the wind that sculpted the dunes into fantastic forms was gentle and almost warm. I remember that Web's bird circled over us twice, crying forlornly, and then went back to the sea. The presence of his Wit-beast reminded me savagely of the absence of mine, and sent me into a fresh pit of mourning. I did not sob but the tears ran down my face in a steady flow.

Emotion can be more exhausting than physical endeavor. By the time Peottre announced that we would set our tents, I no longer cared about anything. I was without volition as I stood and watched them put up the tents. Vaguely, I remember that Peottre apologized to Chade because his "courage rations" had so incapacitated me. Chade accepted the apology in an offhand way, replying that I had always had an unpredictable temperament and been prone to abusing herbs. I knew why he said such words, yet they struck to my heart like a dagger. I could not bring myself to eat the bowl of porridge that Web eventually brought me. I went to my blankets while everyone else was still awake. I did not sleep, but stared up at the shadows of the tent's recesses and tried to imagine why my father had ever lain with my mother. It seemed an evil thing they had done. I heard Web playing his little instrument for Thick outside the tent, and I suddenly missed the funny little man's Skill-music. Eventually, I must have slept, and heavily.

When I awoke, it was late in the day. All around me were the tousled pallets of the men-at-arms, empty. I wondered why they had not wakened me and why we had not struck camp and begun our day's march. I crawled shivering from my blankets, grimaced at the robe I still wore, and hastily pulled on my coat and outer trousers. I stuffed the robe into my pack, still wondering at the silence of the camp. I dreaded that some threat of the weather had forced us to delay our journey.

I emerged from the tent into a steady sweep of mild wind, laden with tiny crystals of snow swept down from the bulging shoulder of glacier that loomed over us. Around me, the camp seemed almost deserted. Web was tending a kettle of food on a tripod over a tiny fire in a clay pot. The pot was settling into the snow as its heat melted the ice around it. "Ah, you're awake," Web said with a welcoming smile. "I trust you're feeling better."

"I . . . yes, I am," I replied, somewhat surprised to find it was true. The unreasoning blackness of yesterday's mood had lifted. I did not feel cheery; the loss of my Skill still weighted me heavily and the task before us daunted me, but the deep despair that had led me to wishing to end my life had lifted. Slowly, a dull anger began to rise in me. I hated Peottre for what he had put me through. I knew that Chade's strategy with the man required me to refrain from any vengeance, but I refused to believe that those "rations" held an ordinary amount of elfbark that his comrades could consume without devastating effects. I'd been deliberately poisoned. Again. I hoped that sometime before I returned to the Six Duchies, fate would afford me the chance to even things with Peottre. All my training as an assassin forbade me the luxury of vengeance. Ever since King Shrewd had first made me his, I had been taught that my talents were used at the will of the Crown, not at my personal judgment or for private vengeance. Once or twice I'd strayed outside those guidelines, with devastating results. I reminded myself of that several times as I surveyed the area around me.

Our camp was pitched on a gentle slope of snow. Not far away, a ridge of black rock broke jaggedly through the snow's crust. Above me towered a steep mountain. It was like a cup with a piece broken out of its lip. Here and there, black stone outcropped from the snow crust. Its bowl cupped ice and snow, a frozen cascade that sloped down toward us. We were camped on the final, flattest spread of the spill.

"You're very quiet," Web observed gently. "Are you in pain?"

"No. Thank you for your concern. I've just been given a great deal to think about."

"And your Skill Magic has been stolen from you."

At the glance I gave him, he held up a fending hand. "No one else has deciphered that secret. Thick was the one who accidentally explained it to me. He was quite distressed for you. Annoyed by you too, but worried for you. Last night, he tried to explain to me that it wasn't just your bleak mood and constant talking and fidgeting that alarmed him, but that you were gone from his mind. He told me a story from when he was small. His mother let go of his hand one night on a crowded street during a fair. He was lost for hours, and he could not find her, not with his eyes or his mind. From the way he told his tale, I think she abandoned him, and then thought better of it later that night and came back for him. But he took a long time to explain to me that he knew his mother was there, but she wouldn't let him touch her thoughts. With you, he says, you are just gone. As if you were dead, as his mother is dead now. And yet you walk around and he sees you. You frighten him, now."

"Like a Forged One I must seem to him."

Web winced sympathetically. I knew then that he had experienced the chilling presence of Forged Ones, for he said, "No, my friend. I feel you still, with my Wit. You have not lost that magic."

"And yet what use is it to me, without a partner?" I asked the question bitterly.

He was silent for a moment, then spoke resignedly. "And that is yet another thing I could teach you, if ever you have the time to sit and learn."

There seemed little I could say to that. So I asked a question. "Why haven't we moved on yet today?"

He gave me a quizzical look, then smiled. "We are here, my friend. This is as close a camping site as we shall find. Peottre says the dragon used to be hazily visible in the ice near here. Prince Dutiful and Chade and the others are following Peottre and the Narcheska up to the dragon. The Hetgurd witnesses have gone with them. Up there." He pointed.

The glacier's polished and sculpted surface was deceptive. Where it appeared smooth and continuous, there were actually many falls and rises in its surface. Now, as I watched, our people emerged in a long line like a trail of ants higher on the icy hillside. I spotted Peottre in his furs leading them, with the Narcheska at his heels. Everyone was there, following Peottre up the hillside immediately above us. Only Web and I had remained in camp. I commented on that.

"I didn't want you to wake alone. Riddle said you had spoken of ending your own life." He shook his head sternly. "I believed better of you. And yet, having seen your black mood yesterday, I did not want to take the chance."

"I would not kill myself. That was a passing madness, the herb's toxin speaking rather than any true thought of mine," I excused myself. In truth, looking back on the wild words I had uttered the night before, I was ashamed that I had even spoken such a thought aloud. Suicide has always been deemed a coward's act in the Six Duchies.

"And why would you use such an herb, knowing it would affect you so?" he asked severely.

I bit my tongue, wishing that I knew what Chade had said of my debilitation. "I've used it in the past, for great pain or weariness," I said quietly. "This time, the dose was far stronger than I thought."

Web sighed in a great breath. "I see," he said, and no more than that, but his disapproval was strong.

I ate the congealing mass in the kettle. It was Outislander food, stinking of oily fish. They made a soup from sticky dry cubes of cooked fish mashed with oil to bind it. Heated with snow water, it made a greasy chowder. Despite the foul flavor, I felt more myself after I had eaten it. There was still a strange absence all around me. It was more than Thick's music silenced. I had grown accustomed to threads of awareness that extended to Dutiful, Chade, the Fool, and Nettle. I had been torn free of that web of contact.

Web watched me eat, and then clean the kettle. I

banked the tiny fire in the clay pot with small hope it would survive. Then, "Shall we join them?" he invited me, and I nodded grimly.

Peottre had marked a trail with bright scraps of red fabric on sticks driven into the snow both to the left and right. Web and I followed the meandering path up the face of the glacier. At first, we spoke little. Then, as we walked, Web began to speak to me, and finally, I listened.

"You asked what the use of the Wit is, when you do not have a companion. I understand that you mourn your wolf still, and that is only fitting. I'd think less of you if you rushed into another bonding simply for the sake of assuaging your own loneliness. That is not the Old Blood way, any more than a widowed man should wed someone simply to provide a mother for his bereaved children and someone to warm his bed. So, you are right to wait. But in the meantime, you should not turn your back on your magic.

"You speak little to the rest of us Witted ones. Those who do not know you share our magic think you avoid us because you despise it, Swift included. Even if you do not wish to let them know you too are Old Blood, I think you should correct that impression. I do not understand, fully, why you keep both your magics a secret. The Queen has said she will no longer allow persecution of the Witted, and I have seen that you fall under her protection in any case. And if you have the Farseer magic, the Skill, as I believe you do, well, that has always been an honorable and well-regarded magic in the Six Duchies. Why cloak that you serve your queen and prince with it?"

I pretended that I was too winded to answer immediately. The climb was steep and steady, but I was not that taxed by it. Finally, I surrendered to his silence. "I'd be giving away too many pieces of who I am. Someone will put them all together, look at me, and say, *The Witted Bastard lives. The killer of King Shrewd, the ungrateful bastard who turned on the old man who sheltered him.* I do not think our queen's policy of tolerance toward the Witted is ready for that yet."

"So you will live out all the rest of your years as Tom Badgerlock."

"It seems likely to me." I tried to keep the bitterness out of my voice and failed.

"Do you feel that?" Web asked me suddenly.

"I feel it's the wisest thing to do, if not the easiest," I replied reluctantly.

"No, no. Open your Wit, man. Do you feel something, something more immense than you've ever felt before?"

I halted and stood silent. The Wit is like any other sense. One becomes so accustomed to the sounds of the day or the smells of the cook fires that one ceases to pay full attention to them. Now I stood still, as if listening, but actually unfolding my awareness of the life-net around me. There was Web, warm and hearty and near. Farther up the trail, I sensed the others, a confused string of beings emanating various degrees of fatigue and discomfort. My sensation of those who were Witted was slightly sharper and clearer than for the ordinary folk of the party. I could not feel Web's bird; I suspected she was out over the water, feeding. "Only the ordinary—" I began to say, and then stopped. Had I felt something? A very large, subtle swelling of the Wit? It was as if a door had opened briefly and then closed again. I grew more still, and closed my eyes. No. "Nothing," I commented, opening them again.

He had been watching my face. "You felt it," he told me. "And I feel it still. Next time you sense it, hook on to it."

"Hook on to it?"

He shook his head regretfully. "Never mind. That is one of those things that 'one day' you'll have time to learn from me."

It was the closest he had come to a rebuke, and I was surprised by how much it stung. I knew I deserved it. I found the strength to be humble and asked, "Do you think you could explain it to me as we walk?"

He turned his head and lifted his eyebrows in gentle mock surprise. "Why, yes, Fitz. I could do that, now that you ask me to. Choose someone in the party ahead of us, someone unWitted, and I'll try to explain to you how it is done. Some Old Bloods theorize that it is how pack hunters settle on one animal in a herd and mark it out as their prey. Perhaps you've seen young wolves or other predators that fail to make that first step in hunting. Instead of selecting a single animal to hunt, they charge the entire herd or flock, and all prey evades them. That is, of course, one of the strengths of a herd. Prey animals cloak their individuality from the hunters, and hide in plain sight of them."

And so, very belatedly, began my lessons with Web. By the time we had caught up with the others, I had been able to single out Chade and be aware of him, even at the moments when he was not in my line of sight. I had also felt, twice more, that immense heave of presence in my Witsense. But unlike Web, I had felt such a sensation before. I kept that piece of knowledge to myself, though it made my heart sink to do so. I knew a dragon when I felt one. I expected the wide shadow of wings to sweep over me, for I knew of no other way to explain how I could sense so large a creature, and then feel no trace of it. But the skies above me remained blue, clear and empty.

When we reached the others, they were standing in the scant shelter of an outcropping of rock. Outislander runes were cut into the surface of it in a wavering line that wandered back beneath the ice level. The Hetgurd witnesses stood near the rock, and their displeasure at being here was writ large on their faces. Yet most of them looked sourly amused, too. I wondered why. One of their men was on his knees, doggedly digging at the ice that had pushed up against the rock. His tool was his belt knife, and he clashed the iron blade against the stubborn ice as if he were stabbing someone. He'd make a dozen strokes and then brush away a negligible amount of chipped ice. It seemed a futile task, but he was intent on it.

Longwick's men had brought their tools up with them. They carried shovels and picks and pry bars, but as yet they had not put any of them to work. They stood at the ready, bored and uninterested as any good soldiers usually are, and waited to be assigned their task. I did not wonder long why they had not yet begun. As we approached, Chade and Dutiful were face-to-face with the Narcheska and Peottre. The other members of the Wit coterie stood idly nearby. Thick had sat down in the snow behind them and was humming aloud to himself, nodding his head in a rhythmic counterpoint.

"Yes, but where?" Chade demanded, and from his tone, I knew it was not the first time he had asked his question.

"Here," Peottre replied patiently. "Here." He swept one arm wide, indicating the small plateau we stood on. "As the runes on the rock say, 'Here sleeps the dragon Icefyre.' I have brought you to him, as we agreed we would do, and the Narcheska has accompanied us to witness your task. Now, it is up to you. You are the ones who must unearth him and take his head. Is not that the task the Prince agreed to, within his own mothershouse?"

"Yes, but I didn't think he'd have to chip a whole glacier into shards to do it! I thought there would be some indication of where he was. There's nothing here, just ice and snow and rock. Where do we begin?"

Peottre lifted his shoulders in a heavy shrug. "Anywhere you like, I suppose." One of the Hetgurd witnesses gave a bitter chuckle at his words. Chade glanced about almost wildly. His brief look acknowledged that I was finally present but he seemed to think I would not be of much use. He tried again with Peottre.

"The last time you were here and could see the dragon, where was he?"

Peottre shook his head slowly. "I've only been here twice before, with my aunt, when I was a boy. She brought me here to teach me the way. But we never saw the dragon, only the writing that marks his place. It has been at least a generation since the dragon was visible through the ice."

This seemed to spark something in the Owl clanmember, for he suddenly stepped forward from the huddle of Hetgurd witnesses. He smiled slightly when he spoke, nodding to himself. "My grandmother saw him, when she was a girl. I shall tell you what she told me, and perhaps you will gain wisdom from it. She came here with her own mother's mother, to leave a gift for Icefyre and ask for greater fertility amongst our sheep. When they got here, her mother's mother showed her a dark shadow, just visible through the ice when the day's sun was strongest. 'There he is,' she told my grandmother. 'He used to be much easier to see, but every year the ice grows and he sinks farther away. Now he is only a shadow, and there will come a time when people will doubt he ever existed. So look well, and make sure that no descendant of ours shames us by doubting the wisdom of their own people.'" The bard ceased his telling as abruptly as he had begun it. He stood, his cheeks reddened by the wind that blew his long hair, and nodded to himself, pleased.

"And would you know, then, where we would begin to look for the dragon?"

The Owl laughed. "I do not know. And I would not tell you if I did."

"I am curious," the Prince said more gently. "What was the offering made to the dragon, and how did he accept it?"

"Blood," Owl replied promptly. "They cut a sheep's throat and let it bleed out on the ice. The mothers studied the shape of the puddle it made and where it sank in and where it pooled on the surface. They judged that they had pleased Icefyre with their gift. Then they left the sheep's carcass here for the Black Man, and went home. The next spring, many of our sheep dropped two lambs instead of just one, and none of them were touched by the flux. We had a good year." Owl glanced sourly around at us. "That is the sort of luck we used to receive for honoring Icefyre. Dishonor and doubt him, and I dread to think of the misfortune that will befall your houses."

"And our houses too, like as not, for being present," Seal observed sullenly.

Peottre did not look at them as he reminded them, "Our mothershouse has accepted all that may come from this. It will not fall upon you."

"So you say!" Owl snorted disdainfully. "Yet I doubt you speak for Icefyre, you who would destroy him for a woman's whim!"

"Where is the dragon?" Chade broke in, his exasperation complete. His answer came from an unexpected source.

"He's here," Swift said quietly. "Oh, yes, he is. His presence ebbs and surges like a wild tide, but there's no denying he's here." The boy swayed as he spoke and his voice was far away. Cockle set his hand to the young man's shoulder, and Web left me to hasten to Swift's side.

"Look at me!" he commanded the boy, and when Swift was slow to comply, he gave the lad a shake. "Look at me!" he urgently ordered him again. "Swift! You are young and never-bonded. You may not understand what I'm telling you, but keep yourself to yourself. Do not go to him, and do not let him come into you. This is a powerful presence that we feel, splendid and awe-inspiring. But do not become absorbed in that. I feel in this creature the charm of a great cat, the beckoning wile that can bond a youngster whether he would or no."

"You can feel the dragon? He is definitely here, and alive?" Chade was incredulous.

"Oh, yes," Dutiful replied unwillingly. For the first time, I realized how pale he was. The rest of us were ruddy-cheeked with the cold. Dutiful stood very still and slightly apart from us. He looked at the Narcheska as he spoke.

"The dragon Icefyre is indeed here. And he is alive, though I do not understand how that can be so." He paused as if thinking deeply, his eyes going afar. "I can just brush my mind against his. I reach for him, but he ignores me. Nor do I grasp how I can be aware of him one moment, and then feel him fade beyond my reach the next."

I tried not to gape as the Prince carelessly revealed that he was Witted. I was also surprised that he seemed to be sensing the dragon with his Wit when I could barely perceive him. Some time ago, I had realized that the Prince's Wit ability was not as strong as my own. Had his lessons with Web sharpened it? Then an alternative shocked me. Did he speak of the Wit, or of the Skill? In my dreams, the dragon Tintaglia had touched me with the Skill. I suspected that she had used the Skill Magic to find Nettle, as well. I transferred my gaze to Chade. The old man looked deeply thoughtful, and frustrated. It was Thick who decided me. He seemed completely absorbed in his humming, nodding his head in time. I wished that I could hear his Skill-music, and wished even more that I could provoke him to raise his Skill-walls. I had never seen the little man so enraptured.

"Do not go groping after him!" Web gave the command without regard for the Prince's rank. "There are legends, very old Wit tales, of the fascination of dragons. It is said they can infatuate the unguarded mind, inspiring a nearly slavish devotion. The oldest songs warn of breathing of the exhaled breath of a dragon." He turned suddenly, putting me in mind of a commander ordering his troops as he said to Cockle, "You know the song I speak of, do you not? Tonight, it would be a good song for all to hear. In my youth, I gave little thought to such old songs, but in my older years, I have learned that much truth can be hidden in the old poetry. I would hear it again."

"As would I," Chade unexpectedly agreed. "And any other songs you know that may have to do with dragons. But for now, if our prince's Wit coterie can sense this dragon, perhaps they can guide us in where we should begin our digging."

"Tell you where he is, so you can dig down to kill him? No! I, for one, won't do it!" Swift uttered the words with sudden, wild passion. He looked more distressed than I had ever seen him. Chade rounded on him immediately.

"Do you so quickly forget your vow to your prince?"

"I—" The boy could find no words. His face flushed and then paled. I watched him struggle to find his loyalty, and wished I could help him. But I knew, possibly better than anyone there, how torn he might be.

"Stop this," Web said quietly as the old assassin fixed Swift with his stern stare.

"It is nothing to do with you," Chade said quietly, and for the first time, I saw Web's anger. It came as a physical bunching of his muscles and a swelling of his chest. He contained himself, but I saw how difficult it was for him. So did my prince.

"Stop this," Dutiful echoed Web's words, but he gave them the inflection of royal command. "Swift, be calm. I do not doubt your loyalty to me. I will not test it this way, setting one of my men to decide between what his heart says is right and what he has vowed to do. I do not judge that I can honorably lay that burden upon him. Nor is my own will certain in this." He swung his gaze suddenly to the Narcheska. She did not meet his gaze but looked out over the snowy plain below us. He surprised me by going to her and standing before her. Peottre took a step as if to intervene, but Dutiful did not offer to touch her. Instead, he said quietly, "Will you look at me, please?"

She turned her head and lifted her chin to meet his eyes. Her face was still, save for one brief flash of defiance in her eyes. For a moment, Dutiful said nothing, as if hoping she would speak to him. All was silent save for the shushing of the wind as it stirred the old ice crystals on the glacier's face and the crunching of snow underfoot as the men-at-arms shifted their weight in readiness. Even

Thick's humming had ceased. I spared him a glance. He looked perplexed, as if he were trying to recall something. When the Narcheska held her silence, Dutiful sighed.

"You know more of this dragon than you have ever revealed to me. And I have never mistaken this task you have given me for a maiden's challenge to her suitor. There is no woman's whim in what you ask me to do, is there? Will not you tell me the greater import of this task you have laid upon me, so that I may judge what best to do?"

I thought he had won her, until he added that last phrase. I could almost feel her distress that he might flinch from doing what he had said he would. I saw her retreat from the honesty that had tempted her into a pique worthy of any court-bred young noblewoman. "Is it thus that you fulfill your pledges, Prince? You said you would do this thing. If it daunts you now, speak so plainly, so all may know the moment at which your courage slipped."

She did not have her heart in the challenge. I saw that and so did Dutiful. I think it hurt him all the more that she flogged his pride with such a merciless dare and it did not even come from her heart. He took a deep breath and squared his shoulders. "I keep my word. No. That is not the exact truth of it. I have given my word to you, and you choose to keep it. You could give it back to me and release me from this task. But you do not. So, by the honors of both my mother's and my father's houses, I will do what I have sworn to do."

Web spoke. "This is not a stag you hunt for meat, my prince. It is not even a wolf that you slay to protect your flocks. This is a creature, as intelligent as yourself if the legends be true, that has given you no provocation to kill it. You must know—" And then Web halted his words. Even as provoked as he was, he would not betray his prince's secret Wit. "You must know what I shall now tell you. He lives, this Icefyre. How he does, I do not know, nor can I say how robust the spark that lingers in him. He flickers in and out of my awareness like a flame dying on a final coal.

It may be that we have come all this way and arrived only in time to witness his passing from the world. There would be no dishonor in that. And I have traveled far enough at your side that I think it is not in you to slay any creature that lies defenseless at your feet. Perhaps you shall prove me wrong. I hope not. But"—and here he turned to his Witted companions—"if we do not fulfill our prince's request to help him locate the dragon, if we do not unearth Icefyre from this ice that grips him, I believe he will die just as surely as if our prince took his head. The rest of you may do as you will in this. But I shall not hesitate to use what magic Eda has blessed me with to discover the dragon's prison and free him from it." He lowered his voice. "It would, of course, be much easier if you all helped me."

During all of this, the Hetgurd contingent had held themselves apart. I stole a glance at them, and was only mildly surprised to see the Fool standing, not with them, but beside them, as if to show plainly where his loyalties lay. The Owl, their bard, had that listening look so familiar to me from my days with Starling. Every word uttered here would be fixed in his memory, to be later set in the swinging, lurching rhymes of the Outislander bard's tongue. Speculation and dread played over the faces of the others. Then Bear, their leader, thudded a fist on his chest to draw everyone's attention to him.

"Do not forget us, nor forget why we are here. If it is as your wizards say, if the dragon lives but only feebly and you unearth him, we will witness that. And if this Six Duchies farmer-prince kills our dragon when he is in sickness and unwarlike, then all the wrath of every clan will fall, not just on Narwhal and Boar clans for condoning such a cowardly act, but upon the Six Duchies. If the young Prince does this to make an alliance and stave off further war with the God's Runes folk, then he must be sure that he does it in the manner agreed upon. He was to meet our dragon in fair combat, not ignobly take his head as he lies ailing. There is no honor in taking a battle token from a warrior who is already dying and not by your own hand."

The Fool stood silent through the Bear's declaration, and yet something in his stance made it seem the man was his spokesman. He did not have his arms crossed on his chest, nor did he scowl forbiddingly. Instead he looked deeply at Dutiful, the White Prophet pondering the man who might be his antagonist in his quest to set the world on a better path. The look sent a chill up my back.

As if aware of my gaze on him, he suddenly turned his eyes to mine. The question in them was plain. What would I do, how did I choose? I looked away from him. I could not choose, not yet. When I saw the dragon, I thought to myself, then I would know. And a cowardly part of myself muttered, "If he dies before we chip him out of the ice, then all is solved, and I need never stand in opposition to Chade or the Fool." It was no comfort that I suspected they were both aware of that secret hope.

Peottre spoke in reply to the Bear. He said, in the weary way of a man who explains something for the hundredth time to a stubborn child, "The Narwhal mothershouse accepts all consequences of this act to our own. Be it so, if the dragon rises against us and curses our descendants. If our kin and fellows turn against us, be it so. We accept that we have brought it upon ourselves."

"You can bind yourself!" Bear declared angrily. "But your words and gestures cannot bind Icefyre! Who is to say he will not rise to take his vengeance on any who came here to witness his betrayal?"

Peottre looked down at the snow in front of his feet. He seemed to brace himself, as if preparing to shoulder a heavier burden on top of what he already bore. Then he spoke slowly, clearly, as if saying his lines in a ritual, yet his words were plain as bread. "When the time comes to take sides, lift your weapons against me. I vow I will stand and face them all. If I am defeated, let every man of you bloody his weapon in me before I die."

Midway through his speech, Elliania had gasped in a sharp breath and surged forward as if to stand in front of him. He thrust her aside roughly, a harsher treatment of her than I had ever seen him make, and he held her out from him at arm's length with a firm grip on her upper arm, as if to hold her apart from whatever he had just taken onto himself. Her body heaved as if she stifled sobs or screams as she hid her face in both her hands as he spoke on.

"If Icefyre is all the legends say he is, then he will recognize that you have championed his cause, and he will not hold you or your mothershouses responsible for what we did here. Does that satisfy you?"

When his words were finished, Peottre abruptly drew Elliania close to his side and embraced her, muttering words into her hair as he bent over her, words I could not catch. A terrible gravity had seized every Outislander face at Peottre Blackwater's words. Again, I was left groping after the full meaning of some foreign gesture. I felt that somehow he had once again bound them as well as himself. Was there some shameful attachment to what he had offered them? I did not know, but could only guess.

Dutiful was a white-faced witness. Chade stood motionless and silent, and I longed to once more have the Skill in me. It seemed to me that there were suddenly too many ways the dice could fall now. If the dragon was dead when we unearthed him, if he was alive, if he fought, if he didn't, if we slew the dragon and took his head, but Peottre died keeping his word . . . I suddenly found myself sizing up the Hetgurd witnesses as warriors, estimating who I could kill by fair means and who must fall to foul. A glance at Longwick showed him issuing soft-spoken commands to his men, and I suspected that the Prince would now have a shadow at every moment of the day and night.

But strangest of all, perhaps, were the actions of Web, Cockle, Swift, and Civil. Ignoring all else, they walked a random, searching pattern over the snow and ice, looking intently down as if each had lost a diamond and must find it amongst the sparkling crystals of snow. Web was the first to find a stopping place. He was silent and motionless, waiting. Swift came to a halt perhaps a dozen paces away from him. A ship's length from him, Civil scrambled down a steeper piece of ice and then stood still. Cockle was the last to choose his place. He had an uncertain look on his face. He moved slowly, hands outstretched and seeking, as if feeling for rising warmth where none could exist. Slowly he walked away from all of them until he came to a halt about fifteen paces away from Web. The minstrel appeared uncertain as he looked up for Web's approval. Web nodded slowly. "Yes. I believe you are right. He is immense, larger than any creature I have ever seen. Here beneath my feet, I feel him strongest. But if that is where his slow heart beats or where his head rests, I cannot say. Perhaps it is only where his tail tip is closest to the surface. Each of you others, drop a token to mark where you stand. Then walk toward me and tell me if you judge it as I have."

Cockle pulled off his mitten and let it drop into the snow where he stood, while Civil plunged his staff in and let it stand. Then each made his careful way back to Web. Dutiful and I exchanged a glance, and then, as if simply curious, walked toward the Witmaster. I watched Dutiful's face, but I do not think he was as aware of the sensation as I was. It came and went, flickering like a guttering candle. Even when I stood at my prince's shoulder near Web, my Wit-sense of the dragon was not consistent. But I agreed with Web. When I did sense him, I sensed him more strongly here.

Web and the others of the Wit coterie had kept their eyes down, as if they could see through the snow. Now, one by one, they lifted their gazes. Dutiful waited until Web's eyes met his. I do not know what passed between them in that stare; perhaps they measured one another. But when Web nodded slowly, the Prince dipped his head once in agreement. He turned to Chade.

"This is where we will begin the digging," he said.

chapter XVIII

ICE

My lady Queen,
You know I remain your most loyal servant. I do not
question the wisdom of your judgment, but ask that you
temper that wisdom with the reflection that perhaps what
we have endured has pushed us past the bounds of justice
into retribution. I assure you that the report of a
"massacre of Piebalds" is a gross overstatement. If we of
the Old Blood have erred, it is in that we have held back
our hands so long from taking the actions that will
convince the renegades amongst us that we will no longer
tolerate their incursions against their own folk. This is,
in a sense, a cleaning of our own house, and the filth
that we must scrub out of our blood shames us. Look
aside, we beg you, whilst we scour from our bloodlines
those who degrade us.

        ❦ UNSIGNED LETTER, FOLLOWING THE
              GRIMSTON BLOODBATH

And so we dug in the ice.

Longwick sent Riddle and Hest down to our camp to
bring up the shovels, picks, and pry bars. While they were
gone, Longwick asked the Prince solemnly, "How big a

hole do you wish, my lord?" Dutiful and Chade drew it out on the snow, an area large enough for four men to work in without getting in one another's way. Riddle, Hest, and I were the diggers. Longwick worked alongside us, to my surprise. I suppose he felt that his reduced company of guardsmen made it essential that he take a hand, as well. The guardsmen worked with a will, but awkwardly. They were fighters, not farmers, and though they knew the essentials of throwing up emergency earthworks, they had never had to work on a glacier before. Neither had I. It was an enlightening experience.

Digging ice is not like digging in soil. Soil is made of particles, and particles give way before the blade of a shovel. Ice forms alliances and holds tight to itself. The top layer of loose snow was the most annoying, for it was like shoveling fine flour. There was little weight to each load, but it was difficult to control where each shovelful landed. The next layer was not so bad. It was like digging old packed snow once we broke through the icy crust. But the deeper we went, the more difficult the digging became. We could not shove a spade in and lift and throw out a shovelful of snow. Instead, we used picks to break the ice into chunks, and in the process sent shards and chunks of it flying at one another. Once the ice was loosened, we could scoop it up and toss it up and out of the hole, where the others loaded it onto one of the sleds and hauled it away from the hole's edge. If I kept on my coat, my back ran sweat. Taking it off meant that frost collected on my shirt.

We did not work alone. A compromise had been reached, for the Prince's Witted coterie were the ones to haul the ice from the hole's edge. After a time, the two groups took turns at the picks, the shovels, and the hauling. By the first nightfall, we had a hole that was shoulder deep with no sign of a dragon in the bottom of it.

As evening fell, the winds rose, sending flurries of loose ice crystals scurrying across the surface of the glacier. As we gathered at our camp below, to eat our lukewarm food as we clustered about the tiny potted fires, I wondered uneasily how much snow the winds would sweep into our excavation.

Although our earlier division had been forgotten in the day's labor, camp that night recalled it. We all huddled in the scanty protection of the circled tents, which broke the wind somewhat and gave an illusion of shelter on the bare and windswept ice. It was not a large space, yet within it we assorted ourselves. The Hetgurd warriors were friendlier toward the Witted and the Fool than they had been, trading rations and conversation with one another. Their skinny bard, Owl, sat next to Cockle while he performed for us. Cockle sang two songs without accompaniment, for he was not willing to risk either his hands or his instruments by exposure to the chilling wind. One was about a dragon who so charmed a man that he left his family and home and never more was seen. If there was some great truth hidden in it, I did not find it. As Web had mentioned, it spoke of the man breathing of the dragon's breath, and in that moment giving his heart to the creature. The other song had an even more obscure reference to dragons, yet all kept silent and listened to them thoughtfully as Cockle's solo voice battled with the sweeping winds. The only competing voice was Thick's. He sat near Dutiful, humming and rocking to himself. Although Chade tried several times to shush him, a few minutes later, the little man would take up his music again. It worried me, but there was nothing I could do.

I had glimpsed Peottre and the Narcheska earlier in the day, looking down on our work. Both of their faces seemed very still, caught between hope and dread. Dutiful had gone to speak to them, but I had not heard his words nor any reply from them. The Narcheska had stared at him as if he were a stranger accosting her when her mind was full of other matters. Tonight, they did not join us for the evening food and fire, but went directly to their tent. The

dim light of a candle glowing within it was the only reminder of their presence.

When Cockle's song was finished and we had thanked
him, I was full ready for bed. As much as I wanted private
talk with Chade, Dutiful, and the Fool, I longed for sleep
more. My body had not fully recovered from my elfbark
excess, and the afternoon of heavy work in the cold had
exhausted me.

I rose, stretching, and Chade beckoned me to his side.
When I went to him, he asked me to bring Thick to the
Prince's tent and help him prepare for bed. I thought at first
it was an excuse to have quiet time to speak to me, but
when I stood over Thick, my concern deepened. Thick
rocked from side to side, humming continuously. His eyes
were closed. I hesitated to touch him, just as a burned child
hesitates to reach again toward the fire. Then the deadness
of my Skill persuaded me that any leap of his mind to mine
would actually be a relief rather than a shock. So I set my
hand to his shoulder and shook him gently. Not only was
there no jolt of Skill, but Thick gave no sign of rousing. I
shook him again, more firmly, and finally had to drag him
to his feet before he showed any sort of wakefulness. Then
he blubbered like a suddenly wakened babe, and I felt like
a beast as I steered him toward the Prince's tent. As I tugged
off his snow-caked boots and outer garments, all he did was
mutter semicoherent complaints about the cold. Without
prompting, he crawled into his blankets and I tucked them
down around him.

I had just finished when Chade and the Prince came
into the tent. "I'm worried about him," I said quietly, tipping my head toward Thick. From beneath the mounded
blankets, a soft humming had already commenced.

"It's the dragon," Chade said darkly.

"We think," Dutiful amended wearily. He sat down on
the edge of his pallet and bent over to drag off his boots.
"We can't be sure. We try to Skill to Thick, and it seems as
if he is there, but he just ignores us."

I delivered the news I had carried all day like a stone. "I've had no indication that I'm recovering. My Skill is gone."

The Prince nodded heavily, unsurprised. "I reach for you, and it's like you are not there at all. It's a strange sensation." He lifted his eyes to meet mine. "It makes me realize that for most of my life, you *have* been there. A tiny presence in the corner of my mind. Did you know that?"

"I feared that," I admitted. "Chade and I discussed it. He said that you had had strange dreams when you were small, dreams of a wolf and a man."

For an instant, Dutiful looked startled. Then a slow smile dawned on his face. "Was that you? And Nighteyes?" He suddenly took a deep breath and looked aside from me. "They were some of the best dreams I ever had. Sometimes at night, when I was young, I would try to have the same dreams when I was falling asleep. I never had the same dream twice, but sometimes I'd have a new one. Hm. Even then, you were teaching me to Skill, how to reach out and find you. And Nighteyes. Oh, Eda, Fitz, how you must miss him! In those dreams, you were one creature. Did you know that?"

Sudden tears ambushed me. I turned and brushed at my face before they could fall. "I suspected so. Nettle sees me so, still, as a wolf-man."

"Then you went into her dreams, too?"

Was there a note of jealousy in the Prince's voice? "Not intentionally. For either of you. I never imagined that I was teaching either of you to Skill. Nettle, I sometimes deliberately looked in on, trying to see Burrich and Molly. Because I loved them, and I missed them. And because Nettle was my daughter."

"And me?"

For that solitary instant, I was glad my Skill was gone. I never wanted the Prince to know the role I had played in his conception. Verity might have used my body to get him, but he was still my king's son. Not mine. Not mine in any way, save the way his mind had called to mine. Aloud, I said, "You were Verity's son. I did not consciously seek you out, and I was not aware of your sharing my dreams. Not until much later."

I glanced at Chade and was surprised to see that he was barely following our conversation. He seemed to be looking into a distance and not seeing what was before his eyes. "Chade?" I asked him worriedly. "Are you all right?"

He drew a sudden breath, as if I'd wakened him. "I think it is the dragon that is fascinating Thick. I was trying to get his attention, but his music is strong and all-consuming. Neither the Prince nor I can sense the dragon with the Skill. Yet, when I reach after Thick with the Skill, I can sense something there. But it's odd . . . it's like seeing the shadow of a man, but not the man himself. I cannot tell anything about him, other than that he's there. Dutiful says that from time to time his Wit catches a whiff of Icefyre, only to have him vanish like a scent when the wind changes."

I stood still for a moment and sent my Wit questing. After a time, I came back to them. "He's there. And then he isn't. I can't tell if it's something that he is doing deliberately, some sort of Wit-camouflage, or if, as Web suggested, he's very close to death."

I glanced at Dutiful, but his thoughts had followed a different track. I wondered if he had heard what Chade and I had said at all. "I'm going to try to Skill to Nettle tonight," he announced suddenly. "We need a real link with Buckkeep and she's our only hope of one. I also think that if any one of us can distract Thick from the dragon, if that is what is fascinating him, then she can. Even if it isn't the dragon, she may be our best chance of reaching him."

I was stunned. I didn't want him to try this. I did. "Do you think you can reach her?"

"Perhaps. It would be a lot easier to do if I actually knew her." The emphasis he placed on those last words made it plain it was my fault that he didn't. I think he had heard my reluctance in my question, and been stung by it. I swallowed that, and let him speak on. "I only brushed minds with her that one time, and that was through you. Reaching her on my own is going to be difficult."

Anxiety gnawed at me. I knew I should not ask the question of him, but I did. "If you do, what will you tell her?"

He stared at me bleakly before replying, "The truth. I know it's a novel idea, but I thought that at least one Farseer should try it."

I knew he was trying to provoke me. The events of the day had been difficult for him, and my prince was abruptly behaving like a petulant fifteen-year-old, trying to find someone to put the blame on. I tried again to let it go past me. "The truth is a large thing. Which part of the truth do you plan to tell her?" I asked, and tried to smile as I awaited his answer.

"For now, only the parts that belong to me. That I am Prince Dutiful and I desperately need her to pass on tidings to my mother, and then convey to me her advice. I want my mother to know about Sydel and her parents. As much to be wary of them as to rescue Sydel, I'll admit. And if she will listen to that message and accept it, then I will tell her my fears for Thick: that a dragon is stealing what little mind he has. Then I'll ask her to distract him from it, if she can reach him." He sighed suddenly. "I suppose I shall be lucky if I get that far in a conversation with her." He gave me another doleful look.

I think at that instant I felt most keenly the loss of my Skill. I did not want Dutiful to speak to my daughter out of my hearing and awareness. I feared what he might accidentally reveal. He might influence how she thought of me before I had a chance to let her know me on her own. He answered my thought as if he had heard it.

"You'll have to trust me, won't you?"

I took a breath. "I do trust you," I said, and tried to make that statement not a lie.

"I'll be with the lad," Chade told me, and then laughed

aloud at the dismay on my face. "No, don't say you trust me. I don't think I could stand it."

"But I have to trust you," I pointed out, and Chade nodded. I asked, "What did you think of what went on today? Do you think that the Hetgurd folk will turn on us and attack if the dragon is unearthed alive and we attempt to take his head?"

"Yes," Dutiful replied. "Without doubt. I think that the absence of the Black Man's approval has inflamed every superstitious fear that they have."

"I think you are right," Chade agreed. "I noticed that tonight, as we were retiring, they set up yet another offering to him at the outskirts of camp."

I shook my head at Chade. "I know what you are thinking. Even if I could do it, I don't think it would be wise. If the offering was taken now, would not they interpret it as him finally approving of them, because they had spoken out against the Prince's quest? Too late for chicanery in that area, Chade."

"I suppose you are right," he said without apologies. "And if you were caught stealing the offering, it might rouse them to immediate action. No. Best to wait." He sighed and rubbed his arms vigorously. "I am so tired of this cold. I'm too old to be this chilled all the time."

The Prince rolled his eyes silently.

I changed the subject. "Please be careful, both of you, when you reach after Thick. And Dutiful, be very wary contacting Nettle. I am sure I did not imagine what happened to Thick and me that day. Someone was using the Skill to turn us against each other. Whoever it is, he is still out there. He found Thick's mind once. When you Skill to Thick, you may be betraying yourselves to him. And if he follows you, Dutiful, he may find Nettle when you reach for her tonight. Or, you may attract the dragon Tintaglia to yourself." I suddenly felt a coward because I could no longer hope to protect either of them. "Be careful," I said again.

"I will," Dutiful replied irritably, and I was sure he was not giving my warning the weight it deserved. I looked at Chade.

"Have you ever known me to be anything but careful?" my old mentor asked me.

Yes, I have, I nearly said. *When you went after the Skill, you went after it with abandon. I fear you will do so again and risk all I hold dear in the process.* But I held my tongue and contented myself with a nod to his question. "It feels strange to know you have so much to do tonight and there is no way I can help you accomplish it. I feel useless. If you have nothing for me here, then I'll be seeking my bed. I'm exhausted." I rolled my shoulders. "I should have been practicing with a shovel those last months in Buckkeep instead of a sword."

The Prince gave me a grudging chuckle. Chade asked gravely, "Are you going to see the Fool tonight?"

"Yes." I waited, on guard.

"Will you sleep there again?"

I didn't ask how he knew I'd slept in the Fool's tent before. There was no emotion in my voice as I replied, "Possibly. I don't know. If we talk late or if he wants company, I may."

"It looks odd to the others, you know. No, don't scowl at me, that's not my concern. I've known you too long to have any illusions about your preferences in bedmates. I mean only that it may appear to the others that you share his opinion on Icefyre; that we must dig down to the dragon and free it rather than fulfilling the task the Narcheska has put upon our prince."

I stood silent for a moment, pondering that. Then I said quietly, "I can't help what people think, Chade."

"You won't avoid him?"

I met his eyes. "No. He's my friend."

Chade folded his lips for a moment. Then, very cautiously he asked, "Is there any chance that you could persuade him to our way of thinking?"

"To *your* way of thinking?" I corrected him. "I doubt it. This isn't some whim he has suddenly conceived, Chade. All his life, he has believed he is the White Prophet. Part of his mission in life is to restore dragons to the world. I don't think I can persuade him that is not a good idea."

"You've been friends for a very long time. He cares deeply about you," Chade observed delicately.

"Which is exactly why I wouldn't attempt to influence him that way." I pushed my hair back out of my face. The drying sweat from my digging was beginning to chill me. I ached, and not just in body. "Chade. In this, you will have to trust me. I cannot be your tool, and I cannot promise that I will act in a certain way regardless of what we dig up. This one time in my life, I have to be true to myself."

Anger twitched his face, and then in a flash so swift I almost missed it, hurt. He turned aside from me, putting his countenance in shadow as he said, "I see. I had thought your vow to the Farseers meant more to you than that. And, foolishly, I had thought that perhaps we had been friends a long time, perhaps even longer than you and the Fool."

"Oh, Chade." I was suddenly so weary I could scarcely speak. "You are far more to me than friend. You have been my mentor, and my parent and my protector when many hands were lifted against me. Never doubt that I would lay down my life for you."

"And he is a Farseer," Dutiful suddenly interjected, startling both of us. "One whose vow to his family has already cost him many things. So, this time, as your prince, I command this, FitzChivalry Farseer. Keep your vow, to yourself. Be as true to your own heart as you were to Verity's, and to King Shrewd's before him. That is the command of your king."

I looked at him, amazed, not just at the generosity of his command, a freedom that no other Farseer king had ever thought to grant me, but also at his sudden change from sulky fifteen-year-old to heir to the throne. He frowned slightly at my puzzled look, completely unaware of what he had done. I found my tongue. "Thank you, my prince. That is the greatest boon that any Farseer king has ever granted me."

"You're welcome. I just hope that I haven't done something truly foolish. For we must both recall that regardless of what decision you make for yourself, I must hew to my promise to the Narcheska. I am here to take the dragon's head. And much joy may she have of a frozen skull." Abruptly, he was a morose boy again. I looked at him, and was newly reminded of how difficult all this must be for him. He had left stolen kisses behind on Mayle Island. I doubted he had had a private word with Elliania since we'd left her mothershouse. He shook his head to my sympathetic look. "I can only try to do right, and hope that this time I have truly guessed what 'right' is."

"That makes two of us," Chade grumbled.

"No. Three," I contradicted him. He was bent over by the little firepot and had succeeded in waking the embers to a single tongue of flame. He took a small piece of coal and added it to the tiny fire.

"I'm too old to be doing this anymore." He repeated his favorite complaint.

"No. You're not. You'll only be old when you try to stop doing this. I think this trip has done you good." I hunkered down beside him. "Chade. Please believe this of me. This isn't about whether you or the Fool pulls my strings. It isn't a contest of wills between you two to see who holds my heart."

"Then what is it?" he demanded grudgingly.

I tried to give him an answer. "I need to see what is true, before I decide what stance I'll support. We've all known, since before we left Buckkeep, that there is an undercurrent to the Narcheska's request. There may come a time when you are glad I hesitated and did not blindly obey her will. Her handmaid, Henja, was connected somehow to the Piebalds. I'll wager whatever you like on that. She and Peottre and their mothershouse defy the majority of the Hetgurd to put this condition on the Prince. Why? What do they gain? What value to them is a rotting dragon's head?"

"She does not seem pleased with having to ask this of me," Dutiful observed quietly. "She is hard as stone in her determination that I must do this thing for her. Yet she does not seem to regard it with anticipation or eagerness, but dread and reluctance. As if it is not of her will that she asks this."

"Then whose? Peottre's?"

Chade slowly shook his head. "No. His interests run with hers, and she is loyal to him. I think that if she asked this to please him, she would take more pleasure in it. No. So. Fitz asks our basic question. Whose will?"

I gave my best guess. "Henja's. She has power over them somehow. We have seen that. And she is connected to the Piebalds, who have no love for us."

"The Piebalds." Chade pondered this. "Do you discount the Fool's Pale Woman, then?" He asked the question keenly.

"I do not know. What have we seen or heard of her? Nothing save what the Fool has told us. The Outislanders speak of her as an old evil, a malevolence from the past to be avoided, but not with the dread of something that lurks now. Our Six Duchies dragons killed her and Kebal Rawbread, or so I have often heard. Yet the Outislanders still connect them with this island. They say they mined the black stone here to ballast their White Ships. And there is no denying that the aborted stone dragon back at our landing spot stinks of Red Ship Forging." A sudden yawn ambushed me.

"Oh, go to bed," Chade rebuked me. "At least you can rest. Tonight the Prince and I shall reach far and see if we cannot persuade Nettle to aid us. I will admit that I long to know what is passing in the Six Duchies these days. If the Piebalds have stirred to action there, it might tell us that they play a double game."

"Perhaps," Dutiful agreed with a yawn, and I suddenly pitied him. I was going to honest sleep. He had a night's work ahead of him. Yet, as I bade them good night and left their tent, I sensed that he regarded Nettle as a challenge he anticipated as well as dreaded. I set aside worrying about that as I left the tent. It was pointless. I was out of that game for now. Perhaps for always. I felt the earth lurch under me as I considered that thought, and then forced myself to go on. Would it be so terrible to go through the rest of my life unSkilled? Could not I think of it as being free of the Skill?

I made a brief stop at the guardsmen's tent. Longwick kept a weary watch at the opening. He nodded at me silently as I slipped inside amongst the heavily sleeping men-at-arms and then out again. He did not ask what I was about. Chade's man. Chade's men, I corrected myself, looking around at the sleeping forms. Every guardsman on this island with us had been handpicked by him, for both discretion and loyalty. How ruthlessly would they obey his commands?

I was still pondering that question when I paused outside the Fool's tent. I listened for a moment to the sweep of the wind that stirred flurries of ice crystals in a storm at ankle height. Every now and then a gust would propel a stinging onslaught into my face. But wind and rustling ice was all I heard. Within the Fool's tent, all was silent, but the bright figures on the outside of the thin, tight fabric glowed with the life of the tiny fire within. "May I come in?" I asked quietly.

"A moment," he replied as softly. I heard the rustle of fabric, almost indistinguishable from the wind, and after a brief wait, he untied the door flap and admitted me. Clinging frost came with me. It could not be helped, yet the Fool still winced as I brushed it from my clothes. I took the bundled Elderling robe from inside my coat. "Here. I brought it back."

He was reclining on his pallet, the covers already

drawn up around him. The tiny kettle crouched hopefully over the candle fire. He lifted his brows and smiled. "But I thought you looked so fetching in it. Are you sure you won't keep it?"

I sighed. His fey levity was too much at odds with all else I felt that evening. "Chade and Dutiful are going to try to reach Nettle tonight. With the Skill. They fear that the dragon is stealing Thick's mind, and hope that Nettle can distract Thick from Icefyre."

"And you choose not to help them?"

"I cannot. I cannot find a single shred of the Skill inside me. I only know that Thick is troubled because of the way he hums. Always before, he Skilled out his music. Why does he hum and mutter now? It's a change, and I don't like changes, especially changes I don't understand."

"Life is change," the Fool observed placidly. "And death is an even greater change. I think we must resign ourselves to change, Fitz."

"I'm tired of resigning myself to things. My entire life has been one long resignation." I dropped the robe on his pallet and then sat down heavily on the end of it, forcing him to draw his feet up out of the way. I pulled my mittens off and held my hands out to his feeble fire, trying to warm myself.

"Ah, Catalyst, can it be that you do not see all the changes you have made? Some by your resignation and acceptance of circumstance, some by your wild struggles. You can say that you hate change, but you *are* change."

"Oh, please." I folded my arms upon my drawn-up knees and dropped my head onto them. "Don't talk about that tonight. Talk about anything else but that. Please. I can't think about choices and changes tonight."

"Very well." His voice was gentle. "What do you want to talk about?"

"Anything. Something about you. How did you get here, after we left you behind at Buckkeep Town?"

"I told you. I flew."

I lifted my head from my arms to regard him sourly. He was smiling a small challenge at me. It was the Fool's old smile, the one that promised he was telling the truth when he was obviously lying. "No. You did not." I spoke firmly.

"Very well. If you say so."

"Kettricken must have helped you find passage, against Chade's advice. And you came here on a ship with a bird's name." I was guessing wildly, knowing that there would be some small kernel of truth at the bottom of his wild tale.

"Actually, Kettricken counseled me to stay in Buckkeep, in our very brief meeting. I think it taxed her will to say no more to me than that. It was sheer good fortune for me that I encountered Burrich arriving at Buckkeep Castle as I left it. But, as I have agreed to tell this tale, let me tell it in order. Let us go back to the moment at which I last saw you. When I thought that you were hastening to my aid."

I winced, but he went on evenly. "The Harbormaster summoned the City Guard, who were very efficient at removing Lord Golden and his belongings. As you probably have suspected, they detained me until after the ships had sailed. Then I was dismissed, with many apologies and assurances that it had all been a terrible error. But word of the incident spread. By the time Lord Golden returned to his lodgings with his baggage, his creditors had descended, convinced that he had intended to flee the city without paying them. As, indeed, he had. They were happy to confiscate most of his baggage and gear, all save one pack, containing the absolute minimum essentials for his survival, which he'd had the forethought to leave in his Buckkeep chambers."

The little copper kettle was puffing steam. He lifted it from the small flame and poured water into a gaily decorated teapot.

I had to smile. I gestured about the tent. "The bare essentials."

He arched one golden brow. "For civilized adventuring, yes." He put the lid on the teapot. It was shaped like a rose. "And why should one attempt to get by with less? Now. Where was I? Ah, yes. Lord Golden, stripped of his possessions and glamour, was no longer Lord Golden, but only a fleeing debtor. Those who thought they knew him best were astonished at the way he lithely spidered down the outside of his lodgings, to land lightly on his feet and run off into the alleys. I vanished."

He made me wait. He rubbed one eye and smiled at me thoughtfully. I bit the inside of my cheek until he finally gave in and went on.

"I went to Kettricken, by ways and means that I shall leave to your imagination. I think she was quite astounded to encounter me waiting for her in her bedchamber. As I have told you, she urged me to stay at Buckkeep, within the castle, under her wing, until you had completed her mission. I had to decline, of course. And..." Here he hesitated for a time. "I had words with Burrich. I think you know that already, or suspect it. It shocked me that he recognized me immediately, much as you had. He asked me questions, not because he needed answers, but to confirm what he had already ciphered out for himself, from an earlier interview with Kettricken."

He paused so long that I feared he would not go on. Then he said, softly, "At one point he was so furious at what I told him, I thought he would strike me dead. Then, abruptly, he began to weep." And again he halted. I sat there, my tongue turned to ashes in my mouth. Almost I hoped he would not go on. When he did, I knew he left much unsaid.

"Bereft of any support from the castle, I foolishly thought to return to my inn to see what rags of my fortunes my creditors might have left me to aid me in my flight. My stripped apartments looked as if a horde of locusts had despoiled them. Yet worse was to come. The landlord had seen me enter, and he had taken bribes from my creditors to contact them immediately if he heard or saw me. And he earned his greasy coins well. For a second wave of furious former friends appeared. You would have thought that they had honestly earned the money that they had won in wagers from me, so righteously outraged were they!

"So. Once more I fled. This time, I fled the entire city, not so much in fear of my creditors as in fury at my 'friends.' You had betrayed me, Fitz. And yet, perhaps, it was your turn to betray me, given that I had so badly failed you."

"What?"

I was astounded that he could say such a thing. But when our gazes met, I saw ancient shame in his deepening eyes, and recalled a time in the Mountains when my enemies had used him against me. "You know I never counted that against you. It was not you, Fool. It wasn't."

"And perhaps when you betrayed me, it was more Chade than you, but the damage was done, nonetheless. And I was furious and frightened and desolated to think that perhaps I had come so far, only to be defeated by him I most trusted. I fled Buckkeep on foot, eluding my pursuers, yet knowing I could not do so for long and wondering what I might do next. How could it be, I wondered, that the Catalyst could change events so that the White Prophet was so completely defeated? And slowly it came to me that it could not be so; that there was a deeper pattern at work than I had first glimpsed. I resolved to give myself to it, though I could not guess what it might be."

I had turned my head on my arms so I could watch him as he told the story. Now I gave a sigh, and relaxed into my hunch. He reached from beneath the covers to pour a scanty share of tea into a cup and a bowl, then gestured that I should take whichever I wished. The pot had plainly been made for one person, traveling alone, and it touched me that he still offered to share. I lifted the bowl and sipped from it. It tasted like flowers, a mouthful of summer in this land where winter always reigned. The heat of it was fleeing rapidly, briefly warming my hands as it passed through the crockery. The Fool's long elegant fingers wrapped the cup as he drank his share.

"Go on," I urged him when he had let the silence grow. I knew it was a trick of the storyteller to do so, but I did not begrudge him the drama.

"Well. My second horde of creditors had paid heed to the tales of the first. They were soon after me. I ran, and swiftly, but Lord Golden's dress was a bit ostentatious to blend in with a crowd and my pack encumbered me. You recall the hill outside Buckkeep, where the Witness Stones stand still?"

"Of course." I was intrigued. It was the last place I would have fled to. The bare black stones stand upon the barren hillside there as they have always stood, weathered and impervious to all. The folk of the Six Duchies have long used them as an oath place. Lovers pledge to one another there. It is said that if two men duel there, the gods will see that justice is done. The righteous will win there, if nowhere else. It is an oddly solemn place, bereft of brush or clinging vines. There would be no cover there for any hunted creature to hide in. "But why go there?"

He lifted one narrow shoulder in an eloquent shrug. "I knew I could not get far. If I were captured and taken back to Buckkeep, doubtless my creditors would have not only taken my kit but put me to drudgery to work off my debt. I and my mission in the world would be completely undone. So I resolved to rely on fate, and test an idea that I formulated long ago. The Witness Stones are gateway stones, Fitz, just like the Skill-pillars that you have used before when in dire need to flee. Except, of course, that long ago someone or something obliterated the runes from the sides of the Witness Stones. Perhaps they are so old that they wore away naturally; perhaps some ancient Skill-user decided to put an end to their usefulness. In any case, the runes that tell where they lead are gone, leaving only the weathered marks where they used to be. As I ran toward them, my pack heavy on my back, I thought back over what you had told me of your adventures on the Treasure Beach with Prince Dutiful. I knew that I might choose the wrong facet of the stone, and find myself plunged into deep cold water."

I sat up straight in slow cold horror. "Fool, it is far worse than that! What if a stone had fallen facedown and you were flung from it into solid earth? Or what if you chose a destination where the stone had been shattered or—"

"All those thoughts rushed through my mind as I raced toward it. Fortunately, there was no time for me to choose, no time for me even to wonder if there was enough of the Skill left on my fingers to work the stone. I struck the stone, fingertips first, knowing only that I must, I must, I must pass through the portal."

He paused. I was leaning intently toward him, my heart in my throat. To pass through a Skill-portal had always been difficult for me. We knew so little about them, only that some standing stones carved of memory stone and marked with runes could serve as passageways to distant places. I had used them less than a dozen times in my life, and never without dread and uneasiness. Some of Regal's inexperienced Skill-users had lost their minds when they were forced to use the Skill-portals. Using one had jumbled Dutiful's memory of our time on the Treasure Beach and left us both exhausted.

The Fool smiled sweetly at me. "Don't look like that. You know I survived."

"At what cost?" I asked, knowing there must be one.

"Exhaustion. I emerged somewhere, I have no idea where. Nowhere I've ever been before. It was a city in ruins, and still as dead stone can be. There was a river near it. That is as much as I can tell you. I slept, I don't know how long. When I awoke, dawn was all around me. And the Skill-pillar towered over me. This one shone clean of lichen or moss, with each rune standing out as clear as if it had been chiseled yesterday. I studied them a long time, afraid and dreading, and yet knowing they offered me my only hope. I narrowed my choices down to two of them that might possibly be the one I wished. And then I entered the pillar again."

"No." I groaned.

"Exactly how I felt. I emerged feeling as if I had taken a bad beating. But I had come to the right place."

He made me ask the question, enjoying it. "Where?"

"Do you remember the broken plaza, like an ancient market circle? The one where the forest was trying to encroach? I stood on top of a stone pillar there, and for a moment, in a dream, I wore the Rooster Crown. You saw me. You remember it."

I nodded slowly. "It was on our road to the Stone Garden. Where the stone dragons slept, before we roused them and sent them to fight the Red Ships. Where they sleep again now, Verity-as-Dragon amongst them."

"Exactly. Again, I went down that forest path, and I saw him there. But he was not the one I sought. I found Girl-on-a-Dragon there, sleeping, her arms clasping the neck of her dragon, just as you had told me. And I woke her and made her understand that I must come here, and once again I mounted behind her and she flew here with me. And left me. So, you see, old friend, I did not lie to you. I flew here."

I sat bolt upright, suddenly wide awake. A hundred questions swelled in me but I asked the most important one. "How did you wake her? It takes the Wit, the Skill, and blood to wake a stone dragon. Well do I know that!"

"It did. And it does. The Skill I had on my fingertips, and blood was easy enough to come by." He rubbed his wrist, possibly remembering an old cut. "I did not and do not have the Wit. But you may remember that, foolishly, I had already put some of myself into Girl-on-a-Dragon, when I was attempting to complete the carving of her and wake her."

"As did I," I recalled guiltily.

"Yes. I know," he said softly. "It is still in her. You put in the memories you could not stand to recall and the emotions you would not let yourself feel. You gave her your mother abandoning you, and never knowing your father. You gave her Regal's torment of you in his dungeons. You gave her, most of all, the pain of losing Molly and your child, to Burrich, of all people. You put into her your fury and your hurt and your sense of being betrayed." He gave a little sigh. "It is all in her still. The things you could not allow yourself to feel."

"I left all that behind me long ago," I said slowly.

"You cut out a part of yourself and went on, less than you had been."

"I do not see it that way." My reply was stiff.

"You cannot see it that way," he informed me calmly. "Because you cannot truly remember how awful any of it was. Because you put all of it into Girl-on-a-Dragon."

"Can we leave this?" I asked, almost frightened, almost angry, but confused over what would scare or anger me.

"We must. Because you already left it, long years ago. And only I will ever know the full depth of what you felt about those things. Only I fully remember who and what you were before you did it. For we are bound together, not only by Skill and fate, but also because both of us live on, inside Girl-on-a-Dragon. Because I knew what went into her, I could reach her and rouse her. I could convey to her my desperate purpose. And so she brought me to Aslevjal.

"It was a strange journey, wild and wonderful. You know I have ridden with her before. I was with her when she and the other dragons attacked not just the Red Ships that assailed the Six Duchies, but the White Ships that were the cruel tools of the Pale Woman. It was strange for me to be caught up in true battle. I did not like it."

"No one does," I assured him. I put my brow back down on my knees and closed my eyes.

"I suppose not. But this time, flying with her, it was

different. There was no killing to witness, no other dragons flying beside us. Instead, it was just she and I. I sat behind her and put my arms around her slender waist. She is a part of the dragon, you know, not a separate creature at all. Rather like a girl-shaped limb more than anything else. So she did not speak to me, yet, strangely enough, she did smile and from time to time, she would turn to look into my face or gesture to something on the world below us that she wished me to see.

"She flew tirelessly. From the time I climbed up behind her and the powerful beat of her dragon's wings lifted us through the canopy of tree limbs until the moment that we landed on the black sand beaches of Aslevjal, she took no rest. Nor did I. At first, we flew through blue summer skies of the lands beyond Mountain Kingdom. Then higher we flew, until my heart pounded and I was giddy, over the snowy peaks and trodden passes of the Mountains, and then back into summer. We flew over the villages of the Mountain Kingdom. They nestle into the crooks and flanks of the mountains, and their flocks are scattered over the steep pastures like white apple blossoms litter the orchard meadow after a spring windstorm."

I saw it, in my mind, and smiled faintly when he spoke of flying over a Six Duchies hamlet early in the morning, and the one lad who looked up and saw them and ran whooping into his cottage. And on he spoke, of rivers like silver seams in the land and planted fields like patchwork when seen from above, and of the ocean, wrinkling like paper tipped with silver. In my mind, I flew with him.

I must have fallen asleep, lulled by his strange story. When I awoke, night was deep all around us. The camp outside our tent was still, and his pot fire held only a single flickering flame on a wick in the oil. I was huddled beneath one of his blankets, fallen over sideways on his bed. He slept, curled like a kitten, his brow nearly touching mine, on the other end of his pallet. His breathing was deep and

even, and one long hand was palm up on the blankets between us, as if in offering, or beseeching something of me.
Sleepily I reached over and set my hand in his. He did not
seem to wake. Strangely, I felt at peace. I closed my eyes
and sank down into a deep and dreamless slumber.

chapter XIX

BELOW THE ICE

The Outislanders have always been raiders. In the years before the Red Ship War, there were raiding incidents, as it seemed there had always been. Individual ships led by the kaempra of a clan would make a quick strike, carrying off stock, harvested crops, and occasionally captives. Bearns took the brunt of these clashes, and seemed to relish them much as Shoaks enjoyed its border disputes with Chalced. The Duke of Bearns seemed content that they were his concern, and made little complaint of dealing with them.

But with the appearance of the red-hulled ships of Kebal Rawbread, the rules of engagement changed. Suddenly, the ships appeared in groups, and seemed more intent on rape and ruin than on a quick acquisition of goods. They burned or spoiled what they could not carry off, slaughtering herds and flocks, torching grain in the field and storehouses. They killed even those who did not resist them. A new malice had appeared in these raids, one that delighted not just in theft, but also in destruction and devastation.

At that time, we did not even know of the Pale Woman and her influence over Rawbread.

SCRIBE FEDWREN, "A HISTORY OF THE RED SHIP WAR"

In the morning, when we reached the edge of our pit, both Riddle and I groaned. Then we went to work, lifting and flinging the snow that had blown in to half-fill our excavation of the day before. This snow was lighter and unpacked, but for all that, it was frustrating work. It was like shoveling feathers, and half of what we lifted floated free to drift back to the bottom of the hole. It was nearly noon before we had cleared it all down to where we had left off the evening before. Then out came the picks, and we began to break ice and scrape it up and shovel it out again.

I ached at first, and then I didn't, and then I began to hurt in new places. That night, I dropped into an exhausted sleep, deeper than dreams or regret. The wind blew again. Every night, the wind blew. Every morning, we began our task by clearing the previous night's drifted snow. Yet slowly, relentlessly, we toiled and the pit deepened. When we could no longer throw the ice out of the pit, we dug a ramp at one end. After that, we shoveled the ice onto one of the sleds and two men would drag it up out of the pit and away to dump it. The task was beyond tedious. And we found no sign of a dragon in the bottom. Worse, my Witsense of him grew fainter, not stronger.

The workforce grew after the first day. Our first addition was Prince Dutiful rolling back his sleeves and taking up a pickaxe. Chade limited his participation to supervising. He reminded me of Civil's cat, who perched at the edge of the pit and watched us with supreme disinterest.

When the Narcheska entered the pit, Dutiful stopped his work to warn her that the flying ice from his pick might injure her. She gave him an odd little smile, between sad and flirtatious, and cautioned him to be wary of the flying ice that her own pick might free. And then she set to work beside him, swinging her pick with a country girl's competence. "She used to help dig the rocks out, when we were preparing the new fields in spring," Peottre observed. I turned to find him watching her with a mixture of pride and chagrin. "Here, give me your shovel for a time, while you rest yourself."

I saw his aim and surrendered my tool to him. After that, both Narcheska and Peottre worked alongside us, with Peottre taking care that he was never far away from his ward. The Narcheska seemed to take care that she was never far from the Prince. It was the first sign of warmth Elliania had shown toward Dutiful in days and the Prince seemed to take heart from it. They conversed, in quiet, breathless bursts, between pick strokes, and took their rest periods together. Peottre watched over them, sometimes disapproving and sometimes wistful. I think he had come to like our prince despite himself.

The Witted coterie decided that it supported the idea of freeing the dragon, and hence had no qualms about helping with the digging. When the Fool applied his wiry strength to both digging and moving ice, the Hetgurd representatives cautiously came to watch. By the third day, they were helping to drag sledloads of snow and ice from the pit to dump it. I suspect that curiosity to see the ice-encased dragon was as much their motivation as any other.

On the fifth day, Chade sent Riddle and young Hest back to the stored supplies on the beach. Peottre was uncertain about sending them off, and cautioned them many times to follow the flags we had posted along our route and not to wander from it. He looked grave and apprehensive as they set out. They took a sled, for they were to bring back food, and the spare shovels and picks we had brought, now that he had a larger workforce. Chade also told them to bring back all the canvas, in the hopes of rigging a windbreak or cover for the excavation that might block the blowing snow that thwarted our efforts each night. I suspected they would also retrieve the rest of the little kegs of explosive powder. I wanted nothing to do with that when I thought of it in the evenings, but by day, when I was battling the ancient hard ice, I sometimes longed to discover what it might do.

We dug on. If I paused to rest and looked at the sides of our pit, I could see the layers in the ice that marked the passing winters. Every year, more snow had been deposited here, and every following year, yet another layer had blanketed it. It occurred to me that we were digging down through time, and sometimes as I looked at the layers, I wondered when the ice I stood on had fallen as snow. How long had Icefyre been down here, and how had he come to be here? Deeper we dug, and deeper, and still saw not one scale of a dragon. From time to time, Chade and Dutiful would consult with the Witted coterie. Each time, they assured the Prince and his adviser that they still, from time to time, felt the stirring of the dragon's being. I agreed with them. Yet those consultations also made me aware that my own Wit-power was substantially stronger than Dutiful's. I was not as perceptive as Web, but I thought I was at least on a footing with Swift. Cockle was probably a bit stronger than Dutiful, and Civil stronger than the minstrel, but not as sharp as I was. It was odd, to be able to perceive that the Wit might be a strong or weak talent in a man. I had always thought of it as a sense that people either had or didn't. Now I perceived that it was like an aptitude for music or gardening. The strength of it varied widely, just as Skill-ability did.

Perhaps it was Thick's prodigious Skill-strength that kept him latched so firmly to the dragon. The little man seemed to have become a complete idiot, staring vacantly before him and humming. Occasionally, he would pause and make small motions with his hands. Neither the tune he hummed nor his hand motions conveyed anything to me. Once, when I was taking my rest after a digging shift, I sat down next to him. Hesitantly, I set my hand to his shoulder, and tried to find my Skill-ability. I had hoped the fierce Skill-fire that always burned in him would reignite my own talent. But nothing happened except that after a short time Thick shrugged my hand away much as a horse might shudder a fly from his coat. Even his interest in food had waned, which concerned me most of all. Not only Galen, my first Skill instructor, but Verity had warned me of the danger in becoming too absorbed in the Skill. It was always the first hurdle that new initiates had to leap, and for many it had been a deadly one. The Skill-instruction scrolls recounted many sad tales of promising students who were swept away in the Skill-current, losing all touch with our world as they enjoyed the unique contact that the magic provided. Eventually, such people were so enraptured that they lost interest in food and drink, in talking with their fellows, and eventually stopped caring for themselves at all. One warned that such a Skill-user would become "a great drooling babe" and Thick seemed poised on the brink of such a decline. I had always supposed the danger was the fascination with the Skill itself, for I had often felt that pull myself. But if Chade and Dutiful were correct, then Thick was being seduced not by the Skill but by the attraction of another, more powerful mind. I made several fruitless attempts to engage him in conversation, which drew minimal responses from him until finally, in annoyance, he told me to "Go away! Bothering a busy person is not polite!" And then he went back to his staring and rocking.

My Skill remained dead in me.

It was all the more frustrating in that Dutiful had made contact with Nettle. Twice he had touched minds with her, trying to persuade her of who he was and what he needed. The first time, she slammed her walls against him, saying she was in no mood for silly stories and why would a prince be trying to contact her in a dream? The second time, she was more receptive, for I think he had piqued her curiosity. She even tried, with little success, to distract Thick from his preoccupation, though I think she did so more out of concern for him than to please the Prince. Dutiful accompanied her on that mission, but could make little sense of the dream imagery she used. He could explain only that Thick seemed to have gone to a place where his little song was an essential part of a far grander piece of music, and he could not be lured away from it. It was a frustrating analogy. As for conveying the Prince's messages to the Queen, Nettle said she would make mention of her "odd dreams" to Kettricken, if chance afforded her a private moment with Her Majesty, but that she would not risk making a fool of herself before the ladies of the court. She had done that several times already, with her lack of court manners, and had no wish to give them any more amusement than she already had.

That gave me a pang. If I had consented, from the beginning, to letting her know her history and to her visiting the court, she would have grown up in the company of ladies and gentlemen and would not have been shamed by her country ways. I wondered if Kettricken now groomed her, in both studies and manners, so that she might take up a role as secondary heir to the throne. I longed to be able to talk to Nettle, to find out how much they had told her of her heritage, and to give her my explanations for why she had been raised as she had. But my lack of the Skill silenced me, and I could only nightly beg of the Prince that he be circumspect in what he told her.

Daily we continued to dig. The work was backbreaking and the food both limited and boring. Nights were cold and windy, and we looked forward to the men returning with canvas. But they did not. Chade gave them an extra day, and then two. The Hetgurd men claimed to have glimpsed the Black Man circling our camp at night, but their offerings were never taken, and the flowing snow erased any tracks he might have left. In one of our nightly talks, the Fool said that several times he thought he had felt the Black Man's presence and suspected that we were observed. I too had experienced that uneasy sensation of being watched, but could never see anyone spying on us. I suspected that Web did, too, for twice he summoned Risk from her shore-side scavenging and asked her to fly over our camp. He told me that she saw nothing out of the ordinary, just snow, ice, and a few protruding rocks.

In the brief times when we were not digging, eating, or sleeping, Web would find moments in which to work on my Wit with me. He said, without cruelty, that it was actually good that I was currently unpartnered, as it gave me more focus on the magic without making it specific to one creature. He added that Swift too seemed to be benefiting from studying while unencumbered, from which I gathered that the lad's lessons continued as well as mine. When he was with me, Web focused on making me see how the Wit connected all living things, not just those of Old Blood, but all. He showed me how he could extend his Wit and wrap it around Thick, to become more perceptive of his needs and feelings, even though Thick remained unaware of him. It was not an easy discipline to master, for it involved surrendering my own needs and interests to subservience to his. "Watch a mother with an infant, any kind of a mother, human or beast. There you will see this done on the simplest and most instinctive level. If one is willing to work at it, one can extend that same sort of perception to others. It is a worthwhile thing to do, for it conveys a level of understanding of one another that makes hate almost impossible. Seldom can one hate a person if one understands that person."

I doubted that I would ever achieve that level of understanding, but I tried. One evening, as I was eating with Dutiful and Chade in their tent, I tried extending my Wit to include Chade. I let go of my own hunger and aching back and anxiety about my lost Skill and focused myself on the old man. I saw him as clearly as if he were prey. I studied how he sat, his back straight, as if he were too stiff to even slump, and how he kept his gloves on while he spooned up the pallid mush that was our evening repast. His face was a study in contrasts, red nose and cheeks, while his forehead was pale with the cold. Then, as if I suddenly saw his shadow for the first time, I glimpsed an aloneness that trailed back behind him to his earliest years. I suddenly felt his years and the strangeness of a fate that had sent him, in his old age, to camp on a glacier alongside the boy he would make king.

"What?" he demanded suddenly of me, and I started, realizing that I'd been staring at him.

I scrabbled for an answer and then replied, "I was just thinking of all the years and times when I've sat across from you, and wondered if I'd ever truly seen you at all."

His eyes widened, almost as if he feared such a thought. Then he scowled and said, "And I'd hoped you had something useful in your mind. Well, this is what I've been pondering. Riddle and Hest haven't returned with the supplies. They should have been back by now. Today, I asked Web if his bird could seek for them. He said it was difficult to convey to her that we wanted news of two specific men, rather as if I asked you if you had seen two specific gulls. He asked her to look for two men with a sled; he said she did not see them." Chade shook his head. "I fear the worst. We need to send someone back, not just to look for Riddle and Hest, but also to bring back the supplies we needed. Longwick told me tonight we have food for four more days, five if he cuts the rations again." He rubbed his gloved hands together wearily. "I never thought it would take this long to dig out the dragon. All the reports we had seemed to say he was near the surface, even visible years ago. Yet we dig and dig and find nothing."

"He's there," the Prince assured him. "And every day we get closer."

Chade snorted. "And if I took one step southward every day, I'd be getting closer to Buckkeep, but no one could tell me how long it would take me to get there." With a groan he got up. Sitting on the cold earth, even with several layers of bedding beneath him, was obviously uncomfortable. He moved slowly around the cramped tent, cautiously stretching his legs and back. "Tomorrow, I'm sending Fitz to see what became of Riddle and Hest. And I want you to take Thick and the Fool with you."

"Thick and the Fool? Why?"

It was obvious to him. "Who else can I spare from the digging? Removing Thick from the dragon's vicinity may restore him. If it does, then leave him with Churry and Drub on the beach with our supplies. Have him Skill to us from there whatever news he has."

"But why the Fool?"

"Because it takes two men to pull the sled when it's loaded, and I don't think Thick will be of much use to you at that. I suspect you'll have to put Thick on the sled to get him to move from here. And you are one of the few people who can manage Thick at all, so you have to be one of the ones who goes. Fitz, I know it's not an assignment you would choose, but who else can I send?"

I cocked my head at him. "Then you aren't just trying to send the Fool and me away from the digging area before the dragon is uncovered?"

He sighed. "If I sent you and not the Fool, you would ask if I were trying to separate you. If I sent the Fool and not you, I'm sure you'd say the same. I suppose I could ask Web to take Thick and another man for this errand, but he does not understand Thick's Skill-ability. And if something has befallen Riddle and Hest, well, I think you more capable of dealing with a threat than..." He suddenly threw up his hands and said in defeat, "Do what you will, Fitz. You will anyway, and the Fool will only go if you ask him. I've no power to send him anywhere. So you decide."

I felt a bit sheepish. Perhaps I had been looking for motivations that truly didn't exist. "I'll go. And I'll ask the Fool to go with me. To be honest, I'll welcome the change from digging. Make a list of what you want brought back." Privately, I resolved that I'd scavenge any driftwood I could find on the beach and bring it back with me, regardless of how much weight it added to the load. Chade could do with a good roaring blaze, I decided, even if it only lasted one night.

"Be ready at first light, then," Chade advised me.

The Fool was not as pleased to leave the digging as I

was. "But what if they reach the dragon while we are gone? What if I am not here to defend him?"

"The Hetgurd guardians and the Witted coterie oppose killing him as much as you do. Don't you think they'll be enough?"

We were bedded down together, sleeping back to back for the body warmth just as we had in the Mountains so many years ago. Truth to tell, I gained little from it, for the Fool's body had always felt cool to the touch. It was rather like sleeping alongside a lizard, I thought. Yet if he did not give off much warmth, the solid feel of his back against mine was a reassurance of camaraderie that I had not felt since Nighteyes had died. There is security in knowing that a friend has your back, even if he is sound asleep.

"I don't know. I'm too close to where all my visions stopped." He paused, as if he expected me to ask a question, but that was a topic I did not wish to explore. Then, "Do you think we ought to go?" he asked cautiously.

I shifted in the bed, groaning as my aching muscles complained. "I don't think I thought much about it. Chade has been telling me what to do for so long that I simply accepted I should go. But I would like to know what has happened to Riddle and Hest. And I'd like to see if Thick recovers himself when he's moved away from the dragon's influence. And—" I shifted and groaned again. "I wouldn't mind a few days of doing anything other than shoveling."

He was quiet. I was too, pondering his silence. I wondered what was making him take so long to make up his mind. Then I laughed aloud. "Ah, yes. I nearly forgot. I am the Catalyst, the one who makes changes. And this would be a change in what you think you should do. So, you cannot decide whether to oppose it or not."

The silence stretched so long I thought he had fallen asleep. The day had been the warmest we had had so far, making sodden work of our task. I listened to the wind, and hoped the night's cold would crust the surface of the glacier and keep the wind from blowing snow into our excavation.

I had almost dropped off to sleep myself when he said, "You frighten me, sometimes, when you give voice to my thoughts. We will go, tomorrow. We'll take this tent for shelter, shall we?"

"That sounds fine to me," I said as I drowsed off.

And so the next morning we set off. Longwick issued us three days of supplies, which, he told us, should be ample for us to reach the beach. We struck the Fool's elegant tent and packed it on the sled while Longwick gave us last-minute directives. If we reached the beach without encountering the others, we should warn the guard there of our sightings of the Black Man. If we encountered evidence that the others had met with foul play, we should return to the camp immediately and report. If we met the others coming back, we should simply turn around and come back with them. Web's bird would check on us, from time to time. I nodded as I arranged the Fool's tent and bedding for three onto the sled. As predicted, we had to load Thick onto the sled. He could not be persuaded to walk. It was not that he resisted; he simply didn't cooperate. He would take a few steps, and then become lost once more in his musings. Dutiful and Chade both came to bid us farewell. Dutiful snugged Thick's cap down around his ears. I know that he tried desperately to stir Thick with the Skill. I could not feel it, but I saw the intensity in Dutiful's face. Thick turned his head slowly to look at the Prince. "I'm fine," he said sluggishly. And then he stared off in the distance again.

"Take care of him, Tom," the Prince told me gruffly.

"I will, my lord. We'll try to make a quick trip of it." And so saying, with Thick sitting on the great sled bundled up like a cocoon, I took up the lines and began to pull.

The heavily waxed runners moved easily over the snow. Almost too easily, for we were now going downhill rather than up. I had to stop and set the drag to keep the sled from running over the top of me. The Fool went ahead of us, his pack riding high on his shoulders, prodding the snow to make sure our path was sound, even though we were following the line of stakes that Peottre had set up to mark our path for us.

The day was warm, and snow collected, heavy, on my boots. When our path leveled for a time, the runners of the sled began to stick. The sled was cutting a deeper path upon our old one, and as the runners sank into the snow, heavy damp snow began to ride on the tops of the runners. But the day was pleasant and pulling Thick on the sled was still less strenuous than shoveling ice out of a pit. The gaudy sword the Fool had given me tapped against my leg as I strode along, for Longwick had insisted that I, at least, should go armed. We were traversing the trail much more swiftly than we had before, for the path was clearly marked with Peottre's stakes, and there was at least a slight down-hill slope for all of it. Thick's humming, the squeak of the runners, and the crunch of our footsteps on the softened crust of the glacier were not the only sounds. The warmth had wakened the glacier. We heard one distant fall of ice, a thunder that went on for some time. It was followed by lesser creakings and crashes, but always at a distance.

The Fool began to whistle, and I was much cheered when I saw Thick sit up and take notice of the music. He still hummed breathlessly to himself, but I began to make comments on the scenery, uniformly white as it was, and occasionally elicited a response from him. That cheered me unreasonably, but also left me pondering. The Skill was not a magic bounded by distance, and yet Thick seemed to be recovering more of his own awareness of the world the farther we got from the buried dragon. I had no answer to why that might be so, and wished I could discuss it with Dutiful and Chade.

Several times I attempted in vain to reach out with the Skill. A legless man trying to jump would have had more success. The magic was simply gone. If I dwelt on that, I felt a cold pit in the bottom of my belly. I pushed the thought aside. There was nothing I could do about it now.

The daily cycle of warmth and chill combined with the nightly wind had smoothed all the edges of our previous passage's trail. I made a few vain attempts to read it, trying to discern if Riddle and Hest and their sled had passed this way, with no success. We had a wide view of the snowy lands below us. Nothing moved on them, certainly nothing so large as a sled and two men. It was possible that they had lingered at the beach, I told myself, or that some mishap had delayed their return. I tried not to stack their disappearance with the theft of my Skill and the sightings of the Black Man. I had too few facts to make them add up to anything. Instead, I tried to enjoy the freshness of the day. At one point, I heard the high cry of a seabird, and looked up to see a gull describe a wide circle over us. I lifted a hand and waved a greeting at Risk, wondering if that acknowledgment would be relayed to Web.

We passed our previous campsite while we still had plenty of daylight and energy to continue, so we did. That night, we pitched the tent on the trail behind the sled. Thick still periodically hummed to himself, but also expressed both an interest in and then dismay at the simple dinner I prepared. The little tent was a bit more crowded with the three of us, but also warmed more quickly. The Fool told simple children's stories that night until we were all more than ready for sleep. With every passing tale, Thick hummed less and asked more questions. At one time the constant interruptions to the story would have annoyed me. Now they filled me with relief.

"Would you tell Chade and Dutiful good night for me?" I asked Thick as he settled into his blankets.

"Do it yourself," he suggested grumpily.

"I can't. I ate some bad food, and now I can't find them in my mind."

He sat up on one elbow and stared at me. "Oh. Yes. Now I remember. You're gone. That's too bad." He was silent for a time, then said, "They say good night, and thanks for letting them know. And maybe I should stay at the beach, but they'll decide later." He drew a deep, satisfied breath and dropped back into his blankets.

It was my turn to sit up. "Thick. You aren't coughing anymore. Or wheezing."

"No." He rolled over, managing to kick me in the process. I nearly complained but then he said, "He told me, 'Mend yourself. Don't be dumb, mend yourself, don't be annoying.' So I did."

"Who told you that?" I asked, even as I was stricken with guilt. Why hadn't Chade and Dutiful and I thought of trying to heal Thick? It now seemed obvious. I was ashamed we hadn't done it.

"Huh," Thick sighed out consideringly. "His name is a story, too long to tell. I'm sleepy. Stop talking to me."

And that was that. He went off into a deep sleep. I wondered if Icefyre had another name, a dragon name.

I woke once in the night, thinking I heard cautious footsteps outside our tent. I crept to the door flap, and then reluctantly stepped outside into the clear cold. I saw nothing and no one, even when I had made a full circuit of the tent.

When morning came, I made a wider circuit of the camp while the Fool tried to heat water for tea for us. I brought my news back to them. "Someone came to see us last night," I said, trying to keep my voice light. "He walked all around our camp in a big circle. Then he lay down in the snow over there for a while. Then he went away, that way, the same way he came. Do you think I should go see where he went?"

"Why?" Thick asked, even as the Fool said thoughtfully, "I think Lord Chade and Prince Dutiful might want to know about that."

"I think they would, too." I looked at Thick. He sighed wearily, and then turned his gaze inward.

A few moments later, he said, "They said, 'Go to the beach.' Dutiful says he thinks he left maple candy in a bag there. They say we should hurry there, and come back with the stuff, and tell the guards there to come back with us. 'Don't go looking for where the footprints go right now.'"

"Then that is what we'll do." How I wished to be able to hear Chade's thoughts on this for myself.

We packed up the tent and loaded it on the sled. Thick matter-of-factly climbed onto it. I thought it over and decided it was the simplest solution to traveling with him. Dragging him was easier than matching his slow pace. As before, the Fool went on before us, testing the trail while I pulled. The day was fine, a warm wind blowing across the snowy face of the world. I expected that we might reach the beach by the next afternoon if we held our present progress. Thick suddenly spoke.

"Nettle said she missed you. She asked if you hated her."

"I hated— When? When did she say that?"

"At night." Thick waved his hand vaguely. "She said you just went away and never came back at all."

"But that's because I ate the bad food. And I couldn't reach her."

"Ya." Thick dismissed this casually. "I told her you can't talk to her anymore. She was glad to hear it."

"She was glad?"

"She thought you were dead. Or something. She has a friend now, a new girl. Will we stop and eat soon?"

"Not until tonight. We don't have much food, so we have to be careful. Thick, did she—"

My words were interrupted by a whoop of dismay from the Fool. His sounding post had suddenly plunged deep in the snow. He picked it up, took two steps to the left and shoved it in again. Again it sank deep.

"Sit still," I told Thick. I took one of the extra poles from the sled and walked forward to stand beside the perplexed Fool. "Soft snow?" I asked him.

He shook his head. "It's as if there's only a crust, and then nothing. If I hadn't held tight to the pole, it would have dropped right through."

"Let's be very careful." I took hold of his sleeve. "Thick, stay on the sled!" I reminded him again.

"I'm hungry!"

"The food is in the sack behind you. Sit still and eat something." It seemed the easiest way to keep him busy. Tugging the Fool to move with me, we took three steps to the right. This time, I plunged in my pole. I felt what he had told me I would. The crust of snow resisted the pole, and then it shot through into nothingness.

"Peottre's stakes go right across it," the Fool pointed out.

"It wouldn't be that hard to move the stakes," I pointed out.

"Whoever moved them would have had to walk right across, though."

"The crust would be more solid at night. I think." I couldn't decide if we confronted the natural danger of the glacier or if we had followed the line of stakes into a trap. "Let's move back to the sled," I suggested.

"Seems like a very good idea," the Fool agreed.

So it was that as I led him back from the hidden chasm, we plunged downward through the crust. We sank, I to my knees, the Fool to his hips, both yelling in terror. Then, as we stuck there, I laughed out loud at our fright. It was no more than a soft spot in the snow. "Give me your hand," I said as he floundered, trying to get back onto the top of the crust. He took my proffered grasp, and then, as he floundered toward me, we both broke through the second crust below us and went down.

I had a single glimpse of Thick's face contorted in terror. Then his wail of dismay was drowned in the downpour of snow and ice that fell with and after us. I clung to the Fool's hand as I floundered for any sort of solidity anywhere else in the world. There was none. All was white and wet and cold, and we fell in a terrible unending slide of loose snow and ice chunks.

Snow seems a light and fluffy thing when it is falling on a sunlit day. But when it thickens the air to porridge, you cannot breathe it. It flowed inside my clothes like a living thing craving my warmth. It became heavy and relentless. I fought my free hand up to crook my elbow uselessly over my face. We fell still, a slow sliding, and in some part of my mind, I knew that more snow slid down after us. Yet through it all, I held fast to the Fool's hand, and knew that his free hand did not protect his face but clung in a death grip to the shoulder of my coat. There was no free air to breathe.

And then, as if we had passed through the neck of a funnel, we were suddenly falling and sliding more swiftly and freely. I kicked my feet, making vague swimming motions, and felt the Fool likewise struggling alongside me. I felt us sliding to a halt, in cold wet darkness. It terrified me, and I made the final struggle that our bodies demand we make when death clutches us. Then, somehow, against all odds, I was breaking free of the snow. I gasped a breath of almost clear air and floundered toward it, dragging the Fool with me. He came limply and I feared he had already smothered.

All was darkness and cold and cascading snow and ice. I was hip deep, pulling the Fool behind me, and then suddenly the snow let go of me. I waded out of the knee-deep stuff and then blundered clear of it. I heard the Fool take a wheezing gasp of air. I found a breath myself, and then two. Tiny settling crystals of ice still filled the air we breathed, but even so, it seemed such an improvement. We were in darkness.

I shook snow from my hair and dug handfuls of it out of my collar. My hat was gone, and one boot. All was black around us, and the only sounds were the indescribable creaks of settling snow and our own harsh breath. "Where are we?" I gasped, and my little human voice was the muffled squeak of a mouse in a bin full of grain.

The Fool coughed. "Down here." We had let go of one another, but still stood close enough for our bodies to touch. He was huddled at my feet, and I felt him doing something, and then a pale, greenish light opened out from his hands. I blinked, at first seeing no more than the glow, and then realizing that it came from a small box in his hands. "This won't last long," he warned me, his face ghastly in the corpse-light. "At most a day. It is Elderling magic, of the most expensive and rare sort. Not all of my fortune went for gambling and brandy. A good portion of it is right here in my hand."

"Thank the gods for that," I said heartily. For a fleeting instant, I wondered if that was the sole true prayer that Web had once referred to. Dim as the light was, it was still an immeasurable comfort to me. It was just enough to light both our faces as we looked at one another. The Fool's hat had stayed on his head. His pack dangled from one strap, the other torn free from him. I was shocked it had stayed with him at all. My sword belt and sword were gone. As I watched him, he strapped his little pack shut again. We did not speak for a moment or two as we shook snow from our clothing, and then lifted our eyes to peer at our surroundings.

We could see nothing of them. Our light was too dim to show us more than the slide of snow we had emerged from and ourselves. We were in an under-ice hollow or cavern, but the Elderling lantern could not reach the walls of it. No light trickled down from above. I decided that the flood of snow that had followed us had resealed whatever crack we had fallen through. Then, "Thick! Oh, Eda, give him the sense to Skill to Dutiful and Chade what has happened. I hope he just stays where he is on the sled. But when night and cold comes, what then for him? Thick!" I suddenly bellowed the word, thinking of the vague little man left sitting alone on a sled in a world of ice.

"Shush!" The Fool reprimanded me sharply. "If he hears you shout, he may get off the sled and come toward the crack. Be quiet. His danger is less than ours, and I'm afraid you must leave him to face it alone. He'll Skill out, Fitz. His mind is not swift, perhaps, but it works well enough and he will have plenty of time to think what to do next."

"Perhaps," I conceded. My heart felt squeezed. Of all the times to be deprived of my Skill, this was the worst. And then in the next instant, the loss of Nighteyes gutted me again. I missed his instincts and survivor's outlook. My heart caught in my chest. I was alone.

And drowning in self-pity. The thought was as acid as if it had truly come from Nighteyes. *Get up and do something. The Fool's survival depends on you, and possibly Thick's.*

I took a deep breath and lifted my eyes. The fickle green light of the little box showed me nothing, but that did not mean there was nothing to see. If there was no other way out, then we must risk causing another cascade of snow by trying to dig up through it. If there was a way out, then we should find it. It was that simple. Standing here whining like a lost cub would not avail me anything. I reached down and pulled the Fool to his feet. "Come. There is no going back up. Let us see where we are. Moving will keep us warmer."

"Very well." He spoke the words so trustingly that they nearly broke my heart.

I would have welcomed one of our snow poles, but there was no guessing where they were buried now. So, the Fool held his little box of light out in front of us, and we groped our way forward.

We encountered nothing. If we stood still and held our breaths, we could hear water dripping and the bone-deep slow breath of the ice around us. Under our feet, the ice was gritty. We could not see a ceiling above us. We were in a starless night, and our only contact with the world was the solidity under our feet and each other. We did not even see the blackness of a wall before us until we blundered against it.

We both stood touching it for a time, saying nothing. In that stillness, I became aware of the Fool shivering and the shuddering of his breath. "Why didn't you tell me you were that cold?" I demanded of him.

He sniffed, and then laughed weakly. "Aren't you? It seemed a useless thing to speak of it." He dragged in another chattering breath and asked, "Is that ice or rock?"

"Lift the light." He did. I peered at it. "I still can't tell. But it's something we can't pass. Let's follow it."

"It may take us right back to where we came."

"It may, and there's no help for that if it does. If we go all the way round and come right back to here again, at least we'll know there is no way out. Here. A moment." I set my hand to shoulder height on the wall, and then reached for my belt knife. It was gone. Of course. The Fool still had his, and I borrowed it to scratch a rough mark on the wall. It seemed a futile gesture.

"Left or right?" I asked him. I had no sense at all of north or south.

"Left," he said, flapping a hand vaguely in that direction.

"A moment," I said gruffly, and unfastened my cloak. He tried to fend me off when I put it around his shoulders.

"You'll get cold!" he protested.

"I'm already cold. But my body has always warmed itself better than yours. And if you drop from cold, it will not benefit either of us. Don't worry. If I need it back, I'll let you know. Just wear it for now."

I only realized how cold he was when he immediately surrendered. He dropped his pack to the floor and handed me the Elderling light while he fastened the cloak. He was shaking as he held it close around him. I lifted the box and decided it was not just the greenish light that made him such an odd color. He gave me a very small smile. "It's still warm from your body. Thank you, Fitz."

"Thank yourself. That's the one you gave me when I was acting as your servant. Come on. Let's get moving." I lifted his pack before he could. "What else is in here?"

"Nothing of much use, I'm afraid. Only a few personal

things I wouldn't wish ever to lose. There's a little flask of brandy in the bottom. And I think a few honey cakes. I brought them for an emergency, or perhaps a treat for Thick." He gave a strangled laugh. "Emergency. But not this. Even so, I think we should save them as long as we can."

"Likely you're right. Let's go."

He did not move to take the light, but kept his arms wrapped around his body. So I held the light and led the way as we followed the black wall beside us. I could tell by the way he walked that his feet were going numb. Despair threatened to engulf me. Then the wolf in me dismissed it. We were still alive and moving. There was hope.

We trudged on. Endlessly. Time became motion, steps taken in the dark. Sometimes I closed my eyes to rest them from the unnatural light, but even then, I seemed to see it. At such a moment, the Fool asked shakily, "What's that?"

I opened my eyes. "What's what?" I asked him. Blue afterglows danced before my vision. I blinked. They didn't go away.

"That. Isn't that light? Shut the box. See if it's still there or if it's some sort of reflection."

It was hard to get the box to shut. My fingers were cold, and my one unbooted foot was a cold aching lump at the end of my leg. But when the box was closed, a blue shard of light still beckoned to us. It was irregularly shaped and oddly edgeless. I squinted at it, trying to make it assume some familiar aspect.

"It's very strange, isn't it? Let's go toward it."

"And leave the wall?" I asked, oddly reluctant. "There's no way to tell how far away that is."

"Light has to come from somewhere," the Fool pointed out.

I took a breath. "Very well."

We set out toward it. It did not seem to grow larger. The floor became uneven and our pace more shuffling as we groped ahead with numbed feet. Then, in the space of a few steps, our perspective on it changed. A wall to our left had been blocking our view, allowing us to see only a reflection in an icy wall. As we moved past that projection, the blue gleam opened out and became a beckoning corridor of blue and white ice. Hopes renewed, we increased our pace. We hurried around a bend in our black chamber, and suddenly a luminous vista spread before us. The closer we approached, the more my eyes could resolve what we saw. As we angled back toward the illumination, it increased, and after a narrowing in the passage, we emerged into a world of light-suffused ice.

The beam seemed sourceless, as if it had wandered through windows and mirrors and prisms of ice before it found us. We entered into a strange maze of cracks and chasms in a world of palely gleaming walls. Sometimes our way was narrow and sometimes broad. The floor under our feet was never level. Sometimes it seemed we walked in a sharp crack in the ice that had happened yesterday and sometimes it looked as if melting water had slowly sculpted the wandering path we followed. When we came to ways where the passage branched, we always tried to choose the larger way. Often enough, it narrowed shortly after we had made our choice. I did not say to the Fool what I feared; we followed random crackings in the ice of the glacier. There was no reason to expect that any of them led to anything.

The first signs I saw that others had passed this way were subtle. I thought I tricked myself into hope; there seemed to be a scattering of sand where the floor of the passageway was slick. Then, that perhaps the walls had been squared off. My nose caught the scent first: fresh human excrement. In the same instant I was sure of it, the Fool said, "It looks as if steps have been cut into the floor ahead of us."

I nodded. We were definitely ascending, and broad shallow steps had been cut in the icy floor. A dozen steps later, we passed a chamber cut into the ice to our right. A natural fissure had been enlarged into a waste pit, a place to throw rubbish and dump chamber pots. And a grave for the ignominious dead. I saw a naked foot, obscenely pale and bony, projecting from the midden. Another body sprawled facedown upon it, ribs showing through tattered rags. Only the cold made the stench bearable. I halted and asked the Fool in a whisper, "Do you think we should go on?"

"It is the only path," he said tremulously. "We have to follow it."

He stared and stared at the discarded body. He was shaking again. "Are you still cold?" I asked. The passages we were in seemed slightly warmer to me than when we had been in darkness. Light seemed to come from within them.

He gave me a ghastly smile. "I'm scared." He closed his eyes for an instant, squeezing unshed tears onto his golden lashes. Then, "On we go," he said more firmly. He stepped past me to take the lead and I followed him, full of dread.

Whoever was responsible for dumping the slops and chamber pots was a careless fellow. Splotches and splashes marred the icy walls and mottled the ice underfoot. The farther we went, the more obviously man-made or at least hand-modified the passages became. The source of the blue light was revealed when we passed an exposed pale globe that was anchored to the wall overhead. It was larger than a pumpkin, and gave off light but not heat. I halted, staring up at it. Then, as I reached toward it with curious fingers, the Fool caught at my cuff and dragged my hand back down. He shook his head in silent warning.

"What is it?" I asked in a whisper.

He shrugged one shoulder. "I don't know. But I know it's hers. Don't touch it, Fitz. Come on. We have to hurry."

And we did, for a time. Until we came to the first dungeon.

chapter XX

CORRIDORS

*It is said that at one time there was a seer or oracle who
resided on Aslevjal Island. This tale seems to be very
old. Some tell it that there was only one, and she lived
for many generations, but remained young, raven haired
and black eyed. Others say that there was a
mothershouse of oracles, with a Great Mother who
passed on her seer's duties to her elder daughter in turn,
so that a succession of oracles served there. All speak of
them as having lived beyond their Great Mother's day.
There remains no living witness to the truth of this tale.
It was said that the seer lived within the glacier and
emerged only to accept offerings that visitors brought to
Icefyre. If a seeker of truth brought animals to sacrifice,
the seer would do the bloodletting and then fling the
entrails into the air and let them fall smoking to the ice.
The future of the visitor was spelled out in the curling of
the guts. After the reading, in the name of the dragon,
she would claim the sacrificed animal.*

    ❧ COCKLE'S COLLECTED OUTISLANDER TALES

The door was nearly invisible. The Fool had passed it before I perceived what it was and halted him with a touch to

his shoulder. Either the door was made of ice, or was so thickly coated with ice that its original material was unseen. The hinges were vague bulges in the wall, and I saw no sort of handle or lock. It baffled me. There was a narrow slit in the door at about waist height. I stooped to peer into it, and was shocked to see a ragged and battered man crouched in the far corner of a cell. He stared in my direction, mute and expressionless. I staggered back from the sight with an inarticulate cry.

"What?" the Fool whispered and stooped to look in himself. He remained crouched by the door, his face a mask of horror. Then, "We have to let them out. Somehow."

I shook my head wildly, and then found my tongue. "No, Fool. Trust me, please. They're Forged. However heartless it seems to leave them in there, it would be a danger and a cruelty to let them loose. They'd turn on us, for our cloak or for sport. We don't dare let them out."

He stared up at me incredulously. Then he said quietly, "You didn't see them all, did you? Riddle is in there. And Hest."

I didn't want to look. I had to. Heart thundering, breath coming fast, I crept to the door and peered in.

The inside of the cell was dimly lit with the same blue glow as the corridors. I let my eyes adjust to the light until I could see the entire cell. The room was a cavity chopped into the glacier. The floor was crusted with waste. There were five Forged Ones inside, and nothing else. Four of them had taken positions in defensible corners, backs to the walls. Hest, weakened with injuries, sprawled on the floor in the center of the cell. Plainly none of the Forged Ones dared venture forth to attack him, for that would leave their own backs exposed. The three strangers in the cell were Outislanders, starved and scarred and dressed in rags. Their captors had stripped Hest and Riddle of their heavy fur coats, but even so, they were better off than the others. They still had their boots. I quested toward them desperately with the Wit, willing with all my might that I feel something from them. But there was nothing. They crouched, staring with brutish animosity at one another, less than animals. Their connection to the world and society had been stripped from them.

I sagged away from the door, sitting down flat on the icy floor. Misery and sickness flooded through me. Evil memories I had thought long banished clawed at me with scabby fingers. I do not think the Fool could have understood the depth of my horror. He could not feel their absence of connection as I could.

"Is there nothing we can do for them?" he asked softly.

A smile like blight came to my face. I clenched my teeth, refusing to feel the emotions that threatened me. I would not think about this too deeply. I had already thought this through, long ago, and I knew all the final answers. No sense in agonizing my way through lessons I had already learned. I spoke flatly. "I could kill them. Maybe. There are four of them on their feet, and though three of them look starved and weak, I've known Forged Ones to pack up and fight together. For a time, until there were spoils to claim. I don't know if I could kill them all before they pulled me down. Riddle's a good fighter. And he's still healthy."

"But . . . Riddle and Hest?" He pleaded with me.

He should have known better. "Fool. That isn't Riddle or Hest. Their bodies are there, and all the things they knew are there. But that's all. They no longer care about anything or anyone. The only things they'll consider are their own physical appetites. Would Riddle let Hest lie there on the floor, injured and unguarded? No. That isn't Riddle. Not anymore."

"But . . . we have to do something!" His whisper was agonized.

I sighed. "If we open that door, I have to kill them. They'll make me, unless I'm willing to let them kill me."

"Then we have no choice?"

I smiled bitterly. "There are always choices. But

sometimes there are no good ones. I kill them, or they kill us. Or we walk away."

For a long time, the Fool stood silent. Then he turned away from the cell door and walked slowly away. I followed him.

The ice corridors began to show more signs of use. The floor looked trodden and grubby, the icy walls scarred. We passed more dungeons, identical to the first. I peered into each one we passed, sick with horror, but we did not speak of the people we glimpsed inside them. The ones with the woman and the girl in them were the most heartrending for me. The floor of those cells had a layer of straw on it and there were pallets in each corner. Evidently the lives of these captives were to be prolonged. It seemed a crueler fate than Riddle, Hest, and their companions endured. Death would not be swift for the men, but cold ate a man just as steadily as starvation did. They would not suffer long. From the length of the woman's unkempt hair and filthy nails, she had been in there for a long time. Huddled in a filthy bear rug, she crouched in the corner, staring at the wall. In the next cell, a girl of about seven picked at scabs on her ankles. Her eyes flicked once to meet mine as I stared through the crack in the door. The only emotion they showed me was wariness.

Eventually, the corridor of dungeons came to an end. The hall grew wider, and the pale light globes were spaced more frequently. The passageway had been carved rather than chopped out of the ice, and there were grace notes of frozen beauty in the arched walls. The floor was clean and sprinkled with sand for traction. It seemed older to me, as if it had been built to accommodate a greater flow of people, but we had still not glimpsed a soul.

Then we came to a junction that offered us three choices. The main corridor continued before us. To our left, a wide passage descended in shallow steps that wound down and out of sight. To our right, a stairway was cut in the ice, and led steeply upward. Both looked older and far more worn than the path we had been following. The Fool and I halted and exchanged glances.

From the opening on our left, my ears caught a faint shushing sound. It came at distant but regular intervals. I cupped my ear to it. After a short time, the Fool whispered, "It sounds as if something huge is breathing down there."

I widened my nostrils and drew in a deep breath. What I smelled inspired me with hope even as it made the sound instantly recognizable. "No. It's waves, it's the sea. This way leads to a beach. Come on."

His face lit like a man suddenly reprieved. "Yes!" he prayed, and hastened down the broad, wide steps. I followed him and, catching his shoulder, moved him to the inside curve of the steps. "Stay by the wall," I instructed him in a low voice. "If we hear someone coming up, it will give us that one moment to surprise them." Our only weapon, his belt knife, was already in my hand.

We were already weary, with no idea of how long we'd been exploring the ice maze. The steps were shallow and maddeningly irregular. They were gouged too as if heavy objects were often dragged up or down them. As we went deeper, the sea smell became stronger, and the air grew damper. The steps became more slippery, and soon we were negotiating our way down ice steps sheened with water. Someone had thrown sand on them, but it had melted unevenly into the surface, leaving knobs of glistening and slippery ice when least expected. We were forced to go more slowly. Soon the walls were gleaming with slow water, and drops fell from overhead. The smell of the water grew stronger, but the light did not vary from the witchglow of blue that suffused us.

Then we reached the pitted bottom step and saw the futility of our hope. Beyond the ice was a slope of worn black stone that gave onto a beach of black sand. Several metal pegs were driven into it, as if small boats were sometimes moored there. Waves shushed in and out over it, lapping relentlessly higher. And overhead in the cavern, barely visible in the blue glow of the last of the pale globes, was a high ceiling of glistening ice.

"If we had a boat, and if the tide was going out, I'd chance it," I said.

"If," said the Fool, and snickered. I looked at him in shock. He looked terrible, and it was not just the blue light. He took his pack from my arm and sank down on the wet steps with it. For a moment, he hugged it to him as if he were a child hugging a beloved doll. Then he opened it and rummaged to the bottom for the flask of brandy. He opened it and offered it to me first.

I took it, weighed it in my hand, and then drank no more than a quarter of it. It was the same apricot brandy that he had brought to the little house that Hap and I had shared. I swallowed the warmth of a summer day, and then breathed out through my open mouth, tasting apricots and friendship as I held the flask out to him. He took it from me, exchanging a square of black bread for it. It was half the size of my palm. I sat down beside him, and ate it slowly. There were raisins and nuts in it. It was dense and sweet and small, making me more aware of the hunger I'd been ignoring. We ate slowly in silence. After I'd licked the last crumb off my palm, I looked at him. "Up?" I said.

"It won't lead out," he told me softly. "Think about where we are, and the legends we've heard from the Outislanders. This is where they came in under the ice to see the dragon. That little winding staircase must go up to Icefyre. Why else would it be there?"

"Maybe it goes up and out," I said stubbornly. "We won't know until we try it. Maybe that other, wider way goes to the dragon. That would make more sense."

He shook his head. "No. The dragon must be above us, if you could sometimes see him from the surface. The staircase goes to the dragon. Not out." He was adamant. He leaned his head against the icy wall. "There is no way out for me. And I've always known it."

I heaved myself to my feet. The seat of my trousers was wet. Oh, good. "Get up," I told him.

"There's no point to it."

"Get up!" I insisted, and when he didn't move, I seized him by the back of his collar and hauled him to his feet. He did not resist, but only gave me a doleful glance. "We've come this far together, through the years and over many a path and byway. And if we are going to end here, under the ice of Aslevjal, then I'm going to see this damnable dragon that made us come all this way. And so are you."

Is there anything more wearying than shallow steps? Perhaps slippery shallow steps. Nevertheless, we ascended them, and as before, we stayed close to the inner wall and kept our ears perked for sounds of anyone coming our way. We heard the waves growing ever fainter behind us and the random plops of falling drips. Eventually, we reached the place where we intersected with the carved corridor. We halted there, listening, but heard nothing.

I was tired. I was sure we'd gone far past a time when we deserved a night's sleep. My head felt stuffed full of felt and buzzing flies. The Fool looked worse. We crossed the corridor and entered the stairwell. He followed me slowly up the narrow steps. The staircase wound as it climbed. As soon as its curve took us out of sight of the main corridor, I stopped him. "You. Drink the rest of the brandy now. It will warm you and give you a bit of heart, perhaps. In any case, it will do you more good inside your belly than inside the flask."

"Can I sit down?" he asked.

"No. I might not be able to get you up and moving again," I replied heartlessly, but he had already sunk down onto the step. Again he took the brandy flask, opened it, and offered it to me. It wasn't worth an argument. I wet my mouth with it, and then told him, "You finish it."

And he did, in a single deep swallow. He seemed to take a long time to cap the empty flask and put it away. "This is hard," he said, but he did not seem to address his words to me. "I'm too close to the end. I've had glimpses of this, but never clear ones. And now all I know is that I must go on, and that every step I take leads me closer to my death." He met my eyes and said without shame, "I'm terrified."

I smiled. "Welcome to human existence. Come. Let's go see this dragon you came so far to save."

"Why? So I can tell him I've failed him?"

"Why not? Someone should tell him we tried."

It was the Fool's turn to smile. "He won't care. Dragons care nothing for good intentions or failed attempts. He'll only despise us. If he notices us at all."

"Ah! And that will be such a new experience for both of us."

Then he laughed, and I did too, not loud, but in the way men laugh when they know it might be the last opportunity to share a joke with a friend. We were not drunk, at least not on brandy. If the Fool was right, we were drinking the dregs of our lives. I think that whenever a man realizes that, he tries to find every last bit of pleasure in it.

Up we went. The stair wound narrow, and I wondered what madman had carved it. Had there once been a natural feature that someone had ordered into a stairway, or was all of this a sculptor's icy fancy? We went up. At one time, the walls had been decorated with bas-relief ice carvings, but they had been defaced, probably deliberately. All that was left were bits of legs or a hand in a fist, and once a woman's lips and chin. I grew to hate the unevenness of my gait, one foot booted and one in an ice-coated sock. When we stopped to rest, I let the Fool sit down. He leaned against the wall, and I thought that he dozed. When I saw the tears creeping down his cheeks, I roused him. "There's no good in those. Get up. We're moving on now."

My voice was kinder than my words. He nodded to them and hauled himself to his feet. We continued our climb. Like an unending nightmare, the winding steps went on and on. The pale globes could not light every corner of the twisting steps. Every shade of blue and white that could be expressed took a turn. It was a cold and wearying beauty that we traversed. We climbed more slowly, and then rested together, and went on. It seemed that eventually we must break out of the ice, that it could not go on much longer. Then we came to a level gallery carved in the ice. And the dragon.

A thick layer of ice remained between him and us. We saw him through the distortion and haze, yet even so, he was breathtaking. We walked slowly the length of the gallery, paralleling Icefyre. He was bigger than two ships. His wings were folded to his sides and his tail curled back around him. His head was turned back on his long neck, coiled away from us. We gazed at him in awe. The Fool's aching heart was in his eyes. The immense sense of the dragon's life almost overwhelmed my Wit. Never had I been so close to a natural living creature of such great size. Then we came to a crudely bored tunnel that wormed through the ice toward the dragon's breast. I stooped and peered into it. It ended in the darkness of the black dragon. I took a breath. "Lend me your Elderling lantern," I asked the Fool.

"Are you going in there?"

I nodded slowly, unable to say why I must.

"I'll come with you, then."

"There isn't room. Stay here and rest. I'll tell you what I find."

He looked torn between weariness and curiosity. Then the Fool lowered his pack to the floor and opened it. As he gave me the lantern-box, he said, "I have two more pieces of bread. Shall we eat them now?"

"Go ahead. I'll have mine when I come back." Even the mention of food made my mouth suddenly water. Thick came suddenly into my mind. Had he Skilled to Chade and Dutiful, or did he sit woefully awaiting our return? Had he remained safe on the sled, or had it too followed us down in the crush of snow? I pushed the useless questions away. The Fool handed me the little box and I opened it, releasing its peculiar green light.

"Don't be long," he cautioned me as I entered the tunnel. "I want to know what you find there."

The tunnel was not tall enough to stand in. I crawled along it, pushing the box of light before me. The blue light of the gallery faded behind me and soon I traveled only in a pale green light that echoed weirdly in the mirroring ice. The reek of dragon slowly grew until I tasted him as much as smelled him. It strongly recalled the stink of garter snakes when as a curious boy I had captured and handled them. The tunnel became narrower as I went, as if whoever had dug it had been so intent on reaching the dragon that they could not be bothered to keep it a uniform size.

It ended in a wall of dragon, tiled with gleaming black scales, the smallest as large as my spread hand. A neat row of tools rested on a roll of leather on the ice floor before it. Various blades, mallets, drills, and metal picks were there. Two tools, blades broken or blunted, had been discarded. I held the Elderling light closer to the dragon, my gorge rising as I confirmed my suspicion. Someone had crawled along this tunnel to the beast's side, and then attempted to burrow into his heart.

It looked as if his plated scales had defeated the attacks. Some of them were scored, but it looked as if none of the metal implements had managed to penetrate the flesh beneath. A sort of metal wedge was still in place, driven under the overlapping black scales to lift them and create a vulnerable place. I held the light closer. The lifted scales revealed a second layer of creamy scales beneath them, overlapping in a pattern perpendicular to the first layer. A pick like an ice pick had been shoved in under one creamy scale. It had penetrated the leathery hide beneath, but no blood or fluid flowed. I judged that it had been like driving a blade into a horse's hoof. Nonetheless, the sneaking cruelty of such an attack disgusted me.

The dragon lived. Someone had burrowed in here like

a maggot, trying to hack a way into his heart while he was held immobile.

I appreciated the density of his natural armor when it took all my strength to pull the pick from his flesh. I had to hammer sideways at the wedge to get it out of him. The instant it fell free, the scales in that area rippled and writhed and closed up. For a moment, my Wit-sense of his life surged. Then, just as abruptly, it vanished. The scaled wall of flesh before me might have been something pieced together from metal. I hesitated, and then boldly ran a hand over the layered scales. I could not even get a fingernail under the ridged edge of one, so tightly did they clamp, one over another. They were cold too, cold as the ice that encased him.

I gathered the evil tools into their roll of leather and took them with me as I retreated. I had to crawl backward; there was no room to turn around. By the time I reached the gallery, I was sweating, and the reptilian stink of dragon was making me ill.

I found the Fool sound asleep at the end of the gallery closest to the dragon's hidden head. He was seated, his knees drawn up to his chest and his golden head drooped over them. His loosened hair veiled his face. Exhaustion had overcome his curiosity. I sat down on the floor by him and leaned back against the icy wall. In his sleep, he muttered something and shifted closer to lean his weight against me. I sighed and let him be. I wondered why the dragon's assailant hadn't chosen to tunnel into the wall here, closer to the creature's head. Had he feared that even vised in ice, the dragon would have found a way to defend himself?

I looked up at the icy ceiling above me. It was a deep bottomless blue, like staring into deep water. Somewhere up there, I promised myself, Prince Dutiful dug alongside his Wit coterie. I wondered what thickness of ice separated him from us. How long would the Fool and I have to sit here before we heard and then saw the progress of their shovels? An age, I decided. I could hear no sound of shovels or voice, saw no flawing of ice giving way to their efforts. They might as well have been on the other side of the world.

I shifted closer to the Fool. His body trapped my warmth on that side of me. I was so terribly tired and hungry. With one of my new weapons, I chiseled a bit of ice from the wall and sucked on it for water. I put the Elderling light-box back in the Fool's pack. I found the piece of bread he had left me and ate it. It was very good and very small. Then I rested my head on top of the Fool's and closed my eyes for a moment. I suppose we slept.

My own shivering wakened me. I felt as if my bones were trying to rattle themselves out of their sockets. It hurt to unfold myself. The Fool slowly slid down to lie on the ice as I beat my arms and stamped my feet, trying to find feeling in them again. I knelt beside him and pawed at him with hands that were too stiff to work well. He was an awful color. When he groaned softly, I sighed with relief. "Get up," I told him. I kept my voice down, cursing us for having slept so foolishly in such an exposed place. If anyone had come up those stairs, they would have found us unaware and cornered. "Come on. We have to move. We still have to find a way out of here."

He whimpered and curled up more tightly. I prodded at him, feeling both anger and despair. "We can't give up now. Get up, Fool. We have to go on."

"Please." He breathed the word. "A quiet death. A slide into it."

"No. Get up."

He opened his eyes. Something in my face must have told him I would not leave him in peace. He unfolded himself, as stiff and wooden as the puppets he had once carved. He held his hands up before him and looked at them stupidly. "I can't feel them."

"Get up and moving. They'll come back to life."

He sighed. "It was such a good dream. I dreamed that

we both died here and it was all over. There was nothing more we could do, and everyone agreed that we had tried and it wasn't really our fault. They spoke kindly of us." He opened his eyes wider. "How did you stand up?"

"I don't know. Just do it." I did not feel patient.

"I'm trying."

As he made his efforts, I told him what I had discovered at the end of the tunnel. I showed him the tools I had taken, and he shuddered. With every word I spoke, he came back to himself a bit more. Finally, he got to his feet and took a few shuffling steps. We were both shaking with the cold but I had recovered some feeling in my hands. I chafed his roughly, despite his gasps of protest at the pain. When he could open and close his hands again, I handed him a knife. He clutched it awkwardly, but nodded when I told him to keep it ready.

"Once we get down the stairs," I said, blithely ignoring how difficult that might be, "we're going to have to follow the main corridor. It's our only hope now."

"Fitz," he began earnestly, and then at my look, he stopped. I knew he had been going to tell me how hopeless it was. I took a long farewell look at the dragon. He was dormant again, beyond the reach of my Wit to detect his life. *Why*, I silently asked him. *Why are you here and why must Elliania have your head?* Then I turned my back on him, and the Fool followed me as we began our long descent of the stairs.

It was, if anything, more miserable than the ascent had been. We were still tired, hungry, and cold. I lost count of how many times I slipped and fell. The Fool, bereft of his usual grace, stumbled alongside me. I kept expecting that we would encounter someone coming up to torment the dragon, but the stairway remained blue, cold, and silent, and completely indifferent to our suffering. When we grew thirsty, we chipped bits of ice from the wall to suck on. It was the only creature comfort we could offer ourselves.

Eventually we reached the bottom. It seemed almost

sudden when we turned that part of the spiral that exposed the waiting corridor to us. Breath bated, we crept down to peer around the last corner. I sensed no one, but our discovery of the Forged Ones in the dungeons had reminded me that there were dangers my Wit could not make me aware of. But the passageway was wide and empty and silent. "Let's go," I whispered.

"It won't lead us out." The Fool spoke in a normal tone. There was an unhealthy duskiness to the gold of his skin, as if life were already retreating from him, and his voice was dead. "This hall leads to her. It has to. If we follow it, we are going to our deaths. Not that we have many alternatives. As you pointed out before, sometimes all your choices are evil."

I sighed. "What do you suggest then? Go back down to the water's edge and hope someone comes with a boat and we can kill him before he kills us? Or go back to the Forged Ones and give ourselves to them? Or go all the way back to the ice fissures and the dark?"

"I think—" he began uncertainly, and then stiffened. I whirled to see what he pointed at behind me. "The Black Man!" he gasped.

It was he, the same person Thick and I had glimpsed before. He stood at a turning in the wide corridor before us, his hands crossed on his chest as if he were waiting for us to notice him. He was dressed all in black: tunic and trousers and boots. His long hair was as black as his eyes and skin, as if he had been made of all one substance and clad in it, too. And as before, he made no impression on my Wit. For just a moment, he stood and stared at us. Then he turned and swiftly strode away. "Wait!" the Fool cried after him and sprang to the chase. I do not know where he found the energy or agility to run. I only know that I thudded after him, my numb feet shocking me each time they jolted on the icy floor. The Black Man glanced back at us, and then fled. He seemed to run without effort, and yet he did not outdistance us. His feet made no sound.

The Fool ran fleetly for a time and I pounded along behind him. Then his last burst of energy left him, and he suddenly lagged. Still the Black Man did not outdistance us. He remained ahead of us, in sight but unreachable, a taunting phantom. Despite the deep breaths I took as I staggered along beside the Fool, I caught no scent of him.

"He's not real! He's magic, a trick of some kind." I gasped the words to the Fool, wanting to believe them.

"No. He's important." The Fool's breath was ragged and he more stumbled than ran now. He caught at my sleeve and leaned on me briefly, then forced himself up and on. "I've never felt such significance in a man. Please. Help me, Fitz. We have to follow him. He wants us to follow him. Don't you see that?"

I saw nothing save that we could not catch him. We went panting and reeling after him, never catching up yet never losing sight of him. The corridors where he led us grew wider and more elaborate. Vines and blossoms decorated the frozen lintels of the arched entryways we passed. The Black Man did not look to left or right, and gave us no time to do so. We passed a garlanded basin of ice that cupped a sculpted fountain, an arched spray of water trapped in stillness. We traversed the spacious and elegant corridors of a magnificent palace of ice, and saw not a soul nor felt a breath of warmth.

We slowed to a lurching walk, interspersed with a few charging steps to keep him in sight each time the Black Man turned a corner. Neither of us had breath for questions. I do not think the Fool thought of anything except catching him. Useless for me to ask why. Even if I'd formed the question, the Fool would not have answered it. My mouth was dry, my heart thundering in my ears, and still we pursued him. He seemed to be sure of himself as he threaded the warren of passageways. I wondered where we were going and why.

Then he led us into the ambush.

So it seemed to me. He had again chosen a turning,

and as the Fool and I hastened our lagging steps to keep him in sight, we turned a corner and ran full tilt into six men-at-arms. I caught one last glimpse of the Black Man, far down the hall. He halted, and then as the men-at-arms yelled in surprise and fell upon us, he vanished.

There was no question of defending ourselves. We had run too far, on too little food, water, and sleep. I could not have fended off an angry rabbit. As they seized the Fool, all life seemed to go out of him. His knife fell from his nerveless hand. His mouth sagged open but he did not even cry out. I plunged my blade into the wolf-hide tunic of the first man who leaped on me. There it stuck as he bore me down.

The back of my head bounced off the icy floor in a flash of white light.

chapter XXI

IN THE REALM
OF THE PALE WOMAN

*The religion of the White Prophets has never had a
strong following in the north lands, yet for a time it
afforded a most amusing pastime to the nobility of the
Jamaillian court. Satrap Esclepius was quite enamored
of the books of prophecy, and paid great sums to traders
who could bring him copies of those rare manuscripts.
These he entrusted to the priests of Sa, who made yet
more copies of them for him. It was said that he often
consulted them in this fashion. He would make an
offering to Sa, pose his question, and randomly select a
passage from one of the manuscripts. He would then
meditate on that passage until he felt he had resolved the
question.*

*The nobility of his court, ever anxious to mimic
their ruler, soon procured copies of the White Prophecies
for themselves and began to use them in like fashion. For
a time, the pastime enjoyed great popularity until the
head priest of Sa began to decry it as being a portal to
idolatry and blasphemy. At his insistence, most of the
scrolls were gathered and either destroyed or consigned to
the restrictive care of the priesthood.*

*It is rumored, however, that the Satrap's fondness
for the writings was instrumental in winning the aid that*

*he offered to a young boy of strangely pale mien who
wrangled his way into a hearing with the Satrap.
Impressed by the lad's ability to quote from the sacred
writings, and persuaded that his help to the boy had been
foretold by several verses the lad interpreted for him, the
Satrap responded by granting him a free passage on one
of the slaving ships then bound for Chalced.*

❧ "CULTS OF THE SOUTHLANDS," AUTHOR UNKNOWN

I came back to consciousness twice before I could hold fast
to it. The first time I was being dragged, one man to each
arm, down an icy hallway. The second time, I became
aware that I was on my belly and someone was firmly binding my wrists behind my back. The third time, I was again
being dragged by my two guards. This time, I clung stubbornly to wakefulness, however painful. We had entered a
palatial throne room. It had been hewn from the icy interior of the glacier, and the fat fluted columns that had been
left to support its lofty ceiling were blue. On the walls carvings in bas-relief celebrated a woman repeatedly, in one
lofty tableau after another. She was shown with a sword in
her hand, on the bow of a ship with her hair streaming in
the wind; she stood over her crushed enemies, her foot
upon one man's throat; enthroned, she pointed a finger of
judgment at the wretches who cowered before her. All of
the figures were many times life-sized, towering above us,
wrathful and implacable. We had entered the realm of the
Pale Woman.

Yet even here, in the heart of her kingdom, she had a
rival. In the glassy ceiling of the chamber, behind the blue
blurring of thick ice, I glimpsed finally the complete outline of the one I had come so far to see. Our winding path
through the corridors had taken us beneath the dragon. I
thought I could even glimpse a brighter rectangle of light
that might have been our feeble excavation efforts. I wondered if, above us, our friends still labored to chip through

the ice to the trapped dragon. Useless to scream out to them; it would have been like trying to scream through not one, but three or four castle walls.

Scores of the Pale Woman's followers had gathered to watch us brought before her. Immense white globes, suspended from frost-encased chains, lit the hall with an unnatural blue-white light. Heavily clad in furs and skins, her Outislander warriors seemed like dwarves in the overwhelming immensity of the ice palace. They were silent, their faces stoic as we were dragged past them. Their clan tattoos had been obliterated by black blotches. A few wore some sign of regard for their new liege, in the form of dragon or serpent tattoos. They regarded us without pity or hatred or even much curiosity. They did not seem fired with hatred or passion of any kind. The deadness I saw in them went beyond resignation to the beastlike tolerance for suffering that is usually attributed to abused animals. Even my Wit-sense of them was dampened. I wondered if she had discovered some lesser form of Forging, one that tore away their connections to humanity but left them enough fear of her to make them obedient. One of them I recognized. The woman Henja, who had been the Narcheska's servant at Buckkeep, was as uninterested as the rest of them. I turned my head to confirm it. Yes, it was she. Since she'd left Buckkeep Castle, I'd glimpsed her once in Buckkeep Town when the Piebalds nearly killed me, and again when she had spied on the Prince and the Narcheska riding ponies on the hillside of Mayle Island. How did she fit into all of this? I could not make her role clear to myself, but I knew with sudden certainty that she had always been the Pale Woman's tool. Danger threatened my prince as surely as it did me.

I managed to get my feet under me, but I could not keep up with the quick step of my guards. I stumbled between them, and when they finally halted and forced me onto my knees before her, I did not resist. My head was still spinning. I would rest in whatever posture I could, and find my strength in blessed stillness. I tried to turn to look at the Fool, but had only a glimpse of him, head lolling, as his guards held him in a limp obeisance before their ruler. Then a stinging slap from one of my wardens brought my eyes back to my captor.

She was white, as the Fool was once white, and her hair floated unbound around her shoulders. Her eyes were colorless, just as the Fool's had been when he was a boy. Her face was his, softened to a woman's countenance. Her beauty was unearthly, cool as the ice that surrounded her. She sat on overlapping furs, white bear, white fox, and ermine with dangling black tails, on a throne chiseled from ice. Her robe of purest white wool did not conceal the womanly curves of her body. About her throat she wore a necklace of flowers carved from ivory. Diamonds sparkled in their centers. Her long-fingered hands rested in idle relaxation on the fur-draped arms of her throne. Her fingers were ringed with silver, all set with glistening white stones. She looked down at us, held on our knees before her, and appeared neither pleased nor surprised. Perhaps, like the Fool, she had always known it would come to this.

Her throne nestled in the coil of a curved and sleeping carved dragon. The black-and-silver memory stone of his body gleamed in a mountainous arch behind her throne and his folded wings were thick and heavy against him. He was not one single piece of stone, but rather blocks of it, probably painstakingly hauled here from the quarry at the other end of the island, and then fitted tightly together to form a continuous sculpture. The fine seams in the carefully matched stone were barely visible. The dormant dragon was immense, larger than Verity-as-Dragon had been, and yet still not as big as Icefyre. And he was incomplete, soft and slumped and without details, an unformed suggestion of a dragon rather than a reality. His blocky head on his curved long neck rested before the Pale Woman's elevated throne like a step. His eyes were lidded. Even so, I shuddered at his cruel countenance. My Wit clamored with conflicting emotions, fear, hatred, pain, lust, and vengeance. All were trapped within the crudely worked stone.

The source of the dragon's developing essence was plain. Several Outislanders, nearly spent, were chained against his flanks. The captives bore the marks of torture and privation; that would be how the Pale Woman wrung sufficient emotion from them to make them useful to her. Emotions and memories were what a Skill coterie fed into a stone dragon as they created it to hold their joined awareness. I could not understand how she could imagine a creature fed by the discordant memories of tormented wretches could become a sentient creature. What would unite them and give purpose to the dragon's flight? The stone dragons I had seen had been works of single-minded devotion, the crowning glory of the coteries that had created them. Beauty had infused them, no matter how odd the shapes each coterie had selected to represent it. Even the Winged Boar had gained grace in flight. This creature of hers was a mosaic of stolen pain. What temperament would such a creature have? It was obvious to my Wit that the prisoners' humanity had already been Forged away from them, stripped from their souls and forced into the dragon. What she fed it now was the dumb torment of creatures less than beasts. What sort of a dragon would he be, founded on pain and hatred and cruelty?

Between the sleeping dragon's forepaws was another throne, also of ice and also draped with furs. The ice and coverings of that throne were corroded with filth and human waste. A caricature of a human was chained to it, manacled at ankles, wrists, and throat to rings sunk deep in the ice of the royal chair. The black crown he wore looked painfully tight, as if locked to his brow, and his royal robes were stained and tattered. He wore chains of silver about his neck, and the chains that restrained him had been set with jewels, mocking his captivity. His beard and hair were grown long and matted; his nails were yellow and crusted. The ends of his bare toes and fingers were black with frostbite. Discarded bones, picked clean of meat, littered the floor near his feet. Perhaps one was a human armbone. I looked away, unwilling to know what they fed him. He was Forged, but not completely. I could still feel his hate, and how it burned. Perhaps that was the only feeling left to him. And then, like a numbed limb returning to life, I felt an odd tingling of my Skill. I turned my head as if I could capture it, like a man straining after a sound. It came no more clearly to me, but I discerned the source of it. The mad king Skilled at me. His teeth were set in a yellow snarl and his sunken eyes were fixed on me. For an instant, I felt the full force of his Skilled hatred and it struck me like a blow. Then it was gone, not because I shielded myself, but because my ability to feel it faded again. I heaved in a panting breath, shocked at his Skill-strength. Perhaps Thick could have matched him in Skill-power; I knew I never could have.

I managed to lift my head and look back at the woman, and was startled to find her smiling at me. She had been waiting for me, letting me look my fill and reach my own conclusions. A long, graceful hand gestured at her captive king. "Kebal Rawbread. But I'm sure you guessed that only my failed Catalyst could be worthy of such a punishment, FitzChivalry Farseer. Oh, you need not look so aghast. I am only finishing what your Six Duchies dragons began. He foolishly ventured out, to draw his bow and fire at a flight of dragons overhead. But their mere passage above him sapped much of his intelligence. Not that he had much to begin with. He was a useful tool, for a time. He had cunning, ambition, and he knew the ways of war."

She stood, and then descended the dais of her throne, treading on the dragon's head in passing. She strolled over to the soiled throne and the squalid monarch upon it and considered her prisoner. "Nonetheless, he failed me." She stretched out a slender hand to him. His nostrils flared and he bared his teeth as if to snap at her. She shook her head, almost fondly, as a man might over a stallion too spirited to be trusted. Her voice was sweet as she asked him, "Shall I give a bit more of you to the dragon, my pet? Would you like that?"

The muscles around the mad king's deep-set eyes twitched as if he desperately tried to recall something. Then he cringed away from her, raising one shoulder as if that could shelter him. A low moan of "Nooooooo!" oozed from him.

"Not now, perhaps. Eventually, of course, he will have all of you. When there is nothing else to wring from you, I shall fling you on top of him and watch you melt into him. That is how it happens, is it not?" She turned suddenly to confront me. "At the final quickening, are not the sacrifices to the dragon completely absorbed? When your Skill coteries are given to a dragon, do not they vanish completely into its body?"

I held my tongue, as much from shock as from a desire to withhold the information from her. She spoke as if coteries were forced into a dragon, rather than entering one willingly. I would not take her ignorance from her. One of my guards growled and lifted a fist to menace me, but she shook her head and flicked her fingers at him, dismissing my silence as inconsequential.

Instead she transferred her gaze to the Fool, dangling insensible between his captors, and for the first time, a frown marred her sculpted face. "You have not damaged him, have you? I warned you that I wished him brought to me intact. He is the greatest curiosity in the world, that most rare creature, a false White Prophet. Though he scarcely deserves such a title now. Look at him, gone all brown as a withered flower. Is he dead?"

"No, Lady Most High. He has but fainted." The guard who spoke sounded nervous.

"I don't believe it. Shake him a bit. He has the tenacity of a cat, and I'll wager he'd be just as hard to kill as one. Open your eyes, Beloved. Greet me again, with a smile and a little bow, as you did once when you were a pale wisp of a child. Oh, how sweet a creature he was, as if made all of whipped egg white and milk and sugar crystal, a confection of a child. With the tongue of a viper!" She leaned forward suddenly, venom in her voice. As if her hatred warned him of its poison, the Fool gave a sudden gasp and stirred. He wobbled his head upright, and stared blindly about. Then comprehension crashed down around him. I thought he would scream as every muscle in his face went taut. Then he went suddenly still. He looked at me and spoke to me only. "I am so very sorry. So very sorry."

The Pale Woman turned abruptly away from us and re-mounted her throne. She took her time settling herself into her throne, snuggling into her furs. When she was comfortable, she issued her orders. "This day has been long in coming. I see no point in either hurrying or delaying my enjoyment of it. Truth to tell, I had expected that you both would stand before me almost a year ago. The Piebalds had been promised much gold, but only if they delivered both of you, intact. And that they could not seem to do. Some silly personal scheme of vengeance overturned all our arrangements with them. They were unreliable allies, with all their dirty little animals traipsing around after them, tainting their minds with animal thoughts like men forni-cating with sheep! No wonder they failed me. I should never have wasted my time with them. Well. It matters not now. I have you here, by my own maneuvering, and that makes it all the sweeter." She leaned back, steepling her slender hands as she regarded us with satisfaction.

"I have long had quarters prepared for you. Guards, es-cort each of my guests to his proper accommodations, and see that they take full advantage of them. Rest and relax, FitzChivalry. I shall come to call upon you soon. Until then, do you have any questions for me? No? A pity. I do not often offer to answer questions, but for you, I would have. For I think that, the more you know, the more you will see how you have been deceived and misled by our dar-ling little pretender. Take them off, but gently, gently. Harm not a hair of their heads."

At the door of her grand hall they parted us, the Fool's captors taking him in one direction and mine jostling me along in the other. "Fitz!" His sudden shout startled me and made me strain against my guards' grip. One gently twisted my arm higher behind my back. I set my heels to the ice and skidded as they dragged me relentlessly on. The Fool's shout came faint to my ears. "I knew my fate! I chose to meet it! Stay your course and do not doubt! All will be as—" His shout ended in a muffled cry, and then they staggered me around a corner and down yet another icy hall.

"Where are they taking him?" I demanded, and received another example of the Pale Woman's guard's idea of gentleness as a gauntleted fist doubled me over. I could almost take a full breath again when they paused at one of the icy doors. One of the guards produced a long tool and thrust it into a small opening in the ice. He jigged it until I heard a catch give, and then pulled the door open with it. They threw me inside and I landed facedown on some patchy deerskins on the floor. One followed me, and I rolled, trying to escape the punishment sure to come, but he only caught at my bound wrists, pulled them up high and screamingly tight, and then suddenly released them. The knife he had used to cut the bindings nicked my hand in passing. He was not concerned. "Don't make noise!" he warned me. "She doesn't like it, and I don't like having to come and make you be quiet."

The icy door closed behind him before I could think of a reply. The earlier blow to my head had left me woozy. I lifted my head just enough to be sure I was alone in the chamber. As soon as I was reassured that no Forged Ones lurked there, I let my head drop, closed my eyes, and tried to think.

I opened them again. A minute, a day, a week had passed. The light in the chamber remained the same. I had had no useful thoughts, and perhaps I had slept. I got up slowly, feeling various aches. They were washed from my awareness by the tide of anxiety I felt for the Fool. Where had they taken him and what was his fate? It suddenly seemed incomprehensible to me that we had not struggled harder to keep from being separated.

My cell was quickly explored. The bed was a wooden box of straw with several blankets over it. A bucket in the corner for waste. Another bucket held water, skimmed over with ice. A rag by it suggested that perhaps it was for washing. The deer hides on the floor. I patted my clothes. My guards must have taken the dragon tools while I was unconscious. I had no weapons, not even the Fool's little knife. No windows except the low slit in the unyielding door. A light globe was stuck to the ceiling, far out of my reach. No food. No way to measure the passage of time. I moved from the floor to the bed, such as it was. I considered Nighteyes' old advice: when sleep is the only comfort you can take, take it. It will leave you better prepared for whatever might come next.

I closed my eyes and tried to sleep. It didn't work. I tried to Skill. Nothing. I quested out with my Wit. I could vaguely sense other humans nearby, but the prevailing presence was that of the dragon. And then Icefyre was gone again. I sat up and leaned the bruised back of my head against the icy wall of my chamber. It eased the throbbing. I must have dozed, for I woke with my hair frosted to the wall. I pulled free slowly, groaning irritably at myself.

I had explored the slit in the door and the crack that outlined the edges of the door several times when the guard came back. I was sitting on the floor, peering out of my cell. I wondered if I should be flattered that she sent three guards for me. They were different men from the ones that had captured us. "Lie facedown on the floor!" one of them ordered me through the door slit.

I obeyed. Fighting three men would not improve my physical condition. I heard them come in, and one of them matter-of-factly dropped a knee into my back to hold me still while he roped my wrists behind me again. They used the rope and my hair to haul me to my feet. They were a practiced team, with no need to speak as they marched me out of my cell and down the corridor. They marched me grimly down the hall.

"Where is my companion? The tawny man that was with me?"

A punch to my left side, just below my ribs, answered me. They marched on, dragging me until I got my feet under me again. We passed no one else, and I realized that I had lost my bearings. The icy corridors were all too much the same. Even if I had been released that instant, I would not have known where to begin searching for either the Fool or a way out. For now, my only option seemed to be to go with them.

Then we came to an arched portal of ice with doors of polished wood. One of my guards knocked. A woman's voice bade them bring me in. The doors opened and we entered the Pale Woman's bedchamber.

The white orbs that gave off light were placed oddly, on the floor and on a low table, illuminating only the center of the room. An iron brazier burned smokelessly, adding a slight note of warmth. The rest of the chamber softened off into shadow. I glimpsed a large bed crouching at the edge of the light, and a row of servants standing silently, waiting to be summoned. I could not tell how large the chamber was. The Pale Woman had just emerged from a tub of steaming water. The tub itself seemed to be made of very thick glass. The water within it was a cloudy white, and the fragrance of summer flowers rose with its steam. She stood naked on a lush white bearskin, calmly regarding us as two dispassionate maids patted and rubbed her dry. She seemed to feel no discomfort at baring herself to our gaze. She was an even white all over, a woman of snow or marble. Her white hair was painted flat to her skull with water that dripped off the pointed tips of her tresses. The faintest hint of rose showed in the standing nipples on her globular breasts. The tuft of hair at her loins was as white as that on her head. Like the Fool, she was long limbed and limber waisted, but lush of hip and breast. No man could have looked at her and not felt a stirring of lust. She knew that. Yet she showed herself to us, captive and guards alike, as if her ability to flaunt her body and yet remain safe from undesired attentions emphasized her power over us all. Her stone-faced guards made no reaction to seeing their mistress thus. They stood, one on each side of me and one behind me, and waited.

Her handmaidens brought her soft fur boots and draped her in a robe of fine silk, followed by a second, heavier pelisse of wool trimmed with white fur. She took her time seating herself in a low-backed throne of dark wood. A third Outislander woman entered, and I recognized her suddenly as Henja. She carried a fresh towel and brushes and pins. She moved behind the Pale Woman and began to dress her damp hair for her. And all this while, the lady had not spoken a word. She leaned back in the chair, and gave herself over to Henja's attentions with evident pleasure, for her eyes closed to narrow slits as Henja's ivory brush moved slowly through her white mane. When her long hair had been combed out and then braided in a multitude of long plaits and pinned to her head, she opened her eyes and looked about the room. She gazed at me as if noticing me for the first time and gave a small frown.

"He is unwashed! Did not I tell you to provide washwater for him before you brought him to me?"

The guards cowered and one said hastily, "We did, my lady. He ignored it."

"I am not pleased." These simple words to my guards made them pale.

She shifted her gaze to me. "You reek like Kebal Rawbread. I had thought Six Duchies men were cleaner." Her eyes flicked toward the tub. "Remedy it now. There is water in the tub." She lounged back in her throne, challenging me. "Wash, FitzChivalry. You will dine with me, and I desire to smell the food, not you."

I did not move or allow my expression to change. She smiled lazily.

"Do you fear to lose your dignity by undressing and washing? I assure you, most of my servants do not remember what 'human dignity' means, let alone care for yours. You cling to your stench as if it were your pride. I promise you this: you will lose far more than your dignity if you must be forced to bathe. Choose swiftly. I am not patient, and I will not smell such a smell at my table." In an aside to her servants, she observed, "You would think that a king's son, even a bastard, would have more pride in himself."

"My hands are bound," I pointed out stiffly. My mind searched for escape, for advantage in the situation, and found none. Her words had made me aware that I did stink. I felt a moment of shame and then recognized her tactic. Chade had long ago explained the usefulness of breaking a man's pride and self-worth before interrogating him. For some men, it was more effective than torture. Take a man's dignity, imprison him like a beast, and when you offer him back the small comforts of civilization, his gratitude is often disproportionate. Sometimes a man can be won over simply by a small display of kindness. Kept in a cold cell in the dark with no food, a man will perceive a candle and a hot bowl of soup as an offer of amnesty. It is far less work to break a man that way than with torture.

She smiled at me. "Ah, yes. Bound hands would make your task more difficult." She gestured to the guard. "Take him to the tub and cut him free."

I was propelled to the tub in a way that left no doubt that they would force me to do anything she desired. Refusing would give the guards further excuse to beat me. Complying might yield me some advantage, if only that of having my hands free. I gritted my teeth and surrendered my dignity. Once my hands were free, I turned my back to her and stripped. I managed to palm my fox pin from inside my shirt as I did so. I entered the water. I washed quickly, refusing to let the warm water offer me too much comfort.

One of her women brought me soft soap in a bowl. Somehow I found myself gravely thanking her. She made no reply. The water was gray when I stood up from it. Two women advanced on me with towels. I took both towels and turned away from them to dry myself. A moment later, they were back, offering soft shoes of felted wool and a clean white wool robe. My weary Buck garb had vanished. I put on what they offered, concealing my pin inside the collar of the robe, and turned back to my audience. The Pale Woman had had her chair turned so that she could watch me. She smiled a cat's smile now, and observed, "You have some interesting scars. And the body of a warrior. Shave him, Henja. I would see the full face of the man who was almost a king."

It shocked me to hear such words. I had never thought of myself that way. For a moment, the title almost seemed true. Then I rejected it as another tactic of hers. The two women were back, bearing a chair, and Henja appeared with a bowl, soap, and shaving blade. "I'll do it myself," I said hastily. The idea of that woman flourishing a knife near my throat was unbearable.

"That you will not," the Pale Woman informed me, smiling faintly. "I do not underestimate you, FitzChivalry. I know what you were trained to be. Your family made you a killer, not a prince. They never let you see what they cheated you out of. But I will. I will show you the rightful heritage they stole from you. Yet, until I know that you perceive all that I offer you, no weapon will I put in your hand. Sit still now. Henja is a skilled body-servant, but I shall not hold her responsible if you twitch."

I do not think I have ever been more uncomfortable in my life. While Henja shaved my face and then combed back my damp hair, the other women inspected my hands, cleaned my nails and trimmed them. And all the while, the Pale Woman watched me like a cat watches a bird. No one had ever administered to me in such a way before, yet I found this luxury humiliating rather than comforting. I opened my mouth once, to ask, "Where is the Fool?" Henja's blade immediately nicked me. I felt the trickle of blood start from the side of my neck. Henja placed a towel firmly against the cut to staunch it while the Pale Woman replied, "I do believe we are looking at him, are we not?"

At that point, I could scarcely argue with her evaluation. Her guards chuckled dutifully, but a glance from her restored their composure. As her maids fussed over me and her guards stood and stared coldly, other servants brought in a table. They set it with a white cloth and heavy silver implements and dishes. They placed a candelabrum upon it and lit the six tall white candles. Then they brought in covered plates and tureens. Steams and rich odors of food escaped to taunt me. Wine and glasses were brought as well, and finally two cushioned chairs were set at either end of the table. Henja wiped my face and stepped aside to bow to her mistress. The Pale Woman came closer to me, but remained out of arm's reach. She cocked her head and studied me coldly, from head to foot, as if I were a horse she was considering buying. "You are not ill made," she offered me. "Before your family allowed you to be abused, you might have been handsome. Well. Shall we dine?"

She walked to her chair, which one of her guards drew out for her. I rose and followed her to the table, aware that one of her guards shadowed me. A wave of her hand indicated that I should seat myself opposite her. Once I was seated, she waved again. The guard at my back retreated to the shadowed depths of the room. At her command, the pale globes in the room suddenly dimmed. Only the candlelight remained, isolating us in an island of yellow light. It gave a false air of intimacy to the setting, yet I knew that her guards and maids lingered unseen in the dimness, watching us from outside the circle of the candlelight.

The table was small. She ladled soup into a bowl and placed it before me before serving herself from the same tureen. "So you do not think I will poison or drug you," she explained as she took up her spoon. "Eat, FitzChivalry. You will find it very good, and I know you must be hungry. I shall not trouble you with talk just yet." Nonetheless, I waited until I had seen her take two mouthfuls before I picked up my own spoon.

It was very good, a rich and creamy white soup with bobbing chunks of root vegetables and tender meat. It was the best thing I had tasted since I'd left Buckkeep, and I would have wolfed it down if my manners had not stayed me. My self-control seemed to be the only shield I had left, and so I forced myself to eat slowly, to take bread from the basket she offered and butter from the plate. She poured white wine for us, and when the soup was gone, offered me slices of tender pale fowl from a platter. It was delicious, and the food comforted my body despite my desire to stay on guard against her. There was a white pudding for dessert, redolent of vanilla and speckled with warm spices. We spooned it away, and all the while she watched me, silent and speculative. The wine hummed in my blood, relaxing me. I struggled against it, then recognized what I was feeling. I took a deep breath and relaxed into it. Now was not the time to struggle.

She smiled. Had she sensed that surrender? I became more aware of her. She was wearing a perfume, a scent like narcissus.

When we had finished, we stood. A wave of her hand notified the unseen servants. As they emerged from the shadows to clear the table away, the fire in the brazier blazed up as a man set fresh fuel on it. A cushioned couch, curved in a half-circle, had been placed to face it. The Pale Woman walked to it and seated herself, patting the pillows beside her. I followed her and sank down into its comfort. Her kindness was disarming my wariness. Food and wine had filled me and taken my edges away. She would try to get information from me with innocent questions. I kept my thoughts small. My task would be to remain on my guard, and to get as much information from her as I could while giving her as little as possible. She smiled at me, and I feared that she sensed my ploy. But then she curled her legs under her just as the Fool would have and leaned toward me. Her round knees pointed at me. "Do I remind you of him?" she asked suddenly.

It seemed pointless to dissemble. "Yes. You do. Where is he?"

"In a safe place. You are very fond of him, aren't you? You love him?" She replied for me before I could answer. "Of course you do. He has that effect on people, when he chooses to use it. He is so intriguing, so charming. Do not you feel flattered that he offers you even the chance to know him? He dances at the edges of your understanding, offering you tiny hints of who he truly is, like feeding bits of sugar to a dog. With each little bit he offers you, you feel valued that he trusts you so. And all the while, he extracts from you every bit of knowledge that he needs, plunges you into danger and pain for his own ends, and takes from you everything you have to offer."

"He is my dearest friend. I would like to see him and know he is well treated." My words sounded stiff. My heart sank. Her description of the Fool was cruelly accurate. It demoralized me and I saw that she knew it.

"I am sure you would. Perhaps later. After we have talked. Tell me. Do you believe he is truly the White Prophet, come to set the world on a better course?"

I lifted one shoulder. I had never come to a firm answer on that. Yet I felt disloyal to the Fool as I said, "So he has always told me."

"Ah. But he could just as easily tell you that he was the Lost King of the Island of Tales. Would you believe that, also?"

"I've never had reason to doubt him." I tried to speak stoutly, but felt the doubt she sent creeping into my heart.

"Haven't you? I see. Well, I shall have to give you some, then." She reached down and, from an unseen vessel on the floor, took a handful of something. She tossed it onto the flames and a sweet scent rose as it burned. I leaned away from it, and she laughed. "Do you fear I'll try to in-toxicate you? I do not need to. Your own logic and com-mon sense will convince you. So. Our friend has told you he is the White Prophet. Even though he is, undeniably, no longer white. Surely he has told you that true White Prophets remain white, all through their long lives? No? Well, then, I do tell you that now. We are descended, as he may or may not have told you, from the true Whites of leg-ends. They were a wonderful folk, long vanished from this and all other worlds. Pale as milk and wise beyond telling. For they were prescient.

"Now, anyone with two thoughts in their mind can see that no future is set in stone. An infinite number of fu-tures bud at the end of every moment, and each one of them can be changed by a falling rose petal. Even so, some are more likely than others, and a few so likely that they are like fierce channels for time to thunder through. In an-cient days before your people's telling, we saw this, we Whites, and began to see also that by our actions, we could influence which of those futures would come to be. We could not guarantee them, of course, but we could use what we knew to set other, lesser folk onto paths that would gradually divert the flow of time into quieter, safer waters, where all could prosper. Do you understand what I am telling you, FitzChivalry?"

I nodded slowly. Despite her words, the fragrant smoke from the brazier was inclining me toward her. I was aware of her scented skin and of her fine white hair, so sleekly braided. Awareness of her body was slipping into my skin like spring sap moving into buds. I sighed, and she smiled. She seemed to have come closer without moving.

"Yes. That is right. Consider how you came here, walk-ing into my stronghold, delivering yourselves into my hands. I knew that one day I would possess both of you. And yet the devices by which you came into my power were unclear. And so I set out to sway the future, by setting into motion every device that might bring you to me, or make an end of you. My agents traded with Regal, oh yes, to be sure that some tools that might have been useful to you were sent out of your reach. Many that were Forged were given a purpose as well, to find you or Verity, and kill you. All of them failed, but still I labored on. I sent Henja to Buckkeep, and we bribed the Piebalds to capture you both and deliver you. Yet they failed. Again I cast my nets, sending you a cake with delvenbark in it, to quench your magic. But only you partook of it, and that sent that plan awry. I captured the men Chade sent for supplies, knowing well you must come after them. But before I could take you, you vanished from my knowing. Only to walk right into my power. That is the power of the flow of time, FitzChivalry. It was almost inevitable that you would come to me. I could have trusted to luck to bring you here. But it is the White way to try to assure the future we wish to see. And even when we knew our race was vanishing from the world, we tried to reach forward in time to assure that we would not lose all our influence.

"You see, the prescience of the Whites warned them that they would one day perish, and that the world would have to blunder on without them. But one among them, a woman with truer vision even than the rest of her race, knew that their influence could go on, if she would willingly mingle her blood with that of an ordinary mortal. And so she did. She roamed the world, and whenever she found a worthy hero, she bore him a child. Six sons and six daughters did she bear, and each looked as human as could be. But when she went on from the world, she was well satisfied. For she knew that whenever the descendants of her children met and mingled in lovemaking, a White child would be born. Their wisdom and gifts of prophecy would not be lost to the world. Isn't that a lovely tale?"

"The Fool said that only one White Prophet is born at a time."

"The Fool, oh, that is such a charming love-name for him." She smiled, her pale lips arching like an ivory bow.

"And so apt, I'm surprised that he lets you call him that." She gave a little sigh. "I suppose I should be pleased that he was that honest with you. Yes. Only one White Prophet can reign. And for this age, that one is, of course, me. He is a freak of breeding, a throwback born out of his time. I suppose that is why he is darkening. Had he been kept at the temple until he darkened, he could have done no harm. But his keepers were always too soft with him, too trusting of such a charming little fellow. And so he wriggled away from them and went off into the world, working his mischief. Let us see if we can undo a little of it, you and I. Tell me. What is the terrible fate that he so fears for the world, that he must pit his paltry influence against mine?"

I was silent for a time then admitted, "I don't exactly know. A time of darkness and evil."

"Erm." She made a pleased sound, like a settling cat. "Well, I shall speak more plainly to you than he has. He fears an age of man when the strongest shall rule and bring the wildness and disorder of the earth under their dominion. Why he sees that as an evil, I have never understood. For me, it is my goal. Let us have order and productivity, let us see the strong beget strong children to come after them. If I succeed, I shall see that power is balanced in the world. My poor Outislanders lack all good things. They have stony soil to till in their weak and chilly summers, and wring their living from the unforgiving sea. Despite this, they have grown to be a strong people, deserving of better things. I came to try to help them. You cannot deny that would be a great good for the world. But your tawny friend thinks he has finer ideas. He thinks, among other silly things, that he must restore dragons to the world, that the dominion of humanity must be checked by competition. Has he told you that?"

"He has spoken somewhat of it."

"Has he? That surprises me. What great good did he say would come of restoring an immense predator that regards the entire world as its hunting ground? A predator that respects no boundary, concedes no ownership, and regards humanity as, at best, useful and more often as a food source? Tell me. Do you relish the idea of your people becoming cattle for great scaled beasts?"

"Not particularly." It was the only possible answer to such a question, but again I felt traitorous. Her careful words were sending streamers of uncertainty unfurling through me.

She laughed, delighted with my response, and settled herself more closely to me. "Of course not. None of us do. I may be a White, but my parents were human."

I struggled a little. "But you set the Outislanders on my people, to raid us in their Red Ships. They burned and despoiled and Forged my people. That was not a good thing."

"And you think I incited them to that? Oh, what a twisted view. I held them back, dear friend. I restrained them, and did not allow them to claim the lands they had conquered. You have seen Kebal Rawbread. Does he look like a man who carried out his dreams of conquest and plunder? Of course not. Who put him where he is? I did. How can you look at that and think I am the enemy of your people?"

I did not have an answer to that. I turned from her to stare at the brazier. I felt again the tickle of my Skill Magic, and heard, or thought I heard, Thick's distant music. I told myself I imagined it for the Skill was dead in me. I felt the touch of her cool hand on my cheek and she turned me back to meet her eyes. I considered the white column of her throat. How soft it would be beneath my touch.

She held my eyes, speaking. "Your Fool did not lie to you when he said the White Prophets come to divert history from its set course. I've done my best. I could not completely change the course of events, but I tried. The Red Ships raided your coast, but they did not claim your lands." She spoke simply and reasonably. I felt her words close around me like a net. "When traitors within your own land sold Kebal's merchants books of your magic, I could not prevent him from learning it and attempting to turn it against your folk. But some of the blame for that must fall on your own people. They sold the Skill scrolls, did they not? And why? Because a younger son, of undeniably royal lines, desired more power for himself. I know you did not like Regal. He did not care for you. Some part of him recognized how unlikely a creature you were, how rare the occurrence of your birth in all the braided lines of time that might be. Almost instinctively, he tried to do away with you, so that time might flow in its allotted channel. Think of this. Regal traded secretly with the Outislanders. Had he come to power, that trade would have been more open. The Outislanders would have been welcomed to your shores, in trade, not war, for the mutual enrichment of all. Would that have been so terrible? It might have come to be, were it not for the machinations of your Fool. I will be honest with you. Such peace and prosperity would have demanded that your life spark wink out early. But can you honestly say that the price would have been too high? Time and time again, you have been willing to lay down your life for your family. Was not Regal your family, as much a Farseer as you? If you had died but once, swiftly and mercifully, for him, would not that have been an honorable sacrifice?"

She had taken my view of the world and my family and the Six Duchies and twisted it into an unrecognizable form. The silky thread of her telling wrapped around me inexorably, becoming a new truth that bound me. I groped after all I had known but a moment before, and found a flaw in her logic. "If I had not been born, my father would have reigned."

She laughed lightly, but her smile was gentle. "Oh, you quibble, and you know it. Your father would have died, childless, in a hunting accident while he was still a young man. Over and over, I have seen it happen in my visions. Verity would never have wed, and would have perished from a fever the next winter. If you had died, at the right moment, then in time the throne would have passed smoothly to Regal. He would have had his father's favor and guidance, and he would have become a great ruler. Yes, the line would have ended with him, but it would have ended splendidly, in peace and plenty, for the Six Duchies as well as the Out Islands. I have no reason to lie to you about any of this. It is far too late for that future to be, so what could motivate me to lie to you?"

I did not know, and yet I did. My Skill again fluttered at the edges of my awareness. It was a flighty, untrustworthy magic. I knew that; I had always known that. I felt her assure me of it. *Pay no mind to it.* "You're deliberately confusing me. You contradict yourself, and twist my knowledge of truth. You're mocking me."

She laughed, throaty and delighted. "Of course I am. Just as your beloved Fool does. And you love it when he dances his words all around you, offering you a hundred ways to see the world. And so shall I delight you, now that you are mine. For I am taking you. I must. We must work together to put the world back on its true course. Not by your death this time, but by the life I shall give you. You will be my Catalyst now, a Catalyst a thousand times more powerful than Kebal Rawbread. And I shall delight you a thousand times more than your pitiful Fool did. For we are, at last, the perfect fit for one another. We shall be not just Prophet and Catalyst, but male and female, making the whole that turns the world. I will be to you everything that he secretly longed to be to you and could not. Except that I will be perfect, as he was flawed. You will come to see that you are not betraying him, but being true to the world and all that was meant to be. Taste the sweetness of the world as it was meant to be. Taste." Her face had come ever closer to mine as she spoke, and then her mouth touched mine. Her lips were all softness, her tongue a teasing coolness that bade my lips part. And she spoke true. A giddy sweetness, wilder than anything I had ever known, spread through me at her cool touch. I shivered as I put my hands on her shoulders, holding her mouth against mine.

Lust flooded me and the rightness, the inevitability, of the moment pushed aside all other thoughts. I cared not that her guards and maids watched us from outside the circle of candlelight; I cared for nothing except the gleaming white perfection of her body. Only one thing was still lacking in the future she offered me. I let my thoughts stray to it.

"Our child will be beautiful," she assured me as she released me and stood up. "You will delight in our son. I promise you this."

I could feel the truth of her words and they went thrilling through me, like ice and silver in my blood. A child, she would give me a child whom I could hold and cherish. A child who would never be taken from me. She knew all that I most desired and offered it all to me. She created in my thoughts the future that I had always most longed for, tailored to my every need. How, why, could I resist that?

She stood and lifted her robe over her head and let it drop to the floor beside the couch. The silken shift followed it. She stood before me, letting the yellow light of the brazier play over her body. Golden light touched her whiteness, gilding the curves of her body and face. Her white breasts were round and heavy. She lifted them to show me, weighing them in her hands, inviting me to taste them. Slowly she sank down beside me, and then leaned back, opening her arms and her thighs to me. "Come to me. I know everything that you have ever wanted, and I will give it all to you." She lolled her head back against the arm of the couch. Her colorless eyes looked through me and beyond me.

The truth of her words thundered through me with my pounding blood. I stood and fumbled my garments out of the way. She dropped her eyes to see what I would offer her.

And in that instant, I slammed up my Skill-walls

tighter than ever I had before, blocking her insidious tendrils of influence. I flung myself on her, as she had expected, but my hands closed on that milky throat as I brought my knee down sharply onto her gently rounded belly. I felt her Skill batter at me along with her fists. I knew well I had one chance to make good my grip on her, and I knew the icy instant when I had missed it. I should have known that just as she mirrored the Fool in appearance, so also she possessed his uncanny strength. She had no need of her guard as she tucked her chin down tight to thwart my strangle. Her clasped hands came up between my elbows, and then she flung her arms wide, breaking my grip on her throat. She flung me backward off her, and as I fell against the brazier, sending it and hot coals flying in every direction, she lifted her hands. The white globes of light blazed suddenly, flooding the room with illumination. Guards surged at me from all directions, a flood of armed men. It was inevitable that they would take me down, and I would have been wise to let them, to offer them my sudden surrender. Yet my glimpse of the Fool, gagged and spread like a trophy hide on one icy wall, roused in me an anger I had not felt since the days when I had battled Red Ship raiders with an axe.

The tumbled brazier burned my hands as I seized it and flung it at my attackers. I fought them, expecting them to kill me, and thus holding back nothing. I think that is why it took them so long to subdue me. They were more restrained than I was and rendered less damage to me than I did to several of them. I know I broke one man's collarbone, for I heard it crack, and I recall that I spat out a piece of ear, but as with all battles when such a mood is on me, my recollection is disjointed and vague.

I recall clearly that I lost the struggle. I knew it was over when I was down on my belly with three men kneeling on me. There was blood in my mouth, some of it my own. I have never scrupled against using my teeth in a brawl, not since I first bonded with the wolf. My left arm no longer obeyed me. As they hauled me to my feet, that arm flopped and flailed against my side. Wrenched out of its socket, I thought sickly, and waited for that pain to find me.

I had almost made it to the Fool's feet. I lifted my eyes to look at him. He was pinned to the icy wall like a butterfly, his arms spread wide, and even his head held against it with a metal band around his throat. The gag was tight enough to cut his mouth. Blood had leaked in a line from the corner of his mouth to drip down his shirt. They must have ransacked his pack, for he wore the Rooster Crown, the wooden circlet jammed down on his head to the top of his ears. His eyes were open, and I knew he had witnessed all that the Pale Woman had staged for his torment, that that had been the whole point of her attempted seduction of me. I knew too as our eyes met, that he understood that I had never betrayed him. I saw the feeble twitch of the Skilled tips of his fingers on one pinioned hand. He too had sensed her subtle attack on me through my reviving Skill-sense.

"I tried!" I cried out to him as his head bowed as much as his binding would allow it and his eyes began to sag shut. The guards had had their sport with him. Patches of blood seeped through his clothing and streaked his sweaty hair. Now he was held immobile and silenced against the ice, tormented with the cold he had always so hated. Had he foreseen this slow and icy end for himself? Was that why he had always so dreaded the cold?

"Bring them both to my throne room!" The Pale Woman's voice was like ice cracking. I swung my head to look at her. She had retrieved her garments and donned them. Her lower lip was beginning to swell and several loosened plaits dangled by her face. Such were the fruits of my deadly attack upon her. Yet I felt small amusement as my guards seized me roughly, careless that one of my arms hung limp and useless. The piteous cries of the Fool followed me as they tore him from his bindings.

The halls seemed longer and whiter than they had been, as if the lights burned brighter with the anger of the woman who strode ahead of us. We encountered few people, but all we passed cowered or shrank to the side of the corridor as she swept by them. I tried to make note of how we went and what turns we made, telling myself that if the Fool and I escaped, we must know in which direction to run. It was useless, both the effort to memorize the way and the effort to fan hope in myself. It was finished, we were finished and that was the end of it. The Fool was going to die, and I would die alongside him, and all he had worked for would come to a bloody and useless end. "Just as if I had died the very first time that Regal looked at me and proposed to Verity that I meet a discreet end."

I did not know I had spoken aloud until one of the guards gave me a rough shake at the same time he bade me, "Shut your hole."

On we went. It was hard to focus, and harder still to overcome my fear, but I lowered the walls I had raised against the Skill. I gathered my small strength and tried to Skill out to Dutiful, to warn them and to beg for help. I was like a man patting his clothes, trying to find a misplaced pouch. My magic was gone and I could not muster it. Even that last weapon was lost to me.

The Pale Woman had already resumed her throne by the time we entered the hall. A few of her retainers lined the walls. They watched dispassionately as the Fool and I were dragged before them. There we were halted and pushed to our knees as before. For a long time, she looked down on us in silence. Then she gestured at the Fool with her narrow chin. "Give that one to the dragon. He can have Theldo's place. Let the other one watch."

"No!" I cried before a fist to my ear sent me sprawling on the ice. The Fool made not a sound as they dragged him forward. When they were close to one of the chained captives, the guard matter-of-factly drew his blade and plunged it into the wretch. The man did not die swiftly, but neither did he make much noise or fuss about it. I think most of him had already gone into the dragon, and there was little left of his spirit to mourn his body's passing. He fell against the dragon as he died, and slid down the creature's stony flank. For a few moments, his blood was a vivid red smear down the stone. Then, as sand takes in water, the blood was sucked away from the surface, leaving the scales in that area more clearly defined than they had been.

Two guards moved efficiently, careful not to touch the dragon-stone as they unshackled the hapless wretch. One glanced at their queen, and at a nod from her, he cut and disjointed one of the man's arms from his shoulder as neatly as if he were preparing a fowl for the pot. He did not look as he tossed it in Kebal Rawbread's direction. I wished I had not. The mad king lunged the length of his chain, seized the flopping, bloody arm and fell upon it as hungrily as a dog on a joint of fresh meat. He was a noisy eater. I turned aside, sickened.

But a worse sight awaited me. My guards tightened their grips on me, and a third man stepped up to seize my head by my warrior's tail and grip me tight. The Fool's guards moved forward with him. He did not resist. His face looked like that of a man near bled to death, as if he could no longer feel horror or pain, only the encroachment of death. They shackled him, ankle and wrist, to the dragon. By standing in a half-crouch, knees and elbows held out, the Fool could avoid contact with the thirsty stone. It was a posture that was a torment in itself, and one that no man could hold for long. Sooner or later, he must tire, and when he did, he must fall against the dragon and yield something of himself to it.

The Fool faced a slow death by Forging.

"No," I breathed as the reality seeped into me, and then, "NO!" I roared at the Pale Woman. I twisted my head to look up at her, heedless of the hair torn from my head. "Anything!" I promised her. "Anything you want from me, if you let him go!"

She leaned back on her furs. "How tedious. You capitulate much too easily, FitzChivalry Farseer. You didn't even wait to witness the demonstration. Well. I shall not deny myself that pleasure. Dret! Introduce him to my dragon."

The named guard stepped forward, drawing his sword. "No!" I roared, twisting helplessly against my guards as Dret set the point of his blade to the small of the Fool's back and urged him against the stone dragon.

He held him there for only an instant. The Fool did not scream. Perhaps it did not cause pain to his body. But as the man took back his sword, the Fool recoiled from the stone as a hand does from a hot ember. He leaned against the brief length of his chains, trembling but soundless. On the dragon's skin, I saw for an instant the outline of my friend's body as the dragon drank in his memories and emotions. Then his silhouette faded into the stone.

I wondered what the Fool had lost in that brief kiss of stone. A summer's day from his childhood, a moment of watching King Shrewd and Chade talking by the firelight of the hearth in the old King's room? Had it been some moment he and I had shared, now snatched from him and gone forever? He would know such things had happened, but Forging would erase their significance to him. Our friendship and all we had meant to one another slowly would be erased from his mind before he died. When he died, he would not even have memories of having been loved to ease his passage. I lifted my eyes to the Pale Woman. I think she drank in my misery as the dragon had sucked down the Fool's stolen moments.

"What do you want of me?" I asked her. "What?"

She spoke calmly. "Only that you take the easiest path and play the most likely role in the days to come. It will not be difficult for you, FitzChivalry. In almost every future I have foreseen, you accede to my request. Do your prince's bidding, do Chade's bidding, do the Narcheska's bidding. And mine. Take Icefyre's head. That is all. Think of the good you will do. Chade will be pleased, and your queen will win her alliance with the Out Islands. You'll be a hero in their eyes. Dutiful and the Narcheska can consummate their love for one another. I ask nothing difficult of you, only that you do what so many of your friends hope you will do."

"Don't kill Icefyre!" the Fool's low-voiced cry begged me.

The Pale Woman sighed, as exasperated as if interrupted by an ill-mannered child. "Dret. He wishes to kiss the dragon again. Assist him."

"Please!" I shouted as the man again slowly drew his sword. I pulled my head free of my captor's grip to bow it in subservience before her. "Please don't! I'll kill Icefyre. I will."

"Of course you will," she agreed sweetly as the tip of the sword sank into the Fool's back.

He resisted, even as fresh blood soaked his shirt. "Fitz! She has the Narcheska's mother and sister captive here. We saw them, Fitz. They are Forged! Elliania and Peottre do her will to buy their deaths!" And then, the Fool screamed wordlessly as he surrendered to the sword's bite and sagged against the dragon. He twitched all over and the press of the guardsman's blade seemed to hold him there for an eternity. I would have covered my eyes if my hands had been free. I did shut my eyes tightly against the unbearable sight. When the scream ceased and I opened my eyes, my friend's body was outlined in silver on the dragon. More precious than blood, the experiences that made him who he was seeped away into the soulless stone. The Fool stood, muscles taut, straining against his chains to avoid contact with the stone. I heard the gasp of his breath, and prayed he would not speak again, but he did. "She showed them to me! To show me what she could do to me. You can't save me, Fitz! But don't make it all for nothing. Don't do her—"

"Again," she said, between weariness and amusement at his stubbornness. Again Dret stepped forward. Again the sword, again the slow, relentless push. I bowed my head as my friend screamed. If I could have died at that moment, I would have done so. It would have been easier than listening to his torture. Far easier than the terrible, soulless relief that it was not me.

When the echoes of his cries had faded, I did not look up. I could not bear to. I would say nothing more to her or to the Fool, nothing that might tempt him to speak and bring more punishment on himself. I watched the drops of sweat that dripped from my face fall onto the ice and vanish. Just as the Fool was vanishing into the dragon. *Beloved.* I tried to Skill the thought to him, to send him something of my strength, but it was a futile effort. My erratic magic, poisoned by elfbark, was gone again.

"I think I've convinced you," the Pale Woman observed sweetly. "But I'll make it very clear. You choose now. Icefyre's life, or your Beloved's. I'll set you free, to be on your way to kill the dragon. Do my will, and I give your friend back to you. Or as much as is left of him. The more swiftly you go, the more of him there will be for you to reclaim. Delay, and he may be Forged completely. But not dead. I promise you that. Not dead. Do you understand me, FitzChivalry Farseer, little assassin-king?"

I nodded, not lifting my eyes to her. I got a fist in the short ribs for that, and managed to lift my head. "Yes," I said softly. "I understand." I feared to look at the Fool.

"Excellent." Satisfaction burned in her voice. She lifted her eyes to the ceiling of her glassy chamber and smiled. She spoke aloud. "There, Icefyre. He understands. He will deliver you to your death."

She looked back at my guards. "Turn him out from the north chimney. Let him go there." Then, as if she could feel my confusion, she met my eyes and smiled kindly. "I don't know how you find your people again. I only know that you do. And that you kill the dragon. All is so clear before me now. There is no other path. Go, FitzChivalry. Do my will, and buy your Beloved back. Go."

I called no word of farewell to the Fool as they

marched me from the room. I feared he would somehow acknowledge my departure and earn another kiss from her stone dragon. They took me through the icy labyrinth of her lair at a quick march, and up an endless flight of stairs that eventually emerged into a sort of ice cave, a space between the rock and the glacier. Two held me, kneeling, as the third cleared the ice-blown snow and frost that blocked the entry. Then they stood me up and cast me out.

chapter XXII

REUNION

. . . that our King-in-Waiting Chivalry is not at all the
son whom King Shrewd supposed him to be. As you can
well imagine, this has grieved my good husband beyond
telling, but as ever, Prince Regal has done all in his
power to be a comfort to his beloved father. It was my
sad duty to inform both my lord and our wayward prince
that in light of his besprinkling the countryside with
bastards (for where there is one, can we doubt there are
others?) my Dukes of the Inland Duchies have expressed
doubt of Chivalry's worthiness to follow his father as
king. In light of that, Chivalry has been persuaded to
step aside.

I have been less successful in persuading my lord
that the presence of this by-blow at Buckkeep Castle is
an affront to myself and every true married woman. He
maintains that if the child is restricted to the stable and
the stableman's care, it should not concern the rest of us
that this physical evidence of Lord Chivalry's failing is
ever flaunted before us. I have begged in vain for a more
permanent solution . . .

❦ LETTER FROM QUEEN DESIRE TO
LADY PEONY OF TILTH

We had emerged from a crevice that overlooked a steep slope. My guardians laughed. Before I could deduce the reason, I flew through cold darkness, then hit frozen snow. I broke through the crust, found my balance, and rolled to my feet. Darkness surrounded me and when I took a step, I stumbled, fell, slid, regained my feet, fell and slid some more. I was clad only in the wool robe and felted shoes the Pale Woman had given me. It was small protection. Snow found me and clung to me, melting on my sweaty face and then cooling swiftly. My left arm was a thing that flopped and flailed against me. I finally found my footing and looked up and back whence I had come. Clouds obscured the night sky and the usual wind was blowing. I could not see any sign of an entry to the Pale Woman's realm. I knew that the blowing snow would very soon obscure all trace of my tracks.

If I did not go back now, I'd never find it again.

If I went back there now, what good could I do? My left arm hung useless and I had no weapons at all.

But a stone dragon was slowly devouring the Fool.

I stood and staggered up the hill, trying to find my own trail where I had slid. The slope became too steep. I felt I was treading in place, making no uphill progress and all the while getting colder. I swung wide of my trodden trail and tried again to force my way up through the snow. The wool of the robe grew heavy with clinging snow and was no protection at all to my bared legs. I lost my balance and, holding my injured arm tight to my chest, fell and rolled downhill. For a time, I just lay there, panting. Then, as I struggled to my feet, I saw a tiny yellow light in the vale below me.

I stood and stared at it, trying to resolve what it was. It bobbed with the rhythm of a man walking. It was a lantern, and someone was carrying it. It could be one of the Pale Woman's people. What worse could they do to me than what had been done? It might be someone from our camp. It might be a total stranger.

I lifted my voice and shouted through the wind. The lantern halted. I shouted again, and again, and suddenly the lantern began moving again. Toward me. I breathed a prayer, addressed to any god who would help me, and began a staggering slide down the hill. With every step I took, I slid three, and soon I was running, trying to leap through the snow to avoid sprawling facedown in it. The lantern had halted at the bottom of the slope. But, when I was almost close enough to make out the shape of the man holding it, the lantern resumed its bobbing motion. He was walking away and leaving me. I shouted, but he did not pause. A terrible sob welled up in me. I couldn't go on any farther by myself, and yet I must. My teeth were chattering, my whole body aching as the cold stiffened the bruises from my beating, and he was leaving me there. I staggered after him. I shouted twice more, but the lantern didn't pause. I tried to hurry, but I could not seem to get any closer to it. I reached the place where the light-bearer had briefly paused, and after that I followed his broken trail through the snow, finding the going a bit easier.

I don't know how long I walked. The dark, the cold, and the pain in my shoulder made it seem an endless trudge through night and wind. My feet hurt and then grew numb. My calves were scalded with the cold. I followed him across the face of a hill, and along a ridge, down into a dip, plowing through deeper snow, and then began a long, slow climb across another slope. I could not feel my feet and did not know if my flimsy shoes were still on them or not. The robe slapped against me as I walked, whipping my calves with its frosty burden of clinging snow. And with every step I took, I knew the Fool was still shackled to the dragon, hunching wearily away from the stone that would, at a touch, plunder him of his humanity.

Then, miraculously, the swinging of the lantern stopped: Whoever my guide was, he was now awaiting me at the top of the ridge we had gradually ascended. I shouted again from my raw throat and redoubled my efforts. Closer

I drew, and closer, bowing my head against a wind that was angrier along the ridgetop. Then, as I again lifted my eyes to mark my progress, I saw clearly who held the lantern and awaited me.

It was the Black Man.

A nameless dread filled me, and yet, having followed him that far, what else was I to do but go on? I came closer, close enough that when he lifted the lantern, I could briefly make out the aquiline features inside his black hood. Then he set the lantern down by his feet and waited. I clutched my arm to my chest and staggered uphill doggedly. The light grew brighter, but I could no longer see the Black Man standing beside it. When I reached the lantern, I found it resting upon an outcrop of rock that protruded through the shallower snow on the windswept ridge.

The Black Man was gone.

I used my right arm to lower my left hand to my side as gently as I could. My shoulder screamed when my left arm dangled its full weight, but I gritted my teeth and ignored it. I picked up the lantern and held it aloft and shouted. I saw nothing of the Black Man, only blowing snow. I trudged on, following his trail. It ended in a wind-scoured ridge of rock. But in the next valley, not far below me, I saw the dimly lit tents of our camp and I immediately abandoned all thoughts of the Black Man. Below were friends, warmth, and possible rescue for the Fool. I staggered through the snow toward the tents, calling out Chade's name. At my second shout, Longwick roared a challenge up at me.

"It's me, it's Fitz. No, I mean, it's Tom, it's me!" I doubt that he deciphered anything I said. I was hoarse from shouting and competing with the wind. I well recall my deep relief when I saw the other men stumbling from their tents and lanterns being kindled and held aloft. I staggered and slid down the hill toward them as they fanned out to meet me. I recognized Chade's silhouette and then the

Prince's. There was no squat Thick amongst them, and I felt a sob build in my chest. Then I was finally within hearing of the line of men, breathlessly calling, "It's me, it's Tom, let me through, let me in, I'm so cold. Where is Thick, did you find Thick?"

From their midst a broad-shouldered man stepped forth, past Longwick, who tried vainly to motion him back. He ran three strides toward me, and I took a deep, unbelieving breath of his scent just before he enfolded me in a bear hug. Despite the pain to my shoulder, I didn't struggle. I dropped my head on his shoulder, and let him support me, feeling safer than I had in years. Suddenly, it seemed as if everything would be all right, as if everything could be mended. Heart of the Pack was here and he had never let us come to harm.

Over my bent head, Burrich spoke to Chade angrily. "Just look at him! I always knew I never should have trusted him to you. Never!"

In the chaos that had erupted, I stood still on my icy feet, ignoring the shouted questions around me. Burrich spoke by my ear. "Easy, lad. I'm here to take you home, both of you, you and my Swift. You should have come home years ago. What were you thinking? Whatever were you thinking?"

"I have to kill the dragon," I told him. "As soon as possible. If I kill the dragon, she'll let the Fool live. I have to cut off Icefyre's head, Burrich. I must."

"If you must, then you will," he said comfortingly. "But not right this moment." Then, to Swift, "Stop gawking, boy. Fetch dry clothes and make food and hot tea for him. Quickly."

I gratefully surrendered myself to the steady hands I had always trusted. He steered me through the cluster of staring men to the Prince's tent, where my heart nearly broke with relief at the sight of Thick sitting up sleepily on his pallet. He looked none the worse for wear, and even seemed glad to see me until he was told he'd have to move his bed for the night to make room for me. He went off with Longwick in charge of him, but not graciously. Thick had Skilled to Chade and the Prince as soon as we'd vanished in the crevice and Chade had immediately sent Longwick and Cockle to fetch him back. He'd spent a miserable night sitting on the sled in the cold, with only his Skill-contact to sustain him. When his rescuers had reached him the next day, they'd found no sign of Lord Golden and me except for the sunken snow that had filled the crevasse.

I sat down, dazed with cold and exhaustion, on Chade's bedding. Burrich spoke to me as he built up the little fire in the pot. His deep voice and the rhythm of his speech were familiar comforts from my childhood. For a time I heard his voice without paying attention to the words, and then I realized he was reporting to me just as I had once reported to him. Once he had decided he must fetch Swift and me home, he had come as quickly as he could, and he was sorry, so sorry, that he had taken so long to find us. The Queen herself had helped him hire a boat to Aslevjal, but no man of the crew would willingly set foot on the island. When he had landed, he had tried to persuade Chade's guards to guide him to us, but they had righteously refused to leave their tent on the beach and the supplies they guarded. And so he had come on by himself, following Peottre's pennanted poles. He had reached Thick's sled at almost the same time as Cockle and Longwick. Only their shouts of warning had prevented him from plunging into the same abyss that had claimed the Fool and me. Once he had found a safe crossing point, he had come back to the camp with Cockle and Longwick, bearing the news of the loss of Tom Badgerlock and Lord Golden. Chade had brought him to the privacy of the Prince's tent, and quietly told him that those names also belonged to the Fool and me. Burrich had journeyed all the way to Aslevjal, only to hear yet again of my death. His voice was impassive as he related this to me, as if his own pain at hearing such words were of no consequence. "I am glad to see they were wrong. Again." His hands were busy chafing my hands and feet back to painful life.

"Thank you," I said quietly when I could flex my hands again. There was too much to say to Burrich, and no privacy to say it in. So I looked at Chade and asked my most burning question. "How close are we to killing the dragon?"

Chade came to sit beside me on his bed. "We are closer than when you vanished, but not close enough," he said bitterly. "We were divided when you left. Now it's worse. We've been betrayed, Fitz. By a man we had all come to trust. Web sent his gull to Bingtown, bearing a message that tells the Traders everything, and bids them send Tintaglia to keep us from killing Icefyre."

I shifted my gaze to Dutiful and stared in disbelief. "You let him do this?"

Dutiful sat on the end of his pallet, his dark eyes large in his face as he watched us. There were new lines in my prince's face, and his eyes were swollen as if he had wept freely in recent days. I scarce could bear to look at him.

"He did not ask my permission," Dutiful said painfully. "He said no man needs permission to do what is right." He sighed. "Indeed, much has happened in the few days you were gone. In your absence, we continued to dig down into the ice. We reached a point where we could see a huge shadowy body below us. Realizing we had dug down to the torso of the creature, we began to tunnel out from the side of our pit, following the line of his back toward his head. It has been cramped work, but less difficult than excavating the entire area. We believe that what we can see below us now is the dragon's neck and part of his head. But the closer we came to him, the stronger grew the feeling of the Wit coterie that this is a creature which is not ours for the killing; that he harbors both life and intellect, although none of us can reliably sense him. My Old Bloods still dig alongside us each day, but I fear that they will side with the Hetgurd if I attempt to kill Icefyre." He looked away from me, as if shamed that his trust had been betrayed. "Tonight, just before you came into camp, Web admitted to me that he had sent Risk. The contention was hot," he said quietly.

My hope for a swift end to the dragon waned. It required every bit of discipline I had ever been taught to recount my misadventure in detail and in order. Irrational shame burned me as I spoke of how I had walked away from Hest and Riddle. When I told them of the Fool's fate, and of his words about the Narcheska's mother and sister, Dutiful swayed where he sat. "At last, it all comes clear. Too late."

I knew he was right and despair claimed me anew. Even if I knew the way back, even if I could persuade them to muster our entire force and march on the Pale Woman's stronghold, we were too few. She could kill or Forge him in moments, and doubtless would. Nor could I hope to kill the dragon quickly and win his release. Clear the ice, and we must still get past the Hetgurd, our own Old Bloods, and perhaps Tintaglia.

The Pale Woman's promise that he would not die was a thinly disguised threat. The Fool would be Forged. To me would fall the task of taking what remained of his life. I could not contemplate it.

"If we went by stealth to the pit, could we kill Icefyre? In secret? Tonight?" It was the only plan I could think of.

"Impossible," the Prince said. His face and his voice were gray. "The ice between him and us is too thick. There are days of pick-and-shovel work ahead of us before we reach his flesh. And before then, I fear Tintaglia will be here." He closed his eyes for a moment. "My quest has failed. I put my trust in the wrong place."

I looked at Chade. "How much time do we have?" How much time does the Fool have?

He shook his head. "How fast can a gull fly? How swiftly will the Bingtown Traders react to Web's message? How fast can a dragon fly? No one knows those things. But I think the Prince is right. We have lost."

I gritted my teeth. "There is more than one way to move ice," I said and looked at Chade meaningfully. The old man's eyes lit. But before he could reply, Swift's voice was lifted outside the tent.

"Sir! I've brought Tom Badgerlock's pack, and food will follow. May I come in?"

Dutiful nodded at Burrich, and he moved to beckon his son inside.

The boy came in. His bow to his prince was stiffly formal and he did not look at his father or me. It pained me to see how the division between the Prince and his Wit coterie tore the boy. At Burrich's command Swift dug through my pack to pull out dry clothing for me. The lad did not seem well disposed toward his father, but he obeyed him. Burrich saw me observing them, and after the boy had left, he said quietly, "Swift was not exactly glad to see me when I got here. I didn't give him the thrashing he merited, but he's had the length of my tongue several times. He's not said much in reply, for he knew he deserved it. Here. Take off that wet robe."

As I struggled to pull up my leggings, Burrich suddenly leaned into the light, peering at me with his clouded eyes. "What's the matter with you? What's wrong with your arm?"

"It's pulled out of the socket," I choked out. My throat had closed up at the sight of his eyes. I wondered how much he could see anymore. How had he come to find us here, walking with clouded eyes across the snow?

He closed his eyes and shook his head. Then, "Come here," he said tersely. He turned me, and sat me down on the floor at his feet. His fingers walked my shoulder, and the pain they woke was oddly reassuring. He knew what he was doing. I knew it would hurt, but that he would also mend me. I could sense that from his fingers, just as I had when I was a boy, just as I had felt when he restored me after Galen had nearly killed me.

"We've brought the food. May we come in?"

The voice outside the tent was Web's. The Prince

nodded curtly, his mouth a flat line, and again Burrich lifted the door flap. As Web entered, he greeted me with "It's good to see you alive, Tom Badgerlock." I nodded gravely, not trusting myself to find words. He met my eyes and accepted my hostility. The Prince looked aside from the man, his hurt plain in every line of his body. Chade glowered at him. Web's expression remained as kindly and calm as ever.

The small kettle he carried smelled like good beef rather than the fish I'd been expecting. Swift was behind him with a pot of tea. They crowded into the tent to set their burdens down within my reach.

Burrich continued to investigate my shoulder as if they were not there. He ignored Web, but the Witmaster watched Burrich intently. When Burrich spoke, it was to Dutiful. "Prince Dutiful, my lord. You could be of great help to me right now, if you would. I'll need someone to hold him firmly round the chest and brace him while I do what must be done. If you would sit there, and lock your arms around him ... Higher. Like so."

The Prince came to Burrich's request and sat behind me. When Burrich had arranged the Prince's grip around me to his liking, he spoke to me. "This is going to take a sharp tug. Don't look at me while I do it. Look straight ahead, and be as loose as you can. Don't tighten in fear for the pain to come or I'll only have to jerk it harder the second time. Steady. Hold him firm, my lord. Trust me, now, lad. Trust me." As he spoke calmingly, he'd been slowly lifting my arm. I listened to his words, letting them drown out the pain, his touch filling me with calm and trust. "Be easy, be easy, and ... Now!"

I roared with the sudden shock, and in the next instant, Burrich was on his knee on the floor beside me, his big calloused hands holding my arm firmly to my shoulder. It tingled and it hurt, but it hurt the right way, and I leaned against him, weak with the relief of it. Even as I panted, I noticed how he held his game leg out at an angle, the knee scarce bending. I thought of what it had cost him to come all this way, near blind and half-lame, and I felt humbled.

He spoke quietly into my ear as he embraced me. "You're a man grown, all these many years, but when I see you hurt, I swear, you are eight years old and I'm thinking, 'I promised his father I'd look after his son. I promised.'"

"You did," I assured him. "You have."

Web spoke quietly, his voice deep. "I stand amazed. That is a bit of Old Blood magic I thought was lost to us. I saw that kind of healing done on animals a few times when I was a lad, before old Bendry died in the Red Ship War. But I've never seen it used that way on a man, nor so smoothly. Who taught you? Where have you been all these years?"

"I don't use Beast Magic," Burrich said emphatically.

"I know what I just saw," Web replied implacably. "Call it by any dirty name you like. You're a master of it, in a way that is near lost to us. Who taught you, and why have not you passed on the teaching?"

"No one taught me anything. Get out. And stay away from Swift." There was dark threat in Burrich's words, and almost fear.

Web remained calm. "I'll leave, for I think Fitz needs quiet, and a time for private speech with you. But I'll not let your son walk in ignorance. He gets his magic from you. You should have taught him your skills with it."

"My father has the Wit?" Swift looked shocked to his core.

"It all makes sense now," Web said quietly. He leaned toward Burrich, looking at him in a way that went beyond the touch of eyes. "The Stablemaster. And a master in the Wit, as well. How many creatures can speak to you? Dogs? Horses? What else? Where did you come from, why have you hidden yourself?"

"Get out!" Burrich flared.

"How could you?" Swift demanded, suddenly in tears. "How could you make me feel so dirty and low, when it

came from you, when you had it, too? I'll never forgive you.
Never!"

"I don't need your forgiveness," Burrich said flatly.
"Only your obedience, and I'll take that if I have to. Now
both of you, out. I've work to do and you're in my way."

The boy set down the teapot blindly and stumbled
from the tent. I could hear the sobs that wracked him as he
ran off into the night.

Web rose more slowly, setting the kettle of soup down
carefully. "I'll go, man. Now isn't our time. But our time to
talk is going to come, and you'll hear me out, even if we
must come to blows first." Then he turned to me. "Good
night, Fitz. I'm glad you're not dead. I mourn that Lord
Golden did not return with you."

"You know who he is?" The words were torn from
Burrich.

"Yes. I do. And by him, I know who you are. And I
know who used the Wit to pull him back from death and
raise him from the grave. And so do you." Web left on
those words, letting the tent flap fall behind him.

Burrich stared after him, then blinked his clouded
eyes. "That man is a danger to my son," he observed tightly.
"It *may* come to blows between us." Then, he seemed to
dismiss that concern. Turning his head toward Chade and
Dutiful, he said, "I need a strip of cloth or a leather strap
or something to bind his arm to his shoulder for the night,
until the swelling goes down and it holds firm on its own.
What do we have?" Dutiful held up the robe the Pale
Woman had given me. Burrich nodded in approval and
Dutiful began cutting a strip off the bottom of it.

"Thank you." And then, to me, "You can eat with your
right hand while I'm doing this. The hot food will warm
you. Just try not to move too much."

Dutiful gave Burrich the strip of fabric and began dish-
ing the soup from the kettle to a bowl and pouring tea for
me as if he were my page. He spoke as he did so, and yet I
do not think the words were addressed to anyone. "There is

nothing more I can do here. I try to think what I am to do, but nothing comes to me." A time of quiet followed his words. I ate and Burrich worked on my shoulder. When he had finished strapping my arm to my body, he sat back on the pallet, his game leg stretched out awkwardly before him. Chade looked as if he had aged a decade. He had been pondering the Prince's words, for he said slowly, "There are several paths you can take, my prince. We could simply leave tomorrow. That tempts me, I'll admit, if only for the prospect of abandoning all those who deceived and betrayed us. But it would be a petty vengeance, and in the end would win us nothing. Another choice is that we could fall in with Web's plan, and do all we can to free the dragon, abandoning our hopes of an alliance with the Out Islands, and hoping instead to win the goodwill of Tintaglia and the Bingtown Traders."

"Deserting the Fool," I added quietly.

"And Riddle and Hest. Abandoning Elliania's mother and sister, and breaking the word that I gave. Breaking my word, before not just my own dukes, but before the Outislanders as well." He crossed his arms on his chest, looking ill. "A fine king I shall make."

"Abandoning the Fool cannot be helped," Chade said. He spoke the words as gently as he could and yet they stabbed me. "Leaving behind Elliania's relatives and breaking your word can be forgiven, for they used deception to win your promise. As in so many things, much will depend on how it is presented."

Dutiful sounded subdued. "Deception. What would we have done? Elliania's mother and her little sister. No wonder there is so much sorrow in her eyes. And that is why our betrothal ceremony at her mothershouse was so odd, and why her mother has been absent through all our negotiations. I thought Forging was an evil in the past. I never thought it would reach out and touch my life today."

"But it has. And it explains much of Peottre's and the Narcheska's behavior," Chade added.

I flung all discretion to the winds. There was too much at stake for me to sit still through Chade's laborious plotting of possible courses. "We go now, tonight, Dutiful and I only, in secrecy. Chade has created an exploding powder, one that has the force of a lightning bolt. We use it to kill the dragon. We will get our people back, one way or another, from her. And when they are safe"—*dead*, I thought to myself coldly—"then I will find a way to get to her and kill her."

Chade and the Prince stared at me. Then Chade nodded slowly. The Prince looked as if he wondered who I was.

"Think!" Burrich barked at me suddenly. "Think it through for yourself, with no assumptions. There is much here that makes no sense to me, questions that you should answer before you blindly do her wishes, regardless of what threat she holds over you. Why hasn't she simply killed the dragon herself? Why does she bid you do it, and then cast you out of her stronghold, when it would be easier for her to assist you in reaching him?" In an aside to no one, he muttered, "I hate this. I hate thinking this way, the intrigue and the plotting. I always have." He stared blindly into the recesses of the dim tent. "All these intricate balances of power, ambition, and the Farseer drive to set forces in motion and ride them out. All the secrets. That is what killed your father, the finest man I ever knew. It killed his father, and it killed Verity, a man I was proud to have served. Must it kill yet another generation, must it end your whole line before you stop it?" He turned his gaze, and suddenly seemed to see the Prince. "End it, my lord. I beg you. Even at the cost of the Fool's life, even at the cost of your betrothal. End it now. Cut your losses, which are already far too high. Death is all you can buy for the Narcheska's family. Walk away from all of it. Leave here, sail home, marry a sensible woman, and have healthy children. Leave this woeful cup to the Outislanders who brewed it. Please, my prince, blood of my dearest friend. Leave this. Let us go home."

His words shocked all of us, not least the Prince. I could see Dutiful's mind racing as he stared at Burrich. Had it ever occurred to the youngster that he could take such a step? He looked at each of us in turn, then stood up. Something changed in his face. I had never seen it happen, never suspected that perhaps a single moment could carry a boy to manhood. I saw it then. He stepped to the door of the tent. "Longwick!"

Longwick thrust his head inside. "My prince?"

"Fetch me Lord Blackwater and the Narcheska. I wish them to come here, immediately."

"What do you do?" Chade asked in a low voice when Longwick had withdrawn.

Prince Dutiful did not reply directly. "How much of this magic powder do you have? Can it do what Fitz has said it can?"

A light kindled in the old man's eyes, the same light that had used to terrify me when I was his apprentice. I knew that he didn't know completely what his powder could do, but that he was willing to gamble that it would work. "Two kegs, my prince. And yes, I think it will be sufficient."

I heard the crunch of footsteps on the ice outside the tent. We all fell silent. Longwick lifted the flap. "My prince, Lord Blackwater and the Narcheska Elliania."

"Admit them," Dutiful said. He remained standing. He crossed his arms on his chest. It looked forbidding but I suspect he did it to keep his hands from trembling. His face looked as if it had been chiseled from stone. When they entered, he did not greet them or invite them to sit, but merely said, "I know what the Pale Woman holds over you."

Elliania gasped, but Peottre only inclined his head once. "When your man returned, I feared that you might. She has sent me word, saying that she did not intend to divulge that secret, but that now it is known, I may beg you freely to help us." He took a deep breath and I thought I knew what it cost the proud man to sink slowly down on his knees. "Which I do." He bowed his head and waited. I wondered if he had ever before knelt to any man. Elliania's face flared from white to sudden crimson. She stepped forward and put a hand on her uncle's shoulder. Slowly she sank to her knees beside him. Her proud young head drooped until her black hair curtained her face.

I stared at them, wanting to hate them for their intrigues and betrayal. I could not. I knew too well what Chade and I would be capable of, were Kettricken taken as hostage. I thought the Prince would bid her rise, but he only stared at them. Chade spoke. "She has sent you word? How?"

"She has her ways," Peottre said tightly. He remained on his knees as he spoke. "And those I am still forbidden to speak about. I am sorry."

"You are sorry? Why could you not have been honest with us from the beginning? Why could you not have told us that you acted under duress, with no interest in an alliance or a marriage? What makes you guard her secrets still? Forbidden to speak! What worse thing could she have done to you than what she has already done?" The hurt and outrage in the Prince's voice went beyond anything mere words could convey. He knew now, as we all did, that he had been only a tool for the Narcheska, never anyone she could care about. It humiliated him as much as hurt him. I knew then that he had let himself fall in love with her, despite their differences.

Peottre clenched his teeth. His voice grated when he replied. "Exactly the question that keeps me awake at night. You know only of the most recent and vicious attack she has made against Narwhal Clan. For a long time, we stood firm before the blows she dealt us, thinking, 'She has done her worst and we have withstood it. We will not bend to her.' And each time she proved us wrong. What worse can she do to us? We do not know. And that ignorance of where her next blow will land is her most fearsome weapon over us."

"Did you never think that you could have told me that

there were hostages involved? Did you think it would not have moved me to help you?" Dutiful demanded.

Peottre shook his head heavily. "You could never have accepted the bargain she made us. You had too much honor."

The Prince ignored the strange compliment.

"What was the pact?" Chade asked sternly.

Peottre answered in a flat voice. "If we made the Prince kill the dragon, she would kill Oerttre and Kossi. Their torment and shame would end." He lifted his head and looked at me with difficulty, but then spoke honestly. "And if we delivered you and the tawny man to her, alive, she promised to give us their bodies. To return to our motherland."

I groped for my anger and felt only sickness. No wonder they had been so glad to see the Fool awaiting us on Aslevjal. We had been sold like cattle.

"May I speak?" Elliania lifted her head. Perhaps she had always carried that grave sorrow in her, but I had never seen the shame she bore plainly now. She looked younger than I recalled, and yet she had the eyes of a dying woman. She looked at Dutiful and then lowered her eyes before the hurt he did not hide. "I think there is much I could make clear for you. It is long since I had any heart for this vicious sham. But my duty to my family means that first I must speak of this to you. My mother and my sister . . . it is imperative that . . . that we—" She choked for a time. Then she flung up her head and spoke stiffly. "I do not think I can make you understand how important it is. That they must die, and that their bodies must be returned to my mothershouse. For an Outislander, for a daughter of Narwhal Clan, no other choice was ever possible." She clasped her shaking hands in front of her. "There was never an honorable choice," she managed to say before her voice died.

Dutiful spoke quietly. "Sit down, if you can find the space. I think we have all come to the same place now." He did not mean the tent.

We all shifted, trying to make room in the small shelter. Burrich grunted as he tried to move his stiff leg out of the way. As Peottre and Elliania found places to sit, Burrich shook out my shirt and then draped it around me. It almost made me smile. No matter what else might be going on, he still would not let me offend a lady by sitting bare-chested in her presence. The grandson of a slave, he had always been far more aware of the social niceties than I had.

Elliania's voice was shamed and weary. She held her shoulders tightly hunched. "You ask what else she could do to us? Much. We do not know, with certainty, who belongs to her. She has preyed on our men and boys for years. Our warriors go forth and do not return. Young boys vanished while shepherding our flocks, on our own clan lands! Child by child, she has reduced our family. Some she killed. Others went out to play and returned home as soulless monsters." She glanced sideways at Peottre, who stared at nothing. "With our own hands, we have killed the children of our clan," she whispered. The Prince made a small sound at her words. She stopped speaking, then took a ragged breath and went on. "Henja had been in our household for years before she betrayed us. We still do not know how my mother and little sister were snatched so effortlessly from our midst. Just as those two were taken, so others are vulnerable. My Great Mother is elderly, and her mind flickers like a dying candle, as you have seen. All her knowledge should have been passed on to my mother by now. Yet my mother is not there to receive it. So, she lingers, trying her best to mother our house despite the burden of her years. Perhaps you think her pathetic. Nonetheless, if she were taken from us, the center of our mothershouse would be completely destroyed. My family would cease to be. As it is, we have suffered greatly from my mother's absence and the discord it has created. What is a mothershouse, with no mother in it?"

She asked the question as if it were rhetorical, but the Prince suddenly sat very straight. Stiffly, he asked, "But then, if you came to Buckkeep to be my wife, would not you be leaving your mothershouse, that is, who would be the Great Mother when it was your turn to take that role?"

A tiny spark of anger kindled in Elliania's eyes. She spoke disdainfully. "My cousin already fancies herself in that role, as you have seen. She seeks to make others think it is hers by right rather than by default." For a second, I saw the spitfire I had glimpsed on her home island. Then she gave a small sigh and tossed her hands helplessly. "But you are right. I gave up all hope of becoming what I was born to be when I agreed to marry you. That loss is the price I pay to buy the deaths of my sister and mother, and end their torment and degradation." She dwindled back into herself, her shoulders rounding. She clenched her hands, and I saw the sweat start on her brow.

"Why didn't she ask *you* to kill the dragon? Or why doesn't she do it herself?" Chade asked them.

Peottre spoke up. "She believes she is a great prophetess, one who can not only see the future, but one who determines what the future will be. During the war, she said that the Farseer line must perish entirely, or that they would bring the dragons to descend on us, just as they did of old. Some believed her, and tried to do her will. But they failed, and her words came true. You Farseers brought the wrath of the dragons upon us, smashing and destroying our ships and villages."

"But if you had not attacked us with your Red Ships—" Dutiful began, outraged.

Peottre spoke over him. "Now, she says there is still a chance to redeem ourselves. She says our dragon deserves to die, for he failed to rise and protect us. Moreover, she says he deserves to die at a Farseer's hands, since you are the foe that he failed to protect us from. But most of all, she says a Farseer must kill Icefyre because that is what she has seen in her visions of the future. For it to go as she wills it, a Farseer must do this deed."

"Which seems to me to be a very good reason to

consider not doing it," Burrich remarked under his breath to me.

The Prince's ears were keen. He spoke bitterly. "But the best reason to consider not killing the dragon is that it may be impossible. You've been aware that some in my group had begun to doubt my mission. The closer we came to Icefyre, the clearer we could sense him, not just his life that lingers in him still, but his power. His intellect. Now, I discover that my friends have acted against me. Lord Blackwater, Narcheska Elliania, I have failed you. My own trusted friends have sent a message to the Bingtown Traders. They will send their dragon to oppose us. She may already be hastening here."

"I do not understand," Peottre broke in. "I knew there had been resistance in your group to killing the dragon. But what is this talk of 'sensing' him?"

"You are not the only one with secrets, and this I will reserve to myself for now. Just as you reserve the secret of how the Pale Woman has been in contact with you. She prompted you to poison Fit—Tom with the cake you brought to us, did she not?"

Peottre sat up very straight, lips folded. Dutiful gave a sharp nod to himself. "Yes. Secrets. If you had not seen fit to hold yours so tightly, we might have acted as one from the beginning, not against the dragon, but against the Pale Woman. If only you had spoken to me . . ."

The Narcheska suddenly collapsed. She fell onto her side, moaning, and then shuddered into stillness.

Blackwater knelt by her. "We could not!" he exclaimed bitterly. "You cannot even guess what price this little one has paid tonight to speak this plainly to you. Her tongue has been sealed, and mine, too." He looked suddenly at Burrich. "Old soldier, if you have a thread of mercy left in you, will you fetch snow for me?"

"I will," I said quietly, not knowing how much or how little Burrich could see. But he had already risen, taking up an empty cooking pot and going out of the tent. Blackwater rolled Elliania onto her belly and, without ceremony, dragged up her tunic. The Prince gasped at what was revealed and I turned aside, sickened. The dragon and serpent tattoos on her back were inflamed, some oozing droplets of blood, others puffed and wet like freshly burst burns. Peottre spoke through clenched teeth. "She went for a walk one day with Henja, her trusted handmaid. Two days later, Henja brought her stumbling home to us, with these marks on her back and the Pale Woman's cruel bargain for us. Henja spoke it, for Elliania cannot say anything of what befell her without the dragons punishing her. Even the mention of the Pale Woman's name does this to her."

Burrich came back with his pot of snow. He set it down beside the prone woman and peered at her in horror, trying to discern what it was. "An infection of the skin?" he asked hesitantly.

"A poisoning of the soul," Peottre said bitterly. He lifted a handful of the clean snow Burrich had brought and smoothed it across Elliania's back. She stirred slightly. Her eyelids fluttered. I thought she had hovered at the edge of consciousness, but she did not make a sound.

"I free you from all agreements between us," Dutiful said quietly.

Peottre looked at him, stricken. But the Prince spoke on.

"She will not be held by me to any promises she made under duress. Yet I will still kill your dragon," the Prince said quietly. "Tonight. And after we have won clean death for our people, when no one but myself is at risk, then I will do all within my power to finish the Pale Woman's evil forever." He took a great breath, and as if fearing mockery, said, "And if any of us survive, then I will stand before Elliania and ask her if she will have me."

Elliania spoke. Her voice was faint and she did not lift her head. "I will. Freely." The second utterance she added more strongly. I do not think Peottre or Chade approved, but they held their tongues. She motioned away the handful of snow that Peottre held. Instead, she took his hand and managed to sit up. She was still in pain. She looked as if she had taken a death wound.

Chade swung his gaze to me.

"Then we act. Tonight." He looked around at each of us in turn, then almost visibly threw caution to the wind. "We dare not wait, for who among us knows how swift a dragon can fly? If we act together and quickly, then perhaps the deed can be done and we can be gone from here before this Tintaglia even arrives." A flush, almost a blush, suffused the old man's face suddenly. He could not keep down the small smile that came as he announced, "It is true. I have created a powder that has the force of a bolt of lightning. I brought some of it with me, when I came here. I do not have as much of it as I had hoped to apply to this task. Most of my supply remained behind on the beach. But perhaps what I have is enough. When cast into a fire in a sealed container, it explodes violently, like a lightning strike. If we placed it down our tunnel and set it off, it would definitely blow up much ice. By itself, it may kill the dragon. Even if it doesn't, it will give us swifter access to him."

I heaved myself to my feet. "Have you a cloak I can use?" I asked Burrich.

He ignored me, looking only at Chade. "Is this like what you did the night Shrewd died? Whatever you treated the candles with, it did not behave as reliably as you had expected. What do we risk here?"

But Chade's enthusiasm for an immediate test of his wonderful powder had already grown beyond all caution. He was like a boy with an untested kite or boat. "This isn't like that at all. That was a fine measurement, and it had to be done in more haste than I liked. Have you any idea what was involved in treating all those candles and the firewood supply for that evening, with no one the wiser? No one has ever appreciated that, no, nor any of the other wonders I've worked for the Farseer reign. But even so, this is different. It will happen on a much larger scale, and I am free to use as much of the powder as we think necessary. There will be no half-measures this time."

Burrich shook his head at me as I freed my arm from its binding and carefully threaded my left hand into my shirt-sleeve. It was sore, but I could use it. Carefully. The prospect that the dragon might be slain tonight had fired me. A calm part of me knew that all I had was the Pale Woman's word that she would release the Fool as soon as Icefyre was dead. It was scarcely reliable, and yet it was the only chance I had. And if Chade's powder did slay the beast, but did not win the Fool's release, then a second dose of it, used alongside the dragon's body, might very well open up a passageway into her realm under the ice. I kept that thought to myself for now.

"What are the dangers?" Dutiful asked, but Chade waved a dismissive hand.

"I made extensive tests of it. I dug holes on the beach, built fires in the bottom of them, and when it was burning well, put in the box of powder and retreated. When the powder burst, it created a pit on the beach, the size propor-tionate to the amount of powder in the sealed container. Why should ice and snow be any different? Oh, I'll grant you that they are heavier and thicker, but that is why we'll use a larger container of powder. Now as for the fire—"

"Easily done," I said: My mind was already racing. I had found Chade's cloak. I settled it around my shoulders. "A container of some kind, a large cooking pot. That kettle we use for stew and melting snow for water. That will do. Kindling to start a small fire in the bottom of it, and then the Fool's burning oil. He had it with his tent, so it will be there still. I will crawl down the excavated tunnel, get the fire going, and then put in the powder and crawl out. Hastily." Chade and I grinned at one another. I was already infected with his enthusiasm.

Chade nodded, then knit his brows. "But the kettle's not big enough to hold the whole cask. Ah, let me think, let me think. I have it. Several layers of cured leather under the kettle. When you have the fire going well in the kettle, tip it over onto the leather. It will contain it well enough for the short time it will take. Then thrust the cask into the fire. And come out of the tunnel. Quickly." He grinned at me as if it were all a fine jest. Peottre looked alarmed, the Narcheska confused. Burrich was scowling, his face gone black as a thundercloud. Prince Dutiful looked torn between a boy's desire to make things happen and a monarch's need to consider all decisions carefully. When he spoke, I knew which side had won.

"I should do it, not Fi— Tom Badgerlock. His arm is all but useless. And I said I would do it. It's my task."

"No. You're the heir to the Farseer throne. We can't risk you!" Chade forbade it.

"Ah! Then you admit there is a risk!" Burrich growled as I dragged Chade's boots onto my feet. They were too big for me. I had never realized the skinny old man had such long feet.

My mind churned with plans. "I need the kettle, the oil from the Fool's supplies, kindling and tinder, a tinder-box, two treated hides. And the keg of powder."

"And a lantern. You'll need light to see what you're doing down there in the dark. I'll bring the lantern." Dutiful had ignored Chade's warning.

"No. No lantern. Well. Perhaps a small one. We go now and we go silently. If the rest of your Witted coterie gets wind of what we're up to . . . well. We just don't need that to happen." As I had struggled with the boots, I had realized I'd need someone to help me. My shoulder was still twinging at the slightest demand on it. The Prince would be that person. I'd send Dutiful out of the tunnel as soon as I had the fire started. He could stand beside me on the edge of the pit while we waited for the powder to burst. Surely that would be enough to fulfill his word as a Farseer that he would take the dragon's head.

"Witted coterie!" Burrich exploded.

I felt impatient. I spoke as I sorted through Chade's and Dutiful's clothing. I took Chade's fur hat. "Yes. The circle of Witted ones who serve the Farseer King. Did you think the Skill was the only magic that could be employed that way? Ask Swift about it. He's close to being a member of it. And despite Web's betrayal of our plan, I do not think it a bad idea." Then, as Burrich stared at me, both dumbfounded and insulted, I reminded Chade, "Send Longwick to gather those supplies himself. He's tight-lipped and loyal; he won't let a rumor start."

"I'll go with him," Dutiful said. He did not wait for anyone to agree, but snatched up his cloak. He paused briefly near Elliania. His eyes did not meet hers but he offered, "I give you my word. If I can find clean death for your mother and sister, it will be theirs." Then he was gone.

"The Farseer Prince uses magic?" Peottre demanded as he stared after him.

Chade hastily devised a lie. "That was not what Tom said. The Prince has a circle of friends here who can use the Wit, what is sometimes called Old Blood Magic in the Six Duchies. They came with him to help him."

"Magic is dirty stuff," Peottre opined. "At least a sword is honest and a man sees his death coming. Magic is the way the Pale Woman has enchained our folk and shamed us of them. Magic is how she binds us still, to do her low tasks."

Burrich nodded slowly to his words. "Would that the magic of the sword could be worked on her. It is never fitting that a strong man falls to guile, especially the guile of an evil and ambitious woman." I know he thought of my father then, and how Queen Desire had plotted his death. I do not know what Peottre made of his words.

The Narwhal Clan kaempra stood slowly, as if some thought were uncurling uncomfortably in his mind. He nodded, as if to himself. Beside him, the Narcheska stood. "Please tell Prince Dutiful that I said farewell," she said quietly, to no one in particular.

"And I," Peottre said in his deep voice. "I am grieved that it came down to this. Would that there had been a better path for all of us." They left slowly, Peottre moving as if heavily burdened. Dutiful returned quickly, carrying some of the supplies for our mission. A few moments later, Longwick brought the rest. He stood after he had been relieved of the objects. Plainly, he wished to ask questions, but no explanations were offered to him before Chade dismissed him with thanks. The man looked worried. Obviously Dutiful and I were preparing some sort of foray. Little or no explanation of my return had been offered to anyone. Yet, like any good soldier, Longwick accepted the lack of explanation as reasonable and returned to his post outside the tent.

There was some little delay, for Chade had decided that a fire on hides over ice might not burn hot enough to set off his powder. Chade experimented with the kettle to see how large a container of powder would fit into it. This demanded a hasty comparison of packed items to find a container that would both fit within the kettle and sufficiently seal in the powder. At last he settled on a small crock with a pottery stopper that had been full of tea herbs. I suspected the tea was one of his special blends from the way he grumbled over dumping it out. That done, he opened the cask I had carried from the beach and carefully transferred a coarse powder from it into the crock. He did this well away from the tiny candle fire, tamping the powder down with his fingers and muttering to himself as he worked. "It's a little damp," he grumbled as he turned back to me with the sealed crock. "But, well, the flask that we put in your hearth was a bit damp inside too, and it still worked. Not that I had expected it to blow up like it did, but, well, that is how we learn these things, I suppose. Now, keep this well away from kettle fire until it is going very well, as hot as you judge you can get it. Then put this into the kettle, centered, so it doesn't extinguish the fire. Then get out as quickly as you can."

These directions were for me. To the Prince he said, "You are to get out as soon as the fire is started in the kettle. Don't wait for Fitz to put the powder in, get out and away and wait for him well back from the excavation edge. Do you understand me?"

"Yes, yes," Dutiful replied impatiently. He was packing our fire-making supplies into a sack.

"Promise me, then. Promise me that you'll leave as soon as he starts the fire in the kettle."

"I said I would kill the dragon. I should stay at least to see the powder go into the kettle."

"He'll leave before the powder goes into the kettle," I told Chade as I took the sealed crock. "I promise you that. Let's go, Dutiful. We don't have much of the night left."

As we moved toward the door flap, Burrich stood. "Want me to carry some of that?" he asked me.

I looked at him blankly for a moment. Then I understood him and said, "You aren't going, Burrich. Wait here for us. I won't be long."

He didn't sit down. "We need to talk. You and I. About many things."

"And we will. For a long time. There is much I wish to say to you, also. But as it has kept this many years, so it will keep until this task is done. And then we will have time to sit down together. Privately." I emphasized the last word.

"Young men are so confident that there will always be more time, later." He made this observation to Chade. Burrich reached over casually to take part of Dutiful's armload. "Old men know better. We remember all the times when we thought there would be more time, and there wasn't. All the things I thought I would say to your father, someday, remain in my heart, unsaid. Let's go."

I sighed. Dutiful was still standing there with his jaw slightly ajar. I shrugged at him. "There's no use arguing with Burrich. It's like arguing with your mother. Let's go."

We left the tent and moved quietly into the darkness. We moved as silently as Witted ones can, even when one of them won't admit he's Witted. Burrich set a hand lightly on my good shoulder. It was his only concession to his failing vision and I made no comment on it. I glanced back once to see Chade standing in the tent flap in his night robe, peering after us. He seemed embarrassed to have been caught at it; he let the flap drop down into place. But now I knew that he was worried, and I tried not to wonder how well he had tested his exploding powder. Longwick too stared after us.

The path to the excavation was uphill. It had not impressed me as a difficult climb, but the events of the last few days were making themselves felt to me. Now it seemed difficult, and I was blowing by the time we reached the ramp that led down into the pit. We stopped there, and I took the oil from Burrich, wincing a little at the weight of it.

"Wait for us here."

"You needn't worry I'll follow you. I know my vision is gone, and I won't put you in danger by going with you. But I'd have at least a word or two with you before you go. Alone, if you don't mind."

"Burrich. Every moment that I dally, the Fool may lose more of himself to the dragon."

"Son, you know in your heart that we're too late to save him. But I know also that you must go on and do this." He turned his head, not looking at the Prince, but "seeing" him. At a pleading look from me, Dutiful retreated several steps to give us the privacy Burrich sought. He still lowered his voice. "I'm here to bring you and Swift home. I promised Nettle I'd bring her brother home, safe and sound, that I'd kill a dragon to do it if I had to, and that everything would be as it used to be. In some ways, she's still a child, believing that Papa will always be able to keep her safe. I'd like her to go on believing that, at least for a time."

I wasn't sure what he was asking me, but I was in too much of a hurry to quibble. "I'll do my best to let her keep that," I assured him. "Burrich, I have to go."

"I know you do. But...you know that we both believed you were dead. Molly and I. And that we only acted as we did in that belief. You know that?"

"Of course I do. Perhaps we'll talk about it later." I suddenly knew, by both the anger and pain that his words woke in me, that I wanted to talk about it never. That I did not want even to think of talking about it with him. Yet I drew a breath and said the words I'd told myself so often. "You were the better man for her. I slept well at night, knowing that you were there for her and Nettle. And afterward...I didn't come back. Because I never wanted you to feel that, that—"

"That I'd betrayed you," he finished quietly for me.

"Burrich, the sun will be coming up soon. I have to go."

"Listen to me!" he said, suddenly fierce. "Listen to me, and let me say this. These words have been choking me since I was first told what I'd done. I'm sorry, Fitz. I'm sorry for all I took from you, without knowing I had taken it. I'm sorry for the years I can't give back to you. But—but I can't be sorry I made Molly my wife, or for the children and life we had together. Have. I can't be. Because I *was* the better man for her. Just as Chivalry was better for Patience, when all unknowing he took her from me." He sighed suddenly, heavily. "Eda and El. What a strange, cruel spiral we've danced."

My mouth was full of ashes. There was nothing to say.

Very, very softly, he asked me, "Are you going to come back and take her from me? Will you take her from our home, from our children? Because I know that you can. She always kept a place in her heart for the wild boy she loved. I...I never tried to change that. How could I? I loved him, too."

A lifetime spun by on the whirling wind. It whispered to me of might have been, could have been, should have been. Might yet could be. But would not. I finally spoke. "I won't come back and take her from you. I won't come back at all. I can't."

"But—"

"Burrich, I can't. You can't ask that of me. What, do you imagine that I could ride out to visit you, could sit at your table and drink a cup of tea, wrestle your youngest boy about, look at your horses, and not think, not think—"

"It would be hard," he cut in fiercely. "But you could learn to do it. As I learned to endure it. All the times I rode out behind Patience and Chivalry, when they went out on their horses together, seeing them and—"

I couldn't bear to hear it. I knew I'd never have that sort of courage. "Burrich. I have to go. The Fool is counting on me to do this."

"Then go!" There was no anger in his voice, only desperation. "Go, Fitz. But we are going to talk of this, you and I. We are going to untangle it somehow. I promise. I will not lose you again."

"I have to go," I said a final time, and turned and fled from him. I left him standing there, blind in the cold wind, and he stood there alone, trusting that I would return.

chapter XXIII

MIND OF A DRAGON

The Elderlings were a far-flung race. Although few writings have survived from their time, and we cannot read their runes in full, several of our own seem descended from the glyphs they chose to mark on their maps and monoliths. The little we know of them seems to indicate that they mingled with ordinary humans, sometimes residing in the same cities, and much of our knowledge may have come from that association. The Mountain folk have ancient maps that are almost certainly copies of even more ancient scrolls and seem to reflect a familiarity with a much greater territory than those people now claim. Roads and cities marked on those maps either no longer exist or are so distant as to be mythical. Strangest of all, perhaps, is that at least one of those maps shows cities that would today be as far north as Bearns and as far south as the Cursed Shores.

      ✿ FEDWREN'S "TREATISE ON A LOST FOLK"

I didn't say a word as I rejoined Dutiful and he didn't ask. He led the way, small lantern swinging, down the ramp into a pit that had grown substantially deeper and narrower since I had last dug in it. I could see how they had concentrated their efforts once they had glimpsed the shadow of the beast trapped in the ice below them. Again, like being drenched by an unexpected wave, my Wit-sense of Icefyre swelled, and then collapsed and vanished. It unnerved me to be so aware of the one I was coming to kill.

I followed Dutiful as he led me toward the corner of the pit that became a tunnel scratched and scraped into the ice. It started out as taller than a man and two men wide. But it did not go far before it narrowed, and soon I was hunched over, which made my shoulder ache more.

As I followed him, something Burrich had said suddenly rearranged itself in my mind. Burrich had come here to slay a dragon, if he had to, anything to bring Swift home. Nettle had told Thick that her father had gone off to kill a dragon. The two together meant that Nettle didn't know about me. She knew nothing of me. I was torn between relief that I had not said anything to enlighten her and a sick foreboding that I would never really exist in her life. Suddenly the blackness and the ice and cold seemed to close in on me, and for one dizzying instant, I felt squeezed inside the glacier, trapped and wishing I could die, but unable to do even that much for myself. Shame choked me as I tried to will my own death.

Then the suffocating darkness passed and I staggered on. I set Nettle and Burrich and Molly aside, pushed away my past and looked only at the immediate thing that I needed to do: kill this dragon. I followed Dutiful deeper into the ice, telling myself that perhaps I could still save the Fool. Lying to myself.

Dutiful's little lantern showed me nothing except the slickly gleaming walls of ice and Dutiful's silhouette in front of me. The tunnel came to an abrupt end. Dutiful turned to face me and squatted down. "That's his head, down there. We think." Dutiful pointed down at the scuffed ice below us.

I stared at ice he crouched on. "I don't see anything."

"With the bigger lantern and daylight behind you, you

could. Just take my word for it. His head is below us." Awkwardly, he unshouldered his sack onto the floor in front of him. I hunkered down facing him. There would just be room for him to step over the kettle and squeeze past me once we got the fire going.

The cold had crept into my shoulder, stiffening it, and my battered face was a cold, sore mask. It didn't matter. I had my right hand still. How hard could it be to build a fire and put a crock into it? That was something even I could do.

The hides went down first. Dutiful arranged them between us, as if we were soldiers preparing for a dice game. The hides were thick ones, one of ice bear, and one of sea cow. They both stank. I settled the kettle in the middle of them and set the flask of oil carefully aside from it. I put the crock of powder next to it. We had shaved bits of wood for tinder and some scorched linen. I made a tiny nest in the bottom of the kettle. I had struck three futile showers of sparks from the firestone into the kettle before Dutiful asked me curiously, "Couldn't we just light it from the lantern?"

I lifted my eyes and gave him a baleful stare. In response, he grinned at me. The light emphasized his reddened cheeks and cracked lips. I didn't have a smile left in me, but somehow I shaped one for him. I remembered, briefly, that his young shoulders bore burdens too, not the least of which was that killing this dragon was a betrayal, of sorts, of his Old Blood and his Old Blood coterie. Nor would it buy him his own dream. The girl he had come to love was his only as a lure to get him to do the Pale Woman's bidding. She had offered herself to him, not for love, not to secure an alliance, but only to buy her mother's and sister's death. It did not seem a promising foundation for a marriage, and yet, here we were. I rocked back onto my heels. "You do it," I told him. "And then get out of here. Oh. And guide Burrich away from the edge of the excavation for me. He doesn't see well."

"No, really? I thought he was blind." It was a young man's humor, the dark sarcasm that has no fear of ever meeting the fate he mocks. I could no longer smile about it, but perhaps Dutiful didn't notice. He claimed a bit of the scorched linen from the kettle and offered it to the lantern's flame. It licked it hungrily and immediately the fire took. Dutiful hastily dropped it into the kettle on top of the other tinder. It went out.

"Nothing is ever easy for us," I observed after our third try had failed.

I had to turn the kettle on its side, and then Dutiful burnt his fingers poking the last bit of flaming linen under the shaved bits of wood. We held our breaths, waiting, and the tiny flame gripped and clambered over the tinder. I nursed it stronger with curls of wood, deciding that I would not turn the kettle upright and risk dislodging the heart of the fire, but would instead slide the powder into the kettle as if I were putting a loaf of bread into an oven's mouth. I coughed in the gathering smoke from our tiny fire.

"Time for you to go," I told the Prince.

"Just do it and then we'll both go."

"No." I would not say I wanted to be sure he was safely away before I loaded the powder. Instead, I said, "Burrich is very important to me. And very proud. He'll want to wait until I'm with him before he flees. Take his arm and tell him that I'm coming, that you can see me. And get him well away from the pit. We both know that Chade's concoctions sometimes work far better than he expects them to."

"You want me to lie to him?" Dutiful was scandalized.

"I want you to get him to safety. He has a bad knee, and he can't move as swiftly as you or I can. So get him started. I'll give you a moment or two to do that, then I'll load in the powder and get out of here."

It worked. The Prince would not have left me if only his own safety had been at risk. He would for Burrich's. I thanked Kettricken for the heart she had instilled in her son as he stepped gingerly over the hot kettle and clambered past me. I listened to his footsteps in the icy tunnel, trying to gauge when he would leave the pit, reach Burrich, and escort him away. No hurry, I told myself. No need to risk anyone just yet. In a few more minutes, the dragon would be dead. And perhaps the Fool would be safe.

I lay flat on the floor of the tunnel, to avoid the smoke hanging above me and to feed my fledgling fire. I wanted a good bed of coals. Then I'd put in the powder. Reluctantly, I decided I should add the oil at that time too, enough to coax the flames up around the side of the powder container. I opened the flask of oil and set it to hand. It would be safe. It had taken quite a long time before the powder in the flask had exploded in my hearth fire. Of course, that had been before Chade had perfected the powder.

Don't think about that. Don't think about dying here, burnt and crushed, I said to myself. No. I could be trapped and still in the ice, with cold taking me deeper and deeper into blackness, until I was finally gone. I thought of that easing into death. It almost seemed cowardly. And yet what other way was there to go? Alone, mateless, was a death by ice so cruel a fate?

A cold drop from the ceiling fell on the back of my neck, pulling my thoughts back to what I was supposed to be doing. I wondered how my mind had wandered so far. The hides around the blazing kettle were scorching and stinking as it got hotter. I burned my fingers, tipping the lip of the kettle a bit higher so it would hold the oil when the moment came. I cursed and set my burnt fingers against the ice to ease them. And then, like a flood tide, the dragon rushed into me.

I do not believe he intended to. I think he was like a man who holds his breath, thinking he will be able to extinguish his own life. But at the last moment, the body overpowers the will of the mind, and takes that great gasp of air that forces the mind to go on. In that instant when he lost control, we touched. It was not the Wit or the Skill, but something else, and in recognizing it, I knew it was intrinsic to dragonkind. I had felt it before, when Tintaglia invaded my dreams through Nettle. I had thought it was her own peculiar sending, but no. Icefyre echoed it. Tintaglia was better at it, or perhaps having dealt mostly with humans, she had learned to tailor her thoughts to our minds. The dragon swept through my mind and drowned me in his being. It was not phrased in human words or concepts; it was not an attempt at communication with me. In his eruption of thought and emotion and knowledge, I learned far more of him than I wanted to. When the dragon receded from my mind, leaving me beached in my individuality, my elbow gave out, and I found myself belly down on the ice, my face uncomfortably close to the hot kettle.

That brief time of sharing Icefyre's memories seemed more real than my entire life had been. Icefyre was definitely alive. And aware, but his awareness was focused deep within himself. He desired death. He had come here to seek it, deliberately. Death does not come easily to dragons. They may die of disease or injury or in battle with their own kind, but other than those fates, no one knows how many years one may number. Icefyre had been a strong and hearty creature with many years before him. But the skies had become empty, bereft of his kind, and the serpents that should have returned to renew the ranks of the dragons were gone too. The dragons and most of their Elderling servants had perished when the earth shook and split and the mountains belched forth smoke and flame and poisonous winds. The blast had spewed the trees flat and scorched all green from the earth.

Many of the dragons and their attendants had died in the first few days of that cataclysm, burned or choked or smothered in the raining ash. Others had perished in the harsh days that followed, for spring did not come that year, and the previously wide and swift river was a trickling thread groping its way to the sea through a choke of fine ash. The game died off, for the meadows were buried in ash and clinkers and what foliage survived was thin and dusty.

It was a harsh time. Of the dragons that lived, some said they must leave their ancestral lands. A few did, but what became of them, no one knew, for they never returned again. Competition for food weakened many, and resulted in death for others as dragons battled over the scrawny game that remained. Ash lay thick and acid over the once verdant land: no seed unfurled there and few plants pushed up through it. The human folk died off, and even their Elderling kin surrendered to slow death. The herds and flocks of the humans perished beside their two-legged tenders. The few cities that had not been buried stood empty and cracked, broken and licked dry like a nest of raided eggs.

Yet even then, none of them had feared it was the end of the dragons. Humans and Elderling might perish, trees die and game fail, but not dragons. Five generations of serpents remained in the sea. There would be five seasons of migration, and five successions of cocooning. Serpents would emerge as dragons and, eventually, the land must heal. So Icefyre had believed. Even when season after season passed, and he alone spread his wings in the sky, he waited and watched for the serpents to return. But none appeared at the cocooning grounds. He had awaited them, often going without food for fear they would arrive and find no dragons to help them spin their cocoons from the black sand of the cocooning beach and their own saliva. His saliva and venom should have mixed with it, to give to them his memories, the memories that reached back beyond his own life span. The new dragons would be lost without them. Only if he helped them would they gain their full memories of all dragonkind when they emerged from their cocoons in the strong heat of summer.

But the serpents never came.

And when he knew that they would not come, would never return, when he knew he was the last of his kind, he gave thought to how he would end. Not in ignominy, starving to death from a hunting injury, his body becoming carrion for low animals. No. He would choose the hour and place of his death, and would die in such a way that his body would be preserved intact.

Such were his plans when he came to icy Aslevjal. I saw it as he had, as an island almost completely locked under the ice. I recalled his disappointment that it was so, but did not grasp the cause. Perhaps the seas had been lower then, or perhaps the winters colder, for the waters around the island were frozen so that he more felt than saw the sea beneath the ice. He flew over it, as gleaming black as it was white, but could not find the entry he sought. He contented himself at last with a crack in the ice, crawled into it and gave himself over to sleep, knowing that from cold sleep to death was scarce a step for his kind.

But the body always chooses life. It is not swayed by logic or emotion. He passed out of life into a suspension of being, but he could not part from his body. Try as he might, there were moments when awareness seized him again, and clamored that he was cold and stiff and famished with hunger. The closing ice squeezed him and bent his body, but could not break him. He could not break himself.

He longed to die. He dreamed of dying. Again and again, he dived into death, only to have his traitorous body gasp in yet another slow breath, only to have his foolish hearts squeeze out a pulse. Humans came and flitted about him, flies drawn to a dying stag. Some tried to seek his mind, others strove to pierce his flesh. Useless, all of them. They could not even help him die.

I felt myself draw a breath and wondered when I had last taken one. It was as if someone had opened the shutters on a tavern window, to show me all that went on inside, and then as abruptly closed them. I was dazed with all that I suddenly knew about dragons. So completely had the dragon engulfed me that it was as if I had been him. I sprawled on the ice, drenched in my unwelcome awareness of the intellect of the frozen creature trapped below me.

I seized his death wish with relief. I was granting him mercy. I heaved myself up onto my knees, groaning as my injured shoulder took more weight than it wanted. I peered into my kettle oven, then crouched low to blow into it. Red coals glowed. I added a few more small sticks of wood, and carefully arranged the fuel I would tuck in around the powder container.

I knew what it was to long for death. I had tried to die when Regal had me in his power. Tormented, cold, alone, hungry, I would have welcomed a swift death then, by any means. I had come here determined to kill the dragon and now I knew he would welcome that kindness. No reason to hesitate. I picked up the crock of powder and used a stick to make a nest for it in the coals. What difference could one dragon make in the world? He was likely too feeble to survive now, even if we did release him.

Of course, if I had died in Regal's dungeon, as I had hoped, then likely Kettricken would never have found Verity or roused the stone dragons to defend the Six Duchies. No. I took too much significance to myself. She would have gone alone to find her king. But could she have wakened the dragons, if Nighteyes and I had not been there? If we had not gone with her, if Nighteyes had not killed game for her, would she have succeeded? Would Kettle have survived, to aid Verity in carving his dragon? Did, as the Fool had so long insisted, the fate of the whole world hinge on the actions of each man, every day?

The coals in the kettle oven waited and the powder was in my hands. Somewhere in the Pale Woman's hall below me, the Fool strained to hold himself away from the memory stone that continued to Forge him at each touch. I should hurry.

I could not.

I groaned and, yet again, weighed my choices in the balance. Free the dragon, and what did we win? Nothing.

Perhaps Icefyre would rise to mate with Tintaglia; perhaps there would once again be dragons in the world. The Fool had never promised us any great good from that, except for his conviction that dragons and Elderlings were somehow connected. Freeing the dragon guaranteed me nothing except the Fool's slow Forging and the continued degradation of the Narcheska's mother and sister. But if I killed the dragon, Dutiful would win Elliania's love and gratitude. They would consummate their marriage, and reign long with many children and we'd be at peace with the Out Islands...

"Think it through for yourself," Burrich had said to me. "With no assumptions." Blind as he was, he had still seen more clearly than Chade and I had. We had been so fixed on securing the betrothal, so fixed on killing the dragon. But now, almost too late, I applied what Chade had taught me years ago. "Ask yourself, What happens next? Who benefits?" I pushed my thoughts out of their rut as if I were levering out a stuck wagon. Kill the dragon. The Pale Woman grants death to the Narcheska's mother and sister, and releases the Fool to me. And then what? Who benefits?

A Farseer kills the Outislander dragon. What happens next? I saw it as clearly as if I had been granted the Fool's prescience. That insult to the Outislanders not only eliminates all chance of dragons returning to the world, it becomes the incident that unites the Out Islands against the Six Duchies. Far from guaranteeing a marriage that secured a lasting peace, it would be the spark that set off the conflagration of war again. Chade, Dutiful, and I were the last male members of the Farseer line; I doubted that any of us would leave the island alive. And Nettle? If Kettricken revealed my daughter's bloodlines and proclaimed her the Farseer heir, would the Outislanders let her reign in peace? I doubted it. The uncertain peace we had achieved in the last fifteen years would be swept aside. The slaughter would begin here on Aslevjal and spread. There would be no one to rouse the stone dragons this time, no Elderling allies to come to our aid. Destruction and Forging would return to our shores. The Pale Woman would reign, unchallenged, for the future she had made.

My heart was pounding in my chest with what I had nearly done. As the Fool had predicted, the choice had passed to me. I had come so close to fulfilling the Pale Woman's dreams. I set my own fingertips to the marks the Fool had left on my wrist. "Forgive me," I begged him. "Forgive me for doing what you hoped I would do." Then I threw myself flat on the ice, and with every bit of strength I had, I flung my awareness, Wit and Skill, at the dragon.

My Skill was a flapping, fluttering moth, but my Wit was strong. I felt Icefyre become aware of me. I felt the danger of his regard, just as prey lifts its head abruptly, knowing that a predator has focused on it. But I did not quail before him, but roared with my body's strength, like one predator challenging another for territory. With my Wit, I could not convey my thoughts to him, but perhaps he would reach for me. Perhaps if he touched his mind to mine, he could know what I knew. That there was another dragon, a female, and she was even now winging her way toward us guided by a gull.

I know he sensed me, but to him I was a crow, neither prey nor pack, unworthy of his attention. His thoughts rolled over and away from me, and he made another dive into death and oblivion.

I flailed in panic. Just when I needed the Skill most, it had faded to a flickering ember in me. I was not strong enough to reach the dragon's mind on my own. He was too determined to seek his own oblivion. I tried again, honing my Skill to an arrow's point, and jabbing it toward the dragon.

There you are. I thought you were dead! I've been seeking you every night for days now. What is wrong, why did you vanish? Nettle's powerful sending caught my weak Skill like strong hands clutching at a drowning man. She held my thoughts to hers. I pushed her away.

Nettle, not now. Go away. I have no time for you now.

And then, just as she fled in affront and hurt, my stupidity broke over me, and I cried out, *No, come back, wait, I need you!*

She halted at the edge of my awareness. I saw fluttering rags of her dream. She was a hunter, her hair tied back and a game net held at the ready. I lunged at her, pleading, *No, come back! Please! I need your help!*

For what? she demanded coldly.

I'd hurt her by my brusque dismissal of her after so long an absence. I doubt that she recollected that she was the one who had first barricaded her thoughts against mine. I wished I had time for explanations, but I did not. Already my Wit-sense of the dragon was starting to subside. In moments, he'd be beyond my reach. *Help me wake a dragon! I* pleaded with her. *He dives down deep into his dreams, seeking death. But if you can reach down into sleep, perhaps you can reach down into his death dream and pull him back from there.*

But . . . Shadow Wolf? Changer? Is it truly you, bidding me do this? Always before, you cautioned me of the dragon, warning me not to even say her name. Now you would have me wake her for you?

It's a different dragon. And then, knowing how little time there was, I trod heavily where I had never ventured to go before. *Please. If you would only do this thing for me, trusting me, without asking why. There is so little time. I would tell you all if we had time, I will tell you all when it is over. Only, for now, I ask you to trust me. Wake this dragon for me. Help me speak to him.*

What dragon?

This one! I pointed frantically, Wit and Skill, but Icefyre was gone again. *Wait, wait!* I begged her. *He dives deep right now, but he is here, I promise you. Wait and watch with me. In a moment, he'll be back.*

Are you all right? Why haven't you come out yet? Have

you placed the powder? It was a panicky Skilling from Dutiful, breaking into my desperate thoughts to Nettle.

A moment or two longer, my prince. There is something I must do here. Then, as the dragon suddenly surged back into existence below me, I frantically summoned Nettle with, *There! There he is. Wake him, reach him! Tell him he is not the last of his kind, tell him of Tintaglia. Tell him that she comes for him, to wake him and restore dragons to the air and earth.*

Then, like a roll of doom, Chade burst in with *Fitz, what do you do? Would you betray us? Would you betray me, after all these years? Would you betray the Farseer throne and your own blood?*

I do what I must! I Skilled it out wildly, feeling the strength of my magic wobble and fail. I could not tell if anyone heard me. I found I was lying flat on the ice in the tunnel. The dragon had receded again. By my head, the kettle glowed red. The container of powder was by my hand. I summoned my magic, hammered it like red iron, and thrust it out into the world. I begged, hoping Nettle heard my thought. *Tell him to turn away from death and choose life. Choose struggle and toil and pain and lovely, lovely life. Speak to him and tell him that Tintaglia still lives. Speak to him for me.*

I will try, she agreed dubiously. She had held our link. I felt her thought but could no longer see her. *I do not perceive this dragon that you speak of. But if you can show him to me, show me his dream, perhaps I can enter it and find him there.*

I held a feeble Skill-wall against Chade's threats, imprecations, and pleas and Dutiful's confusion while I pressed myself against the floor of ice and sought for the dragon that had no awareness of me. I could not reach him. Time both raced and dragged for me. I needed to reach him soon, before Chade could act against me, physically or with the Skill. I did not doubt that he would stop me if he could.

I recalled there had been a place where our spirits had

touched, the dragon's and mine, and I had entered his dream. I did not want to return to that time and that memory. It had been a turning point in time, not unlike this one, I suddenly realized. It had been one of the Fool's crossroads; a place where a decision made by one had altered all that had followed. Burrich had chosen, for love of me, to use a magic he found hateful. I had chosen to trust the wolf and embrace a death that was not a death. In doing so, I had unwittingly chosen to go on living.

I found the place where my experience matched Icefyre's. I found the cold and the dark and the despair, I found the longing for a death that I could not reach on my own. I returned my soul to Regal's dungeon of beatings and isolation.

It was one thing to know I had been in a place like that. It was another to reach for it, to taste again old blood around my loosened teeth, to smell the stink of my own festering wounds, and feel the numbing cold of the stone walls that was still not enough to dull the aching of my battered flesh. I put my soul back into that trapped body and knew again the despair of reaching for a death that would not come to me. I pushed the life from my body and held it at bay, only to have it flow relentlessly back into my flesh the moment I relaxed my guard against it.

Sweet Eda, was that really you, trapped like that? I thought it but one of your nightmares!

Nettle's horror nearly ripped me from my despair, but in that moment, I felt the dragon once more surge back to the edge of life's shores. In that instant, we touched and duplicated one another. My nightmare and his were the same, and I felt Nettle's awareness flow from my nightmare into the dragon's dark dream.

An instant later, I grasped the fullness of my error. His dream closed around her and took her down as he submerged his life again. I heard Nettle's fading wail at the complete foreignness of the consciousness that now enmeshed her.

I had time only to gasp. Then she was gone, fallen into a tarry darkness that engulfed her.

I Skilled uselessly after her. It was like groping in cold black water. And then even my awareness of the dragon was snatched from me, and my daughter was carried down with him, into the death he so avidly sought.

Once, I had seen a motley-fish leap from the water and seize a seabird in its jaws and bear it down. So had it been. One moment Nettle had been with me, poised at my request to plunge in where I bade her go. And she had and now she was gone, carried down to a place I could not even imagine. I had risked her, weaponless, untrained in the Skill. She had gone at my request. The magnitude of my stupidity gutted me. I could neither blink nor breathe.

I had fed my daughter to a dragon.

I tried to unbelieve that it had happened, to force time back by sheer effort of will. It was impossible that such a terrible thing could have happened so instantaneously, impossible that so dreadful an error could be irreversible. The injustice of it alone would have seemed to make it impossible. She had done nothing to deserve such an end. It was my fault; it should have fallen upon me. Horror hollowed me as I scratched my claws against iron-hard reality. I could not unmake that moment of foolishness. What had possessed me, why hadn't I paused to think before I flung her into the dragon's dream?

Dimly, I was aware of the others.

Where did she go? What happened? This from Dutiful.

She went in the dragon. I been there. The music is big, but he doesn't let you go. He doesn't find you and he doesn't care. You have to be his music, down there. No room for your own music. Thick's Skilling was full of awe and fear.

But worst was Chade's woeful *Oh, Fitz, what have you done? What have you done?*

I wanted to die, if dying could undo my shame and remorse. I needed to die, because I could not live through feeling those things.

And in that horrid place, I again touched the dragon. Touched him, and knew that he had taken my message from Nettle. Taken it and demanded more of her, to know more of things that she did not know. He had torn her wide and emptied her out, a useless juvenile human female, full of their trivial fancies. And so he had discarded her, coughed her out into the Skill, a useless indigestible bit of waste. Like a thoughtless child would wipe the scales of a dead butterfly's wings from his grubby hands, he disposed of her. Unprepared, she dispersed, a drop of pale ink in a rush of water.

And now the dragon found me, wordlessly, roaring into my being, tearing me open to the Skill as if he ripped the scar from an old wound. It was not the Skill that linked our minds, but it was kin to it in some strange way. And in that instant, it was all out of my hands. For I had the knowledge that he wanted, and he took it. He tore my mind open like an old purse, upended my memory as if it were a crock of oddments, and sorted my life impatiently for whatever he wished to know. And even before he was finished, our fate, the fate of all humans, was sealed. For Tintaglia, roaring like a storm wind, suddenly rushed through me, using her awareness of me to find Icefyre. It was as if they converged inside my body; I was the conduit for them, briefly, until they recognized one another. After that, they locked their minds together and cast me aside, unneeded, unnoticed, and unimportant. But their use of me had torn me wide and turned me inside out, emptied me into the wild currents of the Skill. I could no longer find myself, and did not much care to try.

I lay like a flayed fish and the Skill swept past me, carrying off bits of me. It suddenly seemed as if all my walls had not been protection but barriers that had confined me and cut me off from all that was best. It was not even that the Skill-flow was heady and intoxicating; it just seemed inevitable now, the ending I had always been destined for. It would obliterate me and let me forget what I had been and what I had done. That seemed an impersonal kindness, but one I longed for.

Verity was here, somewhere. I could sense him like a fragrance that had almost been forgotten until a sly waft of wind brings a hint of it to the nose. Verity, yes, and others, older and wiser and calm. So calm, the Elders of the Skill-stream. All was peaceful. Then there was a frantic stirring and someone nattering to someone else, speaking so swiftly that I could scarcely follow the thoughts. They were seeking someone who was lost, a girl, no, a man, no, a girl and a man, carried off by the tide. Such a shame, but nothing to do with me. Nothing to do with me. I wished they would stop their worrying of it and let themselves go and join us. Why did they struggle against such peace and oneness as they could know here?

Shame on you. He set his teeth in me and worried me wildly. *Shame on you, letting the cub drown. You would have come after me, and I would have come after you. Shame upon you, letting her go. Are we not pack? If you do this, you leave me behind. Do you know that? Do you care? Were you ever a wolf at all?*

And that question stabbed me sharper than fangs and woke me to the struggle. Chade and Dutiful and Thick were there, linked as a coterie, searching for us. They were doing it all wrong, like a man bailing the sea with a sieve in hopes of catching a fish. Chade made a random search for Nettle, for none of them save Thick knew well the shape of her in the Skill-current, and neither Chade nor Dutiful had thought to ask the little man to locate her. I struggled to find enough of myself to reach them. It was like working in a dream, where the sequences of events make no sense and every moment the reality changes. I touched Thick at last, a touch like a thread settling on his sleeve, and whispered, *Find the woman who helped the kitten. That is what she looks like here. Find her!*

And he did. We had known he was strong, but we had never measured him here, where his navigation of the Skill was all that mattered. He sang the song that was Nettle, and she coalesced around the notes. He did not seek her so much as summon her to fill the shape that he had made for her. And then, as if he were restoring a glass figurine to a shelf, so he carefully restored her to his dream of her. Had ever a woman been regarded as so precious? For a moment I glimpsed the inside of the traveling wagon and then the kitten on the bed told the limp woman sprawled beside him, *It's all right. Rest for now. You know the way home from here. Rest for a time, and then go home. You are safe, now. You know I love you.*

I had only an instant to wonder at what he had done, and so effortlessly. Then he seemed to sense me there and flung me out of his dream. I did not belong there. But even that act of his was a recognition of my shape. He had fixed me into myself again to expel me from their world, and suddenly Dutiful was clutching at me. *Fitz! There you are! We thought you were lost.*

Why did you betray us? What have you done? Where is the girl? Chade demanded.

Nettle is fine. I mended her. Now I'll mend him back together too, Thick suggested pragmatically.

And he slammed me back into my body with no more ceremony than that.

I lay panting on the floor of the ice tunnel. When I found my eyes and opened them, the world was red and black. Then I realized I was looking into the glowing contents of the kettle. I felt the container of powder under my fingers. It rolled under my hand as I scrabbled away from the heat. Thinking about anything seemed like too much trouble. Somewhere, around me and inside me and below me, the dragons spoke to one another. Their communication felt like thunder rolling in my lungs. I did not wish to be a party to that communion. Already I had nearly died of it. I gathered all my strength and managed to pull my knees up under me. Crawling would work, I told myself. I could crawl out.

Three things happened simultaneously. I heard Dutiful shout to me from the entrance of the tunnel. I felt a sudden crack start in the ice beneath my hand. It raced off in a jagged line toward the dawn light that was now seeping into me. And the Pale Woman invaded my mind.

She had the Skill. I should have known and been more careful. Now she looked through my soul with her colorless eyes and pierced me with her hate. Her words slapped me. *You chose, bastard king. You chose a dragon over your Beloved. And you will live with that choice. As will he. At least, for a short time. Until I let you see what you have chosen!*

And then she was gone, leaving me wretched and soiled from that contact with her mind. Such hate and virulence knows no bounds, and I knew that I had won for the Fool every coin of pain she could wring from him before his mind was gone. My spine turned to jelly, and I sprawled on the ground with neither the will nor the strength to move any farther. Again, I felt that vague stirring beneath me, and heard the oddly shrill sounds of complaining ice. Then all was stillness again. I longed to plunge into it as Icefyre had, seeking my death in it, but Dutiful was kneeling by me, shaking me frantically.

"Get up, Fitz. Get up! We have to get out of here. The dragon is stirring and the ice is cracking. He could bring it all down on us. Get up."

And when I could not, he grasped me by the collar and dragged me, out of the tunnel and into the excavation and up the ramp into the world of light and men.

chapter XXIV

TINTAGLIA'S COMMAND

And when the shepherd-turned-warrior had wearied
himself with whetting his blade on the dragon's
impervious hide, he fell back from him, sweating and
panting. Yet the moment he had breath to curse him, he
did so again, saying he would take vengeance times three
on the creature that had eaten his entire flock.

At those words, the dragon seemed to waken from
his sated sleep. Slower than a sunrise, he lifted his head
and opened his eyes. He looked down at the man and his
blade, and his great green eyes swirled and whirled.
Some say they were like whirlpools in the deep, and that
they sucked Herderson's soul down into their depth and
made it the dragon's servant. Others say that Herderson
stood firm before the dragon's gaze, and it was only
when Herderson breathed in the dragon's outblown
breath that he became subject to the creature. It is a hard
thing to bear true witness to, for those who had gathered
to watch Herderson attempt to slay the dragon had come
no closer than the edge of his pasture.

Be it his gaze or his breath, it took the man's heart.
He suddenly flung aside both shield and sword and cried
out, "Forgive me, emerald one, O creature of jewel and
flame and truth. I did not perceive what glory and might

*was yours when I first approached you. Forgive me, and
allow me ever after to serve you and sing your praise."*

   ❦ "THE TALE OF THE DRAGON'S SLAVE"

The world was a bright white place and cold. I found my
feet, got them firmly under me, and remembered how to
make them work. From somewhere, Burrich came, to grab
my other arm. Then Dutiful, Burrich, and I were staggering
and sliding through the dawn light toward the huddled
tents. I saw Chade all but running up the hill toward us. At
a considerable distance behind him, Thick trudged along.
Longwick and his remaining guardsmen were following
them. The Wit coterie had tumbled half-dressed from their
tent, and stood in the snow, pointing up the hillside and
shouting to one another as they pulled on their coats and
boots. The Hetgurd warriors stood apart and staring, nodding to one another as if they had expected a doom like
this all along. Icefyre's first try at breaking free had felt like
a small earthquake, and he continued to make efforts as we
hastened away from the excavation. Behind us, we felt as
much as heard the dragon shuddering to break free of his
icy prison. The cracking ice squeaked and popped and
groaned as he fought it. Even so, it seemed to me that each
effort was feebler than the first one. Then, when we were
halfway down the hill, the creaking of the ice ceased. My
Wit-sense of Icefyre remained as strong, but that awareness
told me of a creature that had expended tremendous effort
and was now on the verge of collapse.

"It would be ironic," I panted to Burrich and Dutiful,
"if after all these years of longing to die, he finally perished
in an attempt to live."

Burrich snorted. "We all perish in our last attempt to
live."

"What went wrong?" Dutiful demanded. "Why did you
wake him instead of just killing him? Did the powder fail?
What changed your mind?"

Before I could answer, Chade was upon us. My old mentor stalked toward me, trembling with his outrage. His questions were harsher.

"How could you?" he demanded, his voice shaking with passion as soon as he was within hearing range of me. "How could you betray your own blood that way? You were sent to kill the dragon. What right do you have to decide against that? How could you turn on your family?"

"I haven't turned on my family. I've let the Fool be Forged for the sake of the Farseers," I said. Speaking that harsh truth aloud, under the bright morning light, suddenly made it real. I had to take a breath. In a quieter voice, I went on. "She's had us watching the puppets, Chade, until we forgot that she was up there, pulling the strings. The Pale Woman wishes the dragon killed, yes. Perhaps if we killed him, she even would have given us back the Fool, but only so that he could witness the destruction of all he'd hoped for. Only so he could witness the end of the Farseer line."

Heedless of the men who were drawing into hearing range, I lined out my logic for Dutiful and him. In their prolonged silence, I heard them trying my reasoning and finding it sound. Into the silence, I said to Dutiful, "I've broken your promise, and lost you your bride. But I cannot tell you I am sorry to have done so. I fear it would have been a marriage founded on death, and death would be the only fruit of it. For now, at least, we've chosen life. Life for the dragon. And possibly a stronger peace between the Six Duchies and the Out Islands than we could have built on the dragon's death."

"Fine words!" Chade fumed. "Grand words, but you've no idea what you've chosen. And neither do I! If that thing breaks out of there and is hungry, will he 'choose life' for us? Or a hearty meal? I admit I've been shortsighted. Perhaps you were wise not to kill him. But that does not mean you were wise to wake him. Who will thank you for this, FitzChivalry, when this long day is done?"

"FitzChivalry?" I heard Civil say, striding up behind Chade. "FitzChivalry? Is that who he means? Tom Badgerlock is FitzChivalry, the Witted Bastard?" He turned to clutch Web's arm incredulously, demanding an answer. His eyes were wide, and he was breathless with shock. Dutiful's friend stared at me as if he had never seen me before, but there was no admiration in his eyes. He was a man cheated of a legend, shown common earth when he had expected the gleam of gold.

"Hush." It was Web, silencing a secret that had outgrown its shroud. "Not now. Later, I'll explain. There is no time now. He has wakened Icefyre. It's up to us to free him." Web measured me with his eyes and seemed pleased with what he saw. He gave me a nod that was almost a bow, and then strode past us.

For the first time, I noted that the Witted coterie carried their digging tools, shovels and pry bars. A new purpose animated them all. Swift and Cockle were bringing up the sled to haul away the ice. Swift did not look at Burrich or me as he passed. Nonetheless, Burrich was aware of him and undeterred by his son's cold silence. "Be careful, son," he admonished him as the boy passed us. "No one knows what Fitz has awakened there, or what his feelings toward us will be."

Then Burrich turned his gaze to me, and I had not known that clouded eyes could still pierce a man. "What *did* you do up there? And why?"

Perhaps it was time for that truth, too. "It wasn't me. Not completely. I knew the dragon was alive, but I couldn't reach him with my Skill, only my Wit. My Skill wasn't strong enough. But then Nettle found me. And—"

"And Nettle waked him up!" Thick announced happily as he finally trudged up to us. "And I saved her and put her safe. She loves me."

"What?" This burst from Burrich, a cry of outrage and pain. "Nettle, my Nettle? Witted? It isn't possible, it cannot be!"

"No. Not Witted. Skilled." Chade sounded impatient. "But untrained. Dangerously untrained. Another consequence for which we must thank Fitz and his whims. We nearly lost her in the Skill-current, but Thick knew her well enough to find her and take her out of it. She's safe now, Burrich. Probably very confused as to what happened to her just then, but safe."

"This is too much. I cannot deal with this." Burrich had been holding my arm, but now I was suddenly supporting him. He shuddered out a breath. "I suspected she had a touch of Chivalry's magic. I suspected for a long time, and when she told me of her wolf dream...that was when I knew I must go to Kettricken, to find out what it meant and to arrange for Nettle to be taught." He gave me a strange smile, torn between pride in her and fear for her future. "She was strong enough to wake a dragon?"

Then all of us were rocked by a blast of thought that sent Chade tottering, and then sinking to his knees. It was dragon speech, reaching into our minds. Tintaglia had found us.

Go and help him! Dig Icefyre out, and harm not a scale upon him. I come swift as flame, for by touch of our minds, I know where he is and no longer need the guidance of a bird! I warn you, I am not far away, and when I arrive, I expect to see him standing to meet me. If he is not, woe upon you all!

It was neither the Skill nor the Wit, and yet it struck my mind with the force of a strong Skill-sending. Icefyre's recent use of my mind had left me raw to the Skill, and the force of Tintaglia's thought physically staggered me. I suspect that those of us versed in the Skill were more susceptible to her thoughts than the others. Certainly it staggered Dutiful's entire Skill coterie. Those of his Wit coterie reacted in a variety of ways, some seeming to take the full import of her words, others looking about as if puzzled, and Cockle showing no awareness of it at all. Civil raised a shout. "You all heard her! Tintaglia commands that we dig

Icefyre out! Let's do it!" He raced up the hill as if leading a charge against an enemy.

Among the Outislanders, at least one prostrated himself, believing that a god or demon had spoken to him. Two of the others stared off in the distance, as if questing after something they might have heard. The others gave no reaction. Burrich, long sealed off to the Skill by my father in order to protect him, looked puzzled for a moment, as if he had almost recalled something. I suspect his Wit made him vaguely aware of a sending without comprehending the thought that had accompanied it.

An instant only I had to absorb all this. Then Thick, with a wide and joyous smile, went racing away from us, up the hill, his short legs pumping as hard as they could. "I'm coming!" he shouted. "I'm coming to dig you out, Icefyre!"

I put his enthusiasm down to Icefyre's earlier influence over his simple mind and his recent success at rescuing Nettle, which must have been a heady experience for the man. I strode after him, Dutiful at my side and Chade at our heels. It was only when I heard Dutiful mutter, "We have moved much of the ice above his back. Surely that is where he will break through first. We have not much more work to do!" that I wondered at his sudden enthusiasm for the task.

"Then you do not share Chade's hope that we could simply leave the dragon where he is, as he was?"

"Yes. I do. I did. But that was...before. Before Nettle woke him. No. Before...But Tintaglia commands this. Tintaglia..." His pace slowed and he looked at me in consternation. "This is, this was, almost like when you commanded me with the Skill. But it isn't. I can set this aside. I think." He caught at my arm and halted me alongside him, an odd expression on his face. "She commanded, and for a moment, I could think of nothing but obeying her. Strange. Is that what they mean by the charm of a dragon?"

Burrich startled me when he spoke. I had almost forgotten him, and yet he had somehow kept pace with us.

"The old tales speak of the charm of a dragon coming from its breath. What have I missed? Some sort of Skill-sending?"

"Something like that," Dutiful pondered. "Almost a Skill-command, I think, but I do not know. I think I wanted to help Icefyre before she commanded it. It seems my own thought to me. Yet—"

And then Chade passed us, muttering, "The powder. The powder will do it; the powder will blast him free. We only have to change where we set it. Or perhaps set it in smaller vessels—"

Dutiful and I exchanged a glance and then caught up with him. I seized his sleeve, but he shook me off. I grabbed hold of him again.

"Chade, you cannot kill him now. It's too late. Tintaglia is nearly here, and too many of our people are intent on digging him free. It won't work."

"I . . . kill him?" He looked shocked at the thought. "No, not kill him. Blast him free, you fool."

I exchanged a worried look with the Prince. "Why?" I asked Chade gently.

He looked as if my ignorance mystified him. Then, for just a moment, I saw another look pass over his face, one that frightened me. He groped. But however Tintaglia had fogged his mind, Chade had long been an expert at fabricating reasons to have me do whatever he decided I should do. "Does it escape you that an angry female dragon is on her way here, one that has been alerted to our presence thanks to you? What have you left us to do? If we kill him now, she'll kill us all. She as much as said so. Unfortunately, that means we must make ourselves useful to a dragon. If we extricate Icefyre before Tintaglia arrives, she may see it as a sign of good intentions on our part. You yourself said we might use her goodwill to build an alliance with Bingtown. Until we know her strength, I judge it best to placate her in any way we can. Don't you?"

"And you think the best way to free him is with your powder?"

"One blast can do the work of ten men with shovels. Trust me on this, Fitz. I know what I'm doing." He now seemed as enthused to blast Icefyre free as he had earlier been to blow him up. How hard had Tintaglia's command hit him? With the force of a Skill-command, which one must unquestioningly obey, regardless of one's own judgment?

Was the Fool Forged yet? Dead? The sudden thought broke abruptly over me like a wave of cold water, dashing me from my present worry. I staggered with the impact of it. I had done what the Fool had hoped I would do. I had wakened the dragon and now all our forces were turned to freeing him and uniting him with Tintaglia. It had even felt like the right thing to do, at the moment that I did it. But now my soul scrabbled at the remorselessness of time. I could not go back and change the decision, yet it suddenly seemed far too heavy and sharp a thing to carry for the rest of my life. His fingerprints burned briefly cold on my wrist.

Still my feet carried me on with the rest of them. When we reached the excavation, we discovered that all the dragon's struggles had done little. The ice over his back was cracked and starred from beneath, and he had collapsed part of the tunnel that had been dug above his neck and head. The Wit coterie had already attacked the cracks in the ice with much enthusiasm and little manpower. As I arrived, the Hetgurd men joined them. For the first time, every man at the camp was united in the task of unearthing the dragon alive. But no amount of excitement could make the work any less arduous.

Chade berated me for being an idiot when we all discovered I had left the powder pot behind when I had fled the tunnel. He put two men to work reopening the tunnel, and then completely confused the suspicious Wit coterie by putting them to work digging deep, narrow holes alongside the dragon. "We'll put smaller loads of powder along the edge of that crack he's made. It won't be enough to harm him, just enough to break the ice up so we can haul it away in larger chunks. Fitz, I'll need you with me to help me measure and package the powder. Dutiful, you too, and bring Longwick. We'll need more vessels suitable for holding the fires. It will be tricky to set them off, but I'm convinced that near-simultaneous blasts will serve us best."

Chade was in his element, organizing and improvising. He burned with a fierce joy at putting his thoughts into action. I realized then that in his own way, he would have been a fine soldier and strategist, much as Verity had been. The times in my life when he had seemed most alive had been when he had finally flung aside all constraints to transform his thoughts into deeds.

Burrich had come with us when we returned to Chade's tent, for he could be of little help with the digging. It was sad to know that he realized that. He reminded me somewhat of an old dog that knows he can no longer keep up with the pack on the scent, and so holds his place at his master's stirrup in faith that he will be there for the kill. I glanced up at him as he sat attentively on Chade's pallet. Chade was opening another small cask of his powder. I knelt on the floor, a clean hide stretched out before me, measuring powder into piles that were approximately the same size as the example that Chade had heaped for me. The consistency of the powder troubled me; it was not a uniform color, and some seemed ground finer than the rest, but Chade had already shrugged aside my questions. "In time I will perfect it. But for now, it will work, and that is all that counts, boy. Where is the Prince? I sent him to scavenge tight containers from any of the tents. He should be back by now. And Longwick, with the kettles. It's going to be a mix-and-match that we must do, and the sooner we begin, the better."

"I'm sure he'll be here soon," I said, and then to Burrich, "You're very quiet. Is it because you came here to kill the dragon, and now we all struggle to save it?"

He knit his dark brows at me. "You thought I came here to slay a dragon?" He gave a snort of amazement and then shook his head. "I didn't believe in this dragon. I thought it a girl's bad dream, and so it was easy for me to assure Nettle that I'd protect her from it. I took her to Buckkeep and there I learned that there might be some vestige of a dragon here. But when I came here, I came to bring you home, you and Swift. Because, regardless of what it might cost you, or me, that is where you belong." He gave a sudden sigh. "I've always been a simple man, Fitz, seeking simple answers to my problems. And here I am, trying to see how to untangle the mess you and I have made of things, and how to protect Nettle from a dragon that knows her name and how to talk sense to Swift about Beast Magic. I'd thought that you had died of the Wit, you know. The Queen tried to give me what she knew of that tale, how a Forged One came to be wearing a shirt I'd sewn for you, with King Shrewd's pin still in the collar…When I think of the anguish I felt as I buried that wretch…"

But his thoughts were interrupted abruptly by Dutiful bursting into the tent. "They've gone! I can't find them anywhere!"

"Containers to put the powder in?" Chade demanded single-mindedly. "What, all gone?"

"No! The Narcheska and Peottre! They are gone, their beds left empty. I do not think they returned to them after we spoke last night. I think they left then and if they did—"

"Then there is only one place they could have gone." Despite Chade's earlier assurances that it didn't matter, he was now scowling and poking at the piles of more finely ground powder. "They went to the Pale Woman. And told her that Fitz had come back to us, and that we now knew the true stakes of the game." He suddenly scowled. "And we spoke of Web's gull in front of them, and Tintaglia coming here. They will have told her. She will now know of our thoughts of her, and what our vulnerabilities are. The Pale Woman will know that if she wishes to move against us, she must act swiftly. Our only recourse is to be even swifter than she is. We must get that dragon out of the ice."

"But why would Elliania and Peottre do that? Why would they turn on us, when they knew I was willing to kill the dragon for them?" The Prince was agonized.

"I don't know." Chade was implacable. "But it's safest for us to assume treachery, to assume that everything we spoke of last night is now being told to the Pale Woman. And we must now see how that leaves us vulnerable."

"But it's all changed since last night! Last night, Fitz and I plotted to do her bidding, to give way to her will. Why go to the Pale Woman to tell her that, why not wait until the deed was done?" Dutiful scowled. "When they left us last night, Peottre did not look like a man about to cower before an enemy."

"I don't know." Chade's concentration didn't waver. "Make the piles only this size when the powder is this fine, Fitz." Then, "I don't know, Dutiful. But it is my duty to assume that they mean you harm, and try to think of what move we could make to forestall them." With a scraper, he corrected one of my piles. "After the dragon is freed," he added, almost to himself. He lifted his eyes back to Dutiful. "We still need those containers."

"I'll get them," the boy replied faintly.

"Good. Set the girl and Peottre out of your mind for a time. If they slipped away last night, they are long gone, and too far away for us to be able to do anything about it. Let us deal with the crisis at hand, and then move on to the next one."

Dutiful nodded distractedly and left. My heart was heavy for him. "Do you really believe they went to report to her?"

"Perhaps. But I don't think so. As I told Dutiful, we must assume the worst, and there draw our lines of defense. And our best defense may be to free the dragon that you have wakened." He knit his brows, pondering it, but then seemed to find his piles of powder more interesting. "We will think more on it when Icefyre is freed."

I feared that Tintaglia's command had sunk deep into his mind. I wanted to believe Chade was thinking clearly, but I was not confident of it.

Longwick came first with the kettles, and then Dutiful with the containers of varying sizes. As soon as he had what he wanted, Chade sent them back to the excavation site, with orders to be sure the six holes he had ordered dug alongside the dragon were progressing. I wondered if he merely intended to keep the Prince busy. Chade seemed very picky to me as he sorted through the containers, first selecting the vessels to hold the powder, making sure of the tightness of the stoppers or lids, and then matching them to their firepots. I offered to help him but he refused. "Eventually, I will devise the perfect container for my powder. It must be one that will yield to fire, but not too swiftly, for whoever sets fire to it must have time to move away. It should be tight enough to keep out moisture, if the powder is to be safely stored in it. And it must be one that can be filled cleanly, with no residual powder clinging to the outside. Eventually, I will fashion a better way to ignite it..."

He was now completely focused on what he was doing, a master still puzzling out his new invention, unwilling to trust it to his journeyman's hands. I withdrew from him a small way, sitting on Dutiful's pallet next to a silent Burrich. He seemed deep in his own thoughts. I still felt a terrible sense of urgency, a desire for it all to be over. I could not decide if Tintaglia had imprinted me with a command, or if it was my agony over the Fool. I could not keep my thoughts from turning to him. I tried not to wonder what he might be enduring, or if he was past enduring anything. The dragon's touch seemed to have restored my Skill, yet when I groped for my silk-thin Skill-bond with the Fool, I could not feel him. It frightened me. "I'm doing what you wanted me to do," I promised the Fool quietly. "I'll try to get the dragon free."

Chade, absorbed in his sorting and loading of the powder vessels, did not appear to hear me, but Burrich did. Perhaps it is as they say, that his fading sight had sharpened his other senses. He set his hand to my shoulder. Perhaps if Web had never spoken of it, I would never have noticed it. But he was right. I felt Burrich's calm flow into me. It was not his thoughts that reached me, but a sense of connection with his being. It did not match the strength of a Wit-bond between man and animal, and yet it was there. He spoke quietly. "You've been doing that for a long time, boy. Doing what others wanted you to do. Taking on tasks no one else wanted." It was a statement, not a judgment.

"So did you."

He was quiet a moment. Then, "Yes. That's true. Like a dog that needs a master, I believe someone once told me."

The cutting words I had once flung at him now brought bitter smiles to both of us. "Perhaps that has been true for me as well," I admitted.

We both sat still and silent for a time, finding a moment of respite in the eye of the storm all around us. Outside, I could hear the muffled noises of the working men. Their voices came distantly through the cold. I heard the dull ring of metal tools against ice, and the deeper thuds of chunks of ice flung into the wooden-bottomed sleds. Closer to hand, Chade muttered to himself and scraped his powder into precise loads. I felt for the dragon, and he was there, but my Wit-sense of him was dimmed as if he conserved his strength and now would do no more for himself than remain alive and await rescue. Burrich's hand was still on my shoulder. I suddenly suspected that, just as I did, he quested out toward the dragon.

"What will you do about Swift?" I asked Burrich, before I was even aware I was going to speak.

Burrich spoke almost casually. "I'll take my son home. Try to raise him to be an upright man."

"You mean, not to use his Wit."

Burrich made a noise that might have been an assent or a request to drop the topic. I couldn't.

"Burrich, all those years in the stables, all your gift for healing and calming and training animals. Was that the Wit? Did you have a bond with Vixen?"

He took his time answering me. Then, he gave me a question instead. "What you are really asking me is, did I do one thing and demand another of you?"

"Yes."

He sighed. "Fitz. I've been a drunk. It was nothing I ever wished to see you or my sons become. I've given in to other appetites, knowing well that no good could come of it. I am a man, and human. But that doesn't mean that I would condone or encourage those things in my boys. Would you? Kettricken told me that you had a foster son. I was glad to hear that you had not been entirely alone. But did raising him not teach you something about yourself? That the faults you find abhorrent in yourself are even more horrifying when you see your son manifest them?"

He had summed it up too neatly. But I still took him round to the jump again, asking him, "Did you use the Wit when you were Stablemaster?"

He took a breath and said shortly, "I chose not to." I thought that was all he would say, but a short time later, he cleared his throat and said, "But it is as Nighteyes said long ago. I could choose not to reply, but I could not choose to be deaf to them. I know what the hounds called me. I've even heard it from your own lips. Heart of the Pack. I knew what they called me and I was aware of their . . . regard for me. I could not conceal from them that I was aware of them, when they cried back to me of the joy of the hunt as they gave tongue to the chase. I shared that joy, and they knew it.

"Long ago, you told me you did not choose Nighteyes. That he chose you and bonded to you and gave you little choice in the matter. So it was with Vixen and me. She was a sickly pup, the runt of an otherwise hearty litter. But she had...something about her. Tenacity. And a mind to find a way around every obstacle. It was not to her mother that she whimpered when her brothers pushed her aside from the nipple, but to me. What was I to do? Pretend I could not hear her plea for a fair share, for a chance at life? So, I saw that she had a chance at the milk. But by the time she was large enough to fend for herself, she had attached herself to me. And in time, I admit, I came to rely on her."

On some level, I had known it. I don't know why I wanted him to admit it. "Then you did forbid me what you yourself did."

"I suppose I did."

"Have you any idea how unhappy you made me?"

He didn't flinch. "About as unhappy as you made me when you didn't obey me. But, then, you probably have no idea what I'm talking about. Doubtless you never forbade anything to your Hap that you yourself were guilty of. And I'm sure he always listens to your wisdom." He was very good. The sarcasm was there only if I looked for it.

That silenced me, for a time. But there was still one more question. "But why, Burrich? Why did you, why do you still so despise the Wit? Web, a man I much admire, sees no harm or danger in his magic. How could your own magic disgust you?"

He smoothed his hair back from his face and then rubbed his eyes. He spoke reluctantly. "Ah, Fitz, it's a long, old tale. My grandmother, when she discovered I had the taint, was horrified. Her father had it. And when he was faced with the choice of saving his wife and small children from slavers or getting his Wit-partner out of a burning stable, he chose his Wit-partner. And because of that, slavers took them. My great-grandmother lived a short, miserable time after that. My grandmother said she was a very beautiful woman. There are few worse traits for a slave to have. Her masters used her and her mistresses abused her out of jealousy. My grandmother and her two sisters witnessed it all. And grew up as slaves, used and abused. Because the man who should have made his primary bond to his wife instead chose a horse over her and his children."

"One man, Burrich. One man making a bad decision. Or who knows what went through his head. Did he think that if he got to the horse, it could carry his wife and children to safety? Or help him battle the slavers? We can't know. But he was only one man. That seems a small foundation upon which to condemn all the Wit."

He exhaled a short breath through his nose. "Fitz. His decision condemned three generations of his family. It did not seem small to anyone who bore that burden. And my grandmother feared that if I were allowed to go on as I had begun, I would do the same. Find an animal, bond to it, and put it above all other considerations. And after she died, for a time, she was right. I did exactly that. As did you. Have you never looked at your own life and said, 'Take the Wit away, and what changes?' Think on it. If Nosey had not come between you and me, would not we have been closer when you were a boy? If you had not bonded to Smithy, would you have done better with your Skill-lessons? If Nighteyes had not been in your life, could Regal have found excuse to condemn you?"

For a moment, I was stymied. Then I replied, "But if the Wit had not been held a shameful thing, none of that would have been true. If you had spoken of it as Old Blood and taught me why I must not bond, if the Wit had been held in esteem as the Skill is, then all would have been well."

His face darkened with rising blood, and for a moment I glimpsed Burrich's old temper. Then, with a patience that only time could have taught him, he said quietly, "Fitz. It is a thing I was taught from the time my grandmother first discovered the taint in me. The Wit is shameful magic, and it shames a man to practice it. Now, you talk of people who practice it openly and find no disgrace in it. Well, I have heard of places where men marry their sisters and have children, where women go about with their breasts showing, where it is not accounted shameful to discard your mate simply because her youth has faded. Yet, would you teach your children that these behaviors are good? Or would you teach them to live as you yourself were taught?"

Chade startled me when he spoke. "There are unspoken rules to every society. Most of us never question them. But surely, Burrich, you must have at some time wondered about what you were taught. Did you never decide that you would determine for yourself if the magic was worth having?"

Burrich turned to regard Chade with his clouded eyes. What did he see? A shape, a shadow, or only his Wit-sense of the old man?

"I always knew it was worth having, Lord Chade. But I was an adult, and I knew the cost of it. Your prince out there; what price would he have to pay for his useful, worthwhile magic if it became known that he was Witted? You deny he has it to shield him from hatred and prejudice. Do you fault me that I tried to shield Chivalry's son?"

Chade looked down at the work of his hands and didn't answer. He had finished. Six containers, everything from flasks to saltboxes, were filled with his explosive powder and resting in kettles or pots. "I'm ready," he said. He lifted his gaze to me and smiled a strange smile. "Let's go and free the dragon."

I could not read his green eyes. I could not decide if he truly intended to free the dragon from the ice or meant to blast it to pieces. Perhaps he himself didn't know. But as if his resolve were contagious, I suddenly felt tight with the need to end this.

"How dangerous is this?" Burrich asked.

"Just as dangerous as it was last night," Chade replied testily.

Burrich put out a hand and ran his fingertips lightly across the pots. "Not six times as dangerous?" he asked. "How will you do it? Will one man set them all, or six?"

Chade thought a moment. "Six men, each to get a

kettle fire going. And then Fitz, to go down the line putting the containers in each pot."

I nodded to the wisdom of that. Six men each judging their own time to put the powder in and flee might end up running into one another. "I'll do it."

I carried three of the pots and Chade carried the other three. Burrich brought the sack of fuel and a smaller kettle of coals from the guards' hoarded night fire. The day seemed very bright to me as we walked up the hill. It was warm, for that place, and the sun glinted off the glistening ice. As we walked up the hill together, Burrich asked me, "Are you sure Nettle is safe now? I do not understand the risk she took, but it seems to have frightened all of you."

I swallowed and admitted my guilt. "I asked her to go into the dragon's dream and wake him. Her strongest Skill-talent is the manipulation of dreams. I never paused to consider that it might be dangerous, that the dreams of a dragon might be a far different challenge than the dreams of a man."

"Yet still she went?" There was quiet pride in Burrich's voice.

"Yes, she did. Because I asked her. I'm ashamed that I risked her."

He was silent for several strides then said, "So. She knows you, and knows you well enough to trust you. For how long?"

"I'm not sure. It's a hard thing to explain, Burrich." I felt a flush rise but forced myself to speak on. "I used to... look in on you. Not often. Only when it got so... It was wrong of me."

His silence was long. Then he said, "That must have been a special torment for you. For the most part, we have been happy."

I took a deep breath. "Yes. It was. Yet I never realized I was involving Nettle to do it. She was my... I don't know, my focus point, I suppose. After a time, she became aware of me. She knew me through her dreams of me, as a, as a wolf-man." I halted, flustered.

Burrich almost kept the amusement out of his voice as he said, "Well. That accounts for some very odd nightmares, when she was small."

"I didn't know I was doing it. Then, after a time, I became aware of her. In my dreams. We talked there, in the dream worlds she made. It took me a while to realize that she was manifesting the Skill, in a way I'd never seen it used before her. But I never... She doesn't, that is, she doesn't know—" And suddenly I couldn't go any further. My throat had crushed the words unsaid.

"I know. If you had told her I wasn't her father, I'd have known."

I nodded wordlessly. It was strange to see how he would perceive such a telling. I thought only of telling her who her father was; Burrich saw it as telling her who was not her father.

He cleared his throat and changed the subject. "She will have to be taught how to manage her magic, or the Skill can steal her mind. I know that is so, from what Chivalry taught me of it."

"Nettle should be taught," I conceded. "It has become dangerous for her to go further without being taught. But she will, if we don't intervene. She must be taught."

"By you?" he asked quickly.

"By someone," I amended. And there we left it. I listened to the sound of tools crunching into snow and ice and the ever-present whooshing of the wind over the glacier. It was like a strange music, one interspersed with the upraised voices of the workers as they exhorted one another. But when we arrived at the lip of the ice quarry, work ceased almost immediately.

Chade stood at the edge of our excavation and spoke to them all, explaining his exploding powder and what he intended to do with it. I felt oddly apart from all of it. I looked from face to uplifted face, seeing concern on Web's

and intrigue on Cockle's. Some of the men reverted to being boys immediately, with boyish enthusiasm for testing
the unknown. Chade went down the ramp with his kettles and I followed with mine. He inspected the holes
that Dutiful and Longwick had caused to be dug. One he
wanted deepened and another he declined, requesting that
a new hole be dug close to the mouth of the caved-in tunnel. All would be in a row, along the deepest fractures that
the dragon had made in the ice. Here Chade judged the ice
to be weakest and that the powder would have the most ef-
ficacy. He chose six men to build the fires in the pots, and
Burrich walked slowly down the line of them, giving each
kindling and fuel and coals from his fire kettle. Then
Chade sent him out of the pit. Chade remained, moving
slowly from firepot to firepot, making sure that each was set
well in its hole in the ice and that the fire would have a
deep foundation of coals for the powder vessels to nestle
into. Several times as his chosen men were kindling the
fires in their pots, he repeated how these were actually
rather small doses of the powder, not enough to do harm to
the dragon, only enough to further crack the ice around
him so that we might move it more swiftly.

Each man stood as he judged that his pot was burning
well enough. In each case, Chade moved down the line,
added more fuel, and then sent the man up to stand with
the others at the edge of the excavation. Each container
of powder was left sitting on the ice, two spans away from
the fire. When Chade and I alone remained in the hole, he
came to me and spoke quietly. "I will join the others at the
edge of the pit. When I nod to you, move swiftly down
the kettles. Drop each container of powder into the kettle
that matches it. Then come quickly to join me. It will take
some little time for the fire to burn through to the powder,
but I judge it best that you do not linger here."

"And I."

He paused as if he would say something more, then
shook his head wordlessly at me. I wondered again if his

will warred with his action. Then I watched him climb up the ramp and join the row of men standing at the edge of the pit looking down at me. It struck me that the walls that had first divided us were gone. Hetgurders, guardsmen, and Wit coterie mingled. Burrich stood beside Chade. Swift was next to Web. Civil's Wit-cat was belly down on the ice, peering down at me curiously.

I took a deep breath, walked to the end of the row, and lifted the first powder vessel. I dropped it into the first burning kettle and sparks flew up around it. The second likewise; the third landed badly and had to be nudged deeper into the flames. I heard the watchers mutter as I did so. The fourth was easy. The fifth stuck to the ice and it seemed to take a year before it gave way to my tugging. Its lid came loose as it did so, and a small quantity of powder leaped from the mouth of it. I put the top back on and brushed it clean. As I set it into its firepot, the flames licked eagerly at the powder-smeared side, sparking and burning white. I reminded myself that quite a lot of time had elapsed before Chade's original flask had exploded in my fireplace. The sixth was as easy as the first, and then I gave in to my impulse and burst into a run. I fled up the ramp and joined the others on the edge of the pit. The fifth pot suddenly burst into a fountaining roar of flames, sparks, and sulfurous fumes. I heard gasps of amazement and fear from the watchers, but as I gained the lip of the pit, the leaping white fire grew less and subsided. The pot that had held it cracked loudly and we heard a hiss as melted water met fire.

When I reached Chade's side, he was shaking his head. "That is one wasted," he said tersely. "El's balls! I wish I'd had more time to test the powder and devise the right sort of container for it. But again, consider how the flame traveled up the powder to reach the main dose of it. Could we use that? I had believed that the powder had to be inside a vessel for it to—"

And then the first explosion went off. It wasn't in the first pot. I think it was the second, that perhaps that container had burned through more swiftly. It was hard to tell, for as shards and lumps of ice burst up from the floor of the pit and rained down around us, one of the other pots, or perhaps two, burst simultaneously.

The second blast was much louder than the first, deafening me. I had never experienced anything like it. The very air seemed to slap my skin and my ears felt as if they had been boxed. Fine ice stung my face. I blinked, thinking I'd been blinded, but it was a mist of impossibly fine snow hanging in the air.

Around me, men were yelling, deep-voiced cries of anger and dismay, as they retreated from the lip of the pit. Civil's terrified cat bolted past me, his master in frantic pursuit. From the buried dragon, I felt a wave of outrage. *We're trying to free you!* I Skilled at him, but felt no response. Beside me, Burrich gripped my shoulder and stared about frantically, his face twisted with panic.

I seized Burrich's arm to guide him back from the lip of the pit but he twisted free of me, crying, "Swift! Where is my son?" as the next explosion slapped the earth against our feet. I found myself driven to my knees and Burrich prone beside me. The air was thick with drifting crystalline ice, and Burrich choked and spat and shouted out, "Swift! Swift, where are you, boy?"

"I'm here, Papa!" the boy cried out, and he came bounding to us through the hanging fog, hurtling into Burrich's embrace. His eyes were huge.

"Thank Eda, you're safe! Stay close by me, now. Damn my eyes. Fitz, what is happening? I expected flame and sparks and smoke, not this! What has that madman done?"

"It's like a log bursting apart in the fire, Burrich, no more than that. The powder has burst, breaking the ice that surrounded it. I did not think it would be like this, but it's over now. Be calm." But even as I spoke the words, seeking to reassure myself as much as him, the earth heaved a second time under our feet. At the same moment, I felt a furious mental onslaught.

You will pay, you puny treacherous grubs! Your blood will be shed, a bucket for every loosened scale on his flesh. I come! Tintaglia's wrath is upon you! All of you will die!

"*We're trying to help him, not harm him!*" I flung the words wide, voice, Wit, and Skill. She made no reply.

But as I blinked the clinging mist of ice from my lashes and peered down into the pit, something stirred there. The settling flurry of ice crystals concealed it, but within that haze, something dark bucked and heaved, showing above the settling mist like a breaching whale. I heard the squeal and crack of breaking ice, and a smell came to me, a stench of trapped and scabrous flesh, a reptilian stench. I scrabbled to my feet and then ventured closer to the edge of the pit, peering down.

A slow and mammoth struggle was taking place down there. Parts of the dragon's emaciated back were exposed. His tail humped and twitched, almost a separate creature as it strove to free its lashing tip from the ice. One immense hind leg was free, the overgrown claws of the long-captive dragon scoring deep gashes in the ice as it strove to free the rest of its body. Then a wing unfolded, clumps of ice flung wide as it lifted like the tattered canvas of a derelict ship. It flapped desperately, and the waft of unhealthy animal gagged me. Icefyre struggled there, his head and neck still encased in ice. As the mist of ice crystals settled, the humans straggled back to the edge of the pit and stared down, some gawking, some transfixed with horror. Chade's face was a picture. I could not decide if his awe was for the destruction his powder had wrought or for the size of the creature he had partially bared.

Burrich spoke first. "That poor beast." He lifted both his hands, the fingers wide, and pushed gently at the air before him. So often I had seen him gesture as he approached an uneasy horse. Now I wondered if quelling calm emanated from his hands. He raised his voice suddenly. "He needs our help. Shovels and picks, but I want you all to go carefully. It would be as easy to harm him now as to help him. Don't encourage him to struggle." One hand clamped onto Swift's shoulder, and the other stretched out a little before him as he stumbled toward the edge of the pit. "Easy, easy down there," he was already calling, and his words, freighted with soothing Wit, were for the dragon. "We're coming. Still your struggles, you'll only hurt yourself. Or us. Be easy now. We'll help you."

Again, I was aware of the flow of comfort that went with those words. The dragon too seemed affected by them. Or perhaps it was exhaustion that made his struggles slow and then cease.

"Mind the edge of the pit, man. The ramp is this way. Swift, guide your father down there. We'll need him." Web's brow was bleeding from a glancing blow from a chunk of flung ice. He strode past us, unmindful of his own hurt, shovel in hand. For the first time, I became aware that the blast had injured some of us. One Hetgurd man was down, unconscious in the snow, blood trickling from his nose and ears. One of his fellows knelt by him in bewilderment. Civil had caught his hissing cat and held him in an awkward hug, trying to calm the struggling animal. I looked around for Dutiful, and saw him already hurrying down the ramp toward the trapped dragon, using a pry bar as a stave as he descended. The floor of the pit had been broken, reminding me of ice floes on a restless sea.

"My prince! Be careful! He may be dangerous!" Chade bellowed after him, and then he went hastening down the ramp and into the pit. Witted and unWitted alike converged on the trapped creature and began removing the loosened chunks of ice. It was hazardous, for the dragon continued to buck and heave as he struggled to free himself.

The stench was terrible. Starvation and dormant snake fouled the air. Burrich seemed unfazed by it as he stepped forward and then set his hands calmingly on the creature's black and scaly hide. "Be easy. Let us clear away the loosened ice before you struggle any more. Breaking a wing now will not help you."

He stilled. It was not Skill but Wit that carried to me the dragon's panicky suffocation. I sensed Icefyre's attention was focused elsewhere now, and suspected that he communicated with Tintaglia. I hoped he would tell her that we were trying to help him.

"We need to get his head free. He can't get enough air to struggle," Burrich told me as I came closer.

"I know. I feel it, too." I tried not to smirk as I added, "I am Witted, you know."

I had not realized that Swift would overhear me. Perhaps, because my ears were still ringing, I had spoken more loudly than I thought. But he stared at me, avid and intent. "Then you *are* FitzChivalry, the Witted Bastard. And it's true that my father raised you in the stables?" There was a strange lilt in his voice, as if he had suddenly discovered a link to fame and legend in his own family. I suppose he had, but I did not think it was healthy.

"We'll discuss it later," Burrich and I said at almost the same instant. Swift gaped at us and then gave a strangled laugh.

"Clear that loose ice from around his left shoulder," Web called as he strode by, and men hastened to obey him, Swift among them.

But Web halted beside us, pick in hand. A sharp motion of his hand halted Swift beside him. Quietly he observed to Burrich, "Later will not wait forever, for either of you. A time will come when both of you will have to explain yourselves to this lad." Yet his words were not a rebuke, and I almost thought that a small smile played across his face when he spoke to us. He bowed to Burrich and went on, "Forgive me if I offend. I know that your sight is failing you, but your shoulders and back still look strong. If your son guided you, you could be most useful helping to pull the sleds full of ice chunks away from the worksite. Would you help us, Burrich?"

I thought Burrich would refuse. I knew he still wished to avoid Web and all he stood for. But the request had been made courteously, and it was a way in which Burrich could be genuinely helpful. I could guess how it chafed him to stand by a trapped animal while others labored to free him. Web's offer was also putting Swift right at Burrich's side, under his paternal authority. I saw Burrich make a difficult compromise. He spoke, not to Web, but to Swift, saying, "Guide me to the sled, lad, and let's put our backs into it."

I was left standing alone as Swift and Burrich, father and son, departed to do Web's bidding. I watched them take up the hauling lines alongside Civil and Cockle. They leaned into their work, and despite Burrich's bad leg, his brawn was much the greatest there. The laden sled moved steadily up the ramp and out of the pit. It had been neatly done, that throwing together of them, and I think Burrich welcomed it as much as Swift did not. Did Web try to mend the rift between them, even as he sought to mellow Burrich's attitude toward the Wit?

I was still pondering the permutations of that when the final blast went off.

I now believe that the little kettle I had carelessly left burning when I retreated from the dragon's head had continued to burn. Did it eventually ignite the hides it rested upon, spreading fire to the oil flask and to the powder container? Or had the flask of oil spilled when the earlier, smaller blasts overset it on the hides near the powder and kettle? I have spent far too much time wondering about such useless questions.

It was a larger charge of powder, intended to kill. The explosion from it burst the icy roof of the tunnel up into the air at the same time that it blew loose chunks of ice out of the tunnel's mouth and into the pit where we all worked. Men and ice were flung in the slamming concussion of that blast. I myself was thrown across the excavation. In the wake of that blast, ice sharper than arrows rained down and pierced some of us. I felt the falling chunks, but all was white before me. I thought I had been blinded as well as deafened. Then the fine ice mist began to settle, revealing a soundless chaos. I saw Web stumbling past me, his hands clasped over his ears. I saw Eagle crumpled in a broken heap under immense chunks of ice. I saw men screaming but did not hear them. I wondered if I would ever hear anything ever again.

I lifted my eyes and saw Chade and Dutiful looking down in horror. They had not been in the pit, and an instant later I realized that the men dragging out the sleds would also have escaped the worst effects of the blast. But just as I found my feet and decided that none of my bones were broken, a second trembling shook me. The ground beneath me shifted, pieces of ice heaving beneath my feet, and new cracks gaped wide and then suddenly gave way. Black flesh heaved to the top through broken fragments of ice.

Free!

It was the most coherent thought I had received from Icefyre, and it was more a sensation of triumph than a word.

His immense black head lifted on a serpentine neck. His wings, half-opened, served him as additional limbs as he levered his way up out of the clinging ice. The sight of his long-trapped body woke pity in me, even in the midst of my horror at what had befallen my fellows. His flesh barely coated his bones, and his scaled skin was tattered and sagging like badly sewn garments. When he opened his wings, there were rents and gaps in them, a fine cloak snagged by brambles.

He wallowed up from the ice, pausing several times to roar and struggle to free a leg and then a wingtip. He was heedless of the men who lay dazed about him, but that did not reassure me, for his sudden great hunger radiated like heat from him. For the first time, I knew on an instinctive level that I was prey to this far larger predator. My words to him would have no more effect on his thoughts than the wild frenzy of a rabbit had on a wolf's thoughts. Nighteyes and I had never tried to speak to our meals while they were alive; neither would this creature. "Fool, what have you turned loose on this world?" I groaned.

The dragon gave another lurching heave and emerged more fully from the tumbled ice. His size only became more impressive as he did so. As Icefyre gained footholds on the shifting wreckage of his tomb, he drew his tail up and out of the ice. It just kept coming, impossibly long, until it lay around him on the broken surface like a whip's curled lash. He threw back his head suddenly and let out a wild cry that began as a deep roar and then climbed until it was beyond reach of my hearing. It was my first perception of sound since the blast, and it seemed a new sense to me as the creature's trumpeting shook the lungs inside my body.

Then I saw his nostrils flare, and his wedged head dipped down toward Eagle's body. Even though the man was dead, what was about to befall him appalled me. Icefyre nosed the body, dislodging it from the ice boulders that had crushed it. He lipped it carefully, and then lifted Eagle up and shook the remaining ice fragments from him, like Nighteyes worrying dead leaves from a fish. The dragon ate like a gull, tossing the meat that had been a man up into the air and opening his maw wide so that the falling body was halfway down his gullet before he gulped. Then Eagle was no more than a lump sliding down that long throat.

The wolf in me was nonjudgmental: a dead man might as well be meat as anything else, and the dragon had done no more than eat carrion. I myself had done it in times of great hunger, and had been glad to steal a share of a bear's kill while the owner slept off his gluttony. But Eagle had been a man and a leader of men, someone who had eaten beside me and met my eyes over a fireside. It upset my order in the world that he could suddenly be no more than food for this creature we had wakened.

In that instant, I dimly grasped the immense scale on which our actions had reordered the world. This was no dragon of stone, imbued with the souls of heroes, awakened to save us. This was a huge creature of flesh, with appetites and drives and the will to sate them for the sake of his own survival, with no regard for what it might cost us humans.

I lifted dazed eyes to look for escape. I was not immediately in front of Icefyre, but I was among his closest available prey. I was shocked to see the bleeding men who had staggered forward to line the edges of the pit and stare down in amazement at what we had freed. Burrich was there, his hand clamped on Swift's shoulder, and Cockle with his greedy minstrel's eyes and Civil. His cat by his knee was twice his normal size, every hair on his body standing up. I looked in vain for Chade and Dutiful and feared they had perished. I saw one booted foot not far from me, and hoped a body was still attached to it under the flung snow. Who was it? I saw Swift's arm lift, his finger pointing at me urgently as he spoke to Burrich, and then that great fool moved his mouth and I knew the words he shouted out, "Fitz! Fitz, get out of there, flee!"

And the dragon's head turned toward that shout. I saw his whirling eyes of silver and black focus on the man who had raised me, I saw his head lift at the end of that long neck, and "No!" I roared out, my own words little more than a whisper to my ears.

He seemed to know he had drawn the dragon's attention to himself, for Burrich turned and gave Swift a savage shove that sent him flying to sprawl facedown in the snow. He turned, weaponless, to face the dragon.

And then a second shock threw me from my feet. Suddenly the earth seemed to be giving way under me. Icefyre was also abruptly struggling to keep his footing. He spread his tattered wings wide and clawed at the edges of the pit. Men fled before him as he scrabbled at the edge of it and then hauled himself up out of it. As he did so, the ice beneath him fell away into a gaping hole. Even as I clung to the edges of the pit, some part of my mind recognized what had happened. His struggles to free himself and perhaps

Chade's exploding powder had weakened the ceiling of the Pale Woman's grand throne room. It was caving in on her. I savagely hoped she would be crushed under the fall. I looked down at the collapsing ice chunks, draining in ponderous boulders into the palace below. I wondered if some opening to the chamber below would suddenly be revealed, wondered if I could enter that way and survive such a fall amid the cascading ice and somehow free the Fool while he still lived. More likely was that the collapse of the ice ceiling into the chamber below would fill and obliterate it. A quick end for him, some part of me suggested, but I roared out, "No! No, no, no! Beloved Fool! No!"

As if in answer to my cry, something shifted in the ice below me. I stared at it, unable to comprehend the strength of whatever bucked and heaved beneath that avalanche. The movement subsided.

I clung to the icy ledge, and cried out in shock as Dutiful's hand suddenly gripped my wrist. "Come up!" he bellowed at me, and I suddenly knew he had been calling to me before this, trying to get my attention away from the fall of ice and the struggling dragon. Icefyre was almost free of the pit. The others seemed to have fled, save for two limp bodies that I could not identify.

I gave Dutiful my weight and he grunted as he took it, bracing to allow me to scrabble up the edge of the pit and out. "Where is Chade? We must flee!" I bellowed at him. He made a wide gesture that seemed to indicate that the others had fled downhill, toward the camp. Then he opened his mouth wide and then wider as his eyes popped from their sockets in terror. I twisted to look back over my shoulder, for he was staring down into the pit. In the bottom of the collapsed pit of ice, churning his way to the top like a toad emerging from an icy hibernation, was the Pale Woman's dragon. Life had imparted no grace to him. He was still a creature crudely carved and fashioned of many discordant lives, a murky gray color like unfired clay. My Wit sensed his roaring hunger. He was hollow with appetite and I knew he would devour anything within his reach. Then the blast of his Skill-thrust hit me, and I quailed before it. It was not just the hunger of a ravenous beast. One personality had come to dominate the dragon that wallowed and roared beneath us. I knew that she must have flung him to her stone dragon in a last wild effort to wake it. And the Pale Woman had succeeded.

Rawbread comes! I come to conquer and kill and devour. I hunger for farmers' flesh. Revenge shall be mine today! His gaze snagged on Icefyre. *Six Duchies dragon, today you die!* The stone dragon lunged, his great jaws closing on the base of Icefyre's tail. He braced his stubby legs and began to drag the black dragon back into the pit with him.

chapter XXV

DRAGONS

During the Red Ship War, many of the mothershouses paid unwilling tribute to Kebal Rawbread and the Pale Woman, in the form of a sacrifice of the males of their clans. Those who refused Rawbread's forced muster of their warriors were punished by what is called here in the Six Duchies "Forging." The Forging was mainly carried out against the women and female children of the clans. This left the males in an untenable position. The Forged females were a shame and a disgrace to the clan, yet no mothershouse could allow a male of the house to slay a female without exacting the same fate against him. It was better for the men to embark as warriors for Rawbread than to risk the complete destruction of their clan. The men who did eventually return to their mothershouses were changed creatures. Many of them apparently died in their sleep after the war. Some say their own mothershouse women poisoned them, for they no longer had the spirits of righteous sons.

                                                      ～ COCKLE'S "BRIEF HISTORY OF THE
OUT ISLANDS' RED SHIPS"

A blue and silver lightning bolt fell from the cloudless sky. She plunged directly into the pit, all lashing tail and darting head, her wide-held jaws revealing rows of daggerlike teeth. She landed on the dragon that had been Kebal Rawbread like a furious cat and her jaws closed on his neck just behind his blocky head. Her claws screeched and clattered over his scales as she sought to make good her grip on him and stay on top of his back. His shock at the attack broke his concentration on Icefyre. He opened his jaws to roar, and Icefyre jerked away from him.

Get clear of him. Clamber away, take flight. Do not seek to battle this one on the ground!

Sounds came from Tintaglia. It was not language, but meaning rode with the sounds and I perceived it as speech. I do not think that all humans there grasped that she spoke. Certainly Icefyre knew that she spoke to him, and he bugled back to her, but I did not grasp his meaning fully. Perhaps my earlier exposures to Tintaglia had increased my comprehension of her. Whatever the reason, I saw the ragged dragon clamber to the edge of the pit, away from the lashing tangle of true dragon and stone dragon below him. I knew Tintaglia could not hold Rawbread long. She was a female, and I suspected it was a disparity of gender that made her so much smaller than Icefyre.

The stone dragon was massive and blocky, thick where Tintaglia was slender and flexible, heavy where she was light. In comparison to Rawbread, she was an attacking falcon pitted against a bull. She was quickness itself, yet she could not seem to damage him. Her teeth had sunk into his neck, but I saw no flow of blood. The scoring of her powerful clawed hindquarters down his flanks left only white scratches, as if a boy had scraped one stone down another. He did not appear to take hurt from them. He shook himself heavily, trying to dislodge her, but she gripped him fast, futilely battling him with weapons that did him no harm. Her claws were a woman's fingernails pitted against a warrior's leather armor.

I wondered, did he have blood to shed? Or was he all stone animated by will?

And what could kill such a stone dragon? If his hide was impervious to a powerful creature like Tintaglia, what could stop him?

Wave after wave of Skilled hate emanated from Rawbread. I sensed his confusion and frustration as he tried to adapt to his unwieldy but powerful body. Quickened he might be, yet he was still somehow incomplete. His legs churned beneath him in the broken ice without propelling him from the pit. He unfolded one wing awkwardly but could not seem to flap it or even to tuck it back to his body. It remained outflung and useless. He whipped his heavy head ponderously from side to side in a futile effort to loosen the determined female.

Tintaglia's silver eyes rolled to watch Icefyre's progress. It was pitiably slow. He heaved himself out of the pit. When he rocked back onto his hind legs, the ravages of his long encasement in the ice were made even plainer. I could see his keeled breastbone through the sag of his scaly hide. He reminded me of a bird's carcass, all eaten away by ants. He lifted his ragged wings wide. When he shook them experimentally, a waft of stinking sickly animal washed past me. He limbered his long neck and lashed his tail several times, like a man settling himself into clothes he had long outgrown. He seemed to take his time to do all this, as if the struggle in the pit did not concern him at all. He nosed over his wings, almost like a bird preening. Then he extended his wings and rattled them like a beggar crow settling his feathers back into place. He flapped them once, slowly, and again, and then the third time he drove them down with a force that sent snow whisking away from him and wind whistling through the rents in them. Suddenly he leaned into his wings, his muscled hind legs driving him forward and up. He lifted from the ice heavily like an awkward seabird, but once his claws left the ground, it was as if he were released from its bonds. He rose steadily.

I caught a glimpse of Risk, circling high above us, and wondered how she must feel to see such an immense being rising toward her. Tintaglia, apparently deciding that Icefyre was now safely away from the awkward stone dragon, abruptly released her grip on Rawbread. She leaped, light as a lizard, into the air. Her silvery blue wings spread gracefully wide and in two beats of them she began to climb toward the sky.

Belatedly, Rawbread seemed to realize the attack on him had ceased. He threw back his head, roaring his hatred at us, then craned his neck to turn a mud-colored eye toward the sky. His neck was shorter and thicker than that of the true dragons. A rolling, viscous rumble came from his throat.

The Pale Woman's Skilling to him carried the force of fury. I was not the target of her thought and I felt but the brush of its passage yet had no problem discerning the message. Her power of Skill seemed less than it had been, as if the freeing of the dragon had exhausted her. She forced her thoughts through a quagmire of pain.

Kill the dragons, one of them, or both of them, but kill at least one! Never mind the humans. They cannot harm you. Later, you can devour them at your will. But for now, take your revenge on the Six Duchies. Kill their dragons, Rawbread!

And in that instant, he turned his heavy head and snapped at Tintaglia's tail, closing his rocky jaws on its lashing tip. It jerked her from the grace of flight into a wild fall. She cried out and I saw Icefyre tip his wings and felt his gaze sweep over the struggle on the ground. He tilted and then dived sharply. The stone dragon had finally mastered how to spread his wings and he sought at first to brake Tintaglia's flight, but in that awkward effort, some vague idea of how to use them seemed to come to him. Never relinquishing his hold on Tintaglia's tail, he beat his wings savagely, making abortive lunges into the air. The struggling queen dragon was jerked about like a kite on a string. She screamed, shrill as a sword being drawn, and suddenly coiled back to attack her attacker. It was a mistake. For all her size, she was a butterfly battering herself against a lizard. The wind of her wildly fluttering wings sprayed icy snow into my face and drove me down, but did not impress Rawbread at all. He buffeted her with his heavy wings, slamming blows that sounded heavy slaps like a slaughter-house hammer against her flesh.

He would kill her.

An instant later, the consequence of that thought came to me. The Pale Woman would still have won. Despite all, she would have put an end to dragons in the world. And no man could stop it from happening now. If Tintaglia's claws had not even scored the stone dragon's flesh, what could any weapon of ours do against him?

A lifetime had passed in a heartbeat. I became aware of the Prince standing frozen beside me and cursed my fool-ishness. I shook him and bellowed, "Get out of here! There's nothing we can do. Run!"

And still he stood and gaped, transfixed by the battle before us.

Then Icefyre struck, a bolt of black lightning. The force of that immense body striking the stone dragon shook the earth like one of Chade's explosions. Dutiful and I were flung to the earth. When I managed to get to my knees and clear my eyes, Tintaglia was clear of the battle. She crawled away from it, wings and feet dragging her across the snowy ground. Where her thick blood fell on the snow, it smoked. My Wit sensed the waves of pain that flowed from her. I do not think she had ever felt such agony; the outrage and horror of it stunned her.

Impossibly, the two battling males rose, clawing and flapping, from the pit of tumbled ice. The battering force of their wingbeats drove the Prince and me to our knees over and over again as we stumbled and fought to get clear of their combat. I dragged Dutiful back, shouting, "If a stone dragon overshadows you for long, he can Forge you! We must flee!" Then the force of the wind from their wings lessened. Dutiful stumbled as I thrust him away from me, but I halted and looked back. And up.

Locked in battle, yet still they rose, wings beating almost in unison. It appeared a strange and twisting dance they performed, claws seeking grips and their heads repeatedly striking like darting snakes. But it was the strength of Icefyre's battered wings that bore them up more than the stone dragon's efforts. Clenched together, they rose screaming, until they were black silhouettes in the blue sky.

"Fitz! Look!" Dutiful's shout was a whisper to my buffeted, ringing ears, but I could not ignore the way he shook me. The idiot had come back. He was pointing down into the pit full of collapsed ice. There was a small opening at one end of it where the sliding ice had not quite filled the palatial chamber beneath it. A small gap remained open. Coming up that tumbled and shifting slope of ice was Elliania. She gripped a shrieking, struggling girl by the chains about her wrist and dragged her behind her as she determinedly plowed her way up toward us. The girl's hair was matted to her head with filth and a ragged shift barely covered her, but for all that, the family resemblance was strong. Elliania had captured her sister. Peottre was behind her, half-crawling as he emerged from the hole. A drawn and bloody sword was in his hand, and he towed a limp and emaciated woman behind him. Blood from a scalp wound sheeted one side of his face. As soon as he could stand, he seized the woman and tried to race up the slope, but the treacherous chunks of ice shifted and slid under his feet. He gained a span or two and then went down on one knee. He was breathing in gasps as if he were nearly at the end of his strength. As we watched, he suddenly dropped his sister to the ground and turned to face his pursuers as they emerged on their hands and knees from the hole. Oerttre Blackwater fell limply, unconscious or dead, and began to slide back down toward the gap.

Elliania had reached us. She glanced back and shrieked as she saw Peottre brought to bay. "Hold this!"

she commanded Dutiful, and flung the chain at him. He caught it by reflex, gaping at his disheveled intended. Blood had run from one of her nostrils, outlining that side of her mouth in a caked line, and her wild hair hung loose around her face. Then she spun from him, short-sword in her hand, and charged back toward Peottre. Dutiful was left gripping the Forged girl's chain.

"Hold this!" Dutiful suddenly echoed her and flung the chain at me. It fell to the earth before I could catch it, but I stepped forward to trap it under my foot before she could flee. But she didn't wish to flee. Instead, she flung herself at me, mouth gaping wide. To my Wit, she wasn't there, but as I caught her and tried to fend off her attack, my flesh felt the impact of her blows. I have fought many men, but never had I reckoned on dealing with an emaciated ten-year-old girl with absolutely no fears or concerns for her own survival. Teeth and nails and knees, she sought determinedly to rip or pound my flesh from my bones, and made some fair headway at doing so, clawing my face and sinking her teeth into my wrist before I managed to fling her down in the snow. I covered her with my body, pressing her to the ice until I could roll her onto her belly. I reached under her and seized her elbows and then jerked her back against me, so that her arms were crossed on her own chest. She continued to kick at me, but she was barefoot and the heavy leather of my trousers muted those blows. She ducked her head then and seized my sleeve in her teeth, worrying it as if it were prey, but good wool was all she gripped, so I let her chew at it. When her biting did not bring her release, she flung her head back, thudding it against my chest. It was not pleasant, but as long as I kept my chin up, I could withstand it.

Having so bravely immobilized my scrawny opponent, I craned to see what was happening below me. In the pit of sliding snow, Elliania had reached her mother. She crouched over Oerttre, blade ready, her last line of defense as Peottre fought two of the Pale Woman's dead-eyed guards. I did not know if Elliania was poised to hold off attackers or deal her mother's death blow before she could be taken again. For a heart-stopping moment, I could not see Dutiful. Then I caught a glimpse of him past Peottre. He stood squarely in the mouth of the hole from which the Narcheska and Peottre had emerged. His knife was red and whoever was down there was not getting past him.

We are attacked! Chade's Skilled warning reached me at the same moment that shouts turned my head. I looked down toward our camp. From somewhere, the Pale Woman's minions had appeared, to fall upon our reduced and rattled party. It looked as if they were trying to prevent anyone from going to Tintaglia's aid, though none of them were yet brave enough to attack the fallen dragon. I had a glimpse of my old mentor as I had never before seen him. Feet braced, blade in hand, Chade stood beside Longwick. Thick crouched behind them, wailing, his arms wrapped protectively over his head.

Thick! Push at them, like you push at me! Not all of them will give way, but some will. Fight back! Tell them, Go away, and don't see us! Please, Thick! Despair washed over me as I gripped the still-struggling girl to me. I dared not let her go, but while I held her, I was useless to do anything else.

Thick had not reacted to my suggestion, I thought. And then, I saw the little man lift one of his arms and peer out like a fearful child. Then I felt a faint wash of the Skill he directed at their attackers.

Go away, go away, go away, go away!

I saw at least two of the Pale Woman's warriors do just that, abruptly turning their backs on the battle and striding away as if they had suddenly remembered urgent business elsewhere. Several others seemed to lose the momentum of their attacks, reduced to defending themselves as they suddenly wondered why they were there and attacking us.

Do it again, Thick! Help me! I could feel Chade's failing wind in that Skilling. His sword weighed as much as the earth, and he had never liked seeing a man's eyes when he killed him. Then I felt a red wash of pain as a blade slipped up the top of his forearm. I saw Thick spring back, gripping his own arm.

Chade! Block your pain! Thick is feeling it. Thick! Tell the pain to go away. Give it to the bad men. You can do it!

Then a buffet of wind from above me made me crouch like a field mouse that feels the wash of an owl's wings above him. The dragons were back, fighting in terrible silence save for the battering rush of their wings and the dull impacts they dealt to one another. They had soared high, locked in their frenzy. Cowering, I stared up at them and thought I knew Rawbread's strategy. He clung to Icefyre, his jaws clenched on the back of the other dragon's neck. Icefyre was expending most of his energy in an effort to stay aloft. Well he knew he could not hope to defeat the stone dragon on the ground. The frailer dragon twisted and writhed, trying to escape the stone dragon's deadly grip.

They could come down on top of us!

"Get out of there!" I roared down at Dutiful. "The dragons are falling!"

Dutiful looked up, startled, and then leaped back to avoid his opponent's blade. The Prince shouted something toward Peottre and the Narcheska. Peottre had finished one of his men and the other was retreating from him. The Narcheska seized her mother's ankle and began to drag her out of the pit, all the while keeping her blade at the ready. I reached a hand to her as she got closer to me, then seized her by her sword wrist and hauled her up and over the edge of the pit. She dragged her mother gracelessly behind her. An instant later, I had to make good my grip on her little sister again as she spat and struggled. Elliania dragged her mother away from the edge and then screamed, "Get out of there! They're falling!"

She was right. The dragons were a struggling knot that was plummeting larger and larger toward us. Dutiful and Peottre both fled their battles, the treacherous ice tumbling and sliding under their feet as they struggled to move uphill and out of the collapsed pit. Elliania, dragging her mother by her ankles, was beating her own retreat, desperately shrieking at Dutiful and Peottre to hurry, hurry. I stooped, seized the little girl, and followed her. I knew there was nothing else I could do and yet I felt a coward as I ran. Then, his boots pounding the ice, Dutiful passed me. He reached the Narcheska, and stooping, scooped up her mother and threw her across his shoulders. A moment later, Peottre's hand fell heavily on my shoulder, pushing me faster as we fled together. The shadows of the falling dragons spread wider around us. I felt stupefied and dizzy for a moment, and then staggered on. We caught up to Dutiful and the women. Elliania pointed upward wordlessly.

Icefyre had shaken free of Rawbread. His frantically beating wings bore him higher and higher as Rawbread plummeted gracelessly back toward the earth, his outspread wings able to do little more than break the force of his heavy body's descent.

The crash of his impact shook the icy earth. He had landed half in the pit and half on the edge where I had been standing but moments before. I hoped he was dead, but he slowly rolled to his feet and shook out his wings. His blunt head quested on his thick neck, turning this way and that. Then like a squat lizard digging his way out of mud, his powerful limbs moved and he crawled out of the pit on his belly, his tail lashing angrily as it churned the snow behind him. He seemed to stare right at me and my entrails turned to ice in that glare. Then, like a sharply reined horse, he flung back his head and shook it in frustration. His eyes, lackluster in contrast to Tintaglia's whirling silver, looked past me and fixed on the downed female dragon. He diverted from us and lumbered toward her, snorting angrily. I became aware of the Pale Woman's Skilled exhortations to him to kill the female and all would be well, that he then could sate his anger and hunger as he pleased. But first, kill the female. Nothing stood between him and triumph now. She could not fight him.

But the Pale Woman was wrong. My heart fell as I perceived that Tintaglia still had two defenders. Blind Burrich stood next to the dragon, his folded cloak pressed hard to her neck as he sought to quell her bleeding. The smoking of the fabric made me wonder of what stuff dragon blood was made. Burrich was intent on his task, and Tintaglia's head on her long neck was coiled back protectively toward her body. They both seemed unaware of the lumbering death that made his ponderous way down the hill toward them.

But Swift was not. He stood before her, an ant protecting a castle. The Fool's brightly painted arrow flew from his bow, to splinter uselessly against the stone dragon. Undaunted, he drew another from his quiver, nocked it and drew it back. From some reserve of courage that seemed too large for such a small boy to contain, he took two steps forward, toward the dragon. He let fly again, with as futile a result. Still, he stood his ground as he pulled out yet another arrow. To reach Tintaglia, Rawbread would have to trample him. I saw Swift call a warning back to his father over his shoulder. An arrow was set to Swift's bow. And all I could do was watch helplessly as the stone dragon's relentless gaze fixed on the boy. Abruptly, Rawbread broke into a clumsy gallop. Swift looked up at his death and his mouth stretched wide in a scream that was both terror and defiance. His bow shook in his hands, the head of the gray arrow wobbling wildly, but he stood his ground.

Burrich lifted his head. He turned. Even now, I recall every instant of that moment. I saw him draw breath and heard through the ringing of my ears the deep roar of his outrage that anything would threaten his son.

I had never seen him move so swiftly. He threw himself toward Swift and the dragon, his boots throwing up clumps of snow as he ran. Tintaglia lifted her head slightly, feeble witness to his charge. Then Burrich was between his boy and the dragon, drawing his belt knife as he ran. It was the most ridiculous and the most courageous attack I've ever witnessed. As he sprang to meet the suddenly bewildered dragon's charge, he drew back his knife. I saw the blade splinter as he drove it against the stony flesh. At the same moment, I felt the blast of Wit *repel* that he leveled at the creature. It was like one of Chade's explosions. It was the fierceness of a stallion defending his herd, the savagery of a wolf or bear that protects its cubs, compounded more from love of what he protected than hatred of what he battled. It was targeted at the dragon, and the prodigious force of that blast dropped the stone beast to his knees.

But as Rawbread fell, a wild flap of his heavy wing swatted Burrich, flinging the man to one side as if he were nothing. His body spun as he flew. "No!" I cried, but it was done. He hit the frozen snow badly, bending like a flung rag doll, and then skidding away across the ice, spinning as he went. Rawbread lumbered back onto his clawed black feet. He shook his heavy head and I saw him gasp for breath. Then he advanced, openmouthed, on both Swift and Tintaglia.

Swift had turned his head to watch the shattering of his father's body. Now he turned back to the dragon, and the roar that stretched his mouth wide was hatred, pure and simple. With that strength, he drew his bowstring back and back, until I thought the bow itself would splinter. I saw him become his arrow as he locked eyes with the dragon lumbering toward him.

He let his shaft fly.

True as a father's love, the shining gray missile flew. It struck the dragon's eye and sank in, nearly vanishing. I saw Rawbread begin to lift a forefoot to paw at it. Then he halted abruptly, as if listening to someone. I was aware of the Skill the Pale Woman directed at him, as she hysterically commanded him to finish it, kill the bowman, kill the she-dragon, and then he could do whatever he wished, whatever he wished at all. I thought Rawbread paused to listen to her. But he did not move again. The drab color of life fled his skin, as a dull patina of stone settled over him.

He remained as he was, wings half-lifted, forepaw about to claw the arrow from his eye, jaws agape. A silence of disbelief settled over the whole battle. The stone dragon was dead.

An instant later, the girl in my arms came back to life. My Wit-sense of her blossomed into full bloom. She had stopped struggling at the moment of the dragon's death. Now she suddenly curled into my arms. "I'm so cold. I'm so hungry," she wailed, and then, as I looked down in astonishment at her, she burst into childish tears.

"A moment, a moment," I told her, and hated that I had to set her little bare feet down on the snow. I tore Chade's cloak from my body and settled it around her. It came all the way down to her toes, and as I picked her up again, she pulled her feet up into it gratefully, huddling into a shivering ball in my arms. "Give her to me, give her to me!" Peottre demanded. Tears were streaming down his face, cutting through the blood.

"Oh, little fish, oh, my Kossi! Elliania, look, look, our Kossi has come back to us. She is herself!" The old warrior turned to his niece, and then as if joy had drained his strength from him, he fell to his knees, holding the child to his chest and murmuring over her.

Elliania looked over at us, her heart in her eyes, and then looked down at the woman who sprawled in the snow at her feet. She dropped to her knees by her mother and her tears came as she said, "We saved one of them. At least we saved one of them. Mother, I did my best. We tried so hard."

Dutiful looked over at her from where he knelt on the other side of the woman. Gentle as a nurse, he pushed the filthy hair back from her emaciated face. "No. You saved both of them. She's unconscious, Elliania, but she's back, too. I can feel her with my Wit-sense. Your mother has come back to you, too."

"But...how can you know this?" She stared down at the woman's face, not daring yet to hope.

Dutiful smiled at her. "I promise you, I know this is so. It's an old Farseer magic, a gift of my father's lineage." He stooped again to take up the lax woman. "Let's get her to warmth and shelter. And food. The battle seems to be over, for now."

They all just stopped fighting when the dragon died, Chade confirmed for me as I stood and peered out over the battlefield below us. *It was as if they all just suddenly lost heart.*

No. They regained it. It's hard to explain, Chade, but I feel it with the Wit. Her servants were partially Forged, but with the dragon's death, all that was taken and put into him came back to them. The same thing happened to the Narcheska's mother and sister. They're no longer Forged. Have the Outislanders speak to those we fought. Offer them food and welcome. And comfort them. They may be very confused.

I allowed my eyes to wander over the battlefield below me, and saw the truth of my own thought. The Pale Woman's soldiers, to a man, had dropped their weapons. One man stood, his hands clapped over his ears, weeping. Another had seized one of his fellows by the shoulder and was laughing wildly as he spoke to him. A small group of men stood clustered around the stone dragon. Lifeless, it had settled unevenly into the glacier, an ugly statue set awry.

But strangest of all was that Tintaglia had come to her feet. She walked stiff-legged as a stalking cat toward the stone dragon. Cautiously, she extended her head on her gracile neck. She sniffed the monster, nosed it cautiously, and then without warning, struck it a ringing blow with her clawed forepaw. The stone dragon rocked stiffly in the snow but did not fall over. Nonetheless, Tintaglia lifted her head high on her long neck and trumpeted her triumph over her foe. Blood might still ooze from the bites and scratches he had dealt her, but she claimed victory as hers. And around her, men raised their voices to join their cries of triumph to hers. If ever there had been a stranger sight

than this dragon celebrating amidst human cheering, then
no minstrel has ever told it.

From high above, a trumpeting call echoed hers. Battered and tattered, Icefyre circled in a wide spiral above us.
He banked his wings and slid down the sky, swooping over
us in a lower circuit. On the ground, Tintaglia threw back
her head and bugled again. Around her throat, panels of
her scales suddenly stood up like a mane and a crest on her
head, scarcely noticeable before, stood erect and silver like
a crown. A wash of color went over her, from deepest blue
to brightest silver. The men who had gathered around her
drew back. When she leaped from the ground to the air it
was effortless in the manner of a cat floating from the floor
up to a tabletop. Her wings opened as she sprang, and with
three beats of them she was climbing.

Icefyre immediately tipped his wings and stroked them
frantically, but the female easily outdistanced him as they
climbed. He trumpeted after her lustily, but she did not
bother to reply. Her wings carried her up and up, until to
my straining eyes she might have been a silver gull winging
overhead. Icefyre, almost twice her size, starved and tattered, battered his way through the sky in pursuit of her. I
blinked as they passed before the sun.

Then they were spiraling together. His deep cries were
a challenge to all the world, but her higher calls were a defiance and mockery of him alone. He was above her for a
moment, and then she tipped her wings and slid away from
him. So I thought. Instead he clapped his wings to his body
and fell upon her, his wide-open jaws so scarlet that even at
that distance I perceived it before his teeth clamped onto
her outstretched neck. Then his larger wings overshadowed hers, and suddenly their beating synchronized. He
pulled her tight against him, his longer tail wrapping hers
as he arched around her.

I knew what I witnessed. By that mating flight, there
would be dragons in our skies again. I stared up at that

wonder, at their casual flaunting of their return to life, and wondered what we had restored to the world.

"I do not understand!" the Narcheska exclaimed in horror. "She came all this way to save him and now he attacks her. Look at them fight!"

Dutiful cleared his throat. "I don't think they're fighting."

"Then . . . Yes they are! Look how he bites her! Why does he seize her like that, if not to hurt her?" Elliania shaded her eyes with one hand as she looked up in wonder at them. Her dark hair fell tangled down her shoulders and back and her uplifted chin bared the long straight column of her neck. Her tunic strained over her breasts. Dutiful made a small sound in his throat. He lifted his eyes from looking at her and his gaze went from me to Peottre. Her uncle had one arm around his sister's shoulders and held Kossi in his other. I think the Prince decided that our opinion of the matter no longer concerned him. He stepped closer to Elliania and took her in his arms. "I'll show you," he said to her astonishment. He clasped her firm and close, and lowered his mouth to hers.

Despite all that had befallen me that day, despite every loss I had sustained, I found myself smiling. That which surged between the dragons above must affect any man sensitive to the Skill. The Narcheska broke the kiss at last. Lowering her brow to his shoulder, she laughed softly. "Oh," she said. Then she lifted her face again to be kissed. I looked aside.

Oerttre did not. She was scandalized. Despite her rags and filth, her reaction was regal. "Peottre! You allow a farmer to kiss our narcheska?"

He laughed aloud. I was shocked to realize it was the first time I'd ever heard the man laugh. "No, my sister. But she does, and she allots to him what he has earned. There is much explaining to do yet. But I promise you, what happens there is not against her will." He smiled. "And what is a man that he should oppose the will of a woman?"

"It is not proper," Oerttre replied primly, and despite

her stained dress and caked hair, her words were that of a narcheska of the Out Islands. It struck me how completely she had come back to herself.

Abruptly it came to me that if the Fool still lived, then with the dragon's death, whatever Forging had been done to him would have come undone as well. Wild hope leaped in me and the world lurched around me. "The Fool!" I exclaimed, and then when Peottre looked at me in disapproval, to see if I mocked the Prince, I clarified, "The tawny man. Lord Golden. He might yet live!"

I turned and ran over the crusted snow. I reached the edge of what had been our pit and tried to find a safe way down into it. The upheaval of the dragons had made it a treacherous place. The opening that Peottre and the Narcheska had emerged from was gone. Rawbread's final landing in the side of the pit and his struggles to get out of it had obscured that gap into the Pale Woman's palace. But I knew where it had been and surely, surely, it could not be buried that deeply. I set out down the unstable slope, trying to hurry and yet keep my footing as the broken ice crunched and then cascaded past me. I halted and forced myself to walk more carefully. I picked my way down the sliding slope, hating the delay. Every chunk of ice I dislodged now was yet another I must move. The opening had been at the deepest end of the pit. I was nearly to it when I heard someone call my name. I halted and looked over my shoulder. Peottre stood at the edge of the excavation, looking down on me. He shook his head, his eyes full of pity. He spoke bluntly.

"Give it up, Badgerlock. He's dead. Your comrade is dead. I'm sorry. We saw him when we were searching the cells for our people. I had promised myself that if he were still alive, we would try to steal him, too. But he wasn't. We were too late. I'm sorry."

I stood staring up at him. Suddenly I couldn't see him. The contrast between the brightness of the day and his dark silhouette seemed to blind me. Cold crept up me, followed by a wave of numbness. I thought I would faint. I sat down very slowly in the ice. I hated the stupid words that came from my mouth. "Are you sure?"

Peottre nodded, and then said reluctantly, "Very sure. They had—" He stopped speaking suddenly. When he resumed, he said flatly, "He was dead. He could not have lived through that. He was dead." He took a breath and then sighed it out slowly. "They are calling for you, down at the camp. The boy, Swift, he is with the dying man. They want you there."

The dying man. Burrich. He jolted back into my thoughts like one of Chade's explosions. Yes. I would lose him, too. It was too much, far too much. I put my face down in my hands and curled up, rocking back and forth in the snow. Too much. Too much.

"I think you should hurry." Blackwater's voice reached me from some distant place. Then I heard someone else say quietly, "You go tend to your own people. I'll see to mine."

I heard someone working his way down the slope of ice to me, but I didn't care. I just sat there, trying to die, trying to let go of a life where I failed everyone I cared about. Then a hand fell heavily on my shoulder and Web said, "Get up, FitzChivalry. Swift needs you."

I shook my head childishly. I would never, never, let anyone depend on me again.

"Get up!" he said more sternly. "We've lost enough people today. We're not going to lose you, too."

I lifted my head and looked up at him. I felt Forged. "I was lost a long time ago," I told him. Then I took a deep breath, stood up, and followed him.

chapter XXVI

HEALINGS

The Chalcedean practice of tattooing one's slaves with a
special mark of ownership began as a fashion among the
nobility. In the early days of it, only the most valuable
slaves, slaves one expected to own for a lifetime, were so
marked. The custom seems to have escalated when Lord
Grart and Lord Porte, both powerful nobles in the
Chalcedean court, entered a rivalry to display their
wealth. Jewelry, horses, and slaves were the measure of
wealth at that time, and Lord Grart chose to have all of
his horses prominently branded and all of his slaves
tattooed. Ranks of both accompanied him everywhere he
went. It is said that Lord Porte, in imitation of his rival,
actually bought hundreds of cheap slaves of little or no
standing as craftsmen or academics, simply for the
purpose of tattooing them as his and displaying them.

At that time in Chalced, some slave craftsmen and
artisans and courtesans were allowed by their masters to
accept outside commissions. Occasionally one of these
privileged slaves would earn enough to purchase his
freedom. Many masters were understandably reluctant
to let such valuable slaves go. As tattoos of ownership
could not be removed from the slave's face without
substantial scarring, and freedom papers were widely

*falsified, it was difficult for former slaves to prove they
had earned their freedom. Slave owners took advantage
of this by creating expensive "freedom rings," earrings of
gold or silver, often with jewels, the design unique to
each noble family, that indicated a particular slave had
earned his freedom. Often it took a slave years of
service, after he had bought his freedom, to purchase the
expensive earring that showed he was truly free to move
about Chalced as he pleased, on his own recognizance.*

         FEDWREN'S "HISTORY OF CHALCED'S
SLAVE CUSTOMS"

I am no stranger to the aftermath of battle. I've walked
across bloody earth and stepped over hacked bodies. Yet
never before had I been in a place where the futility of war
was so clearly illustrated. Warriors bound up the wounds
they had dealt to one another, and Outislanders who had
fought us now anxiously asked the Hetgurd men for news
of relatives and clan lands left years ago. Like men waked
from a legendary sleep they were, groping after lost lives,
trying to cross a rift of years. It was too clear that they well
remembered all that they had done as servants of the Pale
Woman. I recognized one of the guards who had dragged
me before her. He looked hastily aside from my gaze, and I
did not confront him. Peottre had already told me the only
thing I needed to know.

I made my way through our camp. With an almost un-
seemly haste, it was being struck. Two badly injured men,
both from the Pale Woman's force, were already loaded
on the sleds, and the tents were coming down. A hasty
ice cairn was being assembled over three dead men. All of
them had belonged to her. Icefyre had eaten Eagle, the
Hetgurd man who had fallen to the dragon. There would be
no entombment for him. The other two men we had lost,
Fox and Deft, had already been buried in the collapse of the
pit. No sense digging them up only to bury them again, I

suppose. It seemed a hasty and irreverent way to leave our fallen, but I sensed the emotion that drove it. There was an aura of haste to this departure, as if the sooner we could leave this place, the faster the Pale Woman would become a creature of the past. I hoped that she too was entombed beneath the immense fall of ice.

❧   ❧   ❧

Web walked beside me and Chade came hurrying to meet me. Someone had bandaged his arm. "This way," he told me, and led me to where Burrich lay in the snow. Swift knelt beside him. They had not tried to move him. There was a wrenching wrongness to how his body lay. The spine is not meant to twist like that. I dropped to my knees beside him, surprised to find his eyes open. His hand spidered feebly against the snow. I slipped mine underneath it. He was breathing shallowly, as if hiding from the pain lurking in the lower half of his body. He managed a single word. "Alone."

I looked at Web and Chade. Without a word, they withdrew. Burrich's eyes met Swift's. The boy looked stubborn. Burrich took a slightly deeper breath. There was a color in his skin around his mouth and eyes, a strange darkening. "Just a moment," he said huskily to his son. Swift bowed his head slightly and walked away from us.

"Burrich," I said, but an almost sharp movement of his hand against mine bade me stop.

I saw him gather the remnants of his strength. He paced himself, taking a breath for each phrase he uttered. "Go home," he said. And then, commanding me, "Take care of them. Molly. The lads." I started to shake my head as he asked the impossible of me, and for a moment his hand tightened on mine, a shadow of his old grip. "Yes. You will. You must. For me." Another breath. He furrowed his brow, as if making an important choice. "Malta and Ruddy. When she comes in season. Not Brusque. Ruddy." He wagged one finger at me, as if I had thought to argue that decision. He took a deeper breath. "Wish I would see that foal." He blinked his eyes slowly, then, "Swift," he said, painfully.

"Swift!" I shouted and saw the loitering boy lift his head and start to run back to us.

Just before he reached us, Burrich spoke again. He almost smiled as he said, "I was the better man for her." A breath. In a whisper, "She still would have chosen you. If you'd come back."

Then Swift flung himself to his knees in the snow beside Burrich and I gave my place over to him. Chade and Web had come back with a heavy blanket. Web spoke. "We're going to try to scoop out the snow under you and sling you in the blanket to put you on the sled. The Prince has already released the bird that will summon the ships to fetch us back to Zylig."

"Doesn't matter," Burrich said. His hand closed on Swift's as he shut his eyes. A few moments later, I saw his hand go lax.

"Move him now," I suggested. "While he's unconscious."

I helped them, digging in the snow under Burrich's body and sliding the blanket beneath him. Despite our efforts to be gentle, he moaned as we moved him, and my Wit-sense of him faded a notch. I said nothing of that but I am sure that Swift was as aware of it as I was. The situation didn't need words. We loaded him onto the sled with the other two injured men. Just before we left that place, I looked up into the clear sky, searching. But there was no sign of either dragon.

"Not even a thank-you," I commented to Web.

He shrugged wordlessly and we set out.

For the rest of that day, I either walked beside Burrich or took turns pulling the sled. Swift walked always where he could see his father, but I do not think Burrich's eyes opened again that day. Thick rode on the tail of the sled, huddled in a blanket and staring. Kossi and Oerttre rode on the other sled, well bundled against the cold. Peottre pulled it, humming a tune as he trudged along, while the Narcheska and Dutiful walked alongside it. They were in front of us. I could not hear what the Narcheska was telling her mother, but I could guess. Her eye, when it fell on Dutiful, was slightly less disapproving, but mostly her gaze lingered on her daughter, with pride. The remaining Hetgurd men led us, probing the snow for cracks as we went. Web and then Chade came to walk alongside me for a time. There was nothing to say and that was what we said.

I counted it up to myself, mostly because I could not stop my mind from doing so. My prince had led here one dozen men plus Swift and Thick. Six Hetgurd men had come to oversee us. Twenty in all. Plus the Fool and Burrich. Twenty-two. The Pale Woman had killed Hest and Riddle and the Fool. Burrich was dying from the injury her dragon had dealt him. Eagle had died in the rain of ice from Chade's explosion. Fox and Deft were likewise lost. Sixteen of us would return to Zylig. Assuming that Churry and Drub had survived on the beach alone. I drew a deep breath. We were bringing the Narcheska's mother and sister home. Surely that counted for something. And eight Outislanders would be going back to their homes, men their families had long believed dead. I tried to feel some sort of satisfaction, but could not find it. This last and briefest battle of the Red Ship War had been the most costly to me.

Peottre called a halt in the gray of evening and we made a quiet camp. We used two of the tents to erect a makeshift shelter around the sled that the injured men were on so we would not have to move them. The other two were able to speak and eat, but Burrich was still and quiet. I brought Swift food and drink, and sat with him for a time, but after a while, I sensed that he wished to be alone with his father. I left him there and went out to walk under the stars.

There is no true dark to a night in that land. Only the

brightest of the stars showed. The night was cold and the constant wind blew, heaping loose snow against the shelters. I could not think of anywhere I wanted to be or anything I wanted to do. Chade and the Prince were crowded into the Narcheska's tent with Peottre's family. There was triumph and rejoicing there; both were foreign emotions to me. The Hetgurd men and the recovered Outislanders were having a reunion of sorts. I walked past a tiny fire where Owl was matter-of-factly burning a dragon-and-serpent tattoo off a man's forearm. The smell of roasting flesh rode the wind while the man grunted and then roared with the pain. Dutiful's Wit coterie, sans Swift, had also crammed themselves into a small tent. I heard Web's deep voice as I went past and caught the gleam of a cat's eye peering out. Doubtless they shared the Prince's triumph. They had freed the dragon and he'd won the Narcheska's regard.

Longwick sat alone before a small fire in front of a darkened tent. I wondered where he had got the brandy I smelled. I nearly walked past him with a silent nod, but something in his face told me that here was where I belonged tonight. I hunkered down and held my hands over the tiny fire. "Captain," I greeted him.

"Of what?" he retorted. He rolled his head back with a crackling sound, and then sighed. "Hest. Riddle. Deft. Doesn't say much for me that all the men who accompanied me here are dead and I still live."

"I'm still alive," I pointed out to him.

He nodded. Then he gestured with his chin toward the tent and said, "Your half-wit's in there, asleep. He looked a bit lost tonight, so I took him in."

"Thanks." I knew a moment of guilt, and then asked myself if I should have left Burrich to tend Thick. And reflected that perhaps having someone to oversee had been the best thing for Longwick. He shifted, and then offered me a brandy flask. It was a soldier's flask, dented and scratched, his own hoard of spirits, and a gift to be respected. I drank from it sparingly before returning it to him.

"Sorry about your friend. That Golden fellow."

"Yes."

"You went back a ways."

"We were boys together."

"Were you? Sorry."

"Yes."

"I hope that bitch died slow. Riddle and Hest were good men."

"Yes." I wondered if she had died at all. If she were still alive, could she be any threat to us? Dragon, Rawbread, and Forged servants had all been taken from her. She was Skilled, but I could think of no way she could use that against all of us. If she was alive, she was as alone as I was. Then I sat for a time, wondering which I hoped: whether she was dead or alive and suffering? Finally, it came to me. I was too tired to care.

Some time later, Longwick asked me, "Are you really him? Chivalry's Bastard?"

"Yes."

He nodded slowly to himself, as if that explained something. "More lives than a cat," he said quietly.

"I'm going to bed," I told Longwick.

"Sleep well," he said, and we both laughed bitterly.

I found my pack and bedding and took it into Longwick's tent. Thick stirred slightly as I made my bed alongside him. "I'm cold," he mumbled.

"Me, too. I'll sleep against your back. That will help."

I lay down in my blankets but I didn't sleep. I wondered useless things. What had she done to the Fool? How had she killed him? Had he been completely Forged before she killed him? If she'd sent him into the dragon, did that mean he'd felt some final pain when the stone dragon died? Stupid, stupid questions.

Thick shifted heavily against my back. "I can't find her," he said quietly.

"Who?" I asked sharply. The Pale Woman was large in my thoughts.

"Nettle. I can't find her."

My conscience smote me. My own daughter, the man who had raised her dying, and I hadn't even thought of reaching out to her.

Thick spoke again. "I think she's afraid to go to sleep."

"Well. I can't blame her." Only myself.

"Are we going back home now?"

"Yes."

"We didn't kill the dragon."

"No. We didn't."

There was a long pause and I hoped he had gone back to sleep. Then he asked me quietly, "Are we going home on a boat?"

I sighed. His childish concern was the only thing that could have weighed me heavier. I tried to find sympathy for him. It was difficult. "It's the only way we can go home, Thick. You know that."

"I don't want to."

"I don't blame you."

"Me, neither." He sighed heavily. After a time he said, "So this was our adventure. And the prince and the princess get married and live happily ever after, with many children to warm them in their old age."

He had probably heard that phrase thousands of times in his life. It was a common way for a minstrel to end a hero tale.

"Perhaps," I said cautiously. "Perhaps."

"What happens to the rest of us?"

Longwick came into the tent. Quietly he began to make up his bed. From the way he moved, I suspected he had finished his brandy.

"The rest of us go on with our lives, Thick. You'll go back to Buckkeep and serve the Prince. When he becomes the King, you'll be at his side." I reached to find his happy ending. "And you'll live well, with pink sugar cakes and new clothes whenever you need them."

"And Nettle," he said with satisfaction. "Nettle is at Buckkeep now. She's going to teach me how to make good dreams. At least, that's what she said. Before the dragon and all."

"Did she? That's good."

With that, he seemed to settle for the night. In a short time, his breathing took on the slower rhythm of sleep. I closed my eyes and wondered if Nettle could teach me how to make good dreams. I wondered if I'd ever have the courage to meet her. I didn't want to think about her right now. If I thought about her, then I had to think about telling her about Burrich.

"What will you do, Lord FitzChivalry?" Longwick's question in the dark was like a voice out of the sky.

"That isn't me," I said quietly. "I'll go back to the Six Duchies and be Tom Badgerlock."

"Seems like a lot of people know your secret now."

"I think they are all men who know how to hold their tongues. And will do so, at Prince Dutiful's request."

He shifted in his blankets. "Some might do so merely at Lord FitzChivalry's request."

I laughed in spite of myself, then managed to say, "Lord FitzChivalry would greatly appreciate that."

"Very well. But I think it's a shame. You deserve better. What of glory? What of men knowing what you have done and who you are, and giving you the acclaim you deserve for your success? Don't you want to be remembered for what you've done?"

I didn't need to think long. What man has not played that game, late at night, staring into the fire's embers? I had been down the road of what might have been so often that I knew every crossroad and pitfall in it. "I'd rather be forgotten for the things people think I've done. And I'd give it all if I could forget the things I failed to do."

And there we left it.

I suppose I must have slept at some point, because I awoke in the predawn gray. I crawled from my blankets to keep from disturbing Thick and went immediately to Burrich's bedside. Swift slept curled beside him, holding his father's hand. My Wit-sense of the Stablemaster told me that he was sinking away from us. He was going to die.

I went to Chade and Dutiful and woke them. "I want something from you," I told them. Dutiful peered at me blearily from his blankets. Chade sat up slowly in his bedding, alerted by my voice that this was a serious matter.

"What?"

"I want the coterie to try to heal Burrich." When no one spoke, I added, "Now. Before he slips any further away."

"The others are going to realize that you and Thick are more than what you seem," Chade pointed out to me. "It is why I have left my own injury alone. Not that it compares to Burrich's."

"All my secrets seem to have spilled out on this island anyway. If I must live with those consequences, then I'd like to have something to show for it. For all I've lost here. I'd like to send Swift home to Molly with his father."

"Her husband," Chade reminded me quietly.

"Don't you think I know that, don't you think I see all the possible consequences?"

"Go wake Thick," the Prince suggested as he threw back his blankets. "I know you want to hurry, but I suggest you get him a good breakfast before we try this. He can't focus on anything when he's hungry. And mornings are not his best time. So let's at least feed him."

"Shouldn't we think this through a bit before—" Chade began, but Dutiful cut him off.

"This is the only thing Fitz has ever asked of me. He's getting it, Lord Chade. And he's getting it now. Well, as close to now as I can manage. As soon as Thick has had some breakfast." He began to dress, and with a groan, Chade threw back his blankets.

"You act as if I hadn't thought of this myself. I have.

Chivalry sealed Burrich to the Skill. Doesn't anyone besides me remember that?" Chade asked wearily.

"We can try," Dutiful replied stubbornly.

And we did. It seemed to take an eternity to get a breakfast made for Thick, and while he consumed it in his careful and thorough way, I tried to explain to Swift what I wanted to do. I feared to give him too much hope, and at the same time, I wanted him to understand the risks of what we did. If our attempt at mending Burrich's crumpled body was too much for his physical reserves and he died, I did not want the lad to think we had killed him recklessly.

I had thought it would be a difficult thing to explain. More difficult was getting Swift to pause and consider what I was telling him. I tried to call him aside to speak to him, for the Bear was not far away, tending the Outislander injured. But Swift refused to leave his father's side for even a moment so finally I spoke to him where he sat. At the first mention that Prince Dutiful might be able to use the Farseer magic to mend his father's body, Swift became so avid that I am sure my cautions and warnings of possible failure went right past him. The boy looked like a castaway, his eyes dark-circled and sunken in grief. Whatever sleep he had taken last night had not rested him. When I asked him if he had eaten, he just shook his head as if such an idea exhausted him.

"When will you start?" he demanded of me for the third time, and I surrendered. "As soon as the rest of them get here," I told him, and almost at that moment, Chade lifted the flap of the rough tent we had erected over the sled and entered. Dutiful and Thick crowded in behind him. The number of people in the crude shelter now threatened to collapse it, and with an impatient gesture, Dutiful suggested, "Let's get this down and out of the way. It will be more distraction than shelter while we work."

So, while Swift chewed his lip impatiently, Longwick and I took down the screening canvas and bundled it up for transport. By the time we had finished, rumor of what we were doing had begun to trickle through the camp and all gathered to watch. I did not relish working in front of everyone, let alone revealing to all how intimate my connection to the Prince was. Yet there was no help for it.

We gathered around Burrich's body. It was hard to persuade Swift to step aside and let me put my hands on him, yet Web at last drew him back. He stood behind the lad and held him as if he were a much younger boy. Wit and arms, he wrapped him in a comforting embrace, and I sent him a grateful look. He nodded to me, acknowledging it and bidding me begin.

Chade and Dutiful and Thick joined hands, looking like men about to play some child's game. I shivered with dread of what we were about to attempt and tried to ignore the avid attention of the onlookers. Cockle the minstrel was wide-eyed and tense with focus. The Outislanders, both Hetgurders and rescued, watched us with suspicion. Peottre stood at a slight distance, his women around him, his face solemn and intent.

When I was a few years older than Swift I had tried, at Burrich's suggestion, to draw Skill-strength from him as my father had. I had failed, and not just because I had not known what I was doing. My father had used Burrich as a King's Man, as a source of physical strength for his Skill-work. But any man so used also becomes a conduit to the user, and so Chivalry had sealed Burrich off to other Skill-users, so that no one could use him as a means to attack Chivalry or spy on him. Today, I would pit my strength and that of Dutiful's coterie against my father's ancient barricade and see if I could break past it into Burrich's soul.

I reached a hand toward the coterie and Thick took it. I set my other hand on Burrich's chest. My Wit told me that he lingered in his body reluctantly. The animal that Burrich dwelt in was hopelessly injured. If his body had been a horse, Burrich would have put it down by now. That was an unsettling thought and I pushed it aside. Instead, I tried to set my Wit aside and hone my Skill to the sharpness of a blade. I banished all other thoughts and sought for some place to pierce him with that awareness.

I found none. I sensed the rest of the coterie, sensed their anxiety and hovering readiness, but I could find no place to apply that eagerness. I could sense Burrich there, but my awareness of him skated over the surface, unable to penetrate. I did not know how my father had sealed him and had no idea how to undo it. I do not know how long I strove to break past his walls. I only know that at length, Thick dropped my hand, to wipe a sweaty palm down the front of his jerkin. "That one's too hard," he proclaimed. "Do this easy one instead."

He did not ask anyone permission, but leaned in past Burrich to set his hand on the shoulder of one of the injured Outislanders. I was not even holding Thick's hand, but in that instant I knew the Outislander. He had been the Pale Woman's slave for he knew not how many years. He wondered if his son had prospered in his mother's house, and wondered too about his sister's three sons. He had promised to teach them swordmanship, all those years ago. Had anyone stepped forward to do that duty for him?

These thoughts tormented him as much as his injury, a sweeping sword wound that Bear had dealt him. It had laid open the flesh of his chest and bitten deep into his upper arm. He'd lost a lot of blood and that weakened him. If he could find the strength to live, his body would heal. Then, without regard to that, his flesh began to knit itself up. The man gave a roar and lifted a hand to clutch at his closing wound. Just like a rent garment sewing itself up, his flesh reached for the severed ends of itself. Bits that were dead or past repair were expulsed from him. In a sort of horror, I watched the pads of flesh on the man's face melt away. Luckily for us, he was a burly man, possessed of the reserves that his body now burned.

He sat up suddenly on his pallet, and wrenched the caked bandages from his body, throwing them aside. All the witnesses gasped. His newly healed flesh shone, not with the poreless sheen of a scar but with the health of a child's body. It was a pale and hairless stripe down his swarthy body. He stared down at himself, and then, with a rough laugh of amazement, he thumped himself on the chest as if to convince himself of its soundness. A moment later, he had swung his legs over the side of the sled and hopped off it, to caper barefoot in the snow. An instant later, he was back, to sweep Thick off his stubby legs and swing him in a wide circle before setting the astonished little man back on his feet. In his own language, he thanked him, calling him Eda's Hands, an Outislander phrase I did not understand. It conveyed something to Bear, though, for he instantly went to the other wounded man on the sled and, throwing back the man's coverings, gestured at him, for Thick to come to him.

Thick didn't even glance at the rest of us. I scarcely had a thought to spare for him or what he did. My gaze was fixed on Swift, who stared at me with eyes gone blank and hopeless. I held out a useless hand to him, palm up. He swallowed and looked away from me. Then he came, not to me, but to Burrich. He took his place beside his father and picked up his darkening hand. He looked at me, a question in his eyes.

"I'm sorry," I said, through the exclamations of amazement as the second Outislander stood, healed of his injuries. "He is sealed. My father closed him off to other Skill-users. I cannot get in to help him."

He looked away from me, his disappointment so deep that it bordered on hatred; not necessarily hatred of me, but of the moment, of the other men who were rising, renewed, and of those who rejoiced over them. Web had moved away from Swift, to allow him his anger. I saw no sense in trying to speak any more to him just then.

Thick seemed to have mastered the knack of Skill-healing, and with moderate supervision from Dutiful he moved on to heal the two men who had burned off their Pale Woman tattoos the night before. Pale smooth skin replaced oozing and blistered flesh. From being an object of disdain, Thick was suddenly the prince of their regard and a living embodiment of Eda's Hands. I heard the Bear begging Prince Dutiful's pardon for their former disrespect of his servant. They had not realized that he possessed Eda's gift, and now they understood the great value the Prince placed on him and why he would have brought him to a battle. It hurt me to see Thick suddenly bask in their approval just as he had cringed before their disdain. I felt somehow betrayed that he could so swiftly forget how they had spurned him. Yet, I was glad that he could, even as I recognized the contradiction of it. Almost, I wished I could be as simple as he was, and accept that people truly meant the expressions they wore.

Chade came up behind me and set his hand lightly on my shoulder. I turned to him with a sigh, expecting some task. Instead, the old man put his arm around me. His grip tightened and he spoke softly by my ear. "I'm sorry, boy. We tried. And I'm sorry too for the Fool's death. We did not always agree, he and I. But he did for Shrewd what no one else could have done, and the same for Kettricken. If we opposed one another this last time, well, be assured I had not forgotten those former times. As it was, he still won." He glanced up at the sky, as if he almost expected to see dragons overhead. "Won, and left us to deal with whatever it was he won for us. I don't doubt that it will be as unpredictable as he was. And that, I am sure, would please him."

"He told me he would die here. I never completely believed him. If I had, there are things I would have said to him." I sighed, suddenly filled with the futility of such thoughts, and of all the things I had meant to do and never done. I groped within myself trying to find some meaningful thought or sentiment. But there was nothing to think or to say. The Fool's absence filled me, leaving no room for anything else.

We moved on that day, and most of us were in high spirits. Burrich rode alone on the sled now, silent and unmoving, fading more as the day passed. Swift walked on one side of him and I on the other, and we spoke not at all. On our rest halts, I trickled a little water into Burrich's mouth. Each time, he swallowed it. Even so, I knew that he was dying, and I didn't lie to Swift about it.

Night came and we halted, and made food. Thick had no lack of friends now ready to look after him, and he loved the attention. I tried not to feel abandoned by him. All the days that I had wished to be free of his care, and now that I was, I wished I had the distraction of it again. Web came to Swift and me, bringing food for the boy and nodding to me that I should take a rest from my vigil. Yet walking apart from Burrich and Swift only made the night seem colder.

I found myself at Longwick's fire, where he shared his harvest of gossip with me. Some of the freed Outislanders had been with the Pale Woman since the Red Ship War. Once, there had been scores of them, but she had relentlessly fed them to the dragons. At first, the main settlement had been on the shore near the quarry site, but after the war she had begun to fear that the Outislanders would turn on her. She had also been determined, from the beginning, that she would make an end of the dragon Icefyre. Legend said that the halls and tunnels beneath the glacier had existed for generations. She had waited for the year's low tide to discover the fabled under-ice entry to it. Once within, she had put her men to chipping out the icy ceiling of the treacherous passage, to create a hidden access that could be used at almost any low tide. When she destroyed her beach settlement, she had ordered her servants to transport the larger of the two stone dragons and reassemble him in the great hall of ice. It had been a prodigious task, but she cared nothing for how many men or how much time it consumed.

In the years since the war, she had dwelt there, extracting tribute from the clans that still feared her or hoped to regain their hostages from her. She struck cruel bargains;

for a shipment of food, she might return a body. Or a promise that the hostage would never be released to shame his family. When I asked Longwick if he thought that knowledge of her habitation was widespread in the Out Islands, he shook his head. "I got the sense that it was a matter of shame. No one who paid the bribes would have spoken of it." I nodded to myself at that. I doubted that many of the Narwhal Clan knew the full tale of what had become of Oerttre and Kossi, only that they were missing. Well did I know that very large secrets could still remain secrets.

So the Pale Woman's kingdom had been built, from the labor of half-Forged warriors. When one became injured, or old, or intractable, he was given to the dragon. Many lives had gone into the stone in her futile efforts to animate it. We had arrived at the waning of her power. Scores served her where once there had been hundreds. Her dragon and the forced labor had consumed them.

The Pale Woman had made efforts of her own to kill Icefyre but had never succeeded in more than tormenting him. She feared to remove the ice that held him and had never discovered a weapon that effectively pierced his overlapping scales and thick hide. Her hatred and her fear of him had been legendary among her slaves.

"I still don't understand," I said to Longwick quietly as we watched the small flames of his fire dying. "Why did they serve her? How did she get Forged Ones to obey her? The ones I saw in Buck were without loyalties of any kind."

"I do not know. I soldiered in the Red Ship War, and I know what you speak about. The men I talked to said that their memories of their time serving her are dulled. They recall only pain, no pleasure, no scent, no taste of food. Only that they did what she bade them, because it was easier than being disobedient. The disobedient were fed to the dragon. I think here we see a more sophisticated use of Forging than any we knew in the Six Duchies. One man told me that, when she took all his loyalty and love of his home and family away, it seemed to him that she was the only thing he could serve. And serve he did, though even the blunted memories of what he did for her shame him now."

When I left Longwick and went back to where Burrich rested on the sled, I caught a glimpse of Prince Dutiful and the Narcheska between the tents. They stood, their hands entwined and their heads close together. I wondered how her mother regarded their marriage to come. To her, it must seem a strange and sudden alliance with an old enemy. Would she support it when it meant her daughter must leave her mothershouse to reign in a distant land? I wondered how Elliania herself felt about it; she had only recently regained her mother and sister. Would she now wish to leave them and travel to the Six Duchies?

Web was sitting with Swift and Burrich when I returned to them. Grief had aged the boy to the edge of manhood. I sat down quietly beside them on the edge of the sled. A makeshift tent draped it to keep the night winds at bay and a single candle lit it. Despite the blankets that swathed Burrich, his hands were cold when I took one in mine.

Swift looked defeated already as he asked me quietly, "Couldn't you try again? Those others...they healed so quickly. And now they sit and talk and laugh with their fellows around the fire. Why can't you heal my father?"

I'd told him. I repeated it anyway. "Because Chivalry closed him to the Skill, many years ago. Did you know that your father has served Prince Chivalry? That he served him as a King's Man, a source of strength for when the King chose to do his magic?"

He shook his head, his eyes full of regret. "I know little of my father, other than as my father. He's a reserved man. He never told us tales of when he was a boy like Mother tells us stories of Buckkeep Town and her father. He taught me about horses and caring for them, but that was before—" He halted, then forced himself to go on. "Before he knew I was Witted. Like him. After that, he tried to keep me out of the stables and away from the animals as much as possible. That meant I had little time with him. But he didn't talk about the Wit much either, other than to tell me he forbade me to touch minds with any beast."

"He was much the same way with me, when I was a boy," I agreed with him. I scratched my neck, suddenly weary and uncertain. What belonged to me? What belonged to Burrich? "When I got older, he spoke to me more, and explained things more. I think that as you got older, he would have told you more about himself, too."

I took a deep breath. Burrich's hand was in mine. I wondered if he would forgive me what I was about to do, or if he would have thanked me. "I remember the first time I saw your father. I was about five years old, I think. One of Prince Verity's men took me down the hall to where the guardsmen were eating in the old quarters at Moonseye. Prince Chivalry and most of his guard were away, but your father had remained behind, still recovering from the injury to his knee. The one that makes him limp. The first time he was hurt there, it was because he jumped down between a wild boar and my father, to save my father from being gutted by the animal's tusks. So. There was Burrich, in a kitchen full of guardsmen, a young man in his fighting prime, dark and wild and hard-eyed. And there was I, suddenly thrust into his care, with no warning to either of us. Can you imagine it? Even now, I wonder what must have gone through his mind when the guardsman first set me down on the table in front of him and announced to all that I was Chivalry's little bastard, and Burrich was to have the care of me now."

Despite himself, a very small smile crept over Swift's face. So we eased into the night, with me telling him the stories of the rash young man who had raised me. Web sat by us for some time; I am not sure when he slipped away. When the candle guttered, we lay down on either side of Burrich to keep him warm, and I talked on quietly in the darkness until Swift slept. It seemed to me that my Wit-sense of Burrich beat stronger in those hours, but perhaps it was only that I had recalled to myself all that he had been to me. Mixed in with my memories of how he had encouraged and disciplined me, of the times when he had righteously punished me and praised me, I now saw more clearly the times when a young single man had curtailed his life for the sake of a small boy. It was humbling to realize that my dependency on him had probably shaped his life as much as his had influenced me.

The next morning when I gave Burrich water, his eyelids fluttered a bit. For an instant, he looked out at me, trapped and miserable. Then, "Thanks," he wheezed, but I do not think it was for the water. "Papa?" Swift asked him eagerly, but he had already faded again.

We made good time in our travel that day, and when evening came we decided to push on and try to be off the glacier before we stopped for the night. We were full of enthusiasm for that idea. I think we were all weary of camping on ice, but the distance yet to travel proved farther than we had believed. On we went, and on, past weariness into that stubborn place where we refused to admit we had misjudged.

It was deep into the night before we approached the beach. We saw the welcome sight of watch fires, and before it sank in to my weary mind that one fire should have sufficed for two guards, we heard Churry's challenge ring out. Prince Dutiful answered it, and we heard a glad cry of several voices raised. But none of us were prepared to hear Riddle shouting a welcome to us. When I recalled how I had last seen him, it raised the hackles on the back of my neck. I knew one wild moment of irrational hope that the Fool too would somehow be there. Then I recalled what Peottre had told me and sorrow drenched me.

We were among the last to reach the beach camp. By the time we arrived, all was in an uproar of welcome and storytelling. Nearly an hour passed before I managed to get the tale out of someone. Riddle and seventeen Outislander survivors of the Pale Woman's palace were there. They had come to themselves, probably at the moment of the dragon's slaying. Riddle and his fellow prisoners had been rescued from their dungeon by one of her guard, when his sensibilities had come back to him. They had joined forces to find a way out, and Riddle had managed to lead them back to the beach. They were all very confused as to what had led to the recovery of their senses and their liberation. It took all the rest of that night for us to splice the story together for them.

Chade summoned me to his tent the next day, to be present when Riddle made his full report to the Prince and him. I listened to his account of how the Pale Woman's soldiers had fallen upon Hest and him, capturing both of them. Their mistake had been in seeing some of her guards emerge from a hidden entrance to her realm. They could not be allowed to bear that information back to the Prince. He was not able to describe coherently how he had been Forged. It had to do with the dragon, but every time he attempted to tell about it, he began to tremble so violently that he was unable to go on. At last and to my relief, Chade gave up on attempting to wring that knowledge out of him. Truly, I thought it was information better lost than discovered.

He was astonished to know that the Fool and I had glimpsed him in the dungeon. He said he did not blame me for leaving him there; that if I had forced the door, he would certainly have attacked me for the sake of getting my warm clothing. Yet there was something in his eyes, so deep a shame that someone he knew had seen him in that state, that I doubted our fledgling friendship would survive. I did not think I could ever be comfortable again, looking at the man I had left behind to die.

I wondered if Riddle would ever again be the light-hearted man he had been. He had seen into a dark corner of himself, and ever after would have to carry those memories with him. He admitted, before us all, that he was the one who had finally killed Hest. He had used his shirt to wrap his hands against the cold. He could recall how carefully he had planned to kill the wounded man and take advantage of the spoils from his body while the other Forged Ones in the dungeon slept. He also told us that he recalled the Pale Woman telling them it was a sort of test; that those who survived the fortnight would be given the freedom to serve her, and regular meals. He grinned madly as he told it, his teeth clenched as if to hold back sickness, saying that, at that moment, he could imagine no better fate than to serve her and have regular meals.

Two of the Outislanders who had returned with Riddle were men of the Narwhal Clan, long missing and presumed dead. Peottre welcomed them with joy. The Pale Woman had preyed on their clan for over a decade, decimating their men before she finally reduced them to despair by stealing both the reigning Narcheska and her younger daughter. The restoration of these warriors to the clan only increased the Prince's status as a hero in their eyes.

When Chade had finished with his questions, I asked the three that had burned in me. The answers were all disappointing. Riddle had not seen the Fool at any time in his captivity or during his escape. He had not seen the Pale Woman, not even her body, after he was freed from the dungeon.

"But I don't think we have to be concerned about her. The man who came and freed me, Revke, saw her end. Something made her suddenly go mad. She screamed that everyone had failed her, everyone, and now only her dragon would win the day for her. She must have ordered at least a score of men dragged forward. One after another, they were forced against the stone dragon, and slaughtered there. Revke said their blood soaked into the stone. But even that didn't content her. She became furious, shouting that they were supposed to go into the dragon completely, that it would not rise unless someone went into the dragon whole."

He looked around at our transfixed faces, perplexed. "I don't speak Outislander as well as I should. I know it sounds mad, that she wanted someone to go into a stone dragon. But that was what Revke seemed to be saying to me. I could be wrong."

"No. I suspect you are exactly right. Go on," I begged him.

"She finally ordered Kebal Rawbread given to the dragon. Revke said that when they unshackled him, the guards underestimated the old warrior's strength and his hatred of the Pale Woman. The guards had hold of him and were dragging him toward the dragon, and he was fighting them all the way. Then suddenly he lunged in the other direction, toward the Pale Woman. He caught her by the wrists, and he was laughing and shouting that they'd go into the dragon together and rise in triumph for the Out Islands. That it was the only way to win. And then Rawbread dragged her toward the dragon, shrieking and kicking. And then..." He halted again. "I'm just telling the tale as Revke told it to me. It makes no sense, but—"

"Go on!" Chade commanded him hoarsely.

"Rawbread walked backward into the dragon. He sort of melted into it, and he held tight to the Pale Woman and dragged her in after him."

"She went into the dragon?" I exclaimed.

"No. Not all the way. Rawbread disappeared into the dragon, and he was pulling her after, so her hands and her wrists went in. She was shrieking at her guards to help her, and finally two seized hold of her and pulled her back. But...but her hands were melted away. Gone into the dragon."

The Prince had his hand clamped tight over his mouth. I found I was trembling. "Is that all?" Chade asked. I wondered where he got his calm.

"Mostly. What was left of her hands was sort of burnt. Not bleeding, just charred away, Revke said. He said, she just stood there, looking at her stumps. The dragon was coming to life by then. When it started to move, it lifted its head too high, and big chunks of the ceiling came down. Revke said everyone ran, both from the falling ceiling and from the dragon. And that he was still hiding from the dragon when he suddenly got himself back." Riddle halted suddenly, and then said with difficulty, "I can't explain to you what it feels like. I was in my cell, back to the wall, trying to stay awake because if I slept the others would kill me. And then I glanced down and saw Hest dead on the floor. And suddenly I cared that he was dead, because he'd been my friend." He shook his head and his voice went to a whisper. "Then I remembered killing him."

"It wasn't your fault," the Prince said quietly.

"But I did it. It was me, I—"

I cut into his words before he could give any more thought to what he had done. "And how did you get out?" I asked quietly.

Riddle seemed almost grateful for the question. "Revke opened the door for us and led us out and through her palace. It's like a huge maze under the ice. We finally walked out of an opening that looked like a crack in an ice wall, right onto the glacier's flank. Once we were out, no one knew what to do next. The others knew no other place on the island where we could seek shelter. But I could just glimpse the sea from where we were. I told them that if we made our way to the sea and followed the beach, we'd have to eventually come to this base camp, even if we walked clear round the island first. As it was, we were lucky. We chose the shorter route and arrived here even before you did."

There was one last question, but he answered it before I spoke. "You know how the wind blows at night, Tom. Drifting snow has probably covered all our tracks by now. Even if I wanted to, I don't think I could find my way back." He took a deep breath, and then added reluctantly, "Perhaps one of the Outislanders would be willing to try.

But not me. Never. I don't ever want even to get close to that place again."

"No one will ask you to," Chade assured him, and he was right. I left it at that.

Dawn was breaking when I returned to Burrich and Swift. Swift slept beside Burrich's body. I noticed that he had moved, that one of his hands now lay outside his blankets. In tucking it in again, I discovered that Burrich clutched a wooden earring in his hand. I recognized it; the Fool had carved it, and I knew that inside it I would find the slave's freedom earring that Burrich's grandmother had won at such hardship to herself. That he had found the strength to take it off told me how important it was to him. I thought I knew his intentions for it.

Dutiful had released the homing pigeon that would fly back to Zylig to let the Hetgurd know that our quest was over. Nonetheless, it would take some days for the boats to reach us; in the meanwhile, we faced the prospect of short rations spread out over a larger party. It was not a pleasant thing to contemplate, yet I think most of us shrugged it off after all we had been through.

I found a quiet time with Swift, sitting beside the ever-dwindling Burrich. I told him the tale of the earring while I struggled to get it out of its wooden enclosure. In the end, the Fool's handiwork proved too sophisticated for me. I had to break it to open it. Within lay the earring, shining as blue and silver as when Patience had first presented it to me. As she had that day, I used the pin of it to pierce Swift's ear so he could wear it. I was slightly kinder to him than she had been to me; we numbed his earlobe with snow before I thrust the pin through it. "You wear this always," I told the boy. "And you remember your father. As he was."

"I will," Swift replied quietly. He touched it with cautious fingers; well did I remember its weight swinging from my raw earlobe. Then he wiped his bloody fingertips on his trouser leg and said, "I'm sorry I used it, now. If I still had it, I'd give it to you."

"What?"

"The arrow that Lord Golden gave me. I thought it was ugly when he gave it to me, but I took it to be polite. Then, when all the others bounced off the dragon, the gray one struck and sank. I never saw anything like that before."

"I doubt that anyone ever has," I replied.

"Maybe he had. He said it was an ugly bit of wood, but that it might still serve me well in time of need. He said he was a Prophet, that night. Do you think he knew the gray arrow would kill the dragon?"

I managed a smile. "Even when he was alive, I never knew when he truly knew something before it happened and when he was just cleverly reconstructing his words to make it seem that he did. In this case, however, he seems to have been right."

"Yes. But did you see my father? Did you see what he did? He dropped that dragon in his tracks. Web says he'd never felt strength like that before, strength to *repel* a dragon." He looked at me, challenging me to forbid it to him as he added, "He says that strength like that sometimes runs in Old Blood families. That perhaps I'll inherit it, if I use my magic with discipline and judgment."

I reached to cup the boy's jaw, the earring cold against my palm. "Let's hope you do. This world needs strength such as that."

Longwick thrust his head inside our shelter. "Prince Dutiful has need of you, Tom," he apologized.

"I'll be right there," I assured him, and then, to Swift, "You don't mind?"

"Go. There's nothing either of us can do here save keep watch."

"I'll be back," I promised, and then stepped from the tent to follow Longwick through our camp.

The Prince's tent was crowded. He, Chade, and Thick were there, with Peottre, Oerttre, Kossi, and the Narcheska. Thick's lip was thrust out and I sensed his upset. The Narcheska sat on the floor, a blanket clasped around her shoulders and her back to me. I made my courtesies to all and then waited.

The Prince spoke. "We are having a bit of a problem with the Narcheska's tattoos. She would like them removed, but they haven't yielded to Thick's Skill. Chade thought that, as you'd dealt with your own scars, perhaps you might be able to help."

"A scar is very different from a tattoo," I replied, "but I'm willing to try."

The Prince leaned down to her. "Elliania? May he see them?"

She made no response. Her back was very straight as she sat there, and disapproval was plain on her mother's face. Then, slowly, without a word, Elliania dropped her head forward and allowed the blanket to slide down her back. I knelt down and lifted the light to see more plainly. And then I gritted my teeth and understood why they'd thought of me.

The gleaming beauty of the serpents and dragons was gone. The tattoos were sunken into her back, the skin drawn tight as if they'd been branded in. I suspected it was the Pale Woman's last act of vengeance. "They still cause her pain, from time to time," the Prince said quietly.

"I'm speculating," I admitted. "Perhaps Thick can't heal her easily because this isn't a recent injury. It's one thing to aid the body in doing what it's already attempting to do. But these are old, and her body has accepted them."

"Your scars went away when we healed you," the Prince pointed out.

"They aren't hers," Thick observed sullenly. "I don't want to touch them."

I let Thick's cryptic remark go by. "I think the Fool restored me to how he had always seen me. Unscarred." I did not want to say more of that just then, and I think they all knew that.

Elliania's voice shook only slightly as she said, "Then burn them off, and heal the burn. I care not what it takes. I only want them gone. I will not wear her marks upon my body."

"No!" the Prince said in horror.

"Wait. Please," I said. "Let me try." I lifted a hand and then remembered to ask, "May I touch you?"

She dropped her head lower and I saw every muscle in her back go tight. Then she gave a single nod. Peottre towered over us, his arms crossed on his chest. I looked up at him and met his gaze. Then I sat down on the floor behind the Narcheska and carefully laid both my hands flat to her back. By an act of will, I kept them there. The palms of my hands felt the warm back of a young girl, but my Skill felt dragons and serpents writhing beneath my fingers. "More than ink is beneath her skin," I said, but did not know what it was that I sensed there.

Elliania spoke with an effort. "She made the inks from her own blood. So that they would always belong to her and obey her."

"She's bad," Thick said darkly.

Elliania had given us the piece of knowledge we needed. Even so, it was a grueling evening of Skill-work. I did not know Elliania well, and Thick was loath to touch her. He lent us his strength, but every intricate figure had to be separately driven out from her. Her mother and sister sat and watched silently. Peottre stayed a time, then went out and walked, came back, and then went out again. I did not blame him. I wished I did not have to witness it. Foul-smelling ink oozed reluctantly from the pores on her back. Worse, it hurt her. She clenched her teeth, and then pounded wordlessly on the earth. Her long black hair, pulled forward to be out of our way, grew heavy with perspiration. Dutiful sat facing her, his hands on her shoulders to brace her, while I painstakingly traced each illustration with my fingertip, calling on her skin to push out the Pale Woman's foulness. As I did so, I saw again the Fool's back, so exquisitely and cruelly marked, and thanked the fates that his had been forced on him before the Pale Woman had gained and perverted the Skill-learning. I could not understand why her tattoos so resisted us. By the time the last clawed foot had been forced from her skin, I was exhausted, but her back was smooth and clear.

"It's done," I said wearily, and lifted the blanket to drape her again. She took in a breath that was almost a sob and Dutiful gingerly gathered her into his arms.

"Thank you," he said to me quietly, and then, to Elliania, "It's all finished. She can never hurt you again."

I knew a moment's uneasiness, wondering if that were true. But before I could voice any doubts, we heard a welcome cry from outside the tent. "Sail! Sail sighted, two sails. One flies the Boar and the other is the Bear!"

chapter XXVII

DOORS

The more I delve into the affairs and associations of Lord and Lady Grayling, the more I am convinced that your suspicions are well founded. Although they have conceded to the Queen's "invitation" for young Lady Sydel to spend time at the Buckkeep Court, they did not do so graciously or eagerly. Her father was more determined to be hard-hearted in this matter than her mother. Her mother was truly scandalized that he sent her off with no garb fit for an ordinary day at court, let alone for feasting or dancing. The allowance he allotted her is also insufficient for a milkmaid. I believe he hopes that she will embarrass herself at court sufficiently to be sent home.

The woman he chose as her maid is not to be trusted. I suggest that a grievance against Opal be discovered and that she be dismissed from Buckkeep as swiftly as possible. Take care that her gray housecat leaves with her.

Sydel herself seems guilty of little more than being young and flighty. I do not think, for those reasons, that she even knows her parents have declared as Piebalds, let alone is privy to any of their plotting.

🙠 SPY'S REPORT, UNSIGNED

Favorable tides had brought the ships to us sooner than we had expected. But if we were surprised to see the ships so soon, the crews of the ship were equally shocked at the size of the party that awaited them on the shore. The boats they put over to come to shore were crowded with folk anxious to discover the news. So many of our men met them on the beach that the boats were literally picked up clear of the water and run far up the sand before the crews could disembark. The uproar sounded like a battle as every man strove to tell the tale his own way to our amazed transport. There was laughter, chest thumping, and shoulder slapping as each man strove to be the first to tell the tale. Above all was the joyous roar of Arkon Bloodblade as he shared the Narwhal triumph. His reunion with Oerttre was more restrained and formal than I had expected it to be. Father he might be to Elliania, but he had never been formally wed to Oerttre, nor had he sired Kossi. So he rejoiced in their return as a friend, not as a father and husband, and it seemed more the satisfaction that a warrior took in the triumph of an ally.

Later, I would discover that the Narcheska had promised much to her father in terms of crops, trade, and other favors. The Boar Clan lands were rocky and steep, fine lands for grazing swine but not for growing field crops. Bloodblade had eight young nieces of his own clan to provide for, and these Boar youngsters would prosper because of the Narwhal triumph.

But all I knew at the time was that once more, rejoicing and triumph surrounded young Swift and me, making our sorrow all the deeper in comparison. Worse, I had made a resolution last night, one that felt so precisely correct that I knew nothing would turn me aside from it. So, while men whooped outside and overshouted one another telling their portions of the tale, I spoke quietly to Swift as we sat in dimness under draped canvas beside his unresponsive father.

"I won't be going back with you. Can you take care of your father without me?"

"Can I...what do you mean, you won't be coming back with us? What else can you do?"

"Stay here. I need to go back to the glacier, Swift. I want to find a way into her underground palace. At the least, I want to find my friend's body and burn it. He hated to be cold. He would not wish to be entombed forever in ice."

"And what else do you hope to do? There is something you are not saying."

I took a deep breath, thought of a lie, and then set it down. Enough lies for one lifetime. "I hope to look on the Pale Woman's body. I hope to find her dead, to know that she died for all she has done to us. And if I find her living, I hope to kill her."

It was a small and simple promise I'd made to myself. I doubted it would be easy to carry out, but it was the only comfort I could find to offer myself.

"You look a different man when you talk like that," Swift said in a hushed voice. He leaned close to me. "When you talk like that, you have a wolf's eyes."

I shook my head and smiled. At least, my teeth showed. "No. No wolf wastes time on vengeance, and that is what this is. Vengeance, pure and simple. When people look most vicious, what you are seeing is not their animal side. It is the savagery that only humans can muster. When you see me loyal to my family, then you see the wolf."

He touched a finger to his dangling earring. He knit his brows and asked, "Do you want me to stay with you? You should not face this alone. And, as you have seen, I did not lie. I am good with a bow."

"You are indeed. But you have other duties, more pressing ones. Burrich has no chance at all if he stays here. Get him onto the ship and back to Zylig. They may have skilled healers there. At the very least, they will have a place that is warm, with decent food and a clean bed for him."

"My father is going to die, FitzChivalry. Let us not pretend otherwise."

Oh, the power that lurks in the naming of names. I let go. "You are right, Swift. But he need not die in the cold, under a piece of flapping canvas. That much we can give him."

Swift scratched his head. "I want to do my father's will in this. I think he would tell me to stay with you. That I cannot be as useful to him as I could be to you."

I thought about it. "Perhaps he would. But I do not think your mother would tell you that. I think you need to be with him. He may rally again, before the end, and what words he may have for you could be precious ones. No, Swift. Go with him. Be with him, for me."

He did not reply, but bowed his head to my words.

Even as we spoke, men were dismantling our camp and loading it aboard the ship. I think it shocked Swift when it was the Outislanders who came for him and Burrich. Bear came, to incline his head gravely to the boy and ask the honor of transporting him and his father aboard the Hetgurd ship. "Demon-slayers," he named both of them, and I think it shocked Swift to realize that he had been left to grieve in isolation out of respect, not out of negligence. The Owl, their bard, sang them aboard the Bear ship, and though he twisted the words in their bard's tongue, still I heard with throat-choking pride of the man who had brought the dragon-demon to its knees and the boy who slew it to set the Pale Woman's hostages free. Web, I noted, rode out in the boat with them, and would be taking ship with Swift. This comforted me. I did not want the lad to be alone among strangers, no matter how they might honor him when Burrich died, and I feared he would not live to see Zylig port.

Then the Prince was at my side, demanding to know which ship I was embarking upon. "You are welcome on either, but it will be close quarters no matter which you choose. They did not expect to carry off this many people. We shall be packed like salt fish in a keg. Chade, in his wisdom, has chosen to separate me from the Narcheska, so I will be on the Bear ship. Chade goes on the Boar ship with Peottre and his women, for he hopes to further advance the final negotiations of our alliance during the voyage."

I had to smile, despite my heavy heart. "Alliance, you still call it? It has begun to look like a wedding to me. And have you given Chade reason to think it best to separate you from Elliania for the voyage to Zylig?"

He raised an eyebrow, the corner of his mouth quirking. "Not I! It was Elliania who proclaimed she was satisfied as to her challenge to me to be worthy of her, and declared that she now regarded me as her husband. I do not think her mother was entirely pleased, but Peottre declined to oppose her. Chade has tried to explain to Elliania the necessity of my vowing to her in my 'mothershouse,' but she will have none of that. She asked him, 'And what is a man, to oppose a woman's will in this matter?'"

"I would have loved to hear his reply to that," I said.

"He said, 'Truly, lady, I do not know. But my queen's will is that her son shall not bed with you until you have stood before her and her nobles in her house, and proclaimed that you are satisfied he is worthy of you.'"

"And did she accept that?"

"Not graciously." The Prince was obviously flattered by his bride-to-be's eagerness. "But Chade has extracted a promise from me that I will act with restraint. Not that Elliania has made that easy for me. Ah, well. So I sail on the Bear ship and she on the Boar. Chade will be on the Boar, and we think Thick, for the Outislanders have made much of him and his Eda's Hands. So. Which one for you? Come on the Bear. You can be with Burrich and Swift and me."

"Neither ship will I board. But I'm glad to hear you'll

be on the Bear ship with Swift. This is a hard time for him. He may bear it better among friends."

"What do you mean, neither?"

Time to announce it. "I'm staying here, Dutiful. I need to go back and try to find the Fool's body."

He blinked, considering it, and then, in an act of understanding that warmed me, simply accepted that I had to do it. "I'll stay with you, of course. And you'll need some men, if you're hoping to tunnel down through the dragon pit."

It touched me that he did not argue the necessity of it, and that he offered to delay his own triumph. "No. You go on. You've a narcheska to claim and an alliance to create. I'll need no one, for I'm hoping to go back in where Riddle and the others came out."

"That's a fool's errand, Fitz. You'll never find it again. I listened to Riddle's answers as closely as you did."

I smiled at his choice of words. "Oh, I think I will. I can be tenacious about things like this. All I ask is that you leave me what food you can spare and any extra warm clothing you have. It may take me some time to accomplish this."

He looked uncertain at those words. "Lord FitzChivalry, forgive me for saying this, but this may be a rash risk of yourself, for no gain. Lord Golden is beyond feeling anything. There is little chance you will find a way back in, let alone find his body. I do not think I am wise to allow this."

I ignored his final statement. "And that is another thing. You will be going back to enough chaos. You scarcely need Lord FitzChivalry's resurrection in the midst of it. I suggest that you meet quietly with your Wit coterie and still all their tongues about me. I've already spoken to Longwick. I don't think I need worry about Riddle. Everyone else is dead."

"But . . . the Outislanders know who you are. They've heard you called by that name."

"And it has no significance for them. They won't recall

my true name any more than I can recall Bear's or Eagle's. I'll simply be the crazy one who stayed on the island."

He threw his hands wide in a gesture of despair. "And we are still back to you remaining on this island. For how long? Until you starve? Until you find that your quest is as futile as mine was?"

I pondered it briefly. "Give me a fortnight," I said. "Then arrange for a boat to come back here for me. If I haven't succeeded in a fortnight, I'll give it up and come home."

"I don't like this," he grumbled. I thought he would argue further, but then he countered with "A fortnight. And I won't wait to hear from you, so do not Skill to me to beg for more time. In a fortnight, there will come a boat to this beach to take you off. And regardless of your success or failure, you will meet it and board it. Now, we have to hurry, before they've finished loading everything."

But in the end, that was an idle fear. The crews were actually unloading things from the ships to make more room for the extra passengers. Chade grumbled and swore at my stubbornness, but in the end, he had to give way to me, mostly because I would not change my mind and everyone else was in a great rush to leave on the change of the tide.

It was still surpassing strange to stand on the shore and watch the ships borne away on the tide's change. Heaped behind me on the beach was a miscellaneous dump of equipment. I had far too many tents and sleds for one man to use, and an adequate if very uninteresting supply of food. In the time between the ships' vanishing and the fall of night, I picked through what they had left me, loading what I thought I'd actually use into my own battered old pack. I put in extra clothing, as much food as I thought I would need, and my feathers from the Others beach. Longwick had left me a very serviceable sword; I think it had been Deft's. I had Longwick's own belt knife. The Fool's tent and bedding I kept, setting it up for my night's shelter, and his cooking supplies, as much because they were his as because they were the lightest to pack. Chade, I found to my amusement, had left me a small keg of his blasting powder. As if I'd risk tinkering with that again! My hearing was still not what it should have been. Yet, in the end, I did put a pot of it into my pack.

I built up a good fire for myself that night. Driftwood was not plentiful on the beach, but there was only one of me to warm, so I indulged myself. I had expected to find the peace that isolation usually brought to me. Even when my spirits were darkest, solitude and the natural world had always comforted me. But tonight, I did not feel that. The restless humming of the submerged stone dragon was like a simmering reminder of the Pale Woman's evil. I wished there were a way to still it, to cleanse the evil carving back to honest stone again. I made up a generous pot of hot porridge for myself and recklessly sweetened it with some barley sugar that Dutiful had left for me.

I had just taken my first mouthful when I heard footsteps behind me. I choked and sprang to my feet, drawing my sword. Thick stepped into the circle of my firelight, grinning sheepishly. "I'm hungry."

I swayed with the shock of it. "You can't be here. You're supposed to be on the ship, going back to Zylig."

"No. No boats for me. Can I have some dinner?"

"How did you stay behind? Does Chade know? Does the Prince? Thick, this is impossible! I have things to do, important things to do. I can't look after you right now."

"They don't know yet. And I'll look after myself!" he huffed. I'd hurt his feelings. As if to prove he could, he went to the heap of abandoned cargo and rummaged until he came up with a bowl. I sat, staring at the flames, feeling completely defeated by fate. He came back into my firelight and sat down on a stone across from me. As he dished up more than half the porridge for himself, he added, "It was easy to stay. I just sent *with Chade, with Chade* at

Prince, and *with Prince, with Prince* at Chade. They believed me and got on the boats."

"And no one else noticed you were missing?" I asked skeptically.

"Oh. I went *don't see me, don't see me* at the others. It was easy." He resumed eating with pragmatic enjoyment of the food. He was obviously pleased with how clever he'd been. Between mouthfuls he asked, "How did you trick them into letting you stay?"

"I didn't trick them. I stayed because I had a task I had to do. I still do. They'll be back for me in a fortnight." I put my head into my hands. "Thick. You've done me a bad turn. I know you didn't mean to, but it's bad. What am I going to do with you? What did you plan to do when you stayed here?"

He shrugged and spoke through the porridge. "Not get on a boat. That's what I planned. What did you plan to do?"

"I planned to go on a long walk, back to the icy place. And kill the Pale Woman if I could find her. And bring back Lord Golden's body, if I could find it."

"All right. We can do that." He leaned forward and looked into the porridge pot. "Are you going to eat that?"

"It seems not." My appetite had fled, along with all thoughts of peace. I watched him eat. I had two choices. I knew I could not leave him alone on the beach while I went off to hunt the Pale Woman. It would have been like leaving a small child to look after himself. I could remain here with him on the beach for a fortnight until the boat that Dutiful had promised to send back for me arrived. Then I could send Thick off with it, and try to resume my tasks. By then, autumn would be upon this northern island. Falling snow would join the blowing snow to obscure all signs of passage. Or I could drag him along with me, proceeding at his plodding, torturous pace, taking him into danger. And taking him, also, into a very private part of my

life. I did not want him to be there when I recovered the
Fool's body. It was a task I wished and needed to do alone.

Yet there he was. Depending on me. And unwanted,
there came to me the memory of Burrich's face when I had
first been thrust into his care. So it had been for him. So it
was for me now. I watched him scraping the last of the porridge from the kettle and licking the sticky spoon.

"Thick. It's going to be hard. We have to get up early
and travel fast. We are going up into the cold again. Without much fire, and with very boring food. Are you sure you
want to do this?"

I don't know why I offered him the choice.

He shrugged. "Better than getting on a boat."

"But eventually, you will have to get on a boat. When
the boat comes back for me, I'm leaving this island."

"Nah," he said dismissively. "No boats for me. Will we
sleep in the pretty tent?"

"We need to let Chade and the Prince know where
you are."

He scowled at that, and I thought he might try to use
the Skill to defeat me. But in the end, when I reached for
them, he was with me, very much enjoying the prank he
had played on them. I sensed their exasperation with him
and their sympathy for me, but neither offered to turn back
the ships. In truth, they could not. A tale such as they bore
would not await the telling. Neither ship could turn back.
For either the Prince or the Narcheska to be absent would
not be acceptable to the Hetgurd. They must go on. Chade
offered grimly to send back a boat for us the moment they
docked in Zylig, but I told him to wait, that we would Skill
to them when we were ready to leave. *Not on a boat,* Thick
added emphatically, and none of us had the will to argue
with him just then. I was fairly certain that when he saw
me leave, he would depart with me. By then, he would
probably be very weary and bored with survival here. I
could not imagine him desiring to stay on the island alone.

And as the night wore on, I reflected that perhaps it

was better for me that he was there, in some ways. When I bedded down in the Fool's tent that night, Thick seemed an intruder there, as out of place as a cow at a harvest dance. Yet, if he had not been there, I know I would have sunk into a deep melancholy, and dwelt on all I had lost. As it was, he was a distraction and an annoyance, and yet also a companion. In caring for him, I did not have time to examine my pain. Instead, I had to create a pack for him with a share of supplies that I thought he could carry. Into his pack I put mostly warm clothing for him and food, knowing he would not abandon food. But as I prepared for sleep, I already dreaded the morrow and dragging him along with me.

"Are you going to sleep now?" Thick demanded of me as I pulled my blankets up over my head.

"Yes."

"I like this tent. It's pretty."

"Yes."

"It reminds me of the wagon, when I was little. My mother made things pretty, colors and ribbons and beads on things."

I kept silent, hoping he would doze off to sleep.

"Nettle likes pretty things, too."

Nettle. Shame washed through me. I had sent her into danger and nearly lost her. And since that moment, I had made no effort to contact her. The way I had risked her shamed me, and I was shamed that I had not been the one to save her. And even if I'd had the courage to beg her forgiveness, I did not have the courage to tell her that her father was dying. Somehow, it felt like that was my fault. If I had not been here, would Burrich have come? Would he have challenged the dragon? This was the measure of my cowardice. I could go off, sword in hand, hoping to kill the Pale Woman. But I could not face the daughter I had wronged. "Is she all right?" I asked gruffly.

"A little bit. I'm going to show her this tent tonight, all right? She will like this."

"I suppose so." I hesitated, and then ventured one step closer. "Is she still afraid to go to sleep?"

"No. Yes. Well, but not if I'm there. I promised her I wouldn't let her fall in there again. That I'll watch her and keep her safe. I go into sleep first. Then she comes in."

He spoke as if they were meeting in a tavern, as if "sleep" were a room across town, or a different village down the road. When he spoke again, my mind struggled to comprehend what the simple words meant to him. "Well. I have to go to sleep now. Nettle will be waiting for me to come for her."

"Thick. Tell her...no. I'm glad. I'm glad you can be there like that."

He leaned up on one stubby elbow to tell me earnestly, "It will be all right, Tom. She'll find her music again. I'll help her." He took a long breath and gave a sleepy sigh. "She has a friend now. Another girl."

"She does?"

"Um. Sydel. She comes from the country and is lonely and cries a lot and doesn't have the right kind of clothes. So she is friends with Nettle."

That told me far more than I'd wanted to know. My daughter was afraid to sleep, unhappy at night, lonely, and befriending a disowned Piebald. I was suddenly certain that Hap was doing just as well as Nettle was. My spirits sank. I tried to be satisfied that Kettricken had removed Sydel from her undeserved isolation. It was hard.

The Fool's tiny oil firepot flickered between us and died away to nothing. Darkness, or what passes for darkness in that part of the world on a summer night, cupped our tent under her hand. I lay still, listening to Thick's breathing and the wash of the waves on the beach and the disquieting mutter of the disjointed dragon under the water. I closed my eyes, but I think I was afraid to sleep, fearful both that I'd find Nettle or that I wouldn't. After a time, it seemed to me that sleep truly was a place and I'd forgotten the way there.

Yet, I must have slept eventually, for I awoke to dawn light shining in through the colors of the Fool's tent. I'd slept far longer than I intended, and Thick slumbered still. I went outside, relieved myself, and brought washwater to heat from the icy stream. Thick did not get up until he smelled the morning's porridge cooking. Then he emerged, stretching cheerfully, to tell me that he and Nettle had hunted butterflies all night, and she had made him a hat out of butterflies that flew away just before he woke up. The gentle silliness cheered me, even as it made a sharp contrast with my plans.

I tried to hurry Thick along, with small success. He walked idly on the beach while I struck the tent and loaded it onto my back. It took some persuasion to get him to take up his own pack and follow me. Then we set off down the beach in the direction from which Riddle and his fellows had come. I had listened intently to Riddle's tale. I knew they had followed the beach for about two days. I hoped that if I did the same and then watched for where they had climbed down onto the beach, I'd find my way back to the crevasse where they had emerged from the Pale Woman's realm.

Yet I had not reckoned with having Thick with me. At first he followed me cheerfully down the beach, investigating tide pools and bits of driftwood and feathers and sea-weed as we went. He wet his feet, of course, and grumbled about that, and was soon hungry. I'd thought of that, and had travelers' bread and some salt fish in a pouch. It was not what he had hoped for, but when I made it clear that I was going to continue hiking regardless of what he did, he took it and chewed as we walked.

We did not lack for fresh water. Rivulets of it cut the beach or dampened the stony cliff faces. I kept an eye on the rising tide, for I had no wish to be caught by it on a section of beach where we could not escape it. But the tide did not come up far, and I was even rewarded by footprints above the tideline. These traces of Riddle's passage cheered me, and we trudged on.

As night came closer, we picked up the sparse bits of driftwood that the beach yielded to us, set up our tent well above the high water line, and built our fire. If I had not had such a heavy heart, it would have been a pleasant evening, for we had a bit of moon and Thick was inspired to take out his whistle and play. It was the first time I'd ever been able to give myself over completely to both his musics, for I was as aware of his Skill-music as I was of the whistle's piping. His Skill-music was made of the ever-present wind and the keening of the seabirds and the shush of waves on the shore. His whistle wove in and out of it like a bright thread in a tapestry. Because I had access to his mind, it was a comprehensible music. Without the Skill, I am sure it would have been annoying, random notes.

We ate a simple meal, a soup made from dried fish with some fresh seaweed added from the beach and travelers' bread. It was filling; that was possibly the kindest thing that could be said for it. Thick ate it, mainly because he was hungry. "Wish we had cakes from the kitchen," he said wistfully while I scrubbed out the pot with sand.

"Well, we won't have anything like that until we travel back to Buck. On the boat."

"No. No boat."

"Thick, there is no other way for us to get there."

"If we just kept walking, we might get there."

"No, Thick. Aslevjal is an island. It has water all around it. We can't get back home by walking. Sooner or later, we have to get on a ship."

"No."

And there it was again. He seemed to grasp so many things, but then we would come to the one that he either refused or could not accept. I gave it up for the night and we went to our blankets. Again, I watched him slip into sleep as effortlessly as a swimmer enters water. I had not had the courage to speak to him about Nettle. I wondered what she thought of my absence, or if she noticed it at all. Then I closed my eyes and sank.

By that second day of hiking, Thick was bored with the routine. Twice he let me get so far ahead of him that I was nearly out of his sight. Each time, he came huffing and hurrying over the wet sand to catch up with me. Each time, he demanded to know why we had to go so fast. I could not think of an answer that satisfied him. In truth, I knew only my own urgency. That this was a thing that must be finished, and that I would know no peace until I did. If I thought of the Fool as dead, if I thought of his body discarded in that icy place, the pain of such an image brought me close to fainting. I knew that I would not truly realize his death until I saw it. It was like looking down at a festering foot and knowing it must come off before the body could begin to heal. I hurried to face the agony.

That night caught us on a narrow beach along a cliff face hung with icicles. Sheeting water ran down the rock face. I judged there was just room to pitch the tent and that we would be fine, as long as no storm rose to drive the tide higher. We set up our tent, using rocks to hold it in the sand, and made our fire and ate our plain provender.

The moon was a little stronger, and we sat for a time under the stars looking out over the water. I found time to wonder how Hap was doing, and if my boy had overcome his dangerous affection for Svanja or succumbed to it completely. I could only hope he had kept his head and his judgment. I sighed as I worried about that and Thick asked sympathetically, "You got a gut ache?"

"No. Not exactly. Worrying about Hap. My son back in Buckkeep Town."

"Oh." He did not sound very interested. Then, as if this was a thing he had pondered for a long time, he added, "You're always somewhere else. You never do the music where you are."

I looked at him for a moment, and then lowered my perpetual guard against his music. Letting it in was like letting the night into my eyes when twilight came over the land and it was a good time to hunt. I relaxed into the moment, letting the wolf's enjoyment of the now come into me, as I had not for far too long. I had been aware of the water and the light wind. Now I heard the whispering of blowing sand and snow, and deep behind it, the slow groaning creak of the glacier across the land. I could suddenly smell the salt of the ocean and the iodine of the kelp on the beach and the icy breath of old snow.

It was like opening a door to an older place and time. I glanced over at Thick and suddenly saw him as complete and whole in this setting, for he gave himself to it. While he sat here and enjoyed the night, he lacked nothing. I felt a smile bend my mouth. "You would have made a good wolf," I told him.

And when I went to sleep that night, Nettle found me. It took me some time to become aware of her, for she sat at the edge of my dream, letting the wind off the sea ruffle her hair as she stared out of the window of my boyhood bedchamber at Buckkeep. When I finally looked at her, she stepped out of the window and onto my beach, saying only, "Well. Here we both are."

I felt all the apologies and explanations and excuses rise in me, crowding to be the first words out of my mouth. Then she sat down beside me on the sand and looked out over the water. The wind stirred her hair like a wolf's ruff rippling in the breeze. Her stillness was such a contrast to all the jumbled communication inside me that I suddenly felt what a tiresome fellow I was, always filling the air with the rattle of words and anxieties. I found that I was sitting beside her with my tail neatly curled around my forefeet. And I said, "I promised Nighteyes that I would tell you tales of him, and I have not."

Silence spun a web between us and then she said, "I think I would like to hear one tonight."

So I told her about a clumsy, blunt-nosed Cub springing high to land on hapless mice and how we had learned to trust one another and to hunt and think as one. And she listened through the night, and to some tales I told, she cocked her head and said, "I think I remember that."

I came awake to dawn seeping in through the bright beasts that cavorted on the tent walls, and for a moment I forgot that I was weighted with sorrow and vengeance. All I saw was a gleaming blue dragon, wings spread wide as he rocked on the wind while below him scarlet and purple serpents arched through the water. Slowly I became aware of Thick snoring and that the waves were very close to the door of our tent. That sound woke alarm in me, and I scuttled to the door to peer out. At first, I was relieved, because the water was retreating. I had slept through the real danger, when the sea had reached within two steps of our door.

I crawled out of the tent and then stood, stretching and looking out over the waves. I felt an odd sense of peace. My dolorous mission was still before me, but I had reclaimed a part of my life that I thought I had spoiled. I walked a little away from the tent to relieve myself, almost enjoying the chill of the packed wet sand under my bare feet. But when I turned back to the tent, all my equanimity fled.

Twisted into the sand, inches from the tent flap, was the Fool's honey jar.

I recognized it in that instant, and recalled well how it had disappeared from outside my tent on my first night on this island. I scanned the beach hastily and then the cliffs above us, looking for any sign of another person. There was nothing. I crept up on the honey jar as if it might bite me, all the while searching for even the tiniest sign of who had come and left so silently in the night. But the encroaching waves had wiped the beach clean of any sign of his passage. The Black Man had once more eluded me.

At last I picked it up. I took out the stopper, expecting I knew not what, but found it perfectly empty, with not even a trace of its former sweetness left within. I took it inside the tent and packed it carefully away with the Fool's other possessions, even as I pondered what it might mean. I thought of Skilling of my strange discovery to Chade and Dutiful, but at length I decided I would say nothing of it to anyone for now.

I found little wood that morning, and so Thick and I had to be content with salt fish and cold water for breakfast. The supplies that had seemed more than adequate for one man now seemed to be dwindling all too swiftly. I took a deep breath and tried to be a wolf. For now, there was fine weather and enough food for the day, and I should take advantage of that to continue my journey without whining for more. Thick seemed in a genial mood until I began to pack up the tent. Then he complained that all I wanted to do was to walk down the beach every day. I bit my tongue and did not remind him that he was the one who had chosen, uninvited, to stay behind and link his life to mine. Instead, I told him that we did not have much farther to go. That seemed to encourage him, for I did not mention that I would be looking for whatever marks Riddle and the others might have left when they clambered down to the sand. He had mentioned a cliff, and I hoped their passage had left some trace that wind and tide had not yet obscured.

So on we tramped, and I tried to take pleasure in the freshness of the day and the ever-changing countenance of the sea, even as I kept one eye on the cliffs that backed us. Yet the sign that suddenly greeted me was, I was sure, no doing of Riddle or of his companions. It was freshly scratched on the stone of the cliffs, unweathered by wind or water, and its meaning was unmistakable. A crude dragon cavorted over an arched serpent. Above them, an arrow pointed straight up.

It seemed to me that whoever had made the marks had chosen for us a fairly easy climb from the beach to the clifftops. Even so, I went up first and unencumbered while Thick waited placidly on the beach below. At the top of the wind-scoured cliffs, there was a thin edge of bare ground. Stubborn grasses tufted there amidst a crunchy sort of moss. A sort of shallow meadow bloomed beyond it, of grasses and lichen-crusted rocks and pessimistic bushes. I had climbed up, knife in teeth, but no one, friend or enemy, awaited me there. Instead, there was only the barren sweep of cold wind from the crouching glacier.

I returned to the beach, to bring up first our packs and then Thick. He did well enough at climbing, but was hampered by his shorter stature and stockier girth. Eventually, however, we stood on the clifftop together. "Well," he exclaimed when he had finished puffing. "And now what?"

"I'm not sure," I said, and looked about, guessing that whoever had left us such a plain sign on the cliff would not abandon us now. It took me a moment to see it. I do not think it was intended to be subtle, but rather that there was little to work with. A row of small beach stones was set in a line. One end of it pointed toward the place we had just climbed up. The other end pointed inland.

I handed Thick his pack and then settled my own on my shoulders. "Come on," I said. "We're going that way." I pointed.

He followed my finger with his eyes and then shook his head in disappointment. "No. Why? There's nothing there but grass. And then snow."

I had no easy explanation. He was right. In the distance, the plain of stubby grass gave way to snow and then looming ice. Beyond them, a rock face shone with a frosting of ice and snow. "Well, that's where I'm going," I said. And I struck out. I set an easy pace, but avoided looking back. Instead, I listened, and with my Wit, quested for an awareness of him. He was following, but grudgingly. I slowed my pace enough to allow him to catch up. When he was alongside me, I observed companionably, "Well, Thick, I think that today we will have answers to at least a few of our questions."

"What questions?"

"Who or what is the Black Man?"

Thick looked stubborn. "I don't really care."

"Well. It's a lovely day. And I'm not just hiking on the beach anymore."

"We're hiking toward the snow."

He was right, and soon enough we reached the outlying edges of it. And there, plainly, were the tracks of the Black Man, going and coming. Without commenting on them, I followed them, Thick trudging at my heels. After a short time, Thick observed, "We aren't poking the snow. We might fall right through."

"As long as we follow these tracks, I think we're safe," I told him. "This isn't the true glacier yet."

By early afternoon, we had followed the tracks across a windswept plain of snow and ice to a rocky cliff wall. Towering and forbidding, it defied the wind. Ice made columns down its face and had wedged cracks into it. At the base of it, the tracks turned west and continued. We followed. Night grayed the sky and I pushed on doggedly, giving Thick sticks of salt fish when he complained of being hungry. As the twilight grew deeper around us, even my curiosity lagged along with my energy. At length, we halted. I felt sheepish as I turned to Thick and said, "Well, I was wrong. We'll set up the tent here for the night, shall we?"

His tongue and lower lip pouted out and he beetled his brows at me in disappointment. "Do we have to?"

I glanced around, at a loss for what else I could offer him. "What would you like to do?"

"Go there!" he exclaimed and pointed. I lifted my eyes to follow the stubby finger. My breath caught in my chest.

I had been keeping my eyes on the tracks. I had not lifted my gaze to the looming cliff wall. Ahead of us, and halfway up the bluff, a wide crack had been fitted with a door of gray wood. The rest of the crack had been filled in with rocks of various sizes. The door had been left ajar and yellow firelight shone within. Someone was in there.

With renewed haste, we followed the tracks to where they suddenly doubled back to follow a steep footpath that worked up and across the face of the cliff. Calling it a footpath was generous. We had to go in single file and our packs bumped against the rock as we negotiated it. Nevertheless, it was a well-used trail, kept free of debris and treacherous ice. Where trickles of ice from above had attempted to cross the path, they had been chopped off short and brushed away. It appeared to be a recent effort.

Despite these signs of hospitality, I was full of trepidation when I stood at last before the door. It had been constructed of driftwood, hand-planed and pegged together painstakingly. Warmth and an aroma of cooked food wafted out from it. Although it was ajar and the space in front of it small, still I hesitated. Thick didn't. He shoved past me to push the door open. "Hello!" he called hopefully. "We're here and we're cold."

"Please, enter do," someone replied in a low and pleasant voice. The accent on the words was odd, and the voice seemed husky as if from disuse, but the welcome was plain in the tone. Thick didn't hesitate as he stepped inside. I followed him more slowly.

After the dimness of the night, the fire in the stone hearth seemed to glare with light. At first, I could make out no more than a silhouette seated before the fire in a wooden chair. Then the Black Man slowly stood and faced us. Thick drew in his breath audibly. Then, with a show of recovery and manners that astounded me in the little man, he said carefully, "Good evening, Grandfather."

The Black Man smiled. His worn teeth were as yellow as bone in his black, black face. Lines wreathed his mouth and his eyes nestled deep in their sockets, like shining ebony disks. He spoke, and after a time my mind sorted out his badly accented Outislander. "I know not how long I've been here. Yet this I know. This is the first time that anyone has entered and called me 'Grandfather.'"

When he stood, it was without apparent effort, and his spine was straight. Yet age was written all over his countenance, and he moved with the slow grace of a man who protects his body from shocks. He gestured to a small table. "Guests I seldom have, but my hospitality I would offer despite what is lacked. Please. Food I have made. Come."

Thick didn't hesitate. He shrugged out of his pack, letting it slide to the floor without regret. "We thank you," I said slowly as I carefully removed my own and set both of them to one side. My eyes had adjusted to the light. I do not know if I would have called his residence a cave or a large crevice. I could not see a ceiling, and I suspected that smoke traveled up but not out. The furnishings were simple but very well made, with both the craft and attention of a man who had much time to learn his skills and apply them. There was a bedstead in a corner, and a larder shelf, a water bucket and a barrel, and a woven rug. Some of the items appeared to have been salvaged, windfalls from the beach, and others were obviously made from the scanty resources of the island. It bespoke a long habitation.

The man himself was as tall as I was, and as solidly black as the Fool once had been white. He did not ask our names or offer his, but served soup into three stone bowls that he had warmed by the fire. He spoke little at first. Outislander was the language we used; yet it was not native to any of us. The Black Man and I worked at communicating. Thick spoke Duchy-tongue but managed to make himself understood. The table was low, and our chairs were cushions with woven reed covers stuffed with dry grass. It was good to sit down. His spoons were made of polished bone. There was fish in the soup, but it was fresh, as were the boiled roots and meager greens. It tasted very good after our long days of dried or preserved food. The flat bread that he set out with it startled me and he grinned when he saw me looking at it.

"From her pantry to mine," he said, with no apology. "What I needed I took. And sometimes more." He sighed. "And now it is done. Simpler, my life will be. Yours, lonelier, I think."

It suddenly seemed to me that we were in the middle of a conversation, with both of us already knowing, without words, why we had come together. So I simply said, "I have to go back for him. He hated the cold. I cannot leave his body there. And I must be sure that this is finished. That she is dead."

He nodded gravely to the inevitable. "That would be your path, and you that path must tread."

"So. You will help me, then?"

He shook his head, not regretfully but inevitably. "Your path," he repeated. "The path of the Changer belongs to you only."

A shiver ran down my back that he called me that. Nevertheless, I pressed him. "But I do not know the way into her palace. You must know a way, for I saw you there. Cannot you at least show me that?"

"The path will find you," he assured me, and smiled. "In darkness it cannot hide itself."

Thick held up his empty bowl. "That was good!"

"More, then?"

"Please!" Thick exclaimed, and then heaved a great sigh of pleasure as the man refilled his bowl. He ate his second serving more slowly. There was no talk as the Black Man rose and set a battered old kettle full of water over the fire. He fed the fire larger, and I watched the driftwood catch and burn with occasional licks of odd colors in the flames. He went to a shelf and carefully considered three little wooden boxes there. I arose hastily and went to my pack.

"Please, allow us to contribute something to the meal. I have tea herbs here."

When he turned to me, I saw that I had guessed correctly. It was as if I had offered another man jewels and gold. Without hesitation, I opened one of the Fool's little packets and offered it to him. He leaned over it to smell it, and then closed his eyes as a smile of purest pleasure came over his face.

"A generous heart you have!" he exclaimed. "A memory of flowers grows here. Nothing brings to mind the memories so much as fragrance."

"Please. Keep it all, to enjoy," I offered him, and he beamed with delight, his black eyes shining.

He made tea with a rare caution, crumbling the herbs to powder and then steeping them in a tightly covered container. When he removed the lid and the fragrance of the tea steamed up, he laughed aloud in delight, and, just as people do when a small child laughs, Thick and I joined in for sheer pleasure in his enjoyment. There was an immediacy about him that was very charming, so that it was almost impossible for me to find the focus to worry and fret. He shared out the tea, and we drank it in tiny sips, savoring both the fragrance and the flavor. By the time we were finished, Thick was yawning prodigiously, which somehow increased my own weariness.

"A place to sleep," our host announced, and gestured Thick toward his own bedstead.

"Please, we have our own bedding. You need not give up your bed to us," I assured him, but he patted Thick on the shoulder and again gesticulated at the bed.

"You will be comfortable. Safe and sweet the dreaming. Rest well."

Thick needed no other invitation than that. He had already taken off his boots. He sat down on the bed and I heard the creak of a rope framework. He lifted the coverlet and crawled in and closed his eyes. I believe he went to sleep in almost that instant.

I had already begun to spread out our bedding near the fire. Some of it was the Fool's Elderling-made stuff, and the old man examined it carefully, rubbing the thin coverlet between his finger and thumb wistfully. Then, "So kind you are, so kind. Thanks you." Then he looked at me almost sadly and said, "Your path awaits. May fortune be kind, and the night gentle." Then he bowed to me in what was obviously a farewell.

In some confusion, I glanced at his door. When I looked back at him, he nodded slowly. "I will keep the watch," he assured me, gesturing toward Thick.

Still I stood staring at him, confused. He took a breath and then paused. I could almost see him pushing his thoughts into words I could understand. He touched both hands to his cheeks and then held his black palms out to me. "Once, I was the White. The Prophet." He smiled to see my eyes widen, but then sadness came into his dark gaze. "I failed. With the old ones, I came here. We were the last ones and we knew it. The other cities had gone empty and still. But I had seen there was still a chance, a slight chance, that all might go back to what had been. When the dragon came, at first he gave me hope. But he was full of despair, sick with it like a disease. Into the ice he crawled. I tried. I visited him, I pleaded, I . . . encouraged. But he turned from me to seek death. And that left nothing for me. No hopes. There was only the waiting. For so long, I had nothing. I saw nothing. The future darkened, the chances narrowed." He put his hands together and looked through their cupped palms as if peering through a crack, to show me how limited his visions had become. He lifted his gaze back to me. I think my confusion disappointed him. He shook his head, and then with an obvious effort, pushed on. "One vision is left to me. A tiny peer . . . no! A tiny glimpse of what could be. It was not certain, ever, but it was a chance. Another might come. With another Catalyst." He held a hand out to me, formed a tiny aperture with his fist. "The smallest chance, maybe there is. So small, so unlikely. But there is that chance." He looked at me intently.

I forced myself to nod, though I was still not certain I understood all he told me. He had been a White Prophet who failed? Yet he had foreseen that eventually the Fool and I would come here?

He took encouragement from my nod. "She came. At first, 'She is the one!' I think. Her Catalyst she brings. Hope comes to me. She says she seeks the dragon. And I am a fool. I show her the way. Then, the betrayal. She seeks to kill Icefyre. I am angry, but she is stronger. She drove me out, and I had to flee, by a way she cannot follow. She thinks me dead and makes all here her own. But I return, and here I make a place for myself. To this side of the island, her people do not come. But I live and I know she is false. I want to throw her down. But to be the change-maker is not my role. And my Catalyst..." His voice suddenly went hoarser. He spoke with difficulty. "She is dead. Dead so many years. Who could imagine that death lasts so much longer than life? So, only I remained. And I could not make the change that was needed. All I could do was wait. Again, I waited. I hoped. Then I saw him, not white, but gold. I wondered. Then you came after him. Him I knew, at first glance. I recognized you when you left the gift for me. My heart..." He touched his chest and then lifted his hands high. He smiled beatifically. "I longed to help. But I cannot be the Changer. So limited what I may do, or down it all falls. You understand this?"

I replied slowly. "I think I do. You are not allowed to be the one who makes the changes. You were the White Prophet of your time, not the Changer."

"Yes. Yes, that it is!" He smiled at me. "And this time is not mine. But it is yours, to be the Changer, and his to see the way and guide you. You did. And the new path found is. He pays the cost." His voice sank, not in sorrow, but in acknowledgment. I bowed my head to his words.

He patted my shoulder and I looked up at him. He smiled the smile of age. "And on we go," he assured me. "Into new times! New paths, beyond all visions. This is a time I never saw, nor she, she who me deceived. This, she never seen has. Only your Prophet has seen this way! The new path, beyond the dragons rising." He gave a sudden deep sigh. "High the price was for you, but it has been paid.

Go. Find what is left of him. To leave him there..."
The ancient man shook his head. "That is not to be." He
gestured again. "Changer, go. Even now, I dare not the
change-maker be. While you live, it is only for you. Now,
go." He gestured at my pack and at his door. He smiled.

Then, without any further talk, he eased himself down
onto the Fool's bedding and stretched out before the fire.

I felt oddly torn. I was weary and the Black Man created just such an isle of rest as the Fool would have. And
yet, in that comparison, I once more felt the urgency to put
it all to a final end. I wished I had known I was leaving him;
I would have warned Thick what to expect. Yet somehow,
I did not think he would be alarmed to awaken here and
find me gone.

Leaving him felt inevitable. I put on my still chilly
outer garments, and shouldered my pack again. I looked
once more around the Black Man's tiny home and could
not help but contrast it to the splendor of the Pale
Woman's glacial domain. Then, my heart smote me that
my friend's body was still discarded in that icy place. I went
out quietly into the deep gray of the night, shutting the
door firmly behind me.

chapter XXVIII

CATALYST

*In a backwater of the river there, not far from the Rain
Wilders' city, lie huge logs of what is known as Wizard
Wood. The sailor told me that it is a sort of husk that the
serpents make in the process of becoming dragons. Much
magical power is ascribed to this so-called wood.
Artifacts made from it may eventually acquire a life of
their own; it is said that the Liveships of the Bingtown
Traders were originally made from such wood. Ground
to a dust and exchanged by lovers, it is said to allow
them to share dreams. Ingested in a larger quantity, it is
said to be poisonous. When I asked why such valuable
stuff would be left lying in a riverbed, the sailor told me
that the dragon Tintaglia and her litter guard it as if it
were gold. It would be worth a man's life, he told me, to
steal so much as a sliver of the stuff. My effort to bribe
him to get me some met with resounding failure.*

    ⁂ SPY'S REPORT TO CHADE FALLSTAR, UNSIGNED

The Black Man was right. No night could hide my path
from me.

    Nevertheless, it was a challenge to tread his narrow
cliffside trail in the darkness. While I had lingered inside,

slow rills of water had crept across it to become serpents of ice under my feet. Twice I nearly fell, and when I was at the bottom, I looked back up, marveling that I had descended without a mishap.

And I saw my way. Or, at least, the start of it. Higher in the cliff face and past the Black Man's door, a very pale blush of light emanated from the ice-draped stone. I shuddered at its dreadful familiarity. Then with a sigh, I turned back to the steep footpath.

Even by day, it would have been a nasty climb. My brief rest in the Black Man's cavern seemed to have more sapped my energy than restored it. I thought, more than once, of going back into the warmth and comfort of his home, to sleep until morning. I did not think of it as something I could do but rather as something that I wished I could do. Now that I was so close to my goal, I was oddly reluctant to confront it. I had put a little wall of time between my grief and me. I knew that tonight, I would look my loss in the face and embrace the full impact of it. In strange anticipation, I wanted it to be over.

When I finally reached the softly glimmering crack in the wall, I found that the opening was barely large enough for me to enter. The slow slide of water down the rock face was icing it gradually closed. I suspected that it must be a near daily task for the Black Man to keep this entrance clear enough to use.

I drew my belt knife and clashed away enough of the icy curtain that I could just squeeze through. My pack scraped. Once I was inside, I still had to turn my body sideways and edge forward toward the pale light, dragging my pack behind me. The crack widened very gradually, and when I looked back the way I had come, it did not look like a promising exit. If I had not known otherwise, I would have said that the crack came to an end with no outlet. The crack narrowed and then bent slightly before it intersected with a corridor of worked stone. One of the Pale

Woman's globes gleamed there; it was the straying light from that orb which had beckoned me into this place.

I surveyed the corridor carefully before I stepped out of the crack. All was still in both directions, so still that I could hear the slow distant drip of water, and then the soft groaning of the glacier shifting somewhere. My Wit told me all was deserted, but in this place, that was small comfort. What assurance did I have that all the Forged had been freed? I lifted my nose, scenting like a wolf, but smelled only ice-melt and faint smoke. I stood debating which way to go, and then impulsively chose to go left. Before I went, I scratched a mark at eye level on the stone wall by my crack, that small act affirming that I expected to return.

Once more, I traveled the chill corridors of the Pale Woman's realm. The halls were horribly familiar and yet unfamiliar in their stark similarity. They reminded me of somewhere I had been, and yet I could not summon the memory. In that realm, I had no way to measure the passage of time. The light of the bulbous globes was uniform and unwavering. I found myself walking lightly and silently, and approaching each corner with caution. I felt I explored a tomb, and not just because I sought the Fool's body. Perhaps it was the movement of air in the cold tunnels, but there seemed always to be a whispering at the edge of my hearing.

This portion of the Pale Woman's stronghold showed signs of long disuse. Most of the chambers that opened onto the corridor were bare. One held a scattering of useless debris: a worn sock, a broken arrow, a tattered blanket end, and a cracked bowl were left behind on the dusty stone floor. In another, small cubes of memory stone were scattered all over the floor, obviously tumbled from the long narrow shelves that lined the walls. I wondered who had populated these chambers and when? Had this been a fortress for the Red Ships crews when they were not raiding? Or was it as the Black Man had told, had other people created these rooms and inhabited them? I decided that the habitation was far older than the Red Ship War. High on the wall, above the reach of casual destruction, the remains of bas-relief carvings showed me glimpses of a woman's narrow face, of a dragon on the wing, of a tall and slender king. Only disconnected fragments of them remained, and I wondered if the Pale Woman had ordered them destroyed or if it was merely the idle pastime of Forged Ones to eradicate beauty. Knowledge seeped into me slowly, but eventually I wondered, Had she wished to erase all evidence that these passages had once belonged to the Elderlings? Were they the "old ones" that the Black Man had seen perish here?

The corridor I followed merged seamlessly with one of ice. I stepped from black stone onto blue ice. Another dozen steps, and a carved portal admitted me into an immense vaulted chamber of ice. Flowering vines of ice were carved on the massive ice pillars that had been left in place to support the blue ceiling. Time had softened their line as the slow melt had eased them back into obscurity, but their grace remained. It was a place of dusk, a moonlit garden of ice, with a large glowing crescent moon embedded in the ceiling and the constellations spelled out in smaller light orbs overhead. The Women's Gardens of Buckkeep Castle would have fitted twice into this chamber. It was obviously intended as a place of beauty and peace. Yet the lower reaches of the garden, the fantastically sculpted ice fountains, and the decorative benches all showed signs of malicious vandalism. It was the sort of desecration that bespoke anger and resentment more than idleness. Only the body of a dragon poised on a pillar of ice remained. His wings had been broken away, his head shattered in a dozen pieces. The smell of old urine was strong and the foundation pillar that supported him was corroded with yellow, as if merely destroying the dragon's image had not been enough for them.

I crossed the ice gardens and found a winding stairwell

that led down. At one time, there had likely been carved
ice steps going down and a balustrade, perhaps, but time
and slow melt had changed the steps to an uneven and
treacherous slope. I fell several times, clawing at the walls
to slow my sliding and biting my cheek to endure the pain
silently. The destruction in the chamber above had reminded me of the Pale Woman's capacity for hate. I still
feared that she might lurk somewhere in this ice labyrinth.
I reached the bottom bruised and discouraged. I did not
want to consider how I would ascend it again.

A wide corridor headed straight into a blue distance.
Light globes at intervals illuminated the empty niches in
its walls. As I passed them, I noted stumps of legs in one. In
another, the stub of a vase remained. At one time, then,
they had held sculptures and this had been a sort of gallery,
I supposed. A plain and functional side passage opened off
from it, and I took it, almost relieved to leave the broken
beauty behind me. I followed it for what seemed like a long
time. It sloped gently down. At the next turning, I went
right, for I thought I knew where I was.

I was wrong. The place was a warren of intersecting ice
passages. Doors lined some passages, but they were frozen
shut and windowless. I made my marks at junctions, but
soon wondered if I would ever find my way out again. I
tried always to choose the path that was more used or
wider, showing the recent dirt of human usage. Evidence of
that became more obvious as I worked my way ever lower
into the city of ice. Such I was now certain it had been.
Looking back, I wonder if the Elderlings had simply accepted and shaped the ice when it overtook the city or if
they had deliberately built in the stone of this island and
then extended their dwelling into the glacier. I felt that as
I found the passages and chambers that the Pale Woman
and her Forged minions had used, I left behind the beauty
and grace of the Elderlings and descended into the grubbi-
ness and destruction of humanity and I felt ashamed of my
kind.

The chambers began to show signs of recent habitation. Unemptied slop buckets stood in corners of what might have been barracks rooms. Sleeping-hides were scattered on the floor among the casual litter of a guardroom. Yet I saw none of the touches that soldiers usually kept in their sleeping places: no dice or gaming pieces, no luck charms given by their sweethearts, no carefully folded shirt set aside for an evening in the tavern. The rooms bespoke a hard and bare life, stripped of humanity. Forged. It stirred in me a fresh surge of pity for the men who had lost years of their lives in her service.

More luck than memory led me at last to her throne room. When I saw the double door, a wave of sick anticipation swept through me. That was where I had had my final glimpse of the Fool. Would his chained body still sprawl on the floor there? At that thought, I felt a surge of dizziness and, for a moment, blackness closed in at the edges of my vision. I halted where I stood and breathed slowly, waiting for my weakness to pass. Then I forced my legs to carry me on.

One of the tall doors of the chamber stood ajar. A shallow spill of snow and ice had been vomited out into the hall. At the sight of it, my heart stood still. Perhaps my quest would be thwarted here, the entire immense chamber collapsed and full of ice. The spilled snow was a ramp into the room; the days and nights that had passed since its collapse had seized the snow and ice in an icy grip and stilled it. Only the top third of the entry remained clear. I climbed up the fall of ice and peered into the chamber. For a moment I stood in awe in the muted bluish light.

The center of the chamber ceiling had given way. Snow and ice had collapsed into it from above, filling the middle of the room but cascading to shallowness at the edges. Light came from a few remaining globes and peered out uncertainly from beneath the fall of ice. I wondered how long those unnatural lanterns would continue to burn.

Was their magic that of the Pale Woman, or were those, too, remnants of an Elderling occupation of this place?

I went cautious as a rat exploring a new room, creeping around the perimeter of the walls where the fall of ice was shallowest. I clambered up and down over chunks and drifts of ice, fearing that I would eventually find my way blocked. But I finally reached the throne end of the room and could see what remained of the Pale Woman's great hall.

The crush of falling ice had spared that end of the chamber, its rush depleted. The wave of avalanching ice had stopped short of her throne. It was overturned and broken, but I suspected that had happened when the stone dragon had stirred to life. He seemed to have made his exit through the middle of the chamber's ceiling rather than from this end. The remains of two men protruded from the avalanche. Perhaps those were the fighters Dutiful had battled, or perhaps they had merely been in the dragon's way as he charged off to do battle. Of the Pale Woman, there was no sign. I hoped that she had shared their fate.

The fallen and muted light globes lit this area uncertainly. All was ice and blue shadow. I circled the toppled throne and tried to remember exactly where the Fool had been chained to the dragon. In retrospect, it seemed impossible that the dragon had been as immense as I recalled him. I looked in vain for fallen shackles or my friend's body. At last, I climbed up on icy rubble and from that vantage studied the room.

Almost immediately, I glimpsed a swirl of familiar colors and shapes. My belly churned as I slowly clambered down and walked over to it. I stood staring down at it, unable to feel any grief, only burning horror and disbelief. The overlay of frost could not disguise it. At length, I went to my knees, but I do not recall if I knelt to see it better or if my shaking legs simply gave out under me.

Dragons and serpents tangled and tumbled in the discarded folds of it. Scarlet frost outlined it. I did not need to touch it; I could not have brought myself to touch it, but it needed no touch to know that it was frozen solidly into the floor of the chamber. As body warmth had departed it, it had sunk into the ice and become one with it.

They had flayed the tattooed skin from his back.

I knelt beside it like a man in prayer. Doubtless it had been a slow and careful skinning to take it off intact. Despite the way it had wrinkled as it fell, I knew it was one continuous flap of skin, his entire back. To take it off like that would not have been easy. I did not want to imagine how they had restrained him, or who had lovingly wielded the blade. A second thought displaced that horrid image. This would not have been how she vindictively ended his life when she realized that I had defied her and wakened the dragon. Rather, she had done this to amuse herself, at her leisure, probably beginning the slow lifting of skin from flesh almost as soon as I had been taken from the room. Flung to one side, the wrinkled layer of skin was frozen to the floor like a dirty shirt cast aside. I could not stop staring at it. I could not keep myself from imagining every slow moment of his death. This was what he had foreseen; this was the end he had dreaded to face. How many times had I assured him that I would give up my life before I saw his torn from him? Yet here I knelt, alive.

Sometime later, I came back to myself. I had not fainted and I do not know where my thoughts had gone, only that I seemed to awaken from a time of utter blackness. I rose stiffly. I would not try to free her grisly trophy and bear it off with me. That was no part of my Fool. It was the cruel mark she had put upon him, his daily reminder that eventually he must come to her and yield back to her what she had etched upon his skin. So let it lie there, frozen forever. With ever-darkening hatred of her and ever-deepening grief, I knew with sudden certainty where I would find my friend's body.

As I stood, I caught sight of a curved sheen of gray. It was not far from where his skin lay upon the floor. I knelt beside it and brushed a layer of frost away to reveal a blood-smeared shard of the carved Rooster Crown. A single gem winked up from a carved bird's eye. That I did take with me. That had belonged to him and me, and I would not leave it behind.

I left the demolished room and threaded my way through corridors as frozen as my heart. In all directions, the halls looked the same, and I could not focus my mind to recall how I had been dragged to her, let alone the location of the dungeon where they had confined me. I knew now, with certainty, where I had to go. I needed to find my way back to the first corridor the Fool and I had entered.

I know it took me more than the rest of the night. I wandered until I was past weariness. The cold nudged at me and my ears strained after imagined sounds. I saw no sign of any living creature. Eventually, when my eyes ached from remaining open, I decided to rest. I set my pack down in the corner of a small room where firewood had been stored. I put my back to the corner and sat on my pack. I clutched my sword in my hand as I drooped my head over my knees. I dozed fitfully until nightmares awoke me and drove me on again.

Eventually, I found her bedchamber, her frozen braziers draped with icicles. The lights burned brightly there and I could see the whole chamber, the carved wardrobes of rich wood, and the elegant table that held her mirror and brushes, her sparkling jewelry gleaming on a silvery tree. Someone, perhaps, had plundered as he fled, for one of the wardrobes stood open, and garments trailed from it across the floor. I wondered how they had missed taking the jewels. The sleek furs of her bed were hoared with frost. I did not linger there. I did not want to gaze at the empty shackles affixed to the wall across from her bed, or on the bloody stains they framed on the icy wall.

Beyond her bedchamber, another door gaped. I glanced in as I passed, then halted and went back to it. There was a table in the middle of the room, and scroll racks lined the walls. They were neatly filled, the scrolls rolled and tied in the Six Duchies fashion. I walked over to them, knowing what I had found, but feeling oddly emotionless about it. I pulled out a scroll at random and opened it. Yes. It was by Master Treeknee. This one had to do with rules of conduct for candidates-in-training. It strictly forbade the playing of pranks that involved the use of Skill. I let it fall to the icy floor and chose another at random. This was newer, and I recognized Solicity's rounded hand and sloping letters. The words squirmed before my tearing eyes, and I let it fall to join its fellow. I lifted my gaze to look around the room. Here was the missing Skill library of Buckkeep Castle, surreptitiously sold away by Regal to finance his lush lifestyle at Tradeford. Traders who were agents for the Pale Woman and Kebal Rawbread had bought from the youngest Prince the knowledge of the Farseer magic. Our inheritance had come north, to the Outislanders and eventually to this room. Here the Pale Woman had learned how to turn our own magic against us, and here she had studied how to make a stone dragon. Chade would have given his eyeteeth for a single afternoon in this room. It was a treasure trove of lost knowledge. It would not buy what I most desired, a chance to do things differently. I shook my head and turned and left it there.

Eventually, I found the dungeons that had held the Narcheska's mother and sister. Peottre had left those doors ajar when he had snatched his women free of them. The next dungeon showed me a more grisly sight. Three dead men sprawled within it. I wondered if they had died as Forged Ones, fighting amongst themselves, or if the death of the dragon had restored them to themselves, so that they perished of cold and hunger while in full possession of their sensibilities.

The door of the cell that had held Riddle and Hest stood open. Hest's plundered body lay face up on the floor. I forced myself to look down into his face. Cold and death had blackened his countenance, but I saw there still the

young man I had known. After a moment's hesitation, I
stooped and seized his shoulders. It was hard work, but I
pried his body from the floor. It was not a pleasant task, for
he was well frozen to it. I dragged him back to the room
that had held the Narcheska's mother and placed him on
the wooden bed. I gathered from that room and her daughter's cell anything that I thought might burn, old bedding
and straw from the floor. I heaped it around his body, and
then sacrificed half of the flask of oil that I had brought
with me for burning the Fool's body. It took some little
time to get a bit of the straw to light, but once it did, the
flames licked eagerly at the oil and clambered over the
wood and straw. I waited until a curtain of flames had risen
around his body. Then I cut a lock of my hair and added it
to his funeral pyre, the traditional Six Duchies sacrifice to
say farewell to a comrade. "Not in vain, Hest. Not in vain,"
I told him, but as I left him burning, I wondered what we
had truly accomplished. Only the years to come would tell
us, and I was not yet ready to say that the freeing of the
dragon was a trumph for humanity.

And that left the last chamber. Of course. It would
have been her final degradation of him, her final mockery
and triumphant discarding of him. In a chamber spattered
with human waste and garbage, by a heap of offal and filth,
I found my friend.

He had been alive when they dumped him here. She
would have wanted him to be aware of this final indignity
offered him. He had crawled to the corner of the room that
was least soiled. There, huddled in a piece of dirty sacking,
he had died. My Fool had been such a clean man in his life
that I did not doubt that dying among filth had been an additional torment for him. I do not know if someone had
flung the old sacking over him or if he had sought it himself
in the time before he finally died, curled in a tight ball on
the icy floor. Perhaps whoever had disposed of him here
had bundled him in it to make his body easier to drag.
Blood and fluids had soaked the coarse and crusty weave of

the fabric, freezing it tight to his diminished body. He had drawn up his knees and tucked his chin tight to his chest, and his face was locked in an expression of pain. His gleaming hair was loose and tattered, with mats of blood in it.

I set my hand on his cold clenched brow. I had not known I was going to do it until I did it. With all the Skill I could muster, I reached and sought for him. I found only stillness. I set both my hands to his cheeks and forced my way in. I explored his corpse, pushing my way through the passages where life had once flowed effortlessly. I tried to heal it, to awaken it again to life. *Go!* I commanded his blood and *Live!* I commanded his flesh.

But his body had been still too long. Reluctantly, I learned too well what all hunters know. At the instant of death, the decay begins. The tiny bits that make up the flesh begin the slide into carrion, letting go of one another so that they can find the freedom to become other things. His blood was thick, the skin that once held out the world had become a sack that held in the separating flesh. Breathless, I pushed at it, willing life into it, but it was like pushing on a hinge rusted closed. The pieces that used to move separately had become a single unmoving entity. Function had become stillness. Other forces were at work here now, disassembling the tiniest pieces, breaking them down like grinding grain into flour. All the little links that bound them were coming undone. Nevertheless, I tried. I tried to move his arm; I tried to force his body to take a breath.

What are you doing?

It was Thick, mildly annoyed that I had broken into his sleep. I was suddenly frantically glad to feel him with me. *Thick, I have found him, the Fool, my friend, Lord Golden. I have found him. Help me heal him. Please, lend me your strength.*

He was sleepily tolerant of my request. *All right. Thick will try.* I felt the wide yawn he did not disguise. *Where is he?*

Here! Right here! With my Skill, I indicated the still body before me.

Where?

Right here! Here, Thick. Under my hands.

There's no one there.

Yes there is. I'm touching him, right here. Please, Thick. Then, in my despair, I threw my plea wider. *Dutiful, Chade. Please. Lend me strength and Skill for a healing. Please.*

Who is hurt? Not Thick! Chade was with me abruptly, full of panic.

No, I am fine. He wants to heal someone who isn't there.

He is here. I've found the Fool's body, Chade. Please. You all brought me back. Please. Help me heal him, help me bring him back!

Dutiful spoke, calmingly. *Fitz, we are all here, and you know we will do this for you. It may be harder, as we are separated, but we will try. Show him to us.*

He is here! Right here, I'm touching him. I was suddenly furiously impatient with them. Why were they being so stupid? Why wouldn't they help me?

I don't sense him, Dutiful said after a long pause. *Touch him.*

But I am! I bent over him and put my arms around his curled body. *I'm holding him. Please. Help me heal him.*

That? That isn't a person. Thick was obviously puzzled. *You can't heal dirt!*

Rage filled me. *He isn't dirt!*

Dutiful spoke gently. *It's all right, Thick. Don't be upset. You said nothing wrong. I know you didn't mean it that way.* Then, to me, *Oh, Fitz, I am so sorry. But he's dead. And Thick is right, in his own blunt way. His body is becoming . . . something else. I cannot sense it as a body. Only as . . .* He halted, unable to say the words. Carrion. Rot. Degenerating meat. Dirt.

Chade spoke as calmly as if he were reminding me of an obvious lesson. *Healing is a function of the living body, Fitz. The Skill can urge it, but the body does it. When it is alive.*

That is not the Fool you hold, Fitz. It is his empty shell. You cannot make it live any more than you could make a rock live. There is no calling him back into it.

Thick spoke pragmatically. *Even if you made it work again, there's no one to put in it.*

I think it finally became real then. The corpse that was no longer his body. The absence of his spirit.

A long, long time seemed to pass. Then Chade spoke again softly. *Fitz. What are you doing now?*

Nothing. Just sitting here. Failing. Again. Just as I did with Burrich. He died, didn't he?

I could almost see the resignation on the old man's face. I knew how he would draw a breath and sigh that I insisted on stacking all my pain in one pile, facing it all at once. *Yes. He did. With his son beside him. And Web. All of us honored him. We halted the ships, to be together when they slid him over the side and let him go. Just as you must let the Fool go.*

I did not want to agree with that or to answer it at all. The habits of a lifetime are strong. I diverted Chade's attention. *I found the Skill scrolls. The stolen library. It is here, in the Pale Woman's stronghold. Only I do not think this place was truly hers. I have seen things here that make me think it was a place where Elderlings abided.*

Chade surprised me. *Later, Fitz. Later is plenty of time to consider recovering the scrolls. For now, listen to me. Honor your friend's body, however you see fit. Release it. Then both you and Thick hurry back to the beach. I will come back on the ship that I send for you. I misjudged what you intended to do. I do not think you should be alone with this sort of grief.*

But he was wrong. Grief makes its own solitude, and I knew that I must endure it. I compromised, knowing it was the only way to make him leave me alone. *Thick and I will be on the beach when the ship arrives. You don't need to come back for us. I won't let any harm come to us. But for now, I would be alone. If you don't mind.*

No boats! Thick said decisively. *Not ever. No. I'll stay right here where I am before I go on a boat. Forever.*

Thick isn't with you now? Chade sounded anxious.

No. He will explain. I still have a task to do, Chade. Thank you. All of you. Thank you for trying. I pulled up my walls, closing myself off from them. I felt Dutiful try to reach for me, but I could not tolerate even his gentle touch right then. I walled them out, even as Thick sleepily told them that the Black Man made wonderful food. Before my walls closed, I felt a tenuous touch that might have been Nettle, trying to send me comfort.

There was no comfort for me and I would not expose her to my pain. She would have enough of her own, soon enough. I closed my walls. It was time to deal with death.

I peeled the Fool's corpse from the floor, leaving an outline of his coiled body and a handful of golden strands of his hair to mark where he had died. He was a solid, cold weight in my arms. In death, he seemed to weigh less than he had in life, as if the departure of his spirit had taken most of him with it.

I held him curled against my chest, the soiled mat of his golden hair under my chin, the coarse sacking against my fingers. I walked empty through the ice halls. We passed the chamber where Hest still burned. The smoke of his flesh crawled along the ceiling above us, tainting the still air with the aroma of cooking meat. I could have put the Fool's body with his, but it did not feel right. My friend should burn alone, in a private farewell between us. I walked on, past the other cell doors.

After a time I became aware that I was speaking aloud to him. "Where? Where would you want me to do this thing? I could place you on her bed and burn you in the midst of all her heaped wealth . . . would you want that? Or would you think that contact with anything of hers would soil you? Where would I want to be burned? Under the night sky, I think, sending my own sparks up to the stars. Would you like that, Fool? Or would you prefer to be within the Elderling tent, with your own things around you, closed in with the privacy you always cherished? Why didn't we ever talk about these things? It seems something a man should know about his best friend. But in the end, does it matter at all? Gone is gone, ash is ash . . . but I think I would prefer to loose your smoke to the night wind. Would you laugh at me for that? Gods. Would that you could laugh at me for anything again."

"How touching."

The lilt of mockery, the knife's edge of sarcasm, and the voice so like his made my heart stop and then lurch on. I slammed my Skill-walls tight, but felt no assault against them. I turned, teeth bared, to confront her. She stood in the door of her bedchamber. She was mantled in ermine, white fur with tiny black tails interrupting it in a scattered pattern. It hung from her shoulders to the floor, draping her entire body. Despite the richness of her garb, she looked haggard. The perfect sculpting of her face had sunken to her bones and her pale hair, ungroomed, lagged and wisped like dry straw around her face. Her colorless eyes seemed almost dull, the eyes of a beached fish.

I stood before her, clutching the Fool's corpse to my breast. I knew he was dead and she could no longer hurt him, and yet I backed away from her, as if I still needed to protect him from her. As if I had ever been able to protect him from her!

She lifted her chin, baring the white column of her throat. "Drop that," she suggested, "and come and kill me."

Was it because she had suggested it that my first thought now seemed like such a bad idea? "No," I replied, and suddenly I wanted only to be left completely alone. This was an intimate death I held. She, of all people, should not witness or take satisfaction in my grief. "Go away," I said, and did not know the low growl of my own voice.

She laughed, icicles shattering on stone. "Go away? Is that all? Go away? Such a keen vengeance for FitzChivalry

Farseer to take upon me! Ah, that shall go down in tales and songs! 'And then he stood, holding his *beloved* and said to their enemy, 'Go away!'" She laughed, but there was no music in it. It was like rocks rattling down a hillside, and when I made no response to it, her laughter trailed away into silence. She stared at me, and for a moment she looked confused. She had truly believed that she could make me drop him and attack her. She tipped her head, staring at me, and after a moment, spoke again. Her voice was lower now.

"Wait. I see. You have not yet unwrapped my little gift to you. You have not yet seen all that I did to him. Wait until you see his hands, and those clever, graceful fingers of his! Oh, and his tongue and teeth, which spoke so wittily for your amusement! I did that for you, FitzChivalry, that you might fully regret your disdainful rejection of me." She paused very briefly and then said, as if reminding me, "Now, Fitz. This is when you promise to kill me if I follow you."

I had been about to utter those words. I bit down on them. She had made them empty and childish. Perhaps those words were always empty and childish. I shifted my burden in my arms and then turned and walked away from her. My Skill-walls were up and tight, but if she made any assault against them, it was too subtle for me to feel. My back felt exposed and I'll admit that I wanted to run. I asked myself why I did not kill her. The answer seemed too simple to be true. I did not want to put his body down on her floor while I did it. Even more, I did not want to do anything that she expected me to do.

"He called out for you!" She sang the words after me. "He thought he was close to dying, I imagine. Of course, he was not. I am more adept than that! But he thought the pain would kill him, and he cried out for you. 'Beloved! Beloved!'" Her mockery of his agonized voice was perfect. The hair on the back of my neck stood up as if he had spoken to me from beyond the grave. Despite my resolve, my steps slowed. I held his body closer and bowed my head more tightly over his. I hated that her words could bring tears to my eyes. I should kill her. Why didn't I kill her?

"He did mean you, did he not? Well, of course he did, though you may not know it. I doubt you know the custom of the people he came from; how they exchange names to denote the lifelong bonds they form? Did you ever call him by your name, to show him that he was as dear to you as your own life? Did you? Or were you too much of a coward to let him know?"

I wanted to kill her then. But I would have had to set his body down and I would not do that. She could not make me abandon him again. I would not set him down and I would not look back at her. I hunched my back against her pelted words and trudged away.

"Did you? Did you? Did you?"

I had expected to hear her voice fade as I walked away. Instead, she lifted it, and her tone became even angrier as she flung the hateful question at me. After a time, I knew she was following me. The words were a hoarse shriek now, the cawing of crows as they summon one another to the rich pickings of a battlefield. "Did you? Did you? Did you?"

Even when I heard her running footsteps behind me and knew that she would attack me, I could not bring myself to drop the Fool's body. I held him and turned, hunching a shoulder to her maddened onslaught. I do not think it was what she expected. Perhaps she had hoped I would face her with a drawn blade. She tried to stop but the icy floor betrayed her. She slid into me. I kept my grip on the Fool's body as I slammed against the wall, and somehow managed to stay on my feet. She did not. She sprawled on her side, gasping hoarsely in her pain. I looked at her dumbly, wondering how a fall could have caused her that much agony. Then, as she tried to rise, I saw what she had concealed from me.

Riddle's telling had been true. I stared at the blackened and shriveled forearms that she struggled to use. She could neither rise nor cover them again beneath the robe. I met her colorless eyes and spoke my words coldly. "You are the coward. At the last minute, you could not give up yourself, not even to complete your vision of what the world should be. You lacked his courage. He accepted the price fate decreed for him. He took his pain and his death and he won. He triumphed. You failed."

She made a sound, between a shriek and a yelp, full of hatred and fury. It battered at my Skill-wall, but she could not get through. Had her strength for that magic been drawn from Kebal Rawbread? I watched her try to get to her feet. The long mantle hindered her, for she knelt on the hem of it. The black sticks that had been her arms and hands were of no use to her. From the elbow down, her arms were shrunken to bones that ended in charred and tapering ends. I could see the remains of the dual bones in her forearms. There was no sign of her hands and fingers. Those, at least, the dragon had claimed before she had managed to drag herself free of him. I recalled how Verity had gone, and Kettle, melting into the dragon they had fashioned so lovingly for the good of their people. Then I turned and walked away from her.

"Stop!" she commanded me. There was outrage in her voice. "You kill me here! I have seen this, a hundred times in my nightmares. You kill me now! It was my certain fate if I failed. I dreaded it but I now command it! My visions have always been true. You are fated to kill me."

I spoke over my shoulder, scarcely considering my words at all. "I am the Catalyst. I change things. Besides. The time we are in now is the time the Fool chose. It is his future I live in. In his vision of the future, I walk away from you. You die slowly. Alone."

Another dozen steps, and then she screamed. She screamed until her breath was gone, and then I heard her ragged panting. I walked on.

"You *are* the Catalyst still!" she shrieked after me. There was nothing but desperation and amazement in her voice now. "If you will not kill me, then come back and use your Skill to heal me. I will be subject to you in all ways! You could use me as you wished, and I could teach you all I have learned from the Skill scrolls! You have the strength to wield that magic! Heal me, and I will show you the path to power. You will be the rightful King of the Six Duchies, of the Out Islands, of all the Cursed Shores! All. I will give you all your dreams, if only you come back!"

My dream was dead in my arms. I continued to walk.

I heard her scratching the blackened stubs of her melted arms against the ice. It reminded me of an overturned beetle frantically scrabbling in a washbasin. I did not look back. I wondered, briefly, if she had ever foreseen this moment, if she had ever imagined the look of my back as I walked away. No, I suddenly knew. The Black Man had told me. I walked in the Fool's world now, the future he had shaped. She could see nothing, prophesy nothing here. This time was not hers. It was the time he had chosen.

I do not think I am by nature a cruel man, and yet I have never been able to feel any sort of compunction over what I did. I heard her scream once, like an animal screams from a trap, but I did not look back. I turned a corner and walked on, back the way I had come.

I was unutterably weary and cold and hungry. Yet none of those things consumed me as much as my grief. At some point, tears came to me. They fell on the Fool's golden hair and misted my vision of the tunnels to a pale maze. Perhaps in my daze, I missed one of my marks on the wall. I realized it, and turned back, but found myself in an unfamiliar corridor. I came to an eroded ice staircase and attempted to go up it, but found that, burdened as I was, I could not. I turned back again and trudged on, hopelessly lost.

At one point, I spread my cloak out on the floor and slept for a time, my arm flung protectively across his frozen body. When I awoke, I searched through my pack and found a bit of travelers' bread and ate it. I drank from my flask, and then wet the edge of my cloak and wiped some of the blood and filth from his contorted face. I could not

wipe the pain from his brow. Then I rose and took him up
and walked on, completely disoriented in the unchanging
pale light. I was, perhaps, a trifle mad.

I reached a place where one wall was of ice and one of
stone. I should have turned back, but like a moth drawn
toward light, I followed the passageway that was leading
me upward. I came to stairs cut in the stone and followed
them up. The bluish light of the gleaming orbs did not waver, never brightening or dimming, so that I bore his body
through a timeless maze of gentle stairs that wound ever
upward. I halted for breath on a landing. There was a
wooden door there, the wood gone splintery and dry. I
pushed it open, thinking of finding fuel for his burning.

If I had doubted at all that once this icy realm had belonged to the Elderlings, that chamber dispelled it. I had
seen furniture like this before, tottering in the deserted ruins of the city by the river. I had seen a map such as this
room held, though this seemed to be of a world rather than
of a city and the surrounding countryside. It was on a table
in the center of the room. It was round, but it was not flat,
nor drawn upon paper. Each island, each coast, each wave
tip had been sculpted. Tiny mountains jutted in ranges,
and the sea crinkled. Gleaming rivers meandered through
grasslands to the sea.

An island, most likely Aslevjal, was in the exact center of it. Other islands dotted the sea around it. To the
south and west, I saw the coast of the Six Duchies, though
it was subtly wrong in many places. To the north was a land
I had no name for, and across a wide sea, on the eastern
edge of the map, I saw a coastline where tradition told me
there was only endless ocean. Tiny gems had been set randomly into the map, each marked with a rune. Some
seemed to glow with an inner light. One glittered white on
Aslevjal. Four, set in a minute square, sparkled in Buck,
near the mouth of the Buck River. There were a handful of
others throughout the Six Duchies, some bright and some
dull. There were more in the Mountain Kingdom, and a

line of them, carefully spaced, along the Rain Wild River, though many of those were quenched. I nodded slowly to myself. Of course.

Dimly, I was aware that my arms and back ached. Yet it never occurred to me that I might wish to set down my burden and rest for a time. Inevitable as sunset, there was the door to another stairwell in the corner. I entered it. It was narrower than the first and the stairs were steeper. I marched slowly up it, my feet scuffing as I found each step unseeing. The light changed slowly as I went. The bluish glow faded, slowly replaced with the murky light of true day. Then I emerged into a tower room walled with glass. One panel of it had cracked, and all of the windows were coated with frost. The ceiling spoke of a steep spire overhead, with sheltering eaves. I put my eye to the crack in the window and peered out. Snow. Blowing snow. I could see no more than that.

In the center of the room was a Skill-pillar. The runes carved into the sides of it were as cleanly chiseled as the day they had been cut. I walked a slow circuit around them until I came to the one that I had known would be there. I nodded to myself. I held him close to me and said softly into his blood-matted hair, "Let's go back, then."

I opened one hand and we walked into the Skill-pillar.

Perhaps my recent practice of the Skill had strengthened me, or perhaps this pillar worked better than others I had known. The Fool in my arms, I stepped from winter to summer, from a stone tower to what remained of a market plaza. All around me, a summer day hummed in the forest that had encroached to the edges of it. I took two more steps and then went to my knees, both in weakness and gratitude. Here, suddenly, it did not feel like blasphemy to deposit him on the clean stone and earth. I sat down flat beside him and rested. For a time, all was still, save for the calls of birds and the buzzing of busy insects. I looked down the overgrown road, like a tunnel through the greenery of the forest, that would, if I followed it, lead me to the Stone

Garden where all the Elderling dragons slept. I looked up at the worn pillar, where once a young Fool had perched and I had seen him transformed into a white girl wearing a rooster crown. "This is a good place," I said softly. "I'm glad we came back here." I leaned back and closed my eyes. I slept.

It took time for the warmth of the afternoon to seep into me. When I awoke, I was too warm. The Fool's frozen body was thawing and loosening in the sunlight. I peeled my winter garments from my body as if I were shedding an outworn skin until I wore only my tunic and leggings. Now that we were here, alone and together, I felt my urgency leave me. There was time here, time that belonged only to him and me, time in which I could do things properly.

I fetched water from the stream where once we had drunk. I gently washed his face, wiping the blood from his lips and smoothing the hair over his torn ear. When I could do so, I peeled the sacking away from his raw flesh. What I saw dizzied me at first. Yes. She was right. I did regret that I had turned away from her instead of dealing her the agonizing death she deserved. But as I straightened, as much as I could, his tormented and stiffened limbs and wiped away with green leaves and clean grass the filth and clotted blood, all hatred seeped away from me. Here was my Fool, and if I could not save him from death, I could send him from this life with dignity.

He had curled protectively around his last treasure. He gripped the Rooster Crown in his lifeless hands. I pried its dull gray wood carefully from his nailless fingers. His tormentors had broken the crown, probably in the course of beating him, but he had repaired it before he died. When I saw how he had done it, how he had used his own congealing blood as a binder to hold the pieces together, I choked for a time. Its circle had a gap in it. I wondered if that had grieved him as he died.

Slowly I took from my pouch the shard they had left on the floor of the throne room. It only lacked that one piece to make it complete. I dipped the edges of it into his thawing blood, and joined it to its fellows to complete the crown. Dampened with blood, the wood swelled and seized and held, almost as if it had never been broken. I did not know what this treasure was, exactly. Whatever it had meant to him, I would send him from this world wearing it.

I set it to one side as I gathered evergreen boughs and dry fallen limbs, dead twigs and dry grasses, for his funeral pyre. Evening was hovering before it was built. When it was ready, I spread my cloak over it. Overhead, a deep blue sky shimmered, and summer seemed to hold its breath around us, awaiting the first stars of evening. The sparks of his burning would join them. I lifted him and placed him on the cloak. Experience told me the evergreen boughs would burn well and consume him. With a heavy heart, I sat down on the stone beside his pyre, the Rooster Crown in my lap. It lacked but one thing to be complete.

From my pack I took a bundled packet. Gently I unrolled the fabric. One at a time, I set out the feathers from the Others beach. As I handled each one, I marveled anew at the intricate workmanship that had gone into their carving. Despite all the long way they had traveled with me, they were unharmed. Why someone had chosen such a lusterless wood for such fine work escaped me. It was as plain and dull as the arrow the Fool had given Swift.

It took some moments for me to fit each feather into its proper place. I noticed now what I never had before, that the end of each feather's shaft was notched. Each would slide only into its proper aperture in the crown. As I pushed the last one into place, it seemed to my weary eyes that a wave of colors washed over both crown and feathers. Perhaps it was only a rainbow caught for an instant in the sudden tears that brimmed my eyes. I dashed them away impatiently. Time to be done with all this.

The crown whispered uncomfortably against my fingers, like a trapped fly buzzing in a fist. I wondered what I held. What potent Elderling magic was trapped here, denied for

all time by the Fool's death? For a moment, my eyes lingered
on the softened carvings of roosters' heads that ringed the
crown. Either the Fool had never got round to painting it as
we recalled it, or it had refused to hold the paint. Chips of
color still clung in the deeper corners of the carving. Tiny
gems still winked in two of the carved eyes; the others were
blank and empty. There were dark seams in the ring of the
crown where it had been broken and then glued back into a
whole with the Fool's blood. I tapped one of the seams cautiously, testing the strength of the bond. It held and suddenly
he leaped into my mind, my memory of him so poignant and
whole that I felt disemboweled with sorrow.

I sat down heavily on the pyre beside him. Rigor had
kept his body in its defensive curl. I could do nothing about
that. I wished that I could have smoothed the lines of terror and pain from his face before I sent him on his way. I
pushed his golden hair back from his tawny forehead. "Oh,
Beloved," I said. I bent and kissed his brow in farewell.
And then, grasping the rightness of that foreign tradition, I
named him as myself. For when I burned him, I knew I
would be ending myself, as well. The man I had been would
not survive this loss. "Good-bye, FitzChivalry Farseer." I
took the crown in both hands to ease it onto his brow. I felt
suddenly as if all my life had been funneling me toward this
moment. It seemed cruel that the strongest current of my
life would propel me toward this moment of absolute end
and loss. But there were no other choices left for me. Some
things could not be changed. It was time to crown the
king's jester and send him on his way.

I stopped.

I halted my hands, and it felt as if by doing so, I stood
alone against fate and defied the flow of all time. I knew
what I was meant to do. I should crown my Fool and then
drench the pyre with the remaining oil. A spark, at most
two, would be enough for the summer-dry tinder. He would
burn away to nothing, his smoke rising on the summer
wind of the land beyond the Mountain Kingdom. I would

go back, through the pillar, to Aslevjal. I would collect Thick and go back to the little bay and wait for a ship to come and fetch us. It was right, it was inevitable, it was the channel in which the entire world wished to flow. Life would go on without the Fool, because he had died. I could see it all so clearly, as if I had always known it would come to this.

He was dead. Nothing could change that.

But I was the Changer.

I stood suddenly. I lifted the humming crown high overhead in my hands and shook it at the sky. "NO!" I roared. I still do not know to whom I spoke. "No! Let it be different! Not this way! Whatever you want from me, take it! But don't let it all end like this! Let him take my life and give me his death. Let him be me and I be him. I take his death! Do you hear me? I take his death for my own!"

I lifted the crown to the sun. Through my flowing tears, it shone iridescent, and the feathers seemed to waver gently in the summer breeze. Then, with an almost physical wrench, I tore it out of time's destined path. I clapped it firmly upon my own brow. As the world spun around me, I lay my body down on my funeral pyre, wrapped my arms around my friend, and gave myself over to whatever awaited me beyond it.

chapter XXIX

FEATHERS IN A FOOL'S CAP

*She was the richest girl in the world, for not only had she
a noble father, and many silk gowns and so many
necklaces and rings that not even a dozen little girls could
have worn them all at once, but she had also a little gray
box, carved from a dragon's womb. And inside it,
ground to fine powder, were all the happy memories of
the wisest princesses who had ever lived. So, whenever
she got the least bit sad, all she had to do was open her
little box and take a tiny bit of the memory snuff, and,
kerchoo! She was as happy as a girl could be again.*

                ➤ OLD JAMAILLIAN TALE

I missed a step in the dark. It was like that, that unexpected
lurch.

"Blood is memory." I swear someone whispered that by
my ear.

"Blood is who we are," a young woman agreed with
him. "Blood recalls who we were. Blood is how we will be
remembered. Work it well into the womb wood."

Someone laughed, an old woman with few teeth. "Say
that six times swiftly!" she cackled. And she did. "Work it
well into the womb wood. Work it well into the womb

wood. Work it well into the womb wood. Work it well into the womb wood. Work it well into the womb wood. Work it well into the womb wood."

The others laughed, amused at her tripping tongue. "Well, you try it!" she challenged us.

"Work it well into the womb wood," I said obediently. But it wasn't me.

There were five other people there inside me, looking out of my eyes, running my tongue over my teeth, scratching at my beard with my unkempt nails. Breathing my breath, and rejoicing in the taste of the forest on the night air. Shaking out my hair, alive again.

Five poets, five jesters. Five tellers of tales. Five jumbling, tumbling minstrels, leaping and whirling in gratitude for their release, shaking out my fingers, limbering my voice, and already squabbling and vying for my attention.

"What is your need? A birthday anthem? I've a host of them at my beck and call, and it's no trouble, no trouble at all, to adapt one to your recipient's name!"

"Hackery! Shameless hackery, this chopping and splicing of old relics, this dressing of bones anew! Let me have your voice and I'll sing you a song to rouse your warriors and make your maidens tremble with newborn lust!" This was a man, and he filled my lungs to bursting to roar out his words. Each set of words, each voice came from my own throat. I was a puppet for them, a pipe to be played.

"Lust is but a wet moment, a surge and a splat!" she said disdainfully. She was a young woman, and she remembered freckles across the bridge of her nose. Strange to hear her words pipe from my throat. "You want a love song, don't you? Something timeless, something older than the fallen mountains, and newer than a seed unfurling in rich soil. Such is love."

"Good luck!" someone exclaimed in dismay. He tinged his words with a fop's disdain. "Listen. Fa, la, la, la, la, la— oh, hopeless! This one has the pipes of a sailor, and a body of wood. The finest song ever sung will be a crow's croaking when it comes from this throat, and I'll wager he never turned a handspring in his life. Who is this, and how came he by our treasure?"

"Minstrels," I said dully. "Minstrels, tumblers, and bards. Oh, Fool, this *would* be your treasure. A circle of jesters. There is no help for us here." I put my head down into my hands. I felt the rough wood of the crown beneath my fingers. I pushed at it, but it clung stubbornly in place. It had tightened to my brow.

"We've only just arrived," the toothless crone complained. "We've no intention of leaving already. We are a great gift, a magnificent gift, only awarded to the one most pleasing to the King. We are a chorus of voices, from all ages, we are a rainbow of history. Why would you refuse us? What sort of a performer are you?"

"I'm not a performer at all." I sighed heavily. For a moment, I regained full awareness of my body. I stood by the funeral pyre. I didn't recall getting up from it. Night was dark around us and chirring insects were tuning their voices. In the cooling air, I smelled the rich leaf mold of the forest. The Fool's degenerating body added its own note of sweet rot. All his life, he had been the Scentless One to Nighteyes. Now, in death, I smelled him. It did not sicken me. There was still wolf enough in me that how he smelled was simply how he smelled. It was the change that gave me a pang, for it was irrefutable evidence that his body was going back to the earth and the natural web of rot and rebirth all around me. I tried to pause for long enough to take some comfort in that, but the five within me were too impatient for stillness. They turned me in a slow circle, lifting my arms, testing the spring of my feet, filling my lungs with air. I sensed how those within me lapped eagerly at the night, the taste, the smell, the sound, and the feel of the forest air on my face. They were avid for life.

"What help do you need?" the freckled girl asked me, and in her voice I heard sympathy and a readiness to listen. And under it, scarcely cloaked, lurked the hunger that all minstrels have for the tale of another's woe. She wanted that part of life back as well. I did not wish to share mine.

"No. Go away. You can't help me." And then, against my will, I told them anyway. "My friend is dead. I want to bring him back to life. Can a minstrel help with that?"

For one respectful instant, they were silent as I gazed down on the Fool's corpse. Then, the freckle-nosed girl said tremulously, "He's very dead, isn't he?"

"Yes, he is," the bull-throated one declared, but added, "I can make you such a song as will have him remembered a thousand years hence. It is the only way ordinary mortals can transcend the flesh. Give me your memories of him, and I'll get started."

The crone spoke sense to me. "Did we know how to undo death, would we be what we are, feathers in a fool's cap? We are lucky to have this much of life left to us. A pity that your friend did not have the favor of a dragon, or perhaps he too could share this boon."

"What are you?" I demanded.

"We are sweet preserves of song, stored away so that in the winter of our deaths you can taste again the tang of our summers." It was the young man, so conscious of his imagery that he ruined it for me.

"Someone else!" I begged when the young man fell silent.

"We were favored of dragons," a calm voice said. She was one who had not spoken before. Her voice was a deep calm pond, huskier than the voice of most women. I heard it in my mind even as my own throat rusted her words. "I lived by the river of black sand, in a little town called Junket. I went one day to fetch water from the river, and there I met my dragon. She was a young thing, just at the end of her first summer, and I was in the spring of my years. Oh, she was green, a thousand greens, with eyes like deep pots of melted gold. She stood in the river and the waters rushed by her. Then she looked at me, and my heart fell into her whirlpool eyes, never to surface again. I had to sing to her; speaking would not have been enough. So she charmed me and I sang to her, and charmed her in return. I was her minstrel and her bard for all the days of my life. And when my time to end was approaching, she came to me, with the gift that only a dragon may give. It was a sliver of wood from a dragon's womb…do you know whereof I speak? The cradles they spin for the serpents to sleep in until they emerge as dragons? Sometimes, there is one who does not survive that stage, who dies in the sleep between serpent and dragon. Slow is the womb wood to erode, and the dragons forbid that humans touch any of it, save by their leave. But to me, fair Smokewing brought a sliver of it. She bid me wet it well with my own blood, and work the blood into it with my fingers, all the while thinking of a feather.

"I knew what such a favor meant. It was rarely granted, even to minstrels who had served their dragons well. It meant I would take a place in the crown of minstrels, so that my songs and words and my way of thinking would go on, long after I died. The crown is the property of the Ruler of all the River Lands. The Ruler alone declares who may wear the crown and sing with the voices of minstrels long dead. It is a great honor, for only a dragon can select you to become a feather, and only the Ruler can bestow the gift of wearing the crown. Such an honor. I remember how I clasped my feather as I died…for die I did. Just like your friend. A pity that your friend was not favored of dragons, to have been granted such a boon."

I was hammered by the irony of it. "He should have been. He died to waken a dragon, the last male dragon in the world, so that Icefyre might rise to partner Tintaglia, the last female. So that there might be dragons again in this world."

The moment of silence told me that I had impressed them. "Now, here is a tale worth the telling! Give us the memories of that, and each of us will make you a song, for surely there are at least a score of songs in such an event!"

It was the crone who spoke, my mouth going soft with her words.

"But I don't want a song about him. I want the Fool as he was, alive and whole."

"Dead is dead," the bull-voiced man said. But he said it gently. "If you wish to open your memories to us, we will weave you songs. Even with your voice, they will be songs that will live, for true minstrels will hear you sing them, and wish to sing them as they should be sung. Do you want to do that?"

"No. Please, Fitz, no. Leave it be. Let it be over."

It was a whisper against my senses, scarce a breathing of the words. I shivered to it, wild with hope and fear.

"Fool," I breathed, praying there would be some response.

Instead, there was a cacophony, the thoughts indistinguishable from one another, as the five feather minstrels all shouted a dozen unanswerable questions at me. At last, Bull-throat roared through them with a reply.

"He's here! With us. In the crown, of all places. He put his blood in the crown!"

But from the Fool, there was no reply. I spoke for him. "The crown was broken. He used his blood to mend it."

"The crown was broken?" The crone was aghast. "It would have ended all of us! Forever!"

"He cannot stay in the crown! He was not chosen. Besides, the crown belongs to all of us. If he takes it, we shall not be able to speak, save through him." The young man was outraged at the Fool's rash assumption of his territory.

"He must go," the bull-voiced man concluded. "We are very sorry, but he must go. It is not right or fitting that he be here."

"He was not chosen."

"He was not invited."

"He is not welcome."

They gave me no time to express an opinion. The crown was tight to my brow and suddenly it became tighter. I lifted my hands to it, for they seemed to have retreated from my body into the crown, to do whatever they were doing now. For the nonce, my body was my own again. I tried to tear the crown from my head, but I could not get so much as a nail between it and my skin. In a wave of horror, I realized it was melding to my flesh, melting into me like a coterie seeping into a stone dragon. "No!" I roared. I shook my head and clawed at it. It would not budge. Worse, it no longer felt like wood beneath my fingers. It felt like a band of flesh. When I queasily lifted my fingers to investigate the feathers, they flexed softly as cockerel plumes against my fingers. I felt sick.

Trembling, I went back to the funeral pyre and sank down onto it beside the Fool. I sensed no battle in the crown, only a concerted effort by the five minstrels. The Fool did not resist them; he simply did not know how to do what they demanded of him. I no longer had any voice in what they did. Theirs was a quarrel heard across the market, a conflict I was aware of but had no part in. They would force him out of the crown, and then he would be truly gone, forever. I could not stop it.

I took his body in my lap and held it. It had passed through stiffness now to laxness. His hand flopped to one side, and I lifted it by the wrist to fold it back in to his chest. Something in the way it moved so lifelessly woke an ancient memory. I scowled after it. It was not my recall. It was Nighteyes, and he saw it through a wolf's eyes. We were in hunting light and the colors were muted. Yet I had been there. Somehow. And then it came back to me.

The Gray One, Chade, leaning on a shovel, his breath white in the cold air. He stands some distance away, so as not to frighten us. Heart of the Pack is the one who sits on the edge of my grave. His feet dangle in the hole before him, my splintered coffin at his feet. He holds my corpse in his lap. He waves the hand of it at me, beckoning the wolf in closer. His Wit is strong, and Nighteyes cannot bring himself to disobey Heart of the Pack. Heart of the Pack is speaking to us, a steady stream of calm words. "Come back to this. This is yours, Changer. Come back to it."

Nighteyes lifts a lip and snarls. We know death when we smell it. That body is dead. It is carrion, not fit for an honest meal. Nighteyes conveys the message to Heart of the Pack. "It smells bad. It is spoiled meat, we do not want it. There is better meat by the pond than that."

"Come closer," Burrich bids us. For that moment, I perceive him as both Burrich and Heart of the Pack. I slide sideways from the wolf's perception of him into my human memory of that moment. I had long suspected that I had truly died, despite Chade's assurances that his poisons had only feigned my death. My body had been too battered to withstand any amount of poison. In the memory, my wolf's nose is mercilessly truthful. That body was dead. But the wolf's keener Wit-awareness tells me what I had never guessed before. Heart of the Pack does more than hold my flesh. He has prepared it for me; it is ready to begin again, if only he can coax me into it. Nighteyes is a reassuring whisper against my senses.

The Wit. Not the Skill. Burrich did it with the Wit. But he was much stronger in that magic than I was, and far more wise. I stroked the Fool's slackening face, willing his body to align with mine, but I could not find a way into him. He did not have the Wit. Was that the difference? I did not know. But I knew that there was a way, once, a place where we had linked, he and I. Once, he had dragged me from the wolf's body back into my own. I turned my own wrist up to the faltering moonlight and found there the duskiness of his fingerprints. I took his mangled hand in mine. The fingernails had been peeled from three of his slender, delicate fingers. I pushed away my awareness of that agony he had endured. My hand overshadowed his as I carefully set each fingertip of his to each print on my wrist. I groped for the slender Skill-link, spun between us so many years before.

And it was there, faint as gossamer, but there. I gathered my courage, knowing well that I was going into death itself. But go I would. Had not I just said that I would, that I would take his death for him? I could feel that the crown minstrels were forcing him out, expelling him into my own flesh, but I had no time to wait and make explanations for him. I took a deep breath and trickled down the Skill-link, leaving my body to his awakening awareness and entering the ruin of his.

For the briefest moment, my perception was doubled. The Fool was in my flesh, looking out of my eyes. He stared down aghast at his own lax corpse in my arms. He lifted a hand to touch my whiskered chin. "Beloved!" he groaned. "Oh, Beloved, what have you done? What have you done?"

"It's all right," I assured him quietly. "If I fail, take my life and live it. I willingly take your death." Then, like a stone falling into muck, I sank into the Fool's lifeless flesh.

I was in a body that was dead, that had been dead for days.

This body had no life left in it, and hence it was no longer a body. Lifeless as a rock, it was separating into its components and going back to the earth. My Skill did not know what to make of such a situation. I pushed aside my impulse to use it, to cry out to Thick and Chade and Dutiful. They would only have forced me back into my own body to save me.

The Wit is the awareness of life all around us. It is a web, a net that connects us to every living creature. Some were vital and complex, large healthy beasts that demanded my recognition. Trees and plants were subtler, but even more essential to the continuation of life than creatures that moved. They were the warp the world is woven upon, and without them we would all snarl and fall. Even so, I had successfully ignored them for most of my life, other than a passing interest in the green shadow life of the oldest trees. But beyond and beneath it all, there flowed an even more nebulous life.

It was death.

Death, the knots in the net that connected us all, was

not death at all. In that twisting and tightening noose, life was re-formed, not destroyed. The Fool's body rioted with life. It was a simmering cauldron of life, bubbling its way to rebirth. Every element that had united to make his body a living creature was still there. The question was, could I persuade it to assume its old alignment rather than the simpler forms it was now reducing itself to?

Breathless, voiceless, senseless, I gave myself over to it. It was like a Skill-stream in its own way, for it plucked and tugged at the strings of the Fool's body, carrying away bits of him that it would use elsewhere. It fascinated me, this orderly dispersal, this re-sorting and reordering. It was rather like watching a well-played game of Stones. The bits moved in a pattern. I tried to coax one back to its old position, but it flowed away from me to join its fellows.

It is the old game again. Still, you will not see it. They are not individual hunters, but a pack. You do not set your will against the individuals. There are too many of them. You cannot stop them. So drive them. Use them. What they have made new, put back in place of the old.

It was a wolf's wisdom. As Black Rolf had told me it could be, so it was. Nighteyes was with me, not as he had been, but as we had been. It was his vision I used that night, his simple wolf's awareness that when one ate meat, one ate life as much as flesh. The elegant balance of the predator and the prey applied here as much as it did when we had hunted together. Death feeds life. What the body takes apart, it assembles again.

This was not a Skill-healing. It was a guiding of the changes, a herding of the bits into the alignment I recalled. I doubt that I was as adept as Burrich had been in my restoration. Time and again, the flows I had corrected reversed themselves and had to be persuaded again to build up, not tear down. Nor was the Fool completely human. That night, I confronted completely his strangeness. I thought I had known him. In those hours of rebuilding, I realized and accepted him as he was. That, in itself, was a revelation. I had always believed we were more alike than different. It simply was not true. He was human only in the same way that I was a wolf.

I stayed with my work, past the moment when I felt the blood begin to once more flow within his veins, beyond the slow perception that I could once more draw breath into his lungs. Some of his body had been repaired in the act of restoring it. Two of his ribs had been broken. Those bone ends had found their mates and begun knitting themselves together. Gossamer stitches of flesh closed the worst rents in his skin. But there was little I could do about the places where flesh or bone or nail was simply missing. Delicately, I set in motion his own healing. I dared not urge it much past its own careful reconstruction. He had already burned the reserves of his body. I closed the raw flesh of his back against the agonizing kiss of the air. I coaxed his split tongue into a whole again. Two of his teeth were missing, and there was nothing I could do about that. When I knew I had done all I could for his body, I drew a deeper breath into his lungs. I opened his eyes.

Night was fading into dawn. The weaker stars had already given way to the creeping light of day. A bird sang a dawn call. Another one challenged it. An insect hummed past my ear. I became aware of my body more slowly. Blood moved through me and I tasted air sliding from my lungs. It was good. There was pain, a great deal of pain. But pain is the body's messenger, the warning that something is wrong and must be repaired. Pain says that you are still alive. I heeded that message and reveled in it. For a long time, it seemed enough.

I blinked my eyes and shifted my gaze. Someone cradled me in his arms. His arm beneath my raw back was a scarlet welt of agony, but I lacked the strength to move away from it. I looked up into my own face. It was different from seeing myself in a mirror. I was older than I thought. He had taken off the crown, but there was a standing welt on my brow where it had scored my flesh with its grip. My eyes were closed and tears from beneath the closed lids slid down my cheeks. I wondered why I wept. How could anyone weep on such a dawn? With great effort, I lifted one hand slowly and touched my own face. My eyes snapped open and I stared at them in wonder. I had not known they were so dark or that they could be so wide. I looked down at myself incredulously. "Fitz?" The inflection was the Fool's but the hoarse voice was mine.

I smiled. "Beloved."

His arms closed around me almost convulsively. I arched away from that pain but he seemed unaware of it. Sobs shook him. "I don't understand!" he wailed to the sky. "I don't understand." He looked around, my face wild with his uncertainty and fear. "I have never seen this moment. I am out of my time, beyond where I ended. What has happened? What has become of us?"

I tried to move, but I had so little strength. For a time, I had to ignore his weeping while I assessed myself. There was a lot of damage, but the body was striving to repair. I felt terribly, terribly frail. I drew a breath, and told him quietly, "The skin on my back is new and tender yet."

He gulped for air. Breath ragged, he protested, "But I died. I was in that body, and she sliced the skin free from my back. I died." His voice cracked on the words. "I remember it. I died."

"It was your turn to die," I agreed. "And my turn to bring you back."

"But how? Where are we? No, I know where, but when? How can we be here, alive? How can we be like this?"

"Be calm." I had the Fool's voice. I tried for his lilt of amusement, and almost found it. "All will be well."

I found my wrist with his hand. The fingertips knew where to fall. For a moment, our gazes held as we mingled in unity. One person. We had always been one person. Nighteyes had voiced it long ago. It was good to be whole again. I used our strength to pull myself up, to press his brow to mine. I did not close his eyes. Our gazes locked. I felt my frightened breath against his mouth. "Take your body back from me," I bade him quietly. And so we passed, one into the other, but for a space we had been one. The boundaries between us had melted in the mingling. "No limits," I recalled him saying, and suddenly understood. No boundaries between us. Slowly I drew back from him. I straightened my back and looked down at the Fool in my arms. For an instant, he gazed clear-eyed at me with only wonder in his face. Then the pain of his wracked body demanded his attention. I saw him clench his eyes to it and wince away from my touch. "I'm sorry," I said softly. I eased him down onto the cloak. The evergreen boughs that had been his funeral pyre were his mattress now. "You did not have the reserves for me to perform a complete healing. Perhaps, in a day or two..."

But he already slept. I lifted a corner of the cloak and draped it over his eyes to shield them from the rising sun. I sniffed the air and it came to me that it would be a good time to hunt.

I took the whole morning for the hunt, and came back with a brace of rabbits and some greens. The Fool still lay as I had left him. I cleaned the rabbits and hung the meat to bleed. I set up his tent in the shade. I found the Elderling robe he had once given to me and laid it out inside the tent. I checked on the Fool. He slept on. I studied him critically. Biting insects had found him. They, and the growing strength of the sun on his skin, convinced me that I should move him.

"Beloved," I said quietly. He made no response. I spoke to him anyway, knowing that sometimes we are aware of the things we hear when we are sleeping. "I'm going to move you. It may hurt."

He made no response. I worked my arms under the cloak and lifted him as gently as I could. Still, he cried out wordlessly, squirming in my arms as he tried to escape the pain. His eyes opened as I carried him across the ancient plaza to the tent in the shade of the trees. He looked at me and through me, not knowing me, not truly awake. "Please," he begged me brokenly. "Please stop. Don't hurt me any more. Please."

"You're safe now," I comforted him. "It's over. It's all done."

"Please!" he cried out again, loudly.

I had to drop to one knee to get him inside the tent. He shrieked as the fabric brushed over his raw back in passing. I set him down as gently as I could. "You'll be out of the sun and away from the insects here," I told him. I don't think he heard me.

"Please. No more. Whatever you want, anything. Just stop. Stop."

"It has stopped," I told him. "You're safe now."

"Please." His eyes fluttered closed again. He was still. He had never truly wakened.

I went out of the tent. I had to be away from him. I was sick at heart for him, and wretched with my own sudden memories. I had known torture. Regal's methods had been crude but effective. But I had had a small shield that the Fool had lacked. I had known that as long as I held out against him, as long as I could refuse to give him proof that I was Witted, he could not simply kill me. So, I had held firm against the beatings and deprivations; I had not given Regal what he wanted. Giving him that would have allowed him to kill me, without compunction, with the sanction of the Dukes of the Six Duchies. And in the end, when I knew that I could not hold out any longer, I had snatched my death from him, taking poison rather than allowing him to break me.

But for the Fool, there had been nothing he could hold back. He had nothing that the Pale Woman wanted, except his pain. What had she made him beg for, what had she made him promise, only to laugh at his capitulation and begin again on his tormented flesh? I didn't want to know. I didn't want to know, and it shamed me that I fled his pain. By refusing to acknowledge what he had suffered, could I pretend it had not happened?

Little tasks are how I have always hidden from my thoughts. I refilled my water skin with clean cold water from the creek. I stole fuel from the former funeral pyre and built a small cook fire from it. When it was burning well, I set one rabbit to roast on a skewer and the other to bubbling in a pot. I gathered up my strewn winter garments, beat some of the dirt from them, and hung them on bushes to air. In the course of my tasks I found the Rooster Crown where the Fool had apparently flung it in a pique. I brought it back and set it just inside the flap of the tent. I went to the stream and scrubbed myself clean with horsetails and then bound my dripping hair back in a warrior's tail. I did not feel like a warrior. I wondered if I would have felt better if I'd killed her. I thought of going back and killing the Pale Woman and bringing her head to the Fool.

I did not think it would help, or quite likely I would have done it.

I set the rabbit soup aside to cool, and ate the roasted one. Nothing quite compares to fresh meat when one has gone a long time without it. It was bloody near the bone and succulent. I ate like a wolf, immersing myself in the moment and in the sensation of feeding. But eventually I had to toss the last gnawed bone into the fire and contemplate the evening ahead of me.

I took the kettle of soup into the tent. The Fool was awake. He lay on his belly and stared at the corner of the tent. The long light of late afternoon shone through the tent's panels and dappled him with color. I had known he was awake. The renewal of our Skill-bond made it impossible for me not to know. I could block most of the physical pain he felt. It was harder to block his anguish.

"I brought you food," I said to him.

After some silence had passed, I told him, "Beloved, you need to eat. And drink. I've brought fresh water."

I waited. "I could make tea for you if you'd like."

Eventually, I fetched a mug and poured the cooling broth into it. "Just drink this, and I'll stop bothering you. But only if you drink this."

Crickets were chirping in the dusk. "Beloved, I mean it. I won't leave you in peace until you at least drink this."

He spoke. His voice was flat and he did not look at me. "Could you not call me that?"

"Beloved?" I asked, confused.

He winced to the word. "Yes. That."

I sat holding the mug of cold broth in both hands. After a time I said, stiffly, "If that is what you wish, Fool. But I'm still not leaving until you drink this."

He moved in the dimness of the tent, turning his head toward me and then reaching a hand for the mug. "She mocked me with that name," he said quietly.

"Oh."

He took the mug awkwardly from me, protecting his torn fingertips from contact. He levered himself up on an elbow, quivering with pain and effort. I wanted to help him. I knew better than to offer. He drank the broth in two long draughts, and then held the mug out to me shakily. I took it and he sank down on his belly again. When I continued to sit there, he pointed out wearily, "I drank it."

I took the kettle and the mug out into the night with me. I added more water to the kettle of soup and set it near the fire. Let it simmer until morning. I sat staring into the fire, recalling things I didn't want to think about and chewing on my thumbnail until I bit it too close to the quick and tore it. I grimaced, and then, staring out into the night, shook my head. I had been able to retreat into being a wolf. As a wolf, I had not been humiliated and degraded. As a wolf, I'd kept my dignity and power over my life. The Fool had nowhere to go.

I'd had Burrich, and his calm, familiar ways. I'd had isolation and peace and the wolf. I thought of Nighteyes, and rose, and went to the hunt.

My first night's luck did not hold. I came back to the

camp after sunrise, with no meat, but a shirt full of ripe plums. The Fool was gone. A kettle of tea had been left to stay warm by the fire. I resisted the urge to call out his name and waited, almost patiently, by the fire until I saw him coming up the path from the stream. He wore the Elderling robe and his hair was slicked flat to his skull with water. He walked without grace in a lurching limp and his shoulders were bowed. With difficulty, I restrained myself from going to him. He reached the fire at last and, "I found plums," I told him.

He took one solemnly and bit into it. "They're sweet," he said, as if it surprised him. With an old man's caution, he lowered himself to the ground. I saw him run his tongue around the inside of his mouth and winced with him when he found the gap of missing teeth on one side. "Tell me what happened," he requested quietly.

So I did. I began with her guards throwing me out into the snow, and reported in as much detail as if it were Chade sitting there, nodding to my words. His face changed slowly as I began to speak about the dragons. Slowly he sat up straighter. I felt the Skill-link between us intensify as he reached for my heart to confirm what he was hearing, as if mere words could not be enough to convey it to him. Willingly, I opened myself to him and let him share my experience of that day. When I told him that Icefyre and Tintaglia had mated in flight and then disappeared, a sob shook him. But he was tearless as he asked me incredulously, "Then...we triumphed. She failed. There will be dragons in the skies of this world again."

"Of course," I said, and only then realized that he could not have known that. "We walk in your future now. On the path you set for us."

He choked again, audibly. He rose stiffly and paced a turn or two. He turned back to me, his heart in his eyes. "But...I am blind here. I never foresaw any of this. Always, in every vision, if there was triumph, I bought it with my death. I always died."

He cocked his head slowly and asked me, as if for confirmation, "I did die?"

"You did," I admitted slowly. But I could not help the grin that crept over my face. "But, as I told you in Buckkeep, I am the Catalyst. I am the Changer."

He stood still as stone, and when comprehension seeped into him, it was like watching a stone dragon come to wakefulness. Life infused him. He began to tremble, and this time I did not fear to take his arm and help him sit down. "The rest," he demanded shakily. "Tell me the rest."

And so I told him, the rest of that day, as we ate plums and drank his tea and then finished the rabbit broth from the night before. I told him what I knew of the Black Man, and his eyes grew wide. I spoke of searching for his body, and reluctantly told how I had found him. He looked aside from me as I spoke and I felt our Skill-link fade as if he would vanish from my sight if he could. Nonetheless, I told him, and told him too of my encounter with the Pale Woman. He sat rubbing his arms while I spoke of her, and when he asked, "Then, she lives still? She did not die?" his voice shook.

"I did not kill her," I admitted.

And, "Why?" he demanded shrilly, incredulously. "But why didn't you kill her, Fitz? Why?"

That outburst shocked me and I felt stupid and defensive as I said, "I don't know. Perhaps because I thought she wanted me to." The words seemed foolish to me, but I said them anyway. "First the Black Man and then the Pale Woman said I was the Catalyst for this time. The Changer. I did not want to cause any change to what you had done."

For a time, silence held between us. He rocked back and forth, very slightly, breathing through his mouth. After a time, he seemed to calm, or perhaps he only deadened. Then with an effort he tried to conceal, he said, "I'm sure you did what was best, Fitz. I don't hold it against you."

Perhaps he meant those words, but I think it was hard

for either of us to believe them just then. It dimmed the glow of his triumph and made a small shadowy wall between us. Nevertheless, I continued my account, and when I spoke of how we had come here through a Skill-pillar I'd found in the ice palace, he grew very still. "I never saw that," he admitted with a shade of wonder. "Never even guessed it."

The rest was quickly told. When I came to the Rooster Crown and my shock that it was not some powerful magical talisman, but only five poets frozen in time, he lifted one shoulder as if to excuse his desiring such a frivolous item. "It wasn't for me that I wanted it," he said quietly.

I sat silent for a moment, waiting for him to enlarge on that. When he did not, I let it go. Even when my tale was done and he realized how completely he had won, he seemed oddly muted. His triumph might have been years ago instead of mere days. The way he accepted it made it seem inevitable instead of a battle hard-won.

Evening had crept up on us. My tale was done, but he made no effort to tell me of what had befallen him. I did not expect him to. Yet the quiet that followed and fell between us was like a telling. It spoke of humiliation, and the bafflement that something done to him could make him feel shamed. I understood it too well. I understood too that if I had tried to tell him that, I would have sounded condescending. Our silences lasted too long. The small sentences, my telling him that I would fetch more firewood, or his observation that the chirring of the insects was actually pleasant after our silent nights on the glacier, seemed to float like isolated bubbles on the quiet that separated us.

At last he said that he was going to bed. He entered the tent and I did the small tasks one does around a camp at night. I banked the fire so the coals would survive until the morning and tidied away our clutter. It was only when I approached the tent that I found my cloak outside it, neatly folded on the ground. I took it and made my own bed near the fire. I understood that he still struggled, and that he wished to be alone. Yet, still, it stung, mostly because I wanted him to be more healed than he was.

Night was deep and I was sleeping soundly when the first shriek burst from the tent. I sat up, my heart pounding and my hand going immediately to the sword on the ground beside me. Before I could draw it from the sheath, the Fool burst from the tent, eyes wide and hair wild. The panic of his breathing shook his entire body and his mouth hung wide in his effort to gulp down air.

"What is it?" I demanded, and he started again, flinching back from me. Then he appeared to come to himself and to recognize my shadow by the banked fire.

"It's nothing. It was a bad dream." And then he clutched his elbows and bent over his crossed arms, rocking slightly as if some terrible pain gnawed at his vitals. After a moment, he admitted, "I dreamed she came through the pillar. I woke up and thought I saw her standing over me in the tent."

"I don't think she knows what a Skill-pillar is, or how it works," I offered him. Then I heard how uncertain a reassurance that was, and wished I had said nothing.

He did not reply. Instead he came shivering through the mild night to stand close to the fire. Without asking him, I leaned over and put more wood on it. He stood, hugging himself and watching as the flames woke and took hold of the fuel. Then he said apologetically, "I can't go back in there tonight. I can't."

I didn't say anything, but spread my cloak wider on the ground. Cautious as a cat, he approached it. He did not speak as he lowered himself awkwardly to the ground and stretched out between me and the fire. I lay still, waiting for him to relax. The fire mumbled to itself, and despite myself, my eyes grew heavy again. I was just starting the slide toward sleep when he spoke quietly.

"Do you ever get over it? Did you ever get past it?" He

asked me so earnestly for there to be a tomorrow that did not possess that shadow.

I told the hardest truth I had ever had to utter. "No. You don't. I didn't. You won't. But you do go on. It becomes a part of you, like any scar. You will go on."

That night, as we slept back to back beneath the stars on my old cloak, I felt him shudder, and then twitch and fight in his sleep. I rolled to face him. Tears slid gleaming down his cheeks and he struggled wildly, promising the night, "Please, stop. Stop! Anything, anything. Only please, please stop!"

I touched him and he gave a wild shriek and fought me savagely for an instant. Then he came awake, gasping. I released him and he immediately rolled free of me. On hands and knees, he scuttled away from me, over the stone of the plaza to the forest edge, where he hung his head like a sick dog and retched, over and over, trying to choke up the cowardly words he had said. I did not go to him. Not then.

When he came back, walking, I offered him my water skin. He rinsed his mouth, spat, and then drank. He stood, looking away from me, staring into the night as if he could find the lost pieces of himself there. I waited. Eventually, silently, he came back and sank down onto the cloak beside me. When he finally lay down, he lay on his side, huddled in a ball, facing away from me. Shudders ran over him. I sighed.

I stretched out beside him. I edged closer to him and, despite his resistance, carefully turned him to face me and took him into my awkward embrace. He was weeping silently and I thumbed the tears from his cheeks. Mindful of his raw back, I drew him close, tucked his head under my chin, and wrapped my arms around him. I kissed the top of his head gently. "Go to sleep, Fool," I told him gruffly. "I'm here. I'll take care of you." His hands came up between us and I feared he would push me away. Instead, he clutched the front of my shirt and clung tightly to me.

All that night, I cradled him in my arms, as closely as if he were my child or my lover. As closely as if he were my self, wounded and alone. I held him while he wept, and I held him after his weeping was done. I let him take whatever comfort he could in the warmth and strength of my body. I have never felt less of a man that I did so.

chapter XXX

WHOLE

I write this in my own pen, and plead that you excuse the Mountain hand with which I ink the Six Duchies characters. A formal writ is being prepared by our esteemed Scribe Fedwren, but in this scroll I desired to write to you myself, widow to widow and woman to woman, so that you may know well that I understand that no grant of land or title can make any easier the loss that you have suffered.

Your husband spent most of his life in service to the Farseer reign. Truly, he should have been rewarded years ago for all he did for his kings. His was a song which should have been sung in every hall. It was only by his risking of his life that I survived that dark night when Regal the Pretender turned upon us. In his modesty, he begged that his deeds remain unsung. It seems a callous thing that only now, when he has suffered death in our service, does the Six Duchies throne recall all that we owe to him.

I was seeking to select Crown lands that would amply reward Burrich's service when a courier arrived from Lady Patience. Truly, ill news seems to fly swiftly, for she had already been informed of your husband's passing. She wrote to me that he was among the most *cherished of friends to the late Prince Chivalry, and that she was certain her lord would have wished to see his estate at Withywoods pass into your family's stewardship. Title to these lands shall be immediately conveyed to you, to remain with your family forever.*

❦ LETTER, FROM QUEEN KETTRICKEN
TO MOLLY CHANDLER BURRICHSWYF

"I dreamed I was you." He spoke softly to the flames of the fire.

"Did you?"

"And you were me."

"How droll."

"Don't do that," he warned me.

"Don't do what?" I asked him innocently.

"Don't be me." He shifted in the bedding beside me. Night was a canopy over us, and the wind was warm. He lifted thin fingers to push the golden hair back from his face. The dying light of the fire could almost conceal the bruises fading from his face, but his cheekbones were still too prominent.

I wanted to tell him that someone had to be him, as he himself had stopped doing it so completely. Instead, I asked him, "Why not?"

"It unnerves me." He took a deep breath and sighed it out. "How long have we been here?"

It was the third time he'd awakened me that night. I'd grown accustomed to it. He did not sleep well at night. I didn't expect him to. I recalled clearly how I had chosen to sleep only by day and when Burrich was near me, watching over me, in the days of my recovery from Regal's dungeons. There are times when it is comforting to sleep with sunlight on your eyelids. And times when quiet talk at night is better than sleep, no matter how weary you are. I tried to think how much time had passed since I'd carried his body through the pillar. It was strangely difficult. The interrupted nights and the sun-dappled days of rest seemed to multiply themselves. "Five days, if we count days. Four nights, if we count nights. Don't fret about it. You're still very weak. I don't want to try the Skill-pillar until you are stronger."

"I don't want to try the Skill-pillar at all."

"Um." I made a sound of agreement. "But eventually, we have to. I cannot leave Thick with the Black Man forever. And I told Chade that we would be on the beach, ready to greet the ship when it arrived. That should be in, oh, in about five days. I think." I had lost track of time in the ice labyrinth. I tried to be concerned about it. I had blocked all Skill-contact with the coterie since our failed healing attempt. Several times, I'd felt vague scratching at my door, but I'd determinedly ignored them. They were probably concerned for me. I said aloud, to convince myself, "I have a life to get back to."

"I don't." The Fool sounded rather satisfied about that. That encouraged me. There were still moments in the day when he halted, motionless, as if listening for futures that no longer beckoned to him. I wondered what it was like for him. For his entire life, he'd endeavored to set the track of time into the path that he perceived as best. And he had achieved that; we lived in the future that he had devised. I think he alternated between satisfaction with the future he had created and anxiety about his role in it. When he gave thought to such things. Sometimes he simply sat, his damaged hands cradled in his lap as he looked at the soil just beyond his knees. His eyes were afar then, his breathing so slow and shallow that his chest scarce moved with it. I knew that when he sat so, he was trying to make sense of things that were inherently senseless. I did not try to talk him out of it. But I did try, as now, to be optimistic about the days to come.

"That's right. You don't have a life that you must return to; no burden to take up, no harness to resume. You died. See how pleasant it can be, to have died? Once you've died, no one expects you to be a king. Or a prophet."

He propped himself up on one elbow. "You speak from experience." He spoke pensively, ignoring my jesting tone.

I grinned. "I do."

He eased himself back onto my cloak beside me and stared up at the sky. He had not smiled. I followed his gaze. The stars were fading. I rolled away from him and came lightly to my feet. "Time to hunt soon. Dawn is coming. Do you feel strong enough to come with me?"

I had to wait for his answer. Then he shook his head. "In all honesty, no. I'm more tired than ever I've been in my life. What did you do to my body? I've never felt this weak and battered."

You've never been tortured to death before. That did not seem a good answer to give him, so I stepped aside from it. "I think it will take you time to recover, that's all. If you had a bit more flesh on your bones, we could use the Skill to heal you."

"No." He flatly forbade it. I let it go by.

"In any case, I'm tired of Outislander travel rations, and we haven't much left of them anyway. Some fresh meat would do you good. Which I shan't get for you by lazing here. If you want it cooked, try to wake the fire before I get back."

"Very well," he agreed quietly.

I hunted poorly that dawn. Concern for the Fool clouded my thoughts. I nearly stepped on one rabbit and it still managed to elude my frantic spring. Luckily, there were fish in the stream, fat and silver and easy to tickle. I came back in the early light, wet to the shoulders, with four of them. We ate them as the sun grew strong, and then I insisted we walk together to the stream to wash the smoky grease from our hands and faces. Belly full, I was ready to sleep after that, but the Fool was pensive. He sat by the fire and poked at it. The third time that he sighed, I rolled over onto my back and asked him, "What?"

"I can't go back."

"Well, you can't stay here. It's a pleasant enough place now, but take my word for it. Winter here is hard."

"And you speak from experience."

I smiled. "I was a couple of valleys away from here. But yes, again, experience."

He admitted, "For the first time in my life, I don't know what to do. You have carried me forward, to a place in time that is past my death. Every day when I awaken, I am shocked. I have no idea what will happen to me next. I don't know what I should be doing with my life. I feel like a boat cut loose and left to drift."

"Is that so terrible? Drift for a time. Rest, and grow strong. Most of us long for a place in our lives to do that."

He sighed again. "I don't know how. I've never felt like this before. I can't decide if it's bad or good. I've no idea what to do with this extra life you've given me."

"Well, you could probably stay here for the rest of the summer, if you learned to fish for yourself and hunt a bit. But you cannot hide forever from your life and friends. Eventually, you must face it again."

He almost smiled. "This, from the man who spent over a decade being dead. Perhaps I should follow your example. Find a quiet cottage and live like a hermit for a decade or two. Then come back as someone else."

I chuckled. "Then, in a decade, I could come ferret you out. Of course, I'll be an old man by then."

"And I shall not," he pointed out quietly. He met my eyes as he said it and his face was solemn.

It was an unsettling thought, and I was just as glad to leave it. I did not want to think too deeply on such things. There would be enough difficult things for me to face when I went back. Burrich's death. Swift. Nettle. Hap. Eventually, Molly, Burrich's widow. Her now fatherless little boys. Complications I didn't want and had no idea how to deal with. It was far easier not to think about them. I pushed them aside, and probably succeeded better than the Fool at walling myself off from the world that awaited my return, for I was practiced at it. For the next two days, we lived as wolves, in the now. We had meat and water and the weather continued fair. Rabbits were plentiful and we still had dry travelers' bread in my pack, so we ate well enough. The Fool continued to heal, and though he did not laugh, there were times when he seemed almost relaxed. I was accustomed to his need for privacy, but now there was a dullness to his avoidance of me that saddened me. My efforts at banter woke no like response from him. He did not scowl or ignore them. He had always been so quick to find humor in even the most dismal circumstances that I felt that even in his presence, I missed him. Even so, he grew stronger and moved with less caution. I told myself that he was getting better and that there was nothing more to desire. Even so, I began to feel restless, and when he said one morning, "I am strong enough, now," I did not argue with him.

There was little enough to prepare for us to leave. I tried to take down his Elderling tent, but he shook his head, almost wildly, and then said hoarsely, "No. Leave it. Leave it." That surprised me. True, he had not slept in it since the nightmare, preferring to sleep between me and the fire, but I had thought he would want it. Nonetheless, I did not argue with him. In fact, as I gave it a last glance, and saw how the dragons and serpents on the fine fabric rippled in the light breeze, I found I could think only of his peeled skin on the ice. I shuddered and turned away from it.

In passing, I picked up the Rooster Crown from the ground. It had returned to its wooden state, if indeed it had ever been otherwise save in my imagination. The silvery gray feathers stood up in their stiff row around the circlet. It still seemed to whisper and buzz in my hand. I held it out to him and asked, "What of this? A circle of jesters. Do you want it still? Shall we leave it on top of the pillar, to remember she who once wore it?"

He gave me an odd look, and then said softly, "I told

you. I did not want it for myself. It was for a bargain I struck, long ago." He looked at me very carefully and nodded very slightly as he said, "And I think it is time that I honored it."

And so we did not go straight to the pillar, but walked again down that fading path under the overarching trees, past the creek and back to the Stone Garden. It was as long a hike as I recalled, and little stinging midges found us once we had entered the shade. The Fool made no comment at them, but only pressed on. Birds flitted overhead, moving shadows that crossed our path. The forest teemed with life.

I recalled my wonder the first time I had glimpsed the stone dragons hidden in their sleep under the trees. I had been terrified, literally awestruck by them. Even though I had walked amongst them several times since then, and even seen them called to life and flight to battle the Red Ships for us, I still found them no less astounding. I quested ahead of us with my Wit-sense, and found them, dark green pools of waiting life beneath the shadowing trees.

This was the resting place of all the carved dragons that had awakened to defend the Six Duchies from the Red Ships. Here we had found them, here we had wakened them with blood, Wit, and Skill, and here they had returned when the year of battle was over. Dragons I had called them and called them still, from long habit, but not all of them took that shape. Some spoke of other fancies or of heraldic beasts of legend. Vines draped the immense figures of carved stone, and the winged boar had a cap of last year's leaves on his head. They were stone to the eye and alive to my Wit-touch, gleaming with color and detail. I could sense the life that teemed deep within the stone, but could not rouse it.

I walked amongst them with more knowledge now than when I had first discovered them here, and even fancied I could tell which ones had been worked by Elderling hands and which were the work of Six Duchies Skill coteries. The Winged Buck was a Six Duchies dragon and no mistake. Those that were more dragonlike in form, I now suspected were the Elderlings' work. I went first, of course, to Verity-as-Dragon. I did not torment myself with trying to rouse him from whatever stone dream held him. I did take off my shirt and dust the forest debris from his scaled brow and muscled back and folded wings. Buck blue he gleamed in the dappling sunlight after I had polished the length of he who had been my king. After all I had endured lately, the sleeping creature looked peaceful to me now. I hoped he truly was.

The Fool had gone, of course, to Girl-on-a-Dragon. As I approached them, I saw that he stood quietly before her, the crown in one hand. The other hand rested lightly on the dragon's shoulder, and I noted that his Skilled fingers touched the creature. His face was very still as he looked up at the figure of the girl astride the dragon. She was breathtakingly lovely. Her hair was more golden than the Fool's; it fell to her shoulders and caressed them with its loose curls. Her skin was like cream. She wore a jerkin of hunter green, but her legs and feet were bare. Her dragon was even more glorious, his scales the shining green of dark emeralds. He possessed the lax grace of a sleeping hunting cat. When last I had seen her, she had been posed in sleep upon the dragon, her rounded arms wrapped around his lithe neck. Now she sat upright on her mount. Her eyes were closed, but she lifted her face as if she could feel the errant sunbeams that touched her cheek. A very faint smile curved her lips. Crushed green plants beneath her sleeping steed indicated how recently she had flown. She had carried the Fool to Aslevjal Island, and then returned here, to rejoin her fellows in sleep.

I thought I had walked quietly, but as I approached, the Fool turned his head and looked at me. "Do you recall how we attempted to free her, that night?"

I bowed my head. I felt a bit ashamed, still, that I had ever been so young and rash.

"I've repented it ever since." I had touched her with

the Skill, thinking it might be enough to free her. Instead, it had only roused her to her torment.

He nodded slowly. "But what about the second time you touched her? Do you remember that?"

I sighed heavily. It had been the night I had Skill-walked, and seen Molly take Burrich as her man. Later that evening, I had worn Verity's body, for he had borrowed mine, to get himself a son. To get Dutiful upon Queen Kettricken. I had not known that had been his intent. In an old man's aching body, I had wandered the memory stone quarry. Wandered it until Nighteyes and I had come upon the Fool at his forbidden task. He had been chipping at the stone around the dragon's feet, trying to finish the dragon so it might be set free. I had felt sorry for him, so great was his empathy with the creature. I had known too what it truly took to quicken a dragon: not just the work of a man's hands, but the surrender of his life and his memory, his loves and his pains and his joys. And so I had set Verity's Skill-silvered hands to the rocky flesh of Girl-on-a-Dragon, and I had poured forth into her all the misery and pain of my short life, that she might take it and take life with it. Into the dragon I had poured my parents' abandonment of me to the care of strangers, and all I had suffered at Galen's hands and in Regal's dungeon. I had given those memories to the dragon to keep and to hold and to shape herself with. I had given her my loneliness as a child and every sharp-edged misery of that night. Given it willingly, and felt my pain ease even as the world dulled around me and my love of it dimmed slightly. I would have given far more if the wolf had not stopped me. Nighteyes had re-buked me, saying that he had no wish to be bonded to a Forged One. I had not, at that time, grasped what he meant. Having seen the warriors who served the Pale Woman, I thought I understood better now.

I thought I understood too what the Fool had in mind and why he had come here. "Don't do it!" I pleaded with him, and when he looked at me in sharp surprise, I said, "I know you are thinking of putting your memories of her torture of you into the dragon. Girl-on-a-Dragon could drain them out of you and keep them forever locked away where they cannot stab you. It would work. I know that. But there was a cost to that surcease from pain, Fool. When you dull pain and hide it from yourself..." My words trickled away. I did not want to sound self-pitying.

"You dull your joys as well." He said it simply. He looked away from me for a time, his lips folded. I wondered if he weighed the one against the other. Would he decide to be rid of night terrors at the expense of taking fresh joy in every morning? "I saw that in you, afterward," he said. "I felt guilty. If I had not been chipping away at Girl-on-a-Dragon, you never would have done it. I wished to undo it. Years later, when I came to see you at your cottage, I thought, 'Surely he will be healed by now. Surely he will have recovered.'" He swung his gaze to meet me. "But you had not. You had just...stopped. In some ways. Oh, you were older and wiser, I suppose. But you had not made any move on your own to reach out to life again. But for your wolf, I think it would have been even worse. As it was, you were living like a mouse in a wall, off the crumbs of affection that Starling tossed to you. As thick-skinned as she is, even she could see it. She gave you Hap and you took him in. But if she had not brought him to your doorstep and dumped him there, would you have sought out anyone to share your life?" He leaned closer to me and said, "Even after you came back to Buckkeep and your old world, you held yourself apart from it. No matter what I did or offered. Myblack. You couldn't even connect to a horse."

I stood very still. His words stung but they were also true. "Done is done," I said at last. "The best I can do now is to say, if that is what you came here to do, don't do it. It wasn't worth it."

He sighed. "I'll admit I thought of it. I admit I longed for it. I will even tell you that this is not the first time I have visited Girl-on-a-Dragon since we came here. I thought of offering her my memories. I know she would take them, just as she took yours. But... in a way... although I did not see this future, almost it seems as if it were meant to be. Fitz. What do you recall of her story?"

I took a breath. "Verity told me that she was part of a coterie making a dragon. I recall her name. Salt. I discovered that, the night I gave her my memories. But Salt could not give herself willingly to the dragon. She sought to remain a part of the coterie, and yet separate, to be only the Girl of Girl-on-a-Dragon. And with that, she doomed them. Because she held back too much, they did not have enough life to take flight as a dragon. They nearly quickened, but then mired down in stone. Until you freed them."

"Until *we* freed them." After a long time, he said, "It is like an echo of a dream to me. Salt was the leader of the coterie, and so it was called Salt's Coterie. But, when it came to the carving, the one willing to give heart to the dragon was Realder. So. When all believed that the dragon would be quickened, it was announced as Realder's Dragon." He looked at me quietly. "You saw her. Crowned with the Rooster Crown. A rare honor, and even rarer for a foreigner. But she had come a long way to seek her Catalyst. And like me, she had taken on the role of performer. Jester, minstrel, tumbler." He shook his head. "I had only that moment of being her. Just that brief dream, when I stood upon the pillar. I was, as I am, a White Prophet, and I stood high above the crowd and announced the flight of Realder's Dragon to the people of this Elderling town. But not without regrets. For I knew that my Catalyst would do that day what he had always been destined to do. He would enter a dragon, so that years hence, he could work a change." He stopped and smiled a bittersweet smile, the first I had seen on his face in days. "How it must have grieved her, to see Realder's Dragon mire and fail due to Salt's hesitation. She probably thought that she had failed, too. But if Realder had not made a dragon, and if that dragon had not failed, and if we had not found them there, still, in the quarry... what then, FitzChivalry Farseer? You looked far back that day, to see a White Prophet clowning on top of a Skill-pillar. Did you see all that?"

I blinked slowly. It was like awakening from a dream, or perhaps returning to one. His words seemed to wake memories I could not possibly hold.

"I will give Realder's Dragon the Rooster Crown. That was the price he named for me, the first time I flew with him. He said that he wished to wear forever the crown the White Prophet wore, on the day his beloved said farewell to him right before he entered this dragon."

"The price for what?" I asked him, but he did not answer. Instead, he looped the crown over one of his wrists and then began his cautious climb up the dragon. It saddened me to see him move so stiffly and cautiously. Almost I could feel the tightness of the new skin that pulled across his back. But I did not offer him my hand; I think that would have made it worse for both of us. Once he stood behind her on the dragon's haunches, he balanced himself. Then, taking the crown in both hands, he settled the circle on her brow. For a moment, it remained as it was, silvery wood. And then, color flowed into it from the dragon. The crown gleamed gold, the rooster heads that ringed it shone red, and their jeweled eyes winked. The feathers themselves took on the gloss of real feathers and lost all stiffness, to bow just as real cockerel plumes would have nodded.

A deeper flush seemed to suffuse the Girl's cheeks. She seemed to draw a breath. I was transfixed with amazement. And then her eyes opened, as green as her dragon's scales. She gave no look to me, but twisted in her seat to look up at the Fool still standing on the dragon's haunches behind her. She reached back a hand to cup his jaw. Her eyes locked with his. He leaned closer to her, captured by her gaze. Then her hand moved to the back of his head, and she pulled his mouth down onto hers.

She kissed him deeply. I had to witness the passion of

what she shared with him. Yet it did not seem like gratitude, and as she prolonged the kiss, I think the Fool would have broken away if he could. He stiffened, and the muscles of his neck stood out. He never embraced her, but his hands went from wide open and forbidding to clenched fists clutched against his chest. And still she kissed him, and I feared to see him either melt into her or turn to stone in her embrace. I feared what he gave and feared more what she took from him. Had not he heard a word of what I had said to him? Why hadn't he heeded my warning?

And then, as suddenly as she had stirred to life, she released him. As if he no longer mattered, she turned away from him and once more stretched her face up to the sunlight. It seemed to me that she sighed once, deeply, and then closed her eyes. Stillness crept over her. The gleaming Rooster Crown had become a part of Girl-on-a-Dragon.

But the Fool, released from that unwelcome intimacy, was limp and falling. In a near swoon, he toppled from the dragon's back, and I was barely able to catch him and keep him from tearing loose all his newly healed hurts. Even so, he cried out as I closed my arms around him. I could feel him shuddering, like a man in an ague. He turned to me, his eyes blind, and cried out piteously, "It is too much. You are too human, Fitz. I am not made for such as this. Take it from me, take it, or I shall die of it."

"Take what?" I demanded.

Breathlessly, he replied, "Your pain. Your life."

I stood frozen and uncomprehending as he lifted his mouth to mine.

I think he tried to be gentle. Nonetheless, it was more like a serpent's strike than a tender kiss as his mouth fastened to mine and the venom of pain flowed. I think that if there had not been his love mixed with the anguish he gave back to me, I would have died of it, human or not. It was a searing, scalding kiss, a flow of memories, and once they began, I could not deny them. No man, in the fullness of his years, should have to experience afresh all the passion that a youngster is capable of embracing. Our hearts grow brittle as we age. Mine near shattered in that onslaught.

It was a storm of emotion. I had not forgotten my mother. Never forgotten, I had banished her to a part of my heart and refused to open the door to it, but she was there, her long gold hair smelling of marigolds. And I remembered my grandmother, also of Mountain stock, but my grandfather had been no more than a common guardsman, posted too long at Moonseye and taking on the Mountain ways. All that I knew in a flash, and recalled how my mother had summoned me in from the pastures where, even at five, I had a share of the shepherding. "Keppet, Keppet!" her clear voice would ring out, and I would run to her, barefoot over wet grass.

And Molly... how had I ever banished the smell and taste of her, honey and herbs, and the way her laugh rang like chimes when I had chased down the beach after her, her red skirts whipping wildly around her bare calves as she ran, or the feel of her hair in my hands, the heavy strands of it tangling and snagging on the rough skin of my palms? Her eyes were dark, but they'd held the light of the candles when I'd looked down on them below me as I made love to her in her servant's room in the upper reaches of Buckkeep Castle. I had thought that light seen there would always belong only to me.

And Burrich. He'd been father to me in every way he could, and friend to me when I'd been tall enough to stand at his side. A part of me understood how he had fallen in love with Molly when he'd thought I was dead, but a part of me was outraged and hurt beyond common sense or rationality that he could have taken to wife the mother of my daughter. In ignorance and passion, he had stolen from me both woman and child.

Blow after blow rained on me. I was pounded iron on an anvil of memory. I languished again in Regal's dungeons. I smelled the rotting straw on the floor and felt the cold of the stone against my smashed mouth and pulped cheek as I lay there, trying to die so he could not hurt me anymore. It was a sharp echo of the beating Galen had given me years before, on the stone tower top we had called the Queen's Garden. He had assaulted me physically and with the Skill, and to finish the task, he had crippled my magic, putting it firmly in my mind that I had no ability and would do better to kill myself than live on in shame to my family. He had given me, forever, the memory of teetering on the brink of taking my own life.

It was new, it all happened to me afresh, flaying my soul and leaving me bared to a salty wind.

I came back to summer and the sun's slackening strength. The shadows were darker under the trees. I sprawled on the forest humus, my face hidden in my hands, beyond tears. The Fool sat next to me in the leaves and grass, patting my back as if I were an infant and singing some gentle, silly song in his old tongue. Slowly it caught my attention and my shuddering breaths calmed. When at last I was still, he spoke to me quietly. "It's all right now, Fitz. You're whole again. This time, when we go back, you'll go all the way back to your old life. All of it."

After a time, I found I could breathe deeply again. Gradually I got to my feet. I moved so cautiously that the Fool came to take my arm. But it was not weakness but wonder that slowed my steps. I was like a man given back his sight. The edges of every leaf stood out when I glanced at it, and there, the veins, and a lacy heart where insects had fed. Birds called overhead and answered, and my Wit of them was so keen that I could not focus on the soft questions the Fool kept asking me. Light broke in streams through the canopy of leaves overhead, sending shafts of gold arrowing through the forest. Floating pollen sparked briefly in those beams. We came to the stream and I knelt to drink its cold, sweet water. But as I bent over it, the rippling of the water over the stones suddenly captured me and drew me in to the clear, darkling world beneath the moving water. Silt was layered in patterns over the smoothed pebbles and water plants swayed gently in the current of water. A silver fingerling angled through the plants to disappear beneath a trapped brown leaf. I poked at it with a finger and had to laugh aloud at how he darted away from me. I looked up at the Fool, to see if he had also seen it, and found him looking down on me fondly but solemnly. He set his hand to my head as if he were a father blessing a child and said, "If I think of all that befell me as a linked chain that brings me finally to this place, with you kneeling by the water, alive and whole, then . . . then the price was not too high. To see you whole again heals me."

He was right. I was whole again.

We did not leave the forest plaza that evening. Instead, I built a new fire, and stared into it for most of the night. As if I were sorting scrolls or storing herbs for Chade, I went through all the years since I had given half my life away, and reordered my experience of them. Half-passions. Relationships in which I had invested nothing and received it in return. Retreats and evasions. Withdrawal. The Fool lay between the fire and me, pretending to sleep. I knew he kept vigil with me. Toward dawn, he asked me, "Did I do you a wrong?"

"No," I said quietly. "I did myself a wrong, long ago. You've put me on the path to righting it." I did not know how I would do it, but I knew I would.

In the morning, I scattered the ashes of our fire on the plaza. We left the Elderling tent billowing in the wind and fled a promised summer squall. We shared out my winter clothing between us, and then, his fingers pressed to my wrist, and Skill-linked, we entered the pillar.

We stepped out into the pillar room of the Pale Woman's ice castle. The Fool gasped and went to his knees after two staggering steps into the room. The trip through the pillar did not affect me as badly, though I knew a moment's vertigo. Almost immediately, the chill of the place seized me. I helped the Fool to his feet. He stared around himself in wonder, hugging himself against the cold. I gave him some time to recover, and time to explore the frost-rimmed windowpanes, the snowy view, and the Skill-pillar that dominated the room, and then told him quietly, "Come on."

We went down the stairs, and halted again in the map room. He looked down at the world portrayed there. His long fingers wandered over the rippling sea and then returned, to hover over Buck. Without touching them, he indicated the four jewels set near Buckkeep. "These gems... they indicate Skill pillars?"

"I think so," I replied. "And those would be the Witness Stones."

He touched, a wistful caress, the coast of a land far to the south and east of Buckkeep. No gem winked there. He shook his head. "No one who knew me lives there anymore. Silly even to think of it."

"It's never silly to think of going home," I assured him. "If I asked Kettricken, she—"

"No, no, no," he said quietly. "It was but a passing fancy, Fitz. I cannot go back there."

When he had finished gazing at the map, we went down the stairs, deeper into the pale blue light of the labyrinth. I felt as if we descended back into old nightmare. As we went, I saw his trepidation grow. He grew paler, not just from the cold. The half-healed bruises on his face stood out like shadows of the Pale Woman's power over us. I tried to stay to the stone passages and find some egress from there, without success. As we wandered from room to room, the beauty of the place touched me even as I worried about the Fool's growing silence and weariness. Perhaps we had misjudged, and he was not yet ready to confront the place where he had been so tormented.

Many of the chambers on this stone level seemed untouched by the vandalism and degradation I had seen elsewhere in the ice fortress. Themes of forest and flowers or fish and birds were lovingly chiseled into the stone lintels, and were echoed in the friezes within the chambers. The friezes seemed exotic and foreign, the colors either too pastel or too smoky for my Six Duchies taste. The figures of the humans were elongated, with fancifully colored eyes and strange markings on their faces. They called to mind Selden, the Bingtown Trader, with his unnatural growth and scaled face. I said as much to the Fool, and he nodded. Sometime later, as we walked down yet another stone passageway, he asked me, "Have you ever seen a white rose that has grown for years in proximity to a red?"

"Probably," I said, thinking of the gardens at Buckkeep. "Why?"

His mouth quirked to one side. "I think you have looked at them without truly seeing them. After years of such closeness, there is an exchange. It shows most plainly in the white roses, for they may take on a rosy blush, or exhibit faint tendrils of red in what used to be snowy white blossoms. It happens because there has been an exchange of the very stuff of their beings."

I gave him a curious look, wondering if his mind was wandering and I should be concerned. He shook his head at me. "Be patient. Let me explain. Dragons and humans can live side by side. But when they do so for a long period, they influence one another. Elderlings show the effect of having been exposed to dragons for generations." He shook his head a bit sadly and added, "It is not always a graceful transformation. Sometimes, there is too much exposure, and the children do not survive much past birth, or suffer a shortened life span. For a few, life may be extended, at the expense of fertility. The Elderlings were a long-lived race, but they were not fecund. Children were rare and treasured."

"And we are responsible for bringing dragons back into the world, so they may wreak this change upon us again?" I asked him.

"Yes. We are." He seemed quite calm about it. "Humanity will learn the cost of living in proximity to dragons. Some will pay it gladly. Elderlings will return."

We walked for a time in silence and another question came to me. "But what of dragons? Do they take no effect from their exposure to us?"

He was silent for a longer time. Then he said, "I suspect they do. But they find it shameful and banish such beings. You have been to Others Island."

That boggled my thoughts. I could think of nothing to say. Again we came to a junction of corridors, one of ice and two of stone. I chose one of the stone ones at random. As we paced along it, I tried to reconcile the Fool's notion of Elderlings with what I had experienced of them.

"I thought Elderlings were close to gods," I said at last. "Far loftier than humans in both spirit and mind. So they have seemed when I've encountered them, Fool."

He gave me a quizzical look.

"In the Skill-current. Bodiless beings, of great power of mind."

He threw up his head suddenly and I halted beside him, listening. He turned to look at me, his eyes huge. My hand went to my sword. For a time, we stood frozen. I heard nothing. "It's all right," I told him. "Air moves in these old passages. It sounds like someone whispering in the distance."

He nodded, but it took several minutes for his breath to slow. Then he said, "I suspect that the Skill is what remains to you from an older time. That it is the trailing end of a talent that developed between dragons and humans, as a way to communicate. I do not understand what you speak of when you talk of the Skill-current, but perhaps the ability can allow one to transcend the need for a physical body. You have already shown me that it is a far more powerful magic than I ever suspected. Perhaps it was a result of living alongside the dragons, and perhaps it lingered. So that even after dragons were gone, the descendants of the Elderlings kept that ability, and passed it down to their children. Some inherited little of it. In others"—he gave me a sideways glance—"the Elderling blood ran stronger."

When I was silent for a time, he asked, almost mockingly, "You can't quite admit it aloud, can you? Not even to me."

"I think you are wrong. Would not I know such things if they were true, would not I feel them? You seem to be saying that I am descended, somehow, from the Elderlings. And that would mean that, in a sense, I am part dragon myself."

He gave a snort of laughter. It was so welcome a sound from him that I treasured it, even at my expense. "Only you would put it that way, Fitz. No. Not that you are part dragon, but rather that, somewhere, the stuff of dragons entered your family line. Some ancestor of yours may have 'breathed the dragon's breath,' as the old tales say. And it has come down to you."

We walked on, our feet scuffing on stone. The passages echoed oddly, and several times the Fool glanced back over his shoulder. "Like a long-tailed kitten born from a long line of stump tails?" I asked him.

"I suppose you could think of it that way."

I nodded slowly to myself. "That would account for the Skill cropping up in odd places. Even in the Outislanders, it would seem."

"What's this?"

His eyes had always been sharper than mine. His long fingers touched a mark scratched on the wall. Incredulous, I stepped closer to peer at it. It was one of mine. "It's the way home," I told him.

chapter XXXI

DRAGON'S HEAD

And dark Oerttre, mother to them all, lifted her eyes and
    shook her head.
"It cannot be," she said with grave resolve. "We are not
    bound by what mere men have said.
My eldest must remain here, to reign after me. Woman
    to woman is our power passed.
You would take our Narcheska to be your Queen? Of all
    our treasure, she would be the last
That we would forfeit, no matter what your deed. Show
    me in fact how you have fulfilled
The letter of your promise. In blood you wrote your vow
    that you'd do as she had willed.
O Farseer Prince, recall now the boast that you did say:
On these hearthstones of our mothershouse, Icefyre's
    head you'd lay."

          ▸"THE DRAGON'S HEAD," COCKLE LONGSPUR

We followed my marks backward through the Elderling
maze, and emerged eventually from the crack in the icy
wall into a bright day. The wind was brisk and blowing ice
crystals filled the air, peppering our skins and making the
steep path treacherous underfoot. The clear light of true

day made my eyes tear. The Fool went before me down the steep path. Here, exposed to the wind and cold, his weakness showed plain, and I muttered at my own stupidity. This had overtaxed him. The second time he slipped, I took a firm grip on the back of his collar and kept him upright on his feet until we reached the Black Man's door. "Knock!" I told him, but when he only stared back at me, bleary-eyed with exhaustion, I reached past him to thud my fist against the wood.

The door was opened so swiftly that I had to believe that he had been waiting for us. Even then, the Fool stood frozen, staring at the smiling Black Man who confronted us. "He's cold, and very weary," I excused him, and then thrust him into the room in front of me. Once inside I pushed the door firmly shut behind us and then turned back gratefully to the cozy room. I blinked, letting my eyes adjust to the dimness after the brightness of full daylight. I saw the small hearth fire first, and then I found the Black Man staring at the Fool in mutual incredulity.

"He was dead," the Black Man told me firmly. "He died." His eyes were very wide.

"Yes. He was." I confirmed it for him. "But I am the Catalyst. I change things."

And then Thick sprang up from the hearth and grasped me in a short-limbed hug. He danced like a little bear as he shouted, "You're back! You're back! I thought you would never come back. Chade said, 'The ship is coming,' and I said, 'But he's not here and I won't get on a ship.' Then he said, 'It's coming anyway.' And it did, but no one was there and it went back, because I said, 'No, I am not walking back all alone, all alone, and I don't want to get on a ship anyway!'" He halted his dance and then told me with a satisfied grin, "Either you are dead or Chade is so mad at you that you'll wish you were. That was what he said. Dutiful. Oh, and the dragon head, I forgot to tell the dragon head part. Nettle did it! She sent the dragon head to the mothershouse and it was a big surprise for everyone.

Except me. She told me she could do it, could talk to Tin-taglia and make her sorry if she didn't. So she did. And everything is good again now."

The last he said so confidently that it was difficult to look down into the cheerful round-eyed face and say, "I don't think I understood half of what you just told me. And I think I have been away longer than I thought. But I'm glad to be back." I extricated myself from his hug. A strange silence had fallen in the other half of the room. The Black Man and the Fool regarded one another, not with animosity, but disbelief. Looking at the two of them together, I could see a kinship, but it was one of ancient lineage rather than a close family resemblance. The Black Man was the first to speak.

"Welcome," he said faintly.

"I never saw you," the Fool said wonderingly. "In all the futures I glimpsed, in all that might be, I never saw *you*." He abruptly began to tremble and I knew he was at the end of his strength. The Black Man seemed to sense this also, for he pushed a cushion closer to the fire and motioned hastily that the Fool should be seated. The Fool more collapsed than sat down. I took my cloak from around him, telling him, "The warmth will reach you faster if you let it in."

"I don't think I'm that cold," he said faintly. "I'm just . . . I'm outside of my time, Fitz. I'm a fish in the air or a bird beneath the sea. I'm past my life and I grope forward through each day, wondering what I am meant to do with myself. It's hard. It's very hard for me." His voice dwindled as he said the words. He looked up at the Black Man as if begging for help. His head wavered on his neck.

I did not know what to say to him. Did he resent that I had sought more life for him? It hurt to think so, but I held my tongue. I watched the Black Man grope for words. "This, I can teach . . ." The Black Man's voice slowly faded away. A smile slow as sunrise came to his face. He cocked his head at the Fool and said something in another tongue.

The Fool opened to him as a flower turns to light. A tremulous smile lit his face and he replied hesitantly in the same language. The Black Man whooped aloud in delight to hear him. He gestured at himself and said something rapidly, and then, as if remembering his manners, took up the kettle and a cup and with a graceful flourish, poured tea for the Fool and set it before him. The Fool thanked him extravagantly. Their language seemed to take many words to say simple things. Not one syllable of it resembled any tongue I'd ever heard before. The Fool's voice grew fainter. He took a breath and then finished what he was saying.

I felt an adolescent pang of exclusion. Almost as if the Fool sensed it, he turned slowly to me. He pushed his hair back from his face with fingers that shook. "I have not heard the language of my childhood since, well, since I left home. It is like balm to hear it again."

Chade and Dutiful must have known through Thick that I had returned, for I felt then such a battering against my Skill-walls as might have been a siege. I decided reluctantly that it was time to let them in. I took the cup of tea the Black Man had just poured for me and sat down by his fire and then, seeing the Fool well occupied with our host, I surrendered and lowered my Skill-walls.

Chade's blast of fury, fear, and frustration preceded all thought, shaking and cuffing me as if I were an errant serving boy. When he was finished, I think it annoyed him even more that I laughed at his onslaught, even as my reaction cheered Dutiful.

Not much can be wrong with you if you can laugh like that! I've never felt such a carelessness of spirit from you. I caught the boy's sense of amazement and wonder.

An instant later, Chade echoed it. *What has come over you? Are you drunk?*

No. I am whole and well healed. And so is the Fool. But my tale will keep. Does all go well with you? Has our prince well and truly won his bride? Thick has told me a wild bit of tale about a dragon's head on the mothershouse hearth. Is it true? Who killed Icefyre?

No one killed the dragon. It was just his head he placed there. But, yes, it seems to be done and settled, Chade replied with grim satisfaction. *Now that we know you are safe, we can sail tomorrow. That is, if Dutiful can find the courage to tell his bride she must come home with him.*

I but allow her time to be sure it is her will that she follows in this, Dutiful replied sternly.

I do not understand. Would someone start at the beginning and tell the tale?

And then it was that I heard in full, from both Chade and Dutiful, with excited asides from Thick, of how Nettle had bedeviled and nagged Tintaglia, troubling her dreams and her waking hours, importuning her to pay back the puny humans who had suffered so much so that Icefyre could fly free. Tintaglia in her turn had driven Icefyre much as a pigeon drives his mate to the nest, back to Zylig, where the dragons presented themselves to the Hetgurd still convened there, and then on to Mayle Island and Wuislington.

There the dragons had landed before Elliania's mothershouse. I gathered that there had been some structural damage in the process, but nonetheless the immense Icefyre had forced his way into the mothershouse, where he ungraciously placed his head, very briefly, upon the hearthstones, so that Dutiful's promise to Elliania might be completely carried out.

I thought that Elliania had professed herself satisfied that Dutiful had fulfilled his promise and proven himself worthy of her when he aided in the rescue of her mother and sister. I was a bit confused as to why all this had been necessary.

Oh, she has shown herself well satisfied, *for some days now,* Chade replied acidly, and I suspected that perhaps Dutiful's virtue had not been proof against the girl's importuning. *It is her mother who has proven difficult, much to Peottre's woe. Oerttre told us, before we were even docked in*

Zylig, that she did not regard any agreement that men had brokered concerning her daughter as binding. She finds it unthinkable that Elliania would leave her home, even to be Queen of all the Six Duchies. She has raised a thousand faults with the arrangement, saying that as she herself was still alive and therefore the true narcheska, all of this was agreed to without the proper consent. She objects to the idea of Lestra inheriting the title of narcheska; she finds the girl unfit to rule after her. And she is horrified at the thought that Elliania and Dutiful's children would remain in the Six Duchies.

Except for our sons, Dutiful interjected.

True, Chade conceded. *She had been more than willing to allow Dutiful and Elliania to, that is, to become, to have—* He could not find a delicate way to verbalize the thought.

Dutiful was more prosaic. *Her mother was willing to allow me to share Elliania's bed. She seemed affronted that anyone might think to thwart her daughter in who she wishes to bed. And the Narcheska Oerttre had offered that any male children so conceived would be given to the Six Duchies. At the age of seven.*

There was a mutual silence as they allowed me to digest that idea. It was untenable. None of his dukes would accept an heir thus created.

And now? Now that Icefyre has fulfilled completely Elliania's challenge to Dutiful?

Narcheska Oerttre was impressed. It is hard not to be impressed when a creature of that size lumbers through your home and places his head on your hearthstones. Especially when some of the framework of your door is still around his neck. I could easily excuse Dutiful's youthful satisfaction at this vindication. I think her objections are at an end. And even if she still has reservations, there were enough members of the Hetgurd here to witness it that they will not stand. They now see it as an honor that Elliania will come to my hearth. To "found a new mothershouse" is how they phrase it.

As if she were conquering all the Six Duchies by becoming Dutiful's queen, Chade complained. *Yet I could hear the* relief in his voice. I foresaw there would be difficulties in future days, as the customs of her land clashed with ours. If she bore a son first, would her relatives be scandalized to see him inherit before her daughters? I set the thought from my mind. There would be enough time to worry about that when it happened.

And how was that brought about?

Ask Thick. He and Nettle seem to have concocted that.

The smile faded from my face. I had to know. *Does Nettle know about Burrich's death?*

Yes. Chade's reply was short and grim.

I would not wish such news to be withheld from me, Dutiful pointed out severely. I knew he was justifying his action to Chade as much as to me. *And so I did as I thought best. Besides, my mother deserved that news, as well, that she can see to the needs of the family of the man who served us so well and so long. Besides. When I stand before my cousin in the flesh, I do not wish to do so with a bag of dirty secrets behind my back.*

That seemed harsh and I sensed that I trod on the edges of a quarrel between Dutiful and Chade. It did not seem a good time to advance my own opinion. Moreover, it was too late to change what had been done. So I tried to change the subject instead. *So. The wedding will now proceed with no further objections.*

Now it can. Dutiful had insisted we remain here until we heard from you. *Or until we decided you were dead, and sent a rescue party back for Thick. Not that he was fond of the idea of being rescued and brought home. But now that you are there, we shall send a boat for both of you immediately. As soon as you arrive here, we can proceed home.*

No boats! Thick insisted.

The Prince ignored him. *Our wait for Fitz has not been wasted time,* Dutiful contradicted Chade. *It would not have been appropriate to immediately snatch the Narcheska from her family. Elliania has been too long separated from her mother and sister. I have enjoyed seeing them together. And when she looks from her sister to me . . . Fitz, she thinks I am a hero. The Outislander bards are making songs of this.*

Very long songs, Chade added. *We've had to listen to them, smiling, nearly every night.*

We simmered into satisfied silence. My prince had won his bride. There would be peace between the Six Duchies and the Out Islands. Then Dutiful added solemnly, *And I was glad that you were allowed some time to deal with your loss. I am sorry, Fitz.*

Chade asked quietly, *You were able to recover the Fool's body?*

It was my moment for triumph. *I recovered the Fool.*

I thought he was dead! Dutiful's gravity dissolved in amazement.

So did I, I replied, and abruptly decided to leave that as my full explanation. It was easy enough to divert them from any more questions regarding the Fool. I simply added, *I am sorry to have missed the ship you sent for us. But you need not bother with another. Thick and I have an easier way back to Buckkeep. One that does not require him to set foot on a deck again.*

Their astonishment at my revelation of the working Skill-pillar could not match Thick's delight at the news he could go home without sailing. He suddenly clutched me about the middle, tugged me to my feet, and capered so wildly about me that I could not hold the focus necessary to Skill. I seized him by his shoulders and braced my feet to stop our dance, and then looked up to find the Black Man regarding us with alarmed amusement. The Fool looked too tired to show any surprise.

"He just realized that we could go home through the Skill-pillars," I explained to them. "Thick hates boats. And he is delighted to know that our journey may be a matter of moments instead of days."

The Black Man looked at me without comprehension. Then the Fool said something to him in his own tongue, and the man made a long "aaaah" of understanding and nodded sagely. The Fool's explanation seemed to bring to his mind some other incident, for the Black Man launched into a long monologue intended for the Fool.

Thick skidded to a sudden halt and cocked his head as if listening. "Skill scrolls, Chade says, bring the Skill scrolls." He paused, frowning as he paid attention to Chade's Skilling. "But not yet! Don't go home yet, not until he has a good way to explain it. But soon. Nettle is getting tired of all the messages. You could do it better."

I had given Chade much to think about, and to my relief, he excused himself from our Skilling to do just that. Dutiful attempted to explain to me how Nettle had persuaded Icefyre to present his head to the Narcheska, but Thick was too excited to permit our conversation. And I sensed restlessness from the Prince that told me he had better ways to pass his time than lingering with me. I sent him off with a stern warning to be circumspect, which I am sure he ignored.

I came back to full awareness to find the Fool nodding wearily to the Black Man's long explanation of something. It was the most foreign babbling I had ever heard, with not a single word that I recognized. Thick insisted on reporting how he had spent his time with the Black Man, with many descriptions of food, of Chade being angry and upset, and of a wonderful sliding place he had discovered not far away. I looked at his round face, beaming with contentment. He was a wonderful man. He accepted, with equanimity, that I had returned, that the Fool was no longer dead, and that soon we would be back home without going on a boat. His joy at sliding on snow was equal to his joy at my return. I envied his easy acquiescence to change and the future.

As he prattled, I tried to decipher what the future held for me. We would go back to Buckkeep and I'd have the task of transporting the Skill library there. Already I dreaded how many trips through the pillars that would entail. Yet that task became simple when I thought of what would follow. I had to introduce myself to Nettle. And reveal to Molly that I lived. Such a wave of longing swept through me at that thought that it near took my breath away. In restoring the full range of memories of her, the Fool had swept my heart back in time to that moment when I first knew I had lost her. The anguish was as fresh, and my love for her as strong. I dreaded the thought of our first meeting, and all the explaining I must do. I dreaded facing her grief for her husband, but I knew I must. Burrich had cared for my daughter when I had "died." Could I do less for his little sons? And yet, it was not going to be easy. None of it was going to be easy. Yet, with an odd sideways tilt of my heart, I realized I was anticipating it, that I believed that beyond the sorrow we would share at Burrich's death, there might eventually be something else. I felt shallow and greedy even as I thought of it, but nonetheless, it was there. It seemed years since I had looked ahead and seen opportunities and possibilities. I suddenly knew that I wanted change and life and the dangers of attempting to win Molly's love again.

Thick shook me by the shoulder. "So?" he asked me delightedly. "So, you want to go now?"

"Yes," I found myself saying, and then discovered that I had been smiling and nodding to his descriptions of sliding on the snow. I'd volunteered to go sliding with him. His delight was too great for me to crush it, and it suddenly came to me that I truly had nothing better to do at the moment. The Fool could do with rest and he seemed to be enjoying his talk with the Black Man. So we bundled up and went outside again. I had planned to slide with him once or twice, just enough to content him, but the slope he had found was as long and sweeping as an otter slide and just as inviting. Thick's use of it over the last few days had polished it smooth. We slid on our bellies and then together, on top of my cloak, whooping like children, heedless of how wet and cold we got.

It was play, pure and simple. Play that I'd had no time for, that I had dismissed as unnecessary and an interruption to all the practical tasks of a well-ordered life. When had I lost sight of taking simple pleasure for the sake of pleasure? I forgot myself in it and came back to the world with a start when I heard my name being called. I had just come to the end of the slide, and as I turned to the Fool's voice, Thick crashed into me from behind. I went flying and landed, mostly unhurt, with Thick on top of me. We floundered to our feet to find the Fool watching us with amusement and fondness that was hard to look upon. Regret and wistfulness were there also. "You should try it," I told him, half-embarrassed to be caught cavorting like a boy in the first snow of the year. I stood and helped Thick to his feet. He was grinning despite his tumble.

"My back," the Fool said quietly, and I nodded, feeling suddenly subdued. I knew it was more than his newly healed back, more than the stiffness of half-healed hurts. His experience had scarred and stiffened more than his body. I wondered how long it would be before his spirit regained its flexibility.

"You'll heal," I assured us both as I walked up to him. I wished I had been more certain.

"Prilkop has made food for us," he told me. "I've come to tell you it's ready. We shouted from the door, but you didn't hear us." He paused. "The walk down looked easy. It wasn't. Now I dread the walk up again."

"It's steep," I agreed as we started back. At the mention of food, Thick had broken into a trot and preceded us. "Prilkop?"

"The Black Man's name." The Fool trudged along beside me as we headed back to the steep cliffside trail. He was breathless. "It took him a moment or two to recall it. It has been long since he had anyone to speak with, and longer still since he has spoken our native tongue."

"You both seemed to be enjoying it," I said, and hoped I did not sound jealous.

"Yes," he agreed. He almost smiled. "It has been so long since he was home that when I told him my childhood memories, he could only marvel at how many things had changed. We both wonder what things are like there now."

"Well, I suppose he could go home now if he wished. I mean, he has no vision to keep him here anymore. Does he?"

"No." We walked a bit in silence and then the Fool said quietly, "Fitz, home is people. Not a place. If you go back there after the people are gone, then all you can see is what is not there anymore." He set his hand on my arm and I halted. "Let me breathe," he begged, and then defeated our pause by speaking. "You are the one who should go home," he told me earnestly. "While you still can. While there are people there who will know you and rejoice in your return. Not just Buckkeep. Molly. And Patience."

"I know. I intend to." I looked at him puzzled, surprised that he had thought I would not.

His face went almost blank with astonishment. "You will? You are?"

"Of course."

"You mean it, don't you?" His eyes searched my face. Almost, I saw a shadow of disappointment there. But then he seized one of my hands in both of his and said, "I am glad for you, Fitz. Truly glad. You had said you would, but you seemed hesitant. I thought perhaps you would change your mind."

"What else would I do?"

He hesitated a moment, as if he would say something. Then he seemed to change his mind. He gave a small snort. "Go find a cave to live in alone for the next decade or so."

"Why would I do that? Retreat from life, and there is no opportunity for anything to get better...Oh."

And then I was rewarded by the slow spread of his old smile across his face. "Help me up the path," he said, and I was glad to do so. He leaned more heavily on my arm than I had expected him to. When we reached Prilkop's cavern, I made him sit down. "Spirits? Brandy?" I asked of Prilkop, and when the Fool had weakly translated my words, the

Black Man shook his head. He came closer to the Fool and bent down to look into his face. He touched the Fool's forehead and then shook his head.

"I will make a tea. For this, a helpful tea."

We ate together and passed the evening telling stories. The Fool and Prilkop seemed to have slaked some of their thirst for conversing in their own tongue. I made up a pallet for the Fool and insisted he lie down near the fire. I tried to tell Prilkop the full tale of how we had come to Aslevjal. He listened intently, nodding, his brow furrowed. From time to time, the Fool would offer a brief explanation to Prilkop of some part of our tale that he did not understand. Mostly he lay still, eyes closed, listening. When he did break into my telling, it was strange to hear how the Fool pieced out our life tale for him, for he made it seem as if always the goal had been to awaken and restore true dragons to the world. I suppose that for him, it had been that. But it was peculiar to see my own life in that light.

It became very late and Thick had dozed off long before Prilkop bade us good night. I knew an odd moment of awkwardness when I spread my blankets separately from the Fool's. There was plenty of bedding here; no need to share anymore. But I had slept beside him for so many nights that I wondered if he would want the comfort of me close by to guard him from his night terrors, but I could not find a way to ask him. Instead, I propped my head on my arm and watched him sleep. His face was slack with exhaustion, yet pain still furrowed his brow. I knew that after all he had been through, he would need time apart from me, time alone with himself to discover once again who he was. Yet, selfishly, I did not want him to grow apart from me again. Not only my love for Molly but my boyish fondness and closeness to the Fool had been rejuvenated, as well. To be the best of friends again, making nothing of one another's differences, to enjoy the days and face hardships optimistically; he represented all that to me, and I vowed I would not let that carelessly slip from my grip again. He and Molly would round out my life to what it should have been. And Patience, I thought with wonder. I would reclaim her too, and never heed the cost.

Perhaps it was that Thick slept close by me, or perhaps it was that for the first time since I'd ventured into the Pale Woman's realm, I slept deeply enough to dream my own dreams. In either case, Nettle found me. Or perhaps I found her. I found myself in an evening place. It was a place I almost remembered, yet it had changed so much that I was not certain of it. Banks of flowers glowed luminously in the dimness. Somewhere, a fountain played, a muted splashing. The evening fragrances of blossoms wafted and blended on the night breeze.

Nettle was sitting on a stone bench, alone. She leaned her head against the wall behind her and stared up at the night sky. I winced when I saw her. Her beautiful hair had been shorn down to her scalp. It was the oldest sign of mourning in the Six Duchies, and not often practiced among women. I came and sat on the paving stones in front of her in my wolf guise. She stirred and looked down at me.

"You know that my father is dead?"

"Yes. I am sorry."

Her fingers toyed with a fold of her dark skirt. "Were you there?" she asked at last.

"When he died, no. When he took the injury that would kill him, yes."

A little silence spun out between us. "Why do I feel so awkward asking this, as if it is improper for me to be curious? I know that the Prince thinks it more appropriate to speak all around it and say only that my father was a hero and fought well. But that is not enough for me. I want to know how he died...was hurt. I want...I need to know every detail. Because they dumped his body in the sea and I will never see him again, dead or alive. Do you know how that feels? Just to be told that your father is dead, and that is all?"

"I know exactly how it feels," I said. "So was it done to me, also."

"But, eventually, they told you?"

"They told me the lie that they told everyone. No. I was never told how he truly died."

"I am sorry," she said, and meant it. She turned her head and looked at me curiously. "You've changed, Shadow Wolf. You...ring. You...like a bell when it is struck. What is the word?"

"Resonate," I suggested, and she nodded.

"I feel you more clearly. Almost as if you were real."

"I am real."

"I mean, real, here."

I wished that I were. "How much of it do you want to know?" I asked her.

She lifted her chin. "All. Everything. He was my father."

"That he was," I was forced to agree. I steeled myself. It was time. Then another thought came to me and I asked her, "Where are you now? When you are awake?"

She sighed. "As you see. In the Queen's Garden, at Buckkeep Castle," she said forlornly. "The Queen allowed me to go home for three days. She apologized to me and to my mother, but said it was as much time as she could spare me now for my mourning. Ever since I learned to dream true, not even my nights have belonged to me. Always I am at the call of the Farseer throne, expected to give my entire life to it."

I phrased it carefully. "In that, you are your father's child."

She blazed up at me suddenly, lighting the garden with her wrath. "He gave his life for them! And what did he get in return? Nothing. Well, some estate, now that he is dead, some Withywoods place I've never heard of. What do I care for land and a title? Lady Nettle, they call me now, as if I were a noble's daughter. And Lady Thornbush they call me, behind my back, simply because I speak my mind in honest words. I care nothing for what they think of me. As soon as I can, I will leave this court and go home. To my real home, the house my father built and its barns and pastures. They can take Withywoods and tear it stone from stone for all I care. I'd rather have my father."

"So would I. But all the same, you have more right to Withywoods than anyone else. Your father served Prince Chivalry, and that estate was one of his favorites. It is almost as if you are Chivalry's heir, that you receive it." And I was sure that was what Patience had intended. She could count the months and years on her fingers, and know that Molly's child was mine. The old woman had done her best to see something of her grandfather's lands passed on to Nettle. It warmed my heart that she had done so. I suddenly knew why Patience had waited until after Burrich's death to see the land go to Nettle. It was because she had respected his claim to Nettle's paternity and would do nothing to make anyone else question it. Now the lands would appear a thing that Burrich had earned for his family rather than an inheritance passed on to a grandchild. The subtleties of my eccentric stepmother would always delight me.

"I would still rather have my father." She sniffed, and turned her face from me. She spoke to the darkness, hoarsely. "Are you going to tell me what happened to him?"

"Yes. I am. But I am trying to decide where to begin that tale." I weighed caution against courage, and then suddenly realized my decision should not rest on my feelings at all. How much should a young woman, alone and in grief, suddenly be confronted with? Now was not the time to change her perception of who she was. She was facing enough changes. Let her grieve unfettered by questions such as my revelations could raise for her.

"Your father took his death wound in service to the Farseer monarchy, it is true. But when by sheer will alone he dropped a dragon to his knees, it was not for his prince.

It was because the stone dragon had threatened his beloved son."

She was incredulous. "Swift?"

"Of course. Swift was why he came here. To get his son and take him safely home. He did not think there would be a real dragon to face."

"There is so much I don't understand. You call the dragon that they faced a 'stone dragon.' What is that?"

She deserved to know. And so I told her a hero's tale, full of the Pale Woman's dark magic and of a man who had come, half-blind and alone, to face down a dragon for the sake of his wayward son. I told her too of how Swift had stood before the dragon's charge, and sped the arrow that slew him. And then I spoke of Swift's loyalty to her father as he lay dying. I even explained the earring that Swift would be wearing when he returned home to them. She wept as I spoke, black tears that vanished as they fell. Her garden faded around us, and the icy glacier wind blew past us and I realized the strength of my telling was such that she saw it, much as I had. Only when my words had faded, did the garden ease back into existence around us. The fragrances were sharper, as if a recent rain had watered them. A moth fluttered by.

"But when will Swift come home?" she demanded anxiously. "It is hard enough for my mother to know her husband is dead. She should not have to worry whether her son will return safely. Why do they linger so long there when their task is done?"

"Swift serves his prince. He will come back when Dutiful returns," I assured her. "They are still negotiating the marriage that will bind our countries in friendship. These things take time."

"What is wrong with that girl?" Nettle demanded angrily. "Is she without a mind or has she no honor? She should live up to the word she gave. She got her dragon's head on the hearthstones. I saw to that!"

"So I have heard," I told her wryly.

"I was so angry with him," she told me confidentially. "It was the only thing I could think of to do."

"You were angry with Icefyre?"

"No! With Prince Dutiful. Dither, dither, dither. Does she like me, does she love me, I won't force her to keep a bargain made under duress, I am so, so very noble... Why does not he tell that fickle Outislander girl, 'I paid the toll and I'll cross the bridge.' I'm sure I would have!" Then her blaze of indignation suddenly dampened as she said, "You don't think I'm traitorous to speak so of him, do you? I mean no disrespect. I am as loyal a subject to our illustrious prince as anyone. It is just that, when you speak with some-one mind to mind, it is hard to remember that he is a prince and far above me. There are times when he seems as thick-witted as one of my brothers, and I just want to shake him!" Despite her earlier protestation of loyalty to her monarch, she suddenly sounded like a girl very exasperated with foolish boys.

"So. What did you do?"

"Well, at that time those Outislander people were making much fuss over his not having put the dragon's head on the hearthstones of her mothershouse. As if rescuing her mother and sister were not worth the weight of a bloody dead animal head stinking in front of your fireplace!" I could feel the effort it took her to restrain herself. "Mind you, I only know of these things as I relay them to the Queen. I am the one who must stand before her each morning and pass on such tidings as they send through me. Does he think that is pleasant? But it occurred to me one dawn, after leaving my queen solemn and heavy of heart because the marriage might not happen at all, that perhaps there was something I *could* do. Despite her bluster and threats, I know Tintaglia well. Perhaps because of those things, I know her well. So, as she had pestered me, dis-turbing my dreams whenever I slept, so I began to do to her. For in all her comings and goings from my sleep, she had worn a sort of path that I could follow back to her. If that makes sense to you."

"It does. But I still marvel that anyone would dare 'pester' such a creature."

"Oh, in the dream world, we are well matched, as I think you might remember. I doubt she would fly all the way here just to trample a mere human. And unlike me, she prefers to sleep heavily after she has eaten or mated. So, those were precisely the times I chose to bother her."

"And you asked her to ask Icefyre to return to Mayle Isle and put his head down on the Narcheska's hearth?"

"Asked her? No. I demanded it. And when she said she would not, I said it was because she could not, that despite all humans had done to rescue him, Icefyre was too petty to acknowledge the debt. And that she durst not make him do it, for though she claims to be a queen, she allowed him to master and drive her. I said that her mating must have addled her brains. That put her into a froth, I can tell you."

"But how did you know it would?"

"I didn't. I just got angry and said what first came to me." I felt her sigh. "It's a fault I have, one that has not made me popular in this court. I am too swift of tongue. But I think it is the best way to speak to a dragon. I told her that if she could not make Icefyre do what was right then she needn't flaunt about so high-and-mighty. I hate it when people lord over you when you know that, given a good scratch, they're no better than you are." She paused, then added, "Or dragons. In all the legends, they are wise, or incredibly powerful or—"

"They *are* incredibly powerful," I interrupted her. "I assure you of that!"

"Perhaps. But Tintaglia, in some ways, she's like . . . me. Sting her pride a bit and she has to prove she can do whatever you've told her she can't. She's a nag, or worse, a bully, when she thinks she can get away with it. And just because she lives so long and was born remembering so much, she acts as if we are moths or ants, with no lives worth honoring."

"It sounds as if you've had more than one conversation with her in this regard."

She paused a trifle. "Tintaglia is an interesting creature. I don't think I'd ever dare call her my friend. She thinks she is, or more accurately, I think she believes I owe her loyalty and duty or worship, simply because she is a dragon. But it is hard to call someone your friend when you know that your death would mean no more to her than a moth flying into a candle means to me. Pftt! Oh, it's gone. Too bad. As if I were just an animal!" She snatched a flower from a nearby bed as if to tear it apart.

I winced. She sensed it.

"No, I meant like a bug or a fish. Not like a wolf." Then, as if the thought had only just come to her, "You aren't as I see you in my mind. I know that now. I know you aren't a wolf. I mean, I don't think of you as just an animal. Did I hurt your feelings?" Hastily, she restored the flower to its broken stem.

She had, but I didn't think I could explain it to myself, let alone her. "It's fine. I know what you meant."

"And when you come back with the others, I'll finally get to meet you and see you as you are?"

"When I come back, it's very likely we'll meet."

"But how will I know you?"

"I'll tell you it's me."

"Good." Hesitantly she added, "I missed you while you were gone. I wanted to talk to you, when they told me my father was dead. But I couldn't find you. Where did you go?"

"Someone very important to me was in trouble. I went to help him. But now that's all settled, and we'll be coming home soon."

"Someone important to you? Will I meet him?"

"Of course. I think you'll like him."

"Who are you?"

I wasn't expecting the question just then. It took me off balance. I didn't want to tell her that I was FitzChivalry or Tom Badgerlock. I found myself saying, unplanned, "I'm someone who used to know your mother, before she met Burrich and married him."

Her reaction was not what I expected. "You're that old?" She was shocked.

"And I think I just got older," I told her, laughing.

But she did not laugh with me. Her reply was stiff. "Then I suppose that when you return, you are more like to be my mother's friend than mine."

There was a complication I had not counted on. Jealousy rang green in her thoughts. I tried to stem it. "Nettle, I have long cared about both of you. And will continue to do so."

Even colder, she asked, "Will you try to take my father's place with her?"

I felt a blundering fool. I groped for an answer and then forced myself to face a truth I'd been avoiding. "Nettle. They were together for, what, sixteen years? They shared seven children. Do you think anyone could take his place with her?"

"Just so you understand that," she replied, somewhat mollified. And then she dismissed me with "Now I must clear my dreams of you in case the Prince wishes to find me. Almost every night, he or Lord Chade has words I must bear to the Queen. I get little time to make my own dreams anymore. Good night, Shadow Wolf."

And then her fragrant garden and gentle twilight world faded away from me and I was left in the darkness. It took a short time for me to realize I was not asleep at all, but was lying on the floor of the Black Man's cave, staring into shadows dimly lit by the embers in his fireplace. I thought over what I had told Nettle, and decided that I had been foolish to let her know that I had once loved Molly. And how could I not have foreseen that Molly's children, including Nettle, might see me as an interloper in their household? I felt discouragement wash over me, and considered a total retreat from all of it.

But in the wake of that, I found iron resolution. No. I would not flee from the chaos I had made of my life. I loved Molly, still, and I thought it possible that she might still have some feelings for me. Even if she didn't, I had told Burrich that I would see to the well-being of his younger children. I would be needed there, even if I were not welcomed at first. I might fail; Molly might even drive me off. But I would not surrender before I had tried.

I was going home.

chapter XXXII

THROUGH STONES

The Witness Stones have stood, time out of mind,
through storm and earthquake, on Witness Hill near
Buckkeep Castle. There is no record of who raised them.
Some say that they are as old as the foundations of
Buckkeep Castle itself. Others say they are older still. A
number of traditions have grown up around them. It is a
popular place for couples to pledge their wedding vows,
for it is said that if someone speaks falsely before the
stones, the gods themselves will punish them. It is also
said that if men meet there, to decide the truth by
contest, the stones will look down and see that the
victory goes to the honorable man.

There are similar standing stones throughout the Six
Duchies and beyond. All seem to be carved of the same
black stone. All seem to have been sturdily set to
withstand all elements. Some are decorated with runes.
Others seem to be plain, but a closer inspection usually
reveals that runes once graced them, and have either
worn away or been chiseled off them.

Although we have not been able to find mention of
them in the Skill scrolls we have, they were almost
certainly used by the Elderlings as a method for swift
transit from one place to another. Herewith, I have set

*out a map of the known Skill-pillars, as I shall call them.
On this map, I have clearly marked a legend that shows
which runes apply to which locations. Although some of
the Skill-pillars may appear to be unmarked, an
experienced Skill-user can still use them for transit. It is
not suggested that younger users of the Skill be allowed
to travel through the stones alone. Indeed, they should
always be accompanied by an experienced user, and
should only use the stones for travel as an absolute
necessity. It can be a taxing experience for the novice
user, leading to exhaustion or, in the case of forced
overuse, madness.*

        ❦ CHADE FALLSTAR'S "ON SKILL-PILLARS"

The Fool's fragile recovery collapsed in the early hours. I
awoke in darkness to the sounds of him tossing and struggling in his sleep. When I tried to wake him, his face was
warm and I could not break him from his nightmares. I sat
beside him, holding his hand and talking to him softly, easing him into quieter dreams. I was uncomfortably aware that
the Black Man had awakened. He lay on his bed and silently
watched me with the Fool. I could not see his eyes, but I felt
them on me. He measured us and I did not know why.

    Toward dawn, I felt Chade's press against my mind.
Reluctantly I admitted him. *You can go home now. This will
be your tale. The Prince and I sent you home early with Thick,
on a trading vessel, as Thick was miserable here and we wished
you to bear tidings to the Queen immediately. I think that will be
believable; just avoid giving any details. I shall be so glad to have
you in place there. Nettle is a fine girl, but we have had to be
very circumspect in our reports through her, and very careful
not to task her beyond her abilities. It is imperative I have someone in place who can be privy to the sort of information that
must be conveyed to the Queen.*

    *I cannot go now, Chade. The Fool has fallen ill. He cannot
travel.*

Chade was silent for a few moments. Then, *But from what you said, you would not have to carry him far. Just to the Skill-pillar, and then whisk him home, to healers and warmth and safety.*

I wish it were that simple. The path to the pillar is very treacherous and cold. And the journey through the Skill-pillar is tasking for him. I dare not risk him. He has already been through too much.

I see. I felt Chade weighing my words. Then, *Do you think he will be better a day from now? I could give you another day.*

I made my thoughts firm. *I do not know. But I will take as many days as he needs, Chade. I will not risk him.*

Very well. The thought oozed annoyance but also acceptance. *If you must.*

Indeed, I must, I replied firmly. *We will travel when the Fool is stronger. Not before.*

Dawn found me hollow with worry. Well I knew that many men who died from battle wounds died days after the battle, from fevers and flux and infection. The journey here had strained his healing and undone many days of rest. The Fool slept heavily, far past midday, and then woke, gummy-eyed and haggard, to drink cup after cup of water. Prilkop insisted that we move him from the floor to his bed. The Fool made the short staggering walk between us, then folded onto the Black Man's bed as if he were exhausted, and almost immediately sank down into sleep. His skin was warm beneath my touch.

"Perhaps it's just one of his changing times," I told Prilkop. "So I hope. It would be better than infection. He will be feverish and weak for several days, and then shed a layer of skin as if he'd been burned. Underneath, his new skin will be darker. If that is what this is, there's little we can do for him now except keep him comfortable and wait."

Prilkop touched both his cheeks with a gesture, and then smiled at me, saying, "This I suspected. To some of us, it happens. The discomfort passes." Then, looking down at the Fool he added, "If that is all of it." He shook his head. "The injuries to him were many."

A question came to me and I asked it without pausing to wonder if it were impolite. "Why did you change? Why is the Fool changing? The Pale Woman remained white."

He lifted his hands, expressing bafflement. "On this, I have thought many times. Perhaps, as we cause change, we change. Other prophets who remain white often speak much, but do little. He and I, in our youths, much change we foretold. Then, out we went and we made changes. And, perhaps, we also changed ourselves."

"But the Pale Woman also did things to try to make changes."

He smiled, grimly satisfied. "She tried. She failed. We prevailed. We changed." Then he tilted his head to one side. "Perhaps. So this old man thinks." Prilkop glanced over at the sleeping Fool and nodded to himself. "Rest is what he needs. Sleep, and good food. And quiet. You and Thick, go fishing. Fresh fish would be good for him."

I shook my head. "I don't want to leave him when he's like this."

Prilkop put a gentle hand on my shoulder. "You make him restless. He feels your worry. To let him rest, you away go."

Thick spoke up from his corner by the hearth. "We should go home. I want to go home."

The Fool startled me when he croaked my name. "Fitz."

I was instantly at his side with water. He did not want to drink it, but I was insistent. When he turned his face from the cup, I took it away. "Was there something else you wanted?"

His eyes were unnaturally bright with fever. "Yes. I want you to go home."

"He doesn't know what he's saying," I told Prilkop. "I couldn't take him like this."

The Fool drew a deep breath. He spoke with an effort. "Yes. I do. Know what I'm saying. Take Thick. Go home. Leave me here." He coughed and then motioned for more water. He drank it in sips, and then pulled in another deep breath. I let him lie back in his blankets.

"I won't leave you like this," I promised him. "I'll take as much time as we need here. Don't worry about anything. I'll be right here."

"No." He seemed irritable, in that weary way the sick do. "Listen to me. I need to stay. Here. For a time. With Prilkop. I need to understand . . . when I am, where I am . . . I need to . . . Fitz, he can help me. You know I will not die of this. It is only my changing time. But what I need to learn, I must learn alone. Be alone, for a time. I need to think, alone. You understand. I know you do. I was you." He lifted thinning fingers to rub at his face and cheeks. The dry skin rippled and rolled under his fingers, flaking away from newer, darker skin beneath. He rolled his eyes to Prilkop. "He should go," he said, as if Prilkop could force me. "He is needed at home. And he needs to be home."

I sat down on the floor by the bed. I did understand. I remembered the long days of my recovery, after my time in Regal's dungeon. I recalled the uncertainty I had felt. Torture shames a man. To break and scream, to beg, to make promises . . . unless a man has endured that, perhaps he cannot forgive it in another. The Fool needed time alone, to reassess how he saw himself. I had not wanted Burrich to ask a thousand questions of me; I had not even wanted him to be solicitous and kind. On some instinctive level, he had known that, and had allowed me my days of sitting and staring, unspeaking, over the meadows and hills. It had been difficult to admit I was a human and not a wolf: it had been harder to admit I was still myself.

The Fool extended a thin hand from under his blankets. He patted my shoulder awkwardly, and then ran his fingers down my bearded cheek. "Go home. And shave while you're there." He managed a faint smile. Then, "Let me rest, Fitz. Just let me rest."

"Very well." I tried not to feel that he dismissed me. I turned to Thick. "I'll take you home, then. Dress warmly, but you needn't pack anything. Before the night is over, we'll be in Buckkeep."

"And warm again?" Thick pressed me. "And with good things to eat? Fresh bread and butter, milk and apples, sweet cakes and raisins? Cheese and bacon? Tonight?"

"I'll do my best. You get ready. And tell Chade for me that we're going home tonight. I'll tell the guard at the gate that we came home early, on the first boat. Because you were cold."

"I am cold," he agreed heartily. "But no boats. You promised."

I hadn't but I nodded anyway. "No boats. Get ready, Thick." I turned back to the Fool. He had closed his eyes again. I spoke softly. "So. You get your way. As you always seem to. I'll take Thick home. I will be gone for a day. At most, two days. But then I'll come back, and I'll bring back food and wine with me. What would you like? What could you eat?"

"Have you any apricots?" the Fool asked me in a wavering voice. Plainly he had not grasped the whole of what I had told him.

"I'll try to bring you some," I said, doubting I could but loath to tell him so. I smoothed his hair back from his warm face. His hair felt stiff and dry. I looked at Prilkop. He nodded slowly to my silent plea. Before I left, I tucked the blankets up over his shoulders. Then I stooped, and despite his closed eyes, I pressed my brow to his. "I'm coming back soon," I vowed. He made no response and perhaps he already slept. I left him there.

Prilkop too made his farewells to us within the cave. "Take care of him," I told the Black Man. "I'll be back to-morrow. Make sure he eats."

He shook his head to my words. "Not that soon," he

cautioned me. "Already, you have used the portals too many times, too close together." He made a motion as if he dragged something out of his chest. "It takes from you, and if you do not have enough left for yourself, it can keep you."

He peered into my eyes, as if trying to be sure I had understood him. I hadn't, but I nodded and assured him, "I'll be careful."

"Farewell, Thick man. Farewell, Fool's Changer." Then, with a tip of his head toward the Fool, he added quietly, "I will watch over him. More than that, none of us can do." And then, as if embarrassed to ask, he said, "The small man said cheese?"

"Cheese. Yes. I will bring you cheese. And tea, and spices and fruit. As much as I can carry."

"When it is safe for you to come again, that would be nice." He was beaming as we thanked him again for all he had done for us, and then left. The wind had come up and the night was chill. Thick had stubbornly refused to abandon his pack, clinging to every single possession in it, so he came laden behind me as we edged up the steep and narrow path to the crack in the rock face. The trickle of moisture had iced it narrow again, and again I had to draw my sword and clash ice away in the darkness. Thick whimpered at the dark and the wind and kept insisting that he wanted to go home, not seeming to connect that I must first open the way so we could.

I was finally able to squeeze through. I pulled Thick after me, though he wedged there for a moment. He followed me in, going slower and slower the closer we came to the unnatural light. "I don't like this," he warned me. "I don't think this is the way home. This is going in a rock. We should go back."

"No, Thick, it's all right. It's just an old magic. We'll be fine. Just follow me."

"You had better be right!" he warned me. He followed me, looking all around himself at every step. The deeper we went, the more cautious he became. When we reached the first Elderling carvings, he gasped and stepped back. "The dragon dreams. Those were in the dragon dreams!" he exclaimed. Then, abruptly, as if I had been tricking him, "Oh, I have been here before. Now I know. But why is it so cold? It didn't used to be so cold."

"Because we are under ice. That makes it cold. Come on, now. Stop walking so slowly."

"Not this cold," he replied cryptically, and followed me again, but no faster than he had before. I thought I had fixed the path in my mind. Despite that, I turned wrong twice. Each time I had to retrace my steps, Thick became more doubtful of me. But eventually, despite his laggard steps and my faulty memory, we reached the map room.

"Don't touch anything," I warned him. I studied the map and the rune by the four tiny gems near Buckkeep. Those gems, I was convinced, represented the Witness Stones. For generations, they had been regarded as a place of power and truth, a gateway to the gods. Now I suspected I knew the origin of that legend. I fixed the rune carefully in my mind. "Come, Thick," I told him. "It's time to go home."

He made no reply, and even when I touched his shoulder, he looked up at me slowly. He had sunk down to sit on the floor. With one hand, he had rubbed the dusty tiles clean to reveal a piece of a pastoral scene. His face had an almost dazed expression. "They liked it here," he said softly. "They played a lot of music."

"Put your walls up, Thick," I bade him, but did not feel that he obeyed me. I took his hand and held it firmly in mine. I wasn't sure he was listening, but as I led him up the stairs to the pillar room, I explained to him several times that we would hold tight to each other and walk through the pillar and be home. His breathing had become deep and even as if he slept heavily. Uneasily I wondered if the city itself were affecting him.

I did not give myself time to wonder if the ancient and

worn Witness Stones would still function as Skill-pillars. The Fool had used one, hadn't he, and his Skill was much less than mine. I drew a deep breath, gave Thick's hand a small shake in an attempt to win his attention, and then stepped determinedly into the pillar, drawing him behind me.

Again there was that breathlessly long pause in my being, almost familiar now. There seemed to pass a star-speckled blackness of indeterminate length and then I stepped out onto the grassy sward of the hillside near Buck-keep. Thick was still with me. I felt a moment's giddiness, and Thick stumbled past me and sat down flat on the turf. The warmth of summer touched our skins and the smells of a summer night filled my nostrils. I stood still, letting my eyes adjust. The four Witness Stones loomed behind me, pointing at the night sky. I drew a deep breath of the warm air. I smelled sheep pastured nearby, and the more distant smell of the sea. We were home.

I went to Thick and put a hand on his shoulder. "You're all right," I told him. "We're home. I told you. Just like stepping through a door." Then a wave of dizziness swept through me and I pitched forward onto my face. For a little time I lay there, trying not to retch.

"We are all right?" Thick asked me miserably.

"In a moment or two," I assured him breathlessly. "In a moment or two, we'll be fine."

"That was as bad as the boat," he said accusingly.

"But much shorter," I told him. "Much shorter a time."

Despite my reassurances, it was some while before we recovered and got to our feet. It was a goodly hike from the Witness Stones to the gates of Buckkeep Castle, and Thick was puffing and complaining long before we got there. The frozen Elderling city and the trip through the pillars seemed to have disoriented him and wearied him. I felt cruel as I hurried him along, tempting him with promises of wonderful food, cold ale, and a warm soft bed. The rising sun lent light to us to avoid most tumbles. Before he had gone far, I was carrying Thick's pack and then his cloak and hat. He would have shed more clothing if I had let him. By the time we reached the gates, we were sweating in our winter clothes on a fair morning.

I think the guards recognized Thick before they did me. I was unshaven and unkempt. I told them we'd been sent home early on a filthy Outislander coastal trader, and that it had been a miserable trip and we were glad to be home. Thick was only too glad to enlarge on my poor opinion of boats. The guards at the gates were full of questions, but I told them that we'd been sent home some time ago and that it had taken us far too long to get here, and that I'd been ordered to report to the Queen before I shared any gossip. They let us through.

It was mostly serving folk and guard up and about at that hour. I got Thick no farther than the kitchens. The men in the guardroom had learned to tolerate the Prince's pet. They would jest with him, roughly, and listen to his tales and measure them by their own. Any brag he made of dragons or magic pillars or Black Men would be taken with a large grain of salt there. I knew I had to leave him and it was perhaps the safest place in the keep for him. Besides, I suspected that his mouth would be too full for much talk. I left him there with a hot meal and the admonition that as soon as he was finished eating, he should either go to bed in his room or seek out Sada, bathe, and let her know, emphatically, that no one on our voyage had died of seasickness.

I took a roll of fresh bread with me and devoured it on my way to the barracks. The warm summer air seemed laden with scent after my long weeks in the cold. Our guards' section of the long, low barracks house was dusty and deserted. I rid myself of my heavy woolen clothes. I longed to stop to wash and shave, but instead simply pulled on a fresh guard's uniform. I longed even more to fall facedown on my bed there but knew that I needed to see the Queen as soon as possible. I knew too that she would not be expecting me yet.

I found my way to the hall that led to the larders and storage rooms for the kitchens. When no one else was in sight I entered the storage room that had the cupboard with the false back in it. It was also where the hams and smoked sausages were stored, and I helped myself to a sausage before I closed the false door behind me and began my weary ascent of the dark stairs. I went by touch, feeling my way, for the steps were pitch-black. I had finished my sausage by the time I reached the entry to Chade's tower room. I opened the door and stepped in.

Darkness and a musty smell greeted me. I encountered the worktable with my hip, cursed the bruise, and then groped my way to the hearth. I found the tinderbox on the end of the mantel. When I finally had a tiny flame going in the neglected hearth, I quickly lit the half-burnt candles from the mantel candelabrum to give me some light. I fed up the fire, more for light than warmth. The room was dismal, dusty and dank after weeks with no fire in the hearth. The flames would freshen the air.

I was aware of Gilly an instant before he burst into the room from one of his own hiding places, full of enthusiasm at the thought that the sausage-bringers had finally returned. When he discovered that I had only the smell and a lick or two of grease on my fingers, he gave me a nip of rebuke and tried to climb up my leg.

"Not now, friend. I'll bring you treats later. First, I must see the Queen." I hastily smoothed my hair back into a short warrior's tail. I wished there was time to do better, but I knew Kettricken would tolerate my unkempt appearance more than she would my dawdling to change it. I entered the secret corridors and made my way to the door that gave onto the Queen's privy room and thence to her private sitting room. I paused to listen carefully at the door before I opened it, not wishing to walk in on her if she had any company. I nearly fell when Kettricken jerked the door open.

"I heard your footstep. I've been waiting for you, oh, it

seems like the entire day. I am so glad you are home, Fitz. So glad to see someone to whom I may speak freely."

Kettricken was not the calm and rational queen I knew. She looked haggard and anxious. The usually serene room was almost disorderly. The wicks of the white candles that burned on her low table needed trimming, and a forgotten wineglass, still a quarter full, idled on the table. There was a pot of tea on the table and cups for us, with a crumble of tea herbs spilled beside it. Two scrolls relating to the Out Islands and their customs were on the corner of the table.

Later, I would discover that it was not just the sporadic and cryptic reports that Chade and Dutiful had sent her through Nettle that had frayed her, but a civil uprising between Old Blood and Piebalds that had erupted in the Six Duchies in our absence. For the last three weeks, she had dealt with murders and retaliations followed by more slaughter. Although there had been no killings reported in the last six days, she still dreaded a knock at her chamber door and a messenger's baton presented to her. It was ironic that she had forced a measure of tolerance for the Witted on her nobles, only to have the Witted turn on one another.

But that was not discussed that morning. She begged a full report of me, so that she might have a better foundation for the decisions Dutiful and Chade were demanding from her. I obediently began it, only to have her interrupt with questions of how my first encounter with the Hetgurd related to what was happening now, and whether I thought Elliania's people would resent our taking of her to be our queen and whether Elliania herself came willingly to Dutiful's side.

After the fifth such interruption, she caught herself. "I am sorry." She had seated herself on a low bench beside the table. I could see her frustration that I had not been a witness to the party's return to Aslevjal and Elliania's mothershouse. I could not give her my view of the Outislander reactions to the dragon, for I had not seen them.

She started to ask another question. I held up a hand. "Why not let me contact Prince Dutiful or Lord Chade? That is why I came home. Let us have them answer your immediate questions, and then, if need be, I will report in full, all that I saw and did."

She smiled. "You take this magic for granted now. It still surprises me. Nettle has done her best for us, and she is a fine young woman. But Chade is so secretive, and Dutiful's messages seem awkward. If you would reach for my son. Please."

There followed for me the most wearying morning of Skilling that I'd ever endured. I had built stamina for the magic, but for the first time in my life, I came to understand just how earlier coteries had served their rulers. Knowing it was closest to her heart, I reached first for Dutiful, who was delighted to find me safely home. There followed from him an outpouring to his mother that I could scarcely keep up with. At first, it was awkward, for he spoke to her as son to mother, with a familiarity that was proper to such a relationship but difficult for me. As he conveyed his thoughts on the events, it was also taxing for me to refrain from correcting him, for it was inevitable that his views did not perfectly coincide with mine.

He revealed that he had offered to release Elliania from their mutual bond. It was after they had come close to quarreling. She saw no reason why they could not be married and yet allow her to remain as Narcheska of the Narwhals, with Dutiful coming and going as the other husbands and lovers did. It had, he confided to his mother through me, deeply hurt her when he said he could not give up his throne to be her husband. *She asked me, why not? Was not that what I was asking of her, that she forsake home, family, and title to become my wife in a strange place, and moreover, to rob her clan of the children that should be rightfully theirs? It was difficult, Mother. She made me see it all in a different light. Even now, when I think of it, I wonder if what we do is right.*

"But she would be Queen, here! Do not they recognize what honor and power would go with such a title?"

And when I had passed Kettricken's words to her son, I felt his regret as he said, *She will not be Clan Narwhal anymore. When, at first, her mother would not release her, she became angry. She threatened to leave her clan without her mother's permission. It was a very ugly moment. Peottre stood by her, but almost all the women of the clan opposed Elliania. Her mother said that if she left, she would be forsaking them, to become a . . . well, they have a word for it. It is not an honorable one to call a woman. It is one who has stolen from her own people to give to strangers. Many of their rules, including their ones for hospitality, insist that family must be provided for first. This, then, is a grave insult.*

I relayed Kettricken's concern. *But it has been resolved, now? She leaves her people with her honor intact?*

I think it has. Her mother and the Great Mother have consented. Still, you know how a thing may be said in words but not meant in the heart. It is like how some of our nobles tolerate the Old Blood. To the letter of the law, but with no heart to be fair to them.

I know well what you mean. It has been difficult here, Dutiful, while you were gone. I have done my best, but I look forward to Web's return. The bloodshed has been appalling, and many of my lesser nobles are muttering that it is as they said, that the Witted are little better than the animals they mate with, and that freed of the curb of punishment, they are happy to slaughter one another. The Old Blood's zeal to eliminate the Piebalds has blackened the reputation of the Witted rather than cleared it.

And so their talk wandered, from one thing to another. After a time, it was almost as if they forgot I was there. I grew hoarse repeating to Kettricken all that Dutiful wished to say to her. I sensed his relief that neither Chade nor Nettle were a party to the conversation. He confided many doubts, and yet also the small, sweet triumphs of his courtship of his bride. There was a particular shade of green that she liked, and he took great pains in describing it, for he hoped that the personal chambers that welcomed her to Buckkeep could incorporate it. He had many minor complaints over how Chade had handled the most recent round of negotiations, and many areas in which he wanted the Queen to rein in her Chief Councilor. Here, Queen and Prince did not precisely agree, and I was again hard put to serve only as go-between without injecting any of my own thoughts.

And gradually, as they employed my magic for the best interests of the Farseer throne, I began to be aware of the Skill-current. It pulled me in a new way. Not the impulsive, dive-into-it-and-be-lost-forever temptation I knew only too well, but like music heard in another chamber, lovely music that draws the attention away from what one is supposed to be doing until one becomes immersed in only it. At first it was distant, like the thunder of rapids heard while one drifts in the calm part of the river. It drew me, but not strongly. I thought I was ignoring it. The Prince's words to the Queen and her replies flowed through me and I scarce had to pay attention to what I said or the thoughts I sent to Dutiful.

It began to seem that the Skill itself was flowing through me, as if I were the river, and I was only jolted from it when the Queen leaned forward and shook me, hard.

"Fitz!" she cried out, and *Fitz!* I dutifully relayed to Dutiful.

Then, "*Wake him however you must. Throw water in his face, pinch him. I fear if I retreat now, he will go under all the way.*"

And even as I spoke Dutiful's words to the Queen, she took up her cup of cooling tea and dashed it in my face. I spluttered, coughed, and was once more fully aware of my surroundings. "I'm sorry," I said, wiping my sleeve over my face. "That has never happened to me before. At least, not in this fashion."

The Queen offered me a kerchief. "We've had some minor difficulties of this type with Nettle. It was one reason Chade wanted you to be here as soon as possible."

"He said something of the kind. I wish he had been more specific. I would have found a way to come sooner."

"She will need instruction in the Skill, Fitz. It should begin soon. Actually, it should have begun long ago."

"I know that, now," I admitted humbly. "A lot of things should have begun long ago. I'm home now, and I intend to begin them soon."

"How about now?" Kettricken asked me levelly. "I could summon my maid, and send for Nettle. You could meet her now."

A wave of dread washed through me. "Not yet!" And then I amended it to "Not like this, my lady, please. Let me be clean and shaven. And rested." I took a breath. "And fed," I added, trying not to make it sound like a remonstrance.

"Oh, Fitz, I am sorry! I have let my own needs and desires run rampant over yours. A selfish act. I apologize."

"A necessary act," I assured her. Then, "Shall I find Dutiful again? Or Chade? I know there is still much you need to know."

"Not just now. I judge it best that you refrain from Skilling for a time."

I nodded. Left alone in my own mind, I felt almost empty, as if I could no longer string together a thought of my own. It must have showed, for she leaned forward to set her hand on mine. "Some brandy, Lord FitzChivalry?"

"Please," I replied, and my queen rose to get it for us.

Sometime later, I twitched my eyes open. A shawl had been put around me and my chin rested on my chest. My brandy waited on the table before me. Kettricken was sitting quietly at the table, looking at her folded hands. I knew she meditated and I did not wish to disturb her. Yet she seemed aware that I had awakened almost as soon as I opened my eyes. She gave me a weary smile.

"My queen, I offer my humblest apologies."

"You have been long without rest." She muffled a small yawn of her own and said, "I sent for breakfast, and let my maid know I am famished. She will wish to tidy this room before she sets it out for me here. Conceal yourself until you hear me knock."

And so I spent some short time sitting on the steps in the darkness behind the concealed panel. I closed my eyes, but did not sleep. Yet it was not the burdens of the Six Duchies throne that weighted my thoughts. I was but a tool to be used in that sorting. I would eat with the Queen, visit the steams and shave, sleep for a short time, and then find a way to slip out of the castle and go back to the Witness Stones. I would raid the storeroom first, I decided, and take with me cheese and fruit and wine for the Fool and the Black Man. Perhaps they would enjoy some fresh bread. I smiled to myself, thinking how they would welcome the change in food. Perhaps the Fool would be better and able to travel. If he was, I could bring them both to Buckkeep, where I would know the Fool was safe. And finally I would be free, to go to Molly, and heal the rift of years. I heard the Queen's tap on the wall.

She had taken advantage of the time to smooth her hair and don a fresh gown. A meal, ample for several people, was set out on the low table. Tea steamed from a flowered pot, and I smelled fresh bread and butter melting on hot porridge beside a pot of thick yellow cream.

"Come and eat," she welcomed me. "And if you have a word left in you, tell me of what you have been through, and how it is that you and Thick have discovered such a swift way to travel."

I realized then the depth of the Queen's faith in me. So much had not been relayed through Nettle for the sake of keeping Chade's secrets. Only by subtle hints had she known to expect me, and yet she had believed we would arrive. And so, as we ate, I found myself reporting to her yet again. She had always been a good listener, and over the years had been my confidante more than once. Perhaps that was why I found myself telling her far more of the truth than I had confided to anyone else. I told her of my search through the city for the Fool's body, and tears ran down her cheek unchecked when I told her where and how I had found him. Her pale eyes brimmed with wonder as I told her how we had returned to the abandoned plaza. To her alone did I confide my venture into death. To her alone did I give a full accounting of our visit to the dragons themselves and the restoration of the Rooster Crown.

Only once did she interrupt. I had told her of brushing the dust and leaves off Verity-as-Dragon. She instantly reached across the table to seize my hand in a cool, hard grip.

"With these pillars, if you held my hand, you could take me to him? Even just once? I know, I know, all that would not be there for me. Yet, even to touch the stone that holds him... Oh, Fitz, you have no idea what that would mean to me!"

"To take an unSkilled person through a pillar... I do not know the full toll it might take on your mind. It could be arduous and dangerous, my queen." I was reluctant, and yet even more reluctant to disappoint her.

"And Dutiful," she said, as if she had not heard my warning at all. "Dutiful should stand, at least once, by the dragon of his father. It would make real his father's sacrifice to him, and he might perceive his own in a kindlier light then."

"Dutiful's sacrifice?"

"Did not you hear what he could not say? That as a man, he could have stayed there with Elliania, and been her husband and welcomed by her family. As a prince, he cannot. It is not a small sacrifice, FitzChivalry. Elliania will follow him here, that is true. But ever, it will be a little wall between them. You yourself have known how sharp that can be, to disappoint the woman you love out of the duty you must yield to your people."

I spoke without considering the wisdom of it. "I will be going back for her, now. The time for that sacrifice is at an end. Burrich is gone and no longer stands between us. I will take Molly again for my own."

A silence followed my words, and I realized I had shocked her. Then she said, gently, "I am glad that, at last, you have found that resolve. I speak now as a woman and your friend. Do not go to Molly too soon. Let her son come home to her first. Let her family heal around their terrible wound. Then, approach her, but as yourself, not as a man coming to take Burrich's place."

I knew her words were wise as soon as I heard them. But my heart howled to rush to Molly as soon as I could, to begin, as soon as possible, to make up the years we had lost. I wanted to comfort her in her grief. I bowed my head, realizing the selfishness of that impulse. Hard as it would be for me to stand to one side and wait, it was what I should do, for the sake of Burrich's sons.

"And the same for Nettle," Kettricken went on implacably. "She will soon know that something has changed when I do not call on her to pass messages to Dutiful for me. Yet, if you will listen to me, do not rush to her. Above all, do not try to replace her father. For such Burrich was to her, Fitz, through no fault of your own. Such he will always be. You will have to find another role in her life, and be content with it."

They were bitter words for me to hear, and more bitter still was it for me to admit, "I know." I sighed. "I will teach her the Skill. That time, I will have with her."

I resumed my tale for the Queen, and by the time I reached the end of it, the pot of tea was gone. I was a bit abashed to see that I had cleared the table of food. I suspected that Kettricken had eaten little of it. I blinked my sandy eyes and tried to stifle a huge yawn. She smiled at me wearily.

"Go and sleep, Fitz."

"Thank you. I shall." Then, well aware I was not

supposed to know her identity, I asked the Queen, "If you would speak to Chade's new apprentice, it would be of great help to me. The third storeroom in the east hall is where he used to have supplies left for Thick to bring up to his tower room. As soon as the Fool can travel, I plan to bring him back to Buckkeep. The tower room might be the best place for him to stay, until he can shed his identity as Lord Golden. Chade's apprentice could stock the room if she—" And there I bit my tongue, knowing I'd betrayed myself in my weariness.

Queen Kettricken gave me a tolerant smile. "I'll tell Lady Rosemary to make the arrangements. And if I need you?"

I pondered briefly, then realized the obvious. "Ask Nettle to contact Thick."

She shook her head. "I plan to send Nettle home to her family for a time. They need her. It is not fair that they be apart at this time."

I nodded. "Thick will be about. You could keep him at your side. It might be a good way to occupy him and keep him from telling too many tales of how he came home."

She nodded gravely. I bowed, suddenly horribly weary.

"Go, Fitz, and take my thanks with you. Oh!" The sharpness of her intake of breath warned me.

"What?"

"Lady Patience is expected. She sent me word of her visit at the same time that she told me she wished to convey Withywoods on Lady Nettle. She also warned me that she wished to 'consult me on serious matters concerning certain inheritances that should be provided for now.'"

There was little point in mincing words. "I am sure she knows that Nettle is my daughter. Eda help the poor child if Patience has decided to take over her education." I smiled ruefully at my remembrance of Patience's instruction of me.

Queen Kettricken nodded to that. Solemnly she

asked, "What is the saying? All your chickens have come home to roost?"

"I think that's it. But strangely enough, my lady queen, I welcome them."

"I am glad to hear you say so." She nodded to me that I was excused.

I left the room, and the climb back up to Chade's tower seemed endless. When I got there, I lay down on the bed. I closed my eyes and tried to sleep, but it suddenly seemed the Skill-current was very near. Perhaps it was because of my long exercise with it that morning. I opened my eyes and became aware I could smell myself. I heaved a sigh and decided that getting cleaned up before I slept would not be a bad idea.

Once more I wound my way through the immense old castle, avoiding the guardroom and the inevitable barrage of questions. I found the steams relatively deserted at that time of day. The two guardsmen there did not know me, and while they greeted me affably enough, they asked no questions. I was as much relieved at that as I was to scrape the whiskers from my face. I gave myself a most thorough scrubbing and then, feeling as if I had been parboiled, emerged clean and ready to sleep.

Nettle was waiting for me outside the steams.

chapter XXXIII

FAMILY

So I shall have to travel to Buckkeep, in the heat of summer, because I dare not trust either the tidings I bring or the items that must be transferred to a courier. My old Lacey has declared she will make the journey with me, despite a weakness of her breath that has taken her lately. I beg that, for her sake, you will find us quarters that do not require the climbing of too many stairs.

I will require a private audience with you, for the time has come when I should reveal a secret I have concealed for many years. As you are not a stupid woman, I suspect you have guessed part of it already, but I should still like to sit down and discuss with you what had best be done for the good of the young woman involved.

▶ MISSIVE FROM LADY PATIENCE
TO QUEEN KETTRICKEN

I knew her at once by her close-cropped head. But there her resemblance to my dream-image of her stopped. The traveling dress she wore was green, cut for riding, and she carried a cloak of sensible brown homespun. Plainly, she saw herself as looking like her mother, for thus she had appeared in my dreams. To my eyes, she more strongly resembled Molly's father but with some Farseer elements thrown into the mix. It was a Farseer gaze that she fixed on me as I emerged, at once dashing my hope that I might walk past her unrecognized. I halted where I stood.

I froze and waited dumbly for what might come. She continued to regard me levelly. After a moment, she said quietly, "Do you think that if you stand very still, I can't see you, Shadow Wolf?"

I smiled foolishly. Her voice was low-pitched, deeper than one might expect in a girl, like Molly's at that age. "I . . . no, of course not. I know you can see me. But . . . how did you know me?"

She came two steps closer. I looked around us and then I walked away from the steams, well aware that for a young noblewoman of the Buckkeep court to be seen casually chatting with an older guardsman might excite gossip. She walked beside me, following me unquestioningly as I led her toward a secluded bench in the Women's Garden. "Oh, it was very easy. You had promised you'd reveal yourself to me, did you not? I knew you were coming home. Dutiful said as much when we spoke last night, that soon I would be freed of these duties for a time. So, when the Queen summoned me and told me I might return home, to comfort my mother for a time, I knew what it meant. That you were here. Then." And she smiled, a genuine smile of pleasure. "I encountered Thick, on his way up to the Queen as I was leaving her. I knew him by his music, as well as by his name. And he knew me, at first glance. Such a hug he gave me! It shocked Lady Sydel, but she will recover. I asked Thick where his traveling companion was. He shut his eyes for a moment, and told me, 'In the steams.' So I came and I waited there."

I wished that Thick had warned me. "And you knew me when you saw me?"

She gave a small *hmph*. "I recognized the dismay on

your face at being found out. None of the other men who have come out gawked at me that way." She gave me a sideways glance, well pleased with herself, but there were little sparks in her eyes. I wondered if mine looked like that when I was angry. She spoke calmly and competently, just as Molly sometimes used to do when she was storing up fuel for a rage. After a moment's reflection, I decided she had the right to be annoyed with me. I had promised to make myself known to her when I returned. And I had intended to evade that promise.

"Well. You've found me," I said lamely, and instantly knew it was exactly the wrong thing to say to her.

"Small thanks to you!" She seated herself solidly on the bench. I stood, well aware of the disparity in our apparent ranks. She had to look up at me, but it did not seem that way when she demanded, "What is your name, sir?"

So I had to give her the name by which I was known when I wore the blue of a Buckkeep Guard. "Tom Badgerlock, my lady. Of the Prince's Guard."

She suddenly looked like a cat with a mouse between her paws. "That's convenient for me. The Queen said she would have a guardsman accompany me on my journey home. I'll take you." It was a challenge flung down.

"I am not free to go, my lady." It sounded like an excuse and I hastily added, "I take over your duties, as you have guessed. I act as go-between for Lord Chade, Prince Dutiful, and our gracious queen."

"Surely Thick could do that."

"His magic is strong, but he has his limits, my lady."

"My lady!" she muttered disdainfully. "And what shall I call you, then? Lord Wolf?" She shook her head, exasperated with me. "I know you are telling me the truth. Worse luck for me." Her shoulders slumped suddenly, and her youth and grief were more apparent. "It is not an easy tale I bring home to my mother and brothers. But they deserve to know the manner of our father's death. And that Swift did not abandon him." Without thinking, she lifted her hands and ran them through her shortened hair until it stood up in spires and peaks all over her head. "This magic of the Skill has not been an easy burden for me. It has snatched me from my home, and kept me here when my mother needs me most." Turning to me accusingly, she demanded, "Why did you choose me, of all people, to give this magic to?"

It shocked me. "I didn't. I didn't choose you. You had it, you were born with the magic. And, for some reason, we connected. I didn't even realize you were there, watching my life, for a very long time."

"There were times when that was obvious," she observed, but before I wondered what I had unwittingly shown her of myself, she added, "And now I have it, like some disease, and it means that I am ever in service to my queen. And to King Dutiful, when he succeeds her. I don't suppose you can even imagine what a burden that could be to me."

"I have some inkling of it," I replied quietly. Then, when she continued to sit unmoving before me, I asked her, "Should not you be on your way? Daylight is the best time for travel."

"We have just met, and you are so anxious for us to be parted." She looked down at the ground beneath her feet. Suddenly, she was Nettle from our dreams as she shook her head and said, "This is not at all how I imagined our first meeting would be. I thought you would be happy to see me, and we would laugh and be friends." She gave a small cough and then admitted shyly, "A long time ago, when I first had dreams about you and the wolf, I used to imagine that we would really meet some day. I pretended you would be my age and handsome, in a wolfish way, and find me pretty. That was silly, wasn't it?"

"I'm sorry to have disappointed you," I said carefully. "I definitely find you pretty, however." She gave me a look that said that such compliments from an aging guardsman made her uncomfortable. Her illusions about me had made a barrier I had not expected. I came closer to her, and then crouched down beside her to look up into her eyes. "Could we, perhaps, begin this again?" I put out a hand to her and said, "My name is Shadow Wolf. And Nettle, you cannot imagine how many years I have longed to meet you." Without warning, my throat closed tight. I hoped I would not get teary. My daughter hesitated, and then set her hand in mine. It was slender, like a lady's hand should be, but brown from the sun and her palm against mine was callused. The touch strengthened our Skill-bond and it was as if she squeezed my heart rather than my fingers. Even if I had wanted to hide what I felt from her, I could not have done so. I think it breached some wall she had held.

She looked up into my face, on a level with hers now. Our eyes met, and suddenly her lower lip trembled like a baby's. "My papa is dead!" she stammered out. "My papa is dead, and I don't know what to do! How can we go on? Chivalry is such a boy still, and Mama knows nothing of the horses. Already, she speaks of selling them off and moving to a town, saying she cannot abide to be where my father so emphatically is not!" She choked and then gasped, "It's all going to fall apart. I'm going to fall apart! I can't be as strong as everyone expects me to be. But I have to." She drew herself up straight and faced me. "I have to be strong," she repeated, as if that would turn her bones to iron. It seemed to work. No tears. Hers was a desperate courage. I caught her in my arms and held her tight. For the first time in her life or mine, I held my daughter. Her cropped hair was bristly against my chin and all I could think was how much I loved her. I opened myself to her and let it flood from me into her. I felt her shock, both at the depth of my feeling and that a relative stranger would touch her so. I tried to explain.

"I will look after you," I told her. "I'll look after all of you. I promised...I promised your papa I would do that, look after you and your little brothers. And I will."

"I don't think you can," she said. "Not as he did." But

trying to gentle her words, she added, "I do believe you will try. But there is no one like my papa in the world. No one."

For a moment longer, she let me hold her. Then, gently, she disentangled herself from me. Subdued, she said, "My horse will be saddled and waiting. And the guardsman the Queen assigned me will be there, also." She took a huge breath, held it, then slowly let it out. "I have to go. There will be a lot to do at home. Mama cannot manage the babies as well as she used to with Papa gone. I'm needed there." She found her kerchief and dabbed unshed tears from her eyes.

"Yes. I'm sure you are." I hesitated, and then said, "There was a message, from your father. You may think it odd or frivolous, but it was important to him."

She looked at me quizzically.

"When Malta comes into season, Ruddy is to stud her."

She lifted a hand to her mouth and gave a strangled little laugh. When she caught her breath, she said, "Ever since the mare came to us, he and Chivalry have argued about that. I'll tell him." She took two steps away from me and repeated, "I'll tell him." Then she whirled and was gone.

I stood for a moment, feeling bereft. Then a sad smile spread over my face. I sat down on the bench and looked out over the Women's Garden. It was summer and the air was rich with the fragrance of both herbs and blossoms, and yet the scent of my daughter's hair was still in my nostrils and I savored it. I stared into the distance over the top of the lilac tree and wondered. It was going to take me longer to get to know my daughter than I had thought. Perhaps there would never be a good time to tell her that I was her father. That piece of information did not seem as important as it once had. Instead, it seemed more important that I find a way to come into their lives without causing pain or discord. It wasn't going to be easy. But I would do it. Somehow.

I must have fallen asleep there. When I awoke, it was

late afternoon. For a moment, I could not recall where I was, only that I was happy. That was such a rare sensation for me that I lay there, looking up at blue sky through green leaves. Then I became aware that my back was stiff from sleeping on a stone bench, and in the following instant, that I had planned to take food and wine back to the Fool today. Well, it was not too late for that, I told myself. I rose and stretched and rolled the kinks out of my neck and shoulders.

The pathway back to the kitchens led through the herb gardens. At that time of year, lavender and dill and fennel grow tall, and this year they seemed even taller than usual. I heard one woman say querulously to another, "Just see how they've let the gardens go! Disgraceful. Pull up that weed, if you can reach it."

Then, as I stepped into view, I recognized Lacey's voice as she said, "I don't think that's a weed, dear heart. I think it's a marigo— Well, it's too late now, whatever it was, you've got it up, roots and all. Give it to me, and I'll throw it in the bushes where no one will find it."

And there they were, two dear old ladies, Patience in a summer gown and hat that had probably last seen the light of day when my father was King-in-Waiting. Lacey, as ever, was dressed in the simple robe of a serving woman. Patience carried her slippers in one hand and the torn-out marigold in the other. She looked at me nearsightedly. Perhaps she saw no more than the blue of a guard's uniform as she declared to me sternly, "Well, it didn't belong there!" She shook the offending plant at me. "That's what a weed is, young man, a plant growing in the wrong place, so you needn't stare at me so! Didn't your mother teach you any manners?"

"Oh, dear Eda-of-the-Fields!" Lacey exclaimed. I thought I might still be able to retreat, but then Lacey, stolid, solid Lacey, turned slowly and fainted dead away into the lavender.

"Whatever are you doing, dear? Did you lose something?" Patience exclaimed, peering at her. And then, when she perceived Lacey was supine and unmoving, she turned on me, asking in outrage, "See what you've done now! Frightened the poor old woman to death, you have! Well, don't stand there, you simpleton. Pluck her out of the lavender before she crushes it completely!"

"Yes, ma'am," I said, and stooping, I lifted her. Lacey had always been a hearty woman, and age had not dwindled her. Nonetheless, I managed to raise her, and even carried her to a shady spot before I set her down on the grass there. Patience had followed us, muttering and shaking her head over how clumsy I was.

"Faints at the drop of a hat she does, now! Poor old dear. Do you feel better now?" She eased herself down beside her companion and patted her hand. Lacey's eyes fluttered.

"I'll fetch some water, shall I?"

"Yes. And hurry. And don't even think of running off, young man. This is all your doing, you know."

I ran to the kitchens for a cup and filled it at the well on my way back. By the time I got there, Lacey was sitting up and Lady Patience was fanning her old servant, alternately scolding and sympathizing. "... and you know as well as I do how the eyes play tricks on us at our age. Why, only last week, I tried to shoo my wrap off the table, thinking it was the cat. It was the way it was curled, you know."

"My lady, no. Look well. It is him or his ghost. He looks just as his father looked at that age. Look at him, do."

I kept my eyes down as I knelt by her and offered her the cup. "A bit of water, ma'am, and I'm sure you'll feel better. It was most likely the heat." Then, as Lacey took the cup from me, Patience reached across her to seize my chin in her hand. "Look at me, young man! Look at me, I said!" And then, as she leaned closer and closer to me, she exclaimed, "My Chivalry never had a nose like that. But his eyes do ... remind me. Oh. Oh, my son, my son. It cannot be. It cannot be."

She let go of me and sat back. Lacey offered her the

cup of water, and Patience took it absently. She drank from it and, turning to Lacey, said calmly, "He wouldn't dare. He wouldn't have."

Lacey still stared at me. "You heard the rumors, same as me, my lady. And that Witted minstrel sang us the song, about the dragons and how the Witted Bastard rose from the grave to serve his king."

"He wouldn't," Patience repeated. She stared at me, and my tongue was frozen to the roof of my mouth. Then, "Help me up, young man. And Lacey, too. She has the fainting spells, these days. Eating too much fish, is what I think brings them on. And river fish at that. Makes her wobbly, so you'll just see us back to our chambers, won't you?"

"Yes, ma'am. I'll be happy to."

"I daresay you'll be happy to. Until we get you behind closed doors. Take her arm, now, and help her along." But that was easier said than done, for Patience clung to my other arm as if a river might sweep her away if she let go.

Lacey was, in truth, swaying as she walked, and I felt very bad indeed to have given her such a shock. Neither one of them said another word to me, though twice Patience pointed out caterpillars on the roses and said they were never tolerated in the old days. Once inside, we still had a long walk through the Great Hall, and then up the wide stairs. I was grateful that it was only one flight, for Patience muttered nasty words as she mastered each riser, and Lacey's knees crackled alarmingly. We went down the hall and Patience waved at a door for me. It was one of the best chambers in Buckkeep, and it pleased me more than I could say that Queen Kettricken had accorded her this respect. Lady Patience's traveling trunk was already open in the middle of the room, and a hat was already perched on the mantel. Kettricken had even recalled that Lady Patience preferred to dine in her chambers, for a small table and two chairs had been placed in the fall of sunlight from the deep-set window.

I saw each of them to a chair, and when they were seated, asked them if there was anything else I could bring them.

"Sixteen years," Patience snapped. "You can fetch me sixteen years! Shut that door. I don't suppose it would be wise for this to be gossip all over Buckkeep. Sixteen years, and not a peep, not a hint. Tom, Tom, whatever were you thinking?"

"More likely, not thinking at all," Lacey suggested, looking at me with martyred eyes. That stung, for always when I had been a boy and in trouble with Patience, Lacey had taken my part. She seemed to have recovered well from her faint. There were spots of color on her cheeks. She ponderously rose from her chair and went into the adjoining room. In a few moments, she returned with three teacups and a bottle of brandy on a little tray. She set it down on the small table between them, and I winced at the sight of her lumpy knuckles and gnarled fingers. Age had crippled those nimble hands that once had tatted lace by the hour. "I suppose we could all do with a bit of this. Not that you deserve any," she said coldly. "That was quite a fright you gave me in the garden. Not to mention years of grief."

"Sixteen years," Patience clarified, in case I had managed to forget in the last few moments. Then, turning to Lacey, she said, "I told you he wasn't dead! When we prepared his body to bury him, even then, washing his cold legs, I told you he couldn't be dead. I don't know how I knew it, but I knew it. And I was right!"

"He was dead," Lacey insisted. "My lady, he had not breath to fog a bit of glass, nor a single thump of his heart. He was dead." She pointed a finger at me. It shook slightly. "And now you are not. You had best have a good explanation for this, young man."

"It was Burrich's idea," I began, and before I could say another word, Patience threw up her hands in the air, crying, "Oh, I should have guessed that man would be at the bottom of this. That's your girl he has been raising all these years, isn't it? Three years after we'd buried you, we heard a rumor. That tinker, Cottlesby, that sells such nice needles, he told us he had seen Molly in, oh, some town, with a little girl at her side. I thought to myself then, how old? For I said to Lacey, when Molly left my service so abruptly she puked and slept like a woman with child. Then, she was gone, before I could even offer to help her with the babe. Your daughter, my grandchild! Then, later, I heard that Burrich had gone with her, and when I asked about, he was claiming all the children as his own. Well. I might have known. I might have known."

I had not been prepared for Patience to be quite so well informed. I should have been. In the days after my death, she had run Buckkeep Castle, and developed a substantial network of folk who reported to her. "I think I could do with some brandy," I said quietly. I reached for the decanter, but Patience slapped my hand away.

"I'll do it!" she exclaimed crossly. "Do you think you can pretend to be dead and vanish from my life for sixteen years and then walk in and pour yourself some of my good brandy? Insolence!"

She got it open, but when she tried to pour, her hand shook so wildly that she threatened to deluge the table. I took it from her, as she began to gasp, and poured some into our cups. By the time I set the bottle down, she was sobbing. Her hair, never tidy for long, had half fallen down. When had so much gray come into it? I knelt down before her and forced myself to look up into her faded eyes. She covered her face with her hands and sobbed harder. Cautiously, I reached up and tugged her hands from her face. "Please believe me. It was never by my choice, Mother. If I could have come back to you without putting the people I loved at risk, I would have. You know that. And the way you prepared my body for burial may have saved my life. Thank you."

"A fine time to call me 'mother,' after all these years,"

she sniffed, and added, "And what would Burrich have known about anything, unless it had four legs and hooves." But she put her tear-wet hands on my cheeks and drew me forward to kiss me on the brow. She sat back and looked down at me severely. The tip of her nose was very pink. "I'll have to forgive you now. Eda knows, I may drop dead tomorrow, and angry as I am with you, I still would not wish you to walk about the rest of your life regretting that I had died before I forgave you. But that does not mean I'm going to stop being angry with you, or that Lacey has to stop being angry with you. You deserve it." She sniffed loudly. Lacey passed her a kerchief. The old serving woman's face rebuked me as she took her seat at the table. More clearly than ever, I saw how the years together had erased the lines between lady and maid.

"Yes. I do."

"Well, get up. I've no desire to get a crick in my neck staring at you down there. Why on earth are you dressed as a guardsman? And why have you been so foolish as to come back to Buckkeep Castle? Don't you know there are still people who would love to see you dead! You are not safe here, Tom. When I return to Tradeford, you shall come with me. Perhaps I can pass you off as a gardener or a wayward cousin's son. Not that I shall allow you to touch my plants. You know nothing about gardens and flowers."

I came to my feet slowly and could not resist saying, "I could help with the weeding. I know what a marigold looks like, even when it isn't in flower."

"There! You see, Lacey! I forgive him and the next word out of his mouth is to mock me!" Then she covered her mouth suddenly, as if to suppress another sob. The tendons and blue veins stood out on the back of her hand. Behind it, she drew a sharp breath, and then said, "I think I'll have my brandy now." She lifted her cup and sipped from it. She glanced at me over the rim, and more tears suddenly spilled. She set the cup down hastily, shaking her head. "You're here and alive. I don't know what I've got to weep about. Except sixteen years and a grandchild, lost to me forever. How could you, you wretch! Account for them. Account for yourself and what you've been doing that was so very important you couldn't come home to us."

And suddenly, all the very good reasons I'd had for not going to her seemed trivial. I could have found a way. I heard myself say aloud, "If I hadn't given my pain to the stone dragon, I think I would have found a way, however risky. Maybe you have to keep your pain and loss to know that you can survive whatever life deals you. Perhaps without putting your pain in its place in your life, you become something of a coward."

She slapped the table in front of her, then exclaimed in pain at her stinging fingers. "I didn't want a moral lecture, I wanted an accounting. With no excuses!"

"I've never forgotten the apples you threw to me through the bars of my cell. You and Lacey were incredibly brave to come to me in the dungeons, and to take my part when few others dared to."

"Stop it!" she hissed indignantly as her eyes filled with tears again. "Is this how you get your pleasure these days? Making old ladies weep over you?"

"I don't mean to."

"Then tell me what happened to you. From the last time I saw you."

"My lady, I would love to. And I will, I promise. But when I encountered you, I was on a pressing errand of my own. One that I should complete before I lose the daylight. Let me go, and I promise that I'll be back tomorrow, to give a full accounting."

"No. Of course not. What errand?"

"You recall my friend the Fool? He has fallen ill. I need to take him some herbs to ease him, and food and wine."

"That pasty-faced lad? He was never a healthy child. Ate too much fish, if you ask me. That will do that to you."

"I'll tell him. But I need to go see him."

"When did you last see him?"

"Yesterday."

"Well, it has been sixteen long years since you've seen me. He can wait his turn."

"But he is not well."

She clashed her teacup as she set it down on the saucer. "Neither am I!" she exclaimed, and fresh tears began to well.

Lacey came to pat her shoulders. Over Patience's head, she said to me, "She is not always rational. Especially when she is tired. We only arrived this morning. I told her that she should rest, but she wanted a bit of air in the gardens."

"And what, pray, is irrational about that?" Patience demanded.

"Nothing," I said hastily. "Nothing at all. Come. I've an idea. Lie down on your bed, and I shall sit beside you where you are comfortable, and begin my tale. And if you drowse off, I shall quietly take my leave, and come back to continue it tomorrow. For sixteen years cannot be told in an hour, or even in a day."

"It will take sixteen years to tell sixteen years," Patience told me sternly. "Help me up, then. I'm stiff from traveling, you know."

I gave her my arm and she leaned on it as I escorted her to her bed. She groaned as she sat down on it, and as the feather bed gave beneath her, she muttered, "Much too soft. I'll never be able to sleep on this. Do they think I'm a hen, setting in a nest?" Then, as she lay back and I helped her lift her feet onto the bed she said, "You've quite ruined my surprise, you know. Here I was, all set to summon a grandchild to me and reveal to her that she was well-born of noble blood, and pass on to her keepsakes of her father. Oh, help me take my shoes off. When did my feet get so far away from my hands?"

"You don't have your shoes on. I think you left your slippers in the garden."

"And whose fault is that? Startling us that way. It's a wonder I didn't forget my head down there."

I nodded, noting but not commenting that her stockings didn't match. Patience had never cared much for detail. "What sort of keepsakes?" I asked.

"It scarcely matters now. As you are alive, I intend to keep them."

"What were they?" I asked, intensely curious.

"Oh. A painting you gave me, don't you know? And, when you were dead, I took a lock of your hair. I've worn it in a locket ever since." While I was speechless, she leaned up on an elbow. "Lacey, come have a lie-down for a bit. You know I don't like you to be too far away if I need you. Your hearing isn't what it used to be." To me, she confided, "They've given her a narrow little bed in a closet of a room. Fine if your maid is a slip of a girl, but hardly appropriate for a mature woman. Lacey!"

"I'm right here, dearie. You needn't shout." The old serving woman came round to the other side of the bed. She looked a bit uncomfortable at the prospect of lying down in front of me, as if I might think it improper that she should share a lady's bed. It made perfect sense to me. "I am tired," she admitted as she sat down. She had brought a shawl, and she spread it over Patience's legs.

I brought a chair to the edge of the bed and sat down backward on it. "Where should I begin?" I asked her.

"Begin by sitting on that chair properly!" And after I had corrected that, she said, "Don't tell me what that vile pretender did to you to kill you. I saw enough of it on your body and I could not bear it then. Tell me, instead, how you survived."

I thought briefly, considering. "You know I am Witted."

"I thought you might be," she conceded. She yawned. "And?"

And so I launched into my tale. I told her of seeking refuge in my wolf, and how Burrich and Chade had called me back to my body. I told her of my slow recovery, and of Chade's visit. I thought she had drowsed off then, but when I tried to rise, her eyes flew open. "Sit down!" she commanded me, and when I had done so, she took my hand, is if to keep me from creeping away. "I'm listening. Go on."

I told her of Burrich leaving, and of the Forged Ones. I explained to her how Burrich had come to believe I had died there, and returned to Molly to protect her and the child she carried. I told her of my long journey from Buck to Tradeford, and of Regal's King's Circle there. She opened one eye. "It's all a garden, now. I've plants and trees and flowers from all over the Six Duchies and beyond. Monkey-tail vine from Jamaillia, and blue-needle bush from the Spice Isles. And a lovely herb-knot in the very middle of where it used to be. You'd like it, Tom. You will like it, when you come to live with me."

"I'm sure I'll like it," I said, scrupulously avoiding the topic of where I might or might not live. "Shall I go on, or do you want to nap now?" A gentle snore buzzed from Lacey's side of the bed.

"Go on. I'm not the least bit sleepy. Go on."

But in the midst of my telling her how I had attempted to kill Regal, she dozed off. I sat still a time longer, waiting until her grip slackened on my hand and I could slip clear of her.

I walked silently to the door. As I lifted the latch, Lacey raised up on one elbow. There was nothing wrong with her hearing, and I suspected that despite her crooked fingers, one would still find a blade up her sleeve. So I nodded to her and left Patience sleeping as I slipped from the room.

I went down to the guardroom and ate heartily. There is nothing like a steady diet of salt fish to make one appreciate bread and butter and cold roast fowl. My enjoyment of the meal was somewhat dampened by the knowledge that evening was drawing on. Guardsmen seemed always hungry, and no one made any comment when I carried off half a loaf of bread and a goodly wedge of cheese with me. From my meal, I went immediately to a storeroom where I helped myself to a carry basket and two sausages. I added the loaf and cheese to the basket. I took my trove up to Chade's tower room. Thick had been there. He had done a cursory dusting of the table and mantel and set out a bowl of fruit. A little fire burned on the hearth. There was a small supply of firewood in the hod, a bundle of tapers on the table, and water in the barrel. I shook my head in wonder at the man. After all he had been through, he was home for one day and still remembered his old duties. I put half a dozen yellow and purple plums into my carry basket and nested a bottle of Chade's wine between the bread and cheese. I was folding feverfew and dried willow bark into a twist of paper when I felt Chade nudge at my mind.

What?

I need to speak to the Queen, Fitz.

Cannot you use Thick instead? I was just on my way to the Skill-pillars.

This will not take long.

I will have to find a way to arrange quiet time with Queen Kettricken.

I have already contacted her, through Thick. The message she sent back was, yes, immediately. If you go to her private sitting room, she will come to you shortly.

Very well.

You seem cross.

I am worried about the Fool. I have some things here I'd like to take back to him. Fresh fruit and herbs for fever.

I understand, Fitz. But this should not take long. Then, you can sleep the night through, and go in the morning.

Very well. I released our contact. Very well. And what else could I have said? He was right. Many of the thoughts Dutiful had conveyed to his mother would have been difficult for Thick to grasp, let alone pass on. I tried not to resent the time it stole from me. The Fool would be fine, I told myself. He had been through the changes before, and who better than the Black Man to tend him? He had even told me that he needed time apart from me, time to think.

Time to think without watching the face of someone who had witnessed what had befallen you. Besides, it was better that I serve this duty than Nettle, I told myself sternly. She needed to be home, with her family, and doubtless her family needed her there. I found a clean piece of cloth and covered the bread. I went down the long dim stairs to wait upon the Queen. It did not take a short time. Chade and Dutiful were quarreling, and Chade had attempted to steal a march upon the Prince by contacting the Queen first. He and the Prince were to board the ship to sail home tomorrow afternoon. The Narcheska was to have come with them, but earlier in the day, she had gone to Dutiful and begged that she might have three more months in the company of her family before she left them to come to Buckkeep. The Prince had granted it to her, privately, without consulting Chade.

Very privately, Chade seethed, and I wondered if he intended that I pass on to the Queen that the asking of the boon and the granting of it had occurred in a setting of an intimacy of which the councilor did not approve.

"Very discreetly was this matter discussed between the Prince and the Narcheska," was what I told her.

"I see," she replied, and I wondered if she did.

As of yet, there has been no public announcement. It is not too late for us to retract this permission. I fear it will throw all our plans awry if the girl is allowed to stay here. For one thing, it will mean that when she arrives, if she keeps her promise to arrive at all, it will be in the storms of winter rather than in time for the nuptials to be celebrated with the autumn harvest. The Prince will be returning to his nobles without a bride, indeed, with nothing visible to show for the time and expense of this expedition. If, as we have hoped, you planned to press for the Dukes to declare him King-in-Waiting, this will be a lackluster event to base it on. Tales of dragons rescued and dragon heads on hearthstones will mean little to nobles who have seen not so much as a scale of a dragon, let alone the bride and alliance won by such valor. And I fear the longer the Narcheska lingers

*among her women here, the harder they will make it for her to
depart from them. Their reluctance to give her up has grown
hourly. They mourn her as one going to her death, as vanishing
from their world forever.*

When these thoughts had been delivered to the
Queen, she suggested to Chade, "Perhaps, then, it would
be wiser to give her more time to bid her people farewell.
Please add many assurances that visitors will always be welcome, and that she will periodically return to visit there, as
well. Have you extended welcome to any of her clan who
wish to accompany her, not just to witness the wedding,
but to stay on that she need not feel so alone here?"

As I passed her words on to Chade, I was reminded
starkly of how alone Kettricken had been when she journeyed from the mountains, without so much as a personal
maid to accompany her. Did she recall her early days of being alone in a foreign court where no one spoke her mother
tongue or recognized her customs?

*It is a part of the difficulty. As I understand it, a woman's
bond to her land is sacred. The women in line to rule their mothershouses seldom leave their homeland at all. They live on it, die
on it, and go back into it. All that goes into a woman or comes
forth from her is expected to stay on her own lands. So, no
women of power will travel with her when she comes to Buckkeep. Peottre will accompany her, and perhaps a couple of her
male cousins. Arkon Bloodblade will come, and a goodly number of leaders from other clans will come, to confirm the trade
alliances they have formed with our visiting nobles. But she will
not have an entourage of servants and ladies.*

"I see," Kettricken replied slowly. We were alone in
her sitting room. She had poured wine for us, and the
glasses rested, neglected, on the low table. The room had
been restored since last I saw it. As ever, Kettricken sought
her peace in simplicity. A single flower floated in a low pottery dish and the candles were shielded to a gentle glow.
The candles released a calming perfume into the air, but
Kettricken was tense as a treed cat. She saw me looking at

her hands clenched on the edge of the table and carefully relaxed them. "Does Chade hear all that I say to you?" she asked me softly.

"No. He is not with me that way, not riding with me as Verity used to do. That takes a great deal of concentration. And demands a total loss of privacy of thought. I have not invited him to do that. So, he hears only what you tell me to say to him."

Her shoulders lowered a trifle as she relaxed. "Sometimes my councilor and I are at odds. When we spoke through Nettle...well. It was difficult, for Chade and I were both being so circumspect, taking care not to involve her in matters far beyond her ability or need to understand. But now you are here." She lifted her head slightly. Almost, she smiled. "I take strength from you, FitzChivalry. In an odd way, when you Skill for me, you serve me as a Queen's Man." She drew herself up straight. "Tell Chade that in this matter, the Prince's word to his affianced one will not be compromised. If he feels winter is not an auspicious time for this wedding, then let us offer to postpone it until spring, when the crossing will doubtless be safer and more pleasant for the Narcheska. In the matter of the Prince being hailed as King-in-Waiting, well, that has always been up to his dukes. If he must bring home a woman as trophy for them to find him worthy of the title, then the title means little to me. He will, eventually, reign over them. It is my opinion that his kindness and consideration to his future bride may well strengthen this alliance rather than be seen as weakness." She paused, as if thinking, pinching her lips firmly together. Then, "Tell him that, please." She took up her wineglass and sipped from it.

This is not wise, Fitz. Cannot you reason with her? The Prince is besotted with Elliania. He must be made to see that it is more important to both their futures that he now gratifies the wishes of his dukes rather than his bride's mother. The sooner this marriage is a reality, the sooner they will see him as a man approaching kingship rather than a boy-prince. He is far too impetuous, following the impulse of his heart when the good of the Six Duchies demands that only his head make his decisions. Make her understand, Fitz, that we have spent the summer doing the Narcheska's will, and now it is time for his dukes to see that they still have his heart, and that their regard is more important to him than the well-wishes of the Out Islands.

I pondered his words for a moment and then opened my eyes to the Queen's anxious gaze. "This is what Chade thinks," I said, and relayed the gist of the message.

The subtlety was not lost on Kettricken. "And what do you think, FitzChivalry?"

I bowed my head to her. "I think you are the Queen. And that Prince Dutiful will someday be King."

"Then you counsel me to ignore my councilor's advice and give support to my son?"

"My lady queen, I am very glad that I do not have to give you advice in this area."

She almost smiled. "You do if I ask you for it."

I was silent for quite a time, thinking furiously.

"Is your chair uncomfortable?" she asked solicitously. "You shift as if it is full of fire ants."

I settled back into it resolutely. "I would find a way between, my lady. It would please his dukes if the Prince were wed and an heir produced, but he is still very young, not even of an age to be a King-in-Waiting. The nuptials and the title can, perhaps, wait. Let the Narcheska have her time with her mother and sister. I have been there and seen how power is wielded. Although Oerttre is Narcheska still, for she is alive, for Elliania to depart will be as profound an abdication as when my father passed the crown to Verity. Some will dispute who should next inherit the title. While she is a presence there, she can make firm her younger sister's claim. And I think it would be in the Six Duchies' best interest to see that her line of the family remains securely in power. Our dukes can be placated in other ways. Trade is what will enrich their coffers, and the Narwhal and Boar clans are not the only ones interested in what we have to offer them. Throw wide the gates. Invite their kaempras, their warrior leaders. Men all, they will not scruple to leave their mothershouses, if by doing so they can gain a trade advantage. Let that be what we celebrate this autumn harvest. Begin now to plan a Harvest Fest that will display for them the riches of our Six Duchies. Encourage the dukes to attend, with their families and nobles of their duchies. Celebrate the trade alliances now, and let the wedding be the capstone when it occurs."

Kettricken leaned back in her chair and regarded me carefully. "And when did you learn to be so sagacious, FitzChivalry?"

"A wise old man taught me that diplomacy is the velvet glove that cloaks the fist of power. Persuasion, not force, works best and lasts longest. Make this alliance in the dukes' best interest and they will be eager to welcome and honor the Narcheska when she arrives."

I did not add that he had taught me that when he had been content to move behind the walls of Buckkeep and manipulate the throne unseen.

"Would that he still recalled that. Tell him your thoughts, but phrase them as if they were mine."

I longed not to be a party to Chade's haggling with the Queen, but there was no way to avoid it. I witnessed, more clearly than I wished, the subtle way in which they wrestled for the power of the Farseer throne. Age and experience of the Six Duchies were on Chade's side. I winced as several times he insisted that it was her Mountain upbringing that blinded Kettricken to the political necessity of showing the Out Islands a strong will. I had known that Chade had amassed power to himself. I do not think he meant any ill; I believe that he genuinely felt that he fought for the best interests of the Six Duchies. Had I manipulated the power of the throne for that long, doubtless I too would have felt a proprietary right to it. At the same time, I saw too clearly that if Kettricken did not stand firm, Dutiful could inherit a hollow crown.

And so, against my will, I began to make suggestions to Kettricken that would outflank Chade and to throw my strength toward her side. It was not long before Chade was aware of it, I am sure. And yet the wily old badger only seemed to relish the game more as he heaped objections and possibilities ever higher. Night deepened and then ventured toward dawn. The old man seemed tireless in his arguments, but I was not, and I watched my queen's pallor grow.

Finally, during a pause in a very convoluted argument in which Chade had been sorting dukes and Outislander kaempras into sets and predicting where each group would side, my weariness got the better of me.

"Just tell him no," I suggested. "Tell him the Prince has given his word to his fiancée, and it will not be abrogated by you or by Chade. Tell him that if it is an error, it is the Prince's error, and learning the consequences of errors is one of the best tutors that any young ruler can have."

My throat was hoarse and my mouth dry with talking. My head seemed too big and heavy for my neck and my eyeballs to have been rolled in sand. I reached for the wine bottle to pour us each a little more, but as I extended my hand, Kettricken seized it in both of her own. I lifted my eyes to hers, startled. Her blue gaze burned as I had never seen it blaze before; it made her eyes seem dark and a little wild.

"You tell him, Sacrifice. Do not say it comes from me. I wish you to tell him it is your decision. That as the rightful if uncrowned King, this is what you decree."

I blinked and stared. "I . . . cannot."

"Why not?"

The answer did not make me feel brave. "If once I take that stance, I cannot step aside from it. If once I declare myself so to Chade, then I must ever guard that right, the right of final say, from him."

"Until Dutiful puts on his full crown. Yes."

"My life would never be my own again."

"This is the life that has always waited for you. This is your life, your own life, which you have never taken up. Take it up now."

"Have you discussed this with Dutiful?"

"He knows that I regard you as Sacrifice. When I told him that, he did not dispute it."

"My queen, I . . ." I pressed the heels of my hands to my throbbing temples. I wanted to say I had never even considered such a role. But I had. I had come two breaths from it on the night King Shrewd died. I had been ready to step up and seize the power of the throne. Not for myself, but to guard it for the Queen until Verity returned. I teetered on accepting the shadow crown she offered. Was it truly hers to give?

Chade pushed into my thoughts. *It is late and I am an old man. Enough of this. Tell her—*

No. It was not hers to give. It was mine to take. *No, Chade. Our prince has given his word, and it will not be abrogated by any of us. If it is an error, it is the Prince's error, and learning the consequences of errors is one of the best tutors that any young ruler can have.*

Those are not the Queen's words.

No. They are mine.

A long absence of thought followed my words. I could feel Chade there, I could almost sense his steady breathing as he stacked up my words and considered them from every angle. When next he touched minds with me, I could feel his smile, and strangely, the welling of his pride. *Well. After fifteen years, do we finally have a true Farseer on the throne again?*

I held my stillness. Waiting. Waiting for mockery or challenge or defiance.

I shall tell the Prince that his decision has been confirmed. And extend our gracious invitation to all the Outislander kaempras. As you will, King Fitz.

chapter XXXIV

COMMITMENTS

Our loss is great, and all for the foolishness of a wager between novices no wiser than children. By order of Skillmaster Treeknee all markings will be removed from the Witness Stones. By order of Master Treeknee, it is forbidden for any Skill candidates or novices to go to the Witness Stones unless the Skillmaster accompanies them. By order of Skillmaster Treeknee, all knowledge of the use of the Witness Stones is hereafter restricted to those who are candidates for Master status.

               — RECOVERED SKILL SCROLL

When I climbed the hidden stairs back up to Chade's tower room that dawn, I was beyond weariness. I could not seem to find a coherent thought of my own. Chade and Prince Dutiful would be on their way home by this afternoon. The invitation to the Harvest Fest would have been passed to every kaempra of every clan. Kettricken would have to set in motion the preparations for the grandest celebration that had ever been held in Buckkeep Castle. The invitations to the dukes and their nobles, the food, the guest housing, the minstrels and jugglers and puppeteers to be hired: it made my head spin and I longed to lie down and sleep. Instead, once in my room, I added a few sticks of dry wood to the failing embers in the hearth. I filled a ewer with water from the barrel, and then poured it into the old washbasin and plunged my face into it. I came up, rubbed at my eyes until they felt less sandy, and then wiped my face dry. I looked into the small glass Chade had always kept there and wondered who it was looking back at me.

I suddenly understood what the Fool had said to me earlier. I had journeyed to a place and time I had never foreseen, one past my death. Futures I had never imagined loomed before me, and I had no idea which one I should aspire to. I had taken a step toward claiming a throne, in essence if not in view. I wondered if that meant that I had pushed any life with Molly out of the possible futures I might claim.

Chivalry's sword rested where I had left it, above the hearth. I took it down. It fitted my hand as if made for it. I flourished it aloft, and then asked the empty chamber, "And what would you think of your bastard now, King Chivalry? But, I forget. You never wore the crown, either. No one ever called you King Chivalry." I lowered the point of the sword to the floor, conceding to fate. "Nor will anyone ever bow the knee to me. All the same, I think I will leave some sign of my passage."

A strange trembling passed through me, leaving calm in its wake. Hastily, I restored the sword to its place and then wiped my sweaty palms down my shirtfront. A fine king, I thought, wiping sweat down his guard's uniform. I needed some sleep, but not yet. King Fitz, the bastard monarch. I made a decision and refused to think any more on it. I added a bottle of good brandy to my basket, covered it with a napkin, took up a heavy cloak and fled.

I left the secret corridors behind me and departed by the guards' entrance. I had to pass the kitchens and almost I stopped to eat. Instead, I helped myself to a little loaf of sweet morning bread from the guards' mess and ate it as I walked. I passed out of the gate with no more than a sleepy nod from the lad on watch there. I thought how I might change that and then pushed the thought aside. I strode on. I diverted from the main road down to Buckkeep Town onto the trodden trail that went first through the woods and then across the gentle roll of a hill. In the early light of day, the Witness Stones stood stark against the blue sky, awaiting me. Sheep cropped the grass around them. As I approached, they regarded me with that lack of curiosity that is sometimes confused with stupidity. They moved away slowly.

I reached the Witness Stones and walked a slow circle around them. Four stones. Four sides to each stone. Sixteen possible destinations. How often had they been used over the years? I stood on the hilltop and looked out around me. Grass and trees and there, if one looked for it, the indentation of an ancient road. If there had ever been the rubble of houses here, it had long ago been swallowed by the earth, or more likely carted off to rise again as a hut elsewhere.

Hands behind my back, I studied the stone faces. I decided the runes had been deliberately effaced, long ago. I wondered why and suspected I would never know. And that was almost a comfort.

The basket on my arm was growing heavy and the sun was warming me too well. I slung the heavy cloak around my shoulders. It would be cold where I was going. I stepped up to the face of the pillar I had emerged from on my last journey, set my hand to it, and passed through it.

I stumbled a bit as I emerged into the pillar room. Then dizziness took me and I sat down flat on the dusty tiles until it passed. "Not enough sleep, and using the stones twice in too short a period of time. Not good," I told myself firmly. "Not wise." I tried to stand up, and then decided to sit down again until the tower stopped spinning. It took several moments of sitting there before I realized something obvious. The floor was no longer cold. I put both hands flat against it, as if to prove it to myself. It was not exactly warm; it was more neutral, neither warm nor cold. I stood, and noticed that the windows were losing their haze of thick frost. I thought I heard whispering behind me and turned quickly. No one was there. Perhaps it was an errant summer wind, a warm wind from the south sweeping the island. Very peculiar. I had no time to dwell on it.

I left the pillar room and, basket on my arm, tried to hasten through the icy labyrinth. My head pounded. I had not imagined the change in temperature. In one corridor, water slipped over the stones of the floor in a shallow running flow. The gentle warming of the chambers and halls lessened and then ceased as I approached the juncture where stone walls met ice. Little black spots danced before my eyes. I stopped and leaned my brow against the icy wall and rested. The spots receded and slowly I felt more myself. The coolness seemed to help. By the time I emerged from the crack in the ice wall onto the narrow path down to the Black Man's cavern, I had my cloak wrapped well about my basket and me.

I made my way down the steep path and knocked again at the Black Man's door. No one answered. I knocked again, hesitated for a time, and then tried the string latch. The door swung open and I entered.

It took a moment for my eyes to adjust to the dim room. The fire had burned low. The Fool was sleeping heavily on a pallet made up near the hearth. There was no sign of Prilkop. I shut the door quietly, put my basket on Prilkop's low table, and took off my cloak. Silently I moved to the Fool's side and, crouching down, peered into his sleeping face. The darkening of his skin was already apparent. I wanted to wake him and ask him how he was. Sternly I resisted that impulse. Instead, I unloaded the basket, finding a wooden platter for the bread and cheese and a basket for the fruit. Prilkop's water barrel was nearly empty. I put water on to heat for tea, and then took his buckets out and down to the place where the trickle down the rock face came to a slight overhang and fell free. I waited while they filled, and then hauled them up again. By that time, the water was hot, and I made fragrant spice tea.

I think the aroma of the tea was what woke the Fool. He opened his eyes and lay still, staring at the awakened fire for a time. He did not move until I said, "Fool? Are you any better?"

Then he gave a small start and turned his head sharply toward me as he jerked his body into a protective ball. I was sorry to have frightened him, and well understood that reflex. I made no comment on it, saying only, "I've come back, and brought food with me. Are you hungry?"

He pushed his blankets back a little and half sat up, and then sagged back down into his bedding. "I'm getting better. The tea smells good."

"No apricots, but I brought you plums."

"Apricots?"

"I thought your mind was wandering a bit when you asked me to fetch you apricots. The fever, you know. Still, if there had been any to hand, I'd have filched some for you."

"Thank you," he said. Then, staring at me, "You look different. More than just being clean."

"I feel different. But the clean helps, too. I wish I could have brought the Buckkeep steams with me for you. I think they'd do you good. But as soon as you can walk at all, I'll get you home. I've told Kettricken that we'll be putting you up in Chade's old tower room for a time, until you've completely recovered and decided who you'd like to become next."

"Who I'd like to become..." He made a small sound of amusement. I could not find the right sort of knife for cutting the bread, so contented myself with tearing off the end of the loaf for him. I took him bread and cheese and a plum, and when the tea had finished steeping, poured him a cup. "Where's Prilkop?" I asked as he sipped at his tea. I was a bit annoyed that he had left the Fool here alone.

"Oh, out and about. He has been investigating the Elderling stronghold, to see what damage has been done to it. We've had more time for talk while you were gone, in the moments when I was awake. There were not many, I think. He told me tales of the old city; they seem interwoven with my dreams. I suspect that is where he is now. He spoke of seeing what damage she had done, and what he could put right. I suspect he did things to make the city less hospitable, in hopes of driving her out. Now he plans to undo them. I asked him, 'For whom?' and he said, 'Perhaps just for the sake of putting it right.' He lived there alone for many years after all the others died. For generations, perhaps. He did not tally the passing years, but I am convinced he has been here a very long time. He welcomed the Pale Woman when she first arrived for he thought she had come with her Catalyst to fulfill Prilkop's goals."

He drew breath and sipped at the tea. "Eat first and then tell stories," I suggested to him.

"Tell me yours while I eat. Something momentous has happened to you. It's in your bearing and eyes."

And so I spoke to him, as I could have to no other, divulging all that had befallen me. He smiled but it seemed weighted with sadness, and nodded to himself as if I were but confirming things that he already knew. When I had finished, he tossed his plum pit into the fire and said quietly, "Well. It is nice to know that my last vision and prophecy was a true one."

"So. I'll live happily ever after, as the minstrels sing?"

He twisted his mouth at me and shook his head. "You'll live among people who love you and have expectations of you. That will make your life horribly complicated and they will worry you sick half the time. And the other half, annoy you. And delight you." He turned away from me and took up his cup and looked into it, like a hedge-witch reading tea leaves. "Fate has given up on you, FitzChivalry Farseer. You've won. In the future that you now have found, it's almost likely that you'll live to a ripe old age, rather than that fate will try to sweep you from the playing board at every opportunity."

I tried to lighten his words. "I was getting a bit tired of being hauled back from death's door and beyond every time I turned around."

"It's nasty. I know how nasty now. You've shown me that." He almost had his old smile as he asked me, "Let's leave it at this and call it even, shall we? One time pays for all?"

I nodded to that. Then, as if he had to say it swiftly before I interrupted, "Prilkop and I have been talking about what should happen next."

I smiled. "A new plan to save the world? One that doesn't involve me dying quite so often?"

"One that doesn't involve you at all," he said quietly. "You could say that we are going home, after a fashion. Back to the place that shaped us."

"You said no one there would remember you; that there was little point to going back there." I was starting to feel alarm.

"Not to the home that birthed me; I am sure I am no longer recalled there. But to the place that prepared both of us to face our destinies. It was a sort of school, you might say. I know I've spoken of it to you, and told you too that I ran away from it when they refused to recognize the truth of what I told them. There, I will be well remembered, and Prilkop also. Every White Prophet who has ever passed through there is well remembered."

"So let them remember you there. It seems to me they did not treat you well. Why go back?"

"To see that it never happens to any child again. To do what has never been done before, to return, and interpret for them the old prophecies in light of what we now know. To expunge from their libraries all that the Pale Woman planted there, or at least to cast it in a different light. To bring back our experiences of the world to them."

I was silent for a long time. "How will you get there?"

"Prilkop says he can use the pillars. Together, we could travel quite a way south before we needed to find another way to travel. We'll get there. Eventually."

"He can use the pillars?" I was stunned. "Why did he remain here, in cold and privation, all those years?"

The Fool looked at me as if it were obvious. "I think he can use them, but he dreads them. Even in our language, there are Elderling concepts he has difficulty in explaining to me. The magic that makes the pillars work takes something from you, each time you use it. Not even the Elderlings used them casually. A courier of an important item might use one or even two pillars to travel, but then the task was passed on to another. But that is not the whole of why he stayed. He stayed to protect the dragon. And to await the coming of the White Prophet and the Catalyst, the ones he had seen who could, perhaps, finish his task. That was, after all, the focus of his life."

"I cannot imagine such devotion."

"Cannot you? I think I can."

I heard the scrape of the door and Prilkop entered. He looked startled to see me there, as well he might, but then exclaimed something to the Fool. The Fool translated. "He is amazed to see you return here so soon, and asks what pressing business had led you to brave the pillars again."

I made a dismissive gesture and spoke to Prilkop. "I wished to bring food for you; see, here is bread and cheese, as you wished, and wine and plums. I had hoped to find you both ready to travel to my home with me. But the Fool still seems weak."

"Travel to your home with you?" he asked me, and I nodded, smiling.

He turned to the Fool and spoke softly to him at length in their tongue. The Fool replied more briefly. Then he turned and spoke reluctantly to me. "Fitz. My friend. Please. Come and sit with me by the fire. I need to talk to you."

He got up stiffly, draped a blanket loosely around his

shoulders, and moved slowly to a grass cushion by the hearth. He eased himself down onto it and I took one beside him. Prilkop was investigating the food. He broke off a piece of cheese, put it into his mouth and then closed his eyes in sheer pleasure. When he opened them again, he bowed his head in thanks to me. I nodded back, pleased to have pleased him. When I turned back to the Fool, he took a deep breath and spoke.

"Prilkop does not intend to go back to Buckkeep with you. And neither do I."

I stared at him, running his words through my mind over and over. They made no sense. "But why? His task here is finished, as is yours. Why remain in such a harsh place? It's cold, and this is summer! Life is hard here, and barren. When winter comes . . . I cannot even imagine wintering here. There is no reason for you to stay here, none at all, and every reason in the world for you to come back to Buckkeep. Why would you want to stay here? I know you wish to return to your 'school' but surely you could come to Buckkeep first. Rest and recover for a time, and then take ship from there."

He looked down at his long hands held loosely in his lap. "I have discussed this at length with Prilkop. There is so much that neither of us knows about this situation, this living beyond our time as White Prophets. He has experienced it longer than I have. He stayed here because it was the last place he had a vision of himself. He stayed in the hopes that his final view of another Prophet and Catalyst coming to finish his task was true. And it was. His last vision was true." He looked into the fire and then leaned over to push the end of a piece of driftwood deeper into it. "I had a final vision, too. Of what would be after my death."

I waited.

"I saw you, Fitz. I saw you in the midst of what you are currently becoming. It did not seem to me that you were always happy, but I thought you were more complete than before."

"What has that got to do with it?"

"It has to do with what I did not see. I was, of course, to be dead. I had seen clearly that my death was a part of your future. No, that sounds cruel, as if my death were a thing you had planned. Rather, say, that my death was a landmark on the journey to where you had gone. You had passed my death and gone on to that life."

"I did pass your death. But, as you have told me so often, I am a Catalyst. I brought you back."

"Yes. You did. I had never foreseen such a thing. Neither had Prilkop. And in all the records we studied and memorized when we were in training, there is nothing that either of us can recall that foreshadows such a thing." He almost smiled. "I should have known that only you could work such a change, a change that may have carried us outside of any future that any White Prophet has ever foreseen."

"But—" I began, and he lifted that long cautioning forefinger to halt me.

"Prilkop and I have discussed this. Neither of us thinks I should risk being around you too much. I could make a serious mistake. There is far less chance of my making a mistake if I do not go back with you."

"I don't understand. A mistake? What mistake? You're feverish still, and not making sense." I was worried and irritated at the same time. I shifted angrily and he reached out a hand and set it on my arm. His touch was almost cool. He was still weak from his changing time but he did not speak from fever. His voice was almost stern, as if he were an old man and I were a willful youngster.

"Yes you do. You understand. You don't want to look at it, but you know it. You are still the Changer, still the Catalyst. Even in the short time you were at Buckkeep, you've proved that. Change is swirling around you like a whirlpool. Restored, you no longer flee it, but seem to attract it. And I, I am blind now, when it comes to seeing what vast changes my influence upon you can cause. So." He was silent for a time. I waited him out. "I will not be coming with you. No, wait, don't speak. Let me talk for a time."

But instead of speaking, he immediately fell silent. I sat and looked at him and thought how he had changed. The pale moon-faced boy, the lithe and narrow youth, was now visibly a young man. Recent privation had sharpened the angles of his face and the bruises around his eyes from his torment were still fading. But that was only his body. His glance had darkened and his solemnity did not seem a temporary mood but a new gravity of spirit. I let him take his time as he mentally sorted his words. I suspected he was working on a decision, and that however resolute he might claim to be, his heart still teetered on a choice.

"Fitz, I faced my death, not bravely perhaps, but determinedly. Because I had seen what might come after it, and judged it worth the cost. I decided to come to this island, and set in motion the events that would end with the dragon rising. I knew I would die, horribly, in pain and cold. But I also saw the chance for the world to know dragons again, a chance for there to be creatures as arrogant and lovely as humans, so that they might balance one another. I dreamed of a world in which men could not dominate all nature and impose their order upon it. It will not be a peaceful world, and it may be that men will curse me for my role in what happened here. But it will be a world in which both men and dragons are so busy with one another that they cannot subvert all nature to themselves. That was what I saw, in the greater scheme of things."

"Fine!" I was weary of his talk of dragons, and uneasy still about what we had loosed on the world. "So now there will be dragons. Lots of them, from what I saw happening over the battlefield. But why can't you come back to—"

"Hush!" he rebuked me sternly. "Do you think this is easy for me? Do you think that lofty reason is my only one?

Do you think it is easy for me to part my ways from yours? No. There is a more personal element that divides my path from yours. It is because of what I glimpsed on a far smaller scale. I saw you, after my death, taking satisfaction in the things and people you had so long denied yourself. Living the life you were meant to have, after my death. You gave me another piece of life. Shall I use it to rob you of yours?" More slowly he added, "I can love you, Fitz, but I cannot allow that love to destroy you and what you are." He rubbed at his face wearily, and then exclaimed in annoyance at the skin that peeled away beneath his fingers. He shook the bits from his fingertips, rubbed his face all over vigorously, and then folded his hands into his lap and looked into the fire. I glowered at him, baffled and waiting.

Behind us, Prilkop moved quietly around the room. I heard a clicking sound and glanced behind me. He had opened the neck of a little sack and was taking small blocks of stone out of it. I recognized it at once. Memory stone, cut into uniform cubes like the ones I had glimpsed in the Elderling chamber. I watched as he held one briefly against his temple, then smiled, and set it aside. He repeated the process, and again. It was soon apparent to me he was sorting the blocks into different stacks. He looked up, realizing the Fool and I were watching him. He smiled and held up a cube of stone. "Music." Another cube. "Some poetry." Another cube. "History. Music, again." He proffered one to me, but I waved it aside, uneasy. The Fool, however, reached out to touch it lightly with one Skilled fingertip. He recoiled from it as quickly as if he had been burned, but then smiled at me. "Music, indeed. Like a rushing flood of it. You should try it, Fitz."

"We were talking," I reminded him quietly. "About your coming back to Buckkeep with me."

"No. We were talking about my not coming back." He tried a smile that failed.

I just looked at him. A short time later he said

something, a request, to Prilkop. At almost the same moment, I felt Chade tug at my thoughts. *I would speak to the Queen.*

I can't right now. Try Thick.

You know all the reasons why that will not work. Please, Fitz. It will not take long.

That is what you said last time. Besides, I am nowhere near the Queen. I went through the pillar. I'm with the Fool.

What? Without warning any of us or consulting with us at all?

I believe my life is still my own.

No. It was a flat denial from Chade. *No, it is not, sir. Last night, you drew a line with me, and I sensed you did it with the Queen's approval. You cannot claim that authority one moment, and then shoulder aside from it the next. Crowns cannot be doffed so lightly.*

I am not truly the King and you know it.

Too late to take that stance, Fitz! Chade sounded angry. *Too late. The Queen offered you the authority and you accepted it.*

I did not capitulate. I could not decide if I agreed with him or not. *Give me some time. By now, you must be at sea. What can be of such immediate importance now that you have sailed?*

It will keep for a time, that is true. But after this, Fitz, you must not absent yourself without warning all of us.

Am I a servant, that my time is never my own?

Worse. You are a king. And Sacrifice to all.

He broke his mind free of mine before I could reply to that. I blinked and realized that I had just heard the door close. Prilkop had left. The Fool was looking at me, somehow aware I had been Skilling and waiting for my attention to come back to him. "I am sorry. Chade, in a rush as always, demanding that he needed contact with the Queen. He claims that if she has recognized me once, even for a moment, as Sacrifice, I now have all the duties and responsibilities of a crowned king. It's ridiculous."

"Is it?"

"You know it is!"

My defense seemed to release a torrent of words from him, as if while he waited the words had mounted up inside him like water behind a dam.

"Fitz. Go back to the life you were meant to have, and love it, without reserve. That was what I saw you doing." He gave a laugh that had hysteria at the edge of it. "It even sustained me while I was dying. To know that you would go on to that life, after I was dead. When the pain was worst, I fixed my thoughts on what I had seen for you, and I let it move through me."

"But . . . she said you called out for me. When she tormented you." I said the words, and then wished I could call them back. He suddenly looked sick and old.

"Probably, I did," he admitted. "I have never claimed to be brave. But the fact that she could wring that from me changes nothing, my friend. Nothing." He looked into the fire as if he had lost something there, and I was ashamed that I had taken him back to his torture. No man should be reminded that he has screamed in front of people who delighted in it. "It should probably serve to teach me that, in many ways, I am not as strong as I wish I were. And I should not put myself in a position in which my weakness could damage both of us."

He suddenly took my hand. It startled me, and when I looked at him, our eyes locked. "Fitz. Please. Do not tempt me to follow you and interfere in the future I saw for you. Do not tempt me to step out of my time and try to take something that was never meant for me." He shivered suddenly, as if a chill had taken him. He let go of my hand and leaned closer to the fire, holding his hands out to it. The nails had just started to regrow. He rubbed his hands together, loosening a layer of skin like white ash. The new skin exposed beneath reminded me of polished wood. Very softly, he asked me, "Could you have been content to live with Nighteyes among the wolves?"

"I would have been willing to try," I said stubbornly.

"Even if his mate could never completely accept you?"

"Could you, for once, simply say whatever it is you are trying to say?"

He looked at me and rubbed his chin as if he were truly considering it. Then he smiled sadly. "No. I can't. Not without damaging something precious to me." As if he were not changing the subject at all, he asked, "Will you ever tell Dutiful that your body fathered his?"

I did not like him to speak that aloud even when it was just we two. My strong Skill-bond with Dutiful made him seem ever close. "No," I said shortly. "He would see too many things differently. It would hurt him, to no good end. It would damage his image of his father, his feelings toward his mother, even his feelings toward me. What purpose could it serve?"

"Exactly. So you will always love him as a son, but treat him as your prince. One step away from where you long to be. Because even if you told him, you could never be his father."

I was starting to get angry again. "You are not my father."

"No." He stared at the fire. "And I'm not your lover, either."

I felt suddenly weary and sour. "Is that what this is about? Bedding with me? You won't return to Buckkeep because I won't bed with you?"

"No!" He did not shout the word, but something in the way he said it stunned me to silence. His voice was low, almost harsh as he spoke. "Always, you bring it back to that, as if that is the only possible culmination of love."

He sighed and abruptly settled back in his chair. He looked at me speculatively, and then asked, "Tell me, did you love Nighteyes?"

"Of course."

"Without reserve."

"Yes."

"Then by your logic, you wished to couple with him?"

"I wished . . . No!"

"Ah. But that was only because he too was male? It had nothing to do with your other differences?"

I gaped at him. A moment longer he managed to keep his face straight in honest inquiry. Then he laughed at me, more freely than I had heard him laugh in a long time. I wanted to be offended, but it was such a relief to hear him laugh, even at my expense, that I could not.

He caught his breath, and said, "There it is. Plainly, Fitz. I told you I set no limits on my love for you. I don't. Yet I never expected you to offer me your body. It was the whole of your heart, all for myself, that I sought. Even though I've never had a right to it. For you gave it away ere ever you saw me." He shook his head. "Long ago, you told me that Molly would never be able to tolerate your bond with the wolf. That she would force you to decide between them. Do you still believe that?"

"I think it likely," I had to reply softly.

"And how do you think she would react to me?" He paused for a heartbeat. "Whom would you choose? And what would you lose, either way, by being forced to make such a choice? Those are the questions I've had to ponder. And if I come back with you, and make that choice a part of your future, what else will my Catalyst change in the process of choosing? If you left the Six Duchies with me, what future would we have set in motion, all unknowing?"

I shook my head and looked away from him. But the flow of his words was relentless and my ears heard them.

"Nighteyes chose. He chose between the pack of wolves that would have accepted him and his bond with you. I do not know if you ever discussed with him what that decision cost him. I doubt it. The little I knew of him makes me think he chose and went forward from there. I do not mean to shame you. But is it not true that Nighteyes paid a higher toll for your bond, for the love that you shared, than you did? What did it cost Nighteyes to be bonded to you? Answer honestly."

I had to look aside, for I *was* ashamed. "It cost him living with a pack, and being a wolf in full. It cost him having a mate and cubs. Just as Rolf later warned us. Because we set no limits on our bond."

"You knew the exhilaration of sharing his wolfness with him. Of being as close to becoming a wolf as a man can. Yet . . . forgive me . . . I do not think he ever sought the human within himself as ardently as you pursued being a wolf."

"No."

He took my hand again and held it in both of his. He turned it over and looked down at the shadows of his fingerprints that I had worn on my wrist for so many years. "Fitz. I have thought long on this. I will not take your mate and cubs from you. My years will be long; by comparison, you have not that many left. I will not take from you and Molly whatever years may remain to you. For I am sure that you will be together, again. You know what I am. You have been within this body, and I in yours. And I have felt, oh, gods help me against that memory, I have felt what it is to be human, fully human, in the moments that I held your love and pain and loss within me. You have allowed me to be as human as it is possible for me to be. What my teachers took away from me, you restored tenfold. With you, I was a child. With you, I grew to manhood. With you . . . Just as Nighteyes allowed you to be the wolf." His voice ran down and we were left sitting in silence, as if he had run out of words. He did not release my hand. The touch sharpened my awareness of the Skill-bond between us. Dutiful nudged at my Skill, seeking my attention. I ignored him. This was more important. I tried to grasp exactly what the Fool feared.

"You think that it would hurt me if you came back to Buckkeep. That it would keep me from a life you had seen."

"Yes."

"You dread that I would grow old and die. And you would not."

"Yes."

"What if I didn't care about those things? About the cost."

"I still would."

I asked my last question, my heart squeezed with hurt, dreading however he might answer it. "And if I said I would follow you, then? Leave my other life behind and go with you."

I think that question stunned him. He drew breath twice before he answered it in a hoarse whisper. "I would not allow it. I could not allow it."

We sat a long time in silence after that. The fire consumed itself. And then I asked the final, awful question. "After I leave you here, will I ever see you again?"

"Probably not. It would not be wise." He lifted my hand and tenderly kissed the sword-callused palm of it, and then held it in both of his. It was farewell, and I knew it, and knew I could do nothing to stop it. I sat still, feeling as if I grew hollow and cold, as if Nighteyes were dying all over again. I was losing him. He was withdrawing from my life and I felt as though I were bleeding to death, my life trickling out of me. I suddenly realized how close to true that was.

"Stop!" I cried, but it was too late. He released my hand before I could snatch it back. My wrist was clean and bare. His fingerprints were gone. Somehow, he had taken them back, and our Skill-thread dangled, broken.

"I have to let you go," he said in a cracked whisper. "While I can. Leave me that, Fitz. That I broke the bond. That I did not take what was not mine."

I groped for him. I could see him, but I could not feel him. No Wit, no Skill, no scent. No Fool. The companion of my childhood, the friend of my youth, was gone. He had turned that facet of himself away from me. A brown-skinned man with hazel eyes looked at me sympathetically.

"You cannot do this to me," I said.

"It is done," he pointed out. "Done." His strength seemed to go out of him with the word. He turned his head away from me, as if by doing that, he could keep me from knowing that he wept. I sat, feeling numbed in the way that one does after a terrible injury.

"I am just tired," he said in a small, quavering voice. "Just tired, still. That is all. I think I will lie down again."

Fitz. The Queen wants you. Thick pushed effortlessly into my mind.

Shortly. I am with the Fool right now.

It's about Old Blood. Soon, please, she says.

Soon, I replied dully.

And no sooner was Thick cleared from my mind than Chade was tapping at my shoulder. I gave him my heed and, *As long as you are there, think to bring back at least some of the Skill scrolls you found there. We'll be in need of them, I think.*

Chade. I will. Please. A time to myself. Please.

Very well. His reply was surly. Then he softened, asking more gently, *What is the problem? Is he that ill?*

Actually, he seems improved. But I need a time for my own thoughts.

Very well.

I turned back to the Fool, but he had either sunk into a true sleep or was pretending one so convincingly that I could not find it in me to try to wake him. I needed a time to think. I thought there must be some way to get him to change his mind, if only I could think of it.

"I'll be back," I told him, and then slung my cloak over my shoulders and went out. I thought I might as well make a trip through the Elderling maze to retrieve some of the Skill scrolls. It would keep me busy while I thought. I have never done my best pondering while sitting still. I climbed the steep path and found I did not have to squeeze quite as much to get into the crack. My comings and goings were wearing it open, I thought to myself. Yet I had not gone far

under the false light of the Elderling globes before I saw
someone coming toward me. It startled me for the instant
before I recognized the Black Man. He had a haunch of
smoked meat on one shoulder, and as we drew near to one
another, he nodded to me and then slung it carefully to the
ground.

"Her supplies, I stole. Many times. Not like this. A little bit here, a little bit there. Now, what I want, I take." He
cocked his head at me. "And you?"

"Somewhat the same. Years ago, scrolls, special writings, were taken from my king. She has them, here, in a
room near her bedchamber. I am to bring them home
again."

"Ah, those. I saw them long ago."

"Yes."

"I will help."

I was not sure I wanted help, but there seemed no
courteous way to refuse him. I nodded my thanks, and we
walked companionably through the halls. He shook his
head at the desecration of the carvings and the missing art
from the empty niches. He spoke to me of the folk who had
lived here in the times he had known. Thick had been
right. Once, the stone hallways had been warmed. Elderlings had come and gone from this place, enjoying the
wonders of the ice and snow that never reached their
warmer lands. I tried to imagine taking pleasure in coming
to a cold place, but the idea was foreign to me.

Prilkop had somehow unharnessed the magic that
gave warmth to the stone. He had sought too to deprive
the Pale Woman of the Elderling light, but had failed at
that. Yet even without warmth, she had stayed. She had
driven Prilkop into hiding, and shown her disdain for him
and the dragon-partnered Elderlings by her encouragement
of the destruction of their art.

"Yet she left the map room alone," I pointed out
to him.

"She did not know of it, perhaps. Or, not knowing the

use, did not care. Of the travel portals, she knew nothing. Once, only once, to flee her I used one." He shook his head at the memory. "So weak, so sick, so—" He put his fists to his temples and made pounding motions. "I could not come back, for many days. When I did"—he shrugged—"she had made my city hers. But now I take it back."

He knew his city well. He took me by a different path, through narrower ways that had, perhaps, been for servants or tradesmen. In less time than I had thought possible, we turned down a hallway that led us past her bedchamber. I glanced in. Someone had been there since I last glimpsed it. I halted and stared. Every item in the room that could have been pushed over or dragged about had been. A cask of jewelry had spilled a stream of pearls and silver chains and glittering white stones across the floor. Some had settled in slow melt into the floor of the chamber. Prilkop saw me staring and calmly entered the room. "This will work," he told me, and pulled a silk coverlet from her bed. As I watched, he knotted the corners to form a very large carry sack. Catching the sense of what he did, I found another and copied him. Then, our makeshift sacks slung across our backs, we went on to the scroll room.

I was not prepared for the sight that met me there. The racks had been deliberately pushed toward the center of the room, so that as they fell, their shelved contents spilled in a messy pile. A broken pitcher lay near them and oil drenched a number of the scrolls. The Pale Woman lay on the floor near them. She was very dead. Her blackened stick arms reminded me of insect legs. Freezing and death had darkened her countenance. She had thrown back her head and died, mouth open like a snarling cat. An Elderling light globe, pried loose from its setting, lay near the oil-soaked manuscripts. It looked battered, as if it had been kicked and beaten. For a time, Prilkop and I stared in silence.

"She tried to make a fire to warm herself," I hazarded

my guess. "She thought something in the light globe might catch the scrolls on fire."

He shook his head in disgust. "No. To destroy. Her whole desire that was. Dragons to destroy. Other Prophets to destroy. Beauty. Knowledge." He nudged one of the oily scrolls that was close to her body. "What she could not control or possess, she destroys." He met my eyes and added, "She could not control your Fool."

He set to work alongside me. The unruined scrolls, we loaded into one sack, taking as much care as we could, for some were very old and fragile. Those that had taken the oil I placed separately from the others. I noticed that we both avoided the Pale Woman. When I had to move her body to get at the scrolls beneath her, Prilkop backed away and looked aside. When every single scroll had been rescued, I looked at her lying there. "Do you want me to do something with her body?" I asked him quietly.

He stared at me, as if uncomprehending. Then he slowly nodded.

So it was that I bundled her into one of the sumptuous fur spreads from her bed and dragged her down the hall behind me. He showed me a door, quite small, that I would not have noticed on my own. It opened onto a chute and the distant rush of waves. He had me push her into this. She vanished from sight, and that seemed to give Prilkop much satisfaction.

We returned to the scroll room for our trove. We walked through the halls, dragging the sacks more than carrying them. Scrolls are surprisingly heavy. I winced at every bump as we took them up the stairs, imagining how Chade would scold me for treating them like this. Well, he would not know what condition they were in when I first found them. With Prilkop's help, I got both sacks up to the pillar room. There we paused to catch our breath. For all his years, the old man seemed as spry as a youngster. For the first time, I pondered how old the Fool might live to be. Then, the even more strange thought came to me, to wonder where he was in his life. Was he still a youngster? Did that have any meaning to him? Once he had told me that he was older than Nighteyes and I put together... I pushed the thought aside uncomfortably. I did not want to consider how different we were, how different we had always been. Our friendship had crossed that line and made us one.

Just as my bond with Nighteyes had made us one. And yet. I sighed as I followed the Black Man down the steps to the map room. And yet it had not made us the same. I was a man, with a man's concerns with this world, unable to live fully in the now as Nighteyes did, or to stretch his years beyond their span.

Was that how the Fool saw me?

I made a small sound in my throat. Prilkop glanced back at me, but said nothing. When we reached the map room, he paused by the image. He rubbed his hands together as he considered it, then, with a raised eyebrow, he gestured at it.

I touched the grouped gems near Buckkeep. "Buckkeep," I told him. "My home."

He nodded sagely. Then, as the Fool had before, he touched a land far to the south. "Home," he said. Then he touched an inlet on the coast of that land and said, "Clerres."

"Your school," I guessed. "Where you wish to return."

He paused, head cocked, then nodded. "Yes. Our school." He gave me a sad look. "Where we must return. That what we have learned may be recorded. For others, yet to come. Very important this is."

"I understand."

The Black Man looked at me kindly. "No. You don't." He studied the map again, and then, as if speaking to himself, said, "The letting go is hard. Yet, this you must do. Both of you. Let go. If not, you will make more changes. Blindly. If, because of him, things you do make changes, what comes of them? No one can say. Even a little thing.

You bring to him bread. He eats. If you do not bring this bread, someone else eats it. See, a change. A little change. To him, you give your time, your talk, your friendship. Who then does not receive your time? Hm? A big change, maybe, I think. Let go, Fool's Changer. Your time together is over. Done."

It was none of his concern and I very nearly told him so. But he looked at me so kindly and sympathetically that my anger died almost as soon as I felt it.

"Let us go back," he suggested. I started to nod and then Thick broke into my thoughts.

Fitz? Have you finished yet? The Queen is still waiting.

I sighed wearily. I'd best go take care of it, and then beg some time for myself. *I've finished. I'll bring the Skill scrolls home with me this time. Meet me at the Witness Stones and help me carry them.*

No! I'm eating raspberry tart! With cream.

After the tart, then. I felt a sudden sympathy for Thick's unwillingness to interrupt his meal to rush and find me. Prilkop had reached the end of the steps. He glanced up at me quizzically. "I have to go back to my home for a time," I told him. "Please tell the Fool that I will come back as soon as I can. I'll bring more food then, fresh fruit and bread."

Prilkop looked alarmed. "Not through the portal stones? So soon? Not wise is that. Foolish, even." He made a beckoning gesture at me. "Come to Prilkop's home. A night, a day, a night, a day, and then go back through the stones. If you must."

"I fear I must go now." I did not want to see the Fool or talk to him again until I had found a way around all his arguments.

"Changer? You can do this? You have done this before?"

"Several times."

He came back up the steps toward me, his brow lined with anxiety. "Never have I seen this done so often, so close together. Be careful, then. Do not come back too soon. Rest."

"I've done this before," I insisted. I recalled how I had been in and out of the Skill-stones with Dutiful on that long-ago day we fled the Others beach. "Do not fear for me."

Despite my brave words, I wondered if I were being foolish in going through the Skill-stones once again. Whenever I look back on that moment, I wonder whatever possessed me. Was it the press of hurt that the Fool had taken our link away? I truly think not. I think it was more likely too little sleep for too many days.

I climbed back up the steps to the Skill-pillar. The Black Man followed me anxiously. "Sure you are? Sure of this?"

I stooped and took up the necks of both bags. "I'll be fine," I assured him. "Tell the Fool I will be back." I gripped the necks of both bags in one hand. I opened my other palm wide and pushed into the pillar. I stepped into a starry night.

chapter XXXV

RESUMPTION

In that last dance of chances
I shall partner you no more.
I shall watch another turn you
As you move across the floor.

In that last dance of chances
When I bid your life good-bye
I will hope she treats you kindly.
I will hope you learn to fly.

In that last dance of chances
When I know you'll not be mine
I will let you go with longing
And the hope that you'll be fine.

In that last dance of chances
We shall know each other's minds.
We shall part with our regrets
When the tie no longer binds.

Fate took a final swipe at me. That is how I have come to think of it. Perhaps the gods wanted to reinforce Prilkop's warning to me.

I felt a very mild surprise. I saw eternal blackness and a scattering of lights of various brightnesses. It was like lying on my back on a tower top and staring up into a summer night. Not that I thought of it that way at the time. At the time, I drifted through stars. But I did not fall. I did not think, I did not wonder. I was simply there. A brighter star there was, and I was drawn to it. I could not tell if I got closer to it, or if it approached me. I could not have told anything, for while I was aware of these things, they did not seem to have any significance. I felt a suspension of life, of interest, a suspension of all feelings. When finally the star was close, I attempted to fasten myself to it. This act did not seem to involve any will or intention on my part. Rather, it was like a smaller drop of water starting to blend with another one close by. But she plucked me free of herself, and in that moment of her considering me, I once more came to awareness of self.

What? You again? Are you really so intent on remaining here? You are far too small, you know. Unfinished. There is not enough of you to exist by yourself here. Do you know that?

Know that? Like a child learning language, I echoed her final words, trying to pin meaning to them. Her kindness to me fascinated me, and I did long to immerse myself in her. To me, she seemed made of love and acceptance. I could let go of my boundaries, if she would allow me, and simply mingle what I had been with what she was. I would know no more, think no more, and fear no more.

Without my speaking, she seemed to know my mind. *And that is what you would truly wish, little one? To stop being yourself, before you have even completed yourself? There is so much more you could grow to be.*

To be, I echoed, and suddenly the simple words took force and I existed again. I knew a moment of full realization, as if I had surfaced from a very deep dive and taken a full deep breath of air. Molly and Nettle, Dutiful and Hap, Patience and Thick, Chade and Kettricken, all of them came back to me in a wave of possibilities. Fear mingled wildly with hope as to what I could become through them.

Ah. I thought perhaps there was something more for you. Then you wish to go back?

Go back.

Where?

Buckkeep. Molly. Nettle. Friends.

I do not think the words had meaning for her. She was beyond all that, beyond the sorting of love into little individual persons or places. But I think my longing was what she could read.

Very well, then. Back you go. Next time, be more careful. Better yet, do not let there be a next time. Not until you are ready to stay.

Very abruptly, I had a body. It sprawled facedown in grass on a chill hillside. Somehow, I still gripped the two bags I had slung over my shoulder. They were on top of me. I closed my eyes. The grass was tickling my face and dust was in my nose. I breathed in the intricacy of earth and grass, sheep and manure, and my amazement at their network stole all my thoughts. I think I slept.

It was dawn when next I came awake. I was shaking with cold, despite the blanketed scrolls on top of me. I was stiff and my skin was wet with dew. I sat up with a groan, and the world spun lazily around me until I lay back down again. The sheep that lifted their heads in surprise to see me stir were fat with wool. I got to my hands and knees and then tottered upright, staring around me like a new foal as I tried to make the ends of my life meet. I took deep slow breaths, but felt little better. I decided that food and a real bed would put me right, and that I'd find that at Buckkeep Castle.

I shouldered one sack and dragged the other. At least, such was my intention. I went three steps and down I went. I felt, if anything, worse than when I had first emerged from the stones. Prilkop was right, I decided grudgingly, and wondered uneasily how long it would be before I dared make a return trip through the portals. But I had more immediate problems to solve.

I groped out with the Skill. I could barely focus enough to wield it, and when I found Thick's music and then Thick, he was already in contact with Dutiful and Chade. I tried to break in and could not. Their thoughts rattled against mine. They did not seem to be passing information, but attempting some Skill-exercise. I became aware of Nettle, floating like a faint perfume. She caught at their circle, almost held, then wafted away again. In the disappointed silence that followed her failed attempt, I found a place for my faint Skilling.

Thick. I'm not well. Can you come to meet me at the Witness Stones? Bring a pony, or even a donkey and cart. I'm not sure I could sit up to ride. I have two large sacks of scrolls.

I felt a wordless blast of amazement from all of them. And then, a pelting of questions: *Where are you?*

Where have you been?

Are you hurt? Were you attacked by something?

Held prisoner?

I just came through the stones. I'm weak. Sick. Prilkop said, don't use the stones too often. And then I let it go, feeling wretchedly nauseous and dizzy. I lay down on my side in the grass. The morning was cold, and I pulled one of the blanket sacks half over me and lay still, shivering.

They all came. I heard sounds and opened my eyes and found myself looking at Nettle's shoes and riding skirt. A healer annoyed me by feeling me all over for broken bones and peering into my eyes. He asked if I had been attacked. I managed to shake my head. Chade said, "Ask him where he has been for the last month. We have been expecting these scrolls since before we arrived back at Buckkeep." I closed my eyes and held my tongue. Then the healer and his helper lifted me into the back of a cart. The bundles of scrolls were placed beside me. The cart lurched off down the tussocky hillside. Chade and Dutiful rode on one side of it, looking grave. Thick came behind on a stocky pony, managing it well enough. Nettle rode a mare, obviously one of Burrich's breeding. Several mounted guards followed, with the edgy look of men who had expected to confront at least a minor enemy and still had dwindling hopes of a skirmish. I had said little, fearing to say too much before ears that should not hear it.

My mind churned like a team stuck in mud. It dragged out the old legends of standing stones. Lovers fled angry parents into them, and returned a year or a decade later, to find all grievances forgotten. They were the gates to the land of the Pecksies, where a year might pass as a day. Or a day as a year. I recalled, hazily, my time in the starry blackness. How much time had passed? A few weeks? Chade had mentioned a month. Obviously enough time had passed that they had returned to Buckkeep from Mayle. For here they were. I smiled faintly at that "swift" leap of logic.

When we reached Buckkeep, Chade led off the guards with the trove of scrolls. The Prince took my hand and thanked me for a job well done, as if I were any guardsman who had completed a difficult task at risk to himself. Hand to hand, he pushed his Skilling into my mind. I could barely hear him. *Come to see you soon. Rest now.*

Nettle and Thick followed him as he strode away and I was assisted into the infirmary, where I was very content to lie still and think of nothing. I believe that several days passed. It was hard to keep track of things like time. The headaches and dizziness passed, but the vagueness lingered. I had been somewhere and experienced something vast and I knew that, but could not find any words for it, even to explain it to myself. It was so large and foreign an event that it challenged all the meaning and order that I gave to the rest of my life. Small things stole my attention: the dance of motes in a beam of sunlight, the twisted wool woven to form my blanket, the grain of the wood in the frame of my bed. It wasn't that I could not Skill; it was more that

I could not see the point of it, nor gather the energy and focus to do it.

They fed me well and let me rest. Visitors came and
went and left almost no impression on me. Once I opened
my eyes to see Lacey looking down on me with stern disapproval. I closed them. The healer could do nothing for me
and often loudly observed in my vicinity that he thought I
was a lazy malingerer. They brought an old, old woman to
see me. After our eyes met, she nodded vigorously and said,
"Oh, yes, he has that Pecksie-nibbled look to him. The
Pecksies took him underground and fed on him. It's known
they have a hole up there, near the Witness Stones. They'll
take a new lamb or a child, or even a strong man if he's in
his cups when he wanders about up there." She nodded
sagely and advised, "Give him mint tea and cook his meat
with garlic until he reeks of it. They can't abide that, and
they'll soon enough let him go. When his nails have grown
long enough to be cut, and he cuts them, that'll set him
free."

And so they fed me a meal of garlicky mutton with
mint tea, and then pronounced me cured and turned me
out of the infirmary. Riddle was waiting for me. He told me
that I looked like a mooncalf. He took me to the steams,
crowded with noisy guardsmen laughing far too loudly, and
then in the guardsmen's act of ultimate purification, took
me to the complete chaos of the guards' tables and effortlessly persuaded me to drink ale with him until I had to
stagger outside and vomit. The level of shouted conversation and laughter made me feel oddly alone. One young
guardsman asked me six times where I had been, and finally
I simply said, "I got lost coming back," which made me the
cleverest fellow at the table for nearly an hour. If he had
expected it to shake loose my tale from me, it failed. Yet,
oddly enough, I felt better, as if my body's violent protest
over the mistreatment had persuaded me that, yes, I was
human and had to make allowances for it. I woke the next
day in the barracks, stinking and sweaty, and went back to

the steams. I scraped my fouled beard from my face and scrubbed myself with salt and then washed all over with cold water. I dressed in a fresh guard's uniform, for my trunk had returned with the rest of the quest's company and gear, and then ate a very simple and small breakfast of porridge in the crowded and noisy guardroom. Just outside the door of the guards' mess, the kitchen rattled and clanged as if a battle were going on there, with whole companies of kitchen help attacking their tasks.

Feeling more like myself than I had in days, I used the concealed door near the laundry court to enter Chade's labyrinth and made my way up to the workroom.

I found the worktable lined with oily scrolls spread out for cleaning and copying. There were fresh apples in a basket by the hearth chairs. They had not been ripe when last I was in this room. That little fact rocked me more than I expected it to. I sat down, focused myself, and reached for Chade. *Where are you? I need to report. I need someone to help me make sense of this.*

Ah! Excellent to hear you. I would very much welcome your report. We are in Verity's tower. Can you make the climb?

I think so. But not swiftly. Wait for me.

I made the climb, but they did have to wait for me. When I emerged from the side of the hearth, I received a shock, for Lady Nettle, unmistakably *Lady* Nettle in her green gown and lace collar, was seated at the great table with Chade, Dutiful, and Thick. She looked only mildly surprised to see me emerge. I lifted a strand of cobwebs from across my eyes and shook it from my fingers into the hearth. Then, uncertain of my role, I offered a guard's courteous bow to all of them and stood as if awaiting orders.

"Are you quite all right?" Dutiful asked me and came to offer me his arm to my seat at the table. I was too proud to take it, and even seated at the table, I was uncertain of how to proceed. Chade marked my furtive glances at Nettle, for he burst into a laugh and said, "Fitz, she's a member of the coterie now. You must have expected it to come to this."

I glanced at her. Her look was like a knife, and her words as cold and sharp as she sank them into me. "I know your name, FitzChivalry Farseer. I even know that I am your bastard daughter. My mother knew no Tom Badgerlock, you see. So, while you were in the infirmary, she went to see who had claimed to be her old friend. Then she came away and told me all. All."

"She does not know 'all,'" I said faintly. Abruptly I could think of no more to say. Chade got up hastily, poured brandy and brought it to me. My hand shook so that I could scarcely raise it to my mouth.

"Well, your mother named *you* well," Dutiful observed acidly to her.

"As did yours," Nettle replied sweetly.

"Enough, both of you. We will set this aside while Fitz tells us where he was while guards combed the entire kingdom for him." Chade spoke quite firmly.

"Molly is here? At Buckkeep?"

"Everyone is here at Buckkeep. The whole world came for Harvest Fest. Tomorrow night." Thick spoke with satisfaction. "I get to help with the apple press."

"My mother is here. And all my brothers. Who know nothing of any of this, and my mother and I have decided it is best that it remain that way. They are here because my father will be honored at Harvest Fest for his role in the slaying of the dragon. As will Swift, and the rest of the Wit coterie."

"Good. I am glad of that," I said, and I was, but my words came out dully. It was not just the shock of discovering that Harvest Fest was tomorrow. I felt plundered of dignity and control of my life. And oddly freed by it. The decision of when and how to tell Molly that I lived had been taken from me. She had seen me. She knew I lived. Perhaps the next move was hers. And the thought that followed that plunged me into an abyss. Perhaps she had already made it. She had walked away from me.

"Fitz?" I became aware that Chade had spoken to me

several times when he touched me on the arm. I twitched and came back to awareness of the people at the table. Dutiful looked sympathetic, Nettle distant, and Thick bored. Chade rested a hand on my shoulder and gave it a gentle squeeze. "Would you report to the coterie on where you have been and what happened to you? I have my suspicions, but I'd like them confirmed."

Habit made me begin from the last time he'd heard from me. I was blithely telling them of entering the Black Man's abode when I suddenly became reluctant to share all the Fool had said. So I looked at my hands on the table and summarized it, leaving out as many of the intimate details as I could. Of those who sat at the table, only Chade perhaps had a glimmering of what my parting from the Fool meant. Without thinking, I said aloud, "But I did not go back, and you say I've been gone over a month. I do not know what they will make of that absence. I want to go back, but now I fear the pillars as I never have before."

"And well you should, if what I have read in the Skill scrolls you brought back is an indicator. But more of that later. Tell the rest."

And so I did, of leaving and claiming the scrolls and disposing of the woman's body. Chade was fascinated by the Elderling magic of lights and warmth, and asked many questions about the cubes of memory stone that I could not answer. I saw him already itching to attempt the trip and explore for himself that magically charged realm. I went on to Prilkop's farewell, and then to my endless passage through the pillars. When I spoke of the being who had rescued me, Dutiful sat up very straight. "Like the ones from our time on the Others beach."

"Like and not like. I think there, our minds were in their world. In the pillars, my body was there, as well. Since I've returned, I've felt . . . strange. More alive in some ways. More connected, to even the tiniest bits of this world. And yet more alone, also." And then I fell silent. There seemed nothing to add to my account. I glanced at

Nettle. She met my gaze with a neutral little look that said I meant nothing to her and never had.

Chade seemed to feel he had enough to ponder, for he pushed back from the table like a man who has finished a substantial meal. "Well. A tale that will take some thought to sort out, and enough lessons for now. All of us have tasks to get to with Harvest Fest just around the corner. There will be a gathering tonight, in the Great Hall, with music and jugglers and dancing and tales. Many of our Outislander friends will be there, as well as all our dukes. I shall see the rest of you there tonight, I am sure."

When they continued to sit and look at him, he added heavily, "And I would speak privately with Fitz now."

Thick stood up. So did Nettle. "After I speak privately with Fitz," Dutiful announced calmly.

Thick looked perplexed, but immediately added, "Me, too."

"Not I," Nettle said coolly as she walked toward the door. "I can't imagine anything I'd ever want to say to him."

Thick stood rooted in place, his eyes darting from Nettle to Dutiful. He was obviously torn. I managed to dredge up a smile for him. "You and I will have lots of time later, Thick. I promise."

"Ya," he agreed abruptly, and managed to catch the door before it had completely closed behind Nettle. He followed her out. Dutiful gave Chade a glance and the councilor retreated to stand by the window looking out over the sea. Plainly it was not what Dutiful wanted. Just as plainly, the power struggle between councilor and prince continued. I looked at Dutiful. He sat down in the chair next to me and drew it closer. He spoke softly and I expected to hear of his concerns with the Narcheska and his betrothal. "I've talked with her a lot about you. She's angry with you right now, but I think if you'll give her time, she can calm down enough to listen to you."

It took me a moment. "Nettle?"

"Of course."

"You talked about me a lot with her?" Better and better, I thought sourly to myself. Dutiful sensed my dismay.

"I had to," he said defensively. "She was saying things like, 'He abandoned my mother when she was pregnant, and never came to see me at all.' I couldn't let her just say things like that, let alone believe them. So I've told her the truth, as you told it to me."

"Fitz?" He spoke a few moments later.

"Oh. Sorry. Thank you." I couldn't even recall what I had been thinking.

"You'll like her brothers. I do. Chivalry's a bit full of himself, but I think it's a bluff to make up for how frightened he is of all the changes. Nimble is nothing like Swift. I've never met two twins less alike. Steady lives up to his name, while Just chatters like a magpie. And Hearth, he's the youngest, all he does is run and giggle and try to get his brothers and Nettle to wrestle with him. He's not afraid of anyone or anything."

"They're all here for Harvest Fest."

"At the Queen's invitation. Because Swift will be recognized and Burrich honored."

"Of course." I looked at the table between my hands. Did I fit anywhere in any of this?

"Well, I suppose that's all I wanted to say. I'm glad you're better. And I think Nettle will come about, if you give her time. She feels tricked. I warned you she would. Oddly enough, I think that what made her angriest was that you disappeared like that. She took it personally, somehow. But I think she'll reconsider her opinion of you, if you give her time."

"I don't think I've much choice in it."

"No, I don't suppose you do. But I didn't want you to think it was hopeless and give up and go off somewhere to avoid seeing her. Your place is at Buckkeep now. So is hers."

"Thank you."

He glanced aside from me. "I can't tell you what it means to me to have her here at court. She's so outspoken and blunt. I never was friends with a girl like I can be with her. I suppose it's because we're cousins."

I nodded, unsure how true it was, but glad of it all the same. If she had the Prince's friendship, she had a powerful protector at court.

"I have to go. I've missed my last two fittings for my Harvest Festival clothing. I swear, they take it out on Thick, poking him with pins 'by accident' if I'm not there to defend him. So I'd best be there."

I nodded to that as well and then somehow he was up and out the door and the room was silent without my much noticing how it had happened. Chade set a cup of brandy down before me with a firm tap on the table. I looked at it and then up at him. "You may need it," he observed mildly. Then he revealed, "The Fool was here, two weeks ago. I'd give a lot to know how he comes and goes from here so unseen, but he managed. I heard a tap at the door of my private sitting room, late at night. And when I opened it, there he was. Changed of course, as you said. Brown as an appleseed, all over. He looked weary and half-sick, but I think that could have been his journey through the pillar. He did not speak of the Black Man, or indeed of anything except you. He obviously expected to find you here. That frightened me."

I set the empty brandy glass down on the table. Without asking, Chade refilled it for me. "When I told him we hadn't seen you, he looked stricken. I told him how thoroughly we'd searched, and that my private premise had been that you'd gone off with him. He asked if we'd used the Skill; I told him that of course we had, but that it had yielded no trace of you. He gave me the name of an inn where he'd be staying for a week, and asked me to send a runner immediately if any news of you came in. At the end of the week, he came back to me again. He looked as if he had aged a decade. He told me he had made inquiries of his own about you, with no positive results. Then he said he had to depart, but that he wished to leave something with me for you. Neither of us expected you'd return to claim it."

I didn't have to ask for it. He set down a sealed scroll, no bigger than a child's closed fist, and a small bag made from Elderling fabric. I recognized it as coming from the coppery robe. I looked at them, but made no move to touch either of them while Chade was watching me. "Did he say anything? As a message for me, I mean."

"I think that is what those things are."

I nodded.

"Hap came to see you while you were in the infirmary. Did you know?"

"No. I didn't. How did he know I was there?"

"I believe he spends a great deal of time at that minstrel tavern these days. When we were searching for you, we put the word out through the minstrels, of course. We were desperate to hear any rumor of you, so he knew that we expected Tom Badgerlock to be at Buckkeep and he wasn't. Then, when you were found, of course the minstrels heard of that, too. So he knew through them. You should see him soon and put his mind at rest."

"He visits the minstrel tavern often?"

"So I've heard."

I didn't ask from whom, or why the Queen's councilor would be kept informed of the habits of a woodworker's apprentice. I merely said, "Thank you for watching over him."

"I told you I would. Not that I've done well at it. Fitz, I am sorry to tell you this. I don't know the details, but I understand he got in a bit of trouble in town and has lost his apprenticeship. He has been staying among the minstrel folk."

I shook my head at that, sick at heart. I should have done better by him. Time, definitely, to take the young man in hand. I decided I'd seek out Starling for gossip on where to find my boy. I felt guilty and remiss that I had not sought him out before this.

"Any other news that I should know?"

"Lady Patience whacked me quite soundly with her fan when she discovered that you had been in the infirmary for some days and no one had informed her."

I laughed in spite of myself. "In public?"

"No. She has gained some discretion in her old age. She summoned me to a private meeting in her chambers. Lacey was waiting for me. I went in, Lacey offered me a cup of tea, and Patience came in and whacked me with her fan." He rubbed his head above his ear and added ruefully, "You might have told me she knew you were alive and disguised as a guardsman. Something that she finds offensive in the extreme, by the by."

"I didn't have a chance. So. Is she angry with me?"

"Of course. But not as angry as she is with me. She called me an 'old spider' and threatened to horsewhip me if I didn't stop interfering with her son. How did she establish a connection between you and me?"

I shook my head slowly. "She's always known more than she lets on."

"Indeed. That was the case even when your father was alive."

"I will go and see Patience also. Well, it seems that my life is as much a tangle as ever. How go things in the greater schemes of Buckkeep?"

"Your plans have succeeded well enough. Those dukes who did not travel to the Out Islands on Prince Dutiful's first sortie are glad to have a chance at making trade agreements with the kaempra who have been arriving. Some think there may be enough profit in it to persuade the Hetgurd to put an end to all raids. I do not know if they can wield that authority, but if all the dukes say, firmly, that trading agreements are contingent on an end to all raiding, it may cease. There has even, you may be surprised to hear, been talk of some marriage offers between Six Duchies nobility and the Out Island clans. So far, it has been all kaempras offering to join our 'mothershouses' and we have had to caution our nobility that the Outislander notion of marriage is sometimes not so permanent as our own. But some may work out. Several of our higher nobles have younger sons they might offer to Outislander clans."

He leaned back in his chair and poured brandy for himself. "It might even be a lasting peace, Fitz. Peace with the Outislanders in my lifetime. Truth to say, I never thought I'd see it." He sipped from his cup and added, "Though I'll not count my chickens before they are hatched. We've still a ways to go. I'd like to see Dutiful hailed as King-in-Waiting before the winter is over, but that may take a bit of doing. The lad is still impulsive and impetuous. I've cautioned him, over and over, that the crown sits on the King's head, not his heart. Nor considerably lower. He needs to show his dukes a man's measured thought, a king's considered opinions, not a boy's passions. Both Tilth and Farrow have said they'd rather see him wed first or with a few more years to steady him before they recognize him as King-in-Waiting."

I pushed my brandy cup toward him and he filled it as well. "You say nothing of the dragons. There have been no problems, then?"

He gave a wry smile. "I think our Six Duchies folk are a bit disappointed that they have not seen so much as a scale of them. They would have relished having Icefyre come crashing through our gates to present his head to our queen. Or they think they would. As for me, I am well contented with that situation. Dragons at a distance are amazing and noble creatures of legend. My closer experience of them makes me suspect they'd burp nobly after consuming me."

"Do you think they went back to Bingtown, then?"

"Most emphatically not. We had a messenger from the Traders last week, seeking word of Tintaglia. From the scroll, I could not tell if they were worried for her well-being, or frantic at having become the sole providers for several earth-bound dragons. I was going to tell them we had no idea of what had become of them after Icefyre made his appearance at the Narwhal mothershouse. Then Nettle spoke up. She said that Tintaglia and Icefyre were feeding and mating and completely engrossed in those two activities. She could not say where; her contact with Tintaglia is intermittent, and a dragon's idea of geography is quite different from ours. But they were feeding on sea bears. So I think that would put them to the north of us. We may yet see something of them if they decide to fly back to Bingtown."

"I've a feeling we've not heard the last of them. But what about closer to home? Have we resolved anything with our Old Blood?"

"Old Blood has shed much blood while we were gone. It has rocked several of our duchies to discover that Old Blood may run stronger in the nobility than was previously admitted. There was even a rumor about Celerity of Bearns, that perhaps she and her hawk saw with the same eyes. Shocking. These revelations come out when vendettas run hot, and one set of murders lead to another. Kettricken has been hard-pressed to keep order. But the gist of it is that Old Blood seems to have thoroughly cleaned their own house of 'the Piebald blight.' Web was horrified at the news he received when he arrived home. He has pressed, more than ever, for Old Blood to make itself known and respectable. In some ways, the bloodletting has been a setback for him. Ironically, he has proposed to create a township for Old Blood, where they may demonstrate their diligence and civility. What once they opposed for fear it would lead to slaughter, they now propose as a way to demonstrate their harmlessness. When unprovoked. The Queen is considering it. Location would require much negotiation. Many fear the Wit more than ever these days."

"Well, not everything can go smoothly, I suppose. At least it may be more out in the open, now." I sat a moment, wondering. Celerity of Bearns, Witted? I did not think so. But looking back, I could not be certain.

"And Lord FitzChivalry Farseer? Will he come out into the sunlight at last?"

"What, only Lord? I thought I was to be King?" And then I laughed, for never had I seen Chade struck dumb before. "No," I decided. "No, I think we will let Lord FitzChivalry Farseer rest in peace. Those important to me know. That was all I ever cared about."

Chade nodded thoughtfully. "I could wish you a minstrel's happy ending to your tale, 'much love and many children,' but I do not think it will come to be."

"It never came true for you, either."

He looked at me and then looked aside. "I had you," he said. "But for you, perhaps I would have died an 'old spider' hiding in the walls. Did you never think of that?"

"No. I hadn't."

"I've things to do," he said abruptly. Then, as he stood, he rested a hand on my shoulder and asked, "Will you be all right now?"

"As well as can be expected," I said.

"I'll leave you, then." He looked down and added, "Will you try to be more careful? It was not easy for me, those days when you went missing. I thought you had fled Buckkeep and the duties of your blood, and then when the Fool came through, I believed you were dead somewhere. Again."

"I'll be just as careful with myself as you are with yourself," I promised him. He lifted one brow at me and then nodded.

I sat for some time after he was gone looking at the package and the scroll. I opened the scroll first. I recognized the Fool's careful hand. I read it through twice. It was a poem about dancing, and a farewell. I could tell he had written it before he discovered my absence. So. He had not changed his mind. He and Prilkop had paused here only to say good-bye to me, not because he'd had a change of heart.

The package was lumpy and rather heavy. When I untied the slithery fabric, a piece of memory stone the size of my fist rolled out on the table. The Fool's Skilled fingers had carved it, I was sure. I poked at it cautiously but felt only stone. I lifted it up to look at it. It had three faces, each blending into the next. Nighteyes was there, and me, and the Fool. Nighteyes looked out at me, ears up and muzzle down. The next facet showed me as a young man, unscarred, eyes wide and mouth slightly ajar. Had I ever truly been that young? And the Fool had carved himself as a fool, in a tailed cap with one long forefinger lifted to shush his pursed lips and his brows arched high in some jest.

It was only when I cupped the carving in my hand that it woke for me and revealed the memories the Fool had imbued in it. Three simple moments it recalled. If my fingers spanned the wolf and myself, then I saw Nighteyes and I curled together in sleep in my bed in the cabin. Nighteyes sprawled sleeping on the Fool's hearth in the Mountains when I touched both Fool and Nighteyes. The last was confusing at first. My fingers rested on the Fool and myself. I blinked at the memory presented to me. I stared at it for some time before recognizing it as another of the Fool's memories. It was what I looked like when he pressed his brow to mine and looked into my eyes. I set it down on the table and the Fool's mocking smile looked up at me. I smiled back at him and impulsively touched a finger to his brow. I heard his voice then, almost as if he were in the room. "I have never been wise." I shook my head over that. His last message to me and it had to be one of his riddles.

I took my treasures and crawled back behind the hearth and set the panel back in place. I went to my workroom and hid them there. Gilly appeared, with many questions about the lack of sausages. I promised him I'd look into it. He told me I should, and bit a finger firmly as a reminder.

Then I left the workroom and slipped back into the main halls of Buckkeep. I knew that Starling would be sniffing over the visiting minstrels, so I went to the lower hall where they usually rehearsed and were generously hosted with viands and drink. The room was stuffed with entertainers, competing with one another in that boisterous and cooperative way they have, but I saw no sign of Starling. I then sought her in the Great Hall and the Lesser, but without success. I had given up and was leaving on my way down to Buckkeep Town when I caught a glimpse of her in the Women's Gardens. She was walking slowly about with several other ladies. I waited until I was sure she had seen me and then went to one of the more secluded benches. I was certain she would find me there and I did not have to wait long. But as she sat down beside me, she greeted me with "This is not wise. If people see us, they will talk."

I had never heard her voice concern over that before and it took me aback, as well as stung my feelings. "Then I will ask my question and be on my way. I'm going to town to look for Hap. I've heard he's been frequenting one of the minstrel taverns and I thought you'd know which one?"

She looked surprised. "Not I! It's been months since I've been to a minstrel tavern. At least four months." She leaned back on the bench, her arms crossed and looked at me expectantly.

"Could you guess which one?"

She considered a moment. "The Pelican's Pouch. The younger minstrels go there, to sing bawdy songs and make up new verses to them. It's a rowdy place." She sounded as if she disapproved. I raised my brows to that. She clarified. "It's fine enough for young folk new to singing and telling, but scarcely an appropriate place for me these days."

"Appropriate?" I asked, trying to master a grin. "When have you ever cared for appropriate, Starling?"

She looked away from me, shaking her head. She did not meet my eyes as she said, "You must no longer speak to me so familiarly, Tom Badgerlock. Nor can I meet you again, alone, like this. Those days are over for me."

"Whatever is the matter with you?" I burst out, shocked and a bit hurt.

"The matter with me? Are you blind, man? Look at me." She stood up proudly, her hands resting on her belly. I had seen bigger paunches on smaller matrons. It was her stance rather than her size that informed me. "You're with child?" I asked incredulously.

She took a breath and a tremulous smile lit her face. Suddenly, she spoke to me as if she were the old Starling, the words bubbling from her. "It is little short of a miracle. The healer woman that Lord Fisher has hired to watch over me says that sometimes, just when a woman's chances for it are nearly gone, she can conceive. And I have. Oh, Fitz, I'm going to have a baby, a child of my own. Already, I love it so that I can scarcely stop thinking of it, night or day."

She looked luminously happy. I blinked. Sometimes, she had spoken of being barren with bitterness, saying that her inability to conceive meant she would never have a se-cure home or a faithful husband. But never had she uttered a word of the deep longing for a child that she must have felt all those years. It stunned me. I said, quite sincerely, "I'm happy for you. I truly am."

"I knew you would be." She touched the back of my hand, briefly, lightly. Our days of greeting one another with an embrace were over. "And I knew you would understand why I must change my ways. No breath of scandal, no hint of inappropriate behavior by his mother should mar my baby's future. I must become a proper matron now, and busy myself only with the matters of my household."

I knew a shocking moment of greenest envy.

"I wish you all the joys of your home," I said quietly.

"Thank you. You do understand this parting?"

"I do. Fare you well, Starling. Fare you well."

I sat on the bench and watched her leave me. She did

not walk, she glided, her arms across her belly as if she already held her unborn child. My greedy, raucous little bird was a nesting mother now. I felt a twinge of loss to watch her go. In her own way, she had always been someone I could turn to when my days were hard. That was gone now.

I thought about my days with Starling on the walk down to Buckkeep Town. I wondered, if I had not given my pain to the dragon, would I ever have given anything of myself to Starling? Not that I had shared much with her. I looked back at how we had come together and wondered at myself.

The Pelican's Pouch was in a new part of Buckkeep Town, up a steep path and then down, and half-built on pilings. It was a new tavern, in the sense that it hadn't existed when I was a lad, yet its rafters seemed well smoked and its tables showed the battering of most minstrel taverns, where folk were prone to leap to a tabletop either to sing or declaim an epic.

It was early in the day for minstrels to be up and about, so the place was mostly deserted. The tavernkeeper was sitting on a tall stool near the salt-rimed window, gazing out over the sea. I let my eyes adjust to the perpetual dimness and then saw Hap sitting at a table by himself in the corner. He had several pieces of wood in front of him and was moving them around as if playing some sort of game with them. He'd grown a little beard, just a fringe of curly hair along his jaw. Immediately, I didn't like it. I walked over and stood across the table until he looked up and saw me. Then he jumped to his feet with a shout that startled the dozing tavernkeeper and came around the table to give me a big hug. "Tom! There you are! I'm so glad to see you! Word went out that you were missing. I came to see you when I heard you'd turned up, but you were sleeping like the dead. Did the healer give you the note I left for you?"

"No, he didn't."

My tone warned him. His shoulders sagged a bit. "Ah. So I see you've heard all the bad news of me, but not the good, I'll wager. Sit down. I'd hoped that you'd read it and I wouldn't have to tell it all again. I get weary of repeating the same words over and over, especially since I do it so much these days." He lifted his voice. "Marn? Could we have two mugs of ale here? And a bit of bread too if there's any out of the oven yet." Then, "Sit down," he said again to me, and took a seat himself. I sat down opposite him. He looked at my face and said, "I'll tell it quickly. Svanja took my money and spent it on pretties that attracted the eye of an older man. She's now Mistress Pins. She married the draper, a man easily twice as old as me. And wealthy, and settled. A substantial man. So. That's done."

"And your apprenticeship?" I asked quietly.

"I lost it," he replied as quietly. "Svanja's father made complaint about my character to my master. Master Gindast said I must change my ways or leave his employ. I was stupid. I left his employ. I tried to get Svanja to run away with me, back to our old cabin. I told her things would be hard, but that we could live simply with our love for each other to make us rich. She was furious that I'd lost my apprenticeship, and told me I was crazy if I thought she wanted to live in the woods and tend chickens. Four days later, she was walking out on Master Pins's arm. You were right about her, Tom. I should have listened to you."

I bit my tongue before I could agree with him. I sat and stared at the tabletop, wondering what would become of my boy now. I'd left him on his own just when he'd needed a father the most. I pondered what to do. "I'll go with you," I offered. "We'll go to Gindast together and see if he will reconsider. I'll beg if I have to."

"No!" Hap was aghast. Then he laughed, saying, "You haven't given me a chance to tell the rest. As usual, you've seized on the worst and made it the only. Tom. I'm here, amongst the minstrels, and I'm happy. Look."

He pushed his bits of wood toward me. The shape was rough yet, but I could see that, pegged together, they'd make a harp. I'd been with Starling long enough to know that the making of a basic harp was among the first steps toward becoming a minstrel. "I never knew I could sing. Well, I knew I could sing, of course, but I mean I never knew I could sing well enough to be a minstrel. I grew up listening to Starling and singing along with her. I never realized how many of her songs and tales I'd got by heart, simply listening to her of an evening. Now, we've had our differences, Starling and I, and she doesn't approve of my taking this path at all. She said you'd blame her for it. But she vouched for me, and she let it be known that I could sing her songs until my own came to me."

The mugs of ale and fresh bread, crusty and steaming, were delivered to our table. Hap tore the bread into chunks and bit into one while I was still trying to grasp it all. "You're going to become a minstrel?"

"Yes! Starling brought me to a fellow named Sawtongue. He has a terrible voice, but a way with the strings that is little short of a god's gift. And he's a bit old, so he can use a young fellow like me to carry the packs and make up a fire on the nights when we're between inns in our traveling. We'll stay in town until after Harvest Fest, of course. He'll play tonight at the lesser hearth, and I may sing a song or two at the earlier revels for the children. Tom, I never knew that life could be this good. I love what I'm doing now. With everything Starling taught me, all unknowing, I've the repertoire of a journeyman already. Though I'm behind on the making of my own instrument, and of course I've few of my own songs yet. But they'll come. Sawtongue says I should be patient, and not try to make songs, but to wait and let them come to me."

"I never thought to see you turn minstrel, Hap."

"Nor I." He lifted a shoulder in a shrug and grinned. "It's a fit, Tom. No one cares who my mother and father were or weren't, or if my eyes don't match. There's not the endless grind of being a woodworker. Oh, I may complain about reciting, over and over, until every single word is exactly as Sawtongue wants it turned, but it's not difficult. I never realized what a good memory I had."

"And after Harvest Fest?"

"Oh. That will be the only sad part. Then I'm away with Sawtongue. He always winters in Bearns. So we'll sing and harp our way there, and then stay with his patron at a warm hearth for the winter."

"And no regrets."

"Only that I'll see even less of you than I have this last summer."

"But you're happy?"

"Hmm. As close to it as a man can get. Sawtongue says that when you let go and follow your fate instead of trying to twist your life around and master it, a man finds that happiness follows him."

"So may it be for you, Hap. So may it be."

And then we talked for a time of incidental things and drank our ale. To myself, I marveled at the knocks he had taken and still struggled back onto his feet. I wondered too that Starling had stepped in to help him as she had, and said nothing of it to me. That she had given him permission to sing her songs told me that she truly intended to leave her old life behind her.

I would have talked the day away with him, but he glanced out of the window and said he had to go wake his master and bring him his breakfast. He asked if I would be at the Harvest Eve revels that night, and I told him I was not sure, but that I hoped he'd enjoy them. He said he'd be certain to, and then we made our farewells.

I took my homeward path through the market square. I bought flowers at one stall, and sweets at another, and racked my brains desperately for any other gifts that might buy me back into Patience's good graces. In the end, however, I could think of nothing and was horrified to realize how much time I'd wasted wandering from booth to booth. As I made my way back to Buckkeep Castle, I was part of the throng going there. I walked behind a wagon full of beer barrels and in front of a group of jugglers who practiced all the way there. One of the girls in the group asked me if the flowers were for my sweetheart, and when I said no, they were for my mother, they all laughed pityingly at me.

I found Patience in her rooms, sitting with her feet up. She scolded me and wept over my heartlessness in making her worry while Lacey put the flowers into a vase and set out the sweets with tea for us. My tale of what had befallen me actually brought me back into her good graces, though she complained still that there were more than a dozen years of my life unaccounted for.

I was trying to recall where I had left off in my telling when Lacey said quietly, "Molly came to visit us a few days ago. It was pleasant to see her again, after all the years." When I sat in stunned silence, Lacey observed, "Even in widow's dress, she's still a fine-looking woman."

"I told her she shouldn't have kept my granddaughter from me!" Patience declared suddenly. "Oh, she had a hundred good reasons for it, but not one good enough for me."

"Did you quarrel with her?" I asked in dismay. Could it become any worse?

"No. Of course not. She did send the girl to see me the next day. Nettle. Now there's a name for a child! But she's straight-spoken enough. I like that in a girl. Said she didn't want Withywoods or anything that might come to her because you were her father. I said it had nothing to do with you, but with the fact that she was Chivalry's granddaughter, and who else was I to settle it on? So. I think she'll come to find that I'm more stubborn than she is."

"Not by much," Lacey observed contentedly. Her crooked fingers played on the edge of the table. I missed her endless tatting.

"Did Molly speak of me?" I asked, dreading the answer.

"Nothing you'd care for me to repeat to you. She knew you were alive; that was no doing of mine, though. I know how to keep a secret. Apparently far better than you do!

She came here ready for a quarrel, I think, but when she found that I too had suffered all those years, thinking you dead, well, then we had much in common to talk about. And dear Burrich, of course. Dear, stubborn Burrich. We both had a bit of a weep over him. He was my first love, you know, and I don't think one ever gets back the bit of heart one gives to a first love. She didn't mind my saying that, that there was still a bit of me that loved that awful head-strong man. I told her, it doesn't matter how badly behaved your first love is, he always keeps a place in your heart. And she agreed that was true enough."

I sat very still.

"That she did," Lacey agreed, and her eyes flickered to me, as if measuring how stupid I could possibly be.

Patience chattered on of this and that, but I found it hard to keep my mind on her words. My heart was elsewhere, walking on windy clifftops with a girl in blowing red skirts. Eventually, I realized she was telling me I had to go; that she must begin to dress for the evening festivities, for it took her longer to do those things than it used to do. She asked if I would be there, and I told her, probably not, that it was still difficult for me to be seen at gatherings of the nobility where someone might dredge up an old memory of me. She nodded to that, but added, "You have changed more than you know, Fitz. If it had not been for Lacey, I might have walked right by you and not known you at all."

I did not know whether to take comfort in that or not. Lacey walked me to the door, saying as we went, "Well, I suppose we've all changed a great deal. Molly, now, I'd have known her anywhere, but I'm not the woman that I used to be. Even for Molly, there are changes, though. She said to me, she said, 'Fancy, Lacey, they've put me in the Violet Chamber, in the south wing. Me, as used to be a maid on the upper floors, housed in the Violet Chamber, where Lady and Lord Flicker used to live. Imagine such a thing!'" Again, her old eyes flickered to mine.

I gave one slow nod.

chapter XXXVI

HARVEST FEST

*As you have requested, I send a messenger to you, to
inform you that the blue queen dragon Tintaglia and the
black drake Icefyre have been seen. They seem to be in
good health and appetite. We conveyed to them that you
were concerned for their well-being and for the well-
being of the young dragons left in your care. We could
not be certain that they understood the gravity or the
urgency of your desire for information about them, as
perhaps you will understand. They seemed very intent
on one another, and little disposed to desire or facilitate
conversation with men.*

MISSIVE FROM QUEEN KETTRICKEN
TO THE BINGTOWN TRADERS COUNCIL

Evening found me at my old post behind the wall. For
once, I was spying for my own curiosity rather than upon
any mission for Chade. I had a bottle of wine, bread, apples, cheese, sausages, and a ferret in a basket beside me,
and a cushion to perch on. I hunched with my eye to a
crack and watched the swirl as Six Duchies and Out Islands met and mingled.

Tonight there was little formality. That would be

tomorrow. Tonight there was food in abundance set out on tables, but the tables edged the walls to leave room for dancing. Tonight there would be opportunity for lesser and younger minstrels, jugglers, and puppeteers to show their skills. Tonight was casual chaos and rejoicing in the harvest prospects. Tonight, commoner and nobles mingled in all the halls and courtyards of the keep. I probably could have safely wandered amongst them, but I had no heart for it. So I hid and peered and took pleasure in the pleasure of others.

I was at my post early enough that I did get to hear Hap sing. He sang for the children, early gathered for they would be early sent to bed, and chose two silly songs, about the man who hunted the moon and the one about the woman who planted a cup to grow some wine and a fork to grow some meat and so on. He'd always laughed at those when Starling sang them to him, and so did his audience now. He seemed to take great and genuine pleasure in that, and his master seemed well pleased. I gave a small sigh. My boy gone off with the minstrels. I'd never imagined that.

I also saw Swift, his head cropped close for mourning, walking about with Web. The lad seemed older than when I last had seen him, not in looks but in bearing. He followed Web and I was glad he had such a man to mentor him. My eyes wandered, and amidst the dancers, I saw young Lord Civil. There was a girl in his arms and, to my shock, it was Nettle. I sat watching and chewing that until the end of the tune, when Prince Dutiful escorted Lady Sydel back to him and claimed the next dance with Nettle for himself. The Prince, I thought, looked a bit forlorn despite his formally pleasant mien. I doubted that it was his friend's lady or his cousin that he truly wished to be dancing with. As for Nettle, she danced well, but self-consciously, and I wondered if she was uncertain of the steps or made awkward by the rank of her partner. Her dress was simple, as simple as the Prince's Harvest Fest attire, and I saw Queen Kettricken's hand in that.

Thinking of the Queen made me look for her, and I found her on a high chair, overlooking the festivities. She looked tired but pleased. Chade was not beside her, and I thought that odd, until I saw that he too was dancing, with a fiery-haired woman who was probably a third of his age.

One by one, my eyes sought and found all the folk who had woven the most important parts of my life. Starling, Lady Fisher now, sat on a cushioned chair. Her lord stood solicitously close by, and fetched her drink and food from the tables himself as if servants could not be trusted with such an essential task. Lady Patience entered, wearing more lace than all the other women combined, with Lacey at her elbow. They found the end of a bench near a puppeteer's stage and sat nudging and pointing and whispering together as if they were two little girls. I spotted Lady Rosemary talking with two Outislander kaempras. I was sure that her charming smile and ample bosom were gathering plenty of information for Lord Chade to ponder on the morrow.

Arkon Bloodblade was there, in a mantle trimmed with red fox fur, discussing something earnestly with the Duchess of Bearns. She seemed to be listening courteously, but I wondered if any trade agreement could ever completely change her heart toward the Outislanders. I saw three others I recognized from the Hetgurd gathering over by the food tables, and several standing and staring perplexedly at a puppet show. My eyes snagged on Nettle again as she drifted alone through the festive throng. A stocky young man approached her. By his close-cropped curls, I deduced that it was Chivalry, Burrich's eldest son. They stood talking in the midst of the noise and laughter. As I watched, a woman in a simple dress of very dark blue approached them, leading a struggling small boy by the hand. I winced at Molly's shorn head, knowing with deep certainty that Burrich would never have approved of what she had done to her tresses. Her bared head made her look oddly young. She gripped Hearth by the hand and was pointing at another young boy, evidently entreating Chivalry to help her gather them up for the night. Instead, Nettle swept her youngest brother up in her arms and whirled him out onto the dance floor, where his squeals of glee at having eluded his mother made more than one couple smile. Chivalry held out a placating hand to Molly, nodding at something she said. Then a troupe of tumblers stacked themselves up in such a way as to precisely block my view. When they were finished with their tricks, I could not see Molly at all.

I sat back in the dimness. At my elbow, Gilly asked, *Sausages?*

I felt about in the basket but discovered only worried bits of meat. He'd taken them all to pieces in the act of killing them. I found one nub larger than the others and offered it to him and he snatched it happily from my hand.

And so my evening passed. On the dance floor, I saw those I cherished most turn and move to music that barely reached my ears through the thick walls. I leaned back from my peephole to ease my aching back. A tiny spot of light reached through it toward me. I caught it in my hand and sat staring at it for a time. A metaphor for my life, I thought. I pushed my self-pity aside and leaned forward again.

Thick was leaving the food table with a stack of tarts in his two hands. His music was loud and joyous and he moved to it, out of step from the tune that all the others heard. But at least he was out there, I thought to myself. At least he was out and amongst them all. I felt the impulse to throw caution to the wind and join him, but it died as swiftly as it had arisen. No.

Molly's children had found a juggler to their liking. They stood in a half-circle, watching him. Nettle held Hearth's and Steady's hands. Just was in Chivalry's arms. Nimble and Swift stood together. I noticed Web behind them, at a distance from them and yet present. My eyes wandered over the crowd, seeking and not finding. I stood.

I left my basket and cushion to the ferret and went unencumbered through the narrow passages.

I knew there was a peephole to the Violet Chamber. I eschewed it. I left my secret warren, spent some small time in a closet slapping dust and cobwebs from myself, and then walked swiftly, eyes down, through the crowded halls of Buckkeep. No one remarked on me, no one called my name or stopped me to ask how I had been. I could have been invisible. As I climbed the stairs, the crowd thinned. By the time I had reached the residential chambers of Buckkeep Castle, the halls were deserted. Everyone was at the festivities below. Everyone but me, and perhaps Molly.

I walked three times past the door of the Violet Chamber. The fourth time, I commanded myself to knock and did, more forcefully than I had intended. My heart was hammering and I was literally shaking in my shoes. There was only silence. Then, when I thought this mustering of courage would be for naught, that no one would answer, I heard Molly ask quietly, "Who is it?"

"It's me," I said stupidly. And then, while I was searching for what name to call myself by, she told me plainly that she knew who was there.

"Go away."

"Please."

"Go away!"

"Please."

"No."

"I promised Burrich I'd look after you and the young ones. I promised him."

The door opened a crack. I could see one of her eyes as she said, "Funny. That was what he told me when he first began to bring things to my door. That he had promised you, before you died, that he'd look after me."

I had no answer to that, and the door started to close. I shoved my foot into it. "Please. Let me in. Just for a moment."

"Move your foot or I'll break it." She meant it.

I decided to risk it. "Please, Molly. Please. After all the years, don't I get one chance to explain? Just one?"

"The time for explaining was sixteen years ago. When it might have made a difference."

"Please. Let me in."

She jerked the door suddenly open. Her eyes were blazing and she said, "I only want to hear one thing from you. Tell me about my husband's last hours."

"Very well," I said quietly. "I suppose I owe you that."

"Yes," she said as she stepped away from the door, holding it just wide enough that I could eel through. "You owe me that. And a lot more."

She wore a night robe and wrapper. Her body was fuller than I remembered it, her figure a woman's rather than a girl's. It was not unattractive. The room smelled of her, not just the perfume she wore, but of her flesh and of beeswax and candle-making. Her dress was neatly folded on top of the chest at the foot of the bed. A trundle bed made up beside hers proclaimed that her boys would sleep here with her. Her brush and comb were set out on a table, more by habit than for any need of them.

The first stupid words out of my mouth were "He would not have wanted you to cut your hair."

She lifted a self-conscious hand to her head. "What would you know about it?" she demanded indignantly.

"The first time he saw you, long before he took you from me, he commented on your hair. 'A bit of red in her coat' is what he said."

"He would put it like that," she said, and then, "He never 'took me' from you. We thought you were dead. You let us think you were dead and I knew despair. I had nothing except a child depending on me for everything. If anyone took anything, I took him. Because I loved him. Because he treated me well and he treated Nettle well."

"I know that."

"I am glad that you do. Sit there. Tell me how he died." So I sat on a chair and she perched on the clothing chest, and I told her of Burrich's last days. It was the last conversation I would have imagined having with her in those circumstances and I hated it. Yet, as I spoke, I felt also a terrible relief. I needed to be telling her these things as much as she needed to be hearing them. She listened avidly as if every word were a moment of his life that she could reclaim for herself. I hesitated to speak of Burrich's Wit, yet there was no way to leave it out of the tale. She must have heard of it before, for she showed no shock or revulsion. I told it in a way that not even Swift could have, for I could say to her that at the end, it was obvious to me how much Burrich loved his son, that there was no rift between them when he died. It was different from telling it to Nettle. Molly understood the full significance of Burrich's asking me to look after her and his little sons. I repeated what he had said to me, that he had been the better man for her, and I repeated to her that I agreed with that.

She sat up straight and spoke bitterly. "Fine. So you both agreed on that. Did either of you ever think to consult with me on it? Did either of you ever pause to consider that perhaps the decision belonged to me?"

And those words opened the door for me to go back down the years, and to tell her what I was doing, and where and how I had learned that she had given herself to Burrich. She looked away from me, chewing on her thumbnail, as I spoke. When my words lapsed to silence she said, "I thought you were dead. If I had known otherwise, if he had known otherwise..."

"I know. But there was no safe way to send word to you. And then, once you had... it was too late. If I had come back, it would have torn all of us apart."

She leaned forward, her chin cupped in both her palms and her fingers over her mouth. Her eyes were closed, but tears welled from under her lashes. "What a mess you made of it. What a mare's nest we made of our lives."

There were a hundred answers to that. I could have

protested that I had not made the mess, that it had befallen all of us. Suddenly, it would have taken more strength than I had. I let it go. I let it all go. "And now it's too late for there ever to be anything for you and me."

"Oh, Fitz." And even in rebuke, for me to hear my name from her lips was a sort of sweetness. "For you, it has always been too late or too soon. Always someday. Always tomorrow, or after you do this one last duty for your king. A woman needs a chance for something to be *now*. I needed that. I'm sorry we had so little of it."

A little time longer we sat there in our own sorry silence. Then she said quietly, "Chivalry will be bringing the little ones to me soon. I promised they could stay until the last puppet show. It would not do for them to find you here. They would not understand and I could not explain."

And so I left her, bowing to her at her door. I had not touched so much as her hand. I felt worse than I had when I had been trying to knock. Then, there had been some shred of possibility. Now, I was left with the reality. Too late.

I descended the stairs, back into the crowds and the noise. Then the noise seemed suddenly louder, and people were talking excitedly, some asking questions, others repeating rumors. "A ship! From the Out Islands!"

"It's late to be docking!"

"A Narwhal banner?"

"The runner just went in! I saw his message baton."

Then I was trapped in the herd of folk crowding back toward the Great Hall. I tried to fight my way to the edge of the corridor, but only succeeded in being elbowed in the ribs, cursed at, and having my feet trodden on. I gave up and let the surge of eager folk carry me into the Great Hall.

A runner had indeed just reached the Queen. It took some little time for awareness of this to settle on the room. The musicians for the dance fell silent first, and then the puppeteers ceased their play. Jugglers stilled their clubs. The crowd hummed like a hive in anticipation as more and yet more folk crowded into the room. The messenger stood before the Queen, panting still, his baton that signaled to all that he was a royal messenger and not to be delayed still clasped in his hand. In a moment, Chade was at Kettricken's side, and then the Prince was climbing the dais to stand beside her. She held out the open scroll so that they both might read it. Then, when she held it aloft, the murmurs and speculation died to near silence.

"Good tidings! A ship with the Narwhal emblem has docked in the harbor," she announced. "It seems that perhaps Kaempra Peottre of the Narwhal Clan of the Out Islands will join us for our Harvest Fest tomorrow."

It was wonderful news and Arkon Bloodblade's shout of enthusiasm was easily heard above the polite mutters of the dukes and duchesses. An Outislander slapped the Duke of Tilth on the back. The Prince nodded his pleasure to the entire assembly and then motioned to the musicians, who launched into a lively and celebratory tune. There was scarcely room to dance; yet folk seemed content to hop or sway in place to the merry tune. Then the crowding in the room eased a bit as some folk fled it for fresh air or space or a chance to spread the gossip further. The puppet show finished and I saw Chivalry and Nettle gather up their smaller siblings and herd them from the room. Other youngsters were being shooed along, as well. Just when I thought that the crowd had eased enough that I could gracefully leave without resorting to elbows to get through the door, a second wave of excited voices reached us from outside. Almost immediately, folk began to spill back into the room. I felt someone tug at my sleeve and turned to find Lacey standing there. "Come sit with us, lad. We'll hide you."

And so I soon found myself on a bench between Patience and Lacey, looking as unostentatious as a fox in the henhouse. I slumped my shoulders and hid my face behind a mug of fresh cider and waited to see what the fresh hubbub was about.

It was Peottre arriving, I thought when I saw him

standing still in the door. And yet the noise outside seemed greater than that would occasion and Peottre himself had a determined look on his face that bespoke something momentous. He lifted both arms over his head and cried out loudly, "Clear a way, if you will! Clear a path."

It was easier said than done in the crowded space, and yet folk tried to give way. He walked in first, setting a measured tread, and then behind him came a vision such as few have ever seen. Elliania wore a hooded blue cloak. The hood was lined with white fur that set off her shining black eyes and hair. The cloak itself was floor length and trailed some little distance in a train. It was Buck blue, and worked all over with bucks and narwhals leaping side by side. Tiny glittering white gems made up their eyes, so that it seemed she wore a summer evening sky as she advanced into the room.

Prince Dutiful had remained upon the dais with his mother. Now he looked down on her and no one in the room could doubt that he beheld her with delight. He did not say a word to either Chade or the Queen. Nor did he bother with the two steps, but leaped straight to the floor. At sight of him, Elliania threw back her hood, and then ran to meet him. They met in the center of the Great Hall. As they clasped hands, her clear and joyous voice carried. "I could not wait. I could not wait for winter and I could not wait for spring. I am here to marry you and I will do my best to live according to your ways, strange though they are."

The Prince looked down at her. I saw his face light with joy, and then I saw his hesitation. I saw him groping for what he must say, for what was correct for him to say before all his gathered people. Elliania looked up at him, and the light in her face began to dim as Dutiful attempted to compose a careful reply.

I Skilled fiercely. *Tell her you cannot wait, either. Tell her you love her and that you will wed her right away. Love that comes so far and at such a price should not be put off! A woman needs to be loved now.*

Chade's face froze in a smile of horror. The Queen stood, and I knew she held her breath. Peottre stood motionless, and his face was very still. I knew he prayed the Prince would not hurt or humiliate the girl.

Dutiful spoke loud and clear. "Then we shall wed, within the week. Not just before my dukes, but before all gathered here. We shall wed, and we shall bring in the harvest as man and wife. Would that please you?"

"El and Eda, the Sea and the Land!" Bloodblade shouted. "The Buck and the Narwhal! At the turning of the year. Good fortune to us all!"

"So it would be!" Peottre cried out and a sort of wonder came into his face.

"That would please me." I saw the words formed by her lips, but did not hear them. Noise had erupted all about me as hundreds of tongues clattered at once. Chade closed his eyes for a moment, then put on a smile and looked with apparent fondness at his impulsive, impetuous prince. Yet the secret sourness of his gaze was defeated and nullified by what shone in Elliania's eyes. If she had ever needed confirmation of her decision, Dutiful had given it. I wondered at what cost to herself and to her clan she had come here. The garment she wore bore both narwhals and bucks, and I doubted she had made it entirely herself. So I deduced some maternal support of her decision.

"They're getting married this week?" Patience asked me, and I nodded in response.

"This will be a Harvest Fest to remember," she observed. "Best send runners out about the countryside. No one will want to miss this. We haven't had a proper wedding in Buckkeep since Chivalry and I married here."

"I don't think this will be one now. They've prepared for Harvest Fest, not a wedding. Cook's going to be very upset!" Lacey warned us.

She was right, of course. I was able to retreat from the chaos I'd created, and actually found a few hours of sleep that night holed up in the workroom. I fear few others did.

The servants worked through the night. It was fortunate they had the feast for the harvest well begun and the castle already decked with autumn garlands. Fortunate too that the Prince's dukes and duchesses had already convened for Harvest Fest, for it would have caused a greater furor if the Prince's haste to wed had caused one of his high nobles to miss the ceremony.

I almost missed my peephole the next day. I stood through the lengthy harvest ceremony in the back row of the Prince's Guard. Longwick had replenished our depleted ranks, yet even so I was painfully aware of the absence of those who had gone to find the dragon with us. Riddle stood beside me, and I think he felt it as keenly as I did. Yet for all that, there was satisfaction in watching our prince and his bride.

They were arrayed as the King and Queen of the Harvest. Long had it been since that old custom was observed, for long had it been since we had had a royal couple in residence. The seamstresses must have worked throughout the night. Elliania wore her cloak of narwhals and bucks, and somehow a doublet that matched it perfectly had been created for the Prince. Dutiful's simple coronet had been replaced with an ornate harvest crown, and in that I saw Chade's subtle hand, for he displayed the Prince as a crowned king before his dukes. Ceremonial it might be, yet it could not fail to leave an impression. Elliania was crowned, as well. Whereas the Prince wore a crown of gilded antlers, hers featured a single narwhal horn enameled in blue and trimmed in silver. When they danced together, alone in the center of the sanded floor, they looked like a couple from a legend sprung to life.

"Like Eda and El themselves," Riddle observed, and I nodded to myself.

Nobility and commoners are alike swayed by pomp and pageantry. Over the next few days, the castle and the town swelled with folk as it had not in years. The ceremony to honor the Prince's Wit coterie was well attended, with far more folk than it would have ordinarily attracted. Cockle had the telling of the tale, and he acquitted himself well and with far more accuracy than I had come to expect of minstrels. Perhaps because he was Witted himself, he did not wish to be seen as embroidering the truth beyond what it would bear. So he told the tale with moving simplicity that made little of the type of magic Burrich and the coterie used and much that they had been willing to sacrifice all for their prince.

Cockle, Swift, Web, and Civil were formally recognized as the Prince's Wit coterie. There was some small grumbling at that, as older nobles recalled well that once the word had only been applied to the circle of Skilled ones who aided a king. Chade assured them that there would indeed eventually be a Skill coterie, as well, as soon as suitable candidates could be tested and selected.

The Queen conveyed Withywoods to Molly rather than Nettle, so that it might be seen as granted to Burrich's line in token of his service. Molly accepted it gravely and I knew that the monies from that estate would provide well for her and all her children. Lady Nettle was presented as the newest of the Queen's circle of ladies, and Swift officially apprenticed to the Witmaster Web. Web spoke briefly but strongly of the power of Burrich's magic, and bemoaned that the man had been forced to hide it rather than educate his son in it. He hoped there would never be such a waste of talent again. Then Web solved for me the riddle that he had given me when first we set out on the voyage. For he said that Burrich briefly rallied before he died, enough to bid his son farewell, and to die with the Warrior's Prayer on his lips. For, "Yes," he had sighed on his dying breath, and all knew that was the ultimate prayer one could offer to life. Acceptance.

I pondered that during the evening when I sat in my workroom. My hands were slick with lamp oil. It had spread through the Skill scrolls, making many of the old letters fuzzy and swollen to my weary eyes. It was a discouraging, tiresome task. I pushed the scroll away from me, wiped my hands on a rag, and poured myself a little more brandy.

I was not certain I agreed with Web's thoughts, and yet it seemed to me that "yes" had been Burrich's word for life. Certainly, there seemed to be very little glory or satisfaction in saying "no" to it. I had said it often enough to have felt fully the truth of that.

I had sought in vain for another opportunity to speak to Molly alone. Always, she seemed surrounded by her children. Slowly it came to me, sitting there alone by my fire, that they were a part of her. Likely there would be very little chance of finding her alone and apart from them. The opportunity I had so long denied myself was here and now, but rapidly slipping away from me.

The next morning, on the eve of the wedding, I went to the steams early in the day. I washed myself and shaved more carefully than I had in years. Back in the tower room, I brushed my hair back into a warrior's tail, and then took out the selection of clothing that the Fool had inflicted on me. I dressed slowly in the blue doublet and the white shirt, finishing it with the Buck blue leggings. I was now definitely a Buckman, but no longer looked like servant or guardsman. I looked at myself in the mirror and smiled ruefully. Patience would approve. I looked dangerously like my father's son. I dared myself, and then moved the silver fox pin from the inside of my doublet to the outside. The little fox winked at me and I smiled back.

I left the secret labyrinth and walked through the corridors of Buckkeep Castle. Several times I felt eyes on me, and once a man stopped dead before me and squinted at me with a frown, as if struggling to remember something. I passed him by. The castle was acrawl with hastening servants and nobles socializing with one another. I made my way to the Violet Chamber and knocked firmly.

Nettle opened the door. I had not been prepared for that, thinking that young Chivalry would have been the first I must confront. She stared at me, and then recognized me with a visible start. She said nothing until I asked, "May I come in? I would speak to your mother and brothers."

"I don't think that's wise. Go away," she said, and began to shut the door, but Chivalry caught the edge of it, asking her, "Who is it?" and then, in an aside to me, "Don't mind her, sir. Dress of a lady and manners of a fishwife."

The room seemed full of children. I had never before realized how many seven children were. Swift and Nimble were sitting on the floor by the hearth, a game of Stones spread out before them, with Steady watching the play. Swift looked up, saw me, and his mouth opened in an O of surprise. I saw his twin poke him, demanding, "What is it? It's your turn." Hearth and Just, wrestling on the bed, ignored me. I suddenly realized the size of the promise that Burrich had demanded of me; it was easily seven times what Chivalry had asked of him when he handed me over to his right-hand man to raise. The blankets were rucked about by the tussling youngsters on the bed and the candelabrum on the night table was in obvious danger of being overset. And then, before Nettle could shut the door on me or Chivalry invite me in, Molly entered from the adjoining chamber. She halted, staring at me.

I think she would have thrown me out if she'd had the chance. Hearth stood up on the bed and made a spring for his brother, who evaded him by rolling away. I took two swift steps and caught the six-year-old before he hit the floor. He wriggled away from me immediately, charging back into battle with his brother. They suddenly reminded me of a litter of puppies, and I smiled as I said, "I promised Burrich that I would look after his sons. I can't do that if I don't know them. I've come to introduce myself."

Swift stood up slowly to face me. The question in his eyes was plain. I took a breath. I found my answer. Yes. "My name is FitzChivalry Farseer. I grew up in the stables of Buckkeep. Your father taught me all things he thought a man should know. I would pass that on to his sons."

Chivalry had caught Nettle's uneasiness, and the

name unsettled him even more. He moved to put his body between the smaller children and me. It was so instinctive of him that I had to smile, even when he said, "I think I can pass my father's teachings on to my brothers, sir."

"I expect that you will. But you will have other things to think of, as well. Who cares for your stock and stables right now, when you are all away?"

"Oxworthy. A man from our village who used to come to help out with the heavy work from time to time. He can manage it well enough, for a few days, though I will have to return to our holdings right after the Prince's wedding."

"It's not his business!" Nettle interjected indignantly.

I knew I had to face her down or let her drive me off. "I made a promise, Nettle. Swift witnessed it. I do not think your father would have asked that of me unless he wished the raising of his small sons to be my business. That sets it out of your hands."

"But not out of mine," Molly interjected firmly. "And for many reasons, I think this unwise."

I took a breath and steeled my will. I turned to look at Chivalry. "I love your mother. I have for years, for years before she chose your father. Yet I promise you, I will not try to take his place with any of you. Only to do what he asked of me. To look after you all." I looked back at Molly. Her face was so white I thought she would faint. "No secrets," I told her. "No secrets among us."

Molly sat down heavily on the bed. Her two youngest boys immediately came to her, Hearth climbing into her lap. She put her arms around him reflexively. "I think you had better go," she said faintly. Steady came to his mother and put a protective arm around her.

Swift stood suddenly. "No secrets? Will you tell them you are Witted, then?" It was a challenge.

I smiled at him. "I believe you just did that for me." I took a breath and looked at Nettle. "I will also be instructing your sister in the Skill." At Chivalry's blank look, I said, "The King's magic, the old magic. She has it. She

talks with dragons. You should chat with her about it sometime. It was why she was first brought here to Buckkeep, to
serve her prince. I believe your father had some ability in
the Skill for he served as King's Man to King-in-Waiting
Chivalry. The man for whom your eldest brother is
named."

Swift was staring at me uncertainly. "Web said we were
not to speak of who you really were. That there were still
some who'd like to see you dead. That your life was in our
hands."

I bowed to him. "Yes. I put my life in your hands." I
looked at Nettle and added, "If you'd truly like to be rid of
me, it would be fairly simple for you."

"Please, Fitz." Molly sounded desperate. "Go. I need to
speak to my children privately. I wish you had not given
such a heavy secret to my younger ones. I scarcely trust
them to wash their necks each day, let alone to preserve
such a confidence."

I felt a bit foolish then, and I bowed, saying only, "As
you will, Molly," and left. I got five steps past the closing of
the door before my knees began to shake so badly that I
had to lean up against the wall for a moment. A passing
servant asked me if I was ill, but I assured her I would be
fine. Yet as I found my strength and walked away down the
corridor, I wondered if I would be.

Then Nettle's sudden Skilling hit me with the force of
a mallet. *The dragons are coming! Tintaglia bids us have live
meat waiting for them, in the "customary" place!*

It was good fortune that brought us dragons on the
Prince's wedding day, but Nettle's inspiration that the tribute Tintaglia had demanded so imperiously be referred to
as the Dragon's Feast. Hapless steers, beribboned with blue
streamers, were penned not far from the Witness Stones,
awaiting their fate. Tintaglia and Icefyre were not present
for the ceremony itself, which was just as well. The well-
wishers who came to witness the Prince and Elliania make
their vows in the center of the Witness Stones crowded

both hillsides. The couple was splendid in blue and white. They stood in the center of the stones under a serendipitously blue sky and spoke their promises loudly and clearly.

I was amongst the guards who stood in a line to keep an area near the cattle pens cleared for the dragons. They appeared as small jewels in the sky just as the Prince had finished his promises to his bride and his dukes. They flew nearer, and the crowd oohed and aahed as if they were an acrobatic troupe brought especially for their pleasure. The dragons grew larger and even larger and soon we had no problems in keeping an area cleared for them to alight as people began to realize the size of the creatures that were approaching. A hush came over the crowd as it became apparent that Tintaglia fled the ardently pursuing Icefyre. Above the Witness Stones, they wheeled and cavorted and mock-battled, swooping low enough that the wind of their wings tousled hair and flapped scarves. Together they soared, gleaming black and silvery blue, up in an abrupt, almost vertical climb, and then Icefyre lunged and caught his mate. They coupled in a display of wanton lust that delighted the gathered witnesses as a good omen for their prince and new princess. No one with even a drop of the Skill in them could have been completely immune to the passions of those great beasts. It infected the crowd with a wave of both sentiment and amorousness that made that evening's festivities a night long and fondly remembered by many.

The dragons cared little for any of that. They coupled several times, with loud trumpeting and mock challenges to one another, and then fell on the bullocks with a zeal for feeding that was horrifying to witness. The pens did not hold the panicky cattle and one guardsman was trampled and several dozen onlookers sent scrambling for safety before Tintaglia and Icefyre completed their slaughter and settled in to feeding. That was bloody and messy enough that even those who had stayed behind to watch the dragons kill the cattle decided to go back to the castle, or to watch from a safer distance.

Yet even though the dragons paid little attention to the occasion, their presence was a triumph for our prince. Before the dukes dispersed to their separate duchies, they met and agreed to recognize Dutiful as King-in-Waiting. It was an end to Dutiful's quest worthy of any minstrel's song, and many were made about it, and sung often in the days to come. The feasting and rejoicing in Buckkeep Castle went on for a full twenty days until the onset of wintry weather convinced the nobility that they ought to seek their own keeps and holdings before travel became completely unpleasant. The castle settled back, very gradually, into a routine. Yet for all that winter, it remained a livelier place than it had in many a year. The King-in-Waiting and his young bride attracted not just the youthful nobility of the Six Duchies, but the younger kaempra of the Out Islands. Alliances were made that had nothing to do with trade, and wedding plans set that spanned the two countries. Among those who announced their intentions were Lord Civil and Lady Sydel.

Yet it was a time of departures, too. I made farewell to Hap and his master, for they would follow their lord back to his keep for the winter. My boy seemed genuinely happy, and if I was not pleased to part with him, I was pleased that he had found a choice that gave him so much satisfaction. Web took Swift off with him, saying it was time the boy got out and met more of his own folk, to understand better all the nuances of the Wit and to make him appreciate the necessity of using it with discipline. My declaration of love for his mother had raised a new wall between Swift and me. I was not sure it was one I could soon breach, and yet I felt better knowing that I had spoken honestly to him. Web tried to talk me into going with them, saying that I too would benefit, but I begged off yet again, promising that truly, truly, one day I would make time. He smiled, and reminded me that no man could make time, but only use that which he was given wisely. I promised him I'd try to do that, and waved them farewell from the gates of Buckkeep.

The dragons departed with the first frost, and we were not sorry to bid them farewell. They were each capable of eating a couple of cattle a day. Nettle warned us early in their visit that if we did not supply them willingly, they would likely take whatever they fancied. Our herds and flocks were well culled before the chill of winter drove them south. I was amused one night to become aware of Nettle and Tintaglia in dream-talk. Nettle dream-rode with Tintaglia. She flew slightly behind Icefyre, heading south as they flew through the night. The sweep of cool wind, the stars overhead, and the rich smells of the slumbering earth below were intoxicating.

And beyond that desert, you will find some of the richest, fattest herds in this part of the world. Or so I have heard so. Nettle was casual with her recommendation.

Desert? Dry sand? I have been longing for a good dust bath. Wet sand clings beneath my scales, and water cannot polish old blood from one's scales like sand does.

I think you will find much there to your liking. I have heard that the cattle of Chalced are easily twice the size of what we raise here, and so fat that the meat catches fire if you try to cook it over an open flame.

Nettle's dream was rich with the smell of roasting meat and dripping fat. It almost made me hungry. *I have never heard of the cattle of Chalced being exceptionally fat or large,* I objected.

We were not conversing with you, Nettle pointed out severely. *And what I know of Chalced, I know from my father's stories of that place. I think they would profit much from a visit from hungry dragons.* And then she tumbled me out of her dream and I awoke on the floor by my bed.

Dutiful, Chade, Nettle, Thick, and I continued to meet in early mornings to study and expand our understanding of the Skill. Nettle was courteous, but spoke to me only as it was necessary. I did not push against that wall, either, but instructed Dutiful, Thick, and her as a group. Soon my paltry advantage over them was apparent, and we proceeded to learn as a coterie. What we learned from the recovered scrolls made us go more slowly rather than more quickly for it rapidly became apparent that we wielded our magic like a boy wields a sword, with little understanding of either the danger or the potential of it. Chade desperately wished to experiment with the Portal Stones, as we began to call them. The Elderling cities and their hints of both treasure and secrets enticed him. Only the extreme aversion that both Thick and I evinced toward them convinced him that he should wait until he had a better mastery of the magic before attempting such a thing. Perhaps the most positive outgrowth of it was that Chade agreed that in spring he would arrange a Calling after the old tradition, and that from among those who came, we would select Skill candidates who would be trained according to the careful procedures outlined in the scrolls.

Despite my duties, winter dragged for me. The day after the wedding, Molly and five of her sons had departed Buckkeep. She did not bid me farewell in any way. I bled inside for three days and then, lacking all other advisers in matters of the heart, took my sorry account of my foolishness to Patience and Lacey. They listened carefully, praised my courage and honesty, condemned my stupidity, and then revealed that Molly had already told them the whole story. After chiding me for rushing in just as they had warned me not to do, Patience announced that I had best return to Tradeford with her for the winter, to keep myself busy and to give Molly some time. I narrowly begged my way out of that. Yet bidding them farewell was difficult for me, and I promised I would come to visit before the year was out.

"If we're still alive," Patience conceded cheerfully. They promised to send me a monthly missive along with the report of the holdings that they sent to the Queen, and I promised to do likewise. I watched them set forth, mounted on horses amidst the guard the Queen had insisted on sending with them, for despite their years they both disdained the comforts of a litter. I stood in the road, staring after them until a curve in the road took them out of sight.

chapter XXXVII

EVER AFTER

*Let the Calling be announced well in advance, for people
deserve a warning before the Skill Magic touches them
for the first time. A Calling issued with no warning can
induce great fear, for some who hold the potential for
Skill will not know what it is, and fear that madness or
worse has come upon them. So let riders be sent out well
ahead of time. But do not tell when the exact day of the
Calling will go forth. In the past, much time has been
wasted trying to wake the Skill in some who came to
Buckkeep, claiming to have heard the Call, when in fact
all they wished to do was escape a life as farmers or
bakers or rivermen.*

*Let the strongest coterie in the keep issue the Call,
making it as far-reaching as possible. A Calling should
be held no more often than every fifteen years.*

▶ TREEKNEE'S "ON THE CALLING OF CANDIDATES"

I tried. But I could not help myself.

One month after Patience had departed, I gave in to
an impulse. I sent a large pot of preserved wintergreen
berries to Molly. I approached Riddle to act as my messenger. He seemed surprised that I even asked if he were busy,

commenting that he had been told several weeks ago to consider himself at my disposal. Chade had undertaken a number of small changes on my behalf since I'd begun to take a more active role in Farseer matters. The pretense that I was an ordinary member of the Prince's Guard was fading, replaced with the unseen acceptance that I served the royal family in more confidential ways. Nominally, I was still Tom Badgerlock but I seldom wore the livery of a guard anymore, and the fox pin rode always on my breast.

Riddle seemed bemused by the errand I gave him but carried the gift and delivered it nonetheless.

"What did she say?" I asked him anxiously when he returned.

He looked at me blankly. "She said nothing to me. I gave it to the lad who came to the door. But I told him it was for his mum. Isn't that what you wanted me to do?"

I hesitated, and then said, "Yes. That was exactly right. Yes."

The next month, I sent a missive saying that I thought Nettle was doing very well with her studies and becoming more comfortable at court. I told the family that Web had sent a bird to inform us that he and Swift would likely winter with the Duke and Duchess of Bearns. Web seemed well pleased with the boy, and I thought Molly would wish to know they were well and doing fine. My letter spoke only of her children. Along with the missive, I sent two jumping jacks and a carved bear and a sack of horehound candies.

Riddle's report from that delivery was slightly more encouraging. "One of the little fellows said horehound was good, but not as good as peppermint."

The next month, a sack of horehound and a sack of peppermint candies, as well as nuts and raisins, accompanied my letter about Nettle. That won me a brief reply from Molly, written on the bottom of my own letter, saying she welcomed news of Nettle but would I kindly stop attempting to make the boys sick with sweets.

My next month's letter duly reported on Nettle and

gave news of Swift, who had taken the blotch-fever along with all the other youngsters at Ripplekeep in Bearns, but had recovered well and seemed none the worse for it. The Duchess herself had taken an interest in the lad and was teaching him much about hawks. Personally, I wondered how much, but left that speculation out of my letter. Instead of sweets, I sent two pouches of baked clay marbles, an exceptionally nice hoofpick in a leather sheath, and two wooden practice swords.

Riddle was amused to report that Hearth had clouted Just with one of the swords before he had even got off his horse, and refused to trade with Nimble for the bag of marbles that had been intended for him. I took it as a good sign that Riddle knew the boys by name now, and that they had all come out of the house to greet him.

The note from Molly was less heartening. Just had suffered a considerable lump to the back of his head, for which she blamed me. The boys had also been disappointed at the lack of sweets with the letter, for which she also blamed me. The letters were welcome but I should stop disrupting her family with inappropriate gifts. There was also a note from Chivalry, stiffly thanking me for the hoofpick. He asked if I knew of a source of saff oil, for one of the mares had a stubborn infection in one hoof and he thought he recalled his father using saff oil.

I did not wait a month. I found saff oil immediately, and sent it back to Chivalry, with instructions to wash out all her hooves with vinegar, move her into a different stall, and then apply saff oil to all four hooves, inside and out. I further suggested that he put a good bed of hearth ash down in her old stall and leave it there for three days before sweeping it out and then mopping the stall with vinegar and letting it dry well before stabling any other horses in it. And with the saff oil and letter to Chivalry, I defiantly sent barley-sugar sticks, with the request that he ration them out so that no one suffered from bellyaches.

He returned a note, thanking me for the oil and saying

he had forgotten about the vinegar portion of the remedy. He asked if I knew the correct proportions for a certain liniment that Burrich used to make, for his attempt at it had come out too runny. And he assured me that the barley sugar would only be distributed as it was earned. Molly sent a note, but it was clearly marked *To Nettle*.

"But Steady told me that they had actually all liked the peppermint better," Riddle informed me as he gave me Chivalry's missive. "Steady seems to me to be the quiet one. You know, the good lad who is often overlooked amongst rowdier boys." With a liar's grin, he added, "I was like that myself, as a lad."

"Surely you were," I agreed skeptically.

"Any response?" Riddle asked me, and I told him I needed some time to think about it.

It took me several days of experiments at the worktable to compound correctly the liniment. It made me realize how much I had forgotten. I made several pots of it and sealed them well. Chade paid one of his rare visits to the old workroom we once had shared. He sniffed the air speculatively and asked what I was concocting.

"Bribes," I answered him honestly.

"Ah," he said, and when he asked no more, I knew that Riddle was still reporting to him, as well. "Made a few changes up here, I see," he added, looking about the room.

"Mostly with a broom and some water. I'd give a great deal to have a window."

He gave me an odd look. "The room next to this one is always left empty. It used to belong to Lady Thyme. I understand there are rumors she haunts it still. Strange odors, you know, and sounds in the night." He grinned to himself. "She was a useful old hag. I bricked up the connecting door years and years ago. It used to be behind that wall hanging. You could probably knock through the wall if you went about it quietly."

"Knock through the wall quietly?"

"It might be a bit difficult."

"A bit. I may try it. I'll let you know."

"Or you could move Nettle out of your old room down below and have the use of it."

I shook my head. "I still hope there may come a time when she would want to use that passage to come up and talk with me of an evening."

"But not much progress there yet."

"No. I'm afraid not."

"Ah, she's as hardheaded as you were. Don't trust her near the mantel with a fruit knife."

I looked at the one that still stood there, driven in as deep as my boyish anger could sink it. "I'll remember that."

"Remember too that you forgave me. Eventually."

I tried to send off the liniment by Riddle with a sack of peppermint drops, some spice tea, and a small marionette of a deer. "That won't do," he told me. "At least put in some tops, so there's something for each of them." And so it was done. He suggested pennywhistles as well, quite innocently, but I pointed out I was trying to win my way in, not provoke Molly to murder me. He grinned, nodded and rode off, and stayed away an extra two days because of a snowstorm.

He brought back letters, one for me and one for Nettle, and the news that he'd eaten with the family and spent the night in the stables after a half-dozen games of Stones with Steady each evening. "I spoke you well, when Chivalry asked after you. Said you spent your nights at your scroll work and were fair to turn into a scribe if you didn't watch yourself. So then Hearth asked, 'What, is he fat, then?' for I gather the scribe at their town is quite a portly man. So I said, no, quite the opposite, that I thought you'd lost flesh and grown quieter of late. And that you spent more time alone than was healthy for any man."

I tilted my head at him. "Could you have made me sound any more pathetic?"

He mimicked the tip of my head. "Is there any of it not true?"

The note was from Chivalry, thanking me for the liniment and recipe.

I don't know what was in Molly's note to Nettle. The next morning, she lingered after the Skill-lesson. Dutiful called to ask if she was coming, for he and Elliania and Civil and Sydel intended to go riding, if she'd care to come. She told him to go ahead and she would catch up easily, for it didn't take her forever to primp her hair before riding out.

She turned back to catch me smiling, and said, "I speak him formal when others are about. It's only here that I talk to him like that."

"He likes it. He was elated when he first discovered he had a cousin. He said it was nice to know a girl who spoke her mind to him."

That stopped her cold, and I regretted the remark, for I thought I had put her off whatever it was she was about to say. But she met my eyes and, lifting her chin, set her fists to her hips. "Oh. And should I speak my mind to you?"

I wasn't sure. "You could," I suggested.

"My mother writes that she is well, and that my little brothers quite enjoy Riddle's visits. She wonders if you are afraid of my brothers, that you don't come yourself."

I slouched back in my chair and looked down at the tabletop. "I'm more likely to be afraid of her. Time was, she had quite a temper." I picked at my thumbnail.

"Time was, I understand you were excellent at provoking it."

"I suppose that is true. So. Do you think she would welcome a visit from me?"

She stood quite a time, not answering. Then she asked, "And are you afraid of my temper, as well?"

"A bit," I admitted. "Why do you ask?"

She walked to Verity's window and stared out over the sea as he used to. In that pose, she looked as much a Farseer as I did. She ran her hands back through her hair distractedly. Truly, she could have given a bit more care to "primping."

Her shortened hair stood up like the hair on an angry cat's back. "Once, I thought we were going to be friends. Then I discovered that you were my father. From that moment on, you haven't much tried even to speak to me."

"I thought you didn't want me to."

"Perhaps I wanted to see how hard you'd try." She turned back to look at me accusingly. "You didn't try, at all."

I sat a long time in silence. She turned and started toward the door.

I stood up. "You know, Nettle, I was raised by a man among men. Sometimes, I think that is the greatest disadvantage a man can have when it comes to dealing with women."

She turned and looked back at me. I spoke from the heart. "I don't know what to do. I want you to at least know me as a person. Burrich was your father and he did well at it. Perhaps it's too late for me to have that place in your life. Nor can I find a place in your mother's life for me. I love her still, just as much as I did when she left me. I thought then that, when all my tasks were done, I would find her and somehow we would be happy together. And here we are, sixteen years later, and I still haven't managed to find my way back to her."

She stood, her hand on the door, looking uncomfortable. Then she said, "Perhaps you are telling these things to the wrong woman." And she slipped quietly out of it, letting it close behind her.

A few days later, Riddle found me at the guards' table eating breakfast. He slid onto the bench opposite me. "Nettle has given me a letter to deliver to her mother and brothers. She said to take it whenever I made my next journey for you." He reached across the table and took a hunk of bread from my plate. He bit into it and asked with his mouth full, "Will that be soon?"

I thought about it. "Tomorrow morning," I suggested.

He nodded. "I thought it might be about then."

I rode Myblack down to the market in Buckkeep Town, chaffering with her all the way. She had had half a year with a stable boy whose idea of exercising her was to take her out and let her run as much as she wanted and then bring her back. She was willful and rude, tugging at her bit and ignoring the rein. I was ashamed of myself for neglecting her. I visited the winter market and rode home with sugared ginger and two arm lengths of red lace. I put them in a basket with a purloined bottle of dandelion wine. I sat all night with a piece of good paper in front of me and managed to find three sentences. "I remember you in red skirts. You climbed up the beach cliffs in front of me, and I saw your bare, sandy ankles. I thought my heart would leap out of my chest." I wondered if she would even remember that long-ago picnic when I had not even dared to kiss her. I sealed the note with a blotch of wax. Four times I unsealed it, trying to think of better words. Eventually, I entrusted it to Riddle as it was, and walked about for the next four days wishing I hadn't.

On the fourth night, I worked the lever that opened the door in Nettle's bedchamber. I did not go in and summon her, as Chade had me. Instead, I went halfway down those steep steps and left a candle burning there. Then I went back up and waited.

The wait seemed to last forever. I do not know which wakened her at last, the light or the draft, but I finally heard her hesitant tread on the stair. I had built up the fire well in the comfortable end of the room.

She peered round the corner of the concealed door, saw me, but still came in cautious as a cat. She walked slowly past the worktable with the stained scrolls stretched out on it, and more slowly past the work hearth with its racks of tongs and measures and stained pans. She came at last to the chairs by the fireside. She had on a nightgown and a woven shawl across her shoulders. She was shivering.

"Sit down," I invited her, and she did, slowly. "This is

where I work," I told her. The kettle was just on the boil and I asked her, "Would you like a cup of tea?"

"In the middle of the night?"

"I do a lot of my work in the middle of the night."

"Most people sleep then."

"I am not like most people."

"That's so." She stood up and studied the items on the mantel above the hearth. There was a carving of the wolf that the Fool had done, and next to it, the memory stone with a similar image turned face out. She touched the handle of the fruit knife embedded there and gave me a puzzled glance. Then she reached up and set her hand to the hilt of Chivalry's sword.

"You can take it down if you like. It was your grandfather's. Be careful. It's heavy."

She took her hand away. "Tell me about him."

"I can't."

"Is it another secret, then?"

"No. I can't tell you because I never knew him. He gave me to Burrich when I was five or six. I never saw him, that I can recall. I believe he looked in on me with the Skill from time to time, through Verity's eyes. But I knew nothing of that, then."

"It sounds like you and me," she said slowly.

"Yes, it does," I admitted. "Except that I have a chance to know you now. If we are both bold enough to take it."

"I'm here," she pointed out, settling deeper into the chair. And then she fell silent and I could not think of anything to say. Then she pointed at the Fool's carving. "Is that your wolf? Nighteyes?"

"Yes."

She smiled. "He looks exactly like I thought you would. Tell me more about him."

And so I did.

Riddle returned three days later, complaining of bad roads and the cold. A storm had followed him home. I scarcely heard him. I took the little roll of bark paper he offered me and carried it carefully up to my lair before I opened it. At first glance, it looked like a drawing. Then I realized it was a hastily sketched map. There were only a few words on the bottom of the page. "Nettle said you were having a hard time finding your way back to me. Perhaps this will help."

A deep wet snow was falling outside Buckkeep Castle. The clouds were heavy; I did not expect it would stop soon. I went to my workroom and stuffed a change of clothing into a saddlebag. I Skilled to Chade, *I'll be gone for a while.*

Very well. We can finish working on that scroll translation tonight.

You misunderstand me. I'll be gone several days at least. I'm going to Molly.

He hesitated and I could feel how badly he wanted to object. There was too much going on for me to leave. There were translations, the refinement of his powder that I'd been helping him with, and the Calling to arrange. The scrolls cautioned that the people of the kingdom had to be prepared for the Calling, lest parents or friends think those who heard voices in their heads were going mad. Yet it also cautioned that the exact day of the Calling be kept secret, to prevent charlatans from wasting the time of the Skill-master.

Irritably I pushed such considerations aside. I waited.

Go then. And good luck. Have you told Nettle?

Now it was my turn to hesitate. *I've told only you. Do you think I should tell her?*

The things you ask my advice on! Never the ones I hope you'll ask me about, always the ones that . . . never mind. Yes. Tell her. Only because not telling her might seem deceptive.

So I reached out to my daughter and said, *Nettle. I've had a note from Molly. I'm going to go visit her.* And then the obvious occurred to me. *Do you want to go along?*

It's storming outside, with worse to come by the look of it. When are you leaving?

Now.

It isn't wise.

I've never been wise. The words echoed oddly in my mind, and I smiled.

Go then. Dress warmly.

I shall. Farewell.

And I went. Myblack was not pleased at being taken from her warm, dry stall to face the storm. It was a cold, wet, and tedious journey. The one inn I stopped at was full of trapped travelers and I had to sleep on the floor near the hearth wrapped in my cloak. The next night, a farmer allowed me to shelter in his barn overnight. The storm did not let up and the journey only became more unpleasant, but I pushed on.

Luck had it that the snow would stop and the clouds blow clear one valley before I reached Burrich's holding. As I pushed Myblack down the buried road toward the house, the place looked like something out of a tale. Snow was heaped on cottage and stable roof. Smoke curled up from the chimney into the blue sky. A path was already worn between the house and the barns. I pulled in Myblack and sat looking down on it. As I watched, Chivalry opened a barn door and then trundled out a barrow of dirty straw. I whistled to give him warning of a visitor and then rode Myblack down the hill. He stood unmoving, watching me come. In the yard before the house I pulled her in and sat still, trying to think of a greeting. Myblack tugged twice at her bit, and then threw her head back irritably.

"That horse wants training," Chivalry observed with disapproval. He came closer, then stopped. "Oh. It's you."

"Yes." The hard words. "May I come in?" He might be barely fifteen, but he was the man of these holdings now.

"Of course." But there was no smile with the words. "I'll take your horse for you."

"I'd rather put her up myself, if you don't mind. I've neglected her and it shows. I'll need to handle her a lot to undo it."

"As you will. This way."

I dismounted and glanced toward the cottage, but if anyone inside was aware of me, it did not show. I led Myblack and followed Chivalry into a well-ordered stable. Nimble and Just were mucking out stalls. Steady came in, carrying buckets of water. They all halted at the sight of me. I suddenly felt surrounded and the ghost of a memory floated to the surface of my mind. Nighteyes, standing at the outskirts of the pack's gathering. Wanting to go in, so badly, but knowing that if he approached them the wrong way they would drive him out.

"I see your father's hands everywhere here," I said, and it was true. I knew at once that Burrich had built this building to meet his own demands. The stalls were larger than the ones at Buckkeep. When the storm shutters were opened, air and light would flood in. I saw Burrich in the way the brushes were stored and the tack put up. I could almost feel him here. I blinked and came back to myself, suddenly aware of Chivalry watching me.

"You can put her in there," he said, gesturing to a stall. They went about their work as I cared for Myblack. I watered her and grained her lightly and left her clean and dry. Chivalry came to look over the door of the stall at her, and I wondered if my work would pass his inspection. "Nice horse," was all he said.

"Yes. She was a gift from a friend. The same one who sent Malta to your father when he knew he wouldn't need her anymore."

"Now there's a mare!" Chivalry exclaimed, and I followed him down the stalls to look at her. I saw Brusque, a four-year-old stallion out of Ruddy that Chivalry had wanted to use to stud her. And I visited Ruddy. I think the old stallion almost remembered me. He came and rested his head against my shoulder for a time. He was old and getting tired.

"This will probably be the last foal he sires," I said quietly. "I think that's why Burrich wanted to use him. One last chance to get that cross of bloodlines. He was a fine stud in his day."

"I remember when he first came. Barely. Some woman came down the hill with two horses and just gave them to my father. We didn't even have a barn then, let alone a stable. Papa moved all the wood out of the woodshed that night so the horses wouldn't be left outside."

"I'll bet Ruddy was glad to see him."

Chivalry gave me a puzzled look.

"You didn't know Ruddy was your father's horse, long before that? Verity gave him the pick of the two-year-olds. He chose Ruddy. He'd known this horse since the day his dam dropped him. The night the Queen had to flee Buckkeep for her life, Burrich put her on this horse. He carried her all the way to the Mountains. Safely."

He was properly amazed. "I didn't know that. Papa didn't talk much about his days at Buckkeep."

And so I ended up helping with the mucking out and the feeding before ever I went in to see Molly. I told stories of horses I had known and Chivalry walked me through the barns with pardonable pride. He'd done a good job of keeping it all up and I told him so. He showed me the mare with the infected hoof, sound now, and then I walked through the shed to the milk cow and the dozen chickens.

By the time Chivalry led me back to the cottage with the lads trooping behind us, I felt I had acquitted myself well with them. "Mother, you've a visitor," Chivalry called as he pushed open the door. I stamped snow and manure from my feet and followed him in.

She had known I was out there. Her cheeks were pink and her shortened hair smoothed back. She saw me looking at it and lifted a self-conscious hand to it. In that moment, we were both reminded of why it was shortened and Burrich's shadow stepped between us.

"Well, chores are done and I'm off to Staffman's," Chivalry announced before I could even greet her.

"I want to go, too! I want to see Kip and play with the puppies," Hearth announced.

Molly bent down to the boy. "You can't always go with Chivalry when he goes to visit his sweetheart," she admonished him.

"He can today," Chivalry announced abruptly. He gave me a sideways glance, as if making sure I knew he was doing me a vast favor. "I'll put him up behind me; his pony can't deal with this snow. Hurry up and get ready."

"Would you like a cup of tea, Fitz? You must be cold."

"Actually, there's nothing like stable chores for warming a man after a long ride. But yes, I would."

"The boys put you to work in the stable? Oh, Chiv, he's a guest!"

"He knows his way around a shovel," Chivalry said, and it was a compliment. Then, "Hurry up, Hearth. I'm not going to wait all day for you."

There were a few moments of noisy chaos that seemed necessary for preparing a six-year-old boy to go anywhere, although no one but me was astonished at it. It made the guards' mess seem a calm place by comparison. By the time the two were out of the door, Steady had already retreated to the loft while Just and Nimble had seated themselves at the table. Nimble pretended to be cleaning his nails, while Just stared at me frankly.

"Fitz, please, sit down. Nimble, move your chair over, make room. Just, I could do with more kindling."

"You're just sending me outside to get me out of the way!"

"How perceptive of you! Now go. Nimble, you may help him. Clear some of the snow from the wood stack, and move some of it into the woodshed to dry."

They both went out, but not quietly or graciously. When the door had closed behind them, Molly took a deep breath. She removed a kettle from the fire, poured hot water over spice tea in a large pot and then brought it to the table. She set out cups for us, and a pot of honey. She sat down across from me.

"Hello," I said.

She smiled. "Hello."

"I asked Nettle if she wanted to come with me, but she didn't want to ride through the storm."

"I can't blame her. And I think it's hard for her to come home, sometimes. Things are far humbler here than at Buckkeep Castle."

"You could move to Withywoods. It's yours now, you know."

"I know." A shadow passed over her face and I wished I hadn't mentioned it. "But it would be too many changes, too fast. The boys are still becoming accustomed to the idea that their father is never coming back. And, as you see, Chivalry is courting."

"He seems very young for that," I ventured.

"He's a young man with a large holding. Another woman in the house would make things much easier for all of us. What should he wait for, if he's found a woman who loves him?" she countered. When I had no answer to that, she added, "If they marry, I don't think Thrift will want to move far from her parents' home. She is very close to her sister."

"I see." And I did. I suddenly saw that Molly was no longer someone's daughter, to be whisked off from her father's house and become mine. She was the center of a world here, with roots and ties.

"Life is complicated, isn't it?" she said to my silence.

I looked at her, in her simple, somber-hued robe. Her hands were no longer smooth and slender; there were lines in her face that had not been there when she was mine. Her body had softened and rounded with the years. She was no longer the girl in the red skirts, running down the beach before me.

"I have never wanted anything so much in my life as I've always wanted you."

"Fitz!" she exclaimed, glancing up at the loft, and I suddenly realized I had spoken the words aloud. Her cheeks glowed and she lifted both hands to cover her mouth with her fingertips.

"I'm sorry," I said. "I know it's too soon. You've told me that. And I will wait. I'll wait however long you want me to wait. I just want to be sure you know that I am waiting."

I saw her swallow. She said huskily, "I don't know how long it will take."

"It doesn't matter." I stretched out my hand, palm up, on the tabletop. She hesitated, and then set hers in it. And we sat, not speaking, until the boys came in with a load of snowy kindling to be scolded by their mother for not wiping their feet.

I stayed until afternoon. We drank tea and I talked about Nettle at the court, and told the boys stories of Burrich when he had been a younger man. I saddled Myblack and bade them farewell before Chivalry and Hearth returned. Molly walked out to say good-bye and kissed me. On the cheek. And I rode three days back to Buckkeep Castle.

Riddle continued to carry letters between her cottage and Buckkeep Castle. They all came up for Spring Fest, and I managed to dance with Molly once. It was the first time I had ever danced with her, and the first time I'd attempted to dance in years. I danced with Nettle, afterward, who advised me never to attempt it again. But she smiled as she said it.

I saw Hap in the early days of spring. He and Sawtongue came through Buck at the beginning of their summer travels. Hap was taller and leaner and seemed content with his life. He'd seen a great deal of Bearns and now was off to Rippon and then Shoaks. He'd made two songs of his own, both humorous, and both seemed well received when he sang them for us at the lesser hearth. Web and Swift came back to Buckkeep later that month. Swift had widened through the shoulders and was more introspective than I recalled him. Web stayed at Buckkeep while Swift went home to spend a week with his family. He returned with news that Chivalry would be getting married in three months.

I went down for the wedding. Watching him stand before Thrift and pledge himself to her while she blushed and smiled, scarcely able to look at him, envy burned in me. It would be so simple for them. They met, they loved, they married. I suspected they'd have a baby in the cradle before the year was out. And I could get no closer to Molly than the touch of her hand and a kiss on the cheek.

Summer grew strong and hot. It was a good summer. Elliania was pregnant and the whole of the Six Duchies seemed abuzz with it. The crops seemed to grow before my eyes. Myblack learned the way to Molly's cottage and back. I helped Chivalry raise the beams on the extra rooms he was building, and watched Molly and Thrift cook companionably together. I watched her as she moved around the room at her simple tasks, watched her laugh and stir the soup and brush her lengthening hair back from her eyes. I had not been so fevered with desire since I was fifteen years old. I could not sleep at night, and when I did, I had to ward my dreams. I could see Molly and speak to her, but it was always in Burrich's house or with Burrich's sons clinging to her hands. There seemed no place in her world that I could claim, and I grew irritable with everyone.

I went to see Patience and Lacey, as I had promised, making the long journey in the hot and dusty days of high summer, and Chade swore I was so fractious that he was glad to be rid of me for a time. I didn't blame him. Lacey had become frailer and Patience had hired two women to help care for her old servant. Walking in her gardens with Patience's worn hand on my arm, seeing how she had converted the bloody soil of Regal's King's Circle to a haven of greenery, beauty, and peace gave me the first rest I had known in a long time. She gave me some of my father's things from her clutter: a plain sword belt he had preferred, letters Burrich had sent to him that mentioned me, and a jade ring. The ring fit my hand perfectly. I wore it home.

Nettle lingered after our Skill-lesson the first morning I was back. Chade did also, but at a look from me, he sighed and left me alone with my daughter. "You were gone a long time. Weeks," she said.

"I hadn't seen Patience in a long time. And she's getting old."

She nodded. "Thrift is pregnant."

"That's wonderful news."

"It is. We're all very excited. But my mother says it makes her feel old, to know she'll be a grandmother soon."

That gave me a moment's pause.

"She said to me, 'Time goes faster when you're older, Nettle.' Isn't that an odd thought?"

"I've known it for some time."

"Do you? I think women know it better perhaps."

I looked at Nettle directly and said nothing. "Perhaps not," she said then, and went away.

Four days later, I saddled Myblack again and set out for Molly's. Chade sternly warned me that I must be back in time for the Calling and I promised him that I would be. The day was fine and Myblack well behaved and in good condition for the journey. The summer evenings were long and I made the journey in two days instead of three. I found myself very welcome, for Chivalry was replacing the posts in the paddock fence. Swift and Steady were helpful in pulling up the old rotted posts and Just and Hearth dug the holes bigger. Chivalry and I came behind, setting each pole straight and tall. He spoke to me about becoming a father and how exciting it was until he realized that my silences were growing longer and longer. Then he declared he was going to take the boys down to the creek and let them swim for a time, for he'd had enough of hot, sweaty work for the day. He asked if I'd come but I shook my head.

I was pouring a bucket of cool water from the well over my head when Molly came out with a basket on her arm.

"Thrift is napping. The heat is hard on her. It is, when you're carrying. I thought we'd leave the house quiet for her, and perhaps find out if there are any blackberries ripe enough to be sweet yet."

We climbed the gentle hill behind the house. The shouts of the boys splashing in the creek below faded. We went past Molly's neat straw hives, gently humming with the warm day. The blackberry tangle was beyond them and Molly led me to the far south side of it, saying the berries always ripened there first. Her bees were busy there too, some among the last blackberry flowers and some after the juice from the bursting ripe fruit. We picked berries until the basket was half-full. Then, as I bent a high prickly branch to bring it down so Molly could reach the top fruit, I offended a bee. It rushed at me, first tangling in my hair and then bumbling down my collar. I slapped at it and cursed as it stung me. I stumbled back from the berry bushes, batting at two others that were suddenly buzzing round my head.

"Move away quickly," Molly warned me, and then came to take my hand and hurry me down the hill.

A second one stung me behind the ear before they gave off the chase. "And we've left the basket back there with all the berries. Shall I try to go back for it?"

"Not yet. Wait a time until they settle. Here, don't rub that, the stinger is probably still in it. Let me see."

I sat down in the shade of an alder and she bent my head forward to look at the sting behind my ear. "It's really swelling. And you've pushed the stinger right in. Sit still, now." She picked at it with her fingers. I flinched and she laughed. "Sit still. I can't get it with my nails." She leaned forward and put her mouth on it. I felt her tongue find the stinger, and then she gripped it between her teeth and pulled it out. She brushed it from her lips onto her fingers. "See. You'd pushed it all the way in. Is there another one?"

"Down my back," I said, and in spite of myself, my voice shook. She stopped and looked at me. She turned her head and looked again at me, as if she had not seen me in a long time. Her voice was husky when she said, "Take your shirt off. I'll see if I can get it out."

I felt dizzy as her mouth once again touched me. She presented me with the second stinger. Then she set her fingers to the arrow scar on my back and said, "What was this?"

"An arrow. A long time ago."

"And this?"

"That's more recent. A sword."

"My poor Fitz." She touched the scar between my shoulder and neck. "I remember when you got this one. You came to my bed, still bandaged."

"I did."

I turned to her, knowing that she was waiting for me. It still took all my courage. Very carefully, I kissed her. I kissed her cheeks, her throat, and finally her mouth. She tasted of blackberries. Over and over, I kissed her, as slowly as I could, trying to kiss away all the years I had missed. I unlaced her blouse and lifted it over her head, baring her to the blue summer sky above us. Her breasts were soft and heavy in my hands. I treasured them. Her skirt slipped away, a blown blossom on the grass. I laid my love down in the deep wild grasses and sweetly took her to me.

It was homecoming, and completion, and a marvel worth repeating. We dozed for a time, and then woke as the shadows were lengthening. "We must go back!" she exclaimed, but, "Not yet," I told her. I claimed her again, as slowly as I could bear to, and my name whispered by my ear as she shuddered beneath me was the sweetest sound I'd ever heard.

We were abruptly guilty adolescents as the raised cries of "Mother? Fitz?" reached our ears. We scrabbled hastily back into our clothing. Molly ventured alone to retrieve our basket of berries. We dusted leaves and bits of grass from our clothing and hair, laughing breathlessly as we did so. I kissed her again.

"We have to stop!" Molly warned me. She returned my kiss warmly, and then lifted her voice to call, "I'm here, I'm coming!"

I took her hand in mine as we went round the bramble and held it as we strode back down the hill to her children.

EPILOGUE

Withywoods is a warm valley, centered on a gently flowing river that carves a wide plain that nestles between gently rising and rolling foothills. It is a wonderful place to grow grapes and grain and bees and young boys. The manor is of timber rather than stone, and there are times when this still seems very strange to me. I sleep now in a room and in a bed that once belonged to my father, and the woman I have loved since I was a boy sleeps beside me at night.

For three years, we were lovers in secret. It was hard for us, and yet somehow all the more delicious. Our trysts were few and uncertain, and I valued them all the more for that. Molly came with her sons to the next Harvest Fest, and I stole her away from the music and dancing and carried her off to my own bed. I had never thought to have her there, and for many nights after, her perfume lingered on my pillows and sweetened my dreams. A visit to her cottage might yield me no more than a swiftly stolen kiss, but each was worth the long ride. I do not think we deceived Chivalry for long, and certainly Nettle's comments let me know that I was not fooling her. But we went carefully, for the sake of her little boys, and I have never regretted taking the time to win their regard.

No one was more surprised than I when Steady answered the Calling. He did not seem to be strongly Skilled at first, but we soon uncovered reserves of strength and calm that made him precisely suited to be a King's Man. Nettle was proud and protective, and I was grateful, for her young son's residence in Buckkeep Castle gave Molly excuses to visit more often. Steady and Nettle became the core of the new King's Coterie, for the bond the brother and sister shared was strong. Twelve others answered the Calling, four with Skill enough to become members of Nettle's coterie and eight of lesser ability. We turned no one away from that first Calling, for as Chade himself pointed out, it sometimes takes time for the Skill to manifest itself completely. Thick and I continue to perform the duties of Solos. Chade, as always, keeps threads tied to us all and tests the boundaries of the magic, risking himself in ways he would deride as foolhardy if anyone else attempted them.

When Chivalry's second son was born, Molly suddenly declared that it was time Thrift had her own hearth and home. She decided to take Hearth and Just to Withywoods. Nimble made the decision to stay with his older brother, for the holding was too much for one man to work alone and he had always enjoyed the horses. Molly privately told me that she thought it had more to do with a certain redheaded girl, the daughter of a wainwright in the closest town.

We wed quietly, making our promises before my king in the presence of Molly's children, Kettricken, Elliania, Chade, Hap, and Riddle. Chade wept, then hugged me fiercely and told me to be happy. Hap asked Nettle if he might kiss his new sister, and was soundly thumped by a protective Hearth for his impertinence. Thick and little Prince Prosper dozed through most of the ceremony.

We traveled to see Patience, who had not been able to make the journey, and to place a flower on Lacey's grave. We stayed a month, and I thought Hearth and Just would wear Patience out with mischief and curiosity. But two days before we were scheduled to depart, Patience abruptly announced that she was tired of Tradeford and too old to run it anymore and that she would come to live with us in Withywoods. To my relief, Molly was pleased at the prospect.

Hearth and Just seem to enjoy the pleasures and absurdities of having such a grandmother. Hearth has promised to seek Molly's permission before there is any more tattooing, and Just has developed a deep interest in plants and herbs that challenges even Patience's knowledge. Riddle turned up at Withywoods when we were scarcely settled, saying that Chade had sent him to be my man. I suspect he still spies on me for the old spider, but that is fine. I am willing to yield to Chade whatever he needs to feel he still has control of his world. Much of his power, I wrested from him, bit by bit, and passed it on to Dutiful as he proved ready for it. If I have never worn the crown of the Six Duchies, I am confident that I have done much to see it passed on intact.

Riddle has demonstrated that he knows much more of hiring servants and running an estate than I ever suspected. It is well, for neither Molly nor I ever expected to have to manage such things, and Patience declares she is far too old to bother. He is a solid man. The last time Nettle visited, I took him to task for being overly familiar with her, until Molly called me aside and told me quietly to mind my own business.

I am summoned often to Buckkeep, and Dutiful and Elliania have come to visit twice to go hawking, for the birding is excellent in our grain fields. I have never cared for that sport, and spent both visits playing with their son while they rode. Prosper is a hearty, healthy boy.

Chade trained arduously as prescribed in the Skill scrolls and then made one venture through the stones. He chose to go to Aslevjal and explore for himself the Elderling ruins there. He stayed ten days and came back with his eyes full of wonder and a sack full of memory cubes. He did not find his way to Prilkop's cave, and if he had, I am sure he would have found it long deserted. I think that when the Fool last visited Chade, he was on his way south, back to their schooling place to bring home all they had learned. I doubt he will come back this way again.

Ours was a ragged and uneven parting. Each of us had intended to see the other again. Each of us had had final words to say. My days with the Fool ended like a half-played game of

Stones, the outcome poised and uncertain, possibilities hovering. Sometimes it seemed to me a cruelty that so much was unresolved between us; at other times, a blessing that a hope of reunion lingered. It is like the anticipation that a clever minstrel evokes when he pauses, letting silence pool before sweeping into the final refrain of his song. Sometimes a gap can seem like a promise yet to be fulfilled.

I miss him often, but in the same way that I miss Nighteyes. I know that such a one will not come again. I count myself fortunate for what I had of them. I do not think I will ever Wit-bond again, or know such a deep friendship as I had with the Fool. As Burrich once observed to Patience, one horse cannot wear two saddles. I have Molly and she is enough for me, and more.

I am content.